THE LOCUS
AWARDS

*Thirty Years of the Best in
Science Fiction and Fantasy*

Edited by

CHARLES N. BROWN AND
JONATHAN STRAHAN

An Imprint of HarperCollinsPublishers

A continuation of the copyright page appears on page 514.

THE LOCUS AWARDS. Collection, introduction, and story notes copyright © 2004 by Locus Publications and Jonathan Strahan. All rights reserved. Printed in the United States of America. No part of this book may be used or reproduced in any manner whatsoever without written permission except in the case of brief quotations embodied in critical articles and reviews. For information address HarperCollins Publishers Inc., 10 East 53rd Street, New York, NY 10022.

HarperCollins books may be purchased for educational, business, or sales promotional use. For information please write: Special Markets Department, HarperCollins Publishers Inc., 10 East 53rd Street, New York, NY 10022.

FIRST EDITION

Eos is a federally registered trademark of HarperCollins Publishers Inc.

Designed by Katherine Nichols

Library of Congress Cataloging-in-Publication Data

The Locus awards : thirty years of the best in science fiction and fantasy / Charles N. Brown and Jonathan Strahan, eds.—1st. ed.
    p. cm.
  ISBN 0-06-059426-8 (acid-free paper)
    1. Science fiction, American. 2. Fantasy fiction, American. I. Brown, Charles N.
  II. Strahan, Jonathan.

PS648.S3L64 2004
813'.0876—dc22   2004042054

04 05 06 07 08 JTC/RRD 10 9 8 7 6 5 4 3 2 1

FOR MARIANNE

AND FOR EVERYONE WHO HAS WORKED

FOR *LOCUS*

CONTENTS

The 1990s

The 2000s

ACKNOWLEDGMENTS

WE WOULD especially like to thank our editors, Stephanie Smith and Diana Gill, for their invaluable work on this book, and artist extraordinaire Michael Whelan, who kindly provided the gorgeous cover art.

We would also like to thank the following people who at various times provided invaluable assistance when needed: Marianne S. Jablon, Jack Dann, Liza Trombi, Gary K. Wolfe, Nick Gevers, Mark R. Kelly, Rich Horton, Justin Ackroyd, Jennifer Brehl, Simon Brown, Ellen Datlow, Terry Dowling, Gardner Dozois, Kirsten Gong-Wong, Jennifer A. Hall, Russell Letson, Jill Wayment, Sean Williams, Jack Womack, and everyone at Westercon who help with the Locus Awards each year.

INTRODUCTION

THIS BOOK CONTAINS some of the finest science fiction and fantasy short fiction ever written. That's all you *really* need to know. The rest of this introduction and the story notes may (or may not) add to your enjoyment, but you can just read the stories and we guarantee you'll be impressed.

All of these stories won the Locus Award in their year of publication. That means they were picked by *Locus* readers from recommendations by *Locus* reviewers, various editors—including the ones who edit the various "best of the year" anthologies—and others as the very best of the year. We've gone through the thirty years of winners and picked what we think are the best, so in essence these stories have been triple-washed for you.

Science fiction and fantasy have evolved considerably over the past thirty years. In the mid-1960s, science fiction existed only on the outer fringes of literature, and commercial fantasy did not exist at all. *The Lord of the Rings* had been published in paperback and was an undergrad college hit in North America, as were the paperbacks of *Dune* and *Stranger in a Strange Land.* *Star Trek* started in 1966; *Star Wars* and the first of the successful Tolkien imitators, *The Sword of Shannara,* were still a decade away.

It was a time when there was a need for new writers to enter the field and reinvigorate it, for new places where science fiction and fantasy could be published, and for a set of benchmarks to be set in place so that the science fiction and fantasy community could recognize excellence within its own ranks. The Hugo Awards existed already, the Nebula Awards were started in 1966, and the World Fantasy Awards began in 1975.

Locus: The Newspaper of the Science Fiction Field started in 1968. It was a modest mimeographed magazine limited to the number of pages that could be mailed with a single 10 cent stamp. It cost a dollar for eight issues and made a modest profit. The magazine kept expanding as the science fiction field expanded. The '60s were an incredible time in SF and in the rest of the world—Vietnam, rock music, student revolts, the Summer of Love, and the first flight to the moon. In science fiction, the older writers, readers, and editors wanted a continuation of strong story values—plot, action, technology-based ideas, a positive view of the future—while those who came into their adulthood in the '60s, the first generation that did not completely grow up with the pulp magazines, wanted to use newer techniques, unreliable narrators, a more negative view of both technology and the universe. Neither side "won," of course, but out of their synthesis came modern science fiction.

Locus was, and is, based on one central idea: science fiction and fantasy are important, and deserve to be treated so; they deserve intelligent consideration and commentary, and careful reportage. That idea attracted readers, writers, editors, and publishers to the *Locus* banner, many of whom became faithful, often lifelong, subscribers. And as *Locus*'s circulation increased, it became clear that its readership was both passionate and well informed about science fiction and fantasy.

By 1971, the field had expanded so much it had become impossible for anybody to read it all. There were 175 books and six regular magazines published in 1970. *Locus* decided to survey its readers annually in order to determine what *they* thought was the best and most important work being published, and then to present that work with awards: the Locus Awards.

Every February, *Locus* publishes a list of the top 100 to 150 books and top 100 to 150 shorter works as recommended by reviewers, editors, and other professionals. The readers vote and the winners are tabulated. Often boasting a voting base larger than the Hugo and Nebula Awards combined, the Locus Awards quickly gained a reputation as a reliable measure of excellence. Unlike most awards, they are not restricted to a shortlist of four or five finalists and a winner. Instead, the winner and a ranked list of all nominees are published in September of each year. What this provides is an accurate picture of how the changes in science fiction and fantasy—the waning of the New Wave, the arrival of cyberpunk, the evolution of the field—are impacting people like you: readers.

And the list of winners! The best, the brightest, the most famous. And *Locus* voters have their favorites. Writer-editor Gardner Dozois—the most influential editor in the field today and second only, perhaps, to *Astounding* editor John W. Campbell as most important editor in the history of the field—has won the Locus Award a record twenty-eight times, while artist Michael Whelan (who provided the gorgeous cover for this volume) has won twenty-three times. Among writers, Harlan Ellison, author of "Jeffry Is Five," has won a staggering eighteen times (a record thirteen times for short fiction); Ursula K. Le Guin, whose "The Day Before the Revolution Came" is reprinted here, has won seventeen times; and author and anthologist Robert Silverberg has been nominated an astounding one hundred and forty-six times in just about every imaginable category. These are the great names of modern science fiction and fantasy.

Which brings us back to this book, *The Locus Awards: Thirty Years of the Best in Science Fiction and Fantasy*. While it can't possibly accommodate all of the many winners or the millions of words of fiction that have been recognized with the award, it does present a rare selection where the popular votes of *Locus*'s readers intersect with the views of its editors: the best and the most popular award winners. You can't ask for a lot more.

Jonathan Strahan & Charles N. Brown
December 2003

The 1970s

THE DEATH OF DOCTOR ISLAND

G ENE WOLFE was born in New York in 1931, served in the Korean War, and graduated from the University of Houston with a degree in mechanical engineering. He worked as an engineer—famously helping to design the machine that makes Pringles potato chips—before becoming the editor of the trade journal *Plant Engineering*. He first came to prominence as a writer in the late '60s with a sequence of short stories—including "The Hero as Werewolf," "Seven American Nights," and "The Island of Doctor Death and Other Stories"—in Damon Knight's *Orbit* anthologies. His first major novels were *The Fifth Head of Cerberus* and *Peace,* but he established his reputation with a sequence of three long multivolume novels—*The Book of the New Sun* (4 vols.), *The Book of the Long Sun* (4 vols.), *The Book of the Short Sun* (3 vols.)—and pendant volume, *The Urth of the New Sun*. Taken together, these dozen books are some of the most important, most consistently impressive science fiction ever written. They have been awarded the Nebula Award, World Fantasy Award, British Science Fiction Award, August Derleth Award, John W. Campbell Memorial Award, Italia Award, and Locus Award. Wolfe has published a number of short story collections, including *The Island of Doctor Death and Other Stories, Endangered Species,* and *Strange Travelers*. He has won the Nebula Award and World Fantasy Award twice, the Locus Award four times, the John W. Campbell Memorial Award, the British Fantasy Award, the British SF Award, and is a recipient of the World Fantasy Award for Lifetime Achievement. Wolfe's most recent book is the fantasy novel *The Knight.* Upcoming is a sequel, *The Wizard,* and a new collection, *Innocents Aboard.*

One of Wolfe's major early achievements was the Archipelago quartet of stories: "The Island of Doctor Death and Other Stories," "The Doctor of Death Island," "Death of the Island Doctor," and the Nebula and Locus Award–winning "The Death of Doctor Island" which follows. It is a powerful and moving look at identity and the dividing line between fantasy and reality.

* * *

I have desired to go
  Where springs not fail,
To fields where flies no sharp and sided hail
  And a few lilies blow.

And I have asked to be
  Where no storms come,
Where the green swell is in the heavens dumb,
  And out of the swing of the sea.

—GERARD MANLEY HOPKINS

A GRAIN OF SAND, teetering on the brink of the pit, trembled and fell in; the ant lion at the bottom angrily flung it out again. For a moment there was quiet. Then the entire pit, and a square meter of sand around it, shifted drunkenly while two coconut palms bent to watch. The sand rose, pivoting at one edge, and the scarred head of a boy appeared—a stubble of brown hair threatened to erase the marks of the sutures; with dilated eyes hypnotically dark he paused, his neck just where the ant lion's had been; then, as though goaded from below, he vaulted up and onto the beach, turned, and kicked sand into the dark hatchway from which he had emerged. It slammed shut. The boy was about fourteen.

For a time he squatted, pushing the sand aside and trying to find the door. A few centimeters down, his hands met a gritty, solid material which, though neither concrete nor sandstone, shared the qualities of both—a sand-filled organic plastic. On it he scraped his fingers raw, but he could not locate the edges of the hatch.

Then he stood and looked about him, his head moving continually as the heads of certain reptiles do—back and forth, with no pauses at the terminations of the movements. He did this constantly, ceaselessly—always—and for that reason it will not often be described again, just as it will not be mentioned that he breathed. He did; and as he did, his head, like a rearing snake's, turned from side to side. The boy was thin, and naked as a frog.

Ahead of him the sand sloped gently down toward sapphire water; there were coconuts on the beach, and sea shells, and a scuttling crab that played with the finger-high edge of each dying wave. Behind him there were only palms and sand for a long distance, the palms growing ever closer together as they moved away from the water until the forest of their columniated trunks seemed architectural; like some palace maze becoming as it progressed more and more draped with creepers and lianas with green, scarlet and yellow leaves, the palms interspersed with bamboo and deciduous trees dotted with flaming orchids until almost at the limit of his sight the whole ended in a spangled wall whose predominant color was black-green.

The boy walked toward the beach, then down the beach until he stood in knee-deep water as warm as blood. He dipped his fingers and tasted it— it was fresh, with no hint of the disinfectants to which he was accustomed. He waded out again and sat on the sand about five meters up from the high-water mark, and after ten minutes, during which he heard no sound but the wind and the murmuring of the surf, he threw back his head and began to scream. His screaming was high-pitched, and each breath ended in a gibbering, ululant note, after which came the hollow, iron gasp of the next indrawn breath. On one occasion he had screamed in this way, without cessation, for fourteen hours and twenty-two minutes, at the end of which a nursing nun with an exemplary record stretching back seventeen years had administered an injection without the permission of the attending physician.

After a time the boy paused—not because he was tired, but in order to listen better. There was, still, only the sound of the wind in the palm fronds and the murmuring surf, yet he felt that he had heard a voice. The boy could be quiet as well as noisy, and he was quiet now, his left hand sifting white sand as clean as salt between its fingers while his right tossed tiny pebbles like beachglass beads into the surf.

"Hear me," said the surf. "Hear me. Hear me."

"I hear you," the boy said.

"Good," said the surf, and it faintly echoed itself: "Good, good, good."

The boy shrugged.

"What shall I call you?" asked the surf.

"My name is Nicholas Kenneth de Vore."

"Nick, *Nick . . . Nick*?"

The boy stood, and turning his back on the sea, walked inland. When he was out of sight of the water he found a coconut palm growing sloped and angled, leaning and weaving among its companions like the plume of an ascending jet blown by the wind. After feeling its rough exterior with both hands, the boy began to climb; he was inexpert and climbed slowly and a little clumsily, but his body was light and he was strong. In time he reached the top, and disturbed the little brown plush monkeys there, who fled chattering into other palms, leaving him to nestle alone among the stems of the fronds and the green coconuts. "I am here also," said a voice from the palm.

"Ah," said the boy, who was watching the tossing, sapphire sky far over his head.

"I will call you Nicholas."

The boy said, "I can see the sea."

"Do you know my name?"

The boy did not reply. Under him the long, long stem of the twisted palm swayed faintly.

"My friends all call me Dr. Island."

"I will not call you that," the boy said.

"You mean that you are not my friend."

A gull screamed.

"But you see, I take you for my friend. You may say that I am not yours, but I say that you are mine. I like you, Nicholas, and I will treat you as a friend."

"Are you a machine or a person or a committee?" the boy asked.

"I am all those things and more. I am the spirit of this island, the tutelary genius."

"Bullshit."

"Now that we have met, would you rather I leave you alone?"

Again the boy did not reply.

"You may wish to be alone with your thoughts. I would like to say that we have made much more progress today than I anticipated. I feel that we will get along together very well."

After fifteen minutes or more, the boy asked, "Where does the light come from?" There was no answer. The boy waited for a time, then climbed back down the trunk, dropping the last five meters and rolling as he hit in the soft sand.

He walked to the beach again and stood staring out at the water. Far off he could see it curving up and up, the distant combers breaking in white foam until the sea became white-flecked sky. To his left and his right the beach curved away, bending almost infinitesimally until it disappeared. He began to walk, then saw, almost at the point where perception was lost, a human figure. He broke into a run; a moment later, he halted and turned around. Far ahead another walker, almost invisible, strode the beach; Nicholas ignored him; he found a coconut and tried to open it, then threw it aside and walked on. From time to time fish jumped, and occasionally he saw a wheeling sea bird dive. The light grew dimmer. He was aware that he had not eaten for some time, but he was not in the strict sense hungry—or rather, he enjoyed his hunger now in the same way that he might, at another time, have gashed his arm to watch himself bleed. Once he said, "Dr. Island!" loudly as he passed a coconut palm, and then later began to chant "Dr. Island, Dr. Island, Dr. Island" as he walked until the words had lost all meaning. He swam in the sea as he had been taught to swim in the great quartanary treatment tanks on Callisto to improve his coordination, and spluttered and snorted until he learned to deal with the waves. When it was so dark he could see only the white sand and the white foam of the breakers, he drank from the sea and fell asleep on the beach, the right side of his taut, ugly face relaxing first, so that it seemed asleep even while the left eye was open and staring; his head rolling from side to side; the left corner of his mouth preserving, like a death mask, his characteristic expression—angry, remote, tinged with that inhuman quality which is found nowhere but in certain human faces.

WHEN HE WOKE it was not yet light, but the night was fading to a gentle gray. Headless, the palms stood like tall ghosts up and down the beach, their tops lost in fog and the lingering dark. He was cold. His hands rubbed his sides; he danced on the sand and sprinted down the edge of the lapping water in an effort to get warm; ahead of him a pinpoint of red light became a fire, and he slowed.

A man who looked about twenty-five crouched over the fire. Tangled black hair hung over this man's shoulders, and he had a sparse beard; otherwise he was as naked as Nicholas himself. His eyes were dark, and large and empty, like the ends of broken pipes; he poked at his fire, and the smell of roasting fish came with the smoke. For a time Nicholas stood at a distance, watching.

Saliva ran from a corner of the man's mouth, and he wiped it away with one hand, leaving a smear of ash on his face. Nicholas edged closer until he stood on the opposite side of the fire. The fish had been wrapped in broad leaves and mud, and lay in the center of the coals. "I'm Nicholas," Nicholas said. "Who are you?" The young man did not look at him, had never looked at him.

"Hey, I'd like a piece of your fish. Not much. All right?"

The young man raised his head, looking not at Nicholas but at some point far beyond him; he dropped his eyes again. Nicholas smiled. The smile emphasized the disjointed quality of his expression, his mouth's uneven curve.

"Just a little piece? Is it about done?" Nicholas crouched, imitating the young man, and as though this were a signal, the young man sprang for him across the fire. Nicholas jumped backward, but the jump was too late—the young man's body struck his and sent him sprawling on the sand; fingers clawed for his throat. Screaming, Nicholas rolled free, into the water; the young man splashed after him: Nicholas dove.

He swam underwater, his belly almost grazing the wave-rippled sand until he found deeper water; then he surfaced, gasping for breath, and saw the young man, who saw him as well. He dove again, this time surfacing far off, in deep water. Treading water, he could see the fire on the beach, and the young man when he returned to it, stamping out of the sea in the early light. Nicholas then swam until he was five hundred meters or more down the beach, then waded in to shore and began walking back toward the fire.

The young man saw him when he was still some distance off, but he continued to sit, eating pink-tinted tidbits from his fish, watching Nicholas. "What's the matter?" Nicholas said while he was still a safe distance away. "Are you mad at me?"

From the forest, birds warned, "Be careful, Nicholas."

"I won't hurt you," the young man said. He stood up, wiping his oily hands on his chest, and gestured toward the fish at his feet. "You want some?"

Nicholas nodded, smiling his crippled smile.

"Come then."

Nicholas waited, hoping the young man would move away from the fish, but he did not; neither did he smile in return.

"Nicholas," the little waves at his feet whispered, "this is Ignacio."

"Listen," Nicholas said, "is it really all right for me to have some?"

Ignacio nodded, unsmiling.

Cautiously Nicholas came forward; as he was bending to pick up the fish, Ignacio's strong hands took him; he tried to wrench free but was thrown down, Ignacio on top of him. "Please!" he yelled. "Please!" Tears started into his eyes. He tried to yell again, but he had no breath; the tongue was being forced, thicker than his wrist, from his throat.

Then Ignacio let go and struck him in the face with his clenched fist. Nicholas had been slapped and pummeled before, had been beaten, had fought, sometimes savagely, with other boys; but he had never been struck by a man as men fight. Ignacio hit him again and his lips gushed blood.

HE LAY A LONG time on the sand beside the dying fire. Consciousness returned slowly; he blinked, drifted back into the dark, blinked again. His mouth was full of blood, and when at last he spit it out onto the sand, it seemed a soft flesh, dark and polymerized in strange shapes; his left cheek was hugely swollen, and he could scarcely see out of his left eye. After a time he crawled to the water; a long time after that, he left it and walked shakily back to the ashes of the fire. Ignacio was gone, and there was nothing left of the fish but bones.

"Ignacio is gone," Dr. Island said with lips of waves.

Nicholas sat on the sand, cross-legged.

"You handled him very well."

"You saw us fight?"

"I saw you; I see everything, Nicholas."

"This is the worst place," Nicholas said; he was talking to his lap.

"What do you mean by that?"

"I've been in bad places before—places where they hit you or squirted big hoses of ice water that knocked you down. But not where they would let someone else—"

"Another patient?" asked a wheeling gull.

"—do it."

"You were lucky, Nicholas. Ignacio is homicidal."

"You could have stopped him."

"No, I could not. All this world is my eye, Nicholas, my ear and my tongue; but I have no hands."

"I thought you did all this."

"Men did all this."

"I mean, I thought you kept it going."

"It keeps itself going, and you—all the people here—direct it."

Nicholas looked at the water. "What makes the waves?"

"The wind and the tide."

"Are we on Earth?"

"Would you feel more comfortable on Earth?"

"I've never been there; I'd like to know."

"I am more like Earth than Earth now is, Nicholas. If you were to take the best of all the best beaches of Earth, and clear them of all the poisons and all the dirt of the last three centuries, you would have me."

"But this isn't Earth?"

There was no answer. Nicholas walked around the ashes of the fire until he found Ignacio's footprints. He was no tracker, but the depressions in the soft beach sand required none; he followed them, his head swaying from side to side as he walked, like the sensor of a mine detector.

For several kilometers Ignacio's trail kept to the beach; then, abruptly, the footprints swerved, wandered among the coconut palms, and at last were lost on the firmer soil inland. Nicholas lifted his head and shouted, "Ignacio? Ignacio!" After a moment he heard a stick snap, and the sound of someone pushing aside leafy branches. He waited.

"Mum?"

A girl was coming toward him, stepping out of the thicker growth of the interior. She was pretty, though too thin, and appeared to be about nineteen; her hair was blond where it had been most exposed to sunlight, darker elsewhere. "You've scratched yourself," Nicholas said. "You're bleeding."

"I thought you were my mother," the girl said. She was a head taller than Nicholas. "Been fighting, haven't you. Have you come to get me?"

Nicholas had been in similar conversations before and normally would have preferred to ignore the remark, but he was lonely now. He said, "Do you want to go home?"

"Well, I think I should, you know."

"But do you want to?"

"My mum always says if you've got something on the stove you don't want to burn—she's quite a good cook. She really is. Do you like cabbage with bacon?"

"Have you got anything to eat?"

"Not now. I had a thing a while ago."

"What kind of thing?"

"A bird." The girl made a vague little gesture, not looking at Nicholas. "I'm a memory that has swallowed a bird."

"Do you want to walk down by the water?" They were moving in the direction of the beach already.

"I was just going to get a drink. You're a nice tot."

Nicholas did not like being called a "tot." He said, "I set fire to places."

"You won't set fire to this place; it's been nice the last couple of days, but when everyone is sad, it rains."

Nicholas was silent for a time. When they reached the sea, the girl dropped to her knees and bent forward to drink, her long hair falling over her face until the ends trailed in the water, her nipples, then half of each breast, in the water. "Not there," Nicholas said. "It's sandy, because it washes the beach so close. Come on out here." He waded out into the sea until the lapping waves nearly reached his armpits, then bent his head and drank.

"I never thought of that," the girl said. "Mum says I'm stupid. So does Dad. Do you think I'm stupid?"

Nicholas shook his head.

"What's your name?"

"Nicholas Kenneth de Vore. What's yours?"

"Diane. I'm going to call you Nicky. Do you mind?"

"I'll hurt you while you sleep," Nicholas said.

"You wouldn't."

"Yes I would. At St. John's where I used to be, it was zero G most of the time, and a girl there called me something I didn't like, and I got loose one night and came into her cubical while she was asleep and nulled her restraints, and then she floated around until she banged into something, and that woke her up and she tried to grab, and then that made her bounce all around inside and she broke two fingers and her nose and got blood all over. The attendants came, and one told me—they didn't know then I did it— when he came out his white suit was, like, polka-dot red all over because wherever the blood drops had touched him they soaked right in."

The girl smiled at him, dimpling her thin face. "How did they find out it was you?"

"I told someone and he told them."

"I bet you told them yourself."

"I bet I didn't!" Angry, he waded away, but when he had stalked a short way up the beach he sat down on the sand, his back toward her.

"I didn't mean to make you mad, Mr. de Vore."

"I'm not mad!"

She was not sure for a moment what he meant. She sat down beside and a trifle behind him, and began idly piling sand in her lap.

Dr. Island said, "I see you've met."

Nicholas turned, looking for the voice, "I thought you saw everything."

"Only the important things, and I have been busy on another part of myself. I am happy to see that you two know one another; do you find you interact well?"

Neither of them answered.

"You should be interacting with Ignacio; he needs you."

"We can't find him," Nicholas said.

"Down the beach to your left until you see the big stone, then turn inland. Above five hundred meters."

Nicholas stood up, and turning to his right, began to walk away. Diane followed him, trotting until she caught up.

"I don't like," Nicholas said, jerking a shoulder to indicate something behind him.

"Ignacio?"

"The doctor."

"Why do you move your head like that?"

"Didn't they tell you?"

"No one told me anything about you."

"They opened it up"—Nicholas touched his scars—"and took this knife and cut all the way through my corpus . . . corpus . . ."

"Corpus callosum," muttered a dry palm frond.

"—corpus callosum," finished Nicholas. "See, your brain is like a walnut inside. There are the two halves, and then right down in the middle a kind of thick connection of meat from one to the other. Well, they cut that."

"You're having a bit of fun with me, aren't you?"

"No, he isn't," a monkey who had come to the water line to look for shellfish told her. "His cerebrum has been surgically divided; it's in his file." It was a young monkey, with a trusting face full of small, ugly beauties.

Nicholas snapped, "It's in my head."

Diane said, "I'd think it would kill you, or make you an idiot or something."

"They say each half of me is about as smart as both of us were together. Anyway, this half is . . . the half . . . the *me* that talks."

"There are two of you now?"

"If you cut a worm in half and both parts are still alive, that's two, isn't it? What else would you call us? We can't ever come together again."

"But I'm talking to just one of you?"

"We both can hear you."

"Which one answers?"

Nicholas touched the right side of his chest with his right hand. "Me; I do. They told me it was the left side of my brain, that one has the speech centers, but it doesn't feel that way; the nerves cross over coming out, and it's just the right side of me, I talk. Both my ears hear for both of us, but out of each eye we only see half and half—I mean, I only see what's on the right of what I'm looking at, and the other side, I guess, only sees the left, so that's why I keep moving my head. I guess it's like being a little bit blind; you get used to it."

The girl was still thinking of his divided body. She said, "If you're only half, I don't see how you can walk."

"I can move the left side a little bit, and we're not mad at each other. We're not supposed to be able to come together at all, but we do: down through the legs and at the ends of the fingers and then back up. Only I can't talk with my other side because he can't, but he understands."

"Why did they do it?"

Behind them the monkey, who had been following them, said, "He had uncontrollable seizures."

"Did you?" the girl asked. She was watching a sea bird swooping low over the water and did not seem to care.

Nicholas picked up a shell and shied it at the monkey, who skipped out of the way. After half a minute's silence he said, "I had visions."

"Ooh, did you?"

"They didn't like that. They said I would fall down and jerk around horrible, and sometimes I guess I would hurt myself when I fell, and sometimes I'd bite my tongue and it would bleed. But that wasn't what it felt like to me; I wouldn't know about any of those things until afterward. To me it was like I had gone way far ahead, and I had to come back. I didn't want to."

The wind swayed Diane's hair, and she pushed it back from her face. "Did you see things that were going to happen?" she asked.

"Sometimes."

"Really? Did you?"

"Sometimes."

"Tell me about it. When you saw what was going to happen."

"I saw myself dead. I was all black and shrunk up like the dead stuff they cut off in the pontic gardens; and I was floating and turning, like in water but it wasn't water—just floating and turning out in space, in nothing. And there were lights on both sides of me, so both sides were bright but black, and I could see my teeth because the stuff"—he pulled at his cheeks—"had fallen off there, and they were really white."

"That hasn't happened yet."

"Not here."

"Tell me something you saw that happened."

"You mean, like somebody's sister was going to get married, don't you? That's what the girls where I was mostly wanted to know. Or were they going to go home; mostly it wasn't like that."

"But sometimes it was?"

"I guess."

"Tell me one."

Nicholas shook his head. "You wouldn't like it, and anyway it wasn't like that. Mostly it was lights like I never saw anyplace else, and voices like I never heard any other time, telling me things there aren't any words for; stuff like that, only now I can't ever go back. Listen, I wanted to ask you about Ignacio."

"He isn't anybody," the girl said.

"What do you mean, he isn't anybody? Is there anybody here besides you and me and Ignacio and Dr. Island?"

"Not that we can see or touch."

The monkey called, "There are other patients, but for the present, Nicholas, for your own well-being as well as theirs, it is best for you to remain by yourselves." It was a long sentence for a monkey.

"What's that about?"

"If I tell you, will you tell me about something you saw that really happened?"

"All right."

"Tell me first."

"There was this girl where I was—her name was Maya. They had, you know, boys' and girls' dorms, but you saw everybody in the rec room and the dining hall and so on, and she was in my psychodrama group." Her hair had been black, and shiny as the lacquered furniture in Dr. Hong's rooms, her skin white like the mother-of-pearl, her eyes long and narrow (making him think of cats' eyes) and darkly blue. She was fifteen, or so Nicholas believed—maybe sixteen. *"I'm going home,"* she told him. It was psychodrama, and he was her brother, younger than she, and she was already at home; but when she said this the floating ring of light that gave them the necessary separation from the small doctor-and-patient audience, ceased, by instant agreement, to be Maya's mother's living room and became a visiting lounge. Nicholas/Jerry said: "Hey, that's great! Hey, I got a new bike—when you come home you want to ride it?"

Maureen/Maya's mother said, "Maya, don't. You'll run into something and break your teeth, and you know how much they cost."

"You don't want me to have any fun."

"We do, dear, but *nice* fun. A girl has to be so much more careful—oh, Maya, I wish I could make you understand, really, how careful a girl has to be."

Nobody said anything, so Nicholas/Jerry filled in with, "It has a three-bladed prop, and I'm going to tape streamers to them with little weights at the ends, an' when I go down old thirty-seven B passageway, look out, here comes that old coleslaw grater!"

"Like this," Maya said, and held her legs together and extended her arms, to make a three-bladed bike prop or a crucifix. She had thrown herself into a spin as she made the movement, and revolved slowly, stage center—red shorts, white blouse, red shorts, white blouse, red shorts, no shoes.

Diane asked, "And you saw that she was never going home, she was going to hospital instead, she was going to cut her wrist there, she was going to die?"

Nicholas nodded.

"Did you tell her?"

"Yes," Nicholas said. "No."

"Make up your mind. Didn't you tell her? Now, don't get mad."

"Is it telling, when the one you tell doesn't understand?"

Diane thought about that for a few steps while Nicholas dashed water on the hot bruises Ignacio had left upon his face. "If it was plain and clear and she ought to have understood—that's the trouble I have with my family."

"What is?"

"They won't say things—do you know what I mean? I just say look, just tell me, just tell me what I'm supposed to do, tell me what it is you want, but it's different all the time. My mother says, 'Diane, you ought to meet some boys, you can't go out with him, your father and I have never met him, we don't even know his family at all, Douglas, there's something I think you ought to know about Diane, she gets confused sometimes, we've had her to doctors, she's been in a hospital, try—' "

"Not to get her excited," Nicholas finished for her.

"Were you listening? I mean, are you from the Trojan Planets? Do you know my mother?"

"I only live in these places," Nicholas said, "that's for a long time. But you talk like other people."

"I feel better now that I'm with you; you're really nice. I wish you were older."

"I'm not sure I'm going to get much older."

"It's going to rain—feel it?"

Nicholas shook his head.

"Look." Diane jumped, bunnyrabbit-clumsy, three meters into the air. "See how high I can jump? That means people are sad and it's going to rain. I told you."

"No, you didn't."

"Yes, I did, Nicholas."

He waved the argument away, struck by a sudden thought. "You ever been to Callisto?"

The girl shook her head, and Nicholas said, "I have; that's where they did the operation. It's so big the gravity's mostly from natural mass, and it's all domed in, with a whole lot of air in it."

"So?"

"And when I was there it rained. There was a big trouble at one of the generating piles, and they shut it down and it got colder and colder until everybody in the hospital wore their blankets, just like Amerinds in books, and they locked the switches off on the heaters in the bathrooms, and the nurses and the comscreen told you all the time it wasn't dangerous, they were just rationing power to keep from blacking out the important stuff that was still running. And then it rained, just like on Earth. They said it got so cold the water condensed in the air, and it was like the whole hospital was right under a shower bath. Everybody on the top floor had to come down because it rained right on their beds, and for two nights I had a man in my room with me that had his arm cut off in a machine. But we couldn't jump any higher, and it got kind of dark."

"It doesn't always get dark here," Diane said. "Sometimes the rain sparkles. I think Dr. Island must do it to cheer everyone up."

"No," the waves explained, "or at least not in the way you mean, Diane."

Nicholas was hungry and started to ask them for something to eat, then turned his hunger in against itself, spat on the sand, and was still.

"It rains here when most of you are sad," the waves were saying, "because rain is a sad thing, to the human psyche. It is that, that sadness, perhaps because it recalls to unhappy people their own tears, that palliates melancholy."

Diane said, "Well, I know sometimes I feel better when it rains."

"That should help you to understand yourself. Most people are soothed when their environment is in harmony with their emotions, and anxious when it is not. An angry person becomes less angry in a red room, and unhappy people are only exasperated by sunshine and birdsong. Do you remember:

"And, missing thee, I walk unseen
On the dry smooth-shaven green
To behold the wandering moon,
Riding near her highest noon,
Like one that had been led astray
Through the heaven's wide pathless way?"

The girl shook her head.

Nicholas said, "No. Did somebody write that?" and then "You said you couldn't do anything."

The waves replied, "I can't—except talk to you."

"You make it rain."

"Your heart beats; I sense its pumping even as I speak—do you control the beating of your heart?"

"I can stop my breath."

"Can you stop your heart? Honestly, Nicholas?"

"I guess not."

"No more can I control the weather of my world, stop anyone from doing what he wishes, or feed you if you are hungry; with no need of volition on my part your emotions are monitored and averaged, and our weather responds. Calm and sunshine for tranquility, rain for melancholy, storms for rage, and so on. This is what mankind has always wanted."

Diane asked, "What is?"

"That the environment should respond to human thought. That is the core of magic and the oldest dream of mankind; and here, on me, it is fact."

"So that we'll be well?"

Nicholas said angrily, "You're not sick!"

Dr. Island said, "So that some of you, at least, can return to society."

Nicholas threw a sea shell into the water as though to strike the mouth that spoke. "Why are we talking to this thing?"

"Wait, tot, I think it's interesting."

"Lies and lies."

Dr. Island said, "How do I lie, Nicholas?"

"You said it was magic—"

"No, I said that when humankind has dreamed of magic, the wish behind that dream has been the omnipotence of thought. Have you never wanted to be a magician, Nicholas, making palaces spring up overnight, or riding an enchanted horse of ebony to battle with the demons of the air?"

"I am a magician—I have preternatural powers, and before they cut us in two—"

Diane interrupted him. "You said you averaged emotions. When you made it rain."

"Yes."

"Doesn't that mean that if one person was really, terribly sad, he'd move the average so much he could make it rain all by himself? Or whatever? That doesn't seem fair."

The waves might have smiled. "That has never happened. But if it did, Diane, if one person felt such deep emotion, think how great her need would be. Don't you think we should answer it?"

Diane looked at Nicholas, but he was walking again, his head swinging, ignoring her as well as the voice of the waves. "Wait," she called. "You said I wasn't sick; I am, you know."

"No, you're not."

She hurried after him. "Everyone says so, and sometimes I'm so confused, and other times I'm boiling inside, just boiling. Mum says if you've got something on the stove you don't want to have burn, you just have to keep one finger on the handle of the pan and it won't, but I can't, I can't always find the handle or remember."

Without looking back the boy said, "Your mother is probably sick; maybe your father too, I don't know. But you're not. If they'd just let you alone you'd be all right. Why shouldn't you get upset, having to live with two crazy people?"

"Nicholas!" She grabbed his thin shoulders. "That's not true!"

"Yes, it is."

"I am sick. Everyone says so."

"I don't; so 'everyone' just means the ones that do—isn't that right? And if you don't either, that will be two; it can't be everyone then."

The girl called, "Doctor? Dr. Island?"

Nicholas said, "You aren't going to believe that, are you?"

"Dr. Island, is it true?"

"Is what true, Diane?"

"What he said. Am I sick?"

"Sickness—even physical illness—is relative, Diane; and complete health is an idealization, an abstraction, even if the other end of the scale is not."

"You know what I mean."

"You are not physically ill." A long, blue comber curled into a line of hissing spray reaching infinitely along the sea to their left and right. "As you said yourself a moment ago, you are sometimes confused, and sometimes disturbed."

"He said if it weren't for other people, if it weren't for my mother and father, I wouldn't have to be here."

"Diane . . ."

"Well, is that true or isn't it?"

"Most emotional illness would not exist, Diane, if it were possible in every case to separate oneself—in thought as well as circumstance—if only for a time."

"Separate oneself?"

"Did you ever think of going away, at least for a time?"

The girl nodded, then as though she were not certain Dr. Island could see her, said, "Often, I suppose; leaving the school and getting my own compartment somewhere—going to Achilles. Sometimes I wanted to so badly."

"Why didn't you?"

"They would have worried. And anyway, they would have found me, and made me come home."

"Would it have done any good if I—or a human doctor—had told them not to?"

When the girl said nothing Nicholas snapped, "You could have locked them up."

"They were functioning, Nicholas. They bought and sold; they worked, and paid their taxes—"

Diane said softly, "It wouldn't have done any good anyway, Nicholas; they are inside me."

"Diane was no longer functioning: she was failing every subject at the university she attended, and her presence in her classes, when she came, disturbed the instructors and the other students. You were not functioning either, and people of your own age were afraid of you."

"That's what counts with you, then. Functioning."

"If I were different from the world, would that help you when you got back into the world?"

"You are different." Nicholas kicked the sand. "Nobody ever saw a place like this."

"You mean that reality to you is metal corridors, rooms without windows, noise."

"Yes."

"That is the unreality, Nicholas. Most people have never had to endure such things. Even now, this—my beach, my sea, my trees—is more in harmony with most human lives than your metal corridors; and here, I am your social environment—what individuals call 'they.' You see, sometimes if we take people who are troubled back to something like me, to an idealized natural setting, it helps them."

"Come on," Nicholas told the girl. He took her arm, acutely conscious of being so much shorter than she.

"A question," murmured the waves. "If Diane's parents had been taken here instead of Diane, do you think it would have helped them?"

Nicholas did not reply.

"We have treatments for disturbed persons, Nicholas. But, at least for the time being, we have no treatment for disturbing persons." Diane and the boy had turned away, and the waves' hissing and slapping ceased to be speech. Gulls wheeled overhead, and once a red-and-yellow parrot fluttered from one palm to another. A monkey running on all fours like a little dog approached them, and Nicholas chased it, but it escaped.

"I'm going to take one of those things apart someday," he said, "and pull the wires out."

"Are we going to walk all the way 'round?" Diane asked. She might have been talking to herself.

"Can you do that?"

"Oh, you can't walk all around Dr. Island; it would be too long, and you can't get there anyway. But we could walk until we get back to where we started—we're probably more than halfway now."

"Are there other islands you can't see from here?"

The girl shook her head. "I don't think so; there's just this one big island in this satellite, and all the rest is water."

"Then if there's only the one island, we're going to have to walk all around it to get back to where we started. What are you laughing at?"

"Look down the beach, as far as you can. Never mind how it slips off to the side—pretend it's straight."

"I don't see anything."

"Don't you? Watch." Diane leaped into the air, six meters or more this time, and waved her arms.

"It looks like there's somebody ahead of us, way down the beach."

"Uh-huh. Now look behind."

"Okay, there's somebody there too. Come to think of it, I saw someone on the beach when I first got here. It seemed funny to see so far, but I guess I thought they were other patients. Now I see two people."

"They're us. That was probably yourself you saw the other time, too. There are just so many of us to each strip of beach, and Dr. Island only wants certain ones to mix. So the space bends around. When we get to one end of our strip and try to step over, we'll be at the other end."

"How did you find out?"

"Dr. Island told me about it when I first came here." The girl was silent for a moment, and her smile vanished. "Listen, Nicholas, do you want to see something really funny?"

Nicholas asked, "What?" As he spoke, a drop of rain struck his face.

"You'll see. Come on, though. We have to go into the middle instead of following the beach, and it will give us a chance to get under the trees and out of the rain."

When they had left the sand and the sound of the surf, and were walking on solid ground under green-leaved trees, Nicholas said, "Maybe we can find some fruit." They were so light now that he had to be careful not to bound into the air with each step. The rain fell slowly around them, in crystal spheres.

"Maybe," the girl said doubtfully. "Wait, let's stop here." She sat down where a huge tree sent twenty-meter wooden arches over dark, mossy ground. "Want to climb up there and see if you can find us something?"

"All right," Nicholas agreed. He jumped, and easily caught hold of a branch far above the girl's head. In a moment he was climbing in a green world, with the rain pattering all around him; he followed narrowing limbs into leafy wildernesses where the cool water ran from every twig he touched, and twice found the empty nests of birds, and once a slender snake, green as any leaf with a head as long as his thumb; but there was no fruit. "Nothing," he said, when he dropped down beside the girl once more.

"That's all right, we'll find something."

He said, "I hope so," and noticed that she was looking at him oddly, then realized that his left hand had lifted itself to touch her right breast. It dropped as he looked, and he felt his face grow hot. He said, "I'm sorry."

"That's all right."

"We like you. He—over there—he can't talk, you see. I guess I can't talk either."

"I think it's just you—in two pieces. I don't care."

"Thanks." He had picked up a leaf, dead and damp, and was tearing it to shreds; first his right hand tearing while the left held the leaf, then turnabout. "Where does the rain come from?" The dirty flakes clung to the fingers of both.

"Hmm?"

"Where does the rain come from? I mean, it isn't because it's colder here now, like on Callisto; it's because the gravity's turned down some way, isn't it?"

"From the sea. Don't you know how this place is built?"

Nicholas shook his head.

"Didn't they show it to you from the ship when you came? It's beautiful. They showed it to me—I just sat there and looked at it, and I wouldn't talk to them, and the nurse thought I wasn't paying any attention, but I heard everything. I just didn't want to talk to her. It wasn't any use."

"I know how you felt."

"But they didn't show it to you?"

"No, on my ship they kept me locked up because I burned some stuff. They thought I couldn't start a fire without an igniter, but if you have electricity in the wall sockets it's easy. They had a thing on me—you know?" He clasped his arms to his body to show how he had been restrained. "I bit one of them, too—I guess I didn't tell you that yet: I bite people. They locked me up, and for a long time I had nothing to do, and then I could feel us dock with something, and they came and got me and pulled me down a regular companionway for a long time, and it just seemed like a regular place. Then they stuck me full of Tranquil-C—I guess they didn't know it doesn't hardly work on me at all—with a pneumo-gun, and lifted a kind of door thing and shoved me up."

"Didn't they make you undress?"

"I already was. When they put the ties on me I did things in my clothes and they had to take them off me. It made them mad." He grinned unevenly. "Does Tranquil-C work on you? Or any of that other stuff?"

"I suppose they would, but then I never do the sort of thing you do anyway."

"Maybe you ought to."

"Sometimes they used to give me medication that was supposed to cheer me up; then I couldn't sleep, and I walked and walked, you know, and ran into things and made a lot of trouble for everyone; but what good does it do?"

Nicholas shrugged. "Not doing it doesn't do any good either—I mean, we're both here. My way, I know I've made them jump; they shoot that stuff in me and I'm not mad anymore, but I know what it is and I just think what I would do if I *were* mad, and I do it, and when it wears off I'm glad I did."

"I think you're still angry somewhere, deep down."

Nicholas was already thinking of something else. "This island says Ignacio kills people." He paused. "What does it look like?"

"Ignacio?"

"No, I've seen him. Dr. Island."

"Oh, you mean when I was in the ship. The satellite's round of course, and all clear except where Dr. Island is, so that's a dark spot. The rest of it's temperglass, and from space you can't even see the water."

"That *is* the sea up there, isn't it?" Nicholas asked, trying to look up at it through the tree leaves and the rain. "I thought it was when I first came."

"Sure. It's like a glass ball, and we're inside, and the water's inside too, and just goes all around up the curve."

"That's why I could see so far out on the beach, isn't it? Instead of dropping down from you like on Callisto it bends up so you can see it."

The girl nodded. "And the water lets the light through, but filters out the ultraviolet. Besides, it gives us thermal mass, so we don't heat up too much when we're between the sun and the Bright Spot."

"Is that what keeps us warm? The Bright Spot?"

Diane nodded again. "We go around in ten hours, you see, and that holds us over it all the time."

"Why can't I see it, then? It ought to look like Sol does from the belt, only bigger; but there's just a shimmer in the sky, even when it's not raining."

"The waves diffract the light and break up the image. You'd see the Focus, though, if the air weren't so clear. Do you know what the Focus is?"

Nicholas shook his head.

"We'll get to it pretty soon, after this rain stops. Then I'll tell you."

"I still don't understand about the rain."

Unexpectedly Diane giggled. "I just thought—do you know what I was supposed to be? While I was going to school?"

"Quiet," Nicholas said.

"No, silly. I mean what I was being trained to do, if I graduated and all that. I was going to be a teacher, with all those cameras on me and tots from everywhere watching and popping questions on the two-way. Jolly time. Now I'm doing it here, only there's no one but you."

"You mind?"

"No, I suppose I enjoy it." There was a black-and-blue mark on Diane's thigh, and she rubbed it pensively with one hand as she spoke. "Anyway, there are three ways to make gravity. Do you know them? Answer, clerk."

"Sure; acceleration, mass, and synthesis."

"That's right; motion and mass are both bendings of space, of course, which is why Zeno's paradox doesn't work out that way, and why masses move toward each other—what we call falling—or at least try to; and if they're held apart it produces the tension we perceive as a force and call weight and all that rot. So naturally if you bend the space direct, you synthesize a gravity effect, and that's what holds all that water up against the translucent shell—there's nothing like enough mass to do it by itself."

"You mean"—Nicholas held out his hand to catch a slow-moving globe of rain—"that this is water from the sea?"

"Right-o, up on top. Do you see, the temperature differences in the air make the winds, and the winds make the waves and surf you saw when we were walking along the shore. When the waves break they throw up these little drops, and if you watch you'll see that even when it's clear they go up a long way sometimes. Then if the gravity is less they can get away altogether, and if we were on the outside they'd fly off into space; but we aren't, we're inside, so all they can do is go across the center, more or less, until they hit the water again, or Dr. Island."

"Dr. Island said they had storms sometimes, when people got mad."

"Yes. Lots of wind, and so there's lots of rain too. Only the rain then is because the wind tears the tops off the waves, and you don't get light like you do in a normal rain."

"What makes so much wind?"

"I don't know. It happens somehow."

They sat in silence, Nicholas listening to the dripping of the leaves. He remembered then that they had spun the hospital module, finally, to get the little spheres of clotting blood out of the air; Maya's blood was building up on the grills of the purification intake ducts, spotting them black, and someone had been afraid they would decay there and smell. He had not been there when they did it, but he could imagine the droplets settling, like this, in the slow spin. The old psychodrama group had already been broken up, and when he saw Maureen or any of the others in the rec room they talked about Good Old Days. It had not seemed like Good Old Days then except that Maya had been there.

Diane said, "It's going to stop."

"It looks just as bad to me."

"No, it's going to stop—see, they're falling a little faster now, and I feel heavier."

Nicholas stood up. "You rested enough yet? You want to go on?"

"We'll get wet."

He shrugged.

"I don't want to get my hair wet, Nicholas. It'll be over in a minute."

He sat down again. "How long have you been here?"

"I'm not sure."

"Don't you count the days?"

"I lose track a lot."

"Longer than a week?"

"Nicholas, don't ask me, all right?"

"Isn't there anybody on this piece of Dr. Island except you and me and Ignacio?"

"I don't think there was anyone but Ignacio before you came."

"Who is he?"

She looked at him.

"Well, who is he? You know me—us—Nicholas Kenneth de Vore; and you're Diane who?"

"Phillips."

"And you're from the Trojan Planets, and I was from the Outer Belt, I guess, to start with. What about Ignacio? You talk to him sometimes, don't you? Who is he?"

"I don't know. He's important."

For an instant, Nicholas froze. "What does that mean?"

"Important." The girl was feeling her knees, running her hands back and forth across them.

"Maybe everybody's important."

"I know you're just a tot, Nicholas, but don't be so stupid. Come on, you wanted to go, let's go now. It's pretty well stopped." She stood, stretching her thin body, her arms over her head. "My knees are rough—you made me think of that. When I came here they were still so smooth, I think. I used to put a certain lotion on them. Because my Dad would feel them, and my hands and elbows too, and he'd say if they weren't smooth nobody'd ever want me; Mum wouldn't say anything, but she'd be cross after, and they used to come and visit, and so I kept a bottle in my room and I used to put it on. Once I drank some."

Nicholas was silent.

"Aren't you going to ask me if I died?" She stepped ahead of him, pulling aside the dripping branches. "See here, I'm sorry I said you were stupid."

"I'm just thinking," Nicholas said. "I'm not mad at you. Do you really know anything about him?"

"No, but look at it." She gestured. "Look around you; someone *built* all this."

"You mean it cost a lot."

"It's automated, of course, but still . . . well, the other places where you were before—how much space was there for each patient? Take the total volume and divide it by the number of people there."

"Okay, this is a whole lot bigger, but maybe they think we're worth it."

"Nicholas . . ." She paused. "Nicholas, Ignacio is homicidal. Didn't Dr. Island tell you?"

"Yes."

"And you're fourteen and not very big for it, and I'm a girl. Who are they worried about?"

The look on Nicholas's face startled her.

AFTER AN HOUR or more of walking they came to it. It was a band of withered vegetation, brown and black and tumbling, and as straight as if it had been drawn with a ruler. "I was afraid it wasn't going to be here," Diane said. "It moves around whenever there's a storm. It might not have been in our sector anymore at all."

Nicholas asked, "What is it?"

"The Focus. It's been all over, but mostly the plants grow back quickly when it's gone."

"It smells funny—like the kitchen in a place where they wanted me to work in the kitchen once."

"Vegetables rotting, that's what that is. What did you do?"

"Nothing—put detergent in the stuff they were cooking. What makes this?"

"The Bright Spot. See, when it's just about overhead the curve of the sky and the water up there make a lens. It isn't a very good lens—a lot of the light scatters. But enough is focused to do this. It wouldn't fry us if it came past right now, if that's what you're wondering, because it's not that hot. I've stood right in it, but you want to get out in a minute."

"I thought it was going to be about seeing ourselves down the beach."

Diane seated herself on the trunk of a fallen tree. "It was, really. The last time I was here it was farther from the water, and I suppose it had been there a long time, because it had cleared out a lot of the dead stuff. The sides of the sector are nearer here, you see; the whole sector narrows down like a piece of pie. So you could look down the Focus either way and see yourself nearer than you could on the beach. It was almost as if you were in a big, big room, with a looking-glass on each wall, or as if you could stand behind yourself. I thought you might like it."

"I'm going to try it here," Nicholas announced, and he clambered up one of the dead trees while the girl waited below, but the dry limbs creaked and snapped beneath his feet, and he could not get high enough to see himself in either direction. When he dropped to the ground beside her again, he said, "There's nothing to eat here either, is there?"

"I haven't found anything."

"They—I mean, Dr. Island wouldn't just let us starve, would he?"

"I don't think he could do anything; that's the way this place is built. Sometimes you find things, and I've tried to catch fish, but I never could. A couple of times Ignacio gave me part of what he had, though; he's good at it. I bet you think I'm skinny, don't you? But I was a lot fatter when I came here."

"What are we going to do now?"

"Keep walking, I suppose, Nicholas. Maybe go back to the water."

"Do you think we'll find anything?"

From a decaying log, insect stridulations called, "Wait."

Nicholas asked, "Do *you* know where anything is?"

"Something for you to eat? Not at present. But I can show you something much more interesting, not far from here, than this clutter of dying trees. Would you like to see it?"

Diane said, "Don't go, Nicholas."

"What is it?"

"Diane, who calls this 'the Focus,' calls what I wish to show you 'the Point.' "

Nicholas asked Diane, "Why shouldn't I go?"

"I'm not going. I went there once anyway."

"I took her," Dr. Island said. "And I'll take you. I wouldn't take you if I didn't think it might help you."

"I don't think Diane liked it."

"Diane may not wish to be helped—help may be painful, and often people do not. But it is my business to help them if I can, whether or not they wish it."

"Suppose I don't want to go?"

"Then I cannot compel you; you know that. But you will be the only patient in this sector who has not seen it, Nicholas, as well as the youngest; both Diane and Ignacio have, and Ignacio goes there often."

"Is it dangerous?"

"No. Are you afraid?"

Nicholas looked questioningly at Diane. "What is it? What will I see?"

She had walked away while he was talking to Dr. Island, and was now sitting cross-legged on the ground about five meters from where Nicholas stood, staring at her hands. Nicholas repeated, "What will I see, Diane?" He did not think she would answer.

She said, "A glass. A mirror."

"Just a mirror?"

"You know how I told you to climb the tree here? The Point is where the edges come together. You can see yourself—like on the beach—but closer."

Nicholas was disappointed. "I've seen myself in mirrors lots of times."

Dr. Island, whose voice was now in the sighing of the dead leaves, whispered, "Did you have a mirror in your room, Nicholas, before you came here?"

"A steel one."

"So that you could not break it?"

"I guess so. I threw things at it sometimes, but it just got puckers in it." Remembering dimpled reflections, Nicholas laughed.

"You can't break this one either."

"It doesn't sound like it's worth going to see."

"I think it is."

"Diane, do you still think I shouldn't go?"

There was no reply. The girl sat staring at the ground in front of her.

Nicholas walked over to look at her and found a tear had washed a damp trail down each thin cheek, but she did not move when he touched her. "She's catatonic, isn't she," he said.

A green limb just outside the Focus nodded. "Catatonic schizophrenia."

"I had a doctor once that said those names—like that. They didn't mean anything." (The doctor had been a therapy robot, but a human doctor gave more status. Robots' patients sat in doorless booths—two and a half hours a day for Nicholas: an hour and a half in the morning, an hour in the afternoon—and talked to something that appeared to be a small, friendly food freezer. Some people sat every day in silence, while others talked continually, and for such patients as these the attendants seldom troubled to turn the machines on.)

"He meant cause and treatment. He was correct."

Nicholas stood looking down at the girl's streaked, brown-blond head. "What is the cause? I mean for her."

"I don't know."

"And what's the treatment?"

"You are seeing it."

"Will it help her?"

"Probably not."

"Listen, she can hear you, don't you know that? She hears everything we say."

"If my answer disturbs you, Nicholas, I can change it. It will help her if she wants to be helped; if she insists on clasping her illness to her it will not."

"We ought to go away from here," Nicholas said uneasily.

"To your left you will see a little path, a very faint one. Between the twisted tree and the bush with the yellow flowers."

Nicholas nodded and began to walk, looking back at Diane several times. The flowers were butterflies, who fled in a cloud of color when he approached them, and he wondered if Dr. Island had known. When he had gone a hundred paces and was well away from the brown and rotting vegetation, he said, "She was sitting in the Focus."

"Yes."

"Is she still there?"

"Yes."

"What will happen when the Bright Spot comes?"

"Diane will become uncomfortable and move, if she is still there."

"Once in one of the places I was in there was a man who was like that, and they said he wouldn't get anything to eat if he didn't get up and get it, they weren't going to feed him with the nose tube anymore; and they didn't, and he died. We told them about it and they wouldn't do anything and he starved to death right there, and when he was dead they rolled him off onto a stretcher and changed the bed and put somebody else there."

"I know, Nicholas. You told the doctors at St. John's about all that, and it is in your file; but think: well men have starved themselves—yes, to death—to protest what they felt were political injustices. Is it so surprising that your friend killed himself in the same way to protest what he felt as a psychic injustice?"

"He wasn't my friend. Listen, did you really mean it when you said the treatment she was getting here would help Diane if she wanted to be helped?"

"No."

Nicholas halted in mid-stride. "You didn't mean it? You don't think it's true?"

"No, I doubt that anything will help her."

"I don't think you ought to lie to us."

"Why not? If by chance you become well you will be released, and if you are released you will have to deal with your society, which will lie to you frequently. Here, where there are so few individuals, I must take the place of society. I have explained that."

"Is that what you are?"

"Society's surrogate? Of course. Who do you imagine built me? What else could I be?"

"The doctor."

"You have had many doctors, and so has she. Not one of them has benefited you much."

"I'm not sure you even want to help us."

"Do you wish to see what Diane calls 'the Point'?"

"I guess so."

"Then you must walk. You will not see it standing here."

Nicholas walked, thrusting aside leafy branches and dangling creepers wet with rain. The jungle smelled of the life of green things; there were ants on the tree trunks, and dragonflies with hot, red bodies and wings as long as his hands. "Do you want to help us?" he asked after a time.

"My feelings toward you are ambivalent. But when you wish to be helped, I wish to help you."

The ground sloped gently upward, and as it rose became somewhat more clear, the big trees a trifle farther apart, the underbrush spent in grass and fern. Occasionally there were stone outcrops to be climbed, and clearings open to the tumbling sky. Nicholas asked, "Who made this trail?"

"Ignacio. He comes here often."

"He's not afraid, then? Diane's afraid."

"Ignacio is afraid too, but he comes."

"Diane says Ignacio is important."

"Yes."

"What do you mean by that? Is he important? More important than we are?"

"Do you remember that I told you I was the surrogate of society? What do you think society wants, Nicholas?"

"Everybody to do what it says."

"You mean conformity. Yes, there must be conformity, but something else too—consciousness."

"I don't want to hear about it."

"Without consciousness, which you may call sensitivity if you are careful not to allow yourself to be confused by the term, there is no progress. A century ago, Nicholas, mankind was suffocating on Earth; now it is suffocating again. About half of the people who have contributed substantially to the advance of humanity have shown signs of emotional disturbance."

"I told you, I don't want to hear about it. I asked you an easy question— is Ignacio more important than Diane and me—and you won't tell me. I've heard all this you're saying. I've heard it fifty, maybe a hundred times from everybody, and it's lies; it's the regular thing, and you've got it written down on a card somewhere to read out when anybody asks. Those people you talk about that went crazy, they went crazy because while they were 'advancing humanity,' or whatever you call it, people kicked them out of their rooms because they couldn't pay, and while they were getting thrown out you were making other people rich that had never done anything in their whole lives except think about how to get that way."

"Sometimes it is hard, Nicholas, to determine before the fact—or even at the time—just who should be honored."

"How do you know if you've never tried?"

"You asked if Ignacio was more important than Diane or yourself. I can only say that Ignacio seems to me to hold a brighter promise of a full recovery coupled with a substantial contribution to human progress."

"If he's so good, why did he crack up?"

"Many do, Nicholas. Even among the inner planets space is not a kind environment for mankind; and our space, trans-Martian space, is worse. Any young person here, anyone like yourself or Diane who would seem to have a better-than-average chance of adapting to the conditions we face, is precious."

"Or Ignacio."

"Yes, or Ignacio. Ignacio has a tested IQ of two hundred and ten, Nicholas. Diane's is one hundred and twenty. Your own is ninety-five."

"They never took mine."

"It's on your records, Nicholas."

"They tried to and I threw down the helmet and it broke; Sister Carmela—she was the nurse—just wrote down something on the paper and sent me back."

"I see. I will ask for a complete investigation of this, Nicholas."

"Sure."

"Don't you believe me?"

"I don't think you believed me."

"Nicholas, Nicholas . . ." The long tongues of grass now beginning to appear beneath the immense trees sighed. "Can't you see that a certain measure of trust between the two of us is essential?"

"Did you believe me?"

"Why do you ask? Suppose I were to say I did; would you believe that?"

"When you told me I had been reclassified."

"You would have to be retested, for which there are no facilities here."

"If you believed me, why did you say retested? I told you I haven't ever been tested at all—but anyway you could cross out the ninety-five."

"It is impossible for me to plan your therapy without some estimate of your intelligence, Nicholas, and I have nothing with which to replace it."

THE GROUND WAS sloping up more sharply now, and in a clearing the boy halted and turned to look back at the leafy film, like algae over a pool, beneath which he had climbed, and at the sea beyond. To his right and left his view was still hemmed with foliage, and ahead of him a meadow on edge (like the square of sand through which he had come, though he did not think of that), dotted still with trees, stretched steeply toward an invisible summit. It seemed to him that under his feet the mountainside swayed ever so slightly. Abruptly he demanded of the wind, "Where's Ignacio?"

"Not here. Much closer to the beach."

"And Diane?"

"Where you left her. Do you enjoy the panorama?"

"It's pretty, but it feels like we're rocking."

"We are. I am moored to the temperglass exterior of our satellite by two hundred cables, but the tide and the currents none the less impart a slight motion to my body. Naturally this movement is magnified as you go higher."

"I thought you were fastened right onto the hull; if there's water under you, how do people get in and out?"

"I am linked to the main air lock by a communication tube. To you when you came, it probably seemed an ordinary companionway."

Nicholas nodded and turned his back on leaves and sea and began to climb again.

"You are in a beautiful spot, Nicholas; do you open your heart to beauty?" After waiting for an answer that did not come, the wind sang:

"The mountain wooded to the peak, the lawns
And winding glades high up like ways to Heaven,
The slender coco's drooping crown of plumes,
The lightning flash of insect and of bird,
The lustre of the long convolvuluses
That coil'd around the stately stems, and ran
Ev'n to the limit of the land, the glows
And glories of the broad belt of the world,
All these he saw."

"Does this mean nothing to you, Nicholas?"

"You read a lot, don't you?"

"Often, when it is dark, everyone else is asleep and there is very little else for me to do."

"You talk like a woman; are you a woman?"

"How could I be a woman?"

"You know what I mean. Except, when you were talking mostly to Diane, you sounded more like a man."

"You haven't yet said you think me beautiful."

"You're an Easter egg."

"What do you mean by that, Nicholas?"

"Never mind." He saw the egg as it had hung in the air before him, shining with gold and covered with flowers.

"Eggs are dyed with pretty colors for Easter, and my colors are beautiful—is that what you mean, Nicholas?"

His mother had brought the egg on visiting day, but she could never have made it. Nicholas knew who must have made it. The gold was that very pure gold used for shielding delicate instruments; the clear flakes of crystallized carbon that dotted the egg's surface with tiny stars could only have come from a laboratory high-pressure furnace. How angry he must have been when she told him she was going to give it to him.

"It's pretty, isn't it, Nicky?"

It hung in the weightlessness between them, turning very slowly with the memory of her scented gloves.

"The flowers are meadowsweet, fraxinella, lily of the valley, and moss rose—though I wouldn't expect you to recognize them, darling." His mother had never been below the orbit of Mars, but she pretended to have spent her girlhood on Earth; each reference to the lie filled Nicholas with inexpressible fury and shame. The egg was about twenty centimeters long and it revolved, end over end, in some small fraction more than eight of the pulse beats he felt in his cheeks. Visiting time had twenty-three minutes to go.

"Aren't you going to look at it?"

"I can see it from here." He tried to make her understand. "I can see every pan of it. The little red things are aluminum oxide crystals, right?"

"I mean, look *inside,* Nicky."

He saw then that there was a lens at one end, disguised as a dewdrop in the throat of an asphodel. Gently he took the egg in his hands, closed one eye, and looked. The light of the interior was not, as he had half expected, gold tinted, but brilliantly white, deriving from some concealed source. A world surely meant for Earth shone within, as though seen from below the orbit of the moon—indigo sea and emerald land. Rivers brown and clear as tea ran down long plains.

His mother said, "Isn't it pretty?"

Night hung at the corners in funereal purple, and sent long shadows like cold and lovely arms to caress the day; and while he watched and it fell, long-necked birds of so dark a pink that they were nearly red trailed stilt legs across the sky, their wings making crosses.

"They are called flamingos," Dr. Island said, following the direction of his eyes. "Isn't it a pretty word? For a pretty bird, but I don't think we'd like them as much if we called them sparrows, would we?"

His mother said, "I'm going to take it home and keep it for you. It's too nice to leave with a little boy, but if you ever come home again it will be waiting for you. On your dresser, beside your hairbrushes."

Nicholas said, "Words just mix you up."

"You shouldn't despise them, Nicholas. Besides having great beauty of their own, they are useful in reducing tension. You might benefit from that."

"You mean you talk yourself out of it."

"I mean that a person's ability to verbalize his feelings, if only to himself, may prevent them from destroying him. Evolution teaches us, Nicholas, that the original purpose of language was to ritualize men's threats and curses, his spells to compel the gods; communication came later. Words can be a safety valve."

Nicholas said, "I want to be a bomb; a bomb doesn't need a safety valve." To his mother, "Is that South America, Mama?"

"No, dear, India. The Malabar Coast on your left, the Coromandel Coast on your right, and Ceylon below." Words.

"A bomb destroys itself, Nicholas."

"A bomb doesn't care."

He was climbing resolutely now, his toes grabbing at tree roots and the soft, mossy soil; his physician was no longer the wind but a small brown monkey that followed a stone's throw behind him. "I hear someone coming," he said.

"Yes."

"Is it Ignacio?"

"No, it is Nicholas. You are close now."

"Close to the Point?"

"Yes."

He stopped and looked around him. The sounds he had heard, the naked feet padding on soft ground, stopped as well. Nothing seemed strange; the land still rose, and there were large trees, widely spaced, with moss growing in their deepest shade, grass where there was more light. "The three big trees," Nicholas said, "they're just alike. Is that how you know where we are?"

"Yes."

In his mind he called the one before him "Ceylon"; the others were "Coromandel" and "Malabar." He walked toward Ceylon, studying its massive, twisted limbs; a boy naked as himself walked out of the forest to his left, toward Malabar—this boy was not looking at Nicholas, who shouted and ran toward him.

The boy disappeared. Only Malabar, solid and real, stood before Nicholas; he ran to it, touched its rough bark with his hand, and then saw beyond it a fourth tree, similar too to the Ceylon tree, around which a boy peered with averted head. Nicholas watched him for a moment, then said, "I see."

"Do you?" the monkey chattered.

"It's like a mirror, only backwards. The light from the front of me goes out and hits the edge, and comes in the other side, only I can't see it because I'm not looking that way. What I see is the light from my back, sort of, because it comes back this way. When I ran, did I get turned around?"

"Yes, you ran out the left side of the segment, and of course returned immediately from the right."

"I'm not scared. It's kind of fun." He picked up a stick and threw it as hard as he could toward the Malabar tree. It vanished, whizzed over his head, vanished again, slapped the back of his legs. "Did this scare Diane?"

There was no answer. He strode farther, palely naked boys walking to his left and right, but always looking away from him, gradually coming closer.

"DON'T GO FARTHER," Dr. Island said behind him. "It can be dangerous if you try to pass through the Point itself."

"I see it," Nicholas said. He saw three more trees, growing very close together, just ahead of him; their branches seemed strangely intertwined as they danced together in the wind, and beyond them there was nothing at all.

"You can't actually go through the Point," Dr. Island Monkey said. "The tree covers it."

"Then why did you warn me about it?" Limping and scarred, the boys to his right and left were no more than two meters away now; he had discovered that if he looked straight ahead he could sometimes glimpse their bruised profiles.

"That's far enough, Nicholas."

"I want to touch the tree."

He took another step, and another, then turned. The Malabar boy turned too, presenting his narrow back, on which the ribs and spine seemed welts. Nicholas reached out both arms and laid his hands on the thin shoulders, and as he did, felt other hands—the cool, unfeeling hands of a stranger, dry hands too small—touch his own shoulders and creep upward toward his neck.

"Nicholas!"

He jumped sidewise away from the tree and looked at his hands, his head swaying. "It wasn't me."

"Yes, it was, Nicholas," the monkey said.

"It was one of them."

"You are all of them."

In one quick motion Nicholas snatched up an arm-long section of fallen limb and hurled it at the monkey. It struck the little creature, knocking it down, but the monkey sprang up and fled on three legs. Nicholas sprinted after it.

He had nearly caught it when it darted to one side; as quickly, he turned toward the other, springing for the monkey he saw running toward him there. In an instant it was in his grip, feebly trying to bite. He slammed its head against the ground, then catching it by the ankles swung it against the Ceylon tree until at the third impact he heard the skull crack, and stopped.

He had expected wires, but there were none. Blood oozed from the battered little face, and the furry body was warm and limp in his hands. Leaves above his head said, "You haven't killed me, Nicholas. You never will."

"How does it work?" He was still searching for wires, tiny circuit cards holding micro-logic. He looked about for a sharp stone with which to open the monkey's body, but could find none.

"It is just a monkey," the leaves said. "If you had asked, I would have told you."

"How did you make him talk?" He dropped the monkey, stared at it for a moment, then kicked it. His fingers were bloody, and he wiped them on the leaves of the tree.

"Only my mind speaks to yours, Nicholas."

"Oh," he said. And then, "I've heard of that. I didn't think it would be like this. I thought it would be in my head."

"Your record shows no auditory hallucinations, but haven't you ever known someone who had them?"

"I knew a girl once . . ." He paused.

"Yes?"

"She twisted noises—you know?"

"Yes."

"Like, it would just be a service cart out in the corridor, but she'd hear the fan, and think . . ."

"What?"

"Oh, different things. That it was somebody talking, calling her."

"Hear them?"

"What?" He sat up in his bunk. "Maya?"

"They're coming after me."

"Maya?"

Dr. Island, through the leaves, said, "When I talk to you, Nicholas, your mind makes any sound you hear the vehicle for my thoughts' content. You may hear me softly in the patter of rain, or joyfully in the singing of a bird— but if I wished I could amplify what I say until every idea and suggestion I wished to give would be driven like a nail into your consciousness. Then you would do whatever I wished you to."

"I don't believe it," Nicholas said. "If you can do that, why don't you tell Diane not to be catatonic?"

"First, because she might retreat more deeply into her disease in an effort to escape me; and second, because ending her catatonia in that way would not remove its cause."

"And thirdly?"

"I did not say 'thirdly,' Nicholas."

"I thought I heard it—when two leaves touched."

"Thirdly, Nicholas, because both you and she have been chosen for your effect on someone else; if I were to change her—or you—so abruptly, that effect would be lost." Dr. Island was a monkey again now, a new monkey that chattered from the protection of a tree twenty meters away. Nicholas threw a stick at him.

"The monkeys are only little animals, Nicholas; they like to follow people, and they chatter."

"I bet Ingacio kills them."

"No, he likes them; he only kills fish to eat."

Nicholas was suddenly aware of his hunger. He began to walk.

HE FOUND IGNACIO on the beach, praying. For an hour or more, Nicholas hid behind the trunk of a palm watching him, but for a long time he could not decide to whom Ignacio prayed. He was kneeling just where the lacy edges of the breakers died, looking out toward the water; and from time to time he bowed, touching his forehead to the damp sand; then Nicholas could hear his voice, faintly, over the crashing and hissing of the waves. In general, Nicholas approved of prayer, having observed that those who prayed were usually more interesting companions than those who did not; but he had also noticed that though it made no difference what name the devotee gave the object of his devotions, it was important to discover how the god was conceived. Ignacio did not seem to be praying to Dr. Island— he would, Nicholas thought, have been facing the other way for that—and for a time he wondered if he were not praying to the waves. From his position behind him he followed Ignacio's line of vision out and out, wave upon wave into the bright, confused sky, up and up until at last it curved completely around and came to rest on Ignacio's back again; and then it occurred to him that Ignacio might be praying to himself. He left the palm trunk then and walked about halfway to the place where Ignacio knelt, and sat down. Above the sounds of the sea and the murmuring of Ignacio's voice hung a silence so immense and fragile that it seemed that at any moment the entire crystal satellite might ring like a gong.

After a time Nicholas felt his left side trembling. With his right hand he began to stroke it, running his fingers down his left arm, and from his left shoulder to the thigh. It worried him that his left side should be so frightened, and he wondered if perhaps that other half of his brain, from which he was forever severed, could hear what Ignacio was saying to the waves. He began to pray himself, so that the other (and perhaps Ignacio too) could hear, saying not quite beneath his breath, "Don't worry, don't be afraid, he's not going to hurt us, he's nice, and if he does we'll get him; we're only going to get something to eat, maybe he'll show us how to catch fish, I think he'll be nice this time." But he knew, or at least felt he knew, that Ignacio would not be nice this time.

Eventually Ingacio stood up; he did not turn to face Nicholas, but waded out to sea; then, as though he had known Nicholas was behind him all the time (though Nicholas was not sure he had been heard—perhaps, so he thought, Dr. Island had told Ignacio), he gestured to indicate that Nicholas should follow him.

The water was colder than he remembered, the sand coarse and gritty between his toes. He thought of what Dr. Island had told him—about floating—and that a part of her must be this sand, under the water, reaching out (how far?) into the sea; when she ended there would be nothing but the clear temperglass of the satellite itself, far down.

"Come," Ignacio said. "Can you swim?" Just as though he had forgotten the night before. Nicholas said yes, he could, wondering if Ignacio would look around at him when he spoke. He did not.

"And do you know why you are here?"

"You told me to come."

"Ignacio means *here*. Does this not remind you of any place you have seen before, little one?"

Nicholas thought of the crystal gong and the Easter egg, then of the micro-thin globes of perfumed vapor that, at home, were sometimes sent floating down the corridors at Christmas to explode in clean dust and a cold smell of pine forests when the children stuck them with their hoppingcanes; but he said nothing.

Ignacio continued, "Let Ignacio tell you a story. Once there was a man— a boy, actually—on the Earth, who—"

Nicholas wondered why it was always men (most often doctors and clinical psychologists, in his experience) who wanted to tell you stories. Jesus, he recalled, was always telling everyone stories, and the Virgin Mary almost never, though a woman he had once known who thought she was the Virgin Mary had always been talking about her son. He thought Ignacio looked a little like Jesus. He tried to remember if his mother had ever told him stories when he was at home, and decided that she had not; she just turned on the comscreen to the cartoons.

"—wanted to—"

"—tell a story," Nicholas finished for him.

"How did you know?" Angry and surprised.

"It was you, wasn't it? And you want to tell one now."

"What you said was not what Ignacio would have said. He was going to tell you about a fish."

"Where is it?" Nicholas asked, thinking of the fish Ignacio had been eating the night before, and imagining another such fish, caught while he had been coming back, perhaps, from the Point, and now concealed somewhere waiting the fire. "Is it a big one?"

"It is gone now," Ignacio said, "but it was only as long as a man's hand. I caught it in the big river."

Huckleberry—"I know, the Mississippi; it was a catfish. Or a sun-fish." —*Finn*.

"Possibly that is what you call them; for a time he was as the sun to a certain one." The light from nowhere danced on the water. "In any event he was kept on that table in the salon in the house where life was lived. In a tank, but not the old kind in which one sees the glass, with metal at the corner. But the new kind in which the glass is so strong, but very thin, and curved so that it does not reflect, and there are no corners, and a clever device holds the water clear." He dipped up a handful of sparkling water, still not meeting

Nicholas's eyes. "As clear even as this, and there were no ripples, and so you could not see it at all. My fish floated in the center of my table above a few stones."

Nicholas asked, "Did you float on the river on a raft?"

"No, we had a little boat. Ignacio caught this fish in a net, of which he almost bit through the strands before he could be landed; he possessed wonderful teeth. There was no one in the house but him and the other, and the robots; but each morning someone would go to the pool in the patio and catch a goldfish for him. Ignacio would see this goldfish there when he came down for his breakfast, and would think, 'Brave goldfish, you have been cast to the monster, will you be the one to destroy him? Destroy him and you shall have his diamond house forever.' And then the fish, who had a little spot of red beneath his wonderful teeth, a spot like a cherry, would rush upon that young goldfish, and for an instant the water would be all clouded with blood."

"And then what?" Nicholas asked.

"And then the clever machine would make the water clear once more, and the fish would be floating above the stones as before, the fish with the wonderful teeth, and Ignacio would touch the little switch on the table, and ask for more bread, and more fruit."

"Are you hungry now?"

"No, I am tired and lazy now; if I pursue you I will not catch you, and if I catch you—through your own slowness and clumsiness—I will not kill you, and if I kill you I will not eat you."

Nicholas had begun to back away, and at the last words, realizing that they were a signal, he turned and began to run, splashing through the shallow water. Ignacio ran after him, much helped by his longer legs, his hair flying behind his dark young face, his square teeth—each white as a bone and as big as Nicholas's thumbnail—showing like spectators who lined the railings of his lips.

"Don't run, Nicholas," Dr. Island said with the voice of a wave. "It only makes him angry that you run." Nicholas did not answer, but cut to his left, up the beach and among the trunks of the palms, sprinting all the way because he had no way of knowing Ignacio was not right behind him, about to grab him by the neck. When he stopped it was in the thick jungle, among the boles of the hardwoods, where he leaned, out of breath, the thumping of his own heart the only sound in an atmosphere silent and unwaked as Earth's long, prehuman day. For a time he listened for any sound Ignacio might make searching for him: there was none. He drew a deep breath then and said, "Well, that's over," expecting Dr. Island to answer from somewhere; there was only the green hush.

The light was still bright and strong and nearly shadowless, but some interior sense told him the day was nearly over, and he noticed that such faint shades as he could see stretched long, horizontal distortions of their objects. He felt no hunger, but he had fasted before and knew on which side of hunger he stood; he was not as strong as he had been only a day past, and by this time next day he would probably be unable to outrun Ignacio. He should, he now realized, have eaten the monkey he had killed; but his stomach revolted at the thought of the raw flesh, and he did not know how he might build a fire, although Ignacio seemed to have done so the night before. Raw fish, even if he were able to catch a fish, would be as bad, or worse, than raw monkey; he remembered his effort to open a coconut—he had failed, but it was surely not impossible. His mind was hazy as to what a coconut might contain, but there had to be an edible core, because they were eaten in books. He decided to make a wide sweep through the jungle that would bring him back to the beach well away from Ignacio; he had several times seen coconuts lying in the sand under the trees.

He moved quietly, still a little afraid, trying to think of ways to open the coconut when he found it. He imagined himself standing before a large and raggedly faceted stone, holding the coconut in both hands. He raised it and smashed it down, but when it struck it was no longer a coconut but Maya's head; he heard her nose cartilage break with a distinct, rubbery snap. Her eyes, as blue as the sky above Madhya Pradesh, the sparkling blue sky of the egg, looked up at him, but he could no longer look into them, they retreated from his own, and it came to him quite suddenly that Lucifer, in falling, must have fallen up, into the fires and the coldness of space, never again to see the warm blues and browns and greens of Earth: *I was watching Satan fall as lightning from heaven.* He had heard that on tape somewhere, but he could not remember where. He had read that on Earth lightning did not come down from the clouds, but leaped up from the planetary surface toward them, never to return.

"Nicholas."

He listened, but did not hear his name again. Faintly water was babbling; had Dr. Island used that sound to speak to him? He walked toward it and found a little rill that threaded a way among the trees, and followed it. In a hundred steps it grew broader, slowed, and ended in a long blind pool under a dome of leaves. Diane was sitting on moss on the side opposite him; she looked up as she saw him, and smiled.

"Hello," he said.

"Hello, Nicholas. I thought I heard you. I wasn't mistaken after all, was I?"

"I didn't think I said anything." He tested the dark water with his foot and found that it was very cold.

"You gave a little gasp, I fancy. I heard it, and I said to myself, *that's Nicholas,* and I called you. Then I thought I might be wrong, or that it might be Ignacio."

"Ignacio was chasing me. Maybe he still is, but I think he's probably given up by now."

The girl nodded, looking into the dark waters of the pool, but did not seem to have heard him. He began to work his way around to her, climbing across the snakelike roots of the crowding trees. "Why does Ignacio want to kill me, Diane?"

"Sometimes he wants to kill me too," the girl said.

"But why?"

"I think he's a bit frightened of us. Have you ever talked to him, Nicholas?"

"Today I did a little. He told me a story about a pet fish he used to have."

"Ignacio grew up all alone; did he tell you that? On Earth. On a plantation in Brazil, way up the Amazon—Dr. Island told me."

"I thought it was crowded on Earth."

"The cities are crowded, and the countryside closest to the cities. But there are places where it's emptier than it used to be. Where Ignacio was, there would have been Red Indian hunters two or three hundred years ago; when he was there, there wasn't anyone, just the machines. Now he doesn't want to be looked at, doesn't want anyone around him."

Nicholas said slowly, "Dr. Island said lots of people wouldn't be sick if only there weren't other people around all the time. Remember that?"

"Only there are other people around all the time; that's how the world is."

"Not in Brazil, maybe," Nicholas said. He was trying to remember something about Brazil, but the only thing he could think of was a parrot singing in a straw hat from the comview cartoons; and then a turtle and a hedgehog that turned into armadillos for the love of God, Montressor. He said, "Why didn't he stay here?"

"Did I tell you about the bird, Nicholas?" She had been not-listening again.

"What bird?"

"I have a bird. Inside." She patted the flat stomach below her small breasts, and for a moment Nicholas thought she had really found food. "She sits in here. She has tangled a nest in my entrails, where she sits and tears at my breath with her beak. I look healthy to you, don't I? But inside I'm hollow and rotten and turning brown, dirt and old feathers, oozing away. Her beak will break through soon."

"Okay." Nicholas turned to go.

"I've been drinking water here, trying to drown her. I think I've swallowed so much I couldn't stand up now if I tried, but she isn't even wet, and do you know something, Nicholas? I've found out I'm not really me, I'm her."

Turning back Nicholas asked, "When was the last time you had anything to eat?"

"I don't know. Two, three days ago. Ignacio gave me something."

"I'm going to try to open a coconut. If I can I'll bring you back some."

WHEN HE REACHED the beach, Nicholas turned and walked slowly back in the direction of the dead fire, this time along the rim of dampened sand between the sea and the palms. He was thinking about machines.

There were hundreds of thousands, perhaps millions, of machines out beyond the belt, but few or none of the sophisticated servant robots of Earth—those were luxuries. Would Ignacio, in Brazil (whatever that was like), have had such luxuries? Nicholas thought not; those robots were almost like people, and living with them would be like living with people. Nicholas wished that he could speak Brazilian.

There had been the therapy robots at St. John's; Nicholas had not liked them, and he did not think Ignacio would have liked them either. If he had liked his therapy robot he probably would not have had to be sent here. He thought of the chipped and rusted old machine that had cleaned the corridors—Maya had called it Corradora, but no one else ever called it anything but *Hey!* It could not (or at least did not) speak, and Nicholas doubted that it had emotions, except possibly a sort of love of cleanness that did not extend to its own person. "You will understand," someone was saying inside his head, "that motives of all sorts can be divided into two sorts." A doctor? A therapy robot? It did not matter. "Extrinsic and intrinsic. An extrinsic motive has always some further end in view, and that end we call an intrinsic motive. Thus when we have reduced motivation to intrinsic motivation we have reduced it to its simplest parts. Take that machine over there."

What machine?

"Freud would have said that it was fixated at the latter anal stage, perhaps due to the care its builders exercised in seeing that the dirt it collects is not released again. Because of its fixation it is, as you see, obsessed with cleanliness and order; compulsive sweeping and scrubbing palliate its anxieties. It is a strength of Freud's theory, and not a weakness, that it serves to explain many of the activities of machines as well as the acts of persons."

Hello there, Corradora.

And hello, Ignacio.

My head, moving from side to side, must remind you of a radar scanner. My steps are measured, slow, and precise. I emit a scarcely audible humming as I walk, and my eyes are fixed, as I swing my head, not on you, Ignacio, but on the waves at the edge of sight, where they curve up into the sky. I stop ten meters short of you, and I stand.

You go, I follow, ten meters behind. What do I want? Nothing.

Yes, I will pick up the sticks, and I will follow—five meters behind.

"Break them, and put them on the fire. Not all of them, just a few."

Yes.

"Ignacio keeps the fire here burning all the time. Sometimes he takes the coals of fire from it to start others, but here, under the big palm log, he has a fire always. The rain does not strike it here. Always the fire. Do you know how he made it the first time? Reply to him!"

"No."

"No, *Patrão!*"

" 'No, *Patrão.*' "

"Ignacio stole it from the gods, from Poseidon. Now Poseidon is dead, lying at the bottom of the water. Which is the top. Would you like to see him?"

"If you wish it, *Patrão.*"

"It will soon be dark, and that is the time to fish; do you have a spear?"

"No, *Patrão.*"

"Then Ignacio will get you one."

Ignacio took a handful of the sticks and thrust the ends into the fire, blowing on them. After a moment Nicholas leaned over and blew too, until all the sticks were blazing.

"Now we must find you some bamboo, and there is some back here. Follow me."

The light, still nearly shadowless, was dimming now, so that it seemed to

Nicholas that they walked on insubstantial soil, though he could feel it beneath his feet. Ignacio stalked ahead, holding up the burning sticks until the fire seemed about to die, then pointing the ends down, allowing it to lick upward toward his hand and come to life again. There was a gentle wind blowing out toward the sea, carrying away the sound of the surf and bringing a damp coolness; and when they had been walking for several minutes, Nicholas heard in it a faint, dry, almost rhythmic rattle.

Ignacio looked back at him and said, "The music. The big stems talking; hear it?"

They found a cane a little thinner than Nicholas's wrist and piled the burning sticks around its base, then added more. When it fell, Ignacio burned through the upper end too, making a pole about as long as Nicholas was tall, and with the edge of a seashell scraped the larger end to a point. "Now you are a fisherman," he said. Nicholas said, "Yes, *Patrão,*" still careful not to meet his eyes.

"You are hungry?"

"Yes, *Patrão.*"

"Then let me tell you something. Whatever you get is Ignacio's, you understand? And what he catches, that is his too. But when he has eaten what he wants, what is left is yours. Come on now, and Ignacio will teach you to fish or drown you."

Ignacio's own spear was buried in the sand not far from the fire; it was much bigger than the one he had made for Nicholas. With it held across his chest he went down to the water, wading until it was waist high, then swimming, not looking to see if Nicholas was following. Nicholas found that he could swim with the spear by putting all his effort into the motion of his legs, holding the spear in his left hand and stroking only occasionally with his right. "You breathe," he said softly, "and watch the spear," and after that he had only to allow his head to lift from time to time.

He had thought Ignacio would begin to look for fish as soon as they were well out from the beach, but the Brazilian continued to swim, slowly but steadily, until it seemed to Nicholas that they must be a kilometer or more from land. Suddenly, as though the lights in a room had responded to a switch, the dark sea around them became an opalescent blue. Ignacio stopped, treading water and using his spear to buoy himself.

"Here," he said. "Get them between yourself and the light."

Open-eyed, he bent his face to the water, raised it again to breathe deeply, and dove. Nicholas followed his example, floating belly-down with open eyes.

All the world of dancing glitter and dark island vanished as though he had plunged his face into a dream. Far, far below him Jupiter displayed its broad, striped disk, marred with the spreading Bright Spot where man-made silicone enzymes had stripped the hydrogen from methane for kindled fusion: a cancer and a burning infant sun. Between that sun and his eyes lay invisible a hundred thousand kilometers of space, and the temperglass shell of the satellite; hundreds of meters of illuminated water, and in it the spread body of Ignacio, dark against the light, still kicking downward, his spear a pencil line of blackness in his hand.

Involuntarily Nicholas's head came up, returning to the universe of sparkling waves, aware now that what he had called "night" was only the shadow cast by Dr. Island when Jupiter and the Bright Spot slid beneath her. That shadow line, indetectable in air, now lay sharp across the water behind him. He took breath and plunged.

Almost at once a fish darted somewhere below, and his left arm thrust the spear forward, but it was far out of reach. He swam after it, then saw another, larger, fish farther down and dove for that, passing Ignacio surfacing for air. The fish was too deep, and he had used up his oxygen; his lungs aching for air, he swam up, wanting to let go of his spear, then realizing at the last moment that he could, that it would only bob to the surface if he released it. His head broke water and he gasped, his heart thumping; water struck his face and he knew again, suddenly, as though they had ceased to exist while he was gone, the pulsebeat pounding of the waves.

Ignacio was waiting for him. He shouted, "This time you will come with Ignacio, and he will show you the dead sea god. Then we will fish."

Unable to speak, Nicholas nodded. He was allowed three more breaths; then Ignacio dove and Nicholas had to follow, kicking down until the pressure sang in his ears. Then through blue water he saw, looming at the edge of the light, a huge mass of metal anchored to the temperglass hull of the satellite itself; above it, hanging lifelessly like the stem of a great vine severed from the root, a cable twice as thick as a man's body; and on the bottom, sprawled beside the mighty anchor, a legged god that might have been a dead insect save that it was at least six meters long. Ignacio turned and looked back at Nicholas to see if he understood; he did not, but he nodded, and with the strength draining from his arms, surfaced again.

After Ignacio brought up the first fish, they took turns on the surface guarding their catch, and while the Bright Spot crept beneath the shelving rim of Dr. Island, they speared two more, one of them quite large. Then when Nicholas was so exhausted he could scarcely lift his arms, they made their way back to shore, and Ignacio showed him how to gut the fish with a thorn and the edge of a shell, and reclose them and pack them in mud and leaves to be roasted by the fire. After Ignacio had begun to eat the largest fish, Nicholas timidly drew out the smallest, and ate for the first time since coming to Dr. Island. Only when he had finished did he remember Diane.

He did not dare to take the last fish to her, but he looked covertly at Ignacio, and began edging away from the fire. The Brazilian seemed not to have noticed him. When he was well into the shadows he stood, backed a few steps, then—slowly, as his instincts warned him—walked away, not beginning to trot until the distance between them was nearly a hundred meters.

He found Diane sitting apathetic and silent at the margin of the cold pool, and had some difficulty persuading her to stand. At last he lifted her, his hands under her arms pressing against her thin ribs. Once on her feet she stood steadily enough, and followed him when he took her by the hand. He talked to her, knowing that although she gave no sign of hearing she heard him, and that the right words might wake her to response. "We went fishing—Ignacio showed me how. And he's got a fire, Diane, he got it from a kind of robot that was supposed to be fixing one of the cables that holds Dr. Island, I don't know how. Anyway, listen, we caught three big fish, and I ate one and Ignacio ate a great big one, and I don't think he'd mind if you had the other one, only say, 'Yes, *Patrão*,' and 'No, *Patrão*,' to him—he likes that, and he's only used to machines. You don't have to smile at him or anything—just look at the fire, that's what I do, just look at the fire."

To Ignacio, perhaps wisely, he at first said nothing at all, leading Diane to the place where he had been sitting himself a few minutes before and placing some scraps from his fish in her lap. When she did not eat he found a sliver of the tender, roasted flesh and thrust it into her mouth. Ignacio said, "Ignacio believed that one dead," and Nicholas answered, "No, *Patrão*."

"There is another fish. Give it to her."

Nicholas did, raking the gob of baked mud from the coals to crack with the heel of his hand, and peeling the broken and steaming fillets from the skins and bones to give to her when they had cooled enough to eat; after the fish had lain in her mouth for perhaps half a minute she began to chew and swallow, and after the third mouthful she fed herself, though without looking at either of them.

"Ignacio believed that one dead," Ignacio said again.

"No, *Patrão,*" Nicholas answered, and then added, "Like you can see, she's alive."

"She is a pretty creature, with the firelight on her face——no?"

"Yes, *Patrão,* very pretty."

"But too thin." Ignacio moved around the fire until he was sitting almost beside Diane, then reached for the fish Nicholas had given her. Her hands closed on it, though she still did not look at him.

"You see, she knows us after all," Ignacio said. "We are not ghosts."

Nicholas whispered urgently, "Let him have it."

Slowly Diane's fingers relaxed, but Ignacio did not take the fish. "I was only joking, little one," he said. "And I think not such good joke after all." Then when she did not reply, he turned away from her, his eyes reaching out across the dark, tossing water for something Nicholas could not see.

"She likes you, *Patrão,*" Nicholas said. The words were like swallowing filth, but he thought of the bird ready to tear through Diane's skin, and Maya's blood soaking in little round dots in the white cloth, and continued. "She is only shy. It is better that way."

"You. What do you know?"

At least Ignacio was no longer looking at the sea. Nicholas said, "Isn't it true, *Patrão?*"

"Yes, it is true."

Diane was picking at the fish again, conveying tiny flakes to her mouth with delicate fingers; distinctly but almost absently she said, "Go, Nicholas."

He looked at Ignacio, but the Brazilian's eyes did not turn toward the girl, nor did he speak.

"Nicholas, go away. Please."

In a voice he hoped was pitched too low for Ignacio to hear, Nicholas said, "I'll see you in the morning. All right?"

Her head moved a fraction of a centimeter.

ONCE HE WAS out of sight of the fire, one part of the beach was as good to sleep on as another; he wished he had taken a piece of wood from the fire to start one of his own and tried to cover his legs with sand to keep off the cool wind, but the sand fell away whenever he moved, and his legs and his left hand moved without volition on his part.

The surf, lapping at the rippled shore, said, "That was well done, Nicholas."

"I can feel you move," Nicholas said. "I don't think I ever could before except when I was high up."

"I doubt that you can now; my roll is less than one one-hundredth of a degree."

"Yes, I can. You wanted me to do that, didn't you? About Ignacio."

"Do you know what the Harlow effect is, Nicholas?"

Nicholas shook his head.

"About a hundred years ago Dr. Harlow experimented with monkeys who had been raised in complete isolation—no mothers, no other monkeys at all."

"Lucky monkeys."

"When the monkeys were mature he put them into cages with normal ones; they fought with any that came near them, and sometimes they killed them."

"Psychologists always put things in cages; did he ever think of turning them loose in the jungle instead?"

"No, Nicholas, though we have . . . Aren't you going to say anything?"

"I guess not."

"Dr. Harlow tried, you see, to get the isolate monkeys to breed—sex is the primary social function—but they wouldn't. Whenever another monkey of either sex approached they displayed aggressiveness, which the other monkeys returned. He cured them finally by introducing immature monkeys—monkey children—in place of the mature, socialized ones. These needed the isolate adults so badly that they kept on making approaches no matter how often or how violently they were rejected, and in the end they were accepted, and the isolates socialized. It's interesting to note that the founder of Christianity seems to have had an intuitive grasp of the principle—but it was almost two thousand years before it was demonstrated scientifically."

"I don't think it worked here," Nicholas said. "It was more complicated than that."

"Human beings are complicated monkeys, Nicholas."

"That's about the first time I ever heard you make a joke. You like not being human, don't you?"

"Of course. Wouldn't you?"

"I always thought I would, but now I'm not sure. You said that to help me, didn't you? I don't like that."

A wave higher than the others splashed chill foam over Nicholas's legs, and for a moment he wondered if this were Dr. Island's reply. Half a minute later another wave wet him, and another, and he moved farther up the beach to avoid them. The wind was stronger, but he slept despite it, and was awakened only for a moment by a flash of light from the direction from which he had come; he tried to guess what might have caused it, thought of Diane and Ignacio throwing the burning sticks into the air to see the arcs of fire, smiled—too sleepy now to be angry—and slept again.

Morning came cold and sullen; Nicholas ran up and down the beach, rubbing himself with his hands. A thin rain, or spume (it was hard to tell which), was blowing in the wind, clouding the light to gray radiance. He wondered if Diane and Ignacio would mind if he came back now and decided to wait, then thought of fishing so that he would have something to bring when he came; but the sea was very cold and the waves so high they tumbled him, wrenching his bamboo spear from his hand. Ignacio found him dripping with water, sitting with his back to a palm trunk and staring out toward the lifting curve of the sea.

"Hello, you," Ignacio said.

"Good morning, *Patrão.*"

Ignacio sat down. "What is your name? You told me, I think, when we first met, but I have forgotten. I am sorry."

"Nicholas."

"Yes."

"*Patrão,* I am very cold. Would it be possible for us to go to your fire?"

"My name is Ignacio; call me that."

Nicholas nodded, frightened.

"But we cannot go to my fire, because the fire is out."

"Can't you make another one, *Patrão?*"

"You do not trust me, do you? I do not blame you. No, I cannot make another—you may use what I had, if you wish, and make one after I have gone. I came only to say goodbye."

"You're leaving?"

The wind in the palm fronds said, "Ignacio is much better now. He will be going to another place, Nicholas."

"A hospital?"

"Yes, a hospital, but I don't think he will have to stay there long."

"But . . ." Nicholas tried to think of something appropriate. At St. John's and the other places where he had been confined, when people left, they simply left, and usually were hardly spoken of once it was learned that they were going and thus were already tainted by whatever it was that froze the smiles and dried the tears of those outside. At last he said, "Thanks for teaching me how to fish."

"That was all right," Ignacio said. He stood up and put a hand on Nicholas's shoulder, then turned away. Four meters to his left the damp sand was beginning to lift and crack. While Nicholas watched, it opened on a brightly lit companionway walled with white. Ignacio pushed his curly black hair back from his eyes and went down, and the sand closed with a thump.

"He won't be coming back, will he?" Nicholas said.

"No."

"He said I could use his stuff to start another fire, but I don't even know what it is."

Dr. Island did not answer. Nicholas got up and began to walk back to where the fire had been, thinking about Diane and wondering if she was hungry; he was hungry himself.

HE FOUND HER beside the dead fire. Her chest had been burned away, and lying close by, near the hole in the sand where Ignacio must have kept it hidden, was a bulky nuclear welder. The power pack was too heavy for Nicholas to lift, but he picked up the welding gun on its short cord and touched the trigger, producing a two meter plasma discharge which he played along the sand until Diane's body was ash. By the time he had finished the wind was whipping the palms and sending stinging rain into his eyes, but he collected a supply of wood and built another fire, bigger and bigger until it roared like a forge in the wind. "He killed her!" he shouted to the waves.

"YES." Dr. Island's voice was big and wild.

"You said he was better."

"HE IS," howled the wind. "YOU KILLED THE MONKEY THAT WANTED TO PLAY WITH YOU, NICHOLAS, AS I BELIEVED IGNACIO WOULD EVENTUALLY KILL YOU, WHO ARE SO EASILY HATED, SO DIFFERENT FROM WHAT IT IS THOUGHT A BOY SHOULD BE. BUT KILLING THE MONKEY HELPED YOU, REMEMBER? MADE YOU BETTER. IGNACIO WAS FRIGHTENED BY WOMEN; NOW HE KNOWS THAT THEY ARE REALLY VERY WEAK, AND HE HAS ACTED UPON CERTAIN FANTASIES AND FINDS THEM BITTER."

"You're rocking," Nicholas said. "Am I doing that?"

"YOUR THOUGHT."

A palm snapped in the storm; instead of falling, it flew crashing among the others, its fronded head catching the wind like a sail. "I'm killing you,"

Nicholas said. "Destroying you." The left side of his face was so contorted with grief and rage that he could scarcely speak.

Dr. Island heaved beneath his feet. "NO."

"One of your cables is already broken. I saw that. Maybe more than one. You'll pull loose. I'm turning this world, isn't that right? The attitude rockets are tuned to my emotions, and they're spinning us around, and the slippage is the wind and the high sea, and when you come loose nothing will balance anymore."

"NO."

"What's the stress on your cables? Don't you know?"

"THEY ARE VERY STRONG."

"What kind of talk is that? You ought to say something like: 'The D-twelve cable tension is twenty-billion kilograms' force. WARNING! WARNING! Expected time to failure is ninety-seven seconds! WARNING!' *Don't you even know how a machine is supposed to talk?*" Nicholas was screaming now, and every wave reached farther up the beach than the last, so that the bases of the most seaward palms were awash.

"GET BACK, NICHOLAS. FIND HIGHER GROUND. GO INTO THE JUNGLE." It was the crashing waves themselves that spoke.

"I won't."

A long serpent of water reached for the fire, which hissed and sputtered.

"GET BACK!"

"I won't!"

A second wave came, striking Nicholas calf-high and nearly extinguishing the fire.

"ALL THIS WILL BE UNDER WATER SOON. GET BACK!"

Nicholas picked up some of the still-burning sticks and tried to carry them, but the wind blew them out as soon as he lifted them from the fire. He tugged at the welder, but it was too heavy for him to lift.

"GET BACK!"

He went into the jungle, where the trees lashed themselves to leafy rubbish in the wind and broken branches flew through the air like debris from an explosion; for a while he heard Diane's voice crying in the wind; it became Maya's, then his mother's or Sister Carmela's, and a hundred others; in time the wind grew less, and he could no longer feel the ground rocking. He felt tired. He said, "I didn't kill you after all, did I?" but there was no answer. On the beach, when he returned to it, he found the welder half buried in sand. No trace of Diane's ashes, nor of his fire. He gathered more wood and built another, lighting it with the welder.

"Now," he said. He scooped aside the sand around the welder until he reached the rough understone beneath it, and turned the flame of the welder on that; it blackened and bubbled.

"No," Dr. Island said.

"Yes." He was bending intently over the flame, both hands locked on the welder's trigger.

"Nicholas, stop that." When he did not reply, "Look behind you." There was a splashing louder than the crashing of the waves, and a groaning of metal. He whirled and saw the great, beetle-like robot Ignacio had shown him on the sea floor. Tiny shellfish clung to its metal skin, and water, faintly green, still poured from its body. Before he could turn the welding gun toward it, it shot forward hands like clamps and wrenched it from him. All up and down the beach similar machines were smoothing the sand and repairing the damage of the storm.

"That thing was dead," Nicholas said. "Ignacio killed it."

It picked up the power pack, shook it clean of sand, and turning, stalked back toward the sea.

"That is what Ignacio believed, and it was better that he believed so."

"And you said you couldn't do anything, you had no hands."

"I also told you that I would treat you as society will when you are released, that that was my nature. After that, did you still believe all I told you? Nicholas, you are upset now because Diane is dead—"

"You could have protected her!"

"—but by dying she made someone else—someone very important—well. Her prognosis was bad; she really wanted only death, and this was the death I chose for her. You could call it the death of Dr. Island, a death that would help someone else. Now you are alone, but soon there will be more patients in this segment, and you will help them, too—if you can—and perhaps they will help you. Do you understand?"

"No," Nicholas said. He flung himself down on the sand. The wind had dropped, but it was raining hard. He thought of the vision he had once had, and of describing it to Diane the day before, "This isn't ending the way I thought," he whispered. It was only a squeak of sound far down in his throat. "Nothing ever turns out right."

The waves, the wind, the rustling palm fronds and the pattering rain, the monkeys who had come down to the beach to search for food washed ashore, answered, "Go away—go back—don't move."

Nicholas pressed his scarred head against his knees, rocking back and forth.

"Don't move."

For a long time he sat still while the rain lashed his shoulders and the dripping monkeys frolicked and fought around him. When at last he lifted his face, there was in it some element of personality which had been only potentially present before, and with this an emptiness and an expression of surprise. His lips moved, and the sounds were the sounds made by a deaf-mute who tries to speak.

"Nicholas is gone," the waves said. "Nicholas, who was the right side of your body, the left half of your brain, I have forced into catatonia; for the remainder of your life he will be to you only what you once were to him—or less. Do you understand?"

The boy nodded.

"We will call you Kenneth, silent one. And if Nicholas tries to come again, Kenneth, you must drive him back—or return to what you have been."

The boy nodded a second time, and a moment afterward began to collect sticks for the dying fire. As though to themselves the waves chanted:

"Seas are wild tonight . . .
Stretching over Sado island
Silent clouds of stars."

There was no reply.

THE DAY BEFORE THE
REVOLUTION

URSULA K. LE GUIN

URSULA K. LE GUIN is one of the most important and respected writers in science fiction today. Born in 1929, daughter of renowned historian Alfred Kroeber, she graduated from Columbia University in 1951. Her first work appeared in the early 1960s and was followed by numerous novels, short story collections, poetry collections, books for children, essays, books in translation, and anthologies. She is the author of the classic Earthsea series of fantasy novels and stories, and the Hainish series of science fiction novels and stories, including landmark award–winning novels *The Left Hand of Darkness* and *The Dispossessed.* Her work has been recognized with the Hugo Award five times, the Nebula Award five times, the World Fantasy Award twice, the James Tiptree Jr. Award three times, the Locus Award sixteen times, and the Theodore Sturgeon Memorial, Ditmar, Endeavour, Prometheus, Rhysling, and Jupiter Awards. Le Guin is an SF Hall of Fame Living Inductee, a recipient of the World Fantasy Award for Lifetime Achievement, and was recently presented with the 2002 PEN/Malamud Award for Short Fiction. Her most recent novel is the "Earthsea" tale *The Other Wind,* and her latest story collection is *Changing Planes.*

The story that follows is an introduction of sorts to the world of *The Dispossessed,* detailing the final recollections of the founder of that society.

* * *

THE SPEAKER'S VOICE was as loud as empty beer-trucks in a stone street, and the people at the meeting were jammed up close, cobblestones, that great voice booming over them. Taviri was somewhere on the other side of the hall. She had to get to him. She wormed and pushed her way among the dark-clothed, close-packed people. She did not hear the words, nor see the faces: only the booming, and the bodies pressed one behind the other. She could not see Taviri, she was too short. A broad black-vested belly and chest loomed up, blocking her way. She must get through to Taviri. Sweating, she jabbed fiercely with her fist. It was like hitting stone, he did not move at all, but the huge lungs let out right over her head a prodigious noise, a bellow. She cowered. Then she understood that the bellow had not been at her. Others were shouting. The speaker had said something, something fine about taxes or shadows. Thrilled, she joined the shouting—"Yes! Yes!"—and shoving on, came out easily into the open expanse of the Regimental Drill Field in Parheo. Overhead the evening sky lay deep and colorless, and all around her nodded the tall weeds with dry, white, close-floreted heads. She had never known what they were called. The flowers nodded above her head, swaying in the wind that always blew across the fields in the dusk. She ran among them, and they whipped lithe aside and stood up again swaying, silent. Taviri stood among the tall weeds in his good suit, the dark grey one that made him look like a professor or a play-actor, harshly elegant. He did not look happy, but he was laughing, and saying something to her. The sound of his voice made her cry, and she reached out to catch hold of his hand, but she did not stop, quite. She could not stop. "Oh, Taviri," she said, "it's just on there!" The queer sweet smell of the white weeds was heavy as she went on. There were thorns, tangles underfoot, there were slopes, pits. She feared to fall, to fall, she stopped.

Sun, bright morning-glare, straight in the eyes, relentless. She had forgotten to pull the blind last night. She turned her back on the sun, but the right side wasn't comfortable. No use. Day. She sighed twice, sat up, got her legs over the edge of the bed, and sat hunched in her nightdress looking down at her feet.

The toes, compressed by a lifetime of cheap shoes, were almost square where they touched each other, and bulged out above in corns; the nails were discolored and shapeless. Between the knob-like anklebones ran fine, dry wrinkles. The brief little plain at the base of the toes had kept its delicacy, but the skin was the color of mud, and knotted veins crossed the instep. Disgusting. Sad, depressing. Mean. Pitiful. She tried on all the words, and they all fit, like hideous little hats. Hideous: yes, that one too. To look at oneself and find it hideous, what a job! But then, when she hadn't been hideous, had she sat around and stared at herself like this? Not much! A proper body's not an object, not an implement, not a belonging to be admired, it's just you, yourself. Only when it's no longer you, but yours, a thing owned, do you worry about it— Is it in good shape? Will it do? Will it last?

"Who cares?" said Laia fiercely, and stood up.

It made her giddy to stand up suddenly. She had to put out her hand to the bed-table, for she dreaded falling. At that she thought of reaching out to Taviri, in the dream.

What had he said? She could not remember. She was not sure if she had even touched his hand. She frowned, trying to force memory. It had been so long since she had dreamed about Taviri; and now not even to remember what he had said!

It was gone, it was gone. She stood there hunched in her nightdress, frowning, one hand on the bed-table. How long was it since she had thought of him—let alone dreamed of him—even thought of him, as "Taviri"? How long since she had said his name?

Asieo said. When Asieo and I were in prison in the North. Before I met Asieo. Asieo's theory of reciprocity. Oh yes, she talked about him, talked about him too much no doubt, maundered, dragged him in. But as "Asieo," the last name, the public man. The private man was gone, utterly gone. There were so few left who had even known him. They had all used to be in jail. One laughed about it in those days, all the friends in all the jails. But they weren't even there, these days. They were in the prison cemeteries. Or in the common graves.

"Oh, oh my dear," Laia said out loud, and she sank down onto the bed again because she could not stand up under the remembrance of those first weeks in the Fort, in the cell, those first weeks of the nine years in the Fort in Drio, in the cell, those first weeks after they told her that Asieo had been killed in the fighting in Capitol Square and had been buried with the Fourteen Hundred in the lime-ditches behind Oring Gate. In the cell. Her hands fell into the old position on her lap, the left clenched and locked inside the grip of the right, the right thumb working back and forth a little pressing and rubbing on the knuckle of the left first finger. Hours, days, nights. She had thought of them all, each one, each one of the Fourteen

Hundred, how they lay, how the quicklime worked on the flesh, how the bones touched in the burning dark. Who touched him? How did the slender bones of the hand lie now? Hours, years.

"Taviri, I have never forgotten you!" she whispered, and the stupidity of it brought her back to morning light and the rumpled bed. Of course she hadn't forgotten him. These things go without saying between husband and wife. There were her ugly old feet flat on the floor again, just as before. She had got nowhere at all, she had gone in a circle. She stood up with a grunt of effort and disapproval, and went to the closet for her dressing gown.

The young people went about the halls of the House in becoming immodesty, but she was too old for that. She didn't want to spoil some young man's breakfast with the sight of her. Besides, they had grown up in the principle of freedom of dress and sex and all the rest, and she hadn't. All she had done was invent it. It's not the same.

Like speaking of Asieo as "my husband." They winced. The word she should use as a good Odonian, of course, was "partner." But why the hell did she have to be a good Odonian?

She shuffled down the hall to the bathrooms. Mairo was there, washing her hair in a lavatory. Laia looked at the long, sleek, wet hank with admiration. She got out of the House so seldom now that she didn't know when she had last seen a respectably shaven scalp, but still the sight of a full head of hair gave her pleasure, vigorous pleasure. How many times had she been jeered at, *Longhair, Longhair,* had her hair pulled by policemen or young toughs, had her hair shaved off down to the scalp by a grinning soldier at each new prison? And then had grown it all over again, through the fuzz, to the frizz, to the curls, to the mane. . . . In the old days. For God's love, couldn't she think of anything today but the old days?

Dressed, her bed made, she went down to commons. It was a good breakfast, but she had never got her appetite back since the damned stroke. She drank two cups of herb tea, but couldn't finish the piece of fruit she had taken. How she had craved fruit as a child badly enough to steal it; and in the Fort—oh, for God's love stop it! She smiled and replied to the greetings and friendly inquiries of the other breakfasters and big Aevi who was serving the counter this morning. It was he who had tempted her with the peach, "Look at this, I've been saving it for you," and how could she refuse? Anyway she had always loved fruit, and never got enough; once when she was six or seven she had stolen a piece off a vendor's cart in River Street. But it was hard to eat when everyone was talking so excitedly. There was news from Thu, real news. She was inclined to discount it at first, being wary of enthusiasms, but after she had read the article in the paper, and read between the lines of it, she thought, with a strange kind of certainty, deep but cold, Why, this is it; it has come. And in Thu, not here. Thu will break before this country does; the Revolution will first prevail there. As if that mattered! There will be no more nations. And yet it did matter somehow, it made her a little cold and sad—envious, in fact. Of all the infinite stupidities. She did not join in the talk much, and soon got up to go back to her room, feeling sorry for herself. She could not share their excitement. She was out of it, really out of it. It's not easy, she said to herself in justification, laboriously climbing the stairs, to accept being out of it when you've been in it, in the center of it, for fifty years. Oh, for God's love. Whining!

She got the stairs and the self-pity behind her, entering her room. It was a good room, and it was good to be by herself. It was a great relief. Even if it wasn't strictly fair. Some of the kids in the attics were living five to a room no bigger than this. There were always more people wanting to live in an Odonian House than could be properly accommodated. She had this big room all to herself only because she was an old woman who had had a stroke. And maybe because she was Odo. If she hadn't been Odo, but merely the old woman with a stroke, would she have had it? Very likely. After all, who the hell wanted to room with a drooling old woman? But it was hard to be sure. Favoritism, elitism, leader-worship, they crept back and cropped out everywhere. But she had never hoped to see them eradicated in her lifetime, in one generation; only Time works the great changes. Meanwhile this was a nice, large, sunny room, proper for a drooling old woman who had started a world revolution.

Her secretary would be coming in an hour to help her despatch the day's work. She shuffled over to the desk, a beautiful, big piece, a present from the Noi Cabinetmakers' Syndicate because somebody had heard her remark once that the only piece of furniture she had ever really longed for was a desk with drawers and enough room on top . . . damn, the top was practically covered with papers with notes clipped to them, mostly in Noi's small clear handwriting: Urgent.—Northern Provinces.—Consult w/R. T.?

Her own handwriting had never been the same since Asieo's death. It was odd, when you thought about it. After all, within five years after his death she had written the whole *Analogy*. And there were those letters, which the tall guard with the watery gray eyes, what was his name, never mind, had smuggled out of the Fort for her for two years. *The Prison Letters* they called them now, there were a dozen different editions of them. All that stuff, the letters which people kept telling her were so full of "spiritual strength"—which probably meant she had been lying herself blue in the face when she wrote them, trying to keep her spirits up—and the *Analogy* which was certainly the solidest intellectual work she had ever done, all of that had been written in the Fort in Drio, in the cell, after Asieo's death. One had to do something, and in the Fort they let one have paper and pens. . . . But it had all been written in the hasty, scribbling hand which she had never felt was hers, not her own like the round, black scrollings of the manuscript of *Society Without Government,* forty-five years old. Taviri had taken not only her body's and her heart's desire to the quicklime with him, but even her good clear handwriting.

But he had left her the Revolution.

How brave of you to go on, to work, to write, in prison, after such a defeat for the Movement, after your partner's death, people had used to say. Damn fools. What else had there been to do? Bravery, courage—what was courage? She had never figured it out. Not fearing, some said. Fearing yet going on, others said. But what could one do but go on? Had one any real choice, ever?

To die was merely to go on in another direction.

If you wanted to come home you had to keep going on, that was what she meant when she wrote "True journey is return," but it had never been more than an intuition, and she was farther than ever now from being able to rationalize it. She bent down, too suddenly, so that she grunted a little at the creak in her bones, and began to root in a bottom drawer of the desk. Her hand came on an age-softened folder and drew it out, recognizing it by touch before sight confirmed: the manuscript of *Syndical Organization in Revolutionary Transition.* He had printed the title on the folder and written his name under it, Taviri Odo Asieo, IX 741. There was an elegant handwriting, every letter well-formed, bold, and fluent. But he had preferred to use a voiceprinter. The manuscript was all in voiceprint, and high quality too, hesitancies adjusted and idiosyncrasies of speech normalized. You couldn't see there how he had said "o" deep in his throat as they did on the North Coast. There was nothing of him there but his mind. She had nothing of him at all except his name written on the folder. She hadn't kept his letters, it was sentimental to keep letters. Besides, she never kept anything. She couldn't think of anything that she had ever owned for more than a few years, except this ramshackle old body, of course, and she was stuck with that. . . .

Dualizing again. "She" and "it." Age and illness made one dualist, made one escapist; the mind insisted, *It's not me, it's not me.* But it was. Maybe the mystics could detach mind from body, she had always rather wistfully envied them the chance, without hope of emulating them. Escape had never been her game. She had sought for freedom here, now, body and soul.

First self-pity, then self-praise, and here she still sat, for God's love, holding Asieo's name in her hand, why? Didn't she know his name without looking it up? What was wrong with her? She raised the folder to her lips and kissed the handwritten name firmly and squarely, replaced the folder in the back of the bottom drawer, shut the drawer, and straightened up in the chair. Her right hand tingled. She scratched it, and then shook it in the air, spitefully. It had never quite got over the stroke. Neither had her right leg, or right eye, or the right corner of her mouth. They were sluggish, inept, they tingled. They made her feel like a robot with a short circuit.

And time was getting on, Noi would be coming, what had she been doing ever since breakfast?

She got up so hastily that she lurched, and grabbed at the chairback to make sure she did not fall. She went down the hall to the bathroom and looked in the big mirror there. Her grey knot was loose and droopy, she hadn't done it up well before breakfast. She struggled with it a while. It was hard to keep her arms up in the air. Amai, running in to piss, stopped and said, "Let me do it!" and knotted it up tight and neat in no time, with her round, strong, pretty fingers, smiling and silent. Amai was twenty, less than a third of Laia's age. Her parents had both been members of the Movement, one killed in the insurrection of '60, the other still recruiting in the South Provinces. Amai had grown up in Odonian Houses, born to the Revolution, a true daughter of anarchy. And so quiet and free and beautiful a child, enough to make you cry when you thought: this is what we worked for, this is what we meant, this is it, here she is, alive, the kindly, lovely future.

Laia Asieo Odo's right eye wept several little tears, as she stood between the lavatories and the latrines having her hair done up by the daughter she had not borne; but her left eye, the strong one, did not weep, nor did it know what the right eye did.

She thanked Amai and hurried back to her room. She had noticed, in the mirror, a stain on her collar. Peach juice, probably. Damned old dribbler. She didn't want Noi to come in and find her with drool on her collar.

As the clean shirt went on over her head, she thought, What's so special about Noi?

She fastened the collar-frogs with her left hand, slowly. Noi was thirty or so, a slight, muscular fellow, with a soft voice and alert dark eyes. That's what was special about Noi. It was that simple. Good old sex. She had never been drawn to a fair man or a fat one, or the tall fellows with big biceps, never, not even when she was fourteen and fell in love with every passing fart. Dark, spare, and fiery, that was the recipe. Taviri, of course. This boy wasn't a patch on Taviri for brains, nor even for looks, but there it was: she didn't want him to see her with dribble on her collar and her hair coming undone.

Her thin, grey hair.

Noi came in, just pausing in the open doorway—my God, she hadn't even shut the door while changing her shirt! She looked at him and saw herself. The old woman.

You could brush your hair and change your shirt, or you could wear last week's shirt and last night's braids, or you could put on cloth of gold and dust your shaven scalp with diamond powder. None of it would make the slightest difference. The old woman would look a little less, or a little more, grotesque.

One keeps oneself neat out of mere decency, mere sanity, awareness of other people.

And finally even that goes, and one dribbles unashamed.

"Good morning," the young man said in his gentle voice.

"Hello, Noi."

No, by God, it was *not* out of mere decency. Decency be damned. Because the man she had loved, and to whom her age would not have mattered—because he was dead, must she pretend she had no sex? Must she suppress the truth, like a damned puritan authoritarian? Even six months ago, before the stroke, she had made men look at her and like to look at her; and now, though she could give no pleasure, by God she could please herself.

When she was six years old, and Papa's friend Gadeo used to come by to talk politics with Papa after dinner, she would put on the gold-colored necklace that Mama had found on a trash heap and brought home for her. It was so short that it always got hidden under her collar where nobody could see it. She liked it that way. She knew she had it on. She sat on the doorstep and listened to them talk, and knew that she looked nice for Gadeo. He was dark, with white teeth that flashed. Sometimes he called her "pretty Laia." "There's my pretty Laia!" Sixty-six years ago.

"What? My head's dull. I had a terrible night." It was true. She had slept even less than usual.

"I was asking if you'd seen the papers this morning."

She nodded.

"Pleased about Soinehe?"

Soinehe was the province in Thu which had declared its secession from the Thuvian State last night.

He was pleased about it. His white teeth flashed in his dark, alert face. Pretty Laia.

"Yes. And apprehensive."

"I know. But it's the real thing, this time. It's the beginning of the end of the Government in Thu. They haven't even tried to order troops into Soinehe, you know. It would merely provoke the soldiers into rebellion sooner, and they know it."

She agreed with him. She herself had felt that certainty. But she could not share his delight. After a lifetime of living on hope because there is nothing but hope, one loses the taste for victory. A real sense of triumph must be preceded by real despair. She had unlearned despair a long time ago. There were no more triumphs. One went on.

"Shall we do those letters today?"

"All right. Which letters?"

"To the people in the North," he said without impatience.

"In the North?"

"Parheo, Oaidun."

She had been born in Parheo, the dirty city on the dirty river. She had not come here to the capital till she was twenty-two and ready to bring the Revolution, though in those days, before she and the others had thought it through, it had been a very green and puerile revolution. Strikes for better wages, representation for women. Votes and wages— Power and Money, for the love of God! Well, one does learn a little, after all, in fifty years.

But then one must forget it all.

"Start with Oaidun," she said, sitting down in the armchair. Noi was at the desk ready to work. He read out excerpts from the letters she was to answer. She tried to pay attention, and succeeded well enough that she dictated one whole letter and started on another. "Remember that at this stage your brotherhood is vulnerable to the threat of . . . no, to the danger . . . to . . . " She groped till Noi suggested, "The danger of leader-worship?"

"All right. And that nothing is so soon corrupted by power-seeking as altruism. No. And that nothing corrupts altruism—no. O for God's love you know what I'm trying to say, Noi, you write it. They know it too, it's just the same old stuff, why can't they read my books!"

"Touch," Noi said gently, smiling, citing one of the central Odonian themes.

"All right, but I'm tired of being touched. If you'll write the letter I'll sign it, but I can't be bothered with it this morning." He was looking at her with a little question or concern. She said, irritable, "There is something else I have to do!"

WHEN NOI HAD gone she sat down at the desk and moved the papers about, pretending to be doing something, because she had been startled, frightened, by the words she had said. She had nothing else to do. She never had had anything else to do. This was her work: her lifework. The speaking tours and the meetings and the streets were out of reach for her now, but she could still write, and that was her work. And anyhow if she had had anything else to do, Noi would have known it; he kept her schedule, and tactfully reminded her of things, like the visit from the foreign students this afternoon.

Oh, damn. She liked the young, and there was always something to learn from a foreigner, but she was tired of new faces, and tired of being on view. She learned from them, but they didn't learn from her; they had learnt all she had to teach long ago, from her books, from the Movement. They just came to look, as if she were the Great Tower in Rodarred, or the Canyon of the Tulaaeva. A phenomenon, a monument. They were awed, adoring. She snarled at them: Think your own thoughts!—That's not anarchism, that's mere obscurantism.—You don't think liberty and discipline are incompatible, do you?—They accepted their tongue-lashing meekly as children, gratefully, as if she were some kind of All-Mother, the idol of the Big Sheltering Womb. She! She who had mined the shipyards at Seissero, and had cursed Premier Inoilte to his face in front of a crowd of seven thousand, telling him he would have cut off his own balls and had them bronzed and sold as souvenirs, if he thought there was any profit in it—she who had screeched, and sworn and kicked policemen, and spat at priests, and pissed in public on the big brass plaque in Capitol Square that said HERE WAS FOUNDED THE SOVEREIGN NATION OF A-IO ETC ETC. Pssssssssss to all that! And now she was everybody's grandmama, the dear old lady, the sweet old monument, come worship at the womb. The fire's out, boys, it's safe to come up close.

"No, I won't," Laia said out loud. "I will not." She was not self-conscious about talking to herself, because she always had talked to herself. "Laia's invisible audience," Tavari had used to say, as she went through the room muttering. "You needn't come, I won't be here," she told the invisible audience now. She had just decided what it was she had to do. She had to go out. To go into the streets.

It was inconsiderate to disappoint the foreign students. It was erratic, typically senile. It was un-Odonian. Psssssss to all that. What was the good working for freedom all your life and ending up without any freedom at all? She would go out for a walk.

"What is an anarchist? One who, choosing, accepts the responsibility of choice."

On the way downstairs she decided, scowling, to stay and see the foreign students. But then she would go out.

They were very young students, very earnest: doe-eyed, shaggy, charming creatures from the Western Hemisphere, Benbili and the kingdom of Mand, the girls in white trousers, the boys in long kilts, warlike and archaic. They spoke of their hopes. "We in Mand are so very far from the Revolution that maybe we are near it," said one of the girls, wistful and smiling: "The Circle of Life!" and she showed the extremes meeting, in the circle of her slender, dark-skinned fingers. Amai and Aevi served them white wine and brown bread, the hospitality of the House. But the visitors, unpresumptuous, all rose to take their leave after barely half an hour. "No, no, no," Laia said, "stay here, talk with Aevi and Amai. It's just that I get stiff sitting down, you see, I have to charge about. It has been so good to meet you, will you come back to see me, my little brothers and sisters, soon?" For her heart went out to them, and theirs to her, and she exchanged kisses all round, laughing, delighted by the dark young cheeks, the affectionate eyes, the scented hair, before she shuffled off. She was really a little tired, but to go up and take a nap would be a defeat. She had wanted to go out. She would go out. She had not been alone outdoors since—when? Since winter! before the stroke. No wonder she was getting morbid. It had been a regular jail sentence. Outside, the streets, that's where she lived.

She went quietly out the side door of the House, past the vegetable patch, to the street. The narrow strip of sour city dirt had been beautifully gardened and was producing a fine crop of beans and *ceeä,* but Laia's eye for farming was unenlightened. Of course it had been clear that anarchist communities, even in the time of transition, must work towards optimal self-support, but how that was to be managed in the way of actual dirt and plants wasn't her business. There were farmers and agronomists for that. Her job was the streets, the noisy, stinking streets of stone, where she had grown up and lived all her life, except for the fifteen years in prison.

She looked up fondly at the façade of the House. That it had been built as a bank gave peculiar satisfaction to its present occupants. They kept their sacks of meal in the bomb-proof money-vault, and aged their cider in kegs in safe deposit boxes. Over the fussy columns that faced the street carved letters still read, "National Investors and Grain Factors Banking Association." The Movement was not strong on names. They had no flag. Slogans came and went as the need did. There was always the Circle of Life to scratch on walls and pavements where Authority would have to see it. But when it came to names they were indifferent, accepting and ignoring whatever they got called, unafraid of being pinned down and penned in, afraid of being absurd. So this best known and second oldest of all the cooperative Houses had no name except The Bank.

It faced on a wide and quiet street, but only a block away began the Temeba, an open market, once famous as a center for blackmarket psychogenics and teratogenics, now reduced to vegetables, secondhand clothes, and miserable sideshows. Its crapulous vitality was gone, leaving only half-paralyzed alcoholics, addicts, cripples, hucksters, and fifth-rate whores, pawnshops, gambling dens, fortune-tellers, body-sculptors, and cheap hotels. Laia turned to the Temeba as water seeks its level.

She had never feared or despised the city. It was her country. There would not be slums like this, if the Revolution prevailed. But there would be misery. There would always be misery, waste, cruelty. She had never pretended to be changing the human condition, to be Mama taking tragedy away from the children so they won't hurt themselves. Anything but. So long as people were free to choose, if they chose to drink flybane and live in sewers, it was their business. Just so long as it wasn't the business of Business, the source of profit and the means of power for other people.

She had felt all that before she knew anything; before she wrote the first pamphlet, before she left Parheo, before she knew what "capital" meant, before she'd been farther than River Street where she played rolltaggie kneeling on scabby knees on the pavement with the other six-year-olds, she had known it: that she, and the other kids, and her parents, and their parents, and the drunks and whores and all of River Street, were all the bottom of something—were the foundation, the reality, the source. But will you drag civilization down into the mud? cried the shocked decent people, later on, and she had tried for years to explain to them that if all you had was mud, then if you were God you made it into human beings, and if you were human you tried to make it into houses where human beings could live. But nobody who thought he was better than mud could understand. Now, water seeking its level, mud to mud, Laia shuffled through the foul, noisy street, and all the ugly weakness of her old age was at home. The sleepy whores, their lacquered hair arrangements dilapidated and askew, the one-eyed woman wearily yelling her vegetables to sell, the half-wit beggar slapping flies, these were her countrywomen. They looked like her, they were all sad, disgusting, mean, pitiful, hideous. They were her sisters, her own people.

She did not feel too well. It had been a long time since she had walked so far, four or five blocks by herself, in the noise and push and striking summer heat of the streets. She had wanted to get to Koly Park, the triangle of scruffy grass at the end of the Temeba, and sit there for a while with the other old men and women who always sat there, to see what it was like to sit there and be old; but it was too far. If she didn't turn back now, she might get a dizzy spell, and she had a dread of falling down, falling down and having to lie there and look up at the people come to stare at the old woman in a fit. She turned and started home, frowning with effort and self-disgust. She could feel her face very red, and a swimming feeling came and went in her ears. It got a bit much, she was really afraid she might keel over. She saw a doorstep in the shade and made for it, let herself down cautiously, sat, sighed.

Nearby was a fruit-seller, sitting silent behind his dusty, withered stock. People went by. Nobody bought from him. Nobody looked at her. Odo, who was Odo? Famous revolutionary, author of *Community, The Analogy,* etc. etc. She, who was she? An old woman with grey hair and a red face sitting on a dirty doorstep in a slum, muttering to herself.

True? Was that she? Certainly it was what anybody passing her saw. But was it she, herself, any more than the famous revolutionary, etc., was? No. It was not. But who was she, then?

The one who loved Taviri.

Yes. True enough. But not enough. That was gone; he had been dead so long.

"Who am I?" Laia muttered to her invisible audience, and they knew the answer and told it to her with one voice. She was the little girl with scabby knees, sitting on the doorstep staring down through the dirty golden haze of River Street in the heat of late summer, the six-year-old, the sixteen-year-old, the fierce, cross, dream-ridden girl, untouched, untouchable. She was herself. Indeed she had been the tireless worker and thinker, but a blood clot in a vein had taken that woman away from her. Indeed she had been the lover, the swimmer in the midst of life, but Taviri, dying, had taken that woman away with him. There was nothing left, really, but the foundation. She had come home; she had never left home. "True voyage is return." Dust and mud and a doorstep in the slums. And beyond, at the far end of the street, the field full of tall dry weeds blowing in the wind as the night came.

"Laia! What are you doing here? Are you all right?"

One of the people from the House, of course, a nice woman, a bit fanatical and always talking. Laia could not remember her name though she had known her for years. She let herself be taken home, the woman talking all the way. In the big cool common room (once occupied by tellers counting money behind polished counters supervised by armed guards) Laia sat down in a chair. She was unable just as yet to face climbing the stairs, though she would have liked to be alone. The woman kept on talking, and other excited people came in. It appeared that a demonstration was being planned. Events in Thu were moving so fast that the mood here had caught fire, and something must be done. Day after tomorrow, no, tomorrow, there was to be a march, a big one, from Old Town to Capitol Square, the old route. "Another Ninth Month Uprising," said a young man, fiery and laughing, glancing at Laia. He had not even been born at the time of the Ninth Month Uprising, it was all history to him. Now he wanted to make some history of his own. The room had filled up. A general meeting would be held here, tomorrow, at eight in the morning. "You must talk, Laia."

"Tomorrow? Oh, I won't be here tomorrow," she said brusquely. Whoever had asked her smiled, another one laughed, though Amai glanced round at her with a puzzled look. They went on talking and shouting. The Revolution. What on earth had made her say that? What a thing to say on the eve of the Revolution, even if it was true.

She waited her time, managed to get up and, for all her clumsiness, to slip away unnoticed among the people busy with their planning and excitement. She got to the hall, to the stairs, and began to climb them one by one. "The general strike," a voice, two voices, ten voices were saying in the room below, behind her. "The general strike," Laia muttered, resting for a moment on the landing. Above, ahead, in her room, what awaited her? The private stroke. That was mildly funny. She started up the second flight of stairs, one by one, one leg at a time, like a small child. She was dizzy, but she was no longer afraid to fall. On ahead, on there, the dry white flowers nodded and whispered in the open fields of evening. Seventy-two years and she had never had time to learn what they were called.

HARLAN ELLISON

HARLAN ELLISON was born in Cleveland, Ohio, in 1934, grew up in nearby Painesville, and attended Ohio State University. He was expelled for shoplifting, poor grades, punching a professor for saying he couldn't write, and driving up the Longwalk onto the statue of William Osley Thompson (all within the space of about ten days) in 1953, before going to New York in 1955 to become a writer.

Science fiction's original *enfant terrible,* Ellison published his first story in 1956 and within a year had published over a hundred fiction and nonfiction pieces, under his own name and under a variety of commercially required pen names. He served in the army between 1957 and 1959, moved to Chicago to edit *Rogue* magazine, and established Regency Books in 1961. Ellison then moved to Los Angeles in 1962 and quickly established himself writing screenplays for popular television shows, most famously the *Star Trek* episode "The City on the Edge of Forever."

Primarily a writer of short fiction, Ellison's most famous stories include "I Have No Mouth, and I Must Scream," "The Beast That Shouted Love at the Heart of the World," "The Deathbird," "Paladin of the Lost Hour," " 'Repent Harlequin!' Said the Ticktockman," and "Jeffty Is Five." His stories are gathered in numerous collections, including *Ellison Wonderland, I Have No Mouth & I Must Scream, Love Ain't Nothing but Sex Misspelled,*

Deathbird Stories, Strange Wine, Shatterday, Angry Candy, and the career retrospective *The Essential Ellison: A Fifty Year Retrospective.* Ellison also had a major influence on the field as an editor when, in 1967, he published the landmark anthology *Dangerous Visions.* If not the herald of science fiction's New Wave movement, it was certainly its most significant statement and showed many of the changes that would dominate the field for the next three decades. His work has been awarded the Hugo Award eight and a half times, the Nebula Award six times, the Bram Stoker Award six times, the World Fantasy Award, the British Fantasy Award, the British Science Fiction Award, and the Locus Award a record eighteen times, thirteen times for short fiction. His career awards include the World Fantasy Award for Life Achievement, the Bram Stoker Award for Life Achievement, the International Horror Guild Living Legend, and the World Horror Grandmaster.

In 1999 *Locus* readers voted in an online poll and named Ellison the top short story writer of all time and "Jeffty Is Five" the best short story.

* * *

WHEN I WAS FIVE years old, there was a little kid I played with: Jeffty. His real name was Jeff Kinzer, and everyone who played with him called him Jeffty. We were five years old together, and we had good times playing together.

When I was five, a Clark Bar was as fat around as the gripping end of a Louisville Slugger, and pretty nearly six inches long, and they used real chocolate to coat it, and it crunched very nicely when you bit into the center, and the paper it came wrapped in smelled fresh and good when you peeled off one end to hold the bar so it wouldn't melt onto your fingers. Today, a Clark Bar is as thin as a credit card, they use something artificial and awful-tasting instead of pure chocolate, the thing is soft and soggy, it costs fifteen or twenty cents instead of a decent, correct nickel, and they wrap it so you think it's the same size it was twenty years ago, only it isn't; it's slim and ugly and nasty tasting and not worth a penny, much less fifteen or twenty cents.

When I was that age, five years old, I was sent away to my Aunt Patricia's home in Buffalo, New York, for two years. My father was going through "bad times" and Aunt Patricia was very beautiful, and had married a stockbroker. They took care of me for two years. When I was seven, I came back home and went to find Jeffty, so we could play together.

I was seven. Jeffty was still five. I didn't notice any difference. I didn't know:

I was only seven.

When I was seven years old, I used to lie on my stomach in front of our Atwater-Kent radio and listen to swell stuff. I had tied the ground wire to the radiator, and I would lie there with my coloring books and my Crayolas (when there were only sixteen colors in the big box), and listen to the NBC Red network: Jack Benny on the *Jell-O Program, Amos 'n' Andy,* Edgar Bergen and Charlie McCarthy on the *Chase and Sanborn Program, One Man's Family, First Nighter;* the NBC Blue network: *Easy Aces,* the *Jergens Program* with Walter Winchell, *Information Please, Death Valley Days;* and best of all, the Mutual Network with *The Green Hornet, The Lone Ranger, The Shadow,* and *Quiet, Please.* Today, I turn on my car radio and go from one end of the dial to the other and all I get is 100 strings orchestras, banal housewives and insipid truckers discussing their kinky sex lives with arrogant talk show hosts, country and western drivel and rock music so loud it hurts my ears.

When I was ten, my grandfather died of old age and I was "a troublesome kid," and they sent me off to military school, so I could be "taken in hand."

I came back when I was fourteen. Jeffty was still five.

When I was fourteen years old, I used to go to the movies on Saturday afternoons and a matinee was ten cents and they used real butter on the popcorn and I could always be sure of seeing a western like Lash LaRue, or Wild Bill Elliott as Red Ryder with Bobby Blake as Little Beaver, or Roy Rogers, or Johnny Mack Brown; a scary picture like *House of Horrors* with Rondo Hatton as the Strangler, or *The Cat People,* or *The Mummy,* or *I Married a Witch* with Fredric March and Veronica Lake; plus an episode of a great serial like *The Shadow* with Victor Jory, or *Dick Tracy* or *Flash Gordon;* and three cartoons; a James Fitzpatrick TravelTalk; Movietone News; and a singalong and, if I stayed on till evening, Bingo or Keeno; and free dishes. Today, I go to movies and see Clint Eastwood blowing people's heads apart like ripe cantaloupes.

At eighteen, I went to college. Jeffty was still five. I came back during the summers, to work at my Uncle Joe's jewelry store. Jeffty hadn't changed. Now I knew there was something different about him, something wrong, something weird. Jeffty was still five years old, not a day older.

At twenty-two, I came home for keeps. To open a Sony television franchise in town, the first one. I saw Jeffty from time to time. He was five.

Things are better in a lot of ways. People don't die from some of the old diseases any more. Cars go faster and get you there more quickly on better roads. Shirts are softer and silkier. We have paperback books, even though they cost as much as a good hardcover used to. When I'm running short in the bank, I can live off credit cards till things even out. But I still think we've lost a lot of good stuff. Did you know you can't buy linoleum any more, only vinyl floor covering? There's no such thing as oilcloth any more; you'll never again smell that special, sweet smell from your grandmother's kitchen. Furniture isn't made to last thirty years or longer because they took a survey and found that young homemakers like to throw their furniture out and bring in all new, color-coded borax every seven years. Records don't feel right; they're not thick and solid like the old ones, they're thin and you can bend them . . . that doesn't seem right to me. Restaurants don't serve cream in pitchers any more, just that artificial glop in little plastic tubs, and one is never enough to get coffee the right color. You can make a dent in a car fender with only a sneaker. Everywhere you go, all the towns look the same with Burger Kings and McDonald's and 7-Elevens and Taco Bells and motels and shopping centers. Things may be better, but why do I keep thinking about the past?

What I mean by five years old is not that Jeffty was retarded. I don't think that's what it was. Smart as a whip for five years old; very bright, quick, cute, a funny kid.

But he was three feet tall, small for his age, and perfectly formed: no big head, no strange jaw, none of that. A nice, normal-looking five-year-old kid. Except that he was the same age as I was: twenty-two.

When he spoke, it was with the squeaking, soprano voice of a five-year-old; when he walked, it was with the little hops and shuffles of a five-year-old; when he talked to you, it was about the concerns of a five-year-old . . . comic books, playing soldier, using a clothes pin to attach a stiff piece of cardboard to the front fork of his bike so the sound it made when the spokes hit was like a motorboat, asking questions like *why does that thing do that like that,* how high is up, how old is old, why is grass green, what's an elephant look like? At twenty-two, he was five.

JEFFTY'S PARENTS WERE a sad pair. Because I was still a friend of Jeffty's, still let him hang around with me in the store, sometimes took him to the county fair or to the miniature golf or the movies, I wound up spending time with *them.* Not that I much cared for them, because they were so awfully depressing. But then, I suppose one couldn't expect much more from the poor devils. They had an alien thing in their home, a child who had grown no older than five in twenty-two years, who provided the treasure of that special childlike state indefinitely, but who also denied them the joys of watching the child grow into a normal adult.

Five is a wonderful time of life for a little kid . . . or it *can* be, if the child is relatively free of the monstrous beastliness other children indulge in. It is a time when the eyes are wide open and the patterns are not yet set; a time when one has not yet been hammered into accepting everything as immutable and hopeless; a time when the hands cannot do enough, the mind cannot learn enough, the world is infinite and colorful and filled with mysteries. Five is a special time before they take the questing, unquenchable, quixotic soul of the young dreamer and thrust it into dreary schoolroom boxes. A time before they take the trembling hands that want to hold everything, touch everything, figure everything out, and make them lie still on desktops. A time before people begin saying "act your age" and "grow up" or "you're behaving like a baby." It is a time when a child who acts adolescent is still cute and responsive and everyone's pet. A time of delight, of wonder, of innocence.

Jeffty had been stuck in that time, just five, just so.

But for his parents it was an ongoing nightmare from which no one—not social workers, not priests, not child psychologists, not teachers, not friends, not medical wizards, not psychiatrists, no one—could slap or shake them awake. For seventeen years their sorrow had grown through stages of parental dotage to concern, from concern to worry, from worry to fear, from fear to confusion, from confusion to anger, from anger to dislike, from dislike to naked hatred, and finally, from deepest loathing and revulsion to a stolid, depressive acceptance.

John Kinzer was a shift foreman at the Balder Tool & Die plant. He was a thirty-year man. To everyone but the man living it, his was a spectacularly uneventful life. In no way was he remarkable . . . save that he had fathered a twenty-two-year-old five-year-old.

John Kinzer was a small man; soft, with no sharp angles; with pale eyes that never seemed to hold mine for longer than a few seconds. He continually shifted in his chair during conversations, and seemed to see things in the upper corners of the room, things no one else could see . . . or wanted to see. I suppose the word that best suited him was *haunted*. What his life had become . . . well, *haunted* suited him.

Leona Kinzer tried valiantly to compensate. No matter what hour of the day I visited, she always tried to foist food on me. And when Jeffty was in the house she was always at *him* about eating: "Honey, would you like an orange? A nice orange? Or a tangerine? I have tangerines. I could peel a tangerine for you." But there was clearly such fear in her, fear of her own child, that the offers of sustenance always had a faintly ominous tone.

Leona Kinzer had been a tall woman, but the years had bent her. She seemed always to be seeking some area of wallpapered wall or storage niche into which she could fade, adopt some chintz or rose-patterned protective coloration and hide forever in plain sight of the child's big brown eyes, pass her a hundred times a day and never realize she was there, holding her breath, invisible. She always had an apron tied around her waist, and her hands were red from cleaning. As if by maintaining the environment immaculately she could pay off her imagined sin: having given birth to this strange creature.

Neither of them watched television very much. The house was usually dead silent, not even the sibilant whispering of water in the pipes, the creaking of timbers settling, the humming of the refrigerator. Awfully silent, as if time itself had taken a detour around that house.

As for Jeffty, he was inoffensive. He lived in that atmosphere of gentle dread and dulled loathing, and if he understood it, he never remarked in any way. He played, as a child plays, and seemed happy. But he must have sensed, in the way of a five-year-old, just how alien he was in their presence.

Alien. No, that wasn't right. He was *too* human, if anything. But out of phase, out of synch with the world around him, and resonating to a different vibration than his parents, God knows. Nor would other children play with him. As they grew past him, they found him at first childish, then uninteresting, then simply frightening as their perceptions of aging became clear and they could see he was not affected by time as they were. Even the little ones, his own age, who might wander into the neighborhood, quickly came to shy away from him like a dog in the street when a car backfires.

Thus, I remained his only friend. A friend of many years. Five years. Twenty-two years. I liked him; more than I can say. And never knew exactly why. But I did, without reserve.

But because we spent time together, I found I was also—polite society—spending time with John and Leona Kinzer. Dinner, Saturday afternoons sometimes, an hour or so when I'd bring Jeffty back from a movie. They were grateful: slavishly so. It relieved them of the embarrassing chore of going out with him, or having to pretend before the world that they were loving parents with a perfectly normal, happy, attractive child. And their gratitude extended to hosting me. Hideous, every moment of their depression, hideous.

I felt sorry for the poor devils, but I despised them for their inability to love Jeffty, who was eminently lovable.

I never let on, of course, even during the evenings in their company that were awkward beyond belief.

We would sit there in the darkening living room—*always* dark or darkening, as if kept in shadow to hold back what the light might reveal to the world outside through the bright eyes of the house—we would sit and silently stare at one another. They never knew what to say to me.

"So how are things down at the plant?" I'd say to John Kinzer.

He would shrug. Neither conversation nor life suited him with any ease or grace. "Fine, just fine," he would say, finally.

And we would sit in silence again.

"Would you like a nice piece of coffee cake?" Leona would say. "I made it fresh just this morning." Or deep dish green apple pie. Or milk and tollhouse cookies. Or a brown betty pudding.

"No, no, thank you, Mrs. Kinzer; Jeffty and I grabbed a couple of cheeseburgers on the way home." And again, silence.

Then, when the stillness and the awkwardness became too much even for them (and who knew how long that total silence reigned when they were alone, with that thing they never talked about any more, hanging between them), Leona Kinzer would say, "I think he's asleep."

John Kinzer would say, "I don't hear the radio playing."

Just so, it would go on like that, until I could politely find excuse to bolt away on some flimsy pretext. Yes, that was the way it would go on, every time, just the same . . . except once.

"I DON'T KNOW WHAT TO DO ANY MORE," Leona said. She began crying. "There's no change, not one day of peace."

Her husband managed to drag himself out of the old easy chair, and he went to her. He bent and tried to soothe her, but it was clear from the graceless way in which he touched her graying hair that the ability to be compassionate had been stunned in him. "Shhh, Leona, it's all right. Shhh." But she continued crying. Her hands scraped gently at the antimacassars on the arms of the chair.

Then she said, "Sometimes I wish he had been stillborn."

John looked up into the corners of the room. For the nameless shadows that were always watching him? Was it God he was seeking in those spaces? "You don't mean that," he said to her, softly, pathetically, urging her with body tension and trembling in his voice to recant before God took notice of the terrible thought. But she meant it; she meant it very much.

I managed to get away quickly that evening. They didn't want witnesses to their shame. I was glad to go.

AND FOR A WEEK I stayed away. From them, from Jeffty, from their street, even from that end of town.

I had my own life. The store, accounts, suppliers' conferences, poker with friends, pretty women I took to well-lit restaurants, my own parents, putting anti-freeze in the car, complaining to the laundry about too much starch in the collars and cuffs, working out at the gym, taxes, catching Jan or David (whichever one it was) stealing from the cash register. I had my own life.

But not even *that* evening could keep me from Jeffty. He called me at the store and asked me to take him to the rodeo. We chummed it up as best a twenty-two-year-old with other interests *could* . . . with a five-year-old. I never dwelled on what bound us together; I always thought it was simply the years. That, and affection for a kid who could have been the little brother I never had. (Except I *remembered* when we had played together, when we had both been the same age; I *remembered* that period, and Jeffty was still the same.)

And then, one Saturday afternoon, I came to take him to a double feature, and things I should have noticed so many times before, I first began to notice only that afternoon.

I CAME WALKING UP TO THE KINZER HOUSE, expecting Jeffty to be sitting on the front porch steps, or in the porch glider, waiting for me. But he was nowhere in sight.

Going inside, into that darkness and silence, in the midst of May sunshine, was unthinkable. I stood on the front walk for a few moments, then cupped my hands around my mouth and yelled, "Jeffty? Hey, Jeffty, come on out, let's go. We'll be late."

His voice came faintly, as if from under the ground.

"Here I am, Donny."

I could hear him, but I couldn't see him. It was Jeffty, no question about it: as Donald H. Horton, President and Sole Owner of The Horton TV &

Sound Center, no one but Jeffty called me Donny. He had never called me anything else.

(Actually, it isn't a lie. I *am,* as far as the public is concerned, Sole Owner of the Center. The partnership with my Aunt Patricia is only to repay the loan she made me, to supplement the money I came into when I was twenty-one, left to me when I was ten by my grandfather. It wasn't a very big loan, only eighteen thousand, but I asked her to be a silent partner, because of when she had taken care of me as a child.)

"Where are you, Jeffty?"

"Under the porch in my secret place."

I walked around the side of the porch, and stooped down and pulled away the wicker grating. Back in there, on the pressed dirt, Jeffty had built himself a secret place. He had comics in orange crates, he had a little table and some pillows, it was lit by big fat candles, and we used to hide there when we were both . . . five.

"What'cha up to?" I asked, crawling in and pulling the grate closed behind me. It was cool under the porch, and the dirt smelled comfortable, the candles smelled clubby and familiar. Any kid would feel at home in such a secret place: there's never been a kid who didn't spend the happiest, most productive, most deliciously mysterious times of his life in such a secret place.

"Playin'," he said. He was holding something golden and round. It filled the palm of his little hand.

"You forget we were going to the movies?"

"Nope. I was just waitin' for you here."

"Your mom and dad home?"

"Momma."

I understood why he was waiting under the porch. I didn't push it any further. "What've you got there?"

"Captain Midnight Secret Decoder Badge," he said, showing it to me on his flattened palm.

I realized I was looking at it without comprehending what it was for a long time. Then it dawned on me what a miracle Jeffty had in his hand. A miracle that simply could *not* exist.

"Jeffty," I said softly, with wonder in my voice, "where'd you get that?"

"Came in the mail today. I sent away for it."

"It must have cost a lot of money."

"Not so much. Ten cents an' two inner wax seals from two jars of Ovaltine."

"May I see it?" My voice was trembling, and so was the hand I extended. He gave it to me and I held the miracle in the palm of my hand. It was *wonderful.*

You remember. *Captain Midnight* went on the radio nationwide in 1940. It was sponsored by Ovaltine. And every year they issued a Secret Squadron Decoder Badge. And every day at the end of the program, they would give you a clue to the next day's installment in a code that only kids with the official badge could decipher. They stopped making those wonderful Decoder Badges in 1949. I remember the one I had in 1945: it was beautiful. It had a magnifying glass in the center of the code dial. *Captain Midnight* went off the air in 1950, and though I understand it was a short-lived television series in the mid-Fifties, and though they issued Decoder Badges in 1955 and 1956, as far as the *real* badges were concerned, they never made one after 1949.

The Captain Midnight Code-O-Graph I held in my hand, the one Jeffty said he had gotten in the mail for ten cents (*ten cents!!!*) and two Ovaltine labels, was brand new, shiny gold metal, not a dent or a spot of rust on it like the old ones you can find at exorbitant prices in collectible shoppes from time to time . . . it was a *new* Decoder. And the date on it was *this* year.

But *Captain Midnight* no longer existed. Nothing like it existed on the radio. I'd listened to the one or two weak imitations of old-time radio the networks were currently airing, and the stories were dull, the sound effects bland, the whole feel of it wrong, out of date, cornball. Yet I held a *new* Code-O-Graph.

"Jeffty, tell me about this," I said.

"Tell you what, Donny? It's my new Capt'n Midnight Secret Decoder Badge. I use it to figger out what's gonna happen tomorrow."

"Tomorrow how?"

"On the program."

"*What* program?!"

He stared at me as if I was being purposely stupid. "On Capt'n *Mid*night! Boy!" I was being dumb.

I still couldn't get it straight. It was right there, right out in the open, and I still didn't know what was happening. "You mean one of those records they made of the old-time radio programs? Is that what you mean, Jeffty?"

"What records?" he asked. He didn't know what *I* meant.

We stared at each other, there under the porch. And then I said, very slowly, almost afraid of the answer, "Jeffty, how do you hear *Captain Midnight?*"

"Every day. On the radio. On my radio. Every day at five-thirty."

News. Music, dumb music, and news. That's what was on the radio every day at 5:30. Not *Captain Midnight.* The Secret Squadron hadn't been on the air in twenty years.

"Can we hear it tonight?" I asked.

"Boy!" he said. I was being dumb. I knew it from the way he said it; but I didn't know *why.* Then it dawned on me: this was Saturday. *Captain Midnight* was on Monday through Friday. Not on Saturday or Sunday.

"We goin' to the movies?"

He had to repeat himself twice. My mind was somewhere else. Nothing definite. No conclusions. No wild assumptions leapt to. Just off somewhere trying to figure it out, and concluding—as *you* would have concluded, as *any*one would have concluded rather than accepting the truth, the impossible and wonderful truth—just finally concluding there was a simple explanation I didn't yet perceive. Something mundane and dull, like the passage of time that steals all good, old things from us, packratting trinkets and plastic in exchange. And all in the name of Progress.

"We goin' to the movies, Donny?"

"You bet your boots we are, kiddo," I said. And I smiled. And I handed him the Code-O-Graph. And he put it in his side pants pocket. And we crawled out from under the porch. And we went to the movies. And neither of us said anything about *Captain Midnight* all the rest of that day. And there wasn't a ten-minute stretch, all the rest of that day, that I didn't think about it.

IT WAS INVENTORY all that next week. I didn't see Jeffty till late Thursday. I confess I left the store in the hands of Jan and David, told them I had some errands to run, and left early. At 4:00. I got to the Kinzers' right around 4:45. Leona answered the door, looking exhausted and distant. "Is Jeffty around?" She said he was upstairs in his room . . .

. . . listening to the radio.

I climbed the stairs two at a time.

All right, I had finally made that impossible, illogical leap. Had the stretch of belief involved anyone but Jeffty, adult or child, I would have reasoned out more explicable answers. But it *was* Jeffty, clearly another kind of vessel of life, and what he might experience should not be expected to fit into the ordered scheme.

I admit it: I *wanted* to hear what I heard.

Even with the door closed, I recognized the program:

"*There he goes, Tennessee! Get him!*"

There was the heavy report of a rifle shot and the keening whine of the slug ricocheting, and then the same voice yelled triumphantly, "*Got him! D-e-a-a-a-d center!*"

He was listening to the American Broadcasting Company, 790 kilocycles, and he was hearing *Tennessee Jed,* one of my most favorite programs from the Forties, a western adventure I had not heard in twenty years, because it had not existed for twenty years.

I sat down on the top step of the stairs, there in the upstairs hall of the Kinzer home, and I listened to the show. It wasn't a rerun of an old program, because there were occasional references in the body of the drama to current cultural and technological developments, and phrases that had not existed in common usage in the Forties: aerosol spray cans, laserasing of tattoos, Tanzania, the word "uptight."

I could not ignore the fact. Jeffty was listening to a *new* segment of *Tennessee Jed.*

I ran downstairs and out the front door to my car. Leona must have been in the kitchen. I turned the key and punched on the radio and spun the dial to 790 kilocycles. The ABC station. Rock music.

I sat there for a few moments, then ran the dial slowly from one end to the other. Music, news, talk shows. No *Tennessee Jed.* And it was a Blaupunkt, the best radio I could get. I wasn't missing some perimeter station. It simply was not there!

After a few moments I turned off the radio and the ignition and went back upstairs quietly. I sat down on the top step and listened to the entire program. It was *wonderful.*

Exciting, imaginative, filled with everything I remembered as being most innovative about radio drama. But it was modern. It wasn't an antique, re-broadcast to assuage the need of that dwindling listenership who longed for the old days. It was a new show, with all the old voices, but still young and bright. Even the commercials were for currently available products, but they weren't as loud or as insulting as the screamer ads one heard on radio these days.

And when *Tennessee Jed* went off at 5:00, I heard Jeffty spin the dial on his radio till I heard the familiar voice of the announcer Glenn Riggs proclaim, "*Presenting Hop Harrigan! America's ace of the airwaves!*" There was the sound of an airplane in flight. It was a prop plane, *not* a jet! Not the sound kids today have grown up with, but the sound *I* grew up with, the *real* sound of an airplane, the growling, revving, throaty sound of the kind of airplanes G-8 and His Battle Aces flew, the kind Captain Midnight flew, the kind Hop Harrigan flew. And then I heard Hop say, *"CX 4 calling control tower. CX-4 calling control tower. Standing by!"* A pause, then, *"Okay, this is Hop Harrigan . . . coming in!"*

And Jeffty, who had the same problem all of us kids had had in the Forties with programming that pitted equal favorites against one another on different stations, having paid his respects to Hop Harrigan and Tank Tinker, spun the dial and went back to ABC, where I heard the stroke of a gong, the wild cacophony of nonsense Chinese chatter, and the announcer yelled, *"T-e-e-e-rry and the Pirates!"*

I sat there on the top step and listened to Terry and Connie and Flip Corkin and, so help me God, Agnes Moorehead as The Dragon Lady, all of them in a new adventure that took place in a Red China that had not existed in the days of Milton Caniff's 1937 version of the Orient, with river pirates and Chiang Kai-shek and warlords and the naive Imperialism of American gunboat diplomacy.

Sat, and listened to the whole show, and sat even longer to hear *Superman* and part of *Jack Armstrong, The All American Boy* and part of *Captain Midnight,* and John Kinzer came home and neither he nor Leona came upstairs to find out what had happened to me, or where Jeffty was, and sat longer, and found I had started crying, and could not stop, just sat there with tears running down my face, into the corners of my mouth, sitting and crying until Jeffty heard me and opened his door and saw me and came out and looked at me in childish confusion as I heard the station break for the Mutual Network and they began the theme music of *Tom Mix,* "When It's Round-up Time in Texas and the Bloom Is on the Sage," and Jeffty touched my shoulder and smiled at me, with his mouth and his big brown eyes, and said, "Hi, Donny. Wanna come in an' listen to the radio with me?"

HUME DENIED THE existence of an absolute space, in which each thing has its place; Borges denies the existence of one single time, in which all events are linked.

Jeffty received radio programs from a place that could not, in logic, in the natural scheme of the space-time universe as conceived by Einstein, exist. But that wasn't all he received. He got mail order premiums that no one was manufacturing. He read comic books that had been defunct for three decades. He saw movies with actors who had been dead for twenty years. He was the receiving terminal for endless joys and pleasures of the past that the world had dropped along the way. On its headlong suicidal flight toward New Tomorrows, the world had razed its treasurehouse of simple happinesses, had poured concrete over its playgrounds, had abandoned its elfin stragglers, and all of it was being impossibly, miraculously shunted back into the present through Jeffty. Revivified, updated, the traditions maintained but contemporaneous. Jeffty was the unbidding Aladdin whose very nature formed the magic lampness of his reality.

And he took me into his world with him.

Because he trusted me.

We had breakfast of Quaker Puffed Wheat Sparkies and warm Ovaltine we drank out of *this* year's Little Orphan Annie Shake-Up Mugs. We went to the movies and while everyone else was seeing a comedy starring Goldie Hawn and Ryan O'Neal, Jeffty and I were enjoying Humphrey Bogart as the professional thief Parker in John Huston's brilliant adaptation of the Donald Westlake novel *Slayground.* The second feature was Spencer Tracy, Carole Lombard and Laird Cregar in the Val Lewton–produced film of *Leiningen Versus the Ants.*

Twice a month we went down to the newsstand and bought the current pulp issues of *The Shadow, Doc Savage* and *Startling Stories.* Jeffty and I sat together and I read to him from the magazines. He particularly liked the new short novel by Henry Kuttner, "The Dreams of Achilles," and the new Stanley G. Weinbaum series of short stories set in the subatomic particle universe of Redurna. In September we enjoyed the first installment of the new Robert E. Howard Conan novel, *Isle of the Black Ones,* in *Weird Tales*; and in August we were only mildly disappointed by Edgar Rice Burroughs's fourth novella in the Jupiter series featuring John Carter of Barsoom— "Corsairs of Jupiter." But the editor of *Argosy All-Story Weekly* promised there would be two more stories in the series, and it was such an unexpected revelation for Jeffty and me that it dimmed our disappointment at the lessened quality of the current story.

We read comics together, and Jeffty and I both decided—separately, before we came together to discuss it—that our favorite characters were Doll Man, Airboy and The Heap. We also adored the George Carlson strips in *Jingle Jangle Comics,* particularly the Pie-Face Prince of Old Pretzleburg stories, which we read together and laughed over, even though I had to explain some of the esoteric puns to Jeffty, who was too young to have that kind of subtle wit.

How to explain it? I can't. I had enough physics in college to make some offhand guesses, but I'm more likely wrong than right. The laws of the conservation of energy occasionally break. These are laws that physicists call "weakly violated." Perhaps Jeffty was a catalyst for the weak violation of conservation laws we're only now beginning to realize exist. I tried doing some reading in the area—muon decay of the "forbidden" kind: gamma decay that doesn't include the muon neutrino among its products—but nothing I encountered, not even the latest readings from the Swiss Institute for Nuclear Research near Zurich, gave me an insight. I was thrown back on a vague acceptance of the philosophy that the real name for "science" is *magic*.

No explanations, but enormous good times.

The happiest time of my life.

I had the "real" world, the world of my store and my friends and my family, the world of profit&loss, of taxes and evenings with young women who talked about going shopping or the United Nations, or the rising cost of coffee and microwave ovens. And I had Jeffty's world, in which I existed only when I was with him. The things of the past he knew as fresh and new, I could experience only when in his company. And the membrane between the two worlds grew ever thinner, more luminous and transparent. I had the best of both worlds. And knew, somehow, that I could carry nothing from one to the other.

Forgetting that, for just a moment, betraying Jeffty by forgetting, brought an end to it all.

Enjoying myself so much, I grew careless and failed to consider how fragile the relationship between Jeffty's world and my world really was. There is a reason why the present begrudges the existence of the past. I never really understood. Nowhere in the beast books, where survival is shown in battles between claw and fang, tentacle and poison sac, is there recognition of the ferocity the present always brings to bear on the past. Nowhere is there a detailed statement of how the present lies in wait for What-Was, waiting for it to become Now-This-Moment so it can shred it with its merciless jaws.

Who could know such a thing . . . at any age . . . and certainly not at my age . . . who could understand such a thing?

I'm trying to exculpate myself. I can't. It was my fault.

IT WAS ANOTHER Saturday afternoon.

"What's playing today?" I asked him, in the car, on the way downtown.

He looked up at me from the other side of the front seat and smiled one of his best smiles. "Ken Maynard in *Bullwhip Justice* an' *The Demolished Man*." He kept smiling, as if he'd really put one over on me. I looked at him with disbelief.

"You're *kid*ding!" I said, delighted. "Bester's *The Demolished Man*?" He nodded his head, delighted at my being delighted. He knew it was one of my favorite books. "Oh, that's super!"

"Super *duper*," he said.

"Who's in it?"

"Franchot Tone, Evelyn Keyes, Lionel Barrymore and Elisha Cook, Jr." He was much more knowledgeable about movie actors than I'd ever been. He could name the character actors in any movie he'd ever seen. Even the crowd scenes.

"And cartoons?" I asked.

"Three of 'em: a *Little Lulu,* a *Donald Duck* and a *Bugs Bunny.* An' a *Pete Smith Specialty* an' a Lew Lehr *Monkeys is da C-r-r-r-aziest Peoples.*"

"Oh boy!" I said. I was grinning from ear to ear. And then I looked down and saw the pad of purchase order forms on the seat. I'd forgotten to drop it off at the store.

"Gotta stop by the Center," I said. "Gotta drop off something. It'll only take a minute."

"Okay," Jeffty said. "But we won't be late, will we?"

"Not on your tintype, kiddo," I said.

WHEN I PULLED into the parking lot behind the Center, he decided to come in with me and we'd walk over to the theater. It's not a large town. There are only two movie houses, the Utopia and the Lyric. We were going to the Utopia and it was only three blocks from the Center.

I walked into the store with the pad of forms, and it was bedlam. David and Jan were handling two customers each, and there were people standing around waiting to be helped. Jan turned a look on me and her face was a horror-mask of pleading. David was running from the stockroom to the showroom and all he could murmur as he whipped past was "Help!" and then he was gone.

"Jeffty," I said, crouching down, "listen, give me a few minutes. Jan and David are in trouble with all these people. We won't be late, I promise. Just let me get rid of a couple of these customers." He looked nervous, but nodded okay.

I motioned to a chair and said, "Just sit down for a while and I'll be right with you."

He went to the chair, good as you please, though he knew what was happening, and he sat down.

I started taking care of people who wanted color television sets. This was the first really substantial batch of units we'd gotten in—color television was only now becoming reasonably priced and this was Sony's first promotion—and it was bonanza time for me. I could see paying off the loan and being out in front for the first time with the Center. It was business.

In my world, good business comes first.

Jeffty sat there and stared at the wall. Let me tell you about the wall.

Stanchion and bracket designs had been rigged from floor to within two feet of the ceiling. Television sets had been stacked artfully on the wall. Thirty-three television sets. All playing at the same time. Black and white, color, little ones, big ones, all going at the same time.

Jeffty sat and watched thirty-three television sets, on a Saturday afternoon. We can pick up a total of thirteen channels including the UHF educational stations. Golf was on one channel; baseball was on a second; celebrity bowling was on a third; the fourth channel was a religious seminar; a teenage dance show was on the fifth; the sixth was a rerun of a situation comedy; the seventh was a rerun of a police show; eighth was a nature program showing a man fly-casting endlessly; ninth was news and conversation; tenth was a stock car race; eleventh was a man doing logarithms on a blackboard; twelfth was a woman in a leotard doing setting-up exercises; and on the thirteenth channel was a badly animated cartoon show in Spanish. All but six of the shows were repeated on three sets. Jeffty sat and watched that wall of television on a Saturday afternoon while I sold as fast and as hard as I could, to pay back my Aunt Patricia and stay in touch with my world. It was business.

I should have known better. I should have understood about the present and the way it kills the past. But I was selling with both hands. And when I finally glanced over at Jeffty, half an hour later, he looked like another child.

He was sweating. That terrible fever sweat when you have stomach flu. He was pale, as pasty and pale as a worm, and his little hands were gripping the arms of the chair so tightly I could see his knuckles in bold relief. I dashed over to him, excusing myself from the middle-aged couple looking at the new 21" Mediterranean model.

"Jeffty!"

He looked at me, but his eyes didn't track. He was in absolute terror. I pulled him out of the chair and started toward the front door with him, but the customers I'd deserted yelled at me, "Hey!" The middle-aged man said, "You wanna sell me this thing or don't you?"

I looked from him to Jeffty and back again. Jeffty was like a zombie. He had come where I'd pulled him. His legs were rubbery and his feet dragged. The past, being eaten by the present, the sound of something in pain.

I clawed some money out of my pants pocket and jammed it into Jeffty's hand. "Kiddo . . . listen to me . . . get out of here right now!" He still couldn't focus properly. *"Jeffty,"* I said as tightly as I could, *"listen* to me!" The middle-aged customer and his wife were walking toward us. "Listen, kiddo, get out of here right this minute. Walk over to the Utopia and buy the tickets. I'll be right behind you." The middle-aged man and his wife were almost on us. I shoved Jeffty through the door and watched him stumble away in the wrong direction, then stop as if gathering his wits, turn and go back past the front of the Center and in the direction of the Utopia. "Yes sir," I said, straightening up and facing them, "yes, ma'am, that is one terrific set with some sensational features! If you'll just step back here with me . . ."

There was a terrible sound of something hurting, but I couldn't tell from which channel, or from which set, it was coming.

MOST OF IT I learned later, from the girl in the ticket booth, and from some people I knew who came to me to tell me what had happened. By the time I got to the Utopia, nearly twenty minutes later, Jeffty was already beaten to a pulp and had been taken to the Manager's office.

"Did you see a very little boy, about five years old, with big brown eyes and straight brown hair . . . he was waiting for me?"

"Oh, I think that's the little boy those kids beat up?"

"What!?! *Where is he?*"

"They took him to the Manager's office. No one knew who he was or where to find his parents—"

A young girl wearing an usher's uniform was kneeling down beside the couch, placing a wet paper towel on his face.

I took the towel away from her and ordered her out of the office.

She looked insulted and snorted something rude, but she left. I sat on the edge of the couch and tried to swab away the blood from the lacerations without opening the wounds where the blood had caked. Both his eyes were swollen shut. His mouth was ripped badly. His hair was matted with dried blood.

He had been standing in line behind two kids in their teens. They started selling tickets at 12:30 and the show started at 1:00. The doors weren't opened till 12:45. He had been waiting, and the kids in front of him had had a portable radio. They were listening to the ball game. Jeffty had wanted to hear some program, God knows what it might have been, *Grand Central Station, Let's Pretend, Land of the Lost,* God only knows which one it might have been.

He had asked if he could borrow their radio to hear the program for a minute, and it had been a commercial break or something, and the kids had given him the radio, probably out of some malicious kind of courtesy that would permit them to take offense and rag the little boy. He had changed the station . . . and they'd been unable to get it to go back to the ball game. It was locked into the past, on a station that was broadcasting a program that didn't exist for anyone but Jeffty.

They had beaten him badly . . . as everyone watched.

And then they had run away.

I had left him alone, left him to fight off the present without sufficient weaponry. I had betrayed him for the sale of a 21″ Mediterranean console television, and now his face was pulped meat. He moaned something inaudible and sobbed softly.

"Shhh, it's okay, kiddo, it's Donny. I'm here. I'll get you home, it'll be okay."

I should have taken him straight to the hospital. I don't know why I didn't. I should have. I should have done that.

WHEN I CARRIED him through the door, John and Leona Kinzer just stared at me. They didn't move to take him from my arms. One of his hands was hanging down. He was conscious, but just barely. They stared, there in the semi-darkness of a Saturday afternoon in the present. I looked at them. "A couple of kids beat him up at the theater." I raised him a few inches in my arms and extended him. They stared at me, at both of us, with nothing in their eyes, without movement. "Jesus Christ," I shouted, "he's been beaten! He's your son! Don't you even want to touch him? What the hell kind of people are you?!"

Then Leona moved toward me very slowly. She stood in front of us for a few seconds, and there was a leaden stoicism in her face that was terrible to see. It said, *I have been in this place before, many times, and I cannot bear to be in it again; but I am here now.*

So I gave him to her. God help me, I gave him over to her.

And she took him upstairs to bathe away his blood and his pain.

John Kinzer and I stood in our separate places in the dim living room of their home, and we stared at each other. He had nothing to say to me.

I shoved past him and fell into a chair. I was shaking.

I heard the bath water running upstairs.

After what seemed a very long time Leona came downstairs, wiping her hands on her apron. She sat down on the sofa and after a moment John sat down beside her. I heard the sound of rock music from upstairs.

"Would you like a piece of nice pound cake?" Leona said.

I didn't answer. I was listening to the sound of the music. Rock music. On the radio. There was a table lamp on the end table beside the sofa. It cast a dim and futile light in the shadowed living room. *Rock music from the present, on a radio upstairs?* I started to say something, and then I *knew* . . . Oh, God . . . *no!*

I jumped up just as the sound of hideous crackling blotted out the music, and the table lamp dimmed and dimmed and flickered. I screamed something, I don't know what it was, and ran for the stairs.

Jeffty's parents did not move. They sat there with their hands folded, in that place they had been for so many years.

I fell twice rushing up the stairs.

THERE ISN'T MUCH on television that can hold my interest. I bought an old cathedral-shaped Philco radio in a second-hand store, and I replaced all the burnt-out parts with the original tubes from old radios I could cannibalize that still worked. I don't use transistors or printed circuits. They wouldn't work. I've sat in front of that set for hours sometimes, running the dial back and forth as slowly as you can imagine, so slowly it doesn't look as if it's moving at all sometimes.

But I can't find *Captain Midnight* or *The Land of the Lost* or *The Shadow* or *Quiet, Please.*

So she did love him, still, a little bit, even after all those years. I can't hate them: they only wanted to live in the present world again. That isn't such a terrible thing.

It's a good world, all things considered. It's much better than it used to be, in a lot of ways. People don't die from the old diseases any more. They die from new ones, but that's Progress, isn't it?

Isn't it?

Tell me.

Somebody please tell me.

THE PERSISTENCE OF VISION

JOHN VARLEY

Born in Austin, Texas, in 1947, John Varley was probably the first writer to be dubbed the "new Robert Heinlein" and it is easy to see why. Varley started his career with a body of short fiction that featured strong female characters in prominent roles, looked at issues of personal liberty, social responsibility and gender, and made up a consistent and detailed future history. Like Heinlein, Varley's career started—with the impressive debut "Picnic on Nearside" (1974)—with a volley of consistently startling and controversial stories that would make up one of the great writing streaks in the history of short science fiction.

The nearly three dozen stories that followed over the next thirty years—including classics like "Retrograde Summer," "Overdrawn at the Memory Bank," "In the Hall of the Martian Kings," "The Barbie Murders," "Blue Champagne," and "Press ENTER"—have been collected in three volumes to date: *The Persistence of Vision, The Barbie Murders,* and *Blue Champagne.* While Varley's major contribution to science fiction is his short fiction, he is also the author of eight novels, most impressively his debut *The Ophiuchi Hotline, Steel Beach,* and *The Gaen Trilogy.* His fiction has won the Hugo Award three times, the Nebula and Seuin Awards twice, as well as the Prometheus, Hayakawa, Apollo, and Jupiter Awards. He has also won the Locus Award nine times. Varley's most recent novel is *Red Thunder,* and upcoming is the retrospective collection *The John Varley Reader* and the new novel *Fuzzy*.

The story that follows, one of Varley's most famous, won the Hugo, Nebula, and Locus Awards. It takes a fresh new look at the country of the blind where who is and is not king is always open to debate.

* * *

IT WAS THE YEAR of the fourth non-depression. I had recently joined the ranks of the unemployed. The President had told me that I had nothing to fear but fear itself. I took him at his word, for once, and set out to backpack to California.

I was not the only one. The world's economy had been writhing like a snake on a hot griddle for the last twenty years, since the early seventies. We were in a boom-and-bust cycle that seemed to have no end. It had wiped out the sense of security the nation had so painfully won in the golden years after the thirties. People were accustomed to the fact that they could be rich one year and on the breadlines the next. I was on the breadlines in '81, and again in '88. This time I decided to use my freedom from the time clock to see the world. I had ideas of stowing away to Japan. I was forty-seven years old and might not get another chance to be irresponsible.

This was in late summer of the year. Sticking out my thumb along the interstate, I could easily forget that there were food riots back in Chicago. I slept at night on top of my bedroll and saw stars and listened to crickets.

I must have walked most of the way from Chicago to Des Moines. My feet toughened up after a few days of awful blisters. The rides were scarce, partly competition from other hitchhikers and partly the times we were living in. The locals were none too anxious to give rides to city people, who they had heard were mostly a bunch of hunger-crazed potential mass murderers. I got roughed up once and told never to return to Sheffield, Illinois.

But I gradually learned the knack of living on the road. I had started with a small supply of canned goods from the welfare and by the time they ran out, I had found that it was possible to work for a meal at many of the farmhouses along the way.

Some of it was hard work, some of it was only a token from people with a deeply ingrained sense that nothing should come for free. A few meals were gratis, at the family table, with grandchildren sitting around while grandpa or grandma told oft-repeated tales of what it had been like in the

Big One back in '29, when people had not been afraid to help a fellow out when he was down on his luck. I found that the older the person, the more likely I was to get a sympathetic ear. One of the many tricks you learn. And most older people will give you anything if you'll only sit and listen to them. I got very good at it.

The rides began to pick up west of Des Moines, then got bad again as I neared the refugee camps bordering the China Strip. This was only five years after the disaster, remember, when the Omaha nuclear reactor melted down and a hot mass of uranium and plutonium began eating its way into the earth, headed for China, spreading a band of radioactivity six hundred kilometers downwind. Most of Kansas City, Missouri, was still living in plywood and sheet-metal shantytowns till the city was rendered habitable again.

The refugees were a tragic group. The initial solidarity people show after a great disaster had long since faded into the lethargy and disillusionment of the displaced person. Many of them would be in and out of hospitals for the rest of their lives. To make it worse, the local people hated them, feared them, would not associate with them. They were modern pariahs, unclean. Their children were shunned. Each camp had only a number to identify it, but the local populace called them all Geigertowns.

I made a long detour to Little Rock to avoid crossing the Strip, though it was safe now as long as you didn't linger. I was issued a pariah's badge by the National Guard—a dosimeter—and wandered from one Geigertown to the next. The people were pitifully friendly once I made the first move, and I always slept indoors. The food was free at the community messes.

Once at Little Rock, I found that the aversion to picking up strangers— who might be tainted with "radiation disease"—dropped off, and I quickly moved across Arkansas, Oklahoma, and Texas. I worked a little here and there, but many of the rides were long. What I saw of Texas was through a car window.

I was a little tired of that by the time I reached New Mexico. I decided to do some more walking. By then I was less interested in California than in the trip itself.

I left the roads and went cross-country where there were no fences to stop me. I found that it wasn't easy, even in New Mexico, to get far from signs of civilization.

Taos was the center, back in the sixties, of cultural experiments in alternative living. Many communes and cooperatives were set up in the surrounding hills during that time. Most of them fell apart in a few months or years, but a few survived. In later years, any group with a new theory of living and a yen to try it out seemed to gravitate to that part of New Mexico. As a result, the land was dotted with ramshackle windmills, solar heating panels, geodesic domes, group marriages, nudists, philosophers, theoreticians, messiahs, hermits, and more than a few just plain nuts.

Taos was great. I could drop into most of the communes and stay for a day or a week, eating organic rice and beans and drinking goat's milk. When I got tired of one, a few hours' walk in any direction would bring me to another. There, I might be offered a night of prayer and chanting or a ritualistic orgy. Some of the groups had spotless barns with automatic milkers for the herds of cows. Others didn't even have latrines; they just squatted. In some, the members dressed like nuns, or Quakers in early Pennsylvania. Elsewhere, they went nude and shaved all their body hair and painted themselves purple. There were all-male and all-female groups. I was urged to stay at most of the former; at the latter, the responses ranged from a bed for the night and good conversation to being met at a barbed-wire fence with a shotgun.

I tried not to make judgments. These people were doing something important, all of them. They were testing ways whereby people didn't have to live in Chicago. That was a wonder to me. I had thought Chicago was inevitable, like diarrhea.

This is not to say they were all successful. Some made Chicago look like Shangri-La. There was one group who seemed to feel that getting back to nature consisted of sleeping in pigshit and eating food a buzzard wouldn't touch. Many were obviously doomed. They would leave behind a group of empty hovels and the memory of cholera.

So the place wasn't paradise, not by a long way. But there were successes. One or two had been there since '63 or '64 and were raising their third generation. I was disappointed to see that most of these were the ones that departed least from established norms of behavior, though some of the differences could be startling. I suppose the most radical experiments are the least likely to bear fruit.

I stayed through the winter. No one was surprised to see me a second time. It seems that many people came to Taos and shopped around. I seldom stayed more than three weeks at any one place, and always pulled my weight. I made many friends and picked up skills that would serve me if I stayed off the roads. I toyed with the idea of staying at one of them forever. When I couldn't make up my mind, I was advised that there was no hurry. I could go to California and return. They seemed sure I would.

So when spring came I headed west over the hills. I stayed off the roads and slept in the open. Many nights I would stay at another commune, until they finally began to get farther apart, then tapered off entirely. The country was not as pretty as before.

Then, three days' leisurely walking from the last commune, I came to a wall.

IN 1964, IN THE UNITED STATES, there was an epidemic of German measles, or rubella. Rubella is one of the mildest of infectious diseases. The only time it's a problem is when a woman contracts it in the first four months of her pregnancy. It is passed to the fetus, which usually develops complications. These complications include deafness, blindness, and damage to the brain.

In 1964, in the old days before abortion became readily available, there was nothing to be done about it. Many pregnant women caught rubella and went to term. Five thousand deaf-blind children were born in one year. The normal yearly incidence of deaf-blind children in the United States is one hundred and forty.

In 1970 these five thousand potential Helen Kellers were all six years old. It was quickly seen that there was a shortage of Anne Sullivans. Previously, deaf-blind children could be sent to a small number of special institutions.

It was a problem. Not just anyone can cope with a deaf-blind child. You can't tell them to shut up when they moan; you can't reason with them, tell them that the moaning is driving you crazy. Some parents were driven to nervous breakdowns when they tried to keep their children at home.

Many of the five thousand were badly retarded and virtually impossible to reach, even if anyone had been trying. These ended up, for the most part, warehoused in the hundreds of anonymous nursing homes and institutes for "special" children. They were put into beds, cleaned up once a day by a few overworked nurses, and generally allowed the full blessings of liberty: they were allowed to rot freely in their own dark, quiet, private universes. Who can say if it was bad for them? None of them were heard to complain.

Many children with undamaged brains were shuffled in among the retarded because they were unable to tell anyone that they were in there behind the sightless eyes. They failed the batteries of tactile tests, unaware that their fates hung in the balance when they were asked to fit round pegs into round holes to the ticking of a clock they could not see or hear. As a result, they spent the rest of their lives in bed, and none of them complained, either. To protest, one must be aware of the possibility of something better. It helps to have a language, too.

Several hundred of the children were found to have IQs within the normal range. There were news stories about them as they approached puberty and it was revealed that there were not enough good people to properly handle them. Money was spent, teachers were trained. The education expenditures would go on for a specified period of time, until the children were grown, then things would go back to normal and everyone could congratulate themselves on having dealt successfully with a tough problem.

And indeed, it did work fairly well. There are ways to reach and teach such children. They involve patience, love, and dedication, and the teachers brought all that to their jobs. All the graduates of the special schools left knowing how to speak with their hands. Some could talk. A few could write. Most of them left the institutions to live with parents or relatives, or, if neither was possible, received counseling and help in fitting themselves into society. The options were limited, but people can live rewarding lives under the most severe handicaps. Not everyone, but most of the graduates, were as happy with their lot as could reasonably be expected. Some achieved the almost saintly peace of their role model, Helen Keller. Others became bitter and withdrawn. A few had to be put in asylums, where they became indistinguishable from the others of their group who had spent the last twenty years there. But for the most part, they did well.

But among the group, as in any group, were some misfits. They tended to be among the brightest, the top ten percent in the IQ scores. This was not a reliable rule. Some had unremarkable test scores and were still infected with the hunger to do something, to change things, to rock the boat. With a group of five thousand, there were certain to be a few geniuses, a few artists, a few dreamers, hellraisers, individualists, movers and shapers: a few glorious maniacs.

There was one among them who might have been President but for the fact that she was blind, deaf, and a woman. She was smart, but not one of the geniuses. She was a dreamer, a creative force, an innovator. It was she who dreamed of freedom. But she was not a builder of fairy castles. Having dreamed it, she had to make it come true.

THE WALL WAS made of carefully fitted stone and was about five feet high. It was completely out of context with anything I had seen in New Mexico, though it was built of native rock. You just don't build that kind of wall out there. You use barbed wire if something needs fencing in, but many people still made use of the free range and brands. Somehow it seemed transplanted from New England.

It was substantial enough that I felt it would be unwise to crawl over it. I had crossed many wire fences in my travels and had gotten in trouble for it yet, though I had some talks with some ranchers. Mostly they told me to keep moving, but didn't seem upset about it. This was different. I set out to walk around it. From the lay of the land, I couldn't tell how far it might reach, but I had time.

At the top of the next rise I saw that I didn't have far to go. The wall made a right-angle turn just ahead. I looked over it and could see some buildings. They were mostly domes, the ubiquitous structure thrown up by communes because of the combination of ease of construction and durability. There were sheep behind the wall, and a few cows. They grazed on grass so green I wanted to go over and roll in it. The wall enclosed a rectangle of green. Outside, where I stood, it was all scrub and sage. These people had access to Rio Grande irrigation water.

I rounded the corner and followed the wall west again.

I saw a man on horseback about the same time he spotted me. He was south of me, outside the wall, and he turned and rode in my direction.

He was a dark man with thick features, dressed in denim and boots with a gray battered Stetson. Navaho, maybe. I don't know much about Indians, but I'd heard they were out here.

"Hello," I said when he'd stopped. He was looking me over. "Am I on your land?"

"Tribal land," he said. "Yeah, you're on it."

"I didn't see any signs."

He shrugged.

"It's okay, bud. You don't look like you out to rustle cattle." He grinned at me. His teeth were large and stained with tobacco. "You be camping out tonight?"

"Yes. How much farther does the, uh, tribal land go? Maybe I'll be out of it before tonight?"

He shook his head gravely. "Nah. You won't be off it tomorrow. 'S all right. You make a fire, you be careful, huh?" He grinned again and started to ride off.

"Hey, what is this place?" I gestured to the wall and he pulled his horse up and turned around again. It raised a lot of dust.

"Why you asking?" He looked a little suspicious.

"I dunno. Just curious. It doesn't look like the other places I've been to. This wall . . ."

He scowled. "Damn wall." Then he shrugged. I thought that was all he was going to say. Then he went on.

"These people, we look out for 'em, you hear? Maybe we don't go for what they're doin'. But they got it rough, you know?" He looked at me, expecting something. I never did get the knack of talking to these laconic Westerners. I always felt that I was making my sentences too long. They use a shorthand of grunts and shrugs and omitted parts of speech, and I always felt like a dude when I talked to them.

"Do they welcome guests?" I asked. "I thought I might see if I could spend the night."

He shrugged again, and it was a whole different gesture.

"Maybe. They all deaf and blind, you know?" And that was all the conversation he could take for the day. He made a clucking sound and galloped away.

I continued down the wall until I came to a dirt road that wound up the arroyo and entered the wall. There was a wooden gate, but it stood open. I wondered why they took all the trouble with the wall only to leave the gate like that. Then I noticed a circle of narrow-gauge train tracks that came out of the gate, looped around outside it, and rejoined itself. There was a small siding that ran along the outer wall for a few yards.

I stood there a few moments. I don't know what entered into my decision. I think I was a little tired of sleeping out, and I was hungry for a home-cooked meal. The sun was getting closer to the horizon. The land to the west looked like more of the same. If the highway had been visible, I might have headed that way and hitched a ride. But I turned the other way and went through the gate.

I walked down the middle of the tracks. There was a wooden fence on each side of the road, built of horizontal planks, like a corral. Sheep grazed on one side of me. There was a Shetland sheepdog with them, and she raised her ears and followed me with her eyes as I passed, but did not come when I whistled.

It was about half a mile to the cluster of buildings ahead. There were four or five domes made of something translucent, like greenhouses, and several conventional square buildings. There were two windmills turning lazily in the breeze. There were several banks of solar water heaters. These are flat constructions of glass and wood, held off the ground so they can tilt to follow the sun. They were almost vertical now, intercepting the oblique rays of sunset. There were a few trees, what might have been an orchard.

About halfway there I passed under a wooden footbridge. It arched over the road, giving access from the east pasture to the west pasture. I wondered, What was wrong with a simple gate?

Then I saw something coming down the road in my direction. It was traveling on the tracks and it was very quiet. I stopped and waited.

It was a sort of converted mining engine, the sort that pulls loads of coal up from the bottom of shafts. It was battery-powered, and it had gotten quite close before I heard it. A small man was driving it. He was pulling a car behind him and singing as loud as he could with absolutely no sense of pitch.

He got closer and closer, moving about five miles per hour, one hand held out as if he was signaling a left turn. Suddenly I realized what was happening, as he was bearing down on me. He wasn't going to stop. He was counting fenceposts with his hand. I scrambled up the fence just in time. There wasn't more than six inches of clearance between the train and the fence on either side. His palm touched my leg as I squeezed close to the fence, and he stopped abruptly.

He leaped from the car and grabbed me and I thought I was in trouble. But he looked concerned, not angry, and felt me all over, trying to discover if I was hurt. I was embarrassed. Not from the examination; because I had been foolish. The Indian had said they were all deaf and blind but I guess I hadn't quite believed him.

He was flooded with relief when I managed to convey to him that I was all right. With eloquent gestures he made me understand that I was not to stay on the road. He indicated that I should climb over the fence and continue through the fields. He repeated himself several times to be sure I understood, then held on to me as I climbed over to assure himself that I was out of the way. He reached over the fence and held my shoulders, smiling at me. He pointed to the road and shook his head, then pointed to the building and nodded. He touched my head and smiled when I nodded. He climbed back onto the engine and started up, all the time nodding and pointing where he wanted me to go. Then he was off again.

I debated what to do. Most of me said to turn around, go back to the wall by way of the pasture and head back into the hills. These people probably wouldn't want me around. I doubted that I'd be able to talk to them, and they might even resent me. On the other hand, I was fascinated, as who wouldn't be? I wanted to see how they managed it. I still didn't believe that they were *all* deaf and blind. It didn't seem possible.

The Sheltie was sniffing at my pants. I looked down at her and she backed away, then daintily approached me as I held out my open hand. She sniffed, then licked me. I patted her on the head, and she hustled back to her sheep.

I turned toward the buildings.

THE FIRST ORDER of business was money.

None of the students knew much about it from experience, but the library was full of Braille books. They started reading.

One of the first things that became apparent was that when money was mentioned, lawyers were not far away. The students wrote letters. From the replies, they selected a lawyer and retained him.

They were in a school in Pennsylvania at the time. The original pupils of the special schools, five hundred in number, had been narrowed down to about seventy as people left to live with relatives or found other solutions to their special problems. Of those seventy, some had places to go but didn't want to go there; others had few alternatives. Their parents were either dead or not interested in living with them. So the seventy had been gathered from the schools around the country into this one, while ways to deal with them were worked out. The authorities had plans, but the students beat them to it.

Each of them had been entitled to a guaranteed annual income since 1980. They had been under the care of the government, so they had not received it. They sent their lawyer to court. He came back with a ruling that they could not collect. They appealed, and won. The money was paid retroactively, with interest, and came to a healthy sum. They thanked their lawyer and retained a real estate agent. Meanwhile, they read.

They read about communes in New Mexico, and instructed their agent to look for something out there. He made a deal for a tract to be leased in perpetuity from the Navaho nation. They read about the land, found that it would need a lot of water to be productive in the way they wanted it to be.

They divided into groups to research what they would need to be self-sufficient.

Water could be obtained by tapping into the canals that carried it from the reservoirs on the Rio Grande into the reclaimed land in the south. Federal money was available for the project through a labyrinthine scheme involving HEW, the Agriculture Department, and the Bureau of Indian Affairs. They ended up paying little for their pipeline.

The land was arid. It would need fertilizer to be of use in raising sheep without resorting to open range techniques. The cost of fertilizer could be subsidized through the Rural Resettlement Program. After that, planting clover would enrich the soil with all the nitrates they could want.

There were techniques available to farm ecologically, without worrying about fertilizers or pesticides. Everything was recycled. Essentially, you put sunlight and water into one end and harvested wool, fish, vegetables, apples, honey, and eggs at the other end. You used nothing but the land, and replaced even that as you recycled your waste products back into the soil. They were not interested in agribusiness with huge combine harvesters and crop dusters. They didn't even want to turn a profit. They merely wanted sufficiency.

The details multiplied. Their leader, the one who had had the original idea and the drive to put it into action in the face of overwhelming obstacles, was a dynamo named Janet Reilly. Knowing nothing about the techniques generals and executives employ to achieve large objectives, she invented them herself and adapted them to the peculiar needs and limitations of her group. She assigned task forces to look into solutions of each aspect of their project: law, science, social planning, design, buying, logistics, construction. At any one time, she was the only person who knew everything about what was happening. She kept it all in her head, without notes of any kind.

It was in the area of social planning that she showed herself to be a visionary and not just a superb organizer. Her idea was not to make a place where they could lead a life that was a sightless, soundless imitation of their unafflicted peers. She wanted a whole new start, a way of living that was by and for the deaf-blind, a way of living that accepted no convention just because that was the way it had always been done. She examined every human cultural institution from marriage to indecent exposure to see how it related to her needs and the needs of her friends. She was aware of the peril of this approach, but was undeterred. Her Social Task Force read about every variant group that had ever tried to make it on its own anywhere, and brought her reports about how and why they had failed or succeeded. She filtered this information through her own experiences to see how it would work for her unusual group with its own set of needs and goals.

The details were endless. They hired an architect to put their ideas into Braille blueprints. Gradually the plans evolved. They spent more money. The construction began, supervised on the site by their architect, who by now was so fascinated by the scheme that she donated her services. It was an important break, for they needed someone there whom they could trust. There is only so much that can be accomplished at such a distance.

When things were ready for them to move, they ran into bureaucratic trouble. They had anticipated it, but it was a setback. Social agencies charged with overseeing their welfare doubted the wisdom of the project. When it became apparent that no amount of reasoning was going to stop it, wheels were set in motion that resulted in a restraining order, issued for their own protection, preventing them from leaving the school. They were twenty-one years old by then, all of them, but were judged mentally incompetent to manage their own affairs. A hearing was scheduled.

Luckily, they still had access to their lawyer. He also had become infected with the crazy vision, and put on a great battle for them. He succeeded in getting a ruling concerning the right of institutionalized persons, later upheld by the Supreme Court, which eventually had severe repercussions in state and county hospitals. Realizing the trouble they were already in regarding the thousands of patients in inadequate facilities across the country, the agencies gave in.

By then, it was the spring of 1986, one year after their target date. Some of their fertilizer had washed away already for lack of erosion-preventing clover. It was getting late to start crops, and they were running short of money. Nevertheless, they moved to New Mexico and began the backbreaking job of getting everything started. There were fifty-five of them, with nine children aged three months to six years.

I DON'T KNOW what I expected. I remember that everything was a surprise, either because it was so normal or because it was so different. None of my idiot surmises about what such a place might be like proved to be true. And of course I didn't know the history of the place; I learned that later, picked up in bits and pieces.

I was surprised to see lights in some of the buildings. The first thing I had assumed was that they would have no need of them. That's an example of something so normal that it surprised me.

As to the differences, the first thing that caught my attention was the fence around the rail line. I had a personal interest in it, having almost been injured by it. I struggled to understand, as I must if I was to stay even for a night.

The wood fences that enclosed the rails on their way to the gate continued up to a barn, where the rails looped back on themselves in the same way they did outside the wall. The entire line was enclosed by the fence. The only access was a loading platform by the barn, and the gate to the outside. It made sense. The only way a deaf-blind person could operate a conveyance like that would be with assurances that there was no one on the track. These people would *never* go on the tracks; there was no way they could be warned of an approaching train.

There were people moving around me in the twilight as I made my way into the group of buildings. They took no notice of me, as I had expected. They moved fast; some of them were actually running. I stood still, eyes searching all around me so no one would come crashing into me. I had to figure out how they kept from crashing into each other before I got bolder.

I bent to the ground and examined it. The light was getting bad, but I saw immediately that there were concrete sidewalks crisscrossing the area. Each of the walks was etched with a different sort of pattern in grooves that had been made before the stuff set—lines, waves, depressions, patches of rough and smooth. I quickly saw that the people who were in a hurry moved only on those walkways, and they were all barefoot. It was no trick to see that it was some sort of traffic pattern read with the feet. I stood up. I didn't need to know how it worked. It was sufficient to know what it was and stay off the paths.

The people were unremarkable. Some of them were not dressed, but I was used to that by now. They came in all shapes and sizes, but all seemed to be about the same age except for the children. Except for the fact that they did not stop and talk or even wave as they approached each other, I would never have guessed they were blind. I watched them come to intersections in the pathways—I didn't know how they knew they were there, but could think of several ways—and slow down as they crossed. It was a marvelous system.

I began to think of approaching someone. I had been there for almost half an hour, an intruder. I guess I had a false sense of these people's vulnerability; I felt like a burglar.

I walked along beside a woman for a minute. She was very purposeful in her eyes-ahead stride, or seemed to be. She sensed something, maybe my footsteps. She slowed a little, and I touched her on the shoulder, not knowing what else to do. She stopped instantly and turned toward me. Her eyes were open but vacant. Her hands were all over me, lightly touching my face, my chest, my hands, fingering my clothing. There was no doubt in my mind that she knew me for a stranger, probably from the first tap on the shoulder. But she smiled warmly at me, and hugged me. Her hands were very delicate and warm. That's funny, because they were calloused from hard work. But they felt sensitive.

She made me to understand—by pointing to the building, making eating motions with an imaginary spoon, and touching a number on her watch— that supper was served in an hour, and that I was invited. I nodded and smiled beneath her hands; she kissed me on the cheek and hurried off.

Well. It hadn't been so bad. I had worried about my ability to communicate. Later I found out she learned a great deal more about me than I had told.

I put off going into the mess hall or whatever it was. I strolled around in the gathering darkness looking at their layout. I saw the little Sheltie bringing the sheep back to the fold for the night. She herded them expertly through the open gate without any instructions, and one of the residents closed it and locked them in. The man bent and scratched the dog on the head and got his hand licked. Her chores done for the night, the dog hurried over to me and sniffed my pant leg. She followed me around the rest of the evening.

Everyone seemed so busy that I was surprised to see one woman sitting on a rail fence, doing nothing. I went over to her.

Closer, I saw that she was younger than I had thought. She was thirteen, I learned later. She wasn't wearing any clothes. I touched her on the shoulder, and she jumped down from the fence and went through the same routine as the other woman had, touching me all over with no reserve. She took my hand and I felt her fingers moving rapidly in my palm. I couldn't understand it, but knew what it was. I shrugged, and tried out other gestures to indicate that I didn't speak hand talk. She nodded, still feeling my face with her hands.

She asked me if I was staying to dinner. I assured her that I was. She asked me if I was from a university. And if you think that's easy to ask with only body movements, try it. But she was so graceful and supple in her movements, so deft at getting her meaning across. It was beautiful to watch her. It was speech and ballet at the same time.

I told her I wasn't from a university, and launched into an attempt to tell her a little about what I was doing and how I got there. She listened to me with her hands, scratching her head graphically when I failed to make my meanings clear. All the time the smile on her face got broader and broader, and she would laugh silently at my antics. All this while standing very close to me, touching me. At last she put her hands on her hips.

"I guess you need the practice," she said, "but if it's all the same to you, could we talk mouthtalk for now? You're cracking me up."

I jumped as if stung by a bee. The touching, while something I could ignore for a deaf-blind girl, suddenly seemed out of place. I stepped back a little, but her hands returned to me. She looked puzzled, then read the problem with her hands.

"I'm sorry," she said. "You thought I was deaf and blind. If I'd known I would have told you right off."

"I thought everyone here was."

"Just the parents. I'm one of the children. We all hear and see quite well. Don't be so nervous. If you can't stand touching, you're not going to like it here. Relax, I won't hurt you." And she kept her hands moving over me, mostly my face. I didn't understand it at the time, but it didn't seem sexual. Turned out I was wrong, but it wasn't blatant.

"You'll need me to show you the ropes," she said, and started for the domes. She held my hand and walked close to me. Her other hand kept moving to my face every time I talked.

"Number one, stay off the concrete paths. That's where—"

"I already figured that out."

"You did? How long have you been here?" Her hands searched my face with renewed interest. It was quite dark.

"Less than an hour. I was almost run over by your train."

She laughed, then apologized and said she knew it wasn't funny to me.

I told her it *was* funny to me now, though it hadn't been at the time. She said there was a warning sign on the gate, but I had been unlucky enough to come when the gate was open—they opened it by remote control before a train started up—and I hadn't seen it.

"What's your name?" I asked her, as we neared the soft yellow lights coming from the dining room.

Her hand worked reflexively in mine, then stopped. "Oh, I don't know. I *have* one; several, in fact. But they're in bodytalk. I'm . . . Pink. It translates as Pink, I guess."

There was a story behind it. She had been the first child born to the school students. They knew that babies were described as being pink, so they called her that. She felt pink to them. As we entered the hall, I could see that her name was visually inaccurate. One of her parents had been black. She was dark, with blue eyes and curly hair lighter than her skin. She had a broad nose, but small lips.

She didn't ask my name, so I didn't offer it. No one asked my name, in speech, the entire time I was there. They called me many things in bodytalk, and when the children called me it was "Hey, you!" They weren't big on spoken words.

The dining hall was in a rectangular building made of brick. It connected to one of the large domes. It was dimly lighted. I later learned that the lights were for me alone. The children didn't need them for anything but reading. I held Pink's hand, glad to have a guide. I kept my eyes and ears open.

"We're informal," Pink said. Her voice was embarrassingly loud in the large room. No one else was talking at all; there were just the sounds of movement and breathing. Several of the children looked up. "I won't introduce you around now. Just feel like part of the family. People will feel you later, and you can talk to them. You can take your clothes off here at the door."

I had no trouble with that. Everyone else was nude, and I could easily adjust to household customs by that time. You take your shoes off in Japan, you take your clothes off in Taos. What's the difference?

Well, quite a bit, actually. There was all the touching that went on. Everybody touched everybody else, as routinely as glancing. Everyone touched my face first, then went on with what seemed like total innocence to touch me everywhere else. As usual, it was not quite what it seemed. It was *not* innocent, and it was not the usual treatment they gave others in their group. They touched each other's genitals a lot *more* than they touched mine. They were holding back with me so I wouldn't be frightened. They were very polite with strangers.

There was a long, low table, with everyone sitting on the floor around it. Pink led me to it.

"See the bare strips on the floor? Stay out of them. Don't leave anything in them. That's where people walk. Don't *ever* move anything. Furniture, I mean. That has to be decided at full meetings, so we'll all know where everything is. Small things, too. If you pick up something, put it back exactly where you found it."

"I understand."

People were bringing bowls and platters of food from the adjoining kitchen. They set them on the table, and the diners began feeling them. They ate with their fingers, without plates, and they did it slowly and lovingly. They smelled things for a long time before they took a bite. Eating was very sensual to these people.

They were *terrific* cooks. I have never, before or since, eaten as well as I did at Keller. (That's my name for it, in speech, though their bodytalk name was something very like that. When I called it Keller, everyone knew what I was talking about.) They started off with good, fresh produce, something that's hard enough to find in the cities, and went at the cooking with artistry and imagination. It wasn't like any national style I've eaten. They improvised, and seldom cooked the same thing the same way twice.

I sat between Pink and the fellow who had almost run me down earlier. I stuffed myself disgracefully. It was too far removed from beef jerky and the organic dry cardboard I had been eating for me to be able to resist. I lingered over it, but still finished long before anyone else. I watched them as I sat back carefully and wondered if I'd be sick. (I wasn't, thank God.) They fed themselves and each other, sometimes getting up and going clear around the table to offer a choice morsel to a friend on the other side. I was fed in this way by all too many of them, and nearly popped until I learned a pidgin phrase in handtalk, saying I was full to the brim. I learned from Pink that a friendlier way to refuse was to offer something myself.

Eventually I had nothing to do but feed Pink and look at the others. I began to be more observant. I had thought they were eating in solitude, but soon saw that lively conversation was flowing around the table. Hands were busy, moving almost too fast to see. They were spelling into each other's palms, shoulders, legs, arms, bellies; any part of the body. I watched in amazement as a ripple of laughter spread like falling dominoes from one end of the table to the other as some witticism was passed along the line. It was *fast*. Looking carefully, I could see the thoughts moving, reaching one person, passed on while a reply went in the other direction and was in turn passed on, other replies originating all along the line and bouncing back and forth. They were a wave form, like water.

It was messy. Let's face it; eating with your fingers and talking with your hands is going to get you smeared with food. But no one minded. *I* certainly didn't. I was too busy feeling left out. Pink talked to me, but I knew I was finding out what it's like to be deaf. These people were friendly and seemed to like me, but could do nothing about it. We couldn't communicate.

Afterwards, we all trooped outside, except the cleanup crew, and took a shower beneath a set of faucets that gave out very cold water. I told Pink I'd like to help with the dishes, but she said I'd just be in the way. I couldn't do anything around Keller until I learned their very specific ways of doing things. She seemed to be assuming already that I'd be around that long.

Back into the building to dry off, which they did with their usual puppy dog friendliness, making a game and a gift of toweling each other, and then we went into the dome.

It was warm inside, warm and dark. Light entered from the passage to the dining room, but it wasn't enough to blot out the stars through the lattice of triangular panes overhead. It was almost like being out in the open.

Pink quickly pointed out the positional etiquette within the dome. It wasn't hard to follow, but I still tended to keep my arms and legs pulled in close so I wouldn't trip someone by sprawling into a walk space.

My misconceptions got me again. There was no sound but the soft whisper of flesh against flesh, so I thought I was in the middle of an orgy. I had been at them before, in other communes, and they looked pretty much like this. I quickly saw that I was wrong, and only later found out I had been right. In a sense.

What threw my evaluations out of whack was the simple fact that group conversation among these people *had* to look like an orgy. The much subtler observation that I made later was that with a hundred naked bodies sliding, rubbing, kissing, caressing, all at the same time, what was the point in making a distinction? There was no distinction.

I have to say that I use the noun "orgy" only to get across a general idea of many people in close contact. I don't like the word, it is too ripe with connotations. But I had these connotations myself at the time, so I was relieved to see that it was not an orgy. The ones I had been to had been tedious and impersonal, and I had hoped for better from these people.

Many wormed their way through the crush to get to me and meet me. Never more than one at a time; they were constantly aware of what was going on and were waiting their turn to talk to me. Naturally, I didn't know it then. Pink sat with me to interpret the hard thoughts. I eventually used her words less and less, getting into the spirit of tactile seeing and understanding. No one felt they really knew me until they had touched every part of my body, so there were hands on me all the time. I timidly did the same.

What with all the touching, I quickly got an erection, which embarrassed me quite a bit. I was berating myself for being unable to keep sexual responses out of it, for not being able to operate on the same intellectual plane I thought they were on, when I realized with some shock that the couple next to me was making love. They had been doing it for the last ten minutes, actually, and it had seemed such a natural part of what was happening that I had known it and not known it at the same time.

No sooner had I realized it than I suddenly wondered if I was right. *Were they?* It was very slow and the light was bad. But her legs were up, and he was on top of her, that much I was sure of. It was foolish of me, but I really had to know. I had to find out *what the hell I was in.* How could I give the proper social responses if I didn't know the situation?

I was very sensitive to polite behavior after my months at the various communes. I had become adept at saying prayers before supper in one place, chanting Hare Krishna at another, and going happily nudist at still another. It's called "when in Rome," and if you can't adapt to it you shouldn't go visiting. I would kneel to Mecca, burp after my meals, toast anything that was proposed, eat organic rice and compliment the cook; but to do it right, you have to know the customs. I had thought I knew them, but had changed my mind three times in as many minutes.

They *were* making love, in the sense that he was penetrating her. They were also deeply involved with each other. Their hands fluttered like butterflies all over each other, filled with meanings I couldn't see or feel. But they were being touched by and were touching many other people around them. They were talking to all these people, even if the message was as simple as a pat on the forehead or arm.

Pink noticed where my attention was. She was sort of wound around me, without really doing anything I would have thought of as provocative. I just couldn't *decide.* It seemed so innocent, and yet it wasn't.

"That's (—) and (—)," she said, the parentheses indicating a series of hand motions against my palm. I never learned a sound word as a name for any of them but Pink, and I can't reproduce the bodytalk names they had. Pink reached over, touched the woman with her foot, and did some complicated business with her toes. The woman smiled and grabbed Pink's foot, her fingers moving.

"(—) would like to talk with you later," Pink told me. "Right after she's through talking to (—). You met her earlier, remember? She says she likes your hands."

Now this is going to sound crazy, I know. It sounded pretty crazy to me when I thought of it. It dawned on me with a sort of revelation that her word for talk and mine were miles apart. Talk, to her, meant a complex interchange involving all parts of the body. She could read words or emotions in every twitch of my muscles, like a lie detector. Sound, to her, was only a minor part of communication. It was something she used to speak to outsiders. Pink talked with her whole being.

I didn't have the half of it, even then, but it was enough to turn my head entirely around in relation to these people. They talked with their bodies. It wasn't all hands, as I'd thought. Any part of the body in contact with any other was communication, sometimes a very simple and basic sort—think of McLuhan's light bulb as the basic medium of information—perhaps saying no more than "I am here." But talk was talk, and if conversation evolved to the point where you needed to talk to another with your genitals, it was still a part of the conversation. What I wanted to know was *what were they saying?* I knew, even at that dim moment of realization, that it was much more than I could grasp. Sure, you're saying. You know about talking to your lover with your body as you make love. That's not such a new idea. Of course it isn't, but think how wonderful that talk is even when you're not primarily tactile-oriented. Can you carry the thought from there, or are you doomed to be an earthworm thinking about sunsets?

While this was happening to me, there was a woman getting acquainted with my body. Her hands were on me, in my lap, when I felt myself ejaculating. It was a big surprise to me, but to no one else. I had been telling everyone around me for many minutes, through signs they could feel with their hands, that it was going to happen. Instantly, hands were all over my body. I could almost understand them as they spelled tender thoughts to me. I got the gist, anyway, if not the words. I was terribly embarrassed for only a moment, then it passed away in the face of the easy acceptance. It was very intense. For a long time I couldn't get my breath.

The woman who had been the cause of it touched my lips with her fingers. She moved them slowly, but meaningfully I was sure. Then she melted back into the group.

"What did she say?" I asked Pink.

She smiled at me. "You know, of course. If you'd only cut loose from your verbalizing. But, generally, she meant 'How nice for you.' It also translates as 'How nice for me.' And 'me,' in this sense, means all of us. The organism."

I knew I had to stay and learn to speak.

THE COMMUNE HAD its ups and downs. They had expected them, in general, but had not known what shape they might take.

Winter killed many of their fruit trees. They replaced them with hybrid strains. They lost more fertilizer and soil in windstorms because the clover had not had time to anchor it down. Their schedule had been thrown off by the court actions, and they didn't really get things settled in a groove for more than a year.

Their fish all died. They used the bodies for fertilizer and looked into what might have gone wrong. They were using a three-stage ecology of the type pioneered by the New Alchemists in the seventies. It consisted of three domed ponds: one containing fish, another with crushed shells and bacteria in one section and algae in another, and a third full of daphnids. The water containing fish waste from the first pond was pumped through the shells and bacteria, which detoxified it and converted the ammonia it contained into fertilizer for the algae. The algae water was pumped into the second pond to feed the daphnids. Then daphnids and algae were pumped to the fish pond as food and the enriched water was used to fertilize greenhouse plants in all of the domes.

They tested the water and the soil and found that chemicals were being leached from impurities in the shells and concentrated down the food chain. After a thorough cleanup, they restarted and all went well. But they had lost their first cash crop.

They never went hungry. Nor were they cold; there was plenty of sunlight year-round to power the pumps and the food cycle and to heat their living quarters. They had built their buildings half-buried with an eye to the heating and cooling powers of convective currents. But they had to spend some of their capital. The first year they showed a loss.

One of their buildings caught fire during the first winter. Two men and a small girl were killed when a sprinkler system malfunctioned. This was a shock to them. They had thought things would operate as advertised. None of them knew much about the building trades, about estimates as opposed to realities. They found that several of their installations were not up to specifications, and instituted a program of periodic checks on everything. They learned to strip down and repair anything on the farm. If something contained electronics too complex for them to cope with, they tore it out and installed something simpler.

Socially, their progress had been much more encouraging. Janet had wisely decided that there would be only two hard and fast objectives in the realm of their relationships. The first was that she refused to be their president, chairwoman, chief, or supreme commander. She had seen from the start that a driving personality was needed to get the planning done and the land bought and a sense of purpose fostered from their formless desire for an alternative. But once at the promised land, she abdicated. From that point they would operate as a democratic communism. If that failed, they would adopt a new approach. Anything but a dictatorship with her at the head. She wanted no part of that.

The second principle was to accept nothing. There had never been a deaf-blind community operating on its own. They had no expectations to satisfy, they did not need to live as the sighted did. They were alone. There was no one to tell them not to do something simply because it was not done.

They had no clearer idea of what their society would be than anyone else. They had been forced into a mold that was not relevant to their needs, but beyond that they didn't know. They would search out the behavior that made sense, the moral things for deaf-blind people to do. They understood the basic principles of morals: that nothing is moral always, and anything is moral under the right circumstances. It all had to do with social context. They were starting from a blank slate, with no models to follow.

By the end of the second year they had their context. They continually modified it, but the basic pattern was set. They knew themselves and what they were as they had never been able to do at the school. They defined themselves in their own terms.

I SPENT MY first day at Keller in school. It was the obvious and necessary step. I had to learn handtalk.

Pink was kind and very patient. I learned the basic alphabet and practiced hard at it. By the afternoon she was refusing to talk to me, forcing me to speak with my hands. She would speak only when pressed hard, and eventually not at all. I scarcely spoke a single word after the third day.

This is not to say that I was suddenly fluent. Not at all. At the end of the first day I knew the alphabet and could laboriously make myself understood. I was not so good at reading words spelled into my own palm. For a long time I had to look at the hand to see what was spelled. But like any language, eventually you think in it. I speak fluent French, and I can recall my amazement when I finally reached the point where I wasn't translating my thoughts before I spoke. I reached it at Keller in about two weeks.

I remember one of the last things I asked Pink in speech. It was something that was worrying me.

"Pink, am I welcome here?"

"You've been here three days. Do you feel rejected?"

"No, it's not that. I guess I just need to hear your policy about outsiders. How *long* am I welcome?"

She wrinkled her brow. It was evidently a new question.

"Well, practically speaking, until a majority of us decide we want you to go. But that's never happened. No one's stayed here much longer than a few days. We've never had to evolve a policy about what to do, for instance, if someone who sees and hears wants to join us. No one has, so far, but I guess it could happen. My guess is that they wouldn't accept it. They're very independent and jealous of their freedom, though you might not have noticed it I don't think you could ever be one of them. But as long as you're willing to think of yourself as a guest, you could probably stay for twenty years."

"You said 'they.' Don't you include yourself in the group?"

For the first time she looked a little uneasy. I wish I had been better at reading body language at the time. I think my hands could have told me volumes about what she was thinking.

"Sure," she said. "The children are part of the group. We like it. I sure wouldn't want to be anywhere else, from what I know of the outside."

"I don't blame you." There were things left unsaid here, but I didn't know enough to ask the right questions. "But it's never a problem, being able to see when none of your parents can? They don't . . . resent you in any way?"

This time she laughed. "Oh, no. Never that. They're much too independent for that. You've seen it. They don't *need* us for anything they can't do themselves. We're part of the family. We do exactly the same things they do. And it really doesn't matter. Sight, I mean. Hearing, either. Just look around you. Do I have any special advantages because I can see where I'm going?"

I had to admit that she didn't. But there was still the hint of something she wasn't saying to me.

"I know what's bothering you. About staying here." She had to draw me back to my original question; I had been wandering.

"What's that?"

"You don't feel a part of the daily life. You're not doing your share of the chores. You're very conscientious and you want to do your part. I can tell."

She read me right, as usual, and I admitted it.

"And you won't be able to until you can talk to everybody. So let's get back to your lessons. Your fingers are still very sloppy."

THERE WAS A lot of work to be done. The first thing I had to learn was to slow down. They were slow and methodical workers, made few mistakes, and didn't care if a job took all day so long as it was done well. When I was working by myself I didn't have to worry about it: sweeping, picking apples, weeding in the gardens. But when I was on a job that required teamwork I had to learn a whole new pace. Eyesight enables a person to do many aspects of a job at once with a few quick glances. A blind person will take each aspect of the job in turn if the job is spread out. Everything has to be verified by touch. At a bench job, though, they could be much faster than I. They could make me feel as though I was working with my toes instead of fingers.

I never suggested that I could make anything quicker by virtue of my sight or hearing. They quite rightly would have told me to mind my own business. Accepting sighted help was the first step to dependence and, after all, they would still be here with the same jobs to do after I was gone.

And that got me to thinking about the children again. I began to be positive that there was an undercurrent of resentment, maybe unconscious, between the parents and children. It was obvious that there was a great deal of love between them, but how could the children fail to resent the rejection of their talent? So my reasoning went, anyway.

I quickly fit myself into the routine. I was treated no better or worse than anyone else, which gratified me. Though I would never become part of the group, even if I should desire it, there was absolutely no indication that I was anything but a full member. That's just how they treated guests: as they would one of their own number.

Life was fulfilling out there in a way it has never been in the cities. It wasn't unique to Keller, this pastoral peace, but the people there had it in generous helpings. The earth beneath your bare feet is something you can never feel in a city park.

Daily life was busy and satisfying. There were chickens and hogs to feed, bees and sheep to care for, fish to harvest, and cows to milk. Everybody worked: men, women, and children. It all seemed to fit together without any apparent effort. Everybody seemed to know what to do when it needed doing. You could think of it as a well-oiled machine, but I never liked that metaphor, especially for people. I thought of it as an organism. Any social group is, but this one *worked.* Most of the other communes I'd visited had glaring flaws. Things would not get done because everyone was too stoned or couldn't be bothered or didn't see the necessity of doing it in the first place. That sort of ignorance leads to typhus and soil erosion and people freezing to death and invasions of social workers who take your children away. I'd seen it happen.

Not here. They had a good picture of the world as it is, not the rosy misconceptions so many other Utopians labor under. They did the jobs that needed doing.

I could never detail all the nuts and bolts (there's that machine metaphor again) of how the place worked. The fish-cycle ponds alone were complicated enough to overawe me. I killed a spider in one of the greenhouses, then found out it had been put there to eat a specific set of plant predators. Same for the frogs. There were insects in the water to kill other insects; it got to a point where I was afraid to swat a mayfly without prior okay.

As the days went by I was told some of the history of the place. Mistakes had been made, though surprisingly few. One had been in the area of defense. They had made no provision for it at first, not knowing much about the brutality and random violence that reaches even to the out-of-the-way corners. Guns were the logical and preferred choice out here, but were beyond their capabilities.

One night a carload of men who had had too much to drink showed up. They had heard of the place in town. They stayed for two days, cutting the phone lines and raping many of the women.

The people discussed all the options after the invasion was over, and settled on the organic one. They bought five German shepherds. Not the psychotic wretches that are marketed under the description of "attack dogs," but specially trained ones from a firm recommended by the Albuquerque police. They were trained as both Seeing-Eye and police dogs. They were perfectly harmless until an outsider showed overt aggression, then they were trained, not to disarm, but to go for the throat.

It worked, like most of their solutions. The second invasion resulted in two dead and three badly injured, all on the other side. As a backup in case of a concerted attack, they hired an ex-marine to teach them the fundamentals of close-in dirty fighting. These were not dewy-eyed flower children.

There were three superb meals a day. And there was leisure time, too. It was not all work. There was time to take a friend out and sit in the grass under a tree, usually around sunset, just before the big dinner. There was time for someone to stop working for a few minutes, to share some special treasure. I remember being taken by the hand by one woman—whom I must call Tall-one-with-the-green-eyes—to a spot where mushrooms were growing in the cool crawl space beneath the barn. We wriggled under until our faces were buried in the patch, picked a few, and smelled them. She showed me how to smell. I would have thought a few weeks before that we had ruined their beauty, but after all it was only visual. I was already beginning to discount that sense, which is so removed from the essence of an object. She showed me that they were still beautiful to touch and smell after we had apparently destroyed them. Then she was off to the kitchen with the pick of the bunch in her apron. They tasted all the better that night.

And a man—I will call him Baldy—who brought me a plank he and one of the women had been planing in the woodshop. I touched its smoothness and smelled it and agreed with him how good it was.

And after the evening meal, the Together.

DURING MY THIRD week there I had an indication of my status with the group. It was the first real test of whether I meant anything to them. Anything special, I mean. I wanted to see them as my friends, and I suppose I was a little upset to think that just anyone who wandered in here would be treated the way I was. It was childish and unfair to them, and I wasn't even aware of the discontent until later.

I had been hauling water in a bucket into the field where a seedling tree was being planted. There was a hose for that purpose, but it was in use on the other side of the village. This tree was not in reach of the automatic sprinklers and it was drying out. I had been carrying water to it until another solution was found.

It was hot, around noon. I got the water from a standing spigot near the forge. I set the bucket down on the ground behind me and leaned my head into the flow of water. I was wearing a shirt made of cotton, unbuttoned in the front. The water felt good running through my hair and soaking into the shirt. I let it go on for almost a minute.

There was a crash behind me and I bumped my head when I raised it up too quickly under the faucet. I turned and saw a woman sprawled on her face in the dust. She was turning over slowly, holding her knee. I realized with a sinking feeling that she had tripped over the bucket I had carelessly left on the concrete express lane. Think of it: ambling along on ground that you trust to be free of all obstruction, suddenly you're sitting on the ground. Their system would only work with trust, and it had to be total; everybody had to be responsible all the time. I had been accepted into that trust and I had blown it. I felt sick.

She had a nasty scrape on her left knee that was oozing blood. She felt it with her hands, sitting there on the ground, and she began to howl. It was weird, painful. Tears came from her eyes, then she pounded her fists on the ground, going "Hunnnh, hunnnh, *hunnnh!*" with each blow. She was angry, and she had every right to be.

She found the pail as I hesitantly reached out for her. She grabbed my hand and followed it up to my face. She felt my face, crying all the time, then wiped her nose and got up. She started off for one of the buildings. She limped slightly.

I sat down and felt miserable. I didn't know what to do.

One of the men came out to get me. It was Big Man. I called him that because he was the tallest person at Keller. He wasn't any sort of policeman, I found out later; he was just the first one the injured woman had met. He took my hand and felt my face. I saw tears start when he felt the emotions there. He asked me to come inside with him.

An impromptu panel had been convened. Call it a jury. It was made up of anyone who was handy, including a few children. There were ten or twelve of them. Everyone looked very sad. The woman I had hurt was there, being consoled by three or four people. I'll call her Scar, for the prominent mark on her upper arm.

Everybody kept telling me—in handtalk, you understand—how sorry they were for me. They petted and stroked me, trying to draw some of the misery away.

Pink came racing in. She had been sent for to act as a translator if needed. Since this was a formal proceeding it was necessary that they be sure I understood everything that happened. She went to Scar and cried with her for a bit, then came to me and embraced me fiercely, telling me with her hands how sorry she was that this had happened. I was already figuratively packing my bags. Nothing seemed to be left but the formality of expelling me.

Then we all sat together on the floor. We were close, touching on all sides. The hearing began.

Most of it was in handtalk, with Pink throwing in a few words here and there. I seldom knew who said what, but that was appropriate. It was the group speaking as one. No statement reached me without already having become a consensus.

"You are accused of having violated the rules," said the group, "and of having been the cause of an injury to (the one I called Scar). Do you dispute this? Is there any fact that we should know?"

"No," I told them. "I was responsible. It was my carelessness."

"We understand. We sympathize with you in your remorse, which is evident to all of us. But carelessness is a violation. Do you understand this? This is the offense for which you are (——)." It was a set of signals in shorthand.

"What was that?" I asked Pink.

"Uh . . . 'brought before us'? 'Standing trial'?" She shrugged, not happy with either interpretation.

"Yes. I understand."

"The facts not being in question, it is agreed that you are guilty." (" 'Responsible,' " Pink whispered in my ear.) "Withdraw from us a moment while we come to a decision."

I got up and stood by the wall, not wanting to look at them as the debate went back and forth through the joined hands. There was a burning lump in my throat that I could not swallow. Then I was asked to rejoin the circle.

"The penalty for your offense is set by custom. If it were not so, we would wish we could rule otherwise. You now have the choice of accepting the punishment designated and having the offense wiped away, or of refusing our jurisdiction and withdrawing your body from our land. What is your choice?"

I had Pink repeat this to me, because it was so important that I know what was being offered. When I was sure I had read it right, I accepted their punishment without hesitation. I was very grateful to have been given an alternative.

"Very well. You have elected to be treated as we would treat one of our own who had done the same act. Come to us."

Everyone drew in closer. I was not told what was going to happen. I was drawn in and nudged gently from all directions.

Scar was sitting with her legs crossed more or less in the center of the group. She was crying again, and so was I, I think. It's hard to remember. I ended up face down across her lap. She spanked me.

I never once thought of it as improbable or strange. It flowed naturally out of the situation. Everyone was holding on to me and caressing me, spelling assurances into my palms and legs and neck and cheeks. We were all crying. It was a difficult thing that had to be faced by the whole group. Others drifted in and joined us. I understood that this punishment came from everyone there, but only the offended person, Scar, did the actual spanking. That was one of the ways I had wronged her, beyond the fact of giving her a scraped knee. I had laid on her the obligation of disciplining me and that was why she had sobbed so loudly, not from the pain of her injury, but from the pain of knowing she would have to hurt me.

Pink later told me that Scar had been the staunchest advocate of giving me the option to stay. Some had wanted to expel me outright, but she paid me the compliment of thinking I was a good enough person to be worth putting herself and me through the ordeal. If you can't understand that, you haven't grasped the feeling of community I felt among these people.

It went on for a long time. It was very painful, but not cruel. Nor was it primarily humiliating. There was some of that, of course. But it was essentially a practical lesson taught in the most direct terms. Each of them had undergone it during the first months, but none recently. You *learned* from it, believe me.

I did a lot of thinking about it afterward. I tried to think of what else they might have done. Spanking grown people is really unheard of, you know, though that didn't occur to me until long after it had happened. It seemed so natural when it was going on that the thought couldn't even enter my mind that this was a weird situation to be in.

They did something like this with the children, but not as long or as hard. Responsibility was lighter for the younger ones. The adults were willing to put up with an occasional bruise or scraped knee while the children learned.

But when you reached what they thought of as adulthood—which was whenever a majority of the adults thought you had or when you assumed the privilege yourself—that's when the spanking really got serious.

They had a harsher punishment, reserved for repeated or malicious offenses. They had not had to invoke it often. It consisted of being sent to Coventry. No one would touch you for a specified period of time. By the time I heard of it, it sounded like a very tough penalty. I didn't need it explained to me.

I don't know how to explain it, but the spanking was administered in such a loving way that I didn't feel violated. *This hurts me as much as it hurts you. I'm doing this for your own good. I love you, that's why I'm spanking you.* They made me understand those old cliches by their actions.

When it was over, we all cried together. But it soon turned to happiness. I embraced Scar and we told each other how sorry we were that it happened. We talked to each other—made love if you like—and I kissed her knee and helped her dress it.

We spent the rest of the day together, easing the pain.

AS I BECAME more fluent in handtalk, "the scales fell from my eyes." Daily, I would discover a new layer of meaning that had eluded me before; it was like peeling the skin of an onion to find a new skin beneath it. Each time I thought I was at the core, only to find that there was another layer I could not yet see.

I had thought that learning handtalk was the key to communication with them. Not so. Handtalk was baby talk. For a long time I was a baby who could not even say goo-goo clearly. Imagine my surprise when, having learned to say it, I found that there were syntax, conjunctions, parts of speech, nouns, verbs, tense, agreement, and the subjunctive mood. I was wading in a tide pool at the edge of the Pacific Ocean.

By handtalk I mean the International Manual Alphabet. Anyone can learn it in a few hours or days. But when you talk to someone in speech, do you spell each word? Do you read each letter as you read this? No, you grasp words as entities, hear groups of sounds and see groups of letters as a gestalt full of meaning.

Everyone at Keller had an absorbing interest in language. They each knew several languages—spoken languages—and could read and spell them fluently.

While still children they had understood the fact that handtalk was a way for deaf-blind people to talk to *outsiders*. Among themselves it was much too cumbersome. It was like Morse Code: useful when you're limited to on-off modes of information transmission, but not the preferred mode. Their ways of speaking to each other were much closer to our type of written or verbal communication, and—dare I say it?—better.

I discovered this slowly, first by seeing that though I could spell rapidly with my hands, it took *much* longer for me to say something than it took anyone else. It could not be explained by differences in dexterity. So I asked to be taught their shorthand speech. I plunged in, this time taught by everyone, not just Pink.

It was hard. They could say any word in any language with no more than two moving hand positions. I knew this was a project for years, not days. You learn the alphabet and you have all the tools you need to spell any word that exists. That's the great advantage in having your written and spoken speech based on the same set of symbols. Shorthand was not like that at all. It partook of none of the linearity or commonality of handtalk; it was not code for English or any other language; it did not share construction or vocabulary with any other language. It was wholly constructed by the Kellerites according to their needs. Each word was something I had to learn and memorize separately from the handtalk spelling.

For months I sat in the Togethers after dinner saying things like "Me love Scar much much well," while waves of conversation ebbed and flowed and circled around me, touching me only at the edges. But I kept at it, and the children were endlessly patient with me. I improved gradually. Understand that the rest of the conversations I will relate took place in either handtalk or shorthand, limited to various degrees by my fluency. I did not speak nor was I spoken to orally from the day of my punishment.

I WAS HAVING a lesson in bodytalk from Pink. Yes, we were making love. It had taken me a few weeks to see that she was a sexual being, that her caresses, which I had persisted in seeing as innocent—as I had defined it at the time—both were and weren't innocent. She understood it as perfectly natural that the result of her talking to my penis with her hands might be another sort of conversation. Though still in the middle flush of puberty, she was regarded by all as an adult and I accepted her as such. It was cultural conditioning that had blinded me to what she was saying.

So we talked a lot. With her, I understood the words and music of the body better than with anyone else. She sang a very uninhibited song with her hips and hands, free of guilt, open and fresh with discovery in every note she touched.

"You haven't told me much about yourself," she said. "What did you do on the outside?" I don't want to give the impression that this speech was in sentences, as I have presented it. We were bodytalking, sweating and smelling each other. The message came through from hands, feet, mouth.

I got as far as the sign for pronoun, first person singular, and was stopped.

How could I tell her of my life in Chicago? Should I speak of my early ambition to be a writer, and how that didn't work out? And why hadn't it? Lack of talent, or lack of drive? I could tell her about my profession, which was meaningless shuffling of papers when you got down to it, useless to anything but the Gross National Product. I could talk of the economic ups and downs that had brought me to Keller when nothing else could dislodge me from my easy sliding through life. Or the loneliness of being forty-seven years old and never having found someone worth loving, never having been loved in return. Of being a permanently displaced person in a stainless-steel society. One-night stands, drinking binges, nine-to-five, Chicago Transit Authority, dark movie houses, football games on television, sleeping pills, the John Hancock Tower where the windows won't open so you can't breathe the smog or jump out. That was me, wasn't it?

"I see," she said.

"I travel around," I said, and suddenly realized that it was the truth.

"I see," she repeated. It was a different sign for the same thing. Context was everything. She had heard and understood both parts of me, knew one to be what I had been, the other to be what I hoped I was.

She lay on top of me, one hand lightly on my face to catch the quick interplay of emotions as I thought about my life for the first time in years. And she laughed and nipped my ear playfully when my face told her that for the first time I could remember, I was happy about it. Not just telling myself I was happy, but truly happy. You cannot lie in bodytalk any more than your sweat glands can lie to a polygraph.

I noticed that the room was unusually empty. Asking around in my fumbling way, I learned that only the children were there.

"Where is everybody?" I asked.

"They are all out ***," she said. It was like that: three sharp slaps on the chest with the fingers spread. Along with the finger configuration for "verb form, gerund," it meant that they were all out ***ing. Needless to say, it didn't tell me much.

What did tell me something was her bodytalk as she said it. I read her better than I ever had. She was upset and sad. Her body said something like "Why can't I join them? Why can't I (smell-taste-touch-hear-see) *sense* with them?" That is exactly what she said. Again, I didn't trust my understanding enough to accept that interpretation. I was still trying to force my conceptions on the things I experienced there. I was determined that she and the other children be resentful of their parents in some way, because I was sure they had to be. They *must* feel superior in some way, they *must* feel held back.

I FOUND THE adults, after a short search of the area, out in the north pasture. All the parents, none of the children. They were standing in a group with no apparent pattern. It wasn't a circle, but it was almost round. If there was any organization, it was in the fact that everybody was about the same distance from everybody else.

The German shepherds and the Sheltie were out there, sitting on the cool grass facing the group of people. Their ears were perked up, but they were not moving.

I started to go up to the people. I stopped when I became aware of the concentration. They were touching, but their hands were not moving. The silence of seeing all those permanently moving people standing that still was deafening to me.

I watched them for at least an hour. I sat with the dogs and scratched them behind the ears. They did that chop-licking thing that dogs do when they appreciate it, but their full attention was on the group.

It gradually dawned on me that the group was moving. It was very slow, just a step here and another there, over many minutes. It was expanding in such a way that the distance between any of the individuals was the same. Like the expanding universe, where all galaxies move away from all others. Their arms were extended now; they were touching only with fingertips, in a crystal lattice arrangement.

Finally they were not touching at all. I saw their fingers straining to cover distances that were too far to bridge. And still they expanded equilaterally. One of the shepherds began to whimper a little. I felt the hair on the back of my neck stand up. Chilly out here, I thought.

I closed my eyes, suddenly sleepy.

I opened them, shocked. Then I forced them shut. Crickets were chirping in the grass around me.

There was something in the darkness behind my eyeballs. I felt that if I could turn my eyes around I would see it easily, but it eluded me in a way that made peripheral vision seem like reading headlines. If there was ever anything impossible to pin down, much less describe, that was it. It tickled at me for a while as the dogs whimpered louder, but I could make nothing of it. The best analogy I could think of was the sensation a blind person might feel from the sun on a cloudy day.

I opened my eyes again.

Pink was standing there beside me. Her eyes were screwed shut, and she was covering her ears with her hands. Her mouth was open and working silently. Behind her were several of the older children. They were all doing the same thing.

Some quality of the night changed. The people in the group were about a foot away from each other now, and suddenly the pattern broke. They all swayed for a moment, then laughed in that eerie, unselfconscious noise deaf people use for laughter. They fell in the grass and held their bellies, rolled over and over and roared.

Pink was laughing, too. To my surprise, so was I. I laughed until my face and sides were hurting, like I remembered doing sometimes when I'd smoked grass.

And that was ***ing.

. . .

I CAN SEE that I've only given a surface view of Keller. And there are some things I should deal with, lest I foster an erroneous view.

Clothing, for instance. Most of them wore something most of the time. Pink was the only one who seemed temperamentally opposed to clothes. She never wore anything.

No one ever wore anything I'd call a pair of pants. Clothes were loose: robes, shirts, dresses, scarves and such. Lots of men wore things that would be called women's clothes. They were simply more comfortable.

Much of it was ragged. It tended to be made of silk or velvet or something else that felt good. The stereotypical Kellerite would be wearing a Japanese silk robe, hand-embroidered with dragons, with many gaping holes and loose threads and tea and tomato stains all over it while she sloshed through the pigpen with a bucket of slop. Wash it at the end of the day and don't worry about the colors running.

I also don't seem to have mentioned homosexuality. You can mark it down to my early conditioning that my two deepest relationships at Keller were with women: Pink and Scar. I haven't said anything about it simply because I don't know how to present it. I talked to men and women equally, on the same terms. I had surprisingly little trouble being affectionate with the men.

I could not think of the Kellerites as bisexual, though clinically they were. It was much deeper than that. They could not even recognize a concept as poisonous as a homosexuality taboo. It was one of the first things they learned. If you distinguish homosexuality from heterosexuality you are cutting yourself off from communication—*full* communication—with half the human race. They were pansexual; they could not separate sex from the rest of their lives. They didn't even have a word in shorthand that could translate directly into English as sex. They had words for male and female in infinite variation, and words for degrees and varieties of physical experience that would be impossible to express in English, but all those words included other parts of the world of experience also; none of them walled off what we call *sex* into its own discrete cubbyhole.

There's another question I haven't answered. It needs answering, because I wondered about it myself when I first arrived. It concerns the necessity for the commune in the first place. Did it really have to be like this? Would they have been better off adjusting themselves to our ways of living?

All was not a peaceful idyll. I've already spoken of the invasion and rape. It could happen again, especially if the roving gangs that operate around the cities start to really rove. A touring group of motorcyclists could wipe them out in a night.

There were also continuing legal hassles. About once a year the social workers descended on Keller and tried to take their children away. They had been accused of everything possible, from child abuse to contributing to delinquency. It hadn't worked so far, but it might someday.

And after all, there are sophisticated devices on the market that allow a blind and deaf person to see and hear a little. They might have been helped by some of those.

I met a deaf-blind woman living in Berkeley once. I'll vote for Keller.

As to those machines . . .

In the library at Keller there is a seeing machine. It uses a television camera and a computer to vibrate a closely set series of metal pins. Using it, you can feel a moving picture of whatever the camera is pointed at. It's small and light, made to be carried with the pinpricker touching your back. It cost about thirty-five thousand dollars.

I found it in the corner of the library. I ran my finger over it and left a gleaming streak behind as the thick dust came away.

OTHER PEOPLE came and went, and I stayed on.

Keller didn't get as many visitors as the other places I had been. It was out of the way.

One man showed up at noon, looked around, and left without a word.

Two girls, sixteen-year-old runaways from California, showed up one night. They undressed for dinner and were shocked when they found out I could see. Pink scared the hell out of them. Those poor kids had a lot of living to do before they approached Pink's level of sophistication. But then Pink might have been uneasy in California. They left the next day, unsure if they had been to an orgy or not. All that touching and no getting down to business, very strange.

There was a nice couple from Santa Fe who acted as a sort of liaison between Keller and their lawyer. They had a nine-year-old boy who chattered endlessly in handtalk to the other kids. They came up about every other week and stayed a few days, soaking up sunshine and participating in the Together every night. They spoke halting shorthand and did me the courtesy of not speaking to me in speech.

Some of the Indians came around at odd intervals. Their behavior was almost aggressively chauvinistic. They stayed dressed at all times in their Levis and boots. But it was evident that they had a respect for the people, though they thought them strange. They had business dealings with the commune. It was the Navahos who trucked away the produce that was taken to the gate every day, sold it, and took a percentage. They would sit and powwow in sign language spelled into hands. Pink said they were scrupulously honest in their dealings.

And about once a week all the parents went out in the field and ***ed.

I GOT BETTER and better at shorthand and bodytalk. I had been breezing along for about five months and winter was in the offing. I had not examined my desires as yet, not really thought about what it was I wanted to do with the rest of my life. I guess the habit of letting myself drift was too ingrained. I was there, and constitutionally unable to decide whether to go or to face up to the problem if I wanted to stay for a long, long time.

Then I got a push.

For a long time I thought it had something to do with the economic situation outside. They were aware of the outside world at Keller. They knew that isolation and ignoring problems that could easily be dismissed as not relevant to them was a dangerous course, so they subscribed to the Braille *New York Times* and most of them read it. They had a television set that got plugged in about once a month. The kids would watch it and translate for their parents.

So I was aware that the non-depression was moving slowly into a more normal inflationary spiral. Jobs were opening up, money was flowing again. When I found myself on the outside again shortly afterward, I thought that was the reason.

The real reason was more complex. It had to do with peeling off the onion layer of shorthand and discovering another layer beneath it.

I had learned handtalk in a few easy lessons. Then I became aware of shorthand and bodytalk, and of how much harder they would be to learn. Through five months of constant immersion, which is the only way to learn a language, I had attained the equivalent level of a five- or six-year-old in shorthand. I knew I could master it, given time. Bodytalk was another matter. You couldn't measure progress as easily in bodytalk. It was a variable and highly interpersonal language that evolved according to the person, the time, the mood. But I was learning.

Then I became aware of Touch. That's the best I can describe it in a single, unforced English noun. What *they* called this fourth-stage language varied from day to day, as I will try to explain.

I first became aware of it when I tried to meet Janet Reilly. I now knew the history of Keller, and she figured very prominently in all the stories. I knew everyone at Keller, and I could find her nowhere. I knew everyone by names like Scar, and She with the missing front tooth, and Man-with-wiry-hair. These were shorthand names that I had given them myself, and they all accepted them without question. They had abolished their outside names within the commune. They meant nothing to them; they told nothing and described nothing.

At first I assumed that it was my imperfect command of shorthand that made me unable to clearly ask the right question about Janet Reilly. Then I saw that they were not telling me on purpose. I saw why, and I approved, and thought no more about it. The name Janet Reilly described what she had been *on the outside,* and one of her conditions for pushing the whole thing through in the first place had been that she be no one special on the inside. She melted into the group and disappeared. She didn't want to be found. All right.

But in the course of pursuing the question I became aware that each of the members of the commune had no specific name at all. That is, Pink, for instance, had no less than one hundred and fifteen names, one from each of the commune members. Each was a contextual name that told the story of Pink's relationship to a particular person. My simple names, based on physical descriptions, were accepted as the names a child would apply to people. The children had not yet learned to go beneath the outer layers and use names that told of themselves, their lives, and their relationships to others.

What is even more confusing, the names evolved from day to day. It was my first glimpse of Touch, and it frightened me. It was a question of permutations. Just the first simple expansion of the problem meant there were no less than thirteen thousand names in use, and they wouldn't stay still so I could memorize them. If Pink spoke to me of Baldy, for instance, she would use her Touch name for him, modified by the fact that she was speaking to me and not Short-chubby-man.

Then the depths of what I had been missing opened beneath me and I was suddenly breathless with fear of heights.

Touch was what they spoke to each other. It was an incredible blend of all three other modes I had learned, and the essence of it was that it never stayed the same. I could listen to them speak to me in shorthand, which was the real basis for Touch, and be aware of the currents of Touch flowing just beneath the surface.

It was a language of inventing languages. Everyone spoke their own dialect because everyone spoke with a different instrument: a different body and set of life experiences. It was modified by everything. *It would not stand still.*

They would sit at the Together and invent an entire body of Touch responses in a night; idiomatic, personal, totally naked in its honesty. And they used it only as a building block for the next night's language.

I didn't know if I wanted to be that naked. I had looked into myself a little recently and had not been satisfied with what I found. The realization that every one of them knew more about it than I, because my honest body had told what my frightened mind had not wanted to reveal, was shattering. I was naked under a spotlight in Carnegie Hall, and all the no-pants nightmares I had ever had came out to haunt me. The fact that they all loved me with all my warts was suddenly not enough. I wanted to curl up in a dark closet with my ingrown ego and let it fester.

I might have come through this fear. Pink was certainly trying to help me. She told me that it would only hurt for a while, that I would quickly adjust to living my life with my darkest emotions written in fire across my forehead. She said Touch was not as hard as it looked at first, either. Once I learned shorthand and bodytalk, Touch would flow naturally from it like sap rising in a tree. It would be unavoidable, something that would happen to me without much effort at all.

I almost believed her. But she betrayed herself. No, no, no. Not that, but the things in her concerning ***ing convinced me that if I went through this I would only bang my head hard against the next step up the ladder.

***

I had a little better definition now. Not one that I can easily translate into English, and even that attempt will only convey my hazy concept of what it was.

"It is the mode of touching without touching," Pink said, her body going like crazy in an attempt to reach me with her own imperfect concept of what it was, handicapped by my illiteracy. Her body denied the truth of her shorthand definition, and at the same time admitted to me that she did not know what it was herself.

"It is the gift whereby one can expand oneself from the eternal quiet and dark into something else." And again her body denied it. She beat on the floor in exasperation.

"It is an attribute of being in the quiet and dark all the time, touching others. All I know for sure is that vision and hearing preclude it or obscure it. I can make it as quiet and dark as I possibly can and be aware of the edges of it, but the visual orientation of the mind persists. That door is closed to me, and to all the children."

Her verb "to touch" in the first part of that was a Touch amalgam, one that reached back into her memories of me and what I had told her of my experiences. It implied and called up the smell and feel of broken mushrooms in soft earth under the barn with Tall-one-with-green-eyes, she who taught me to feel the essence of an object. It also contained references to our bodytalking while I was penetrating into the dark and wet of her, and her running account to me of what it was like to receive me into herself. This was all one word.

I brooded on that for a long time. What was the point of suffering through the nakedness of Touch, only to reach the level of frustrated blindness enjoyed by Pink?

What was it that kept pushing me away from the one place in my life where I had been happiest?

One thing was the realization, quite late in coming, that can be summed up as "What the hell am I *doing* here?" The question that should have answered that question was "What the hell would I do if I *left*?"

I was the only visitor, the only one in *seven years,* to stay at Keller for longer than a few days. I brooded on that. I was not strong enough or confident enough in my opinion of myself to see it as anything but a flaw in *me,* not in those others. I was obviously too easily satisfied, too complacent to see the flaws that those others had seen.

It didn't have to be flaws in the people of Keller, or in their system. No, I loved and respected them too much to think that. What they had going certainly came as near as anyone ever has in this imperfect world to a sane, rational way for people to exist without warfare and with a minimum of politics. In the end, those two old dinosaurs are the only ways humans have yet discovered to be social animals. Yes, I do see war as a way of living with another; by imposing your will on another in terms so unmistakable that the opponent has to either knuckle under to you, die, or beat your brains out. And if that's a solution to anything, I'd rather live without solutions. Politics is not much better. The only thing going for it is that it occasionally succeeds in substituting talk for fists.

Keller *was* an organism. It was a new way of relating, and it seemed to work. I'm not pushing it as a solution for the world's problems. It's possible that it could only work for a group with a common self-interest as binding and rare as deafness and blindness. I can't think of another group whose needs are so interdependent.

The cells of the organism cooperated beautifully. The organism was strong, flourishing, and possessed of all the attributes I've ever heard used in defining life except the ability to reproduce. That might have been its fatal flaw, if any. I certainly saw the seeds of something developing in the children.

The strength of the organism was communication. There's no way around it. Without the elaborate and impossible-to-falsify mechanisms for communication built into Keller, it would have eaten itself in pettiness, jealousy, possessiveness, and any dozen other "innate" human defects.

The nightly Together was the basis of the organism. Here, from after dinner till it was time to fall asleep, everyone talked in a language that was incapable of falsehood. If there was a problem brewing, it presented itself and was solved almost automatically. Jealousy? Resentment? Some little festering wrong that you're nursing? You couldn't conceal it at the Together, and soon everyone was clustered around you and loving the sickness away. It acted like white corpuscles, clustering around a sick cell, not to destroy it, but to heal it. There seemed to be no problem that couldn't be solved if it was attacked early enough, and with Touch, your neighbors knew about it before you did and were already laboring to correct the wrong, heal the wound, to make you feel better so you could laugh about it. There was a lot of laughter at the Togethers.

I thought for a while that I was feeling possessive about Pink. I know I had done so a little at first. Pink was my special friend, the one who had helped me out from the first, who for several days was the only one I could talk to. It was her hands that had taught me handtalk. I know I felt stirrings of territoriality the first time she lay in my lap while another man made love to her. But if there was any signal the Kellerites were adept at reading, it was that one. It went off like an alarm bell in Pink, the man, and the women and men around me. They soothed me, coddled me, told me in every language that it was all right, not to feel ashamed. Then the man in question began loving *me*. Not Pink, but the man. An observational anthropologist would have had subject matter for a whole thesis. Have you seen the films of baboons' social behavior? Dogs do it, too. Many male mammals do it. When males get into dominance battles, the weaker can defuse the aggression by submitting, by turning tail and surrendering. I have never felt so defused as when that man surrendered the object of our clash of wills—Pink—and turned his attention to me. What could I do? What I did was laugh, and he laughed, and soon we were all laughing, and that was the end of territoriality.

That's the essence of how they solved most "human nature" problems at Keller. Sort of like an oriental martial art; you yield, roll with the blow so that your attacker takes a pratfall with the force of the aggression. You do that until the attacker sees that the initial push wasn't worth the effort, that it was a pretty silly thing to do when no one was resisting you. Pretty soon he's not Tarzan of the Apes, but Charlie Chaplin. And he's laughing.

So it wasn't Pink and her lovely body and my realization that she could never be all mine to lock away in my cave and defend with a gnawed-off thighbone. If I'd persisted in that frame of mind she would have found me about as attractive as an Amazonian leech, and that was a great incentive to confound the behaviorists and overcome it.

So I was back to those people who had visited and left, and what did they see that I didn't see?

Well, there was something pretty glaring. I was not part of the organism, no matter how nice the organism was to me. I had no hopes of ever becoming a part, either. Pink had said it in the first week. She felt it herself, to a lesser degree. She could not ***, though that fact was not going to drive her away from Keller. She had told me that many times in shorthand and confirmed it in bodytalk. If I left, it would be without her.

Trying to stand outside and look at it, I felt pretty miserable. What was I trying to *do,* anyway? Was my goal in life *really* to become a part of a deaf-blind commune? I was feeling so low by that time that I actually thought of that as denigrating, in the face of all the evidence to the contrary. I should be out in the real world where the real people lived, not these freakish cripples.

I backed off from that thought very quickly. I was not totally out of my mind, just on the lunatic edges. These people were the best friends I'd ever had, maybe the only ones. That I was confused enough to think that of them even for a second worried me more than anything else. It's possible that it's what pushed me finally into a decision. I saw a future of growing disillusion and unfulfilled hopes. Unless I was willing to put out my eyes and ears, I would always be on the outside. *I* would be the deaf and blind one. I would be the freak. I didn't want to be a freak.

THEY KNEW I had decided to leave before I did. My last few days turned into a long goodbye, with a loving farewell implicit in every word touched to me. I was not really sad, and neither were they. It was nice, like everything they did. They said goodbye with just the right mix of wistfulness and life-must-go-on, and hope-to-touch-you-again.

Awareness of Touch scratched on the edges of my mind. It was not bad, just as Pink had said. In a year or two I could have mastered it.

But I was set now. I was back in the life groove that I had followed for so long. Why is it that once having decided what I must do, I'm afraid to reexamine my decision? Maybe because the original decision cost me so much that I didn't want to go through it again.

I left quietly in the night for the highway and California. They were out in the fields, standing in that circle again. Their fingertips were farther part than ever before. The dogs and children hung around the edges like beggars at a banquet. It was hard to tell which looked more hungry and puzzled.

THE EXPERIENCES AT Keller did not fail to leave their mark on me. I was unable to live as I had before. For a while I thought I could not live at all, but I did. I was too used to living to take the decisive step of ending my life. I would wait. Life had brought one pleasant thing to me; maybe it would bring another.

I became a writer. I found I now had a better gift for communicating than I had before. Or maybe I had it now for the first time. At any rate, my writing came together and I sold. I wrote what I wanted to write, and was not afraid of going hungry. I took things as they came.

I weathered the non-depression of '97, when unemployment reached twenty percent and the government once more ignored it as a temporary downturn. It eventually upturned, leaving the jobless rate slightly higher than it had been the time before, and the time before that. Another million useless persons had been created with nothing better to do than shamble through the streets looking for beatings in progress, car smashups, heart attacks, murders, shootings, arson, bombings, and riots: the endlessly inventive street theater. It never got dull.

I didn't become rich, but I was usually comfortable. That is a social disease, the symptoms of which are the ability to ignore the fact that your society is developing weeping pustules and having its brains eaten out by radioactive maggots. I had a nice apartment in Marin County, out of sight of the machine-gun turrets. I had a car, at a time when they were beginning to be luxuries.

I had concluded that my life was not destined to be all I would like it to be. We all make some sort of compromise, I reasoned, and if you set your expectations too high you are doomed to disappointment. It did occur to me that I was settling for something far from "high," but I didn't know what to do about it. I carried on with a mixture of cynicism and optimism that seemed about the right mix for me. It kept my motor running, anyway.

I even made it to Japan, as I had intended in the first place.

I didn't find someone to share my life. There was only Pink for that, Pink and all her family, and we were separated by a gulf I didn't dare cross. I didn't even dare think about her too much. It would have been very dangerous to my equilibrium. I lived with it, and told myself that it was the way I was. Lonely.

The years rolled on like a caterpillar tractor at Dachau, up to the penultimate day of the millennium.

San Francisco was having a big bash to celebrate the year 2000. Who gives a shit that the city is slowly falling apart, that civilization is disintegrating into hysteria? Let's have a party!

I stood on the Golden Gate Dam on the last day of 1999. The sun was setting in the Pacific, on Japan, which had turned out to be more of the same but squared and cubed with neo-samurai. Behind me the first bombshells of a firework celebration of holocaust tricked up to look like festivity competed with the flare of burning buildings as the social and economic basket cases celebrated the occasion in their own way. The city quivered under the weight of misery, anxious to slide off along the fracture lines of some subcortical San Andreas Fault. Orbiting atomic bombs twinkled in my mind, up there somewhere, ready to plant mushrooms when we'd exhausted all the other possibilities.

I thought of Pink.

I found myself speeding through the Nevada desert, sweating, gripping the steering wheel. I was crying aloud but without sound, as I had learned to do at Keller.

Can you go back?

I SLAMMED THE citicar over the potholes in the dirt road. The car was falling apart. It was not built for this kind of travel. The sky was getting light in the east. It was the dawn of a new millennium. I stepped harder on the gas pedal and the car bucked savagely. I didn't care. I was not driving back down that road, not ever. One way or another, I was here to stay.

I reached the wall and sobbed my relief. The last hundred miles had been a nightmare of wondering if it had been a dream. I touched the cold reality of the wall and it calmed me. Light snow had drifted over everything, gray in the early dawn.

I saw them in the distance. All of them, out in the field where I had left them. No, I was wrong. It was only the children. Why had it seemed like so many at first?

Pink was there. I knew her immediately, though I had never seen her in winter clothes. She was taller, filled out.

She would be nineteen years old. There was a small child playing in the snow at her feet, and she cradled an infant in her arms. I went to her and talked to her hand.

She turned to me, her face radiant with welcome, her eyes staring in a way I had never seen. Her hands flitted over me and her eyes did not move.

"I touch you, I welcome you," her hands said. "I wish you could have been here just a few minutes ago. Why did you go away darling? Why did you stay away so long?" Her eyes were stones in her head. She was blind. She was deaf.

All the children were. No, Pink's child sitting at my feet looked up at me with a smile.

"Where is everybody?" I asked when I got my breath. "Scar? Baldy? Green-eyes? And what's happened? What's happened to you?" I was tottering on the edge of a heart attack or nervous collapse or something. My reality felt in danger of dissolving.

"They've gone," she said. The word eluded me, but the context put it with the *Mary Celeste* and Roanoke, Virginia. It was complex, the way she used the word *gone*. It was like something she had said before: unattainable, a source of frustration like the one that had sent me running from Keller. But now her word told of something that was not hers yet, but was within her grasp. There was no sadness in it.

"Gone?"

"Yes. I don't know where. They're happy. They ***ed. It was glorious. We could only touch a part of it."

I felt my heart hammering to the sound of the last train pulling away from the station. My feet were pounding along the ties as it faded into the fog. Where are the Brigadoons of yesterday? I've never yet heard of a fairy tale where you can go back to the land of enchantment. You wake up, you find that your chance is gone. You threw it away. *Fool!* You only get one chance; that's the moral, isn't it?

Pink's hands laughed along my face.

"Hold this part-of-me-who-speaks-mouth-to-nipple," she said, and handed me her infant daughter. "I will give you a gift."

She reached up and lightly touched my ears with her cold fingers. The sound of the wind was shut out, and when her hands came away it never came back. She touched my eyes, shut out all the light, and I saw no more.

We live in the lovely quiet and dark.

The 1980s

THE WAY OF CROSS AND DRAGON

GEORGE R.R. MARTIN

GEORGE R.R. MARTIN was born in September 1948 in Bayonne, New Jersey, and received a B.S. in journalism from Northwestern University in 1970. A comic book fan and collector in high school, Martin began to write fiction for comic fanzines and made his first professional sale, "The Hero," to *Galaxy* in February 1971. This was followed by the major novella "A Song for Lya," which won the Hugo Award. Other major stories include Nebula Award–winners "Sandkings" and "Portraits of his Children," Bram Stoker Award–winner "The Pear-Shaped Man," and "The Storms of Windhaven" (with Lisa Tuttle). They have been collected in nine volumes to date, including *A Song for Lya and Other Stories, Songs of Stars and Shadows, Sandkings, Songs the Dead Men Sing, Nightflyers, Tuf Voyaging, Portraits of His Children, Quartet,* and *GRRM: A RRetrospective.*

Martin's first science fiction novel, *Dying of the Light,* published in the same year *Star Wars* hit the screens, was a powerful romance about a huge festival on a dying world. It was followed by seven more novels, including the vampire novel *Fevre Dream* and rock 'n' roll novel *The Armageddon Rag.* Martin is best known today for his epic fantasy series "The Song of Ice and Fire," which to date includes *A Game of Thrones, A Clash of Kings,* and *A Storm of Swords.* Upcoming is a fourth volume, *A Feast for Crows.* Martin has won the Hugo Award four times, the Nebula Award twice, the World

Fantasy Award, the Stoker Award, the Seiun Award, and the Locus Award eleven times.

Science fiction, with its ostensibly secular worldview, has often struggled to come to terms with faith and religion, a struggle that has resulted in some of the finest science fiction ever written. In the story that follows, Martin gives us a look at just what the future of heresy might look like.

* * *

"HERESY," HE TOLD ME. The brackish waters of his pool sloshed gently.

"Another one?" I said wearily. "There are so many these days."

My Lord Commander was displeased by that comment. He shifted position heavily, sending ripples up and down the pool. One broke over the side, and a sheet of water slid across the tiles of the receiving chamber. My boots were soaked yet again. I accepted that philosophically. I had worn my worst boots, well aware that wet feet are among the inescapable consequences of paying call on Torgathon Nine-Klariis Tûn, elder of the ka-Thane people, and also Archbishop of Vess, Most Holy Father of the Four Vows, Grand Inquisitor of the Order Militant of the Knights of Jesus Christ, and councillor to His Holiness, Pope Daryn XXI of New Rome.

"Be there as many heresies as stars in the sky, each single one is no less dangerous, Father," the Archbishop said solemnly. "As Knights of Christ, it is our ordained task to fight them one and all. And I must add that this new heresy is particularly foul."

"Yes, my Lord Commander," I replied. "I did not intend to make light of it. You have my apologies. The mission to Finnegan was most taxing. I had hoped to ask you for a leave of absence from my duties. I need rest, a time for thought and restoration."

"Rest?" The Archbishop moved again in his pool; only a slight shift of his immense bulk, but it was enough to send a fresh sheet of water across the floor. His black, pupilless eyes blinked at me. "No, Father, I am afraid that is out of the question. Your skills and your experience are vital to this new mission." His bass tones seemed then to soften somewhat. "I have not had time to go over your reports on Finnegan," he said. "How did your work go?"

"Badly," I told him, "though I think that ultimately we will prevail. The Church is strong on Finnegan. When our attempts at reconciliation were rebuffed, I put some standards into the right hands, and we were able to shut down the heretics' newspaper and broadcast facilities. Our friends also saw to it that their legal actions came to nothing."

"That is not *badly*," the Archbishop said. "You won a considerable victory for the Lord."

"There were riots, my Lord Commander," I said. "More than a hundred of the heretics were killed, and a dozen of our own people. I fear there will be more violence before the matter is finished. Our priests are attacked if they so much as enter the city where the heresy has taken root. Their leaders risk their lives if they leave that city. I had hoped to avoid such hatreds, such bloodshed."

"Commendable, but not realistic," said Archbishop Torgathon. He blinked at me again, and I remembered that among people of his race, that was a sign of impatience. "The blood of martyrs must sometimes be spilled, and the blood of heretics as well. What matters it if a being surrenders his life, so long as his soul is saved?"

"Indeed," I agreed. Despite his impatience, Torgathon would lecture me for another hour if given a chance. That prospect dismayed me. The receiving chamber was not designed for human comfort, and I did not wish to remain any longer than necessary. The walls were damp and moldy, the air hot and humid and thick with the rancid-butter smell characteristic of the ka-Thane. My collar was chafing my neck raw, I was sweating beneath my cassock, my feet were thoroughly soaked, and my stomach was beginning to churn. I pushed ahead to the business at hand. "You say this new heresy is unusually foul, my Lord Commander?"

"It is," he said.

"Where has it started?"

"On Arion, a world some three weeks' distance from Vess. A human world entirely. I cannot understand why you humans are so easily corrupted. Once a ka-Thane has found the faith, he would scarcely abandon it."

"That is well known," I said politely. I did not mention that the number of ka-Thane to find the faith was vanishingly small. They were a slow, ponderous people, and most of their vast millions showed no interest in learning any ways other than their own, nor in following any creed but their own ancient religion. Torgathon Nine-Klariis Tûn was an anomaly. He had been among the first converts almost two centuries ago, when Pope Vidas L had ruled that non-humans might serve as clergy. Given his great lifespan and the iron certainty of his belief, it was no wonder that Torgathon had risen as far as he had, despite the fact that less than a thousand of his race had followed him into the Church. He had at least a century of life remaining to him. No doubt he would someday be Torgathon Cardinal Tûn, should he squelch enough heresies. The times are like that.

"We have little influence on Arion," the Archbishop was saying. His arms moved as he spoke, four ponderous clubs of mottled green-gray flesh churning the water, and the dirty white cilia around his breathing hole trembled with each word. "A few priests, a few churches, and some believers, but no power to speak of. The heretics already outnumber us on this world. I rely on your intellect, your shrewdness. Turn this calamity into an opportunity. This heresy is so spurious that you can easily disprove it. Perhaps some of the deluded will turn to the true way."

"Certainly," I said. "And the nature of this heresy? What must I disprove?" It is a sad indication of my own troubled faith to add that I did not really care. I have dealt with too many heresies. Their beliefs and their questionings echo in my head and trouble my dreams at night. How can I be sure of my own faith? The very edict that had admitted Torgathon into the clergy had caused a half-dozen worlds to repudiate the Bishop of New Rome, and those who had followed that path would find a particularly ugly heresy in the massive naked (save for a damp Roman collar) alien who floated before me, who wielded the authority of the Church in four great webbed hands. Christianity is the greatest single human religion, but that means little. The non-Christian outnumber us five-to-one, and there are well over seven hundred Christian sects, some almost as large as the One True Interstellar Catholic Church of Earth and the Thousand Worlds. Even Daryn XXI, powerful as he is, is only one of seven to claim the title of Pope. My own belief was once strong, but I have moved too long among heretics and non-believers. Now even my prayers do not make the doubts go away. So it was that I felt no horror—only a sudden intellectual interest—when the Archbishop told me the nature of the heresy on Arion. "They have made a saint," he said, "out of Judas Iscariot."

AS A SENIOR in the Knights Inquisitor, I command my own starship, which it pleases me to call the *Truth of Christ.* Before the craft was assigned to me, it was named the *Saint Thomas,* after the apostle, but I did not consider a saint notorious for doubting to be an appropriate patron for a ship enlisted in the fight against heresy.

I have no duties aboard the *Truth,* which is crewed by six brothers and sisters of the Order of Saint Christopher the Far-Traveling, and captained by a young woman I hired away from a merchant trader. I was therefore able to devote the entire three-week voyage from Vess to Arion to a study of the heretical bible, a copy of which had been given to me by the Archbishop's administrative assistant. It was a thick, heavy, handsome book, bound in dark leather, its pages tipped with gold leaf, with many splendid interior illustrations in full color with holographic enhancement. Remarkable work, clearly done by someone who loved the all-but-forgotten art of bookmaking. The paintings reproduced inside—the originals, I gathered, were to be found on the walls of the House of Saint Judas on Arion—were masterful, if blasphemous, as much high art as the Tammerwens and RoHallidays that adorn the Great Cathedral of Saint John on New Rome.

Inside, the book bore an imprimatur indicating that it had been approved by Lukyan Judasson, First Scholar of the Order of Saint Judas Iscariot.

It was called *The Way of Cross and Dragon*.

I read it as the *Truth of Christ* slid between the stars, at first taking copious notes to better understand the heresy I must fight, but later simply absorbed by the strange, convoluted, grotesque story it told. The words of text had passion and power and poetry.

Thus it was that I first encountered the striking figure of Saint Judas Iscariot, a complex, ambitious, contradictory, and altogether extraordinary human being.

He was born of a whore in the fabled ancient city-state of Babylon on the same day that the savior was born in Bethlehem, and he spent his childhood in the alleys and gutters, selling his own body when he had to, pimping when he was older. As a youth he began to experiment with the dark arts, and before the age of twenty he was a skilled necromancer. That was when he became Judas the Dragon-Tamer, the first and only man to bend to his will the most fearsome of God's creatures, the great winged firelizards of Old Earth. The book held a marvelous painting of Judas in some great dank cavern, his eyes aflame as he wields a glowing lash to keep a mountainous green-gold dragon at bay. Beneath his arm is a woven basket, its lid slightly ajar, and the tiny scaled heads of three dragon chicks are peering from within. A fourth infant dragon is crawling up his sleeve. That was in the first chapter of his life.

In the second, he was Judas the Conqueror, Judas the Dragon-King, Judas of Babylon, the Great Usurper. Astride the greatest of his dragons, with an iron crown on his head and a sword in his hand, he made Babylon the capital of the greatest empire Old Earth had ever known, a realm that stretched from Spain to India. He reigned from a dragon throne amid the Hanging Gardens he had caused to be constructed, and it was there he sat when he tried Jesus of Nazareth, the troublemaking prophet who had been dragged before him bound and bleeding. Judas was not a patient man, and he made Christ bleed still more before he was through with Him. And when Jesus would not answer his questions, Judas contemptuously had Him cast back out into the streets. But first, he ordered his guards to cut off Christ's legs. "Healer," he said, "heal thyself."

Then came the Repentance, the vision in the night, and Judas Iscariot gave up his crown, his dark arts, and his riches to follow the man he had crippled. Despised and taunted by those he had tyrannized, Judas became the Legs of the Lord, and for a year carried Jesus on his back to the far corners of the realm he once ruled. When Jesus did finally heal Himself, then Judas walked at his side, and from that time forth he was Jesus's trusted friend and counselor, the first and foremost of the Twelve. Finally, Jesus gave Judas the gift of tongues, recalled and sanctified the dragons that Judas had sent away, and sent his disciple forth on a solitary ministry across the oceans, "to spread My Word where I cannot go."

There came a day when the sun went dark at noon and the ground trembled, and Judas swung his dragon around on ponderous wings and flew back across the raging seas. But when he reached the city of Jerusalem, he found Christ dead on the cross.

In that moment his faith faltered, and for the next three days the Great Wrath of Judas was like a storm across the ancient world. His dragons razed the Temple in Jerusalem, drove the people forth from the city, and struck as well at the great seats of power in Rome and Babylon. And when he found the others of the Twelve and questioned them and learned of how the one named Simon-called-Peter had three times betrayed the Lord, he strangled Peter with his own hands and fed the corpse to his dragons. Then he sent those dragons forth to start fires throughout the world, funeral pyres for Jesus of Nazareth.

And Jesus rose on the third day, and Judas wept, but his tears could not turn Christ's anger, for in his wrath he had betrayed all of Christ's teachings.

So Jesus called back the dragons, and they came, and everywhere the fires went out. And from their bellies he called forth Peter and made him whole again, and gave him dominion over the Church.

Then the dragons died, and so too did all dragons everywhere, for they were the living sigil of the power and wisdom of Judas Iscariot, who had sinned greatly. And He took from Judas the gift of tongues and the power of healing He had given, and even his eyesight, for Judas had acted as a blind man (there was a fine painting of the blinded Judas weeping over the bodies of his dragons). And He told Judas that for long ages he would be remembered only as Betrayer, and people would curse his name, and all that he had been and done would be forgotten.

But then, because Judas had loved Him so, Christ gave him a boon: an extended life, during which he might travel and think on his sins and finally come to forgiveness. Only then might he die.

And that was the beginning of the last chapter in the life of Judas Iscariot. But it was a very long chapter indeed. Once dragon-king, once the friend of Christ, now he was only a blind traveler, outcast and friendless, wandering all the cold roads of the Earth, living still when all the cities and people and things he had known were dead. Peter, the first Pope and ever his enemy, spread far and wide the tale of how Judas had sold Christ for thirty pieces of silver, until Judas dared not even use his true name. For a time he called himself just Wandering Ju', and afterward many other names. He lived more than a thousand years and became a preacher, a healer, and a lover of animals, and was hunted and persecuted when the Church that Peter had founded became bloated and corrupt. But he had a great deal of time, and at last he found wisdom and a sense of peace, and finally, Jesus came to him on a long-postponed deathbed and they were reconciled, and Judas wept once again. Before he died, Christ promised that he would permit a few to remember who and what Judas had been, and that with the passage of centuries the news would spread, until finally Peter's Lie was displaced and forgotten.

Such was the life of St. Judas Iscariot, as related in *The Way of Cross and Dragon.* His teachings were there as well and the apocryphal books he had allegedly written.

When I had finished the volume, I lent it to Arla-k-Bau, the captain of the *Truth of Christ.* Arla was a gaunt, pragmatic woman of no particular faith, but I valued her opinion. The others of my crew, the good sisters and brothers of Saint Christopher, would only have echoed the Archbishop's religious horror.

"Interesting," Arla said when she returned the book to me.

I chuckled. "Is that all?"

She shrugged. "It makes a nice story. An easier read than your Bible, Damien, and more dramatic as well."

"True," I admitted. "But it's absurd. An unbelievable tangle of doctrine, apocrypha, mythology, and superstition. Entertaining, yes, certainly. Imaginative, even darling. But ridiculous, don't you think? How can you credit dragons? A legless Christ? Peter being pieced together after being devoured by four monsters?"

Arla's grin was taunting. "Is that any sillier than water changing into wine, or Christ walking on the waves, or a man living in the belly of a fish?" Arla-k-Bau liked to jab at me. It had been a scandal when I selected a nonbeliever as my captain, but she was very good at her job, and I liked her around to keep me sharp. She had a good mind, Arla did, and I valued that more than blind obedience. Perhaps that was a sin in me.

"There is a difference," I said.

"Is there?" she snapped back. Her eyes saw through my masks. "Ah, Damien, admit it. You rather liked this book."

I cleared my throat. "It piqued my interest," I acknowledged. I had to justify myself. "You know the kind of matter I deal with ordinarily. Dreary little doctrinal deviations; obscure quibblings on theology somehow blown all out of proportion; bald-faced political maneuverings designed to set some ambitious planetary bishop up as a new pope, or wrest some concession or other from New Rome or Vess. The war is endless, but the battles are dull and dirty. They exhaust me spiritually, emotionally, physically. Afterward I feel drained and guilty." I tapped the book's leather cover. "This is different. The heresy must be crushed, of course, but I admit that I am anxious to meet this Lukyan Judasson."

"The artwork is lovely as well," Arla said, flipping through the pages of *The Way of Cross and Dragon* and stopping to study one especially striking plate—Judas weeping over his dragons, I think. I smiled to see that it had affected her as much as me. Then I frowned.

That was the first inkling I had of the difficulties ahead.

SO IT WAS that the *Truth of Christ* came to the porcelain city Ammadon on the world of Arion, where the Order of Saint Judas Iscariot kept its House.

Arion was a pleasant, gentle world, inhabited for these past three centuries. Its population was under nine million; Ammadon, the only real city, was home to two of those millions. The technological level was medium high, but chiefly imported. Arion had little industry and was not an innovative world, except perhaps artistically. The arts were quite important here, flourishing and vital. Religious freedom was a basic tenet of the society, but Arion was not a religious world either, and the majority of the populace lived devoutly secular lives. The most popular religion was Aestheticism, which hardly counts as a religion at all. There were also Taoists, Erikaners, Old True Christers, and Children of the Dreamer, plus adherents of a dozen lesser sects.

And finally there were nine churches of the One True Interstellar Catholic faith. There had been twelve. The other three were now houses of Arion's fastest-growing faith, the Order of Saint Judas Iscariot, which also had a dozen newly built churches of its own.

The Bishop of Arion was a dark, severe man with close-cropped black hair who was not at all happy to see me. "Damien Har Veris!" he exclaimed with some wonderment when I called on him at his residence. "We have heard of you, of course, but I never thought to meet or host you. Our numbers here are small."

"And growing smaller," I said, "a matter of some concern to my Lord Commander, Archbishop Torgathon. Apparently you are less troubled, Excellency, since you did not see fit to report the activities of this sect of Judas worshippers."

He looked briefly angry at the rebuke, but quickly swallowed his temper. Even a bishop can fear a Knight Inquisitor. "We are concerned, of course," he said. "We do all we can to combat the heresy. If you have advice that will help us, I will be glad to listen."

"I am an Inquisitor of the Order Militant of the Knights of Jesus Christ," I said bluntly. "I do not give advice, Excellency. I take action. To that end I was sent to Arion, and that is what I shall do. Now, tell me what you know about this heresy, and this First Scholar, this Lukyan Judasson."

"Of course, Father Damien," the Bishop began. He signaled for a servant to bring us a tray of wine and cheese, and began to summarize the short but explosive history of the Judas cult. I listened, polishing my nails on the crimson lapel of my jacket until the black paint gleamed brilliantly, interrupting from time to time with a question. Before he had half finished, I was determined to visit Lukyan personally. It seemed the best course of action.

And I had wanted to do so all along.

APPEARANCES WERE IMPORTANT on Arion, I gathered, and I deemed it necessary to impress Lukyan with myself and my station. I wore my best boots—sleek, dark hand-made boots of Roman leather that had never seen the inside of Torgathon's receiving chamber—and a severe black suit with deep burgundy lapels and stiff collar. Around my neck was a splendid crucifix of pure gold; my collarpin was a matching golden sword, the sigil of the Knights Inquisitor. Brother Denis carefully painted my nails, all black as ebon, and darkened my eyes as well, and used a fine white powder on my face. When I glanced in the mirror, I frightened even myself. I smiled, but only briefly. It ruined the effect.

I walked to the House of Saint Judas Iscariot. The streets of Ammadon were wide and spacious and golden, lined by scarlet trees called whisperwinds whose long, drooping tendrils did indeed seem to whisper secrets to the gentle breeze. Sister Judith came with me. She is a small woman, slight of build even in the cowled coveralls of the Order of Saint Christopher. Her face is meek and kind, her eyes wide and youthful and innocent. I find her useful. Four times now she has killed those who attempted to assault me.

The House itself was newly built. Rambling and stately, it rose from amid gardens of small bright flowers and seas of golden grass; the gardens were surrounded by a high wall. Murals covered both the outer wall around the property and the exterior of the building itself. I recognized a few of them from *The Way of Cross and Dragon,* and stopped briefly to admire them before walking through the main gate. No one tried to stop us. There were no guards, not even a receptionist. Within the walls, men and women strolled languidly through the flowers, or sat on benches beneath silverwoods and whisperwinds.

Sister Judith and I paused, then made our way directly to the House itself.

We had just started up the steps when a man appeared from within, and stood waiting in the doorway. He was blond and fat, with a great wiry beard that framed a slow smile, and he wore a flimsy robe that fell to his sandaled feet. On the robe were dragons, dragons bearing the silhouette of a man holding a cross.

When I reached the top of the steps, he bowed to me. "Father Damien Har Veris of the Knights Inquisitor," he said. His smile widened. "I greet you in the name of Jesus, and in the name of Saint Judas. I am Lukyan."

I made a note to myself to find out which of the Bishop's staff was feeding information to the Judas cult, but my composure did not break. I have been a Knight Inquisitor for a long, long time. "Father Lukyan

Mo," I said, taking his hand. "I have questions to ask of you." I did not smile.

He did. "I thought you might," he said.

LUKYAN'S OFFICE WAS large but spartan. Heretics often have a simplicity that the officers of the true Church seem to have lost. He did have one indulgence, however. Dominating the wall behind his desk console was the painting I had already fallen in love with: the blinded Judas weeping over his dragons.

Lukyan sat down heavily and motioned me to a second chair. We had left Sister Judith outside in the waiting chamber. "I prefer to stand, Father Lukyan," I said, knowing it gave me an advantage.

"Just Lukyan," he said. "Or Luke, if you prefer. We have little use for hierarchy here."

"You are Father Lukyan Mo, born here on Arion, educated in the seminary on Cathaday, a former priest of the One True Interstellar Catholic Church of Earth and the Thousand Worlds," I said. "I will address you as befits your station, Father. I expect you to reciprocate. Is that understood?"

"Oh, yes," he said amiably.

"I am empowered to strip you of your right to perform the sacraments, to order you shunned and excommunicated for this heresy you have formulated. On certain worlds I could even order your death."

"But not on Arion," Lukyan said quickly. "We're very tolerant here. Besides, we outnumber you." He smiled. "As for the rest, well, I don't perform those sacraments much anyway, you know. Not for years. I'm First Scholar now. A teacher, a thinker. I show others the way, help them find the faith. Excommunicate me if it will make you happy, Father Damien. Happiness is what all of us seek."

"You have given up the faith, then, Father Lukyan," I said. I deposited my copy of *The Way of Cross and Dragon* on his desk. "But I see you have found a new one." Now I did smile, but it was all ice, all menace, all mockery. "A more ridiculous creed I have yet to encounter. I suppose you will tell me that you have spoken to God, that he trusted you with this new revelation, so that you might clear the good name, such that it is, of Holy Judas?"

Now Lukyan's smile was very broad indeed. He picked up the book and beamed at me. "Oh, no," he said. "No, I made it all up."

That stopped me. "What?"

"I made it all up," he repeated. He hefted the book fondly. "I drew on many sources, of course, especially the Bible, but I do think of *Cross and Dragon* as mostly my own work. It's rather good, don't you agree? Of course, I could hardly put my name on it, proud as I am of it, but I did include my imprimatur. Did you notice that? It was the closest I dared come to a byline."

I was speechless only for a moment. Then I grimaced. "You startle me," I admitted. "I expected to find an inventive madman, some poor self-deluded fool, firm in his belief that he had spoken to God. I've dealt with such fanatics before. Instead I find a cheerful cynic who has invented a religion for his own profit. I think I prefer the fanatics. You are beneath contempt, Father Lukyan. You will burn in hell for eternity."

"I doubt it," Lukyan said, "but you do mistake me, Father Damien. I am no cynic, nor do I profit from my dear Saint Judas. Truthfully, I lived more comfortably as a priest of your own Church. I do this because it is my vocation."

I sat down. "You confuse me," I said. "Explain."

"Now I am going to tell you the truth," he said. He said it in an odd way, almost as a cant. "I am a Liar," he added.

"You want to confuse me with a child's paradoxes," I snapped.

"No, no," he smiled. "A *Liar*. With a capital. It is an organization, Father Damien. A religion, you might call it. A great and powerful faith. And I am the smallest part of it."

"I know of no such church," I said.

"Oh, no, you wouldn't. It's secret. It has to be. You can understand that, can't you? People don't like being lied to."

"I do not like being lied to," I said.

Lukyan looked wounded. "I told you this would be the truth, didn't I? When a Liar says that, you can believe him. How else could we trust each other?"

"There are many of you?" I asked. I was starting to think that Lukyan was a madman after all, as fanatical as any heretic, but in a more complex way. Here was a heresy within a heresy, but I recognized my duty: to find the truth of things, and set them right.

"Many of us," Lukyan said, smiling. "You would be surprised, Father Damien, really you would. But there are some things I dare not tell you."

"Tell me what you dare, then."

"Happily," said Lukyan Judasson. "We Liars, like those of all other religions, have several truths we take on faith. Faith is always required. There are some things that cannot be proven. We believe that life is worth living.

That is an article of faith. The purpose of life is to live, to resist death, perhaps to defy entropy."

"Go on," I said, interested despite myself.

"We also believe that happiness is a good, something to be sought after."

"The Church does not oppose happiness," I said dryly.

"I wonder," Lukyan said. "But let us not quibble. Whatever the Church's position on happiness, it does preach belief in an afterlife, in a supreme being and a complex moral code."

"True."

"The Liars believe in no afterlife, no God. We see the universe as it *is*, Father Damien, and these naked truths are cruel ones. We who believe in life, and treasure it, will die. Afterward there will be nothing, eternal emptiness, blackness, nonexistence. In our living there has been no purpose, no poetry, no meaning. Nor do our deaths possess these qualities. When we are gone, the universe will not long remember us, and shortly it will be as if we had never lived at all. Our worlds and our universe will not long outlive us. Ultimately, entropy will consume all, and our puny efforts cannot stay that awful end. It will be gone. It has never been. It has never mattered. The universe itself is doomed, transient, uncaring."

I slid back in my chair, and a shiver went through me as I listened to poor Lukyan's dark words. I found myself fingering my crucifix. "A bleak philosophy," I said, "as well as a false one. I have had that fearful vision myself. I think all of us do, at some point. But it is not so, Father. My faith sustains me against such nihilism. It is a shield against despair."

"Oh, I know that, my friend, my Knight Inquisitor," Lukyan said. "I'm glad to see you understand so well. You are almost one of us already."

I frowned.

"You've touched the heart of it," Lukyan continued. "The truths, the great truths—and most of the lesser ones as well—they are unbearable for most men. We find our shield in faith. Your faith, my faith, any faith. It doesn't matter, so long as we *believe*, really and truly believe, in whatever lie we cling to." He fingered the ragged edges of his great blond beard. "Our psychs have always told us that believers are the happy ones, you know. They may believe in Christ or Buddha or Erika Stormjones, in reincarnation or immortality or nature, in the power of love or the platform of a political faction, but it all comes to the same thing. They believe. They are happy. It is the ones who have seen truth who despair, and kill themselves. The truths are so vast, the faiths so little, so poorly made, so riddled with error and contradition that we see around them and through them, and then we feel the weight of darkness upon us, and can no longer be happy."

I am not a slow man. I knew, by then, where Lukyan Judasson was going. "Your Liars invent faiths."

He smiled. "Of all sorts. Not only religious. Think of it. We know truth for the cruel instrument it is. Beauty is infinitely preferable to truth. We invent beauty. Faiths, political movements, high ideals, belief in love and fellowship. All of them are lies. We tell those lies, among others, endless others. We improve on history and myth and religion, make each more beautiful, better, easier to believe in. Our lies are not perfect, of course. The truths are too big. But perhaps someday we will find one great lie that all humanity can use. Until then, a thousand small lies will do."

"I think I do not care for your Liars very much," I said with a cold, even fervor. "My whole life has been a quest for truth."

Lukyan was indulgent. "Father Damien Har Veris, Knight Inquisitor, I know you better than that. You are a Liar yourself. You do good work. You ship from world to world, and on each you destroy the foolish, the rebels, the questioners who would bring down the edifice of the vast lie that you serve."

"If my lie is so admirable," I said, "then why have you abandoned it?"

"A religion must fit its culture and society, work with them, not against them. If there is conflict, contradiction, then the lie breaks down, and the faith falters. Your Church is good for many worlds, Father, but not for Arion. Life is too kind here, and your faith is stern. Here we love beauty, and your faith offers too little. So we have improved it. We studied this world for a long time. We know its psychological profile. Saint Judas will thrive here. He offers drama, and color, and much beauty—the aesthetics are admirable. His is a tragedy with a happy ending, and Arion dotes on such stories. And the dragons are a nice touch. I think your own Church ought to find a way to work in dragons. They are marvelous creatures."

"Mythical," I said.

"Hardly," he replied. "Look it up." He grinned at me. "You see, really, it all comes back to faith. Can you really know what happened three thousand years ago? You have one Judas, I have another. Both of us have books. Is yours true? Can you really believe that? I have been admitted only to the first circle of the order of Liars, so I do not know all our secrets, but I know that we are very old. It would not surprise me to learn that the gospels were written by men very much like me. Perhaps there never was a Judas at all. Or a Jesus."

"I have faith that that is not so," I said.

"There are a hundred people in this building who have a deep and very real faith in Saint Judas, and the way of cross and dragon," Lukyan said. "Faith is a very good thing. Do you know that the suicide rate on Arion has decreased by almost a third since the Order of Saint Judas was founded?"

I remember rising slowly from my chair. "You are fanatical as any heretic I have ever met, Lukyan Judasson," I told him. "I pity you the loss of your faith."

Lukyan rose with me. "Pity yourself, Damien Har Veris," he said. "I have found a new faith and a new cause, and I am a happy man. You, my dear friend, are tortured and miserable."

"That is a lie!" I am afraid I screamed.

"Come with me," Lukyan said. He touched a panel on his wall, and the great painting of Judas weeping over his dragons slid up out of sight. There was a stairway leading down into the ground. "Follow me," he said.

In the cellar was a great glass vat full of pale green fluid, and in it a thing was floating, a thing very like an ancient embryo, aged and infantile at the same time, naked, with a huge head and a tiny atrophied body. Tubes ran from its arms and legs and genitals, connecting it to the machinery that kept it alive.

When Lukyan turned on the lights, it opened its eyes. They were large and dark and they looked into my soul.

"This is my colleague," Lukyan said, patting the side of the vat, "Jon Azure Cross, a Liar of the fourth circle."

"And a telepath," I said with a sick certainty. I had led pogroms against other telepaths, children mostly, on other worlds. The Church teaches that the psionic powers are one of Satan's traps. They are not mentioned in the Bible. I have never felt good about those killings.

"The moment you entered the compound, Jon read you and notified me," Lukyan said. "Only a few of us know that he is here. He helps us lie most efficiently. He knows when faith is true, and when it is feigned. I have an implant in my skull. Jon can talk to me at all times. It was he who initially recruited me into the Liars. He knew my faith was hollow. He felt the depth of my despair."

Then the thing in the tank spoke, its metallic voice coming from a speaker-grill in the base of the machine that nurtured it. *"And I feel yours, Damien Har Veris, empty priest. Inquisitor, you have asked too many ques-*

tions. You are sick at heart, and tired, and you do not believe. Join us, Damien. You have been a Liar for a long, long time!"

For a moment I hesitated, looking deep into myself, wondering what it was I *did* believe. I searched for my faith—the fire that had once sustained me, the certainty in the teachings of the Church, the presence of Christ within me. I found none of it, none. I was empty inside, burned out, full of questions and pain. But as I was about to answer Jon Azure Cross and the smiling Lukyan Judasson, I found something else, something I *did* believe in, had always believed in.

Truth.

I believed in truth, even when it hurt.

"He is lost to us," said the telepath with the mocking name of Cross.

Lukyan's smile faded. "Oh, really? I had hoped you would be one of us, Damien. You seemed ready."

I was suddenly afraid, and I considered sprinting up the stairs to Sister Judith. Lukyan had told me so very much, and now I had rejected them.

The telepath felt my fear. *"You cannot hurt us, Damien,"* it said. *"Go in peace. Lukyan has told you nothing."*

Lukyan was frowning. "I told him a good deal, Jon," he said.

"Yes. But can he trust the words of such a Liar as you?" The small misshapen mouth of the thing in the vat twitched in a smile, and its great eyes closed, and Lukyan Judasson sighed and led me up at the stairs.

IT WAS NOT until some years later that I realized it was Jon Azure Cross who was lying, and the victim of his lie was Lukyan. I *could* hurt them. I did.

It was almost simple. The Bishop had friends in government and media. With some money in the right places, I made some friends of my own. Then I exposed Cross in his cellar, charging that he had used his psionic powers to tamper with the minds of Lukyan's followers. My friends were receptive to the charges. The guardians conducted a raid, took the telepath Cross into custody, and later tried him.

He was innocent, of course. My charge was nonsense; human telepaths can read minds in close proximity, but seldom anything more. But they are rare, and much feared, and Cross was hideous enough so that it was easy to make him a victim of superstition. In the end, he was acquitted, but he left the city Ammadon and perhaps Arion itself, bound for regions unknown.

But it had never been my intention to convict him. The charge was enough. The cracks began to show in the lie that he and Lukyan had built together. Faith is hard to come by, and easy to lose. The merest doubt can begin to erode even the strongest foundation of belief.

The Bishop and I labored together to sow further doubts. It was not as easy as I might have thought. The Liars had done their work well. Ammadon, like most civilized cities, had a great pool of knowledge, a computer system that linked the schools and universities and libraries together, and made their combined wisdom available to any who needed it.

But when I checked, I soon discovered that the histories of Rome and Babylon had been subtly reshaped, and there were three listings for Judas Iscariot—one for the betrayer, one for the saint, and one for the conqueror-king of Babylon. His name was also mentioned in connection with the Hanging Gardens, and there was an entry for a so-called "Codex Judas."

And according to the Ammadon library, dragons became extinct on Old Earth around the time of Christ.

We finally purged all those lies, wiped them from the memories of the computers, though we had to cite authorities on a half-dozen non-Christian worlds before the librarians and academics would credit that the differences were anything more than a question of religious preference. By then the Order of Saint Judas had withered in the glare of exposure. Lukyan Judasson had grown gaunt and angry, and at least half of his churches had closed.

The heresy never died completely, of course. There are always those who believe no matter what. And so to this day *The Way of Cross and Dragon* is read on Arion, in the porcelain city Ammadon, amid murmuring whisper-winds.

Arla-k-Bau and the *Truth of Christ* carried me back to Vess a year after my departure, and Archbishop Torgathon finally gave me the rest I had asked for, before sending me out to fight still other heresies. So I had my victory, and the Church continued on much as before, and the Order of Saint Judas Iscariot was crushed and diminished. The telepath Jon Azure Cross had been wrong, I thought then. He had sadly underestimated the power of a Knight Inquisitor.

Later, though, I remembered his words.

You cannot hurt us, Damien.

Us?

The Order of Saint Judas? Or the Liars?

He lied, I think, deliberately, knowing I would go forth and destroy the way of cross and dragon, knowing too that I could not touch the Liars, would not even dare mention them. How could I? Who would believe it? A grand star-spanning conspiracy as old as history? It reeks of paranoia, and I had no proof at all.

The telepath lied for Lukyan's benefit, so that he would let me go. I am certain of that now. Cross risked much to snare me. Failing, he was willing to sacrifice Lukyan Judasson and his lie, pawns in some greater game.

So I left, and carried within me the knowledge that I was empty of faith but for a blind faith in truth, a truth I could no longer find in my Church.

I grew certain of that in my year of rest, which I spent reading and studying on Vess and Cathaday and Celia's World. Finally I returned to the Archbishop's receiving room, and stood again before Torgathon Nine-Klariis Tûn in my very worst pair of boots. "My Lord Commander," I said to him, "I can accept no further assignments. I ask that I be retired from active service."

"For what cause?" Torgathon rumbled, splashing feebly.

"I have lost the faith," I said to him, simply.

He regarded me for a long time, his pupilless eyes blinking. At last he said, "Your faith is a matter between you and your confessor. I care only about your results. You have done good work, Damien. You may not retire, and we will not allow you to resign."

The truth will set us free.

But freedom is cold and empty and frightening, and lies can often be warm and beautiful.

Last year the Church finally granted me a new and better ship. I named this one *Dragon*.

JOANNA RUSS

JOANNA RUSS was born in 1937 and was professor of English at the University of Washington until her retirement in the 1990s. She began her writing career with "Nor Custom Stale" in 1959, and published a series of stories in genre magazines through the 1970s, most of which were collected in *The Hidden Side of the Moon.* Her first novel, *Picnic on Paradise,* features series character Alyx, a tough time-traveling mercenary. It was followed by her ambitious second novel *And Chaos Died.* While these works were well received, Russ is best known for her third novel *The Female Man,* probably the most important feminist work to be published as science fiction.

It was followed by five further novels, including *We Who Are About To, The Two of Them,* and *Extra(Ordinary) People*; two further collections, *The Zanzibar Cat* and *The Adventures of Alyx;* and three books of nonfiction, *How to Suppress Women's Writing; Magic Mommas, Trembling Sisters, Puritans and Perverts: Feminist Essays;* and *To Write Like a Woman: Essays in Feminism and Science Fiction.* Russ has won the James Tiptree Jr., Hugo, Nebula, Locus, and Spectrum Awards for her fiction and the Pilgrim Award for her nonfiction.

The story that follows, first published in 1982, won the Hugo Award the following year. It was one of the most striking stories to be published in the '80s and has lost none of its power.

* * *

Deprived of other Banquet
I entertained Myself—

—EMILY DICKINSON

THIS IS THE TALE of the Abbess Radegunde and what happened when the Norsemen came. I tell it not as it was told to me but as I saw it, for I was a child then and the Abbess had made a pet and errand-boy of me, although the stern old Wardress, Cunigunt, who had outlived the previous Abbess, said I was more in the Abbey than out of it and a scandal. But the Abbess would only say mildly, "Dear Cunigunt, a scandal at the age of seven?" which was turning it off with a joke, for she knew how harsh and disliking my new stepmother was to me and my father did not care and I with no sisters or brothers. You must understand that joking and calling people "dear" and "my dear" was only her manner; she was in every way an unusual woman. The previous Abbess, Herrade, had found that Radegunde, who had been given to her to be fostered, had great gifts and so sent the child south to be taught, and that has never happened here before. The story has it that the Abbess Herrade found Radegunde seeming to read the great illuminated book in the Abbess's study; the child had somehow pulled it off its stand and was sitting on the floor with the volume in her lap, sucking her thumb and turning the pages with her other hand just as if she were reading.

"Little two-years," said the Abbess Herrade, who was a kind woman, "what are you doing?" She thought it amusing, I suppose, that Radegunde should pretend to read this great book, the largest and finest in the Abbey, which had many, many books, more than any other nunnery or monastery I have ever heard of: a full forty then, as I remember. And then little Radegunde was doing the book no harm.

"Reading, Mother," said the little girl.

"Oh, reading?" said the Abbess, smiling; "Then tell me what are you reading," and she pointed to the page.

"This," said Radegunde, "is a great *D* with flowers and other beautiful things about it, which is to show that *Dominus,* our Lord God, is the greatest thing and the most beautiful and makes everything to grow and be beautiful, and then it goes on to say *Domine nobis pacem,* which means *Give peace to us, O Lord.*"

Then the Abbess began to be frightened but she said only, "Who showed you this?" thinking that Radegunde had heard someone read and tell the words or had been pestering the nuns on the sly.

"No one," said the child; "Shall I go on?" and she read page after page of the Latin, in each case telling what the words meant.

There is more to the story, but I will say only that after many prayers the Abbess Herrade sent her foster-daughter far southwards, even to Poitiers, where Saint Radegunde had ruled an Abbey before, and some say even to Rome, and in these places Radegunde was taught all learning, for all the learning there is in the world remains in these places. Radegunde came back a grown woman and nursed the Abbess through her last illness and then became Abbess in her turn. They say that the great folk of the Church down there in the south wanted to keep her because she was such a prodigy of female piety and learning, there where life is safe and comfortable and less rude than it is here, but she said that the gray skies and flooding winters of her birthplace called to her very soul. She often told me the story when I was a child: how headstrong she had been and how defiant, and how she had sickened so desperately for her native land that they had sent her back, deciding that a rude life in the mud of a northern village would be a good cure for such a rebellious soul as hers.

"And so it was," she would say, patting my cheek or tweaking my ear; "See how humble I am now?" for you understand, all this about her rebellious girlhood, twenty years back, was a kind of joke between us. "Don't you do it," she would tell me and we would laugh together, I so heartily at the very idea of my being a pious monk full of learning that I would hold my sides and be unable to speak.

She was kind to everyone. She knew all the languages, not only ours, but the Irish too and the tongues folks speak to the north and south, and Latin and Greek also, and all the other languages in the world, both to read and write. She knew how to cure sickness, both the old women's way with herbs or leeches and out of books also. And never was there a more pious woman! Some speak ill of her now she's gone and say she was too merry to be a good Abbess, but she would say, "Merriment is God's flowers," and when the winter wind blew her headdress awry and showed the gray hair—which happened once; I was there and saw the shocked faces of the Sisters with her—she merely tapped the band back into place, smiling and saying, "Impudent wind! Thou showest thou hast power which is more than our silly human power, for it is from God"—and this quite satisfied the girls with her.

No one ever saw her angry. She was impatient sometimes, but in a kindly way, as if her mind were elsewhere. It was in Heaven, I used to think, for I have seen her pray for hours or sink to her knees—right in the marsh!—to see the wild duck fly south, her hands clasped and a kind of wild joy on her face, only to rise a moment later, looking at the mud on her habit and crying half-ruefully, half in laughter, "Oh, what will Sister Laundress say to me? I am hopeless! Dear child, tell no one; I will say I fell," and then she would clap her hand to her mouth, turning red and laughing even harder, saying, "I *am* hopeless, telling lies!"

The town thought her a saint, of course. We were all happy then, or so it seems to me now, and all lucky and well, with this happiness of having her amongst us burning and blooming in our midst like a great fire around which we could all warm ourselves, even those who didn't know why life seemed so good. There was less illness; the food was better; the very weather stayed mild; and people did not quarrel as they had before her time and do again now. Nor do I think, considering what happened at the end, that all this was nothing but the fancy of a boy who's found his mother, for that's what she was to me; I brought her all the gossip and ran errands when I could and she called me Boy News in Latin; I was happier than I have ever been.

And then one day those terrible beaked prows appeared in our river.

I was with her when the warning came, in the main room of the Abbey tower just after the first fire of the year had been lit in the great hearth; we thought ourselves safe, for they had never been seen so far south and it was too late in the year for any sensible shipman to be in our waters. The Abbey was host to three Irish priests, who turned pale when young Sister Sibihd burst in with the news, crying and wringing her hands; one of the brothers exclaimed a thing in Latin which means "God protect us!" for they had been telling us stories of the terrible sack of the monastery of Saint Columbanus and how everyone had run away with the precious manuscripts or had hidden in the woods, and that was how Father Cairbre and the two others had decided to go "walk the world," for this (the Abbess had been telling it all to me for I had no Latin) is what the Irish say when they leave their native land to travel elsewhere.

"God protects our souls, not our bodies," said the Abbess Radegunde briskly. She had been talking with the priests in their own language or in the Latin, but this she said in ours so even the women workers from the village would understand. Then she said, "Father Cairbre, take your friends and the younger Sisters to the underground passages; Sister Diemud, open the gates to the villagers; half of them will be trying to get behind the Abbey walls and the others will be fleeing to the marsh. You, Boy News, down to the cellars with the girls." But I did not go and she never saw it; she was up and looking out one of the window slits instantly. So was I. I had always thought the Norsemen's big ships came right up on land—on legs, I supposed—and was disappointed to see that after they came up our river they stayed in the water like other ships and the men were coming ashore by wading in the water, just as if they had been like all other folk. Then the Abbess repeated her order—"Quickly! Quickly!"—and before anyone knew what had happened she was gone from the room. I watched from the tower window; in the turmoil nobody bothered about me. Below, the Abbey grounds and gardens were packed with folk, all stepping on the herb plots and the Abbess's paestum roses, and great logs were being dragged to bar the door set in the stone walls round the Abbey, not high walls, to tell truth, and Radegunde was going quickly through the crowd, crying, Do this! Do that! Stay, thou! Go, thou! and like things.

Then she reached the door and motioned Sister Oddha, the doorkeeper, aside—the old Sister actually fell to her knees in entreaty—and all this, you must understand, was wonderfully pleasant to me. I had no more idea of danger than a puppy. There was some tumult by the door—I think the men with the logs were trying to get in her way—and Abbess Radegunde took out from the neck of her habit her silver crucifix, brought all the way from Rome, and shook it impatiently at those who would keep her in. So of course they let her through at once.

I settled into my corner of the window, waiting for the Abbess's crucifix to bring down God's lightning on those tall, fair men who defied Our Savior and the law and were supposed to wear animal horns on their heads, though these did not (and I found out later that's just a story; that is not what the Norse do). I did hope that the Abbess or Our Lord would wait just a little while before destroying them, for I wanted to get a good look at them before they all died, you understand. I was somewhat disappointed, as they seemed to be wearing breeches with leggings under them and tunics on top, like ordinary folk, and cloaks also, though some did carry swords and axes and there were round shields piled on the beach at one place. But the long hair they had was fine, and the bright colors of their clothes, and the monsters growing out of the heads of the ships were splendid and very frightening, even though one could see that they were only painted, like the pictures in the Abbess's books.

I decided that God had provided me with enough edification and could now strike down the impious strangers.

But He did not.

Instead the Abbess walked alone towards these fierce men, over the stony river bank, as calmly as if she were on a picnic with her girls. She was singing a little song, a pretty tune that I repeated many years later, and a well-traveled man said it was a Norse cradle-song. I didn't know that then, but only that the terrible, fair men, who had looked up in surprise at seeing one lone woman come out of the Abbey (which was barred behind her; I could see that), now began a sort of whispering astonishment among themselves. I saw the Abbess's gaze go quickly from one to the other—we often said that she could tell what was hidden in the soul from one look at the face—and then she picked the skirt of her habit up with one hand and daintily went among the rocks to one of the men—one older than the others, as it proved later, though I could not see so well at the time—and said to him, in his own language:

"Welcome, Thorvald Einarsson, and what do you, good farmer, so far from your own place, with the harvest ripe and the great autumn storms coming on over the sea?" (You may wonder how I knew what she said when I had no Norse; the truth is that Father Cairbre, who had not gone to the cellars after all, was looking out the top of the window while I was barely able to peep out the bottom, and he repeated everything that was said for the folk in the room, who all kept very quiet.)

Now you could see that the pirates were dumbfounded to hear her speak their own language and even more so that she called one by his name; some stepped backwards and made strange signs in the air and others unsheathed axes or swords and came running towards the Abbess. But this Thorvald Einarsson put up his hand for them to stop and laughed heartily.

"Think!" he said; "There's no magic here, only cleverness—what pair of ears could miss my name with the lot of you bawling out 'Thorvald Einarsson, help me with this oar'; 'Thorvald Einarsson, my leggings are wet to the knees'; 'Thorvald Einarsson, this stream is as cold as a Fimbulwinter!' "

The Abbess Radegunde nodded and smiled. Then she sat down plump on the river bank. She scratched behind one ear, as I had often seen her do when she was deep in thought. Then she said (and I am sure that this talk was carried on in a loud voice so that we in the Abbey could hear it):

"Good friend Thorvald, you are as clever as the tale I heard of you from your sister's son, Ranulf, from whom I learnt the Norse when I was in Rome, and to show you it was he, he always swore by his gray horse, Lamefoot, and he had a difficulty in his speech; he could not say the sounds as we do and so spoke of you always as 'Torvald.' Is not that so?"

I did not realize it then, being only a child, but the Abbess was—by this speech—claiming hospitality from the man, and had also picked by chance or inspiration the cleverest among these thieves and robbers, for his next words were:

"I am not the leader. There are no leaders here."

He was warning her that they were not his men to control, you see. So she scratched behind her ear again and got up. Then she began to wander, as if she did not know what to do, from one to the other of these uneasy folk—for some backed off and made signs at her still, and some took out their knives—singing her little tune again and walking slowly, more bent over and older and infirm-looking than we had ever seen her, one helpless little woman in black before all those fierce men. One wild young pirate snatched the headdress from her as she passed, leaving her short gray hair bare to the wind; the others laughed and he that had done it cried out:

"Grandmother, are you not ashamed?"

"Why, good friend, of what?" said she mildly.

"Thou art married to thy Christ," he said, holding the headdress covering behind his back, "but this bridegroom of thine cannot even defend thee against the shame of having thy head uncovered! Now if thou wert married to me—"

There was much laughter. The Abbess Radegunde waited until it was over. Then she scratched her bare head and made as if to turn away, but suddenly she turned back upon him with the age and infirmity dropping from her as if they had been a cloak, seeming taller and very grand, as if lit from within by some great fire. She looked directly into his face. This thing she did was something we had all seen, of course, but they had not, nor had they heard that great, grand voice with which she sometimes read the Scriptures to us or talked with us of the wrath of God. I think the young man was frightened, for all his daring. And I know now what I did not then: that the Norse admire courage above all things and that—to be blunt—everyone likes a good story, especially if it happens right in front of your eyes.

"Grandson!"—and her voice tolled like the great bell of God; I think folk must have heard her all the way to the marsh!—"Little grandchild, thinkest thou that the Creator of the World who made the stars and the moon and the sun and our bodies, too, and the change of the seasons and the very earth we stand on—yea, even unto the shit in thy belly!—thinkest thou that such a being has a big house in the sky where he keeps his wives and goes in to fuck them as thou wouldst thyself or like the King of Turkey? Do not dishonor the wit of the mother who bore thee! We are the servants of God, not his wives, and if we tell our silly girls they are married to the Christ it is to make them understand that they must not run off and marry Otto Farmer or Ekkehard Blacksmith, but stick to their work, as they promised. If I told them they were married to an Idea they would not understand me, and neither dost thou."

(Here Father Cairbre, above me in the window, muttered in a protesting way about something.)

Then the Abbess snatched the silver cross from around her neck and put it into the boy's hand, saying: "Give this to thy mother with my pity. She must pull out her hair over such a child."

But he let it fall to the ground. He was red in the face and breathing hard.

"Take it up," she said more kindly, "take it up, boy, it will not hurt thee and there's no magic in it. It's only pure silver and good workmanship; it will make thee rich." When she saw that he would not—his hand went to his knife—she *tched* to herself in a motherly way (or I believe she did, for she waved one hand back and forth as she always did when she made that sound) and got down on her knees—with more difficulty than was truth, I think—saying loudly, "I will stoop, then; I will stoop," and got up, holding it out to him, saying, "Take. Two sticks tied with a cord would serve me as well."

The boy cried, his voice breaking, "My mother is dead and thou art a witch!" and in an instant he had one arm around the Abbess's neck and with the other his knife at her throat. The man Thorvald Einarsson roared "Thorfinn!" but the Abbess only said clearly, "Let him be. I have shamed this man but did not mean to. He is right to be angry."

The boy released her and turned his back. I remember wondering if these strangers could weep. Later I heard—and I swear that the Abbess must have somehow known this or felt it, for although she was no witch, she could probe at a man until she found the sore places in him and that very quickly—that this boy's mother had been known for an adulteress and that no man would own him as a son. It is one thing among those people for a man to have what the Abbess called a concubine and they do not hold the children of such in scorn as we do, but it is a different thing when a married woman has more than one man. Such was Thorfinn's case; I suppose that was what had sent him *viking*. But all this came later; what I saw then—with my nose barely above the window-slit—was that the Abbess slipped her crucifix over the hilt of the boy's sword—she really wished him to have it, you see—and then walked to a place near the walls of the Abbey but far from the Norsemen. I think she meant them to come to her. I saw her pick up her skirts like a peasant woman, sit down with legs crossed, and say in a loud voice:

"Come! Who will bargain with me?"

A few strolled over, laughing, and sat down with her.

"All!" she said, gesturing them closer.

"And why should we all come?" said one who was farthest away.

"Because you will miss a bargain," said the Abbess.

"Why should we bargain when we can take?" said another.

"Because you will only get half," said the Abbess. "The rest you will not find."

"We will ransack the Abbey," said a third.

"Half the treasure is not in the Abbey," said she.

"And where is it then?" said yet another.

She tapped her forehead. They were drifting over by twos and threes. I have heard since that the Norse love riddles and this was a sort of riddle; she was giving them good fun.

"If it is in your head," said the man Thorvald, who was standing behind the others, arms crossed, "we can get it out, can we not?" And he tapped the hilt of his knife.

"If you frighten me, I shall become confused and remember nothing," said the Abbess calmly. "Besides, do you wish to play that old game? You saw how well it worked the last time. I am surprised at you, Ranulf's mother's-brother."

"I will bargain then," said the man Thorvald, smiling.

"And the rest of you?" said Radegunde. "It must be all or none; decide for yourselves whether you wish to save yourselves trouble and danger and be rich," and she deliberately turned her back on them. The men moved down to the river's edge and began to talk among themselves, dropping their voices so that we could not hear them any more. Father Cairbre, who was old and short-sighted, cried, "I cannot hear them. What are they doing?" and I cleverly said, "I have good eyes, Father Cairbre," and he held me up to see, so it was just at the time that the Abbess Radegunde was facing the Abbey tower that I appeared in the window. She clapped one hand across her mouth. Then she walked to the gate and called (in a voice I had learned not to disregard; it had often got me a smacked bottom), "Boy·News, down! Come down to me here *at once*! And bring Father Cairbre with you."

I was overjoyed. I had no idea that she might want to protect me if anything went wrong. My only thought was that I was going to see it all from wonderfully close by, so I wormed my way, half-suffocated, through the folk in the tower room, stepping on feet and skirts, and having to say every few seconds, "But I *have* to! The Abbess wants me," and meanwhile she was calling outside like an Empress, "Let that boy through! Make a place for that boy! Let the Irish priest through!" until I crept and pushed and complained my way to the very wall itself—no one was going to open the gate for us, of course—and there was a great fuss and finally someone brought a ladder. I was over at once, but the old priest took a longer time, although it was a low wall, as I've said, the builders having been somewhat of two minds about making the Abbey into a true fortress.

Once outside it was lovely, away from all that crowd, and I ran, gloriously pleased, to the Abbess, who said only, "Stay by me, whatever happens," and immediately turned her attention away from me. It had taken so long to get Father Cairbre outside the walls that the tall foreign men had finished their talking and were coming back—all twenty or thirty of them—towards the Abbey and the Abbess Radegunde, and most especially of all, me. I could see Father Cairbre tremble. They did look grim, close by, with their long, wild hair and the brightness of their strange clothes. I remember that they smelled different from us, but cannot remember how after all these years. Then the Abbess spoke to them in that outlandish language of theirs, so strangely light and lilting to hear from their bearded lips, and then she said something in Latin to Father Cairbre, and he said to us, with a shake in his voice:

"This is the priest, Father Cairbre, who will say our bargains aloud in our own tongue so that my people may hear. I cannot deal behind their backs. And this is my foster-baby, who is very dear to me and who is now having his curiosity rather too much satisfied, I think." (I was trying to stand tall like a man but had one hand secretly holding on to her skirt; so that was what the foreign men had chuckled at!) The talk went on, but I will tell it as if I had understood the Norse, for to repeat everything twice would be tedious.

The Abbess Radegunde said, "Will you bargain?"

There was a general nodding of heads, with a look of: After all, why not?

"And who will speak for you?" said she.

A man stepped forward; I recognized Thorvald Einarsson.

"Ah yes," said the Abbess dryly. "The company that has no leaders. Is this leaderless company agreed? Will it abide by its word? I want no treachery-planners, no Breakwords here!"

There was a great mutter at this. The Thorvald man (he *was* big, close up!) said mildly, "I sail with none such. Let's begin."

We all sat down.

"Now," said Thorvald Einarsson, raising his eyebrows, "according to my knowledge of this thing, you begin. And according to my knowledge you will begin by saying that you are very poor."

"But no," said the Abbess, "we are rich." Father Cairbre groaned. A groan answered him from behind the Abbey walls. Only the Abbess and Thorvald Einarsson seemed unmoved; it was as if these two were joking in some way that no one else understood. The Abbess went on, saying, "We are very rich. Within is much silver, much gold, many pearls, and much embroidered cloth, much line-woven cloth, much carved and painted wood, and many books with gold upon their pages and jewels set into their covers. All this is yours. But we have more and better: herbs and medicines, ways to keep food from spoiling, the knowledge of how to cure the sick; all this is yours. And we have more and better even than this; we have the knowledge of Christ and the perfect understanding of the soul, which is yours, too, any time you wish; you have only to accept it."

Thorvald Einarsson held up his hand. "We will stop with the first," he said, "and perhaps a little of the second. That is more practical."

"And foolish," said the Abbess politely, "in the usual way." And again I had the odd feeling that these two were sharing a joke no one else even saw. She added, "There is one thing you may not have, and that is the most precious of all."

Thorvald Einarsson looked inquiring.

"*My people.* Their safety is dearer to me than myself. They are not to be touched, not a hair on their heads, not for any reason. Think: you can fight your way into the Abbey easily enough, but the folk in there are very frightened of you and some of the men are armed. Even a good fighter is cumbered in a crowd. You will slip and fall upon each other without meaning to or knowing that you do so. Heed my counsel. Why play butcher when you can have treasure poured into your laps like kings, without work? And after that there will be as much again, when I lead you to the hidden place. An earl's mountain of treasure. Think of it! And to give all this up for slaves, half of whom will get sick and die before you get them home—and will need to be fed if they are to be any good. Shame on you for bad advice-takers! Imagine what you will say to your wives and families: Here are a few miserable bolts of cloth with blood spots that won't come out, here are some pearls and jewels smashed to powder in the fighting, here is a torn piece of embroidery which was whole until someone stepped on it in the battle, and I had slaves but they died of illness and I fucked a pretty young nun and meant to bring her back, but she leapt into the sea. And oh yes, there was twice as much again and all of it whole but we decided not to take that. Too much trouble, you see."

This was a lively story and the Norsemen enjoyed it. Radegunde held up her hand.

"People!" she called in German, adding, "Sea-rovers, hear what I say; I will repeat it for you in your tongue," (and so she did): *"People, if the Norsemen fight us, do not defend yourselves but smash everything! Wives, take your cooking knives and shred the valuable cloth to pieces! Men, with your axes and hammers hew the altars and the carved wood to fragments! All, grind the pearls and smash the jewels against the stone floors! Break the bottles of wine! Pound the gold and silver to shapelessness! Tear to pieces the illuminated books! Tear down the hangings and burn them!*

"But" (she added, her voice suddenly mild) "if these wise men will accept our gifts, let us heap untouched and spotless at their feet all that we have and hold nothing back, so that their kinsfolk will marvel and wonder at the shining and glistering of the wealth they bring back, though it leave us nothing but our bare stone walls."

If anyone had ever doubted that the Abbess Radegunde was inspired by God, their doubts must have vanished away, for who could resist the fiery vigor of her first speech or the beneficent unction of her second? The Norsemen sat there with their mouths open. I saw tears on Father Cairbre's cheeks. Then Thorvald Einarsson said, "Abbess—"

He stopped. He tried again but again stopped. Then he shook himself, as a man who has been under a spell, and said:

"Abbess, my men have been without women for a long time."

Radegunde looked surprised. She looked as if she could not believe what she had heard. She looked the pirate up and down, as if puzzled, and then walked around him as if taking his measure. She did this several times, looking at every part of his big body as if she were summing him up while he got redder and redder. Then she backed off and surveyed him again, and with her arms akimbo like a peasant, announced very loudly in both Norse and German:

"What! Have they lost the use of their hands?"

It was irresistible, in its way. The Norse laughed. Our people laughed. Even Thorvald laughed. I did too, though I was not sure what everyone was laughing about. The laughter would die down and then begin again behind the Abbey walls, helplessly, and again die down and again begin. The Abbess waited until the Norsemen had stopped laughing and then called for silence in German until there were only a few snickers here and there. She then said:

"These good men—Father Cairbre, tell the people—these good men will forgive my silly joke. I meant no scandal, truly, and no harm, but laughter is good; it settles the body's waters, as the physicians say. And my people know that I am not always as solemn and good as I ought to be. Indeed I am a very great sinner and scandal-maker. Thorvald Einarsson, do we do business?"

The big man—who had not been so pleased as the others, I can tell you!—looked at his men and seemed to see what he needed to know. He said: "I go in with five men to see what you have. Then we let the poor folk on the grounds go, but not those inside the Abbey. Then we search again. The gate will be locked and guarded by the rest of us; if there's any treachery, the bargain's off."

"Then I will go with you," said Radegunde. "That is very just and my presence will calm the people. To see us together will assure them that no harm is meant. You are a good man, Torvald—forgive me; I call you as your nephew did so often. Come, Boy News, hold on to me.

"Open the gate!" she called then; "All is safe!" and with the five men (one of whom was that young Thorfinn who had hated her so) we waited while the great logs were pulled back. There was little space within, but the people shrank back at the sight of those fierce warriors and opened a place for us.

I looked back and the Norsemen had come in and were standing just inside the walls, on either side the gate, with their swords out and their shields up. The crowd parted for us more slowly as we reached the main tower, with the Abbess repeating constantly, "Be calm, people, be calm. All is well," and deftly speaking by name to this one or that. It was much harder when the people gasped upon hearing the big logs pushed shut with a noise like thunder, and it was very close on the stairs; I heard her say something like an apology in the queer foreign tongue, something that probably meant, "I'm sorry that we must wait." It seemed an age until the stairs were even partly clear and I saw what the Abbess had meant by the cumbering of a crowd; a man might swing a weapon in the press of people but not very far and it was more likely he would simply fall over someone and crack his head. We gained the great room with the big crucifix of painted wood and the little one of pearls and gold, and the scarlet hangings worked in gold thread that I had played robbers behind so often before I learned what real robbers were: these tall, frightening men whose eyes glistened with greed at what I had fancied every village had. Most of the Sisters had stayed in the great room, but somehow it was not so crowded, as the folk had huddled back against the walls when the Norsemen came in. The youngest girls were all in a corner, terrified—one could smell it, as one can in people—and when that young Thorfinn went for the little gold-and-pearl cross, Sister Sibihd cried in a high, cracked voice, "It is the body of our Christ!" and leapt up, snatching it from the wall before he could get to it.

"Sibihd!" exclaimed the Abbess, in as sharp a voice as I had ever heard her use; "Put that back or you will feel the weight of my hand, I tell you!"

Now it is odd, is it not, that a young woman desperate enough not to care about death at the hands of a Norse pirate should nonetheless be frightened away at the threat of getting a few slaps from her Abbess? But folk are like that. Sister Sibihd returned the cross to its place (from whence young Thorfinn took it) and fell back among the nuns, sobbing, "He desecrates Our Lord God!"

"Foolish girl!" snapped the Abbess. "God only can consecrate or desecrate; man cannot. That is a piece of metal."

Thorvald said something sharp to Thorfinn, who slowly put the cross back on its hook with a sulky look which said, plainer than words: Nobody gives me what I want. Nothing else went wrong in the big room or the Abbess's study or the storerooms, or out in the kitchens. The Norsemen were silent and kept their hands on their swords but the Abbess kept talking in a calm way in both tongues; to our folk she said, "See? It is all right but everyone must keep still. God will protect us." Her face was steady and clear and I believed her a saint, for she had saved Sister Sibihd and the rest of us.

But this peacefulness did not last, of course. Something had to go wrong in all that press of people; to this day I do not know what. We were in a corner of the long refectory, which is the place where the Sisters or Brothers eat in an Abbey, when something pushed me into the wall and I fell, almost suffocated by the Abbess's lying on top of me. My head was ringing and on all sides there was a terrible roaring sound with curses and screams, a dreadful tumult as if the walls had come apart and were falling on everyone. I could hear the Abbess whispering something in Latin over and over in my ear. There were dull, ripe sounds, worse than the rest, which I know now to have been the noise steel makes when it is thrust into bodies. This all seemed to go on forever and then it seemed to me that the floor was wet. Then all became quiet. I felt the Abbess Radegunde get off me. She said:

"So this is how you wash your floors up north." When I lifted my head from the wet rushes and saw what she meant, I was very sick into the corner. Then she picked me up in her arms and held my face against her bosom so that I would not see but it was no use; I had already seen: all the people lying about sprawled on the floor with their bellies coming out, like heaps of dead fish, old Walafrid with an axe-handle standing out of his chest—he was sitting up with his eyes shut in a press of bodies that gave him no room to lie down—and the young beekeeper, Uta, from the village, who had been so merry, lying on her back with her long braids and her gown all dabbled in red dye and a great stain of it on her belly. She was breathing fast and her eyes were wide open. As we passed her, the noise of her breathing ceased.

The Abbess said mildly, "Thy people are thorough housekeepers, Earl Split-gut."

Thorvald Einarsson roared something at us and the Abbess replied softly, "Forgive me, good friend. You protected me and the boy and I am grateful. But nothing betrays a man's knowledge of the German like a word that bites, is it not so? And I had to be sure."

It came to me then that she had called him "Torvald" and reminded him of his sister's son so that he would feel he must protect us if anything went wrong. But now she would make him angry, I thought, and I shut my eyes tight. Instead he laughed and said in odd, light German, "I did no housekeeping but to stand over you and your pet. Are you not grateful?"

"Oh very, thank you," said the Abbess with such warmth as she might show to a Sister who had brought her a rose from the garden, or another who copied her work well, or when I told her news, or if Ita the cook made a good soup. But he did not know that the warmth was for everyone and so seemed satisfied. By now we were in the garden and the air was less foul; she put me down, although my limbs were shaking, and I clung to her gown, crumpled, stiff, and blood-reeking though it was. She said, "Oh, my God, what a deal of washing hast Thou given us!" She started to walk towards the gate and Thorvald Einarsson took a step towards her. She said, without turning round: "Do not insist, Thorvald, there is no reason to lock me up. I am forty years old and not likely to be running away into the swamp, what with my rheumatism and the pain in my knees and the folk needing me as they do."

There was a moment's silence. I could see something odd come into the big man's face. He said quietly:

"I did not speak, Abbess."

She turned, surprised. "But you did. I heard you."

He said strangely, "I did not."

Children can guess sometimes what is wrong and what to do about it without knowing how; I remember saying, very quickly, "Oh, she does that sometimes. My stepmother says old age has addled her wits," and then, "Abbess, may I go to my stepmother and my father?"

"Yes, of course," she said, "run along, Boy News—" and then stopped, looking into the air as if seeing in it something we could not. Then she said very gently, "No, my dear, you had better stay here with me," and I knew, as surely as if I had seen it with my own eyes, that I was not to go to my stepmother or my father because both were dead.

She did things like that, too, sometimes.

FOR A WHILE it seemed that everyone was dead. I did not feel grieved or frightened in the least, but I think I must have been, for I had only one idea in my head: that if I let the Abbess out of my sight, I would die. So I followed her everywhere. She was let to move about and comfort people, especially the mad Sibihd, who would do nothing but rock and wail, but towards nightfall, when the Abbey had been stripped of its treasures, Thorvald Einarsson put her and me in her study, now bare of its grand furniture, on a straw pallet on the floor, and bolted the door on the outside. She said:

"Boy News, would you like to go to Constantinople, where the Emperor is and the domes of gold and all the splendid pagans? For that is where this man will take me to sell me."

"Oh yes!" said I, and then, "But will he take me, too?"

"Of course," said the Abbess, and so it was settled. Then in came Thorvald Einarsson, saying:

"Thorfinn is asking for you." I found out later that they were waiting for him to die: none other of the Norse had been wounded but a farmer had crushed Thorfinn's chest with an axe and he was expected to die before morning. The Abbess said:

"Is that a good reason to go?" She added, "I mean that he hates me; will not his anger at my presence make him worse?"

Thorvald said slowly, "The folk here say you can sit by the sick and heal them. Can you do that?"

"To my knowledge, not at all," said the Abbess Radegunde, "but if they believe so, perhaps that calms them and makes them better. Christians are quite as foolish as other people, you know. I will come if you want," and though I saw that she was pale with tiredness, she got to her feet. I should say that she was in a plain brown gown taken from one of the peasant women because her own was being washed clean, but to me she had the same majesty as always. And for him too, I think.

Thorvald said, "Will you pray for him or damn him?"

She said, "I do not pray, Thorvald, and I never damn anybody; I merely sit." She added, "Oh let him; he'll scream your ears off if you don't," and this meant me for I was ready to yell for my life if they tried to keep me from her.

They had put Thorfinn in the chapel, a little stone room with nothing left in it now but a plain wooden cross, not worth carrying off. He was lying, his eyes closed, on the stone altar with furs under him, and his face was gray. Every time he breathed there was a bubbling sound, a little, thin, reedy sound, and as I crept closer I saw why, for in the young man's chest was a great red hole with pink things sticking out of it, all crushed, and in the hole one could see something jump and fall, jump and fall, over and over again. It was his heart beating. Blood kept coming from his lips in a froth. I do not know, of course, what either said, for they spoke in the Norse, but I saw what they did and heard much of it talked of between the Abbess and Thorvald Einarsson later, so I will tell it as if I knew.

The first thing the Abbess did was to stop suddenly on the threshold and raise both hands to her mouth as if in horror. Then she cried furiously to the two guards:

"Do you wish to kill your comrade with the cold and damp? Is this how you treat one another? Get fire in here and some woollen cloth to put over him! No, not more skins, you idiots, *wool* to mold to his body and take up the wet. Run now!"

One said sullenly, "We don't take orders from you, grandma."

"Oh no?" said she. "Then I shall strip this wool dress from my old body and put it over that boy and then sit here all night in my flabby naked skin!

What will this child's soul say to God when it departs this flesh? That his friends would not give up a little of their booty so that he might fight for life? Is this your fellowship? Do it, or I will strip myself and shame you both for the rest of your lives!"

"Well, take it from his share," said the one in a low voice, and the other ran out. Soon there was a fire on the hearth and russet-colored woollen cloth—"From my own share," said one of them loudly, though it was a color the least costly, not like blue or red—and the Abbess laid it loosely over the boy, carefully putting it close to his sides but not moving him. He did not look to be in any pain, but his color got no better. But then he opened his eyes and said in such a little voice as a ghost might have, a whisper as thin and reedy and bubbling as his breath:

"You . . . old witch. But I beat you . . . in the end."

"Did you, my dear?" said the Abbess. "How?"

"Treasure," he said, "for my kinfolk. And I lived as a man at last. Fought . . . and had a woman . . . the one here with the big breasts, Sibihd. . . . Whether she liked it or not. That was good."

"Yes, Sibihd," said the Abbess mildly. "Sibihd has gone mad. She hears no one and speaks to no one. She only sits and rocks and moans and soils herself and will not feed herself, although if one puts food in her mouth with a spoon, she will swallow."

The boy tried to frown. "Stupid," he said at last. "Stupid nuns. The beasts do it."

"Do they?" said the Abbess, as if this were a new idea to her. "Now that is very odd. For never yet heard I of a gander that blacked the goose's eye or hit her over the head with a stone or stuck a knife in her entrails when he was through. When God puts it into their hearts to desire one another, she squats and he comes running. And a bitch in heat will jump through the window if you lock the door. Poor fools! Why didn't you camp three hours' downriver and wait? In a week half the young married women in the village would have been slipping away at night to see what the foreigners were like. Yes, and some un-married ones, and some of my own girls, too. But you couldn't wait, could you?"

"No," said the boy, with the ghost of a brag. "Better . . . this way."

"This way," said she. "Oh yes, my dear, old granny knows about *this* way! Pleasure for the count of three or four and the rest of it as much joy as rolling a stone uphill."

He smiled a ghostly smile. "You're a whore, grandma."

She began to stroke his forehead. "No, grandbaby," she said, "but all Latin is not the Church Fathers, you know, great as they are. One can find a great deal in those strange books written by the ones who died centuries before Our Lord was born. Listen," and she leaned closer to him and said quietly:

"Syrian dancing girl, how subtly you sway
  those sensuous limbs,
Half-drunk in the smoky tavern, lascivious
  and wanton,
Your long hair bound back in the Greek way,
  clashing the castanets in your hands—"

The boy was too weak to do anything but look astonished. Then she said this:

"I love you so that anyone permitted to sit near you and talk to you seems to me like a god; when I am near you my spirit is broken, my heart shakes, my voice dies, and I can't even speak. Under my skin I flame up all over and I can't see; there's thunder in my ears and I break out in a sweat, as if from fever; I turn paler than cut grass and feel that I am utterly changed; I feel that Death has come near me."

He said, as if frightened, "Nobody feels like that."

"They do," she said.

He said, in feeble alarm, "You're trying to kill me!"

She said, "No, my dear. I simply don't want you to die a virgin."

It was odd, his saying those things and yet holding on to her hand where he had got at it through the woollen cloth; she stroked his head and he whispered, "Save me, old witch."

"I'll do my best," she said. "You shall do your best by not talking and I by not tormenting you any more, and we'll both try to sleep."

"Pray," said the boy.

"Very well," said she, "but I'll need a chair," and the guards—seeing, I suppose, that he was holding her hand—brought in one of the great wooden chairs from the Abbey, which were too plain and heavy to carry off, I think. Then the Abbess Radegunde sat in the chair and closed her eyes. Thorfinn seemed to fall asleep. I crept nearer her on the floor and must have fallen asleep myself almost at once, for the next thing I knew a gray light filled the chapel, the fire had gone out, and someone was shaking Radegunde, who still slept in her chair, her head leaning to one side. It was Thorvald

Einarsson and he was shouting with excitement in his strange German, "Woman, how did you do it! How did you do it!"

"Do what?" said the Abbess thickly. "Is he dead?"

"Dead?" exclaimed the Norseman. "He is healed! Healed! The lung is whole and all is closed up about the heart and the shattered pieces of the ribs are grown together! Even the muscles of the chest are beginning to heal!"

"That's good," said the Abbess, still half asleep. "Let me be."

Thorvald shook her again. She said again, "Oh, let me sleep." This time he hauled her to her feet and she shrieked, "My back, my back! Oh, the saints, my rheumatism!" and at the same time a sick voice from under the woollens—a sick voice but a man's voice, not a ghost's—said something in Norse.

"Yes, I hear you," said the Abbess; "you must become a follower of the White Christ right away, this very minute. But *Dominus noster,* please do You put it into these brawny heads that I must have a tub of hot water with pennyroyal in it? I am too old to sleep all night in a chair and I am one ache from head to foot."

Thorfinn got louder.

"Tell him," said the Abbess Radegunde to Thorvald in German, "that I will not baptize him and I will not shrive him until he is a different man. All that child wants is someone more powerful than your Odin god or your Thor god to pull him out of the next scrape he gets into. Ask him: Will he adopt Sibihd as his sister? Will he clean her when she soils herself and feed her and sit with his arm about her, talking to her gently and lovingly until she is well again? The Christ does not wipe out our sins only to have us commit them all over again and that is what he wants and what you all want, a God that gives and gives and gives, but God does not give; He takes and takes and takes. He takes away everything that is not God until there is nothing left but God, and none of you will understand that! There is no remission of sins; there is only change and Thorfinn must change before God will have him."

"Abbess, you are eloquent," said Thorvald, smiling, "but why do you not tell him all this yourself?"

"Because I ache so!" said Radegunde, "Oh, do get me into some hot water!" and Thorvald half led and half supported her as she hobbled out. That morning, after she had had her soak—when I cried, they let me stay just outside the door—she undertook to cure Sibihd, first by rocking her in her arms and talking to her, telling her she was safe now, and promising that the Northmen would go soon, and then when Sihihd became quieter, leading

her out into the woods with Thorvald as a bodyguard to see that we did not
run away, and little dark Sister Hedwic, who had stayed with Sibihd and
cared for her. The Abbess would walk for a while in the mild autumn sunshine and then she would direct Sihihd's face upwards by touching her gen
tly under the chin and say, "See? There is God's sky still," and then, "Look,
there are God's trees; they have not changed," and telling her that the world
was just the same and God still kindly to folk, only a few more souls had
joined the Blessed and were happier waiting for us in Heaven than we could
ever be, or even imagine being, on the poor earth. Sister Hedwic kept hold
of Sibihd's hand. No one paid more attention to me than if I had been a dog,
but every time poor Sister Sibihd saw Thorvald she would shrink away and
you could see that Hedwic could not bear to look at him at all; every time he
came in her sight she turned her face aside, shut her eyes hard, and bit her
lower lip. It was a quiet, almost warm day, as autumn can be sometimes, and
the Abbess found a few little blue late flowers growing in a sheltered place
against a log and put them into Sibihd's hand, speaking of how beautifully
and cunningly God had made all things. Sister Sibihd had enough wit to
hold on to the flowers, but her eyes stared and she would have stumbled and
fallen if Hedwic had not led her.

Sister Hedwic said timidly, "Perhaps she suffers because she has been de-
filed, Abbess," and then looked ashamed. For a moment the Abbess looked
shrewdly at young Sister Hedwic and then at the mad Sibihd. Then she said:

"Dear daughter Sibihd and dear daughter Hedwic, I am now going to tell
you something about myself that I have never told to a single living soul but
my confessor. Do you know that as a young woman I studied at Avignon and
from there was sent to Rome, so that I might gather much learning? Well, in
Avignon I read mightily our Christian Fathers but also in the pagan poets,
for as it has been said by Ermenrich of Ellwangen: 'As dung spread upon a
field enriches it to good harvest, thus one cannot produce divine eloquence
without the filthy writings of the pagan poets.' This is true but perilous; only
I thought not so, for I was very proud and fancied that if the pagan poems
of love left me unmoved that was because I had the gift of chastity right from
God Himself and I scorned sensual pleasures and those tempted by them. I
had forgotten, you see, that chastity is not given once and for all like a wedding ring that is put on never to be taken off, but is a garden which each day
must be weeded, watered, and trimmed anew, or soon there will be only
brambles and wilderness.

"As I have said, the words of the poets did not tempt me, for words are only marks on the page with no life save what we give them. But in Rome there were not only the old books, daughters, but something much worse.

"There were statues. Now you must understand that these are not such as you can imagine from our books, like Saint John or the Virgin; the ancients wrought so cunningly in stone that it is like magic; one stands before the marble holding one's breath, waiting for it to move and speak. They are not statues at all but beautiful naked men and women. It is a city of sea-gods pouring water, daughter Sibihd and daughter Hedwic, of athletes about to throw the discus, and runners and wrestlers and young emperors, and the favorites of kings, but they do not walk the streets like real men, for they are all of stone.

"There was one Apollo, all naked, which I knew I should not look on but which I always made some excuse to my companions to pass by, and this statue, although three miles distant from my dwelling, drew me as if by magic. Oh, he was fair to look on! Fairer than any youth alive now in Germany, or in the world, I think. And then all the old loves of the pagan poets came back to me: Dido and Aeneas, the taking of Venus and Mars, the love of the moon, Diana, for the shepherd boy—and I thought that if my statue could only come to life, he would utter honeyed love-words from the old poets and would be wise and brave, too, and what woman could resist him?"

Here she stopped and looked at Sister Sibihd but Sibihd only stared on, holding the little blue flowers. It was Sister Hedwic who cried, one hand pressed to her heart:

"Did you pray, Abbess?"

"I did," said Radegunde solemnly, "and yet my prayers kept becoming something else. I would pray to be delivered from the temptation that was in the statue and then, of course, I would have to think of the statue itself, and then I would tell myself that I must run, like the nymph Daphne, to be armored and sheltered within a laurel tree, but my feet seemed to be already rooted to the ground, and then at the last minute I would flee and be back at my prayers again. But it grew harder each time and at last the day came when I did not flee."

"Abbess, *you*?" cried Hedwic with a gasp. Thorvald, keeping his watch a little way from us, looked surprised. I was very pleased—I loved to see the Abbess astonish people; it was one of her gifts—and at seven I had no knowledge of lust except that my little thing felt good sometimes when I handled it to make water, and what had that to do with statues coming to life or women turning into laurel trees? I was more interested in mad Sibihd, the way children are; I did not know what she might do, or if I should be afraid of her, or if I should go mad myself, what it would be like. But the Abbess was laughing gently at Hedwic's amazement.

"Why not me?" said the Abbess. "I was young and healthy and had no special grace from God any more than the hens or the cows do! Indeed I burned so with desire for that handsome young hero—for so I had made him in my mind, as a woman might do with a man she has seen a few times on the street—that thoughts of him tormented me waking and sleeping. It seemed to me that because of my vows I could not give myself to this Apollo of my own free will, so I would dream that he took me against my will, and oh, what an exquisite pleasure that was!"

Here Hedwic's blood came all to her face and she covered it with her hands. I could see Thorvald grinning, back where he watched us.

"And then," said the Abbess, as if she had not seen either of them, "a terrible fear came to my heart that God might punish me by sending a ravisher who would use me unlawfully, as I had dreamed my Apollo did, and that I would not even wish to resist him, and would feel the pleasures of a base lust, and would know myself a whore and a false nun forever after. This fear both tormented and drew me. I began to steal looks at young men in the streets, not letting the other Sisters see me do it, thinking: Will it be he? Or he? Or he?

"And then it happened. I had lingered behind the others at a melon-seller's, thinking of no Apollos or handsome heroes but only of the convent's dinner, when I saw my companions disappearing round a corner. I hastened to catch up with them—and made a wrong turning—and was suddenly lost in a narrow street—and at that very moment a young fellow took hold of my habit and threw me to the ground! You may wonder why he should do such a mad thing, but as I found out afterwards, there are prostitutes in Rome who affect our way of dress to please the appetites of certain men who are depraved enough to—Well, really, I do not know how to say it! Seeing me alone, he had thought I was one of them and would be glad of a customer and a bit of play. So there was a reason for it.

"Well, there I was on my back with this young fellow, sent as a vengeance by God, as I thought, trying to do exactly what I had dreamed, night after night, my statue should do. And do you know, it was nothing in the least like my dream! The stones at my back hurt me, for one thing. And instead of melting with delight, I was screaming my head off in terror and kicking at him as he tried to pull up my skirts, and praying to God that this insane man might not break any of my bones in his rage!

"My screams brought a crowd of people and he went running, so I got off with nothing worse than a bruised back and a sprained knee. But the strangest thing of all was that, while I was cured forever of lusting after my Apollo, instead I began to be tormented by a new fear—that I had lusted after *him,* that foolish young man with the foul breath and the one tooth missing!—and I felt strange creepings and crawlings over my body that were half like desire and half like fear and half like disgust and shame with all sorts of other things mixed in—I know that is too many halves, but it is how I felt—and nothing at all like the burning desire I had felt for my Apollo. I went to see the statue once more before I left Rome and it seemed to look at me sadly, as if to say: Don't blame me, poor girl; I'm only a piece of stone. And that was the last time I was so proud as to believe that God had singled me out for a special gift, like chastity—or a special sin, either—or that being thrown down on the ground and hurt had anything to do with any sin of mine, no matter how I mixed the two together in my mind. I dare say you did not find it a great pleasure yesterday, did you?"

Hedwic shook her head. She was crying quietly. She said, "Thank you, Abbess," and the Abbess embraced her. They both seemed happier, but then all of a sudden Sibihd muttered something, so low that one could not hear her.

"The—" she whispered and then she brought it out but still in a whisper: "The blood."

"What, dear, your blood?" said Radegunde.

"No mother," said Sibihd, beginning to tremble, "the blood. All over us. Walafrid and—and Uta—and Sister Hildegarde—and everyone broken and spilled out like a dish! And none of us had done anything but I could smell it all over me and the children screaming because they were being trampled down, and those demons come up from Hell though we had done nothing and—and—I understand, mother, about the rest, but I will never, ever forget it, oh Christ, it is all around me now, oh mother, the *blood*!"

Then Sister Sibihd dropped to her knees on the fallen leaves and began to scream, not covering her face as Sister Hedwic had done, but staring ahead with her wide eyes as if she were blind or could see something we could not. The Abbess knelt down and embraced her, rocking her back and forth, saying, "Yes, yes, dear, but we are here; we are here now; that is gone now," but Sibihd continued to scream, covering her ears as if the scream were someone else's and she could hide herself from it.

Thorvald said, looking, I thought, a little uncomfortable, "Cannot your Christ cure this?"

"No," said the Abbess. "Only by undoing the past. And that is the one thing He never does, it seems. She is in Hell now and must go back there many times before she can forget."

"She would make a bad slave," said the Norseman, with a glance at Sister Sibihd, who had fallen silent and was staring ahead of her again; "You need not fear that anyone will want her."

"God," said the Abbess Radegunde calmly, "is merciful."

Thorvald Einarsson said, "Abbess, I am not a bad man."

"For a good man," said the Abbess Radegunde, "you keep surprisingly bad company."

He said angrily, "I did not choose my shipmates. I have had bad luck!"

"Ours has," said the Abbess, "been worse, I think."

"Luck is luck," said Thorvald, clenching his fists. "It comes to some folk and not to others."

"As you came to us," said the Abbess mildly. "Yes, yes, I see, Thorvald Einarsson; one may say that luck is Thor's doing or Odin's doing, but you must know that our bad luck is your own doing and not some god's. You are our bad luck, Thorvald Einarsson. It's true that you're not as wicked as your friends, for they kill for pleasure and you do it without feeling, as a business, the way one hews down grain. Perhaps you have seen today some of the grain you have cut. If you had a man's soul, you would not have gone *viking*, luck or no luck, and if your soul were bigger still, you would have tried to stop your shipmates, just as I talk honestly to you now, despite your anger, and just as Christ Himself told the truth and was nailed on the cross. If you were a beast, you could not break God's law and if you were a man you would not, but you are neither and that makes you a kind of monster that spoils everything it touches and never knows the reason, and that is why I will never forgive you until you become a man, a true man with a true soul. As for your friends—"

Here Thorvald Einarsson struck the Abbess on the face with his open hand and knocked her down. I heard Sister Hedwic gasp in horror, and behind us Sister Sibihd began to moan. But the Abbess only sat there, rubbing her jaw and smiling a little. Then she said:

"Oh, dear, have I been at it again? I am ashamed of myself. You are quite right to be angry, Torvald; no one can stand me when I go on in that way, least of all myself; it is such a bore. Still, I cannot seem to stop it; I am too used to being the Abbess Radegunde, that is clear. I promise never to torment you again, but you, Thorvald, must never strike me again, because you will be very sorry if you do."

He took a step forward.

"No, no, my dear man," the Abbess said merrily, "I mean no threat—how could I threaten you?—I mean only that I will never tell you any jokes, my spirits will droop, and I will become as dull as any other woman. Confess it now: I am the most interesting thing that has happened to you in years and I have entertained you better, sharp tongue and all, than all the *skalds* at the Court of Norway. And I know more tales and stories than they do—more than anyone in the whole world—for I make new ones when the old ones wear out.

"Shall I tell you a story now?"

"About your Christ?" said he, the anger still in his face.

"No," said she, "about living men and women. Tell me, Torvald, what do you men want from us women?"

"To be talked to death," said he, and I could see there was some anger in him still, but he was turning it to play also.

The Abbess laughed in delight. "Very witty!" she said, springing to her feel and brushing the leaves off her skirt. "You are a very clever man, Torvald. I beg your pardon, Thorvald. I keep forgetting. But as to what men want from women, if you asked the young men, they would only wink and dig one another in the ribs, but that is only how they deceive themselves. That is only body calling to body. They themselves want something quite different and they want it so much that it frightens them. So they pretend it is anything and everything else: pleasure, comfort, a servant in the home. Do you know what it is that they want?"

"What?" said Thorvald.

"The mother," said Radegunde, "as women do, too; we all want the mother. When I walked before you on the riverbank yesterday, I was playing the mother. Now you did nothing, for you are no young fool, but I knew that sooner or later one of you, so tormented by his longing that he would hate me for it, would reveal himself. And so he did: Thorfinn, with his thoughts all mixed up between witches and grannies and whatnot. I knew I could frighten him, and through him, most of you. That was the beginning of my bargaining. You Norse have too much of the father in your country and not enough mother, with all your honoring of your women; that is why you die so well and kill other folk so well—and live so very, very badly."

"You are doing it again," said Thorvald, but I think he wanted to listen all the same.

"Your pardon, friend," said the Abbess. "You are brave men; I don't deny it. But I know your *sagas* and they are all about fighting and dying and afterwards not Heavenly happiness but the end of the world: everything, even the gods, eaten by the Fenris-wolf and the Midgard snake! What a pity, to die bravely only because life is not worth living! The Irish knew better. The pagan Irish were heroes, with their Queens leading them to battle as often as not, and Father Cairbre, God rest his soul, was complaining only two days ago that the common Irish folk were blasphemously making a goddess out of God's mother, for do they build shrines to Christ or Our Lord or pray to them? No! It is Our Lady of the Rocks and Our Lady of the Sea and Our Lady of the Grove and Our Lady of this or that from one end of the land to the other. And even here it is only the Abbey folk who speak of God the Father and of Christ. In the village if one is sick or another in trouble it is: Holy Mother, save me! and: *Mariam Virginem,* intercede for me, and: Blessed Virgin, blind my husband's eyes! and: Our Lady, preserve my crops, and so on, men and women both. We all need the mother."

"You, too?"

"More than most," said the Abbess.

"And I?"

"Oh no," said the Abbess, stopping suddenly, for we had all been walking slowly back towards the village as she spoke. "No, and that is what drew me to you at once. I saw it in you and knew you were the leader. It is followers who make leaders, you know, and your shipmates have made you leader, whether you know it or not. What you want is—how shall I say it? You are a clever man, Thorvald, perhaps the cleverest man I have ever met, more even than the scholars I knew in my youth. But your cleverness has had no food. It is a cleverness of the world and not of books. You want to travel and know about folk and their customs, and what strange places are like, and what has happened to men and women in the past. If you take me to Constantinople, it will not be to get a price for me but merely to go there; you went seafaring because this longing itched at you until you could bear it not a year more; I know that."

"Then you are a witch," said he, and he was not smiling.

"No, I only saw what was in your face when you spoke of that city," said she. "Also there is gossip that you spent much time in Göteborg as a young man, idling and dreaming and marveling at the ships and markets when you should have been at your farm."

She said, "Thorvald, I can feed that cleverness. I am the wisest woman in the world. I know everything—everything! I know more than my teachers; I make it up or it comes to me, I don't know how, but it is real—real!—and I know more than anyone. Take me from here, as your slave if you wish but as your friend also, and let us go to Constantinople and see the domes of gold, and the walls all inlaid with gold, and the people so wealthy you cannot imagine it, and the whole city so gilded it seems to be on fire, and pictures as high as a wall, set right in the wall and all made of jewels so there is nothing else like them, redder than the reddest rose, greener than the grass, and with a blue that makes the sky pale!"

"You are indeed a witch," said he, "and not the Abbess Radegunde."

She said slowly, "I think I am forgetting how to be the Abbess Radegunde."

"Then you will not care about them any more," said he and pointed to Sister Hedwic, who was still leading the stumbling Sister Sibihd.

The Abbess's face was still and mild. She said, "I care. Do not strike me, Thorvald, not ever again, and I will be a good friend to you. Try to control the worst of your men and leave as many of my people free as you can—I know them and will tell you which can be taken away with the least hurt to themselves or others—and I will feed that curiosity and cleverness of yours until you will not recognize this old world any more for the sheer wonder and awe of it; I swear this on my life."

"Done," said he, adding, "but with my luck, your life is somewhere else, locked in a box on top of a mountain, like the troll's in the story, or you will die of old age while we are still at sea."

"Nonsense," she said, "I am a healthy mortal woman with all my teeth, and I mean to gather many wrinkles yet."

He put his hand out and she took it; then he said, shaking his head in wonder, "If I sold you in Constantinople, within a year you would become Queen of the place!"

The Abbess laughed merrily and I cried in fear, "Me, too! Take me too!" and she said, "Oh yes, we must not forget little Boy News," and lifted me into her arms. The frightening tall man, with his face close to mine, said in his strange sing-song German:

"Boy, would you like to see the whales leaping in the open sea and the seals barking on the rocks? And cliffs so high that a giant could stretch his arms up and not reach their tops? And the sun shining at midnight?"

"Yes!" said I.

"But you will be a slave," he said, "and may be illtreated and will always have to do as you are bid. Would you like that?"

"No!" I cried lustily, from the safety of the Abbess's arms, "I'll fight!"

He laughed a mighty, roaring laugh and tousled my head—rather too hard, I thought—and said, "I will not be a bad master, for I am named for Thor Red-beard and he is strong and quick to fight but good-natured, too, and so am I," and the Abbess put me down and so we walked back to the village, Thorvald and the Abbess Radegunde talking of the glories of this world and Sister Hedwic saying softly, "She is a saint, our Abbess, a saint, to sacrifice herself for the good of the people," and all the time behind us, like a memory, came the low, witless sobbing of Sister Sibihd, who was in Hell.

WHEN WE GOT back we found that Thorfinn was better and the Norsemen were to leave in the morning. Thorvald had a second pallet brought into the Abbess's study and slept on the floor with us that night. You might think his men would laugh at this, for the Abbess was an old woman, but I think he had been with one of the young ones before he came to us. He had that look about him. There was no bedding for the Abbess but an old brown cloak with holes in it, and she and I were wrapped in it when he came in and threw himself down, whistling, on the other pallet. Then he said:

"Tomorrow, before we sail, you will show me the old Abbess's treasure."

"No," said she. "That agreement was broken."

He had been playing with his knife and now ran his thumb along the edge of it. "I can make you do it."

"No," said she patiently, "and now I am going to sleep."

"So you make light of death?" he said. "Good! That is what a brave woman should do, as the *skalds* sing, and not move, even when the keen sword cuts off her eyelashes. But what if I put this knife here not to your throat but to your little boy's? You would tell me then quick enough!"

The Abbess turned away from him, yawning and saying, "No, Thorvald, because you would not. And if you did, I would despise you for a cowardly oathbreaker and not tell you for that reason. Good night."

He laughed and whistled again for a bit. Then he said:

"Was all that true?"

"All what?" said the Abbess. "Oh, about the statue. Yes, but there was no ravisher. I put him in the tale for poor Sister Hedwic."

Thorvald snorted, as if in disappointment. "Tale? You tell lies, Abbess!"

The Abbess drew the old brown cloak over her head and closed her eyes. "It helped her."

Then there was a silence, but the big Norseman did not seem able to lie still. He shifted this way and that, stared at the ceiling, turned over, shifted his body again as if the straw bothered him, and again turned over. He finally burst out, "But what happened!"

She sat up. Then she shut her eyes. She said, "Maybe it does not come into your man's thoughts that an old woman gets tired and that the work of dealing with folk is hard work, or even that it is work at all. Well!

"Nothing 'happened,' Thorvald. Must something happen only if this one fucks that one or one bangs in another's head? I desired my statue to the point of such foolishness that I determined to find a real, human lover, but when I raised my eyes from my fancies to the real, human men of Rome and unstopped my ears to listen to their talk, I realized that the thing was completely and eternally impossible. Oh, those younger sons with their skulking, jealous hatred of the rich, and the rich ones with their noses in the air because they thought themselves of such great consequence because of their silly money, and the timidity of the priests to their superiors, and their superiors' pride, and the artisans' hatred of the peasants, and the peasants being worked like animals from morning until night, and half the men I saw beating their wives and the other half out to cheat some poor girl of her money or her virginity or both—this was enough to put out any fire! And the women doing less harm only because they had less power to do harm, or so it seemed to me then. So I put all away, as one does with any disappointment. Men are not such bad folk when one stops expecting them to be gods, but they are not for me. If that state is chastity, then a weak stomach is temperance, I think. But whatever it is, I have it, and that's the end of the matter."

"*All* men?" said Thorvald Einarsson with his head to one side, and it came to me that he had been drinking, though he seemed sober.

"Thorvald," said the Abbess, "what you want with this middle-aged wreck of a body I cannot imagine, but if you lust after my wrinkles and flabby breasts and lean, withered flanks, do whatever you want quickly and then for Heaven's sake, let me sleep. I am tired to death."

He said in a low voice, "I need to have power over you."

She spread her hands in a helpless gesture. "Oh Thorvald, Thorvald, I am a weak little woman over forty years old! Where is the power? All I can do is talk!"

He said, "That's it. That's how you do it. You talk and talk and talk and everyone does just as you please; I have seen it!"

The Abbess said, looking sharply at him, "Very well. If you must. *But if I were you, Norseman, I would as soon bed my own mother.* Remember that as you pull my skirts up."

That stopped him. He swore under his breath, turning over on his side, away from us. Then he thrust his knife into the edge of his pallet, time after time. Then he put the knife under the rolled-up cloth he was using as a pillow. We had no pillow so I tried to make mine out of the edge of the cloak and failed. Then I thought that the Norseman was afraid of God working in Radegunde, and then I thought of Sister Hedwic's changing color and wondered why. And then I thought of the leaping whales and the seals, which must be like great dogs because of the barking, and then the seals jumped on land and ran to my pallet and lapped at me with great icy tongues of water so that I shivered and jumped and then I woke up.

The Abbess Radegunde had left the pallet—it was her warmth I had missed—and was walking about the room. She would step and pause, her skirts making a small noise as she did so. She was careful not to touch the sleeping Thorvald. There was a dim light in the room from the embers that still glowed under the ashes in the hearth, but no light came from between the shutters of the study window, now shut against the cold. I saw the Abbess kneel under the plain wooden cross which hung on the study wall and heard her say a few words in Latin; I thought she was praying. But then she said in a low voice:

" 'Do not call upon Apollo and the Muses, for they are deaf things and vain.' But so are you, Pierced Man, deaf and vain."

Then she got up and began to pace again. Thinking of it now frightens me, for it was the middle of the night and no one to hear her—except me, but she thought I was asleep—and yet she went on and on in that low, even voice as if it were broad day and she were explaining something to someone, as if things that had been in her thoughts for years must finally come out. But I did not find anything alarming in it then, for I thought that perhaps all Abbesses had to do such things, and besides she did not seem angry or hurried or afraid; she sounded as calm as if she were discussing the profits from the Abbey's beekeeping—which I had heard her do—or the accounts for the wine cellars—which I had also heard—and there was nothing alarming in that. So I listened as she continued walking about the room in the dark. She said:

"Talk, talk, talk, and always to myself. But one can't abandon the kittens and puppies; that would be cruel. And being the Abbess Radegunde at least gives one something to do. But I am so sick of the good Abbess Radegunde; I have put on Radegunde every morning of my life as easily as I put on my smock, and then I have had to hear the stupid creature praised all day!— sainted Radegunde, just Radegunde who is never angry or greedy or jealous, kindly Radegunde who sacrifices herself for others and always the talk, talk, talk, bubbling and boiling in my head with no one to hear or understand, and no one to answer. No, not even in the south, only a line here or a line there, and all written by the dead. Did they feel as I do? That the world is a giant nursery full of squabbles over toys and the babes thinking me some kind of goddess because I'm not greedy for their dolls or bits of straw or their horses made of tied-together sticks?

"Poor people, if only they knew! It's so easy to be temperate when one enjoys nothing, so easy to be kind when one loves nothing, so easy to be fearless when one's life is no better than one's death. And so easy to scheme when the success or failure of the scheme doesn't matter.

"Would they be surprised, I wonder, to find out what my real thoughts were when Thorfinn's knife was at my throat? Curiosity! But he would not do it, of course; he does everything for show. And they would think I was twice holy, not to care about death.

"Then why not kill yourself, impious Sister Radegunde? Is it your religion which stops you? Oh, you mean the holy wells, and the holy trees, and the blessed saints with their blessed relics, and the stupidity that shamed Sister Hedwic and the promises of safety that drove poor Sibihd mad when the blessed body of her Lord did not protect her and the blessed love of the blessed Mary turned away the sharp point of not one knife? Trash! Idle leaves and sticks, reeds and rushes, filth we sweep off our floors when it grows too thick. As if holiness had anything to do with all of that. As if every place were not as holy as every other and every thing as holy as every other, from the shit in Thorfinn's bowels to the rocks on the ground. As if all places and things were not clouds placed in front of our weak eyes, to keep us from being blinded by that glory, that eternal shining, that blazing all about us, that torrent of light that is everything and is in everything! That is what keeps me from the river, but it never speaks to me or tells me what to do, and to it good and evil are the same—no, it is something else than good or evil; it *is,* only—so it is not God. That I know.

"So, people, is your Radegunde a witch or a demon? Is she full of pride or is Radegunde abject? Perhaps she is a witch. Once, long ago, I confessed

to Old Gerbertus that I could see things that were far away merely by closing my eyes, and I proved it to him, too, and he wept over me and gave me
much penance, crying, 'If it come of itself it may be a gift of God, daughter,
but it is more likely the work of a demon, so do not do it!' And then we
prayed and I told him the power had left me, to make the poor old puppy
less troubled in its mind, but that was not true, of course. I could still see
Turkey as easily as I could see him, and places far beyond: the squat wild
men of the plains on their ponies, and the strange tall people beyond that
with their great cities and odd eyes, as if one pulled one's eyelid up on a slant,
and then the seas with the great wild lands and the cities more full of gold
than Constantinople, and then the water again until one comes back home,
for the world's a ball, as the ancients said.

"But I did stop somehow, over the years. Radegunde never had time, I
suppose. Besides, when I opened that door it was only pictures, as in a book,
and all to no purpose, and after a while I had seen them all and no longer
cared for them. It is the other door that draws me, when it opens itself but
a crack and strange things peep through, like Ranulf sister's-son and the
name of his horse. That door is good but very heavy; it always swings back
after a little. I shall have to be on my deathbed to open it all the way, I think.

"The fox is asleep. He is the cleverest yet; there is something in him so
that at times one can almost talk to him. But still a fox, for the most part.
Perhaps in time . . .

"But let me see; yes, he is asleep. And the Sibihd puppy is asleep, though
it will be having a bad dream soon, I think, and the Thorfinn kitten is asleep,
as full of fright as when it wakes, with its claws going in and out, in and out,
lest something strangle it in its sleep."

Then the Abbess fell silent and moved to the shuttered window as if she
were looking out, so I thought that she was indeed looking out—but not with
her eyes—at all the sleeping folk, and this was something she had done every
night of her life to see if they were safe and sound. But would she not know
that *I* was awake? Should I not try very hard to get to sleep before she caught
me? Then it seemed to me that she smiled in the dark, although I could not
see it. She said in that same low, even voice: "Sleep or wake, Boy News; it is
all one to me. Thou hast heard nothing of any importance, only the silly
Abbess talking to herself, only Radegunde saying goodbye to Radegunde,
only Radegunde going away—don't cry, Boy News; I am still here—but there:
Radegunde has gone. This Norseman and I are alike in one way: our minds
are like great houses with many of the rooms locked shut. We crowd in a mis-

erable huddled few, like poor folk, when we might move freely among them all, as gracious as princes. It is fate that locked away so much of the Norseman from the Norseman—see, Boy News, I do not say his name, not even softly, for that wakes folk—but I wonder if the one who bolted me in was not Radegunde herself, she and Old Gerbertus—whom I partly believed—they and the years and years of having to be Radegunde and do the things Radegunde did and pretend to have the thoughts Radegunde had and the endless, endless lies Radegunde must tell everyone, and Radegunde's utter and unbearable loneliness." She fell silent again. I wondered at the Abbess's talk this time: saying she was not there when she was, and about living locked up in small rooms—for surely the Abbey was the most splendid house in all the world and the biggest—and how could she be lonely when all the folk loved her? But then she said in a voice so low that I could hardly hear it:

"Poor Radegunde! So weary of the lies she tells and the fooling of men and women with the collars round their necks and bribes of food for good behavior and a careful twitch of the leash that they do not even see or feel. And with the Norseman it will be all the same: lies and flattery and all of it work that never ends and no one ever even sees, so that finally Radegunde will lie down like an ape in a cage, weak and sick from hunger, and will never get up.

"Let her die now. There: Radegunde is dead. Radegunde is gone. Perhaps the door was heavy only because she was on the other side of it, pushing against me. Perhaps it will open all the way now. I have looked in all directions: to the east, to the north and south, and to the west, but there is one place I have never looked and now I will: away from the ball, straight up. Let us see—"

She stopped speaking all of a sudden. I had been falling asleep, but this silence woke me. Then I heard the Abbess gasp terribly, like one mortally stricken, and then she said in a whisper so keen and thrilling that it made the hair stand up on my head: *Where art thou?* The next moment she had torn the shutters open and was crying out with all her voice: *Help me! Find me! Oh come, come, come, or I die!*

This waked Thorvald. With some Norse oath he stumbled up and flung on his sword-belt, and then put his hand to his dagger; I had noticed this thing with the dagger was a thing Norsemen liked to do. The Abbess was silent. He let out his breath in an oof! and went to light the tallow dip at the live embers under the hearth ashes; when the dip had smoked up, he put it on its shelf on the wall.

He said in German, "What the devil, woman! What has happened?"

She turned round. She looked as if she could not see us, as if she had been dazed by a joy too big to hold, like one who has looked into the sun and is still dazzled by it so that everything seems changed, and the world seems all God's and everything in it like Heaven. She said softly, with her arms around herself, hugging herself: "My people. The real people."

"What are you talking of!" said he.

She seemed to see him then, but only as Sibihd had beheld us; I do not mean in horror as Sibihd had, but beholding through something else, like someone who comes from a vision of bliss which still lingers about her. She said in the same soft voice, "They are coming for me, Thorvald. Is it not wonderful? I knew all this year that something would happen, but I did not know it would be the one thing I wanted in all the world."

He grasped his hair. "*Who* is coming?"

"My people," she said, laughing softly. "Do you not feel them? I do. We must wait three days, for they come from very far away. But then—oh, you will see!"

He said, "You've been dreaming. We sail tomorrow."

"Oh no," said the Abbess simply. "You cannot do that for it would not be right. They told me to wait; they said if I went away, they might not find me."

He said slowly, "You've gone mad. Or it's a trick."

"Oh no, Thorvald," said she. "How could I trick you? I am your friend. And you will wait these three days, will you not, because you are my friend also."

"You're mad," he said, and started for the door of the study, but she stepped in front of him and threw herself on her knees. All her cunning seemed to have deserted her, or perhaps it was Radegunde who had been the cunning one. This one was like a child. She clasped her hands and tears came out of her eyes; she begged him, saying:

"Such a little thing, Thorvald, only three days! And if they do not come, why then we will go anywhere you like, but if they do come you will not regret it, I promise you; they are not like the folk here and that place is like nothing here. It is what the soul craves, Thorvald!"

He said, "Get up, woman, for your God's sake!"

She said, smiling in a sly, frightened way through her blubbered face, "If you let me stay, I will show you the old Abbess's buried treasure, Thorvald."

He stepped back, the anger clear in him. "So this is the brave old witch who cares nothing for death!" he said. Then he made for the door, but she was up again, as quick as a snake, and had flung herself across it.

She said, still with that strange innocence, "Do not strike me. Do not push me. I am your friend!"

He said, "You mean that you lead me by a string round the neck, like a goose. Well, I am tired of that!"

"But I cannot do that any more," said the Abbess breathlessly, "not since the door opened. I am not able now." He raised his arm to strike her and she cowered, wailing, "Do not strike me! Do not push me! Do not, Thorvald!"

He said, "Out of my way then, old witch!"

She began to cry in sobs and gulps. She said, "One is here but another will come! One is buried but another will rise! She will come, Thorvald!" and then in a low, quick voice, "Do not push open this last door. There is one behind it who is evil and I am afraid"—but one could see that he was angry and disappointed and would not listen. He struck her for a second time and again she fell, but with a desperate cry, covering her face with her hands. He unbolted the door and stepped over her and I heard his footsteps go down the corridor. I could see the Abbess clearly—at that time I did not wonder how this could be, with the shadows from the tallow dip half hiding everything in their drunken dance—but I saw every line in her face as if it had been full day and in that light I saw Radegunde go away from us at last.

Have you ever been at some great King's court or some Earl's and heard the story-tellers? There are those so skilled in the art that they not only speak for you what the person in the tale said and did, but they also make an action with their faces and bodies as if they truly were that man or woman, so that it is a great surprise to you when the tale ceases, for you almost believe that you have seen the tale happen in front of your very eyes and it is as if a real man or woman had suddenly ceased to exist, for you forget that all this was only a teller and a tale.

So it was with the woman who had been Radegunde. She did not change; it was still Radegunde's gray hairs and wrinkled face and old body in the peasant woman's brown dress, and yet at the same time it was a stranger who stepped out of the Abbess Radegunde as out of a gown dropped to the floor. This stranger was without feeling, though Radegunde's tears still stood on her cheeks, and there was no kindness or joy in her. She got up without taking care of her dress where the dirty rushes stuck to it; it was as if the dress were an accident and did not concern her. She said in a voice I had never heard before, one with no feeling in it, as if I did not concern her or Thorvald Einarsson either, as if neither of us were worth a second glance:

"Thorvald, turn around."

Far up in the hall something stirred.

"Now come back. This way."

There were footsteps, coming closer. Then the big Norseman walked clumsily into the room—jerk! jerk! jerk! at every step as if he were being pulled by a rope. Sweat beaded his face. He said, "You—how?"

"By my nature," she said. "Put up the right arm, fox. Now the left. Now both down. Good."

"You—troll!" he said.

"That is so," she said. "Now listen to me, you. There's a man inside you but he's not worth getting at; I tried moments ago when I was new-hatched and he's buried too deep, but now I have grown beak and claws and care nothing for him. It's almost dawn and your boys are stirring; you will go out and tell them that we must stay here another three days. You are weather-wise; make up some story they will believe. And don't try to tell anyone what happened here tonight; you will find that you cannot."

"Folk—come," said he, trying to turn his head, but the effort only made him sweat.

She raised her eyebrows. "Why should they? No one has heard anything. Nothing has happened. You will go out and be as you always are and I will play Radegunde. For three days only. Then you are free."

He did not move. One could see that to remain still was very hard for him; the sweat poured and he strained until every muscle stood out. She said:

"Fox, don't hurt yourself. And don't push me; I am not fond of you. My hand is light upon you only because you still seem to me a little less unhuman than the rest; do not force me to make it heavier. To be plain: I have just broken Thorfinn's neck, for I find that the change improves him. Do not make me do the same to you."

"No worse . . . than death," Thorvald brought out.

"Ah no?" said she, and in a moment he was screaming and clawing at his eyes. She said, "Open them, open them; your sight is back," and then, "I do not wish to bother myself thinking up worse things, like worms in your guts. Or do you wish dead sons and a dead wife? Now go.

"*As you always do,*" she added sharply, and the big man turned and walked out. One could not have told from looking at him that anything was wrong.

I had not been sorry to see such a bad man punished, one whose friends had killed our folk and would have taken them for slaves—yet I was sorry, too, in a way, because of the seals barking and the whales—and he *was* splendid, after a fashion—and yet truly I forgot all about that the moment he was gone, for I was terrified of this strange person or demon or whatever it was, for I knew that whoever was in the room with me was not the Abbess Radegunde. I knew also that it could tell where I was and what I was doing, even if I made no sound, and was in a terrible riddle as to what I ought to do when soft fingers touched my face. It was the demon, reaching swiftly and silently behind her.

And do you know, all of a sudden everything was all right! I don't mean that she was the Abbess again—I still had very serious suspicions about that—but all at once I felt light as air and nothing seemed to matter very much because my stomach was full of bubbles of happiness, just as if I had been drunk, only nicer. If the Abbess Radegunde were really a demon, what a joke that was on her people! And she did not, now that I came to think of it, seem a bad sort of demon, more the frightening kind than the killing kind, except for Thorfinn, of course, but then Thorfinn had been a very wicked man. And did not the angels of the Lord smite down the wicked? So perhaps the Abbess was an angel of the Lord and not a demon, but if she were truly an angel, why had she not smitten the Norsemen down when they first came and so saved all our folk? And then I thought that, whether angel or demon, she was no longer the Abbess and would love me no longer, and if I had not been so full of the silly happiness which kept tickling about inside me, this thought would have made me weep.

I said, "Will the bad Thorvald get free, demon?"

"No," she said. "Not even if I sleep."

I thought: *But she does not love me.*

"I love thee," said the strange voice, but it was not the Abbess Radegunde's and so was without meaning, but again those soft fingers touched me and there was some kindness in them, even if it was a stranger's kindness.

Sleep, they said.

So I did.

The next three days I had much secret mirth to see the folk bow down to the demon and kiss its hands and weep over it because it had sold itself to ransom them. That is what Sister Hedwic told them. Young Thorfinn had gone out in the night to piss and had fallen over a stone in the dark and broken his neck, which secretly rejoiced our folk, and his comrades did not seem to mind much either, save for one young fellow who had been Thorfinn's friend, I think, and so went about with a long face. Thorvald locked me up in the Abbess's study with the demon every night and went out—or so folk said—to one of the young women, but on those nights the demon was silent and I lay there with the secret tickle of merriment in my stomach, caring about nothing.

On the third morning I woke sober. The demon—or the Abbess—for in the day she was so like the Abbess Radegunde that I wondered—took my hand and walked us up to Thorvald, who was out picking the people to go aboard the Norsemen's boats at the riverbank to be slaves. Folk were standing about weeping and wringing their hands; I thought this strange, because of the Abbess's promise to pick those whose going would hurt least, but I know now that least is not none. The weather was bad, cold rain out of mist, and some of Thorvald's companions were speaking sourly to him in the Norse, but he talked them down—bluff and hearty—as if making light of the weather. The demon stood by him and said, in German, in a low voice so that none might hear: "You will say we go to find the Abbess's treasure and then you will go with us into the woods."

He spoke to his fellows in Norse and they frowned; but the end of it was that two must come with us, for the demon said it was such a treasure as three might carry. The demon had the voice and manner of the Abbess Radegunde, all smiles, so they were fooled. Thus we started out into the trees behind the village, with the rain worse and the ground beginning to soften underfoot. As soon as the village was out of sight the two Norsemen fell behind, but Thorvald did not seem to notice this; I looked back and saw the first man standing in the mud with one foot up, like a goose, and the second with his head lifted and his mouth open so that the rain fell in it. We walked on, the earth sucking at our shoes and all of us getting wet: Thorvald's hair stuck fast against his face and the demon's old brown cloak clinging to its body. Then suddenly the demon began to breathe harshly and it put its hand to its side with a cry. Its cloak fell off and it stumbled before us between the wet trees, not weeping but breathing hard. Then I saw, ahead of us through the pelting rain, a kind of shining among the bare tree-trunks, and as we came nearer the shining became more clear until it was very plain to see, not a blazing thing like a fire at night but a mild and even brightness as though the sunlight were coming through the clouds pleasantly but without strength, as it often does at the beginning of the year.

And then there were folk inside the brightness, both men and women, all dressed in white, and they held out their arms to us and the demon ran to them, crying out loudly and weeping, but paying no mind to the tree-branches which struck it across the face and body. Sometimes it fell but it quickly got up again. When it reached the strange folk they embraced it and I thought that the filth and mud of its gown would stain their white clothing, but the foulness dropped off and would not cling to those clean garments. None of the strange folk spoke a word, nor did the Abbess—I knew then that she was no demon, whatever she was—but I felt them talk to one another, as if in my mind, although I know not how this could be nor the sense of what they said. An odd thing was that as I came closer I could see they were not standing on the ground, as in the way of nature, but higher up, inside the shining, and that their white robes were nothing at all like ours, for they clung to the body so that one might see the people's legs all the way up to the place where the legs joined, even the women's. And some of the folk were like us, but most had a darker color and some looked as if they had been smeared with soot—there are such persons in the far parts of the world, you know, as I found out later; it is their own natural color—and there were some with the odd eyes the Abbess had spoken of—but the oddest thing of all I will not tell you now. When the Abbess had embraced and kissed them all and all had wept, she turned and looked down upon us: Thorvald standing there as if held by a rope and I, who had lost my fear and had crept close in pure awe, for there was such a joy about these people, like the light about them, mild as spring light and yet as strong as in a spring where the winter has gone forever.

"Come to me, Thorvald," said the Abbess, and one could not see from her face if she loved or hated him. He moved closer—jerk! jerk!—and she reached down and touched his forehead with her fingertips, at which one side of his lip lifted, as a dog's does when it snarls.

"As thou knowest," said the Abbess quietly, "I hate thee and would be revenged upon thee. Thus I swore to myself three days ago, and such vows are not lightly broken."

I saw him snarl again and he turned his eyes from her.

"I must go soon," said the Abbess, unmoved, "for I could stay here long years only as Radegunde and Radegunde is no more; none of us can remain here long as our proper selves or even in our true bodies, for if we do we go mad like Sibihd or walk into the river and drown or stop our own hearts, so miserable, wicked, and brutish does your world seem to us. Nor may we come in large companies, for we are few and our strength is not great and we have much to learn and study of thy folk so that we may teach and help without marring all in our ignorance. And ignorant or wise, we can do naught except thy folk aid us.

"Here is my revenge," said the Abbess, and he seemed to writhe under the touch of her fingers, for all they were so light; "Henceforth be not Thorvald Farmer nor yet Thorvald Seafarer but Thorvald Peacemaker, Thorvald War-hater, put into anguish by bloodshed and agonized at cruelty. I cannot make long thy life—that gift is beyond me—but I give thee this: to the end of thy days, long or short, thou wilt know that it is neither good nor evil, as I do, and this knowing will trouble and frighten thee always, as it does me, and so about this one thing, as about many another, Thorvald Peacemaker will never have peace.

"Now, Thorvald, go back to the village and tell thy comrades I was assumed into the company of the saints, straight up to Heaven. Thou mayst believe it, if thou will. That is all my revenge."

Then she took away her hand and he turned and walked from us like a man in a dream, holding out his hands as if to feel the rain and stumbling now and again, as one who wakes from a vision.

Then I began to grieve, for I knew she would be going away with the strange people and it was to me as if all the love and care and light in the world were leaving me. I crept close to her, meaning to spring secretly onto the shining place and so go away with them, but she spied me and said, "Silly Radulphus, you cannot," and that *you* hurt me more than anything else, so that I began to bawl.

"Child," said the Abbess, "come to me," and loudly weeping I leaned against her knees. I felt the shining around me, all bright and good and warm, that wiped away all grief, and then the Abbess's touch on my hair.

She said, "Remember me. And be . . . content."

I nodded, wishing I dared to look up at her face, but when I did, she had already gone with her friends. Not up into the sky, you understand, but as if they moved very swiftly backwards among the trees—although the trees were still behind them somehow—and as they moved, the shining and the people faded away into the rain until there was nothing left.

Then there was no rain. I do not mean that the clouds parted or the sun came out; I mean that one moment it was raining and cold and the next the sky was clear blue from side to side and it was splendid, sunny, breezy, bright, sailing weather. I had the oddest thought that the strange folk were

not agreed about doing such a big miracle—and it was hard for them, too—
but they had decided that no one would believe this more than all the other
miracles folk speak of, I suppose. And it would surely make Thorvald's lot
easier when he came back with wild words about saints and Heaven, as indeed it did, later.

Well, that is the tale, really. She said to me "Be content" and so I am; they
call me Radulf the Happy now. I have had my share of trouble and sickness
but always somewhere in me there is a little spot of warmth and joy to make
it all easier, like a traveler's fire burning out in the wilderness on a cold night.
When I am in real sorrow or distress I remember her fingers touching my
hair and that takes part of the pain away, somehow. So perhaps I got the best
gift, after all. And she said also, "Remember me," and thus I have, every little thing, although it all happened when I was the age my own grandson is
now, and that is how I can tell you this tale today.

And the rest? Three days after the Norsemen left, Sibihd got back her
wits and no one knew how, though I think I do! And as for Thorvald
Einarsson, I have heard that after his wife died in Norway he went to
England and ended his days there as a monk, but whether this story be true
or not I do not know.

I know this: they may call me Happy Radulf all they like, but there is
much that troubles me. Was the Abbess Radegunde a demon, as the new
priest says? I cannot believe this, although he called half her sayings nonsense and the other half blasphemy when I asked him. Father Cairbre, before the Norse killed him, told us stories about the Sidhe, that is the Irish
fairy people, who leave changelings in human cradles, and for a while it
seemed to me that Radegunde must be a woman of the Sidhe when I remembered that she could read Latin at the age of two and was such a marvel of learning when so young, for the changelings the fairies leave are not
their own children, you understand, but one of the fairy-folk themselves,
who are hundreds upon hundreds of years old, and the other fairy-folk always come back for their own in the end. And yet this could not have been,
for Father Cairbre said also that the Sidhe are wanton and cruel and without
souls, and neither the Abbess Radegunde nor the people who came for her
were one blessed bit like that, although she did break Thorfinn's neck—but
then it may be that Thorfinn broke his own neck by chance, just as we all
thought at the time, and she told this to Thorvald afterwards, as if she had
done it herself, only to frighten him. She had more of a soul with a soul's
griefs and joys than most of us, no matter what the new priest says. He never

saw her or felt her sorrow and lonesomeness, or heard her talk of the blazing light all around us—and what can that be but God Himself? Even though she did call the crucifix a deaf thing and vain, she must have meant not Christ, you see, but only the piece of wood itself, for she was always telling the Sisters that Christ was in Heaven and not on the wall. And if she said the light was not good or evil, well, there is a traveling Irish scholar who told me of a holy Christian monk named Augustinus who tells us that all which is, is good, and evil is only a lack of the good, like an empty place not filled up. And if the Abbess truly said there was no God, I say it was the sin of despair, and even saints may sin, if only they repent, which I believe she did at the end.

So I tell myself and yet I know the Abbess Radegunde was no saint, for are the saints few and weak, as she said? Surely not! And then there is a thing I held back in my telling, a small thing and it will make you laugh and perhaps means nothing one way or the other but it is this:

Are the saints bald?

These folk in white had young faces but they were like eggs; there was not a stitch of hair on their domes! Well, God may shave his saints if He pleases, I suppose.

But I know she was no saint. And then I believe that she did kill Thorfinn and the light was not God and she not even a Christian or maybe even human and I remember how Radegunde was to her only a gown to step out of at will, and how she truly hated and scorned Thorvald until she was happy and safe with her own people. Or perhaps it was like her talk about living in a house with the rooms shut up; when she stopped being Radegunde first one part of her came back and then the other—the joyful part that could not lie or plan and then the angry part—and then they were all together when she was back among her own folk. And then I give up trying to weigh this matter and go back to warm my soul at the little fire she lit in me, that one warm, bright place in the wide and windy dark.

But something troubles me even there, and will not be put to rest by the memory of the Abbess's touch on my hair. As I grow older it troubles me more and more. It was the very last thing she said to me, which I have not told you but will now. When she had given me the gift of contentment, I became so happy that I said, "Abbess, you said you would be revenged on Thorvald, but all you did was change him into a good man. That is no revenge!"

What this saying did to her astonished me, for all the color went out of her face and left it gray. She looked suddenly old, like a death's head, even standing there among her own true folk with love and joy coming from them so strongly that I myself might feel it. She said, "I did not change him. I lent him my eyes; that is all." Then she looked beyond me, as if at our village, at the Norsemen loading their boats with weeping slaves, at all the villages of Germany and England and France where the poor folk sweat from dawn to dark so that the great lords may do battle with one another, at castles under siege with the starving folk within eating mice and rats and sometimes each other, at the women carried off or raped or beaten, at the mothers wailing for their little ones, and beyond this at the great wide world itself with all its battles which I had used to think so grand, and the misery and greediness and fear and jealousy and hatred of folk one for the other, save—perhaps— for a few small bands of savages, but they were so far from us that one could scarcely see them. She said: *No revenge? Thinkest thou so, boy?* And then she said as one who believes absolutely, as one who has seen all the folk at their living and dying, not for one year but for many, not in one place but in all places, as one who knows it all over the whole wide earth:

Think again. . . .

OCTAVIA E. BUTLER

O CTAVIA E. BUTLER was born in June 1947 in Pasadena, California. She attended Pasadena City College, where she received an A.A. in 1968. In 1969, she went to California State University at Los Angeles, the University of California at Los Angeles, and attended the 1970 Clarion Science Fiction Writers Workshop. Her first story, "Crossover," appeared in the 1971 Clarion anthology. After working at a number of blue-collar jobs to support herself, she sold the first two novels in her Patternist SF series in 1976: *Patternmaster* and *Mind of My Mind*. After stand-alones *Survivor* and *Kindred,* she returned to the series with *Wild Seed* and the stand-alone *Clay's Ark*. Xenogenesis books *Dawn, Adulthood Rites,* and *Imago* came next. Her most recent novels are the first two volumes in the Parable series, *Parable of the Sower* and *Parable of the Talents*. Much of Butler's small body of short fiction was collected in *Bloodchild and Other Stories*. She won the 1984 Hugo for her short story "Speech Sounds," and the 1985 Hugo, Nebula, and Locus Awards for her novelette "Bloodchild." In 1995, she received a $295,000 MacArthur Foundation Genius award—the first SF writer to do so.

The story that follows, one of Butler's finest works, takes us into a far future where human gender and the alien other become inextricably entwined.

* * *

MY LAST NIGHT of childhood began with a visit home. T'Gatoi's sister had given us two sterile eggs. T'Gatoi gave one to my mother, brother, and sisters. She insisted that I eat the other one alone. It didn't matter. There was still enough to leave everyone feeling good. Almost everyone. My mother wouldn't take any. She sat, watching everyone drifting and dreaming without her. Most of the time she watched me.

I lay against T'Gatoi's long, velvet underside, sipping from my egg now and then, wondering why my mother denied herself such a harmless pleasure. Less of her hair would be gray if she indulged now and then. The eggs prolonged life, prolonged vigor. My father, who had never refused one in his life, had lived more than twice as long as he should have. And toward the end of his life, when he should have been slowing down, he had married my mother and fathered four children.

But my mother seemed content to age before she had to. I saw her turn away as several of T'Gatoi's limbs secured me closer. T'Gatoi liked our body heat and took advantage of it whenever she could. When I was little and at home more, my mother used to try to tell me how to behave with T'Gatoi—how to be respectful and always obedient because T'Gatoi was the Tlic government official in charge of the Preserve, and thus the most important of her kind to deal directly with Terrans. It was an honor, my mother said, that such a person had chosen to come into the family. My mother was at her most formal and severe when she was lying.

I had no idea why she was lying, or even what she was lying about. It *was* an honor to have T'Gatoi in the family, but it was hardly a novelty. T'Gatoi and my mother had been friends all my mother's life, and T'Gatoi was not interested in being honored in the house she considered her second home. She simply came in, climbed onto one of her special couches, and called me over to keep her warm. It was impossible to be formal with her while lying against her and hearing her complain as usual that I was too skinny.

"You're better," she said this time, probing me with six or seven of her limbs. "You're gaining weight finally. Thinness is dangerous." The probing changed subtly, became a series of caresses.

"He's still too thin," my mother said sharply.

T'Gatoi lifted her head and perhaps a meter of her body off the couch as though she were sitting up. She looked at my mother, and my mother, her face lined and old looking, turned away.

"Lien, I would like you to have what's left of Gan's egg."

"The eggs are for the children," my mother said.

"They are for the family. Please take it."

Unwillingly obedient, my mother took it from me and put it to her mouth. There were only a few drops left in the now-shrunken, elastic shell, but she squeezed them out, swallowed them, and after a few moments some of the lines of tension began to smooth from her face.

"It's good," she whispered. "Sometimes I forget how good it is."

"You should take more," T'Gatoi said. "Why are you in such a hurry to be old?"

My mother said nothing.

"I like being able to come here," T'Gatoi said. "This place is a refuge because of you, yet you won't take care of yourself."

T'Gatoi was hounded on the outside. Her people wanted more of us made available. Only she and her political faction stood between us and the hordes who did not understand why there was a Preserve—why any Terran could not be courted, paid, drafted, in some way made available to them. Or they did understand, but in their desperation, they did not care. She parceled us out to the desperate and sold us to the rich and powerful for their political support. Thus, we were necessities, status symbols, and an independent people. She oversaw the joining of families, putting an end to the final remnants of the earlier system of breaking up Terran families to suit impatient Tlic. I had lived outside with her. I had seen the desperate eagerness in the way some people looked at me. It was a little frightening to know that only she stood between us and that desperation that could so easily swallow us. My mother would look at her sometimes and say to me, "Take care of her." And I would remember that she too had been outside, had seen.

Now T'Gatoi used four of her limbs to push me away from her onto the floor. "Go on, Gan," she said. "Sit down there with your sisters and enjoy not being sober. You had most of the egg. Lien, come warm me."

My mother hesitated for no reason that I could see. One of my earliest memories is of my mother stretched alongside T'Gatoi, talking about things I could not understand, picking me up from the floor and laughing as she sat me on one of T'Gatoi's segments. She ate her share of eggs then. I wondered when she had stopped, and why.

She lay down now against T'Gatoi, and the whole left row of T'Gatoi's limbs closed around her, holding her loosely, but securely. I had always found it comfortable to lie that way, but except for my older sister, no one else in the family liked it. They said it made them feel caged.

T'Gatoi meant to cage my mother. Once she had, she moved her tail slightly, then spoke. "Not enough egg, Lien. You should have taken it when it was passed to you. You need it badly now."

T'Gatoi's tail moved once more, its whip motion so swift I wouldn't have seen it if I hadn't been watching for it. Her sting drew only a single drop of blood from my mother's bare leg.

My mother cried out—probably in surprise. Being stung doesn't hurt. Then she sighed and I could see her body relax. She moved languidly into a more comfortable position within the cage of T'Gatoi's limbs. "Why did you do that?" she asked, sounding half asleep.

"I could not watch you sitting and suffering any longer."

My mother managed to move her shoulders in a small shrug. "Tomorrow," she said.

"Yes. Tomorrow you will resume your suffering—if you must. But just now, just for now, lie here and warm me and let me ease your way a little."

"He's still mine, you know," my mother said suddenly. "Nothing can buy him from me." Sober, she would not have permitted herself to refer to such things.

"Nothing," T'Gatoi agreed, humoring her.

"Did you think I would sell him for eggs? For long life? My son?"

"Not for anything," T'Gatoi said, stroking my mother's shoulders, toying with her long, graying hair.

I would like to have touched my mother, shared that moment with her. She would take my hand if I touched her now. Freed by the egg and the sting, she would smile and perhaps say things long held in. But tomorrow, she would remember all this as a humiliation. I did not want to be part of a remembered humiliation. Best just be still and know she loved me under all the duty and pride and pain.

"Xuan Hoa, take off her shoes," T'Gatoi said. "In a little while I'll sting her again and she can sleep."

My older sister obeyed, swaying drunkenly as she stood up. When she had finished, she sat down beside me and took my hand. We had always been a unit, she and I.

My mother put the back of her head against T'Gatoi's underside and tried from that impossible angle to look up into the broad, round face. "You're going to sting me again?"

"Yes, Lien."

"I'll sleep until tomorrow noon."

"Good. You need it. When did you sleep last?"

My mother made a wordless sound of annoyance. "I should have stepped on you when you were small enough," she muttered.

It was an old joke between them. They had grown up together, sort of, though T'Gatoi had not, in my mother's lifetime, been small enough for any Terran to step on. She was nearly three times my mother's present age, yet would still be young when my mother died of age. But T'Gatoi and my mother had met as T'Gatoi was coming into a period of rapid development— a kind of Tlic adolescence. My mother was only a child, but for a while they developed at the same rate and had no better friends than each other.

T'Gatoi had even introduced my mother to the man who became my father. My parents, pleased with each other in spite of their different ages, married as T'Gatoi was going into her family's business—politics. She and my mother saw each other less. But sometime before my older sister was born, my mother promised T'Gatoi one of her children. She would have to give one of us to someone, and she preferred T'Gatoi to some stranger.

Years passed. T'Gatoi traveled and increased her influence. The Preserve was hers by the time she came back to my mother to collect what she probably saw as her just reward for her hard work. My older sister took an instant liking to her and wanted to be chosen, but my mother was just coming to term with me and T'Gatoi liked the idea of choosing an infant and watching and taking part in all the phases of development. I'm told I was first caged within T'Gatoi's many limbs only three minutes after my birth. A few days later, I was given my first taste of egg. I tell Terrans that when they ask whether I was ever afraid of her. And I tell it to Tlic when T'Gatoi suggests a young Terran child for them and they, anxious and ignorant, demand an adolescent. Even my brother who had somehow grown up to fear and distrust the Tlic could probably have gone smoothly into one of their families if he had been adopted early enough. Sometimes, I think for his sake he should have been. I looked at him, stretched out on the floor across the room, his eyes open, but glazed as he dreamed his egg dream. No matter what he felt toward the Tlic, he always demanded his share of egg.

"Lien, can you stand up?" T'Gatoi asked suddenly.

"Stand?" my mother said. "I thought I was going to sleep."

"Later. Something sounds wrong outside." The cage was abruptly gone.

"What?"

"Up, Lien!"

My mother recognized her tone and got up just in time to avoid being dumped on the floor. T'Gatoi whipped her three meters of body off her couch, toward the door, and out at full speed. She had bones—ribs, a long spine, a skull, four sets of limb bones per segment. But when she moved that way, twisting, hurling herself into controlled falls, landing running, she seemed not only boneless, but aquatic—something swimming through the air as though it were water. I loved watching her move.

I left my sister and started to follow her out the door, though I wasn't very steady on my own feet. It would have been better to sit and dream, better yet to find a girl and share a waking dream with her. Back when the Tlic saw us as not much more than convenient, big, warm-blooded animals, they would pen several of us together, male and female, and feed us only eggs. That way they could be sure of getting another generation of us no matter how we tried to hold out. We were lucky that didn't go on long. A few generations of it and we would have *been* little more than convenient, big animals.

"Hold the door open, Gan," T'Gatoi said. "And tell the family to stay back."

"What is it?" I asked.

"N'Tlic."

I shrank back against the door. "Here? Alone?"

"He was trying to reach a call box, I suppose." She carried the man past me, unconscious, folded like a coat over some of her limbs. He looked young—my brother's age perhaps—and he was thinner than he should have been. What T'Gatoi would have called dangerously thin.

"Gan, go to the call box," she said. She put the man on the floor and began stripping off his clothing.

I did not move.

After a moment, she looked up at me, her sudden stillness a sign of deep impatience.

"Send Qui," I told her. "I'll stay here. Maybe I can help."

She let her limbs begin to move again, lifting the man and pulling his shirt over his head. "You don't want to see this," she said. "It will be hard. I can't help this man the way his Tlic could."

"I know. But send Qui. He won't want to be of any help here. I'm at least willing to try."

She looked at my brother—older, bigger, stronger, certainly more able to help her here. He was sitting up now, braced against the wall, staring at the man on the floor with undisguised fear and revulsion. Even she could see that he would be useless.

"Qui, go!" she said.

He didn't argue. He stood up, swayed briefly, then steadied, frightened sober.

"This man's name is Bram Lomas," she told him, reading from the man's armband. I fingered my own armband in sympathy. "He needs T'Khotgif Teh. Do you hear?"

"Bram Lomas, T'Khotgif Teh," my brother said. "I'm going." He edged around Lomas and ran out the door.

Lomas began to regain consciousness. He only moaned at first and clutched spasmodically at a pair of T'Gatoi's limbs. My younger sister, finally awake from her egg dream, came close to look at him, until my mother pulled her back.

T'Gatoi removed the man's shoes, then his pants, all the while leaving him two of her limbs to grip. Except for the final few, all her limbs were equally dexterous. "I want no argument from you this time, Gan," she said.

I straightened. "What shall I do?"

"Go out and slaughter an animal that is at least half your size."

"Slaughter? But I've never—"

She knocked me across the room. Her tail was an efficient weapon whether she exposed the sting or not.

I got up, feeling stupid for having ignored her warning, and went into the kitchen. Maybe I could kill something with a knife or an ax. My mother raised a few Terran animals for the table and several thousand local ones for their fur. T'Gatoi would probably prefer something local. An achti, perhaps. Some of those were the right size, though they had about three times as many teeth as I did and a real love of using them. My mother, Hoa, and Qui could kill them with knives. I had never killed one at all, had never slaughtered any animal. I had spent most of my time with T'Gatoi while my brother and sisters were learning the family business. T'Gatoi had been right. I should have been the one to go to the call box. At least I could do that.

I went to the corner cabinet where my mother kept her large house and garden tools. At the back of the cabinet there was a pipe that carried off waste water from the kitchen—except that it didn't anymore. My father had rerouted the waste water below before I was born. Now the pipe could be turned so that one half slid around the other and a rifle could be stored inside. This wasn't our only gun, but it was our most easily accessible one. I would have to use it to shoot one of the biggest of the achti. Then T'Gatoi would probably confiscate it. Firearms were illegal in the Preserve. There had been incidents right after the Preserve was established—Terrans shooting Tlic, shooting N'Tlic. This was before the joining of families began, before everyone had a personal stake in keeping the peace. No one had shot a Tlic in my lifetime or my mother's, but the law still stood—for our protection, we were told. There were stories of whole Terran families wiped out in reprisal back during the assassinations.

I went out to the cages and shot the biggest achti I could find. It was a handsome breeding male, and my mother would not be pleased to see me bring it in. But it was the right size, and I was in a hurry.

I put the achti's long, warm body over my shoulder—glad that some of the weight I'd gained was muscle—and took it to the kitchen. There, I put the gun back in its hiding place. If T'Gatoi noticed the achti's wounds and demanded the gun, I would give it to her. Otherwise, let it stay where my father wanted it.

I turned to take the achti to her, then hesitated. For several seconds, I stood in front of the closed door wondering why I was suddenly afraid. I knew what was going to happen. I hadn't seen it before but T'Gatoi had shown me diagrams and drawings. She had made sure I knew the truth as soon as I was old enough to understand it.

Yet I did not want to go into that room. I wasted a little time choosing a knife from the carved, wooden box in which my mother kept them. T'Gatoi might want one, I told myself, for the tough, heavily furred hide of the achti.

"Gan!" T'Gatoi called, her voice harsh with urgency.

I swallowed. I had not imagined a single moving of the feet could be so difficult. I realized I was trembling and that shamed me. Shame impelled me through the door.

I put the achti down near T'Gatoi and saw that Lomas was unconscious again. She, Lomas, and I were alone in the room—my mother and sisters probably sent out so they would not have to watch. I envied them.

But my mother came back into the room as T'Gatoi seized the achti. Ignoring the knife I offered her, she extended claws from several of her limbs and slit the achti from throat to anus. She looked at me, her yellow eyes intent. "Hold this man's shoulders, Gan."

I stared at Lomas in panic, realizing that I did not want to touch him, let alone hold him. This would not be like shooting an animal. Not as quick, not as merciful, and, I hoped, not as final, but there was nothing I wanted less than to be part of it.

My mother came forward. "Gan, you hold his right side," she said. "I'll hold his left." And if he came to, he would throw her off without realizing he had done it. She was a tiny woman. She often wondered aloud how she had produced, as she said, such "huge" children.

"Never mind," I told her, taking the man's shoulders. "I'll do it." She hovered nearby.

"Don't worry," I said. "I won't shame you. You don't have to stay and watch."

She looked at me uncertainly, then touched my face in a rare caress. Finally, she went back to her bedroom.

T'Gatoi lowered her head in relief. "Thank you, Gan," she said with courtesy more Terran than Tlic. "That one . . . she is always finding new ways for me to make her suffer."

Lomas began to groan and make choked sounds. I had hoped he would stay unconscious. T'Gatoi put her face near his so that he focused on her.

"I've stung you as much as I dare for now," she told him. "When this is over, I'll sting you to sleep and you won't hurt anymore."

"Please," the man begged. "Wait . . ."

"There's no more time, Bram. I'll sting you as soon as it's over. When T'Khotgif arrives she'll give you eggs to help you heal. It will be over soon."

"T'Khotgif!" the man shouted, straining against my hands.

"Soon, Bram." T'Gatoi glanced at me, then placed a claw against his abdomen slightly to the right of the middle, just below the left rib. There was movement on the right side—tiny, seemingly random pulsations moving his brown flesh, creating a concavity here, a convexity there, over and over until I could see the rhythm of it and knew where the next pulse would be.

Lomas's entire body stiffened under T'Gatoi's claw, though she merely rested it against him as she wound the rear section of her body around his legs. He might break my grip, but he would not break hers. He wept helplessly as she used his pants to tie his hands, then pushed his hands above his head so that I could kneel on the cloth between them and pin them in place. She rolled up his shirt and gave it to him to bite down on.

And she opened him.

His body convulsed with the first cut. He almost tore himself away from me. The sound he made . . . I had never heard such sounds come from anything human. T'Gatoi seemed to pay no attention as she lengthened and deepened the cut, now and then pausing to lick away blood. His blood vessels contracted, reacting to the chemistry of her saliva, and the bleeding slowed.

I felt as though I were helping her torture him, helping her consume him. I knew I would vomit soon, didn't know why I hadn't already. I couldn't possibly last until she was finished.

She found the first grub. It was fat and deep red with his blood—both inside and out. It had already eaten its own egg case but apparently had not yet begun to eat its host. At this stage, it would eat any flesh except its mother's. Let alone, it would have gone on excreting the poisons that had both sickened and alerted Lomas. Eventually it would have begun to eat. By the time it ate its way out of Lomas's flesh, Lomas would be dead or dying—and unable to take revenge on the thing that was killing him. There was always a grace period between the time the host sickened and the time the grubs began to eat him.

T'Gatoi picked up the writhing grub carefully and looked at it, somehow ignoring the terrible groans of the man.

Abruptly, the man lost consciousness.

"Good," T'Gatoi looked down at him. "I wish you Terrans could do that at will." She felt nothing. And the thing she held . . .

It was limbless and boneless at this stage, perhaps fifteen centimeters long and two thick, blind and slimy with blood. It was like a large worm. T'Gatoi put it into the belly of the achti, and it began at once to burrow. It would stay there and eat as long as there was anything to eat.

Probing through Lomas's flesh, she found two more, one of them smaller and more vigorous. "A male!" she said happily. He would be dead before I would. He would be through his metamorphosis and screwing everything that would hold still before his sisters even had limbs. He was the only one to make a serious effort to bite T'Gatoi as she placed him in the achti.

Paler worms oozed to visibility in Lomas's flesh. I closed my eyes. It was worse than finding something dead, rotting, and filled with tiny animal grubs. And it was far worse than any drawing or diagram.

"Ah, there are more," T'Gatoi said, plucking out two long, thick grubs. "You may have to kill another animal, Gan. Everything lives inside you Terrans."

I had been told all my life that this was a good and necessary thing Tlic and Terran did together—a kind of birth. I had believed it until now. I knew birth was painful and bloody, no matter what. But this was something else, something worse. And I wasn't ready to see it. Maybe I never would be. Yet I couldn't not see it. Closing my eyes didn't help.

T'Gatoi found a grub still eating its egg case. The remains of the case were still wired into a blood vessel by their own little tube or hook or whatever. That was the way the grubs were anchored and the way they fed. They took only blood until they were ready to emerge. Then they ate their stretched, elastic egg cases. Then they ate their hosts.

T'Gatoi bit away the egg case, licked away the blood. Did she like the taste? Did childhood habits die hard—or not die at all?

The whole procedure was wrong, alien. I wouldn't have thought anything about her could seem alien to me.

"One more, I think," she said. "Perhaps two. A good family. In a host animal these days, we would be happy to find one or two alive." She glanced at me. "Go outside, Gan, and empty your stomach. Go now while the man is unconscious."

I staggered out, barely made it. Beneath the tree just beyond the front door, I vomited until there was nothing left to bring up. Finally, I stood shaking, tears streaming down my face. I did not know why I was crying, but I could not stop. I went further from the house to avoid being seen. Every time I closed my eyes I saw red worms crawling over redder human flesh.

There was a car coming toward the house. Since Terrans were forbidden motorized vehicles except for certain farm equipment, I knew this must be Lomas's Tlic with Qui and perhaps a Terran doctor. I wiped my face on my shirt, struggled for control.

"Gan," Qui called as the car stopped. "What happened?" He crawled out of the low, round, Tlic-convenient car door. Another Terran crawled out the other side and went into the house without speaking to me. The doctor. With his help and a few eggs, Lomas might make it.

"T'Khotgif Teh?" I said.

The Tlic driver surged out of her car, reared up half her length before me. She was paler and smaller than T'Gatoi—probably born from the body of an animal. Tlic from Terran bodies were always larger as well as more numerous.

"Six young," I told her. "Maybe seven, all alive. At least one male."

"Lomas?" she said harshly. I liked her for the question and the concern in her voice when she asked it. The last coherent thing he had said was her name.

"He's alive," I said.

She surged away to the house without another word.

"She's been sick," my brother said, watching her go. "When I called, I could hear people telling her she wasn't well enough to go out even for this."

I said nothing. I had extended courtesy to the Tlic. Now I didn't want to talk to anyone. I hoped he would go in—out of curiosity if nothing else.

"Finally found out more than you wanted to know, eh?"

I looked at him.

"Don't give me one of *her* looks," he said. "You're not her. You're just her property."

One of her looks. Had I picked up even an ability to imitate her expressions?

"What'd you do, puke?" He sniffed the air. "So now you know what you're in for."

I walked away from him. He and I had been close when we were kids. He would let me follow him around when I was home, and sometimes T'Gatoi would let me bring him along when she took me into the city. But something had happened when he reached adolescence. I never knew what. He began keeping out of T'Gatoi's way. Then he began running away—until he realized there was no "away." Not in the Preserve. Certainly not outside. After that he concentrated on getting his share of every egg that came into the house and on looking out for me in a way that made me all but hate him—a way that clearly said, as long as I was all right, he was safe from the Tlic.

"How was it, really?" he demanded, following me.

"I killed an achti. The young ate it."

"You didn't run out of the house and puke because they ate an achti."

"I had . . . never seen a person cut open before." That was true, and enough for him to know. I couldn't talk about the other. Not with him.

"Oh," he said. He glanced at me as though he wanted to say more, but he kept quiet.

We walked, not really headed anywhere. Toward the back, toward the cages, toward the fields.

"Did he say anything?" Qui asked. "Lomas, I mean."

Who else would he mean? "He said 'T'Khotgif.' "

Qui shuddered. "If she had done that to me, she'd be the last person I'd call for."

"You'd call for her. Her sting would ease your pain without killing the grubs in you."

"You think I'd care if they died?"

No. Of course he wouldn't. Would I?

"Shit!" He drew a deep breath. "I've seen what they do. You think this thing with Lomas was bad? It was nothing."

I didn't argue. He didn't know what he was talking about.

"I saw them eat a man," he said.

I turned to face him. "You're lying!"

"*I saw them eat a man.*" He paused. "It was when I was little. I had been to the Hartmund house and I was on my way home. Halfway here, I saw a man and a Tlic and the man was N'Tlic. The ground was hilly. I was able to hide from them and watch. The Tlic wouldn't open the man because she had nothing to feed the grubs. The man couldn't go any further and there were no houses around. He was in so much pain, he told her to kill him. He begged her to kill him. Finally, she did. She cut his throat. One swipe of one claw. I saw the grubs eat their way out, then burrow in again, still eating."

His words made me see Lomas's flesh again, parasitized, crawling. "Why didn't you tell me that?" I whispered.

He looked startled as though he'd forgotten I was listening. "I don't know."

"You started to run away not long after that, didn't you?"

"Yeah. Stupid. Running inside the Preserve. Running in a cage."

I shook my head, said what I should have said to him long ago. "She wouldn't take you, Qui. You don't have to worry."

"She would . . . if anything happened to you."

"No. She'd take Xuan Hoa. Hoa . . . wants it." She wouldn't if she had stayed to watch Lomas.

"They don't take women," he said with contempt.

"They do sometimes." I glanced at him. "Actually, they prefer women. You should be around them when they talk among themselves. They say women have more body fat to protect the grubs. But they usually take men to leave the women free to bear their own young."

"To provide the next generation of host animals," he said, switching from contempt to bitterness.

"It's more than that!" I countered. Was it?

"If it were going to happen to me, I'd want to believe it was more, too."

"It *is* more!" I felt like a kid. Stupid argument.

"Did you think so while T'Gatoi was picking worms out of that guy's guts?"

"It's not supposed to happen that way."

"Sure it is. You weren't supposed to see it, that's all. And his Tlic was supposed to do it. She could sting him unconscious and the operation wouldn't have been as painful. But she'd still open him, pick out the grubs, and if she missed even one, it would poison him and eat him from the inside out."

There was actually a time when my mother told me to show respect for Qui because he was my older brother. I walked away, hating him. In his way, he was gloating. He was safe and I wasn't. I could have hit him, but I didn't think I would be able to stand it when he refused to hit back, when he looked at me with contempt and pity.

He wouldn't let me get away. Longer legged, he swung ahead of me and made me feel as though I were following him.

"I'm sorry," he said.

I strode on, sick and furious.

"Look, it probably won't be that bad with you. T'Gatoi likes you. She'll be careful."

I turned back toward the house, almost running from him.

"Has she done it to you yet?" he asked, keeping up easily. "I mean, you're about the right age for implantation. Has she—"

I hit him. I didn't know I was going to do it, but I think I meant to kill him. If he hadn't been bigger and stronger, I think I would have.

He tried to hold me off, but in the end, had to defend himself. He only hit me a couple of times. That was plenty. I don't remember going down, but when I came to, he was gone. It was worth the pain to be rid of him.

I got up and walked slowly toward the house. The back was dark. No one was in the kitchen. My mother and sisters were sleeping in their bedrooms— or pretending to.

Once I was in the kitchen, I could hear voices—Tlic and Terran from the next room. I couldn't make out what they were saying—didn't want to make it out.

I sat down at my mother's table, waiting for quiet. The table was smooth and worn, heavy and well crafted. My father had made it for her just before he died. I remembered hanging around underfoot when he built it. He didn't mind. Now I sat leaning on it, missing him. I could have talked to him. He had done it three times in his long life. Three clutches of eggs, three times being opened up and sewed up. How had he done it? How did anyone do it?

I got up, took the rifle from its hiding place, and sat down again with it. It needed cleaning, oiling.

All I did was load it.

"Gan?"

She made a lot of little clicking sounds when she walked on bare floor, each limb clicking in succession as it touched down. Waves of little clicks.

She came to the table, raised the front half of her body above it, and surged onto it. Sometimes she moved so smoothly she seemed to flow like water itself. She coiled herself into a small hill in the middle of the table and looked at me.

"That was bad," she said softly. "You should not have seen it. It need not be that way."

"I know."

"T'Khotgif—Ch'Khotgif now—she will die of her disease. She will not live to raise her children. But her sister will provide for them, and for Bram Lomas." Sterile sister. One fertile female in every lot. One to keep the family going. That sister owed Lomas more than she could ever repay.

"He'll live then?"

"Yes."

"I wonder if he would do it again."

"No one would ask him to do that again."

I looked into the yellow eyes, wondering how much I saw and understood there, and how much I only imagined. "No one ever asks us," I said. "You never asked me."

She moved her head slightly. "What's the matter with your face?"

"Nothing. Nothing important." Human eyes probably wouldn't have noticed the swelling in the darkness. The only light was from one of the moons, shining through a window across the room.

"Did you use the rifle to shoot the achti?"

"Yes."

"And do you mean to use it to shoot me?"

I stared at her, outlined in the moonlight—coiled, graceful body. "What does Terran blood taste like to you?"

She said nothing.

"What are you?" I whispered. "What are we to you?"

She lay still, rested her head on her topmost coil. "You know me as no other does," she said softly. "You must decide."

"That's what happened to my face," I told her.

"What?"

"Qui goaded me into deciding to do something. It didn't turn out very well." I moved the gun slightly, brought the barrel up diagonally under my own chin. "At least it was a decision I made."

"As this will be."

"Ask me, Gatoi."

"For my children's lives?"

She would say something like that. She knew how to manipulate people, Terran and Tlic. But not this time.

"I don't want to be a host animal," I said. "Not even yours."

It took her a long time to answer. "We use almost no host animals these days," she said. "You know that."

"You use us."

"We do. We wait long years for you and teach you and join our families to yours." She moved restlessly. "You know you aren't animals to us."

I stared at her, saying nothing.

"The animals we once used began killing most of our eggs after implantation long before your ancestors arrived," she said softly. "You know these things, Gan. Because your people arrived, we are relearning what it means to be a healthy, thriving people. And your ancestors, fleeing from their homeworld, from their own kind who would have killed or enslaved them—they survived because of us. We saw them as people and gave them the Preserve when they still tried to kill us as worms."

At the word "worms," I jumped. I couldn't help it, and she couldn't help noticing it.

"I see," she said quietly. "Would you really rather die than bear my young, Gan?"

I didn't answer.

"Shall I go to Xuan Hoa?"

"Yes!" Hoa wanted it. Let her have it. She hadn't had to watch Lomas. She'd be proud. . . . Not terrified.

T'Gatoi flowed off the table onto the floor, startling me almost too much.

"I'll sleep in Hoa's room tonight," she said. "And sometime tonight or in the morning, I'll tell her."

This was going too fast. My sister Hoa had had almost as much to do with raising me as my mother. I was still close to her—not like Qui. She could want T'Gatoi and still love me.

"Wait! Gatoi!"

She looked back, then raised nearly half her length off the floor and turned to face me. "These are adult things, Gan. This is my life, my family!"

"But she's . . . my sister."

"I have done what you demanded. I have asked you!"

"But—"

"It will be easier for Hoa. She has always expected to carry other lives inside her."

Human lives. Human young who should someday drink at her breasts, not at her veins.

I shook my head. "Don't do it to her, Gatoi." I was not Qui. It seemed I could become him, though, with no effort at all. I could make Xuan Hoa my shield. Would it be easier to know that red worms were growing in her flesh instead of mine?

"Don't do it to Hoa," I repeated.

She stared at me, utterly still.

I looked away, then back at her. "Do it to me."

I lowered the gun from my throat and she leaned forward to take it.

"No," I told her.

"It's the law," she said.

"Leave it for the family. One of them might use it to save my life someday."

She grasped the rifle barrel, but I wouldn't let go. I was pulled into a standing position over her.

"Leave it here!" I repeated. "If we're not your animals, if these are adult things, accept the risk. There is risk, Gatoi, in dealing with a partner."

It was clearly hard for her to let go of the rifle. A shudder went through her and she made a hissing sound of distress. It occurred to me that she was afraid. She was old enough to have seen what guns could do to people. Now her young and this gun would be together in the same house. She did not know about the other guns. In this dispute, they did not matter.

"I will implant the first egg tonight," she said as I put the gun away. "Do you hear, Gan?"

Why else had I been given a whole egg to eat while the rest of the family was left to share one? Why else had my mother kept looking at me as though I were going away from her, going where she could not follow? Did T'Gatoi imagine I hadn't known?

"I hear."

"Now!" I let her push me out of the kitchen, then walked ahead of her toward my bedroom. The sudden urgency in her voice sounded real. "You would have done it to Hoa tonight!" I accused.

"I must do it to someone tonight."

I stopped in spite of her urgency and stood in her way. "Don't you care who?"

She flowed around me and into my bedroom. I found her waiting on the couch we shared. There was nothing in Hoa's room that she could have used. She would have done it to Hoa on the floor. The thought of her doing it to Hoa at all disturbed me in a different way now, and I was suddenly angry.

Yet I undressed and lay down beside her. I knew what to do, what to expect. I had been told all my life. I felt the familiar sting, narcotic, mildly pleasant. Then the blind probing of her ovipositor. The puncture was painless, easy. So easy going in. She undulated slowly against me, her muscles forcing the egg from her body into mine. I held on to a pair of her limbs until I remembered Lomas holding her that way. Then I let go, moved inadvertently, and hurt her. She gave a low cry of pain and I expected to be caged at once within her limbs. When I wasn't, I held on to her again, feeling oddly ashamed.

"I'm sorry," I whispered.

She rubbed my shoulders with four of her limbs.

"Do you care?" I asked. "Do you care that it's me?"

She did not answer for some time. Finally, "You were the one making the choices tonight, Gan. I made mine long ago."

"Would you have gone to Hoa?"

"Yes. How could I put my children into the care of one who hates them?"

"It wasn't . . . hate."

"I know what it was."

"I was afraid."

Silence.

"I still am." I could admit it to her here, now.

"But you came to me . . . to save Hoa."

"Yes." I leaned my forehead against her. She was cool velvet, deceptively soft. "And to keep you for myself," I said. It was so. I didn't understand it, but it was so.

She made a soft hum of contentment. "I couldn't believe I had made such a mistake with you," she said. "I chose you. I believed you had grown to choose me."

"I had, but . . ."

"Lomas."

"Yes."

"I had never known a Terran to see a birth and take it well. Qui has seen one, hasn't he?"

"Yes."

"Terrans should be protected from seeing."

I didn't like the sound of that—and I doubted that it was possible. "Not protected," I said. "Shown. Shown when we're young kids, and shown more than once. Gatoi, no Terran ever sees a birth that goes right. All we see is N'Tlic—pain and terror and maybe death."

She looked down at me. "It is a private thing. It has always been a private thing."

Her tone kept me from insisting—that and the knowledge that if she changed her mind, I might be the first public example. But I had planted the thought in her mind. Chances were it would grow, and eventually she would experiment.

"You won't see it again," she said. "I don't want you thinking any more about shooting me."

The small amount of fluid that came into me with her egg relaxed me as completely as a sterile egg would have, so that I could remember the rifle in my hands and my feelings of fear and revulsion, anger and despair. I could remember the feelings without reviving them. I could talk about them.

"I wouldn't have shot you," I said. "Not you." She had been taken from my father's flesh when he was my age.

"You could have," she insisted.

"Not you." She stood between us and her own people, protecting, interweaving.

"Would you have destroyed yourself?"

I moved carefully, uncomfortable. "I could have done that. I nearly did. That's Qui's 'away.' I wonder if he knows."

"What?"

I did not answer.

"You will live now."

"Yes." *Take care of her,* my mother used to say. Yes.

"I'm healthy and young," she said. "I won't leave you as Lomas was left—alone, N'Tlic. I'll take care of you."

THE ONLY NEAT
THING TO DO

JAMES TIPTREE JR.

JAMES TIPTREE JR. was born in 1968, but his less well-known creator, Alice B. Sheldon, was born in Chicago, Illinois, in 1915, the only child of author Mary Hastings Bradley and explorer and naturalist Herbert Bradley. Sheldon accompanied her parents on several expeditions during her childhood, including one at age five to the Belgian Congo to study mountain gorillas. She pursued a career as a fine artist and graphic designer before marrying in 1934. In 1941 she became the art critic for the *Chicago Sun* but resigned in 1942 to join the U.S. Army where she met and married second husband Huntington Sheldon. In 1952 she moved to Washington with her husband to assist with setting up the Central Intelligence Agency. She resigned from the CIA in 1955, enrolled at American University and received a bachelor's degree in 1959, then received a doctorate in experimental psychology from George Washington University in 1967.

The story goes that, on the day she completed her doctorate, Sheldon was exhausted and unable to sleep. For relaxation, she wrote a science fiction short story. That story, and a host of other classic stories, began to appear in 1968 under the byline James Tiptree Jr.—a name taken from a popular brand of marmalade. To quote critic John Clute, "she wrote like a man, and a meteor, a flash in the pan, a mayfly angel." The best of her stories—"Houston, Houston, Do You Read?" "Love Is the Plan, the Plan Is

Death," "And I Awoke and Found Me Here on the Cold Hill's Side," and "Her Smoke Rose Up Forever"—are some of the finest in the field. She wrote several novels but is best known for her short fiction, published in the landmark collections *Ten Thousand Light Years from Home, Warm Worlds and Otherwise,* and *Star Songs of an Old Primate.* Sheldon's work was awarded the Hugo Award twice, the Nebula Award three times, the Locus Award twice, and the World Fantasy Award. A collection of her best short fiction, *Her Smoke Rose Up Forever,* is due to be reprinted in 2004.

Sheldon once said of her work, "My true desire is to grab people by the heart or the collar-button and hiss 'Listen! Listen and think, you dolt! Feel how it really is! Let me inscribe a little fable on your nose that will carry more than the words with it when you look in the mirror! . . .' Something like that. Cautionary tales, incarnated in entertainment. . . ."

* * *

H EROES OF SPACE! Explorers of the starfields!
Reader, here is your problem:

Given one kid, yellow-head, snub-nose-freckles, green-eyes-that-stare-at-you-level, rich-brat, girl-type, fifteen-year-old. And all she's dreamed of, since she was old enough to push a hologram button, are heroes of the First Contacts, explorers of far stars, the great names of Humanity's budding Star Age. She can name you the crew of every Discovery Mission; she can sketch you a pretty accurate map of Federation Space and number the Frontier Bases; she can tell you who first contacted every one of the fifty-odd races known; and she knows by heart the last words of Han Lu Han when, himself no more than sixteen, he ran through alien flame-weapons to drag his captain and pilot to safety on Lyrae 91-Beta. She does a little math, too; it's easy for her. And she haunts the spaceport and makes friends with everybody who'll talk to her, and begs rides, and knows the controls of fourteen models of craft. She's a late bloomer, which means the nubbins on her little chest could almost pass for a boy's; and love, great Love, to her is just something pointless that adults do, despite her physical instruction. But she can get into her junior space suit in seventy seconds flat, including safety hooks.

So you take this girl, this Coati Cass—her full name is Coatillia Canada Cass, but everyone calls her Coati—

And you give her a sturdy little space-coupe for her sixteenth birthday.

Now, here is your problem:

Does she use it to jaunt around the star-crowded home sector, visiting her classmates and her family's friends, as her mother expects, and sometimes showing off by running a vortex beacon or two, as her father fears?

Does she? Really?

Or—does she head straight for the nearest ship-fitters and blow most of her credit balance loading extra fuel tanks and long-range sensors onto the coupe, fuel it to the nozzles, and then—before the family's accountant can raise questions—hightail for the nearest Federation frontier, which is the Great North Rift beyond FedBase 900, where you can look right out at unknown space and stars?

That wasn't much of a problem, was it?

The exec of FedBase 900 watches the yellow head bobbing down his main view corridor.

"We ought to signal her folks *c*-skip collect," he mutters. "I gather they're rich enough to stand it."

"On what basis?" his deputy inquires.

They both watch the little straight-backed figure marching away. A tall patrol captain passes in the throng; they see the girl spin to stare at him, not with womanly appreciation but with the open-eyed unselfconscious adoration of a kid. Then she turns back to the dazzling splendor of the view beyond the port. The end of the Rift is just visible from this side of the asteroid Base 900 is dug into.

"On the basis that I have a hunch that that infant is trouble looking for a place to happen," Exec says mournfully. "On the basis that I don't believe her story, I guess. Oh, her ident's all in order—I've no doubt she owns that ship and knows how to run it, and knows the regs; and it's her right to get cleared for where she wants to go—by a couple of days. But I cannot believe her parents consented to her tooting out here just to take a look at unknown stars. . . . On the basis that if they did, they're certifiable imbeciles. If she were my daughter—"

His voice trails off. He knows he's overreacting emotionally; he has no adequate excuse for signaling her folks.

"They must have agreed," his deputy says soothingly. "Look at those extra fuel tanks and long-range mechs they gave her."

(Coati hadn't actually lied. She'd told him that her parents raised no objection to her coming out here—true, since they'd never dreamed of it—and added artlessly, "See the extra fuel tanks they put on my ship so I'll be sure to get home from long trips? Oh, sir, I'm calling her the *CC-One*; will that sound too much like something official?")

Exec closes the subject with a pessimistic grunt, and they turn back into his office, where the patrol captain is waiting. FedBase 900's best depot supply team is long overdue, and it is time to declare them officially missing, and initiate and organize a search.

Coati Cass continues on through the surface sections of the base to the fueling port. She had to stop here to get clearance and the holocharts of the frontier area, and she can top off her tanks. If it weren't for those charts, she might have risked going straight on out, for fear they'd stop her. But now that she's cleared, she's enjoying her first glimpse of a glamorous Far FedBase—so long as it doesn't delay her start for her goal, her true goal, so long dreamed of: free, unexplored space and unknown, unnamed stars.

Far Bases *are* glamorous; the Federation had learned the hard way that they must be pleasant, sanity-promoting duty. So, the farther out a base is, and the longer the tours, the more lavishly it is set up and maintained. Base 900 is built mostly inside a big, long-orbit, airless rock, yet it has gardens and pools that would be the envy of a world's richest citizen. Coati sees displays for the tiny theater advertising first-run shows and music, all free to station personnel; and she passes half a dozen different exotic little places to eat. Inside the rock the maps show sports and dance shells, spacious private quarters, and winding corridors, all nicely planted and decorated, because it has been found that stress is greatly reduced if there are plenty of alternate, private routes for people to travel to their daily duties.

Building a Far Base is a full-scale Federation job. But it conserves the Federation's one irreplaceable resource—her people. Here at Fed 900 the people are largely Human, since the other four spacefaring races are concentrated to the Federation's south and east. This far north, Coati has glimpsed only one alien couple, both Swain; their greenish armor is familiar to her from the spaceport back home. She won't find really exotic aliens here.

But what, and who, lives out there on the fringes of the Rift?—not to speak of its unknown farther shores? Coati pauses to take a last look before she turns in to Fuels and Supply. From this port she can really see the Rift, like a strange irregular black cloud lying along the northern zenith.

The Rift isn't completely lightless, of course. It is merely an area that holds comparatively few stars. The scientists regard it as no great mystery; a standing wave or turbulence in the density-texture, a stray chunk of the same gradients that create the galactic arms with their intervening gaps. Many other such rifts are seen in uninhabited reaches of the starfield. This one just happens to form a useful northern border for the irregular globe of Federation Space.

Explorers have penetrated it here and there, enough to know that the usual distribution of star systems appears to begin again on the farther side. A few probable planetary systems have been spotted out there; and once or twice what might be alien transmissions have been picked up at extreme range. But nothing and no one has come at them from the far side, and meanwhile the Federation of Fifty Races, expanding slowly to the south and east, has enough on its platter without hunting out new contacts. Thus, the Rift has been left almost undisturbed. It is the near presence of the Rift that made it possible for Coati to get to a real frontier so fast, from her centrally located home star and her planet of Cayman's Port.

Coati gives it all one last ardent look, and ducks into the suiting-up corridor, where her small suit hangs among the real spacers'. From here she issues onto a deck over the asteroid surface, and finds *CC-One* dwarfed by a new neighbor; a big Patrol cruiser has come in. She makes her routine shell inspection with disciplined care despite her excitement, and presently signals for the tug to slide her over to the fueling stations. Here she will also get oxy, water, and food—standard rations only. She's saved enough credit for a good supply if she avoids all luxuries.

At Fuels she's outside again, personally checking every tank. The Fuels chief, a big rosy woman whose high color glows through her faceplate, grins at the kid's eagerness. A junior fuelsman is doing the actual work, kidding Coati about her array of spares.

"You going to cross the Rift?"

"Maybe next trip. . . . Someday for sure," she grins back.

A news announcement breaks in. It's a pleasant voice telling them that DRS Number 914 B-K is officially declared missing, and a Phase One search will start. All space personnel are to keep watch for a standard supply tug, easily identifiable by its train of tanks, last seen in the vicinity of Ace's Landing.

"No, correction, negative on Ace's Landing. Last depot established was on a planet at seventeen-fifty north, fifteen-thirty west, RD Eighteen." The voice repeats. "That's far out in Quadrant Nine B-Z, out of commo range. They were proceeding to a new system at thirty-twenty north, forty-two-twenty-eight west, RD Thirty.

"All ships within possible range of this course will maintain a listening watch for one minim on the hour. Anything heard warrants return to Base range. Meanwhile a recon ship will be dispatched to follow their route from Ace's Landing."

The announcer repeats all coordinates; Coati, finding no tablet handy, inscribes the system they're headed to on the inside of her bare arm with her stylus.

"If they were beyond commo range, how did they report?" she asks the Fuels chief.

"By message pipe. Like a teeny-weeny spaceship. They can make up to three *c*-skip jumps. When you work beyond range, you send back a pipe after every stop. There'll soon be a commo relay set up for that quadrant, is my guess."

"Depot Resupply 914 B-K," says the fuelsman. "That's Boney and Ko. The two boys who—who're—who aren't—I mean, they don't have all their rivets, right?"

"There's nothing wrong with Boney and Ko!" The Fuels chief's flush heightens. "They may not have the smarts of some people, but the things they do, they do 100 percent perfect. And one of them—or both, maybe—has uncanny ability with holocharting. If you go through the charts of quadrants they've worked, you'll see how many B-K corrections there are. That work will save lives! And they haven't a gram of meanness or pride between them; they do it all on supply pay, for loyalty to the Fed." She's running down, glancing at Coati to see if her message carried. "That's why Exec took them off the purely routine runs and let them go set up new depots up north . . . . The Rand twins have the nearby refill runs now; they can take the boredom because of their music."

"Sorry," the fuelsman says. "I didn't know. They never say a word."

"Yeah, they don't talk," the chief grins. "There, kid, I guess you're about topped up, unless you want to carry some in your ditty bag. Now, how about the food?"

When Coati gets back inside Base and goes to Charts for her final briefing, she sees what the Fuels chief meant. On all the holocharts that cover the fringes of 900's sector, feature after feature shows corrections marked with a tiny glowing "B-K." She can almost follow the long, looping journeys of the pair—what was it? Boney and Ko—by the areas of richer detail in the charts. Dust clouds, g-anomalies, asteroid swarms, extra primaries in multiple systems—all modestly B-K's. The basic charts are composites of the work of early explorers—somebody called Ponz has scrawled in twenty or thirty star systems with his big signature (B-K have corrected six of them), and there's an

"L," and a lot of "YBCs," and more that Coati can't decipher. She'd love to know their names and adventures.

"Who's 'SS'?" she asks Charts.

"Oh, he was a rich old boy, a Last War vet, who tried to take a shortcut he remembered and jumped himself out of fuel way out there. He was stuck about forty-five standard days before anybody could get to him, and after he calmed down, he and his pals kept themselves busy with a little charting. Not bad, too, for a static VP. See how the SS's all center around this point? That's where he sat. If you go near there, remember the error is probably on the radius. But you aren't thinking of heading out *that* far, are you, kid?"

"Oh, well," Coati temporizes. She's wondering if Charts would report her to Exec. "Someday, maybe. I just like to have the charts to, you know, dream over."

Charts chuckles sympathetically, and starts adding up her charges. "Lots of daydreaming you got here, girl."

"Yeah." To distract him she asks, "Who's 'Ponz'?"

"Before my time. He disappeared somewhere after messaging that he'd found a real terraform planet way out that way." Charts points to the northwest edge, where there's a string of GO-type stars. "Could be a number of good planets there. The farthest one out is where the Lost Colony was. And that you stay strictly away from, by the way, if you ever get that far. Thirty-five-twelve N—that's thirty-five minutes twelve seconds north—thirty-forty west, radial distance—we omit the degrees; out here they're constants—eighty-nine degrees north by seventy west—that's from Base 900, they all are—thirty-two Bkm. Some sort of contagion wiped them out just after I came. We've posted warning satellites. . . . All right, now you have to declare your destination. You're entitled to free charts there; the rest you pay for."

"Where do you recommend? For my first trip?"

"For your first trip . . . I recommend you take the one beacon route we have, up to Ace's Landing. That's two beacons, three jumps. It's a neat place: hut, freshwater lake, the works. Nobody lives there, but we have a rock hound who takes all his long leaves there, with a couple of pals. You can take out your scopes and have a spree; everything you're looking at is unexplored. And it's just about in commo range if you hit it lucky."

"How can places be out of commo range? I keep hearing that."

"It's the Rift. Relativistic effects out here where the density changes. Oh, you can pick up the frequency, but the noise, the garble factor is hopeless.

Some people claim even electronic gear acts up as you really get into the Rift itself."

"How much do they charge to stay at the hut?"

"Nothing, if you bring your own chow and bag. Air and water're perfect."

"I might want to make an excursion farther on to look at something I've spotted in the scope."

"Green. We'll adjust the chart fee when you get back. But if you run around, watch out for this vortex situation here." Charts pokes his stylus into the holo, north of Ace's Landing. "Nobody's sure yet whether it's a bunch of little ones or a great big whopper of a g-pit. And remember, the holos don't fit together too well—" He edges a second chart into the first display; several stars are badly doubled.

"Right. And I'll keep my eyes open and run a listening watch for that lost ship, B-K's."

"You do that. . . ." He tallies up an amount that has her credit balance scraping bottom. "I sure hope they turn up soon. It's not like them to go jazzing off somewhere. . . . Green, here you are."

She tenders her voucher-chip. "It's go," she grins. "Barely."

Still suited, lugging her pouch of chart cassettes, Coati takes a last look through the great view-wall of the main corridor. She has a decision to make. Two decisions, really, but this one isn't fun—she has to do something about her parents, and without giving herself away to anybody who checks commo. Her parents must be signaling all over home sector by now. She winces mentally, then has an idea: Her sister on a planet near Cayman's has married enough credits to accept any number of collect 'skips, and it would be logical— Yes.

Commo is two doors down.

"You don't need to worry," she tells a lady named Paula. "My brother-in-law is the planet banker. You can check him in that great big ephemeris there. Javelo, Hunter Javelo."

Cautiously, Paula does so. What she finds on Port-of-Princes reassures her enough to accept this odd girl's message. Intermittently sucking her stylus, Coati writes:

"Dearest Sis, Surprise! I'm out at FedBase 900. It's wonderful. Will look around a bit and head home stopping by you. Tell folks all O.K., ship goes like dream and million thanks. Love, Coati."

There! That ought to do it without alerting anybody. By the time her father messages FedBase 900, if he does, she'll be long gone.

And now, she tells herself, heading out to the port, now for the big one. Where exactly should she go?

Well, she can always take Charts' advice and have a good time on Ace's Landing, scanning the skies and planning her next trip. She's become just a little impressed by the hugeness of space and the chill of the unknown. Suppose she gets caught in an uncharted gravity vortex? She's been in only one, and it was small, and a good pilot was flying. (That was one of the flights she didn't tell her folks about.) And there's always next time.

On the other hand, she's *here* now, and all set. And her folks could raise trouble next time she sets out. Isn't it better to do all she can while she can do it?

Well, like what, for instance?

Her ears had pricked up at Charts' remark about those GO-type suns. And one of them was where the poor lost team was headed for; she has the coordinates on her wrist. What if she found them! Or—what if she found a fine terraform planet, and got to name it?

The balance of decision, which had never really leveled, tilts decisively toward a vision of yellow suns—as Coati all but runs into the ramp edge leading out.

A last flicker of caution reminds her that, whatever her goal, her first outward leg must be the beacon route to Ace's. At the first beacon turn, she'll have time to think it over and really make up her mind.

She finds that *CC-One* has been skidded out of Fuels and onto the edge of the standard-thrust takeoff area. She hikes out and climbs in, unaware that she's broadcasting a happy hum. This is IT! She's really, really, at last, on her way!

Strapping in, preparing to lift, she takes out a ration snack and bites it open. She was too broke to eat at Base. Setting course and getting into drive will give her time to digest it; she has a superstitious dislike of going into cold-sleep with a full tummy. Absolutely nothing is supposed to go on during cold-sleep, and she's been used to it since she was a baby, but the thought of that foreign lump of food in there always bothers her. What puts it in stasis before it's part of her? What if it decided to throw itself up?

So she munches as she sets the holochart data in her computer, leaving FedBase 900 far below. She's delightedly aware that the most real part of her life is about to begin. Amid the radiance of unfamiliar stars, the dark Rift in her front view-ports, she completes the course to Beacon 900-One AL, and listens to the big *c*-skip converters, the heart of her ship, start the cooling-down process. The *c*-skip drive unit must be supercooled to near absolute zero to work the half-understood miracle by which reciprocal gravity fields will be perturbed, and *CC-One* and herself translated to the target at relativistic speed.

As the first clicks and clanks of cooling resound through the shell, she hangs up her suit, opens her small-size sleep chest, gets in, and injects herself. Her feelings as she pulls the lid down are those of a child of antique Earth as it falls asleep to awake on Christmas morning. Thank the All for cold-sleep, she thinks drowsily. It gave us the stars. Imagine those first brave explorers who had to live and age, to stay awake through all the days, the months, the years. . . .

SHE WAKENS IN what at first glance appears to be about the same starfield, but when she's closed the chest, rubbing her behind where the antisleep injections hit she sees that the Rift looks different.

It's larger, and—why, it's all around the ship! Tendrils of dark almost close behind her. She's in one of the fringy star-clumps that stick out into the Rift. And the starfield looks dull, apart from a few blazing suns—of course, there aren't any nearby stars! Or rather, there are a few very near, and then an emptiness where all the middle-distance suns should be. Only the far, faint star-tapestry lies beyond.

The ship is full of noise; as she comes fully awake she understands that the beacon signal and her mass-proximity indicator are both tweeting and blasting away. She tunes them down, locates the beacon, and puts the ship into a low orbit around it. This beacon, like FedBase, is set on a big asteroid that gives her just enough g's to stabilize.

Very well. If she's going to Ace's Landing, she'll just set in the coordinates for Beacon 900-Two AL, and go back to sleep. But if she's going to look at those yellow suns, she must get out her charts and work up a safe two- or three-leg course to one of them.

She can't simply set in their coordinates and fly straight there, even if there were no bodies actually in the way, because the 'skip drive is built to turn off and wake her up if she threatens to get too deep in a strong gravity field, or encounters an asteroid swarm or some other space hazard. So she has to work out corridors that pass really far away from any strong bodies or known problems.

Decide. . . . But, face it, hasn't she already decided, when she stabilized here? She doesn't need that much time to punch in Beacon Two! . . . Yes.

She *has* to go somewhere really wild. A hut on Ace's Landing is just not what she came out here for. Those unknown yellow suns *are* . . . and maybe she could do something useful, like finding the missing men; there's an off chance. The neat thing to do might be to go by small steps, Ace's Landing first—but the *really* neat course is to take advantage of all she's learned and not to risk being forbidden to come back. Green, go!

She's been busy all this while, threading cassettes and getting them lined up for those GO suns. As Charts had warned her, edges don't fit well. She's working at forcing two holos into a cheap frame made for one, when her mass-proximity tweeter goes off.

She glances up, ready to duck or deflect a sky-rock. Amazed, she sees something unmistakably artificial ahead. A ship? It grows larger—but not large enough, not at the rate it's coming. It'll pass her clean. Whatever can it be? Visions of the mythical tiny ship full of tiny aliens jump to her mind.

It's so small—why, she could pick it up! Without really thinking, she spins *CC-One*'s attitude and comes parallel, alongside the object. She's good at tricky little accelerations. The thing seems to put on speed as she idles up. Touched by chase fever, she mutters, "Oh, no, you don't!" and extrudes the rather inadequate manipulator arm.

As she does so, she realizes what it is. But she's too excited to think, she plucks it neatly out of space, and after a bit of trying, twists it into her cargo lock, shuts the port behind it, and refills with air.

She's caught herself a message pipe! Bound from the gods know where to FedBase. It was changing course at Beacon One, like herself, hence moving slowly. Has she committed an official wrong? Is there some penalty for interfering with official commo?

Well, she's put her spoon in the soup, she might as well drink it. It'll take a while for the pipe to warm to touchability. So she goes on working her charts, intending merely to take a peek at the message and then send the little thing on its way. Surely such a small pause won't harm anything—pipes are used because the sender's out of range, not because they're fast.

She hasn't a doubt she can start it going, again. She's seen that it's covered with instructions. Like all Federation space gear, it's fixed to be usable by amateurs in an emergency.

Impatiently she completes a chart and goes to fish the thing out of the port while it's still so cold she has to put on gloves. When she undogs its little hatch, a cloud of golden motes drifts out, distracting her so that she brushes her bare wrist against the metal when she reaches for the cassette inside. Ouch!

She glances at her arm, hoping she hasn't given herself a nasty cold-burn. Nothing to be seen but an odd dusty scratch. No redness. But she can feel the nerve twitch deep in her forearm. Funny! She brushes at it, and takes out the cassette with more care. It's standard record; she soon has it threaded in her voder.

The voice that speaks is so thick and blurry that she backs up and restarts, to hear better.

"Supply and Recon Team Number 914 B-K reporting," she makes out. Excitedly she recognizes the designation. Why, that's the missing ship! This *is* important. She should relay it to Base at once. But surely it won't hurt to listen to the rest?

The voice is saying that a new depot has been established at thirty-twenty north, forty-two-twenty-eight west, RD Thirty. That's one of the yellow suns' planets, and the coordinates Coati has on her wrist. "Ninety-five percent terraform." The voice has cleared a little.

It goes on to say that they will work back to FedBase, stopping to check a highly terraform planet they've spotted at eighteen-ten north, twenty-eight-thirty west, RD Thirty, in the same group of suns. "But—uh—" The voice stops, then resumes.

"Some things happened at thirty-twenty. There're people there. I guess we have to report a, uh, First Contact. They—"

A second voice interrupts abruptly.

"We did just like the manual! The manual for First Contacts."

"Yeah," resumes the first voice. "It worked fine. They were really friendly. They even had a few words from Galactic, and the signals. But they—"

"The wreck. The wreck! Tell them," says the other voice.

"Oh. Well, yeah. There's a wreck there, an old RB. Real old. You can't see the rescue flag; it has big stuff growing on it. We think it's Ponz. So maybe it's his First Contact." The voice sounds unmistakably downcast. "Boss can decide. . . . Anyway, they have some kind of treatment they give you, like a pill to make you smart. It takes two days; you sleep a lot. Then they let you out and you can understand everything. I mean—everything! It was—we never had anything like that before. Everybody talking and understanding everybody! See how we can talk now? But it's funny. . . . Anyway, they helped us find a place with a level site, and we fixed up a fuel dump really nice. We—"

"What they looked like!" the other voice bursts in. "Never mind us. Tell about them, what they looked like and how they did."

"Oh, sure. Well. Big white bodies with fur all over. And six legs—they mostly walk on the back four; the top two are like arms. They have like long bodies, long white cats, big; when they rear up to look, they're over our heads. And they have. . . ." Here the voice stammers, as if finding it hard to speak. "They have like two, uh, private parts. Two sets, I mean. Some of them. And their faces"—the voice runs on, relieved—"their faces are *fierce*. Some teeth! When they came and looked in first, we were pretty nervous. And big eyes, sort of like mixed-up people and animals. Cats. But they acted friendly, they gave back the signals, so we came out. That was when they grabbed us and pushed their heads onto ours. Then they let go, and acted like something was wrong. I heard one say 'Ponz,' and like 'Lashley' or 'Leslie.'"

"Leslie was with Ponz, I told you," says the second.

"Yeah. So then they grabbed us again, and held on, and that was when they gave the treatment. I think something went into me, I can still hear like a voice. Ko says, him, too. . . . Oh, and there were young ones and some others running around on an island; they said they're not like them until they get the treatment. 'Drons,' they called the young ones. And afterward they're 'Ee-ah-drons.' The ones we talked to. It's sort of confusing. Like the Ee-ah are people, too. But you don't see them." His voice—it must be Boney—runs down. "Is that all?" Coati hears him ask aside.

"Yeah, I guess so," the other voice—Ko—replies. "We better get started, we got one more stop . . . and I don't feel so good anymore. I wish we was home."

"Me, too. Funny, we felt so great. Well, DRS 914 B-K signing off. . . . I guess this is the longest record we ever sent, huh? Oh, we have some corrections to send. Stand by."

After a long drone of coordinate corrections, the record ends.

Coati sits pensive, trying to sort out the account. It's clear that a new race has been contacted, and they seem friendly. Yet something about it affects her negatively—she has no desire to rush off and meet the big white six-legs and be given the "smart treatment." Boney and Ko were supposed to be a little—innocent. Maybe they were fooled in some way, taken advantage of? But she can't think why, or what. It's beyond her. . . .

The other thing that's clear is that this should go to Base, fastest. Wasn't there a ship going to follow Boney and Ko's route? That would take them to the cat planet, which is at—she consults her wrist—thirty-twenty north, et cetera. Oh, dear, must she go back? Turn back, abort her trip to deliver this? Why had she been so smart, pulling in other people's business?

But wait. If it's urgent, she could speed it by calling base and reading the message, thus bypassing the last leg. Then surely they wouldn't crack her for interfering! Maybe she's still in commo range.

She powers up the transponder and starts calling FedBase 900. Finally a voice responds, barely discernible through the noise. She fiddles with the suppressors and gets it a bit clearer.

"FedBase 900, this is *CC-One* at AL Beacon One. Do you read me? I have intercepted a message pipe from Supply Ship DRS 914 B-K, the missing ship, Boney and Ko." She repeats. "Do you read that?"

"Affirmative, *CC-One*. Message from ship 914 B-K intercepted. What is the message?"

"It's too long to read. But listen—important. They are on their way to a planet at—wait a minim—" She rolls the record back and gets the coordinates. "And before that they stayed at that planet thirty-twenty north—you have the specs. There are people there! It's a First Contact, I think. But listen, they say something's funny. I don't think you should go there until you get the whole message. I'm sending it right on."

"*CC-One,* I lost part of that. Is planet at thirty-twenty north a First Contact?"

Garble is breaking up Commo's voice. Coati shouts as clearly as she can, "Yes! Affirmative! But don't, repeat, do—not—go—there—until you get B-K's original message. I—will—send—pipe—at once. Did you get that?"

"Repeating. . . . Do not proceed to planet thirty-twenty north, forty-two-twenty-eight west until B-K message received. Pipe coming soonest. Green, *CC-One*?"

"Go. If I can't make the pipe work, I'll bring it. *CC-One* signing off." She finishes in a swirl of loud static, and turns her attention to getting the pipe back on its way.

But before she takes the cassette out of the voder, she rechecks the designation of the planet B-K are headed for. Eighteen-ten north. Twenty-eight-thirty west. RD Thirty. That's closer than the First Contact planet; that's right, they said they'd stop there on their way home. She copies the first coordinates off on her workpad, and replaces them on her wrist with the new ones. If she wants to help look for Boney and Ko, she could go straight there—but of course she hasn't really made up her mind. As she rolls back her sleeve, she notices that her arm still feels odd, but she can't see any trace of a cold-burn. She rubs the arm a couple of times, and it goes away.

"Getting goosey from excitement," she mutters. She has a childish habit of talking aloud to herself when she's alone. She figures it's because she was alone so much as a child, happily playing with her space toys and holos.

Putting the message pipe back on course proves to be absurdly simple. She blows it clean of the yellow powdery stuff, reinserts the cassette, and ejects it beside the viewports. Fascinated, she watches the little ship spin slowly, orienting to its homing frequency broadcast from Base 900. Then, as if satisfied, it begins to glide away, faster and faster. Sure enough, as well as she can judge, it's headed down the last leg from Beacon One to FedBase. Neat! She's never heard of pipes before; there must be all kinds of marvelous frontier gadgets that'll be new to her.

She has a guilty twinge as she sees it go. Isn't it her duty to go nearer back to Base and read the whole thing? Could the men be in some kind of trouble where every minim counts? But they sounded green, only maybe a little tired. And she understands it's their routine to send a pipe after every stop. If some of those corrections are important, she could never read them straight; her voice would give out. Better they have Boney's own report.

She turns back to figuring out her course, and finds she was fibbing: she has indeed made up her mind. She'll just go to the planet B-K were headed for and see if she can find them there. Maybe they got too sick to move on, maybe they found another alien race they got involved with. Maybe their ship's in trouble. . . . Any number of reasons they could be late, and she *might* be helpful. And now she knows enough about the pipes to know that they can't be sent from a planet's surface. Only from above atmosphere. So if Boney and Ko can't lift, they can't message for help—by pipe, at least.

She's half-talking this line of reasoning out to herself as she works on the holocharts. Defining and marking in a brand-new course for the computer is far more work than she'd realized; the school problems she had done must have been chosen for easy natural corridors. "Oh, gods . . . I've got to erase again; there's an asteroid path there. Help! I'll never get off this beacon at this rate—explorers must have spent half their time mapping!"

As she mutters, she becomes aware of something like an odd little echo in the ship. She looks around; the cabin is tightly packed with shiny cases of supplies. "Got my acoustics all buggered up," she mutters. That must be it. But there seems to be a peculiar delay; for example, she hears the word "Help!" so tiny-clear that she actually spends a few minim searching the nearby racks. Could a talking animal pet or something have got in at Far Base? Oh, the poor creature. Unless she can somehow get it in cold-sleep, it'll die.

But nothing more happens, and she decides it's just the new acoustical re flections. And at last she achieves a good, safe three-leg course to that system at eighteen-ten north. She's pretty sure an expert could pick out a shorter, elegant, two-leg line, but she doesn't want to risk being waked up by some unforeseen obstacle. So she picks routes lined by well-corrected red dwarfs and other barely visible sky features. These charts are living history, she thinks. Not like the anonymous holos back home, where everything is checked a hundred times a year, and they give you only tripstrips. In these charts she can read the actual hands of the old explorers. The man Ponz, for instance—he must have spent a lot of time working around the route to the yellow suns, before he landed on thirty-twenty and crashed and died. . . . But she's dawdling now. She stacks the marked cassettes in order in her computer take-up, and clicks the first one in. To the unknown, at last!

She readies her cold-sleep chest and hops in. As she relaxes, she notices she still has a strange sensation of being accompanied by something or someone. "Maybe because I'm sort of one of the company of space now," she tells herself romantically, and visualizes a future chart with a small "CC" correction. Hah! She laughs aloud, drowsily, in the darkness, feeling great. An almost physical rosy glow envelops her as she sinks to dreamless stasis.

She can take off thus unconscious amid pathless space with no real fear of getting lost and being unable to return, because of a marvelously simple little gadget carried by all jumpships—a time-lapse recorder in the vessel's tail, which clicks on unceasingly, recording the star scene behind. It's accelerated by motion in the field, and slows to resting state when the field is static. So, whenever the pilot wishes to retrace his route, he has only to take out the appropriate cassette and put it up front in his guidance computer. The computer will hunt until it duplicates the starfield sequences of the outward path, thus bringing the ship infallibly, if somewhat slowly, back along the course it came.

SHE WAKES AND JUMPS out to see a really new star scene—a great sprawl of radiant golden suns against a very dark arm of Rift. The closest star of the group, she finds, is eighteen-ten north, just as she's calculated! The drive has cut off at the margin of its near gravity field; it will be a long thrust drive in.

Excitement like a sunrise is flooding her. She's made it! Her first solo jump!

And with the mental joy is still that physical glow, so strong it puzzles her for a minim. Physical, definitely; it's kind of like the buzz of self-stimulation, but without the sticky-sickly feeling that self-stimulation usually gives her. Their phys ed teacher, who'd showed them how to relieve sex tension, said that the negative quality would go away, but Coati hasn't bothered with it all that very much. Now she thinks that this shows that sheer excitement can activate sex, as the teacher said. "Ah, go away," she mutters impatiently. She's got to start thrust drive and run on in to where the planets could be.

As soon as she's started, she turns to the scope to check. Planets—yes! One—two—four—and there it is! Blue-green and white even at this distance! Boney and Ko had said it tested highly terraform. It looks it, all right, thinks Coati, who has seen only holos of antique Earth. She wonders briefly what the missing nonterraform part could be: irregularities of climate, absence of some major life-forms? It doesn't matter—anything over 75 percent means livable without protective gear, air and water present and good. She'll be able to get out and explore in the greatest comfort—on a *new* world! But are Boney and Ko already there?

When she gets into orbital distance from the planet, she must run a standard search pattern around it. All Federation ships have radar-responsive gear to help locate them. But her little ship doesn't have a real Federation searchscope. She'll have to use her eyes, and fly much too narrow a course. This could be tedious; she sighs.

She finds herself crossing her legs and wriggling and scratching herself idly. Really, this sex overflow is too much! The mental part is fairly calm, though, almost like real happiness. Nice. Only distracting. . . . And, as she leans back to start waiting out the run in, she feels again that sense of *presence* in the ship. Company, companionship. Is she going a little nutters? "Calm down," she tells herself firmly.

A minim of dead silence . . . into which a tiny, tiny voice says distinctly, "Hello . . . hello? Please don't be frightened. Hello?"

It's coming from somewhere behind and above her.

Coati whirls, peers up and around everywhere, seeing nothing new.

"Wh-where are you?" she demands. "Who are you, in here?"

"I am a very small being. You saved my life. Please don't be frightened of me. Hello?"

"Hello," Coati replies slowly, peering around hard. Still she sees nothing. And the voice is still behind her when she turns. She doesn't feel frightened at all, just intensely excited and curious.

"What do you mean, I saved your life?"

"I was clinging to the outside of that artifact you call a message. I would have died soon."

"Well, good." But now Coati *is* a bit frightened. When the voice spoke, she definitely detected movement in her own larynx and tongue—as if she were speaking the words herself. Gods—she *is* going nutters, she's hallucinating! "I'm talking to myself!"

"No, no," the voice—her voice—reassures her. "You are correct—I am using your speech apparatus. Please forgive me; I have none of my own that you could hear."

Coati digests this dubiously. If this is a hallucination, it's really complex. She's never done anything like this before. Could it be real, some kind of alien telekinesis?

"But where are you? Why don't you come out and show yourself?"

"I can't. I will explain. Please promise me you won't be frightened. I have damaged nothing, and I will leave anytime you desire."

Coati suddenly gets an idea, and eyes the computer sharply. In fantasy shows she's seen holos about alien minds taking over computers. So far as she knows, it's never happened in reality. But maybe—

"Are you in my computer?"

"Your computer?" Incredibly, the voice gives what might almost be a giggle. "In a way, yes. I told you I am very, very small. I am in empty places, in your head." Quickly it adds, "You aren't frightened, please? I can go out anytime, but then we can't speak."

"In my head!" Coati exclaims. For some reason she, too, feels like laughing. She knows she should be making some serious response, but all she can think of is, this is why her sinuses feel stuffy. "How did you get in my head?"

"When you rescued me I was incapable of thought. We have a primitive tropism to enter a body and make our way to the head. When I came to myself, I was here. You see, on my home we live in the brains of our host animals. In fact, we are their brains."

"You went through my body? Oh—from that place on my arm?"

"Yes, I must have done. I have only vague, primitive memories. You see, we are really so small. We live in what I think you call intermolecular, maybe interatomic spaces. Our passage doesn't injure anything. To me, your body is as open and porous as your landscape is to you. I didn't realize there was so much large-scale solidity around until I saw it through your eyes! Then, when you went cold, I came to myself and learned my way around, and deciphered the speech centers. I had a long, long time. It was . . . lonely. I didn't know if you would ever awaken. . . ."

"Yeah. . . ." Coati thinks this over. She's pretty sure she couldn't imagine all this. It must be *real*! But all she can think of to say is, "You're using my eyes, too?"

"I've tapped into the optic nerve, at the second juncture. *Very* delicately, I assure you. And to your auditory channels. It's one of the first things we do, a primitive program. And we make the host feel happy, to keep from frightening it. You do feel happy, don't you?"

"Happy?—Hey, are *you* doing that? Listen, if that's you, you're overdoing it! I don't want to feel quite so 'happy,' as you call it. Can you turn it down?"

"You don't? Oh, I *am* sorry. Please wait—my movements are slow."

Coati waits, thinking so furiously about everything at once that her mind is a chaos. Presently there comes a marked decrease in the distracting physical glow. More than all the rest, this serves to convince her of the reality of her new inhabitant.

"Can you read my mind?" she asks slowly.

"Only when you form words," her own voice replies. "Subvocalizing, I think you call it. I used all that long cold time tracing out your vocabulary and language. We have a primitive drive to communication; perhaps all life-forms have."

"Acquiring a whole language from a static, sleeping brain is quite a feat," says Coati thoughtfully. She is beginning to feel a distinct difference in her voice when the alien is using it; it seems higher, tighter and she hears herself using words that she knows only from reading, not habitual use.

"Yes. Luckily I had so much time. But I was so dismayed and depressed when it seemed you'd never awaken. All that work would be for nothing. I am so happy to find you alive! Not just for the work, but for—for life. . . . Oh, and I have had one chance to practice with your species before. But your brain is quite different."

However flustered and overwhelmed by the novelty of all this, Coati isn't stupid. The words about "home" and "hosts" are making a connection with Boney and Ko's report.

"Did the two men who sent that message you were riding on visit your home planet? They were two Humans—that's what I am—in a ship bigger than this."

"Oh, yes! I was one of those who took turns being with them! And I was visiting one of them when they left." . . . The voice seems to check itself. "Your brain is really very different."

"Thanks," says Coati inanely. "I've heard that those two men—those two Humans—weren't regarded as exactly bright."

" 'Bright'? Ah, yes. . . . We performed some repairs, but we couldn't do much."

Coati's chaotic thoughts coalesce. What she's sitting here chatting with is an alien—an *alien* who is possibly deadly, very likely dangerous, who has invaded her head.

"You're a *brain parasite!*" she cries loudly. "You're an intelligent brain parasite, using my eyes to see with and my ears to hear with, and talking through my mouth as if I were a zombie—and, and for all I know, you're taking over my whole brain!"

"Oh, please! P-please" She hears her own voice tremble. "I can leave at any moment—is that what you wish? And I damage nothing—nothing at all. I use very little energy. In fact, I have cleared away some debris in your main blood-supply tube, so there is more than ample for us both. I need only a few components from time to time. But I can withdraw right now. It would be a slow process, because I've become more deeply enmeshed and my mentor isn't here to direct me. But if that's what you want, I shall start at once, leaving just as I came. . . . Maybe—n-now that I'm refreshed, I could survive longer, clinging to your ship."

The pathos affects Coati; the timbre of the voice calls up the image of a tiny, sad, frightened creature shivering in the cold prison of space.

"We'll decide about that later," she says somewhat gruffly. "Meanwhile I have your word of honor you aren't messing up my brain?"

"Indeed not," her own voice whispers back indignantly. "It is a beautiful brain."

"But what do you want? Where are you trying to go?"

"Now I want only to go home. I thought, if I could reach some central Human place, we could find someone who would carry me back to my home planet and my proper host."

"But why did you leave Boney and Ko and go with that message pipe in the first place?"

"Oh—I had no idea then how *big* the empty spaces are; I thought it would be like a long trip out-of-body at home. Brrrrr! There's so much I don't know. Can you tell that I am quite a young being? I have not at all finished my instructions. My mentors tell me I am foolish, or foolhardy. I—I wanted adventure?" The little voice sounds suddenly quite strong and positive. "I still do, but I see I must be better prepared."

"Hmm. Hey, can you tell I'm young, too? I guess that makes two of us. I guess I'm out here looking for adventure, too."

"You do understand."

"Yeah." Coati grins, sighs. "Well, I can carry you back to FedBase, and I'm sure they'll be sending parties to your planet soon. It's a First Contact for us, you know; that's what we call meeting a new non-Human race. We know about fifty so far, but no one just like you. So I'm certain people will be going."

"Oh, thank you! Thank you so much."

Coati feels a surge of physical pleasure, an urge—

"Hey, you're doing *that* again! Stop it."

"Oh, I am sorry." The glow fades. "It's a primitive response to gratitude. To give pleasure. You see, our normal hosts are quite mindless; they can be thanked only by physical sensation."

"I see." Pondering this, Coati sees something else, too.

"I suppose you could make them feel pain, too, to punish them, if they did something you didn't like?"

"I suppose so. But we don't like pain; it churns up the delicate brain. Those are some of the lessons I haven't had yet. I had to only once, when my host was playing too near a dangerous cliff. And then I soothed it with pleasure right after it moved back. We use it only in emergencies, if the host threatens to harm itself, rare things like that. . . . Or, wait, I remember, if the host gets into what you call a *fight*. . . . You can see it's complicated."

"I see," Coati repeats. Uneasily she realizes that this young alien passenger might have more control over her than was exactly neat. But it seems to be so well-meaning, to have no intent at all to harm her. She relaxes—unable to suppress a twinge of wonder whether her easy emotional acceptance of its presence in—whew!—her brain might not be a feeling partly engineered by the alien. Maybe the *really* neat thing to do would be to ask her passenger to withdraw, right now. Could she fix some comfortable place for it to stay outside her? Maybe she'll do that, when they get a bit closer to FedBase.

Meanwhile, what about her plan for visiting the planet Boney and Ko were headed for? If she could pick up a trace of them, it would be a real help to FedBase. And wouldn't it be a shame to come all this way without taking a look?

That argument with herself is soon over. And her young appetite is making itself felt. She picks out a ration snack and starts to set the drive course for the planets, explaining between munches what she plans to do before returning to FedBase. Her passenger raises no objection to this delay.

"I am so grateful, so grateful you would think to deliver me," her voice says with some difficulty around the cheese bites.

As Coati opens the cold-keeper, a flash of gold attracts her attention. It's more of that gold dust, clinging to the chilly surface. She bats it away, and some floats to her face.

"By the way, what is this stuff? It came in the message pipe, with you. Can you see it? Hey, it's on my legs, too." She extends one.

"Yes," her "different" voice replies. "They are seeds."

She's getting used to this weird dialogue with herself. It reminds her of a show she saw, where a ventriloquist animated a dummy. "I'm a ventriloquist's dummy," she chuckles to herself. "Only I'm the ventriloquist, too."

"What kind of seeds, of what?" she asks aloud.

"Ours." There's a sound, or feeling, like a sigh, as if a troubling thought had passed. Then the voice says more briskly, "Wait, I forgot. I should release a chemical to keep them off you. They are attracted to—to the pheromones of life."

"I didn't know I knew those words," Coati tells her invisible companion. "I guess you were really into my vocabulary while I slept."

"Oh, yes. I labored."

A moment later Coati feels a slight flush prickling her skin. Is this the "chemical"? Before she can feel alarmed, it passes. And she sees that the floating dust—or seeds—has fallen away from her as if repelled by a charge.

"Good-o." She eats a bit more, finishing the course-set. "That reminds me, what do you call your race? And you, you must have a name. We should get better acquainted!" She laughs for two; all sense of trouble has gone.

"I am of the Eea, or Eeadron. Personally I'm called Syllobene."

"Hello, Syllobene! I'm Coati Cass. Coati."

"Hello, Coati Cass Coati."

"No, I meant, just Coati. Cass is my family name."

"Ah, 'family.' We wondered about that, with the other Humans."

"Sure, I'll be glad to explain. But later—" Coati cuts herself off. "I mean, there'll be plenty of time to explain everything while we slowly approach the planet orbiting that star. And I think I'm entitled to your story first, Syllobene, since I'm providing the body. Don't you agree that's fair?"

"Oh, yes. I must take care not to be selfish, when you do so much."

Somehow this speech for the first time conveys to Coati that her passenger really is a young, almost childish being. The big words it had found in her mind had kept misleading her. But now Syllobene sounds so much like herself reminding herself of her manners. She chuckles again, benignly. Could it be that they are two kids—even two females—together, out looking for adventure in the starfields? And it's nice to have this unexpected companion; much as Coati loves to read and view, she's beginning to get the idea that a lot of space voyaging consists of lonely sitting and waiting, when you aren't in cold-sleep. Of course, she guiltily reminds herself, she could be checking the charts to see if all the coordinates of the relatively few stars out here are straight. But Boney and Ko have undoubtedly done all that—after all, this was their second trip to this sun; on the first one they merely spotted planets. And learning about an alien race is surely important.

She leans back comfortably and asks, "Now, what about your planet? What does it look like? And your hosts—how does that work? How did such a system ever evolve in the first place? Hey, I know—can you make me see an image, a vision of your home?"

"Alas, no. Such a feat is beyond my powers. Making speech is the utmost I can do."

"Well, tell me about it all."

"I will. But first I must say, we have no such—no such material equipment, no such *technology* as you have. What techniques we have are of the mind. I am filled with amazement at all you do. Your race has achieved marvels! I saw a distant world when I looked through your device—a world! And you speak of visiting it as casually as we would go to a lake or a tree farm. A wonder!"

"Yes, we have a lot of technology. So do some other races, like the Swain and the Moom. But I want *yours,* Syllobene! To start with, what's this business of Eea and Eeadron?"

"Ah. Yes, of course. Well, I personally, just myself, am an Eea. But when I am in my proper host, which is a Dron, I am an Eeadron. An Eea by itself is almost nothing. It can do nothing but wait, depending on its primitive tropisms, until a host comes by. It is very rare for Eea to become detached as you found me—except when we are visiting another Eeadron for news or instruction. And then we leave much of ourselves in place, in our personal Dron, to which we return. I, being young, was able to detach myself almost completely to go with the Humans as one of their visitors."

"Oh—were there other Eea inside Boney and Ko when they took off?"

"Yes—one each, at least."

"What would you call that—Eeahumans?" Coati laughs.

But her companion does not seem to join in. "They were very old," she hears herself mutter softly. And then something that sounds like, "no idea of the length of the trip. . . ."

"So you came away when they messaged. Whew—wild act! Oh, Syllobene, I'm so glad I intercepted it and saved you."

"I too, dear Coati Cass."

"But now we've got to get serious about this crazy system of yours. Are you the only people on your planet that have their brains in separate bodies?—Oh, wait. I just realized we should record all this; we'll never be able to go over it twice. Hold while I put in a new cassette."

She gets set up, and bethinks herself to make it sound professional with an introduction.

"This is Coati Cass recording, on board the *CC-One,* approaching unnamed planet at—" She gives all the coordinates, the standard date and time, and the fact that Boney and Ko were last reported to be headed toward this planet.

"Before that they landed on a planet at thirty-twenty north and reported a First Contact with life-forms there. Their report is in a message forwarded to Base before I came here. Now it seems that when they left the planet, some of the life-forms came with them; specifically, two at least of the almost invisible Eea, in their heads. And some seeds, and another Eea, a very young one, who came along, she says, for the adventure. This young Eea moved to the message pipe, not realizing how long the trip would be, and was almost dead when I opened the pipe. She—I call it 'she' because we haven't got sexes, if any, straightened out yet—she moved over to me when I opened the pipe, and is right now residing in my head, where she can see and hear through my senses, and speak with my voice. I am interviewing her about her planet, Nolian. Now remember, all the voice you hear will be mine—but I myself am the one asking the questions. I think you will soon be able to tell when Syllobene—that's her name—is speaking with my voice; it's higher and sort of constricted, and she uses words I didn't know I knew. She learned all that while I was in cold-sleep coming here. Now, Syllobene, would you please repeat what you've told me so far, about the Eea and the Eeadron?"

Coati has learned to relax a little while her own voice goes on, and she hears Syllobene start with a nice little preface: "Greetings to my Human hearers!" and go on to recite the Eea-Eeadron system.

"Now," says Coati, "I was just asking her whether the Eea are the only life-forms on their planet to have their brains in separate animals, so to speak?"

"Oh, no," says her Syllobene voice, "it is general in our, ah, animal world. In fact, we are still amazed that there is another way. But always in other animals, the two are very closely attached. For instance, in the Enquaalons the En is born with the Quaalon, mates when it mates, gives birth when it does, and dies when it dies. The same for all the En—that is what we call the brain animal—except for ourselves, the Eea. Only the Eea are so separate from the Dron, and do not die when their Dron dies. . . . But we have seen aged Endalamines—that is the nearest animal to the Eeadron—holding their heads against newborn Dalamines, as though the En were striving to pass to a new body, while the seed-Ens proper to that newborn hovered about in frustration. We think in some cases they succeed."

"So you Eea can pass to a new body when yours is old! Does that make you immortal?"

"Ah, no; Eea, too, age and die. But very slowly. They may use many Dron in a lifetime."

"I see. But tell about your society, your government, and how you get whatever you eat, and so on. Are there rich or poor, or servants and master Eeadron?"

"No, if I understand those words. But we have farms—"

And so, by random stages and probings, Coati pieces together a picture of the green and golden planet Syllobene calls Nolian, with its sun Anella. All ruled over by the big white Eeadron, who have no wars, and only the most rudimentary monetary system. The climate is so benign that housing is largely decorative, except for shelter from the nightly mists and drizzles. It seems a paradise. Their ferocious teeth, which had so alarmed Boney and Ko, derive from a forgotten, presumably carnivorous past; they now eat plant products and fruits. (Here Coati recollects that certain herbivorous primates of antique Earth also had fierce-looking canines.)

As to material technology, the Eeadron have the wheel, which they use for transporting farm crops and what few building materials they employ. And long ago they learned to control fire, which they regard almost as a toy except for some use in cooking. Their big interest now appears to be the development of a written code for their language; they picked up the idea from

Ponz and Leslie. It's a source of great pleasure and excitement, although some of the older Eea, who serve as the racial memory, grumble a bit at this innovation.

Midway through this account, Coati has an idea, and when Syllobene runs down she bursts out, "Listen! Oh, this is Coati speaking—you said you cleaned out my arteries, my blood tubes. And you cure other hosts. Would you—I mean, your race—be interested in being healers to other races like mine, who can't heal themselves? We call such healers *doctors*. But our doctors can't get inside and really fix what's wrong, without cutting the sick person up. Why, you could travel all over the Federation, visiting sick people and curing them—or, wait, you could set up a big clinic, and people, Humans and others, would come from everywhere to have the Eea go into them and fix their blood vessels, or their kidneys, or whatever was wrong. Oh, hey, they'd *pay* you—you're going to need Federation credits—and everybody would love you! You'd be the most famous, valuable race in the Federation!"

"Oh, oh—" replies the Syllobene voice, sounding breathless, "I don't know your exclamations! We would say—" She gives an untranslatable trill of excitement. "How amazing, if I understand you—"

"Well, we can talk about that later. Now, you learned about Humans from what you call visiting, in the brains of Boney or Ko, is that right?"

"Yes. But if I had not had the experience of visiting my mentor and a few other Eeadron, I would not have known how to enter and live there without causing damage. You see, the brains of the Dron are just unformed matter; one can go anywhere and eat anything without ill effect on the host's brain. In fact, it is up to the Eea to form them. . . . And, I almost forgot, my mentor was old; and was one of those who had known the living Humans Ponz and Leslie. The two who landed violently and died. They were beyond our powers to cure then, but we could abolish their pain. I believe they mated before they died, but no seeds came. My mentor told me how your brains are developed and functioning. We are still amazed."

"Why do you visit other Eeadron?"

"To learn many facts about some subject in a short time. We send out tendrils—I think you have a word, for your fungus plants—mycelia. Very frail threads and knots, permeating the other brain—I believe that is what I look like in your brain now—and by making a shadow pattern in a certain way, we acquire all sorts of information, like history, or the form of landscapes, and keep it intact when we withdraw."

"Look, couldn't you learn all about Humans and the Federation by doing that in my head?"

"Oh, I would not dare. Your speech centers alone frightened me with their complexity. I proceeded with infinite care. It was lucky I had so much time while you slept. I wouldn't dare try anything more delicate and extensive and emotion-connected."

"Well, thanks for your consideration . . ." Coati doesn't want to stall the interview there, so she asks at random, "Do you have any social problems? Troubles or dilemmas that concern your whole race?"

This seems to puzzle the Eea. "Well. If I understand you, I don't think so. Oh, there is a heated disagreement among two groups of Eeadron as to how much interest we should take in aliens, but that has been going on ever since Ponz. A panel of senior councillors—is that the word for old wise ones?—is judging it."

"And will the factions abide by the panel's judgment?"

"Oh, naturally. It will be wiped from memory."

"Whew!"

"And . . . and there is the problem of a shortage of *faleth* fruit trees. But that is being solved. Oh—I believe I know one social problem, as you put it. Since the Eea are becoming personally so long-lived, there is arising a reluctance to mate and start young. Mating is very, ah, disruptive, especially to the Dron body. So people like to go along as they are. The elders have learned how to suppress the mating urge. For example, I and my siblings were the only young born during one whole season. There are still plenty of seeds about—you saw them—but they are becoming just wasted. Wasted . . . I think I perceive something applicable in your verbal sayings, about nature."

"Huh? Oh—'Nature's notorious wastefulness,' right?"

"Yes. But our seeds are very long-lived. Very. And that golden coat, which is what you see, is impervious to most everything. So maybe all will be well."

Her informant seems to want to say no more on this topic, so Coati seizes the pause to say, "Look, our throat—*my* throat—is about to close up or break into flames. "Water!" She seizes the flask and drinks. "I always thought that business of getting a sore throat from talking too much was a joke. It isn't. Can't you *do* something, Dr. Syllobene?"

"I can only block off some of the inflamed channels, and help time do its work. I could abolish the pain, but if we use the throat, it would quickly grow much worse."

"You sound like a doctor already," Coati grumbles hoarsely. "Well, we'll just cut this off here— Oh, I wish I had one of those message pipes! Ouch. . . . Then we'll have some refreshments—I got some honey, thank the gods—and take a nap. Cold-sleep doesn't rest us, you know. Could you take a sleep, too, Syllobene?"

"Excellent idea." That hurts.

"Look, couldn't you learn just to nod my head like this for 'yes' or like this for 'no'?"

Nothing happens for a moment, then Coati feels her head nod gently as if elfin fingers were brushing her chin and brow, yes.

"Fantastic," she rasps. "Ouch."

She clicks off the recorder, takes a last look through the scope at the blue-green-white planet—still far, far ahead—sets an alarm, and curls up comfortably in the pilot couch.

"Sleep well, Syllobene," she whispers painfully. The answer is breathed back, "You, too, dear Coati Cass."

EXCITEMENT WAKES HER before the alarm. The planet is just coming into good bare-eye view. But when she starts to speak to Syllobene, she finds she has no voice at all. She hunts up the med-kit and takes out some throat lozenges.

"Syllobene," she whispers. "Hello?"

"Wha—er, what? Hello?" Syllobene discovers whispering.

"We've lost our voice. That happens sometimes. It'll wear off. But if it's still like this when we get on the planet, you'll *have* to do something so we can record. You can, can't you?"

"Yes, I believe so. But you must understand it will make it worse later."

"Green."

"What?"

"Green . . . means 'I understand, too.' Listen, I'm sorry about your turn to ask questions. That'll be later. For now we'll just shut up."

"I wait."

"Go."

"What?"

"Oh, green, go—that means 'Understood, and we will proceed on that course.' " Coati can scarcely force out the words.

"Ah, informal speech . . . most difficult. . . ."

"Syl, this is killing me. We shut up *now*, green?"

A painful giggle. "Go."

Some hot tea from the snack pack proves soothing. Meanwhile the en-
forced silence for the first time gives Coati a chance to think things over. She
is, of course, entranced by the novelty of it all, and seriously stirred by the
idea that Syllobene's race could provide the most astounding, hitherto inconceivable type of medical help to the others. If they want to. And if a terrible crowd-jam doesn't ensue. But that's for the big minds to wrestle out.

And, like the kid she is, Coati relishes the sensation she fancies her return
will provoke—with a real live new alien carried in her head! But, gods, they
won't be able to *see* Syllobene—suppose they jump to the obvious conclusion that Coati's gone nutters, and hustle her off to the hospital? She and Syl
better talk that over before they get home; Syllobene has to be able to think
of some way to prove she exists.

Funny how firmly she's thinking of Syllobene as "she," Coati muses. Is that
just sheer projection? Or—after all, they're in pretty intimate contact—is this
some deep instinctive perception, like one of Syl's "primitive tropisms"?
Whatever, when they get it unscrambled, it'll be a bit of a shock if Syl's a young
"he" . . . or gods forbid, an "it" or a "them." What was it that Boney had said
about the Dron, that some of them had two sets of "private parts"? That'd be
his modest term for sex organs; he must have meant they were like hermaph-
rodites. Whew. Well, that still doesn't necessarily mean anything about the Eea.

When they can talk, she must get things straightened out. And until then
not get too romantically fixated on the idea that they're two girls together.

All this brings her to a sobering sense of how little she really knows about
the entity she's letting stay in her head—in her very brain. If indeed Syl was
serious about being able to leave. . . . With this sobriety comes—or rather,
surfaces—a slight, undefined sense of trouble. She's had it all along, Coati
realizes. A peculiar feeling that there's more. That all isn't quite being told to
her. Funny, she doesn't suspect Syl herself of some bad intent, of being secretly evil. No. Syllobene is *good,* as good as she can be; all Coati's radar and
perceptions seem to assure her of that. But nevertheless this feeling persists—it's becoming clearer as she concentrates—that something was making
the alien a little sad and wary now and then—that something troubling to Syl
had been touched on but not explored.

The lords know, she and Syl had literally talked all they could; Syl had answered every question until their voice gave out. But Coati's sense of incom-
pleteness lingers. Let's see, when had it been strongest? . . . Around that
business of the seeds in the message pipe, for one. Maybe every time they

touched on seeds. Well, seeds were being wasted. That meant dying. And a seed is a living thing; an encysted, complete beginning of a new life. Not just a gamete, like pollen, say. Maybe they're like embryos, or even living babies, to Syllobene. The thought of hundreds of doomed babies surely wouldn't be a very cheerful one for Coati herself.

Could that be it? That Syl didn't want to go into the sadness? Seems plausible. Or, wait—what about Syl herself? By any chance did she want to mate, and now she can't—or *had* she, and that's the mystery of where those seeds in the message pipe had come from? Whew! Is Syl old enough, is she sexually mature? Somehow Coati doesn't think so, but again, she knows so little—not even that Syl's a she.

As Coati ruminates, her eyes have been on the front view-ports, where the planet is rapidly growing bigger and bigger. She must put her wonderment aside, with the mental note to question Syl at the first opportunity. In a few minim it'll be time to kill the torches and go on antigrav for the maneuvers that will bring her into a close-orbit search pattern. She will have to fly a lot of extra orbits—doing the best she can by eye and with her narrow little civilian radarscope. It'll be tedious; not for the first time, she deplores the unsuitability of a little space-coupe for serious exploration work.

The planet still looks remarkably like holos of Terra. It has two big ice caps, but only three large landmasses set in blue ocean. It looks cold, too. Cloud cover is thin, wispy cirrus. And for many degrees south of the northern ice, the land is a flat gray-green, featureless except for an intricate, shallow lake system, which changes from silver to black as the angle of reflection changes. Like some exotic silken fabric, Coati thinks. The technical name for such a plain is tundra, or maybe muskeg.

No straight lines or curves, no dams, no signs of artificial works appear. The place seems devoid of intelligent life.

Hello, what's this ahead? A twinkling light is rounding the shadowed curve of the planet, far enough out to catch the sun. That's reflected light; the thing is tumbling slowly. Coati slows and turns to the scope. Big sausage tanks! Such tanks must belong to a DRS, a depot resupply ship. Boney and Ko must have left them in orbit before they landed. And they wouldn't fail to pick them up when they left; that means the men are here. Oh, good. That'll give her the enthusiasm to sit out a long, boring search.

She tunes up every sensor on *CC-One* and starts the pattern while she's still, really, too far out. This is going to be a long chore, unless some really wild luck strikes.

And luck does strike! On her second figure eight orbit, she sees an immense blackened swath just south of the northern ice cap. A burn. Can it have been caused by lightning, or volcanism? Or even a natural meterorite?

No . . . on the next pass she can see a central line of scorch, growing as it leads north, with a perceptible zigzag such as no incoming natural object could make. She clicks on the recorder and whispering reports the burn and the tanks in orbit.

On the third pass she's sure. There's a gleam at the north end of the burn scar.

"Oh, the poor men! They must have been sick; they had to correct course with rockets. . . . Syl! Syllobene! Are you awake?"

"Uh—hello?" her voice mumbles. Funny to hear herself sounding sleepy.

"Look, you have to do something about our throat so I can report. I think I've found the men."

"Oh. Yes. Wait . . . I fear I need nourishment. . . ."

"Go right ahead. Be my guest."

For an instant Coati pictures Syl sipping blood, like a vampire; but no, Syl is too small. It'll be more like the little being snagging a red blood corpuscle or two as they rush by. Weird. Coati doesn't feel the least bit nervous about this. Syl had said she's increased the blood flow overall. And in fact Coati herself feels great, very alert and well. They *would* make wonderful healers, she thinks.

The gleam at the end of the burn is definitely a ship; the scope shows her a big Federation supply tug. Her calls on Fed frequencies bring no response. She kills the search pattern and prepares to land on antigrav. The plain beside the strange ship looks good. But maybe there was another reason for their use of torches, she thinks; those two men were super-experienced planetary pilots. Maybe this place has weird mascons or something that had to be corrected for? She'd better keep alert, and be ready to torch if she finds her course going unsteady.

When she calls the supply ship again, her voice is back and her throat suddenly feels great.

"Hey, thanks Syl."

"Coati, why are we landing?"

"The Humans you left are down somewhere on the planet. They were never heard of after you left them; they're officially missing. That means, everybody search. Now I've found their ship, but they don't answer. I have to land and find out what's happening to them. So you'll get to see a strange planet."

The news doesn't seem to cheer her little passenger, who only repeats, "We must land?"

"Oh, yes. Among other things, they may need help."

"Help. . . ." Syllobene's voice repeats, with an odd, almost bitter inflection.

But Coati is too busy to brood over this. "What condition were they in when you left them, Syl?"

"Oh. . . ." her throat sighs. "I do not know your race well enough to tell what is normal. They were speaking of going to cold-sleep when I withdrew and left them. I was trying to hurry because I understood that the message device would soon be sent out. As I said, it's a slow process. As soon as I was dependent on my Eea senses, the men were too large to perceive—for example, I could no longer discern the sound waves of their voices."

Coati thinks this over as she gentles the ship down through thick atmosphere. Her ablation shielding isn't all that good.

"Syl, you have just as much technology in your way as we do. Imagine going back and forth from the molecular to the molar scales!"

"Yes. It *is* a big learning. Very frightening the first time, when we're taught to visit."

"You said there were other Eea in Boney and Ko?"

"Yes . . . but I couldn't establish good contact, and they controlled everything. That's why I slipped away, when I understood about the message device."

Coati grins. "I can understand that, Syl. But you took an awful chance."

She feels the elfin hands nod her head emphatically. "You are my savior."

"Oh, well. I didn't know it. But if I had known it, I would have got you off there, Syllobene. I couldn't have let you die in space."

A feeling of indefinable warmth and real happiness glows within her. Coati understands. There is genuine friendship between her and her tiny alien passenger.

The recorder has been clicking away as they talked. But of course it won't show her feelings. Pity.

"Just for the record," she says formally, "I have, uh, subjective reasons to believe that this alien has sincere feelings of friendship of me. I mean for me, not just as a convenience. I think that's important. I feel the same toward Syl."

It's time to set *CC-One* down. With all care, Coati jockeys her little ship in above the big supply tug and comes down neatly beside it. Nothing unto-

ward shows up. That must mean that Boney and/or Ko were really in wob-
bly condition when they came in.

The atmosphere tests out green, but still she suits up for her first trip out.
As her ports open, she gets her first good look at the DRS.

"Their ramp's down," she tells the 'corder. "And, hey, the port's ajar! Not
good. I'm going in. . . . Hello! Hello in there! . . . Oh!"

Her voice breaks off. Sounds of footsteps, squeaks of ports being pulled.

"Oh, my. What a mess. There were gloves on the ramp—and the inside
looks like they didn't clean anything up for a long time. I see food dishes and
cassettes and a suit—wait, two suits—in a heap on the deck, as if they'd just
jumped out of them. Oh, dear, this looks like trouble . . . I think somebody
threw up here. . . . There're a lot of those goldy seeds around everywhere,
too."

She prowls the cabin, reporting as she checks the sleep chests and anyplace a man-sized body could be. Nothing. And the big cargo hold is empty,
too, except for a carton of supplies bound somewhere.

She comes outside, saying, "I think I should try to find them. The ground
here is soft, like peat, with low vegetation or whatever, and I can see trampled places. There's one big place that looks like a trail leading"—she checks
her bearings—"leading north, of all things. The atmosphere is highly
Human-compatible, lots of oxy. I have my helmet off. So I'm going to try to
follow their trail. But just in case I get into trouble, I think I better send this
record off first. It has all about Syl's planet on it. Lords, I wish I could send
it from the surface. I guess I'll have to lift above atmosphere. I'm taking
some of their message pipes over to my ship. So here goes. It's the only neat
thing to do."

She sighs, clicks off, and gets back into her ship.

Preparing to lift off, she says, "You're very quiet, Syllobene. Are you all
right?"

"Oh, yes. But I am—I am afraid."

"Afraid of what? Walking around on a strange planet? Listen, I do have
a hand weapon in case we run into big, wild, vicious beasts. But I don't think
there's anything like that around here. Nothing for a carnivore to eat."

"No . . . I am not afraid of the planet. I fear . . . what you will find."

Coati is maneuvering her ship up for a fast single orbit and return. "What
do you mean, Syl?" she asks a trifle absently.

"Coati, my friend"—it sounds weird to hear her name in her own
voice—"I wish to wait until you search. Perhaps I am wrong. I hope so."

"Well-ll, green, if you must," Coati is preoccupied with opening a message pipe. "Oh, bother, there're some of those little yellow dust seeds in here. How do I clear them out? I don't want to kill them—you say they can live in space, like you—but I don't think they should get loose in FedBase, do you?"

"No! No!"

"Look, I'm sorry about your seeds. I just want to make them get out of this pipe. How do I do that?"

"Heat. High heat."

"Huh . . . oh, I know." She clicks the recorder on and tells it what she's doing. "I'm going to put the pipe in my food heater and run the heater up to 120 degrees C. That won't hurt the cassette. . . . All right, I'm taking it out with tongs. By the gods, there're a couple of those seeds coming out of the 'corder as it gets near heat. All out, you. I will now end this record as I remove the cassette to send. *CC-One* signing off, before returning to planet to search for B and K."

"Good thing we did that," she tells Syl as she closes the pipe and puts it in the lock to be blown out. "Here goes the air. —And there goes the pipe! I hope the Base frequency reaches this far. . . . Yes, it does. Neat, how the little thing knows where to go. Bye-bye, you. . . . Funny, I'm getting a feeling like we're a long, long ways from anywhere. Being a space adventurer can be a trifle spooky." She noses the ship over into landing mode, thinking, "I'm going down to hike over a strange planet looking for two people who, face it, may be dead. . . .

"Syllobene?"

"Yes?"

"I'm really glad I have you for a friend here. Hey, maybe there's another thing your people could do . . . I mean, for credits: Going with lonely space people on long trips!"

"Ah . . ."

"I was just joking. . . . Or was I?"

Soon they are back on the planet, beside the abandoned DRS. Coati puts on planetary weather gear and tramping shoes. It's sunny but bleak outside. She packs a week's rations and some water, although the ground is spongy-wet. Then she clips the recorder to her shoulder and carefully loads it with a fresh cassette.

A LONG TIME LATER, after Coati has been officially declared missing, that same fresh cassette, its shine somewhat dimmed, is in the hands of the deputy to the exec of FedBase 900. It is about to be listened to by a group of people in the exec's conference room.

Weeks before, the message that Coati had lifted off-planet to send had arrived at FedBase. The staff has heard all about Syllobene and the Eea, and the Eeadron, and the Dron, and all the other features of Syllobene's planet Nolian, and her short trip with Boney and Ko; they have left Coati and her brain passenger about to go back down to the unnamed planet on which sits Boney and Ko's empty ship.

One of the group of listeners now is not of FedBase.

When that first message had come in, the exec had signaled the Cass family, and Coati's father is now in the room. He looks haggard; he has worn out his vocabulary of anger—particularly when he found that no rescue mission was being planned.

"Very convenient for you, Commander," he had sneered. "Letting a teenage girl do your dirty work. I say it's your responsibility to look for your own missing men, and to go get my daughter out of there and free her from that damn brain parasite. You should never have let her go way out there in the first place! If you think I'm not going to report this—"

"How do you suggest I could have stopped her, Myr Cass? She injected herself of her free will into an ongoing search, without consulting anyone. If anyone is to blame for her being out here, it's you. It was your responsibility to have some control over your daughter's travels in that ship you gave her. Meanwhile my responsibility is to my people, and I'm not justified in risking another ship pursuing a Federation citizen on her voluntary travels."

"But that cursed alien in her—"

"Yes. To be blunt about it, Myr Cass, your daughter is already infected, if that's the word, and she has given us evidence of the great mobility and potential for contagion of these small beings. We have probably already lost the men who first visited them. Now I suggest we quiet down and listen to what your daughter has to say. It may be that your concerns are baseless."

Grumblingly, Cass senior subsides.

"This message pipe has been heated, too," says the deputy. "The plastic shows it. From which we can infer that she was compos mentis and possibly in her own ship when she sent it."

The recording starts with a few miscellaneous bangs and squeaks.

"I've decided to take another look at B-K's ship before I start," Coati's voice says. "Maybe they left a message or something."

The 'corder clicks off and on again.

"I've been hunting around in here," says Coati. "No message I can see. There's a holocam focused on the cabin, but it's been turned off. Hey, I bet the Feds like to keep an eye on things, for cases like this. I'll root around by the shell."

Clicks—off, on.

"I've spotted what I think is another holocam up in the bow; I heard it click. . . . How can I get at it? Oh, wait, maybe from outside." Off, on. "Yoho! I got it. It's in time-lapse mode; I think it caught the terrain around the ship. We'll just take it over to my ship and run it."

Click—off.

Exec shifts uneasily. "I believe she's discovered the planetary recorder. I'm not sure the two men knew it was there."

"That must be the additional small cassette in this pipe," the deputy says.

The recorder has come on. "It's really small," Coati is saying. "Hey, it's full of your seeds, Syllobene. Those things must like cassettes. I'm threading it—here we go. Oh, my, oh, my—Syllobene!"

"That is my home," says Coati in what they have come to recognize as the voice of the alien speaking through Coati's throat. "Oh, my beautiful home! . . . But what a marvel, how do you—"

"Later," Coati cuts herself off. "Later we'll look at it all you want. Right now we have to run it ahead to where it shows this planet and maybe the two men we're looking for."

"Yes— Oh, that was my mentor—"

"Oh, gods, I'd love to look. But I'm speeding up now." Sounds of fast clicking, incoherent small sounds from Coati's Syllobene voice.

"See, now they've taken off. It'll be stars for a long time, nothing but the starfield." Furious clicks. "Gods, I hope it doesn't run out."

"No fear," says the deputy. "These things are activated by rapid action in the field. When the action is as slow as a passing starfield, it reverts to its resting rate of about a frame an hour—maybe a frame a day; I forget. Only a passing rock or whatnot will speed them up briefly."

"Here we are," says Coati's voice, "I can see that great string of GO suns. . . . Yes, they seem to be heading in to the planet now; I'd need a scope to tell—ah! It's getting bigger. That's it, all right. . . . Closer, closer . . . they're going into orbit. But Syl, look at that frame wobble. I tell you, whoever's flying is not all right. . . . Oo-oops—that could be changing pilots, or maybe switching over to the rockets. Oh, dear . . . yes, they're coming in like a load of gravel; I'm glad I know they made it. . . . Smoke now, nothing but smoke.

Their torches have hit. Down—I see flames. This must be action-activated; there'll be a pause now, but we can't tell how long. I know this doesn't mean much to you, Syl, but wait till the smoke clears—ah! Look, there's the landscape we saw around the ship, right?"

The alien voice makes a small murmur.

"Action again—that's the edge of the ramp. Here comes one of the men—now the other—which is which? I'll call the tall, thin one Boney. Oh, dear gods, they're staggering. See, they dropped those gloves. And look, the vegetation around the ship outside the burn is all untrampled. This is their first exit, of course—oh, the Boney one fell down! Could the cold-sleep have done that, have they come out too soon? I don't think so: I think they're sick. Look, there's a funny place on Ko's face, over the nose; he keeps scratching. They're not stopping to look around or anything. This isn't good, Syl. . . . Now they're both down on their hands and knees, in the burn. Oh, I wish I could help them. Look, do you see the goldy cloud, like your spores, by the ramp?"

A pause, with small "ohs" and murmurs.

"They're up now; I hope they're not burned—why, they're running or trying to run! Away from the ship. Toward the trampled place we saw, only it isn't trampled now. Oh. Boney is—and Ko—they're *stripping*! What are they trying to do, take a bath? But there's no— Oh! Oh, wait, *what*? Oh, no! Oh! Oh, dear gods, I don't like this much. I thought all spacers operated under the Code. I didn't know recon teams did sex!"

"They don't," growls Exec, startling everybody.

General stirrings in the room as Coati's voice goes on haltingly, "Well, this is weird . . . I don't much want to look at it; it's not happy-looking like our demo teams back at school. Huh . . . I don't think they know what to do, exactly. . . . Their faces look crazy; why, one of them has his mouth open like he was yelling or screaming. They look terrible. . . . Whoever's listening to this, I'm sorry. I hope I'm not saying anything bad. But this is weird, it's like *ugly*. . . . They have to stop soon, I hope. Oh, *no*—" Her voice is shaking on the verge of some kind of outcry.

"Oh, oh, oh—" But it's the other voice that begins sobbing frankly now. The recorder blurs in a confusion of, "Syl! What's the matter? What's wrong?" and "Oh, I was afraid, oh, I'm afraid, oh, Coati, it's terrible—"

"Yeah, it's ugly. That's not the way Humans really mate, Syl."

"No," says Syl's tones, "I don't mean that. I mean we—oh, oh—" And she's sobbing again.

"Listen, Syl!" Coati gulps back alien tears, cuts her off. "I think you know something you aren't telling me! You tell me what's frightening you this instant, or I'll—I'll bash my own brains so hard it'll shake you loose. See?"

There's the sound of a hard slap on flesh, and then a sudden sharp outcry.

"Hey—what—*you hurt me,* Syl. I th-thought you never—"

"Oh, I'm sorry," the alien voice moans. "I p-panicked when you said you would harm yourself—"

"Or harm *you,* huh? Look, I can stand a lot of pain if I have to. You tell me right now what's got into those men. Look, they've collapsed again. *Tell* me!"

"It—it's the young ones."

"The young what?"

"The young Eea—from s-seeds in th-the ship."

"But you said there were grown-up Eea in each of the men. Didn't they keep the seeds off, like you did for me?"

"They— Oh, Coati, I told you, they were very old. They must have died, and the seeds went into the men. I saw them getting feeble. That's when I got frightened and l-left. Before the Humans went in cold-sleep. . . . Oh, Coati, it's so horrible—I feel so bad—"

"Hush up now, Syl, and let me understand. What could seeds do?"

"Seeds hatch, when they're in—they hatched into young ones. With no mentors, no one to train them, they're like wild animals. They grow. They eat—they eat anything. And then in the cold-sleep, some of them must have matured. No teachers, no one to teach them discipline. Oh, the others should have known the seeds and spores would seek hosts, they should have seen that those visitors who went with them were too old. B-but nobody knew how long, how far. . . . When I began to understand how long a time it was going to be, I knew something bad would happen. And I c-couldn't *do* anything; they wouldn't listen to me. So I-I ran away." The alien is convulsing Coati with sobs.

"Well-ll. . . ." Long sigh from Coati. "Oh, dear gods, the poor men. You mean the young ones just ate their brains out?"

"Y-yes, I fear so. As if they were Dron. Worse, because no teachers."

"And that sex stuff—that was the mature ones making them do it?"

"Yes! Oh, yes! Like wild animals. We're taught strictly to control it; we're shown. It takes much training to be fully Eea. Even I am not fully trained. . . . Oh, I wish I'd died there in space instead of seeing this—"

"Oh, no. Brace up, Syl. It's not your fault. Nobody who isn't used to space could grasp how long the distances are. They probably thought it would be like a long trip in your country. . . . Oh, look—the men have gotten up. God, they're holding each other up; their legs keep going out of control. Motor centers gone, maybe. They're going—they went up the path north; only it wasn't a path then. They're making the path, trampling. . . . That's where we go, Syl, unless this shows them coming back. It'll have to be soon; we're almost at where the camera stopped. I wish I knew how long ago this was. The sun looks kind of different, and the colors of the vegetation, but that could be the camera. I'm going to speed up. Syl, stop crying, honey; it's *not your fault.*"

Rapid clicking from the recorder.

"Nothing, nothing," Coati's voice says. "Still nothing. I doubt they came back. Nothing—wait, what's that? Oh, my goodness, it's the wake—it's our ship landing. Well! I don't think I want to see us, do you? Let's take out this cassette and go."

Click.

In the executive office the deputy stops the recorder for a moment.

"Is that clear to everyone?"

Grunts of assent answer him.

"I think this casts a new light on the potentials of Coati's little friend's race," the medical officer says. "I suggest that we all keep a sharp eye open for anything that looks like grains of yellow powder, in case the young woman's heat treatment did not completely clean out this pipe. Or the preceding one. Her initial precautions were very wise."

Before he's finished speaking, Exec has turned on stronger lights. There is a subdued shuffling as people look themselves over, brushing at imaginary golden spots.

"Gods, if a pipeful of that stuff had got loose in here, and nobody warned!" Xenology mutters. "H'mm . . . Boney and Ko."

"Yes," Exec understands Xenology's shorthand. "If we get any indication that their ship lifted off, we have some hard decisions to make. I gather the seeds can affix themselves to the *outside* of space vessels, too. Well, we'd best continue and see what our problem is."

"Right." The deputy douses the top light, restarts the 'corder.

"We are now proceeding north on the trail left by Boney and Ko," says Coati's voice. "We've come about five kiloms. The trail is very plain because the vegetation, or whatever this is, is very delicate and frail. I don't think it's built to have animals walk over it to graze. But the trail isn't all that fresh, because there're little tips of new growth. We haven't seen any animals or birds, only plantlike things and an occasional insect going by fast, like a bullet. It's a pretty cold, quiet, weird place. The ground is almost level, but I think we're headed roughly for one of those lakes we saw from above.

"Syllobene is so shook up by what happened to the men that she won't talk much. I keep trying to tell her it's not her fault. One thing she said shows you—she said the grown-up Eea must have assumed that we could make ourselves immune to the seeds, just as they can, since we're so *complete*. They can't get used to the idea of whole, single animals born that way. And the ship . . . we had so many wild, powerful things. It never occurred to them that the men would be as vulnerable as the Dron. . . . Syl, do you hear what I'm telling my people? Nobody's going to think for a minim that you're at fault. Please brace up, honey, it's awfully lonesome here on this primordial tundra or whatever it is."

". . . After you saved my life," murmurs the Syllobene voice sadly.

"Oh-h-h! Listen, hey Syl, you saved my life, too, for the lords' sake. Don't you realize?"

"I? How?"

"By being on that message pipe, dopus. It was full of seeds, remember? If you hadn't been there, at the risk of your life, if you hadn't been there to keep them off me, I'd have gone just like Boney and Ko. They'd have eaten my brains out. *Now* will you cheer up? You've personally saved my life, too. Hey, Syl, how about that? Hello!"

"Hello . . . oh, dear Coati Cass—"

"That's my Syl. Listen, I've about had the hiking for today; these boots aren't the greatest. I see a little hummock ahead; maybe it's drier. I'll tramp down a flat place and lay out my bag and screen—I don't want one of those bullet-bugs to hit me. I don't think this sun is going to set, either: it must be summer up here, with a big axial tilt." She chuckles. "I've heard of the lands of the midnight sun! Now I've seen one. This is Coati Cass, en route to I don't know where, signing off."

"Your daughter is a remarkable young woman, Myr Cass," Exec says thoughtfully. Cass grunts. Looking more carefully at him, Exec sees that Cass's eyes are wet.

The record continues with a few words by Coati on awakening. Apparently she—they—have slept undisturbed.

"Green, on we go. Now, Syl, I hope you feel better. Think of me, having to lug a Weeping Willie—that means a sad lump of a person—all over the face of this godlost planet. Hey, don't you know any songs? I'd really like that!"

"Songs?"

"Oh, for the gods' sake. Well, explaining and demonstrating will give me something to do. But I don't think our audience needs it."

Click.

In an instant her voice is back again, sounding tired.

"We've been walking eighteen hours total," she says. "My pedometer says we're sixty-one kiloms from the ships. The trail is still clearly visible. We're nearing an arm of one of the glaciers that extend south from the ice cap. I can see a line of low clouds—yes, with rainbows in them!—like a miniature weather front. The men seem to have been making straight toward it. Syl says the seeds have a primitive tropism to cold. That they can live a very, very long time if it's cold enough. I don't think anybody should come near this planet for a very, *very* long time. All right, onward."

Click—off. Click—on.

"The glacier edge and a snowbank are right ahead. I think I see them— I mean, their bodies. . . . There's a cold wind from under the glacier; it smells bad."

Click . . . click.

"We found them. It's pretty bad." The voice sounds drained. "I did what I could. They're like frozen. They crawled under the edge of the ice; it stands off the ground and makes a cave there, with deep green lightcracks. Nothing had been at them that I could tell, but they both have big, nasty-looking holes above their noses, where the sinuses are.

"I don't know their last names, so I just scratched 'Boney and Ko, brave Spacers for the Federation, Fed Base 900' on a slaty piece.

"Oh—they left a message, on the same sort of rock. It says: 'Danger. WE are Infekted. Fatel.' All misspelled, like a kid. I guess the . . . things . . . kept eating their brains out.

"And there are seeds all over around here, like gold dust on the snow. They rise up in a cloud when a shadow falls on them. Syllobene says these are new seeds and spores that the young Eea formed; they mated when the men did, and the seeds grew while the men walked here. Anyway, those holes in their faces are where the new seeds sprouted out in a big clump or stream.

"I got out my glass and looked at a group of seeds. That gold color is their coat or sheath. Syl says it is just about impermeable from outside.

There's a big difference in the seeds, too—some are much, much larger and solid-looking; others are more like empty husks. Syl says the big ones beat out the others when competing for a host, and the earliest big one takes all."
. . . A sigh.

"Let's see, have I said everything? Oh, maybe I should add that I don't think those holes were bad enough to cause the men's deaths. It must have been what went on inside. I didn't see any other wounds, except scratches and bruises from failing down, I think. They . . . they were holding each other by the hand. I fixed them up, but I didn't change that.

"Now I guess that's all. I don't want to sleep here; I'm going to get as far back toward the ships as I can tonight. It may not be night; I told you the sun doesn't set, but it makes some pretty reddish glow colors. Syl is so sad she'll hardly talk at all. . . . Signing off now, unless something drastic happens."

The deputy clicked the 'corder off.

"Is that all?" someone asked.

"Oh, no. I merely wanted to know if everyone is satisfied that they're hearing clearly so far. Did everyone get enough on the men's conditions, or would Doc like me to run back over that?"

"Not at present, thanks," says Medical. "I would assume that the action of forming a large number of embryos requires extra energy, and consequently, during the men's last walk, their parasites were consuming nutrients—brain tissue and blood—at an ever-increasing rate. As to the exact cause of death, it could be a combination of trauma, hypothermia, malnutrition, and loss of blood; or perhaps the parasites attacked brain structures essential to life. We won't know until we can—I guess we won't know, period."

"Anyone else?" says the deputy in his "briefing session" manner.

Coati's father makes an ambiguous throat-clearing noise but says nothing. No one else speaks, despite the sense of large, unuttered questions growing in the room.

"Oh, get on with it, Fred," Exec says.

"Right."

"We're back at the ship, resting up," says Coati's voice. "Syl, you've been very quiet for a long time. Are you all right? Are you still shook from seeing what the young ones did?"

"Oh, yes."

"Well, push it aside, honey. If I can, you can. Try."

"Yes. . . ."

"You don't sound like you're trying. Listen, I can't carry a melancholy, dismal person *in my head* all the way back to FedBase. I'll go nutters, even in cold-sleep. Don't you think you could cheer up a little? Wasn't it fun when we tried singing? After all, the men all happened a long time back; it's all over. There's nothing you can do."

In the room at FedBase, Coati's father recognizes a piece of his own advice to his daughter in long-ago days, and blinks back a tear.

"And we've done something useful—actually invaluable, because only you and I are safe on this planet. Right? So maybe we've saved the lives of whoever might have come to look."

"Um'm. . . ."

"She's right," says Exec.

"Of course, it's only Human lives, but it was the Human men made you sad, wasn't it, Syl. So really, it's all even. And those two had a really nice time on your planet first. Hey, think how good you'll feel when you get home. Would it make you feel better if I showed you the scenes from Nolian when we get going?"

"Yes . . . oh, I don't know."

"Syl, you're hopeless. Or is something else bothering you? I'm getting hunches. . . . Anyway, we've done everything we can here, I'm taking *CC-One* up. I collected Boney and Ko's last charting cassettes; I'll put them in a pipe with this, and with the little cassette from the bow camera. I don't think they have left anything else of value. I closed the door and wrote a sign on the port to stay out. If you at the Fed want to salvage that ship, you're going to have to go in with flamers. Or get an Eea to go in with you. Personally I think it isn't worth the danger: some seeds could be on the outside, and get left wherever you went with the ship. Hey, something I've been thinking—I wonder if possibly this could be the plague that wiped out the Lost Colony. Seeds drifting in from space. This whole great group of suns could be dangerous. Oh, lords. What a blow. . . . Hey, that's something that Syl and I could check someday! Syl, after you get home and have a nice rest-up, how would you like to come with me on another trip? If they'd let me—I'm sure they would, because we'd be their only seedproof scouts! Only, my poor folks. That reminds me: my father may have messaged Far Base; it'd be great if somebody could message him and mother, collect, that all's well and I'm coming back. Thanks a million. My address is Cayman's Port, and all is on record there. Syl, there's another thing we could do—how'd you like to meet my folks? You could learn all about families, and go back and be a big mentor on Nolian. They'd love to meet you, I know . . . I guess. Green. I'm taking the ship up now."

Click. Click.

"We're up, and I'm setting in course for the first leg back to Far Base. Whew, these yellow suns are really beautiful. But Syl is still in a funk. It *can't* be because of what we saw on the planet. I keep feeling sure there's something you aren't telling me, Syl. What is it?"

"Oh, no, I—".

"Syl! Listen, you're thinking with *my* brain, and I can *sense* something! Like every time I suggested something we could do, I got drenched in some kind of sadness. And there's a feeling like a big thing tickling when you won't talk. You've got to tell me, Syl. What *is* it?"

"I . . . oh, I am so ashamed!"

"See, there *is* something you're hiding! Ashamed of what? Go on, Syl, tell me or I'll—I'll bash us both. *Tell me!*"

"Ashamed," repeats the small voice. "I'm afraid, I'm afraid. My training. . . . Maybe I'm not so completely developed as I thought. I don't know how to stop— Ohhh," Coati's voice wails. "I wish my mentor were here!"

"Huh?"

"I have this feeling. Oh, dear Coati Cass, it is increasing; I can't suppress it!"

"What? . . . Don't tell me you're about to have some kind of primitive fit? Did that mating business—?"

"No. Well, maybe, yes. Oh, I *can't*—"

"Syl, you must."

"No. All will be well. I will recollect all my training and recover myself."

"Syl, this sounds terrible . . . . But, face it, you're all alone—*we're* all alone. You can't mate, if that's what's coming over you."

"I know. But—"

"Then that's it. The sooner we get going, the sooner we'll be at FedBase and you can start home. I was going to take a nice nap first, but if you've got troubles, maybe I better just go right into the chest. Couldn't you try to sleep, too? You might wake up feeling better."

"Oh, no! Oh, no! Not the cold! It stimulates us."

"Yes, I forgot. But look, I can't live through all those light-years awake!"

"No—not the cold-sleep!"

"Syl. Myr Syllobene. Maybe you better confess the whole thing *right now*. Just what are you afraid of?"

"But I'm not sure—"

"You're sure enough to be glooming for days. Now you tell Coati exactly what you're afraid of. Take a deep breath—here, I'll do it for you—and start. Now!"

"Perhaps I must," the alien voice says, small but newly resolute. "I don't remember if I told you: If the mating cycle overtakes us when an Eea is alone, we can still . . . reproduce. By—I know your word—spores. Just like seeds, only they are all identical with the parent. And the Eea grows them and gives birth like seeds, as you saw. Then the Eea comes back to itself." Syl's words are coming in a rush now, as from relief at speaking out. "It's very rare, because of course we are taught to stop it when the feeling begins. I— I never had it before. I'm supposed to seek out my mentor at once, to be instructed how to stop it, or the mentor will visit the young one and make it stop. But my mentor is far away! l keep hoping this is not really the feeling that begins all that, but it won't go away; it's getting stronger. Oh, Coati, my friend, I am so afraid—so fearful—" The voice trails off in great sobs.

The Coati voice says, slowly, "Oh, whew. You mean, you're afraid you're going to be grabbed by this mating thing and make spores in my head? And they'll bore a hole?"

"Y-yes." The alien is in obvious misery.

"Wait a minute. Will it make you go crazy and stop being you, like a Human who gets intoxicated? Oh, you couldn't know about that. But you'll act like those untrained young ones? I mean, what will you do?"

"I may—eat blindly. Oh-h-h . . . don't leave me alone in your cold-sleep!"

"Well. Well. I have to think."

Click—the deputy has halted the machine.

"I thought we should take a minim to appreciate this young woman's dilemma, and the dilemma of the alien."

The xenobiologist sighs. "This urge, or cycle is evidently not so very rare, since instructions are given to the young to combat it. Instructions that unfortunately depend on the mentor being available. But it doesn't appear to be a normal part or stage of maturing—more like an accidental episode. I suggest that here it was precipitated by the experience with the two Humans infected by untrained young. That awakened what the Eea seem to regard as part of their primitive system."

"How fast can they get back to that Eea planet, ah, Nolian?" someone asks.

"Not fast enough, I gather," Exec says. "Even if she took the heroic measure of traveling without cold-sleep."

"She's got to get rid of that thing!" Coati's father bursts out. "Cut into her own head and pull it out if she has to! Can't somebody get to her and operate?"

He is met by the silence of negation. The moments they are hearing passed, for good or ill, long back.

"The alien said it could leave," the deputy observes. "We will see if that solution occurs to them." He clicks on.

As if echoing him, Coati's voice comes in. "I asked Syl if she could pull out and park somewhere comfortable until the fit passed. But she says—tell them, Syl."

"I have been trying to withdraw for some time. Early on, I could have done so easily. But now the strands of my physical being have been penetrating so very deeply into Coati's brain, into the molecular and—is atomic the word?—atomic structure. So I have attempted to cut loose from portions of myself, but whenever I succeed in freeing one part, I find that the part I freed before has rejoined. I-I have not had much instruction in this technique, not since I was much smaller. I seem to have grown greatly while with Coati. Nothing I try works. Oh, oh, if only another Eea were here to help! I would do anything, I'd cut myself in half—"

"It's a god-cursed cancer," Coati's father growls. He perceives no empathetic young alien, but only the threat to his child.

"But dear Coati Cass, I cannot. And there is no mistake now; the primitive part of myself that contains this dreadful urge is growing, growing, although I am fighting it as well as I can. I fear it will soon overwhelm me. Is there not something you can do?"

"Not for you, Syl. How could I? But tell me—after it's all passed, and you've, well, eaten my brains out, will you come back to yourself and be all right?"

"Oh—I could never be all right, knowing I had murdered you! Killed my friend! My life would be a horrible thing. Even if my people accepted me, I could not. I mean this, Coati Cass."

"H'mm. Well. Let me think." The recorder clicks off—on. Coati's voice comes back. "Well, the position is: If we carry out our plan to go back to FedBase, I'll be a zombie, or dead, when I get there, and you'll be miserable. And the ship'll be full of spores. I wouldn't be able to land it, but somebody'd probably manage to intercept us. And the people who opened it would get infected with your spores, and by the time things got cleared up, a lot of Humans would have died, and maybe nobody would feel like taking you back to your planet. Ugh."

The alien voice echoes her.

"On the other hand, if we cut straight for Nolian, even at the best, you'd have made spores and they'd have chewed up my brains and it'd be impossible for me to bring the ship down and let you out. So you'd be locked up with a dead Human and a lot of spores, flying on to gods know where, forever. Unless somebody intercepted us, in which case the other scenario would take over. . . . Syl, I don't see any out. What I do see is that this ship will soon be a flying time bomb, just waiting for some non-Eea life to get near it."

"Yes. That is well put, Coati-my-friend," the small voice says sadly. "Oh!" "What?"

"I felt a strong urge to—to hurt you. I barely stopped it. Oh, Coati! Help! I don't want to become a wild beast!"

"Syl, honey . . . it's not your fault. I wonder, shouldn't we sort of say our good-byes while we can?"

"I see . . . I see."

"Syllobene, my dear, whatever happens, remember we were great friends, and had adventures together, and saved each other's lives. And if you do something bad to me, remember I know it isn't really you; it's just an accident because we're so different. I . . . I've never had a friend I loved more, Syl. So good-bye, and remember it all with joy if you can."

A sound of sobbing. "G-good-bye, dear Coati Cass. I am so sad with all my being that it is through me that badness has come. Being friends with you has lifted my life to lightness I never dreamed of. If I survive, I will tell my people how good and true Humans are. But I don't think I will have that chance. One way or another, I will end my life with yours, Coati Cass. Above all, I do not wish to bring more trouble on Humans."

"Syl. . . ." Coati says thoughtfully. "If you mean that about going together, there's a way. Do you mean it?"

"Y-yes. Yes."

"The thing is, in addition to what happens to us, our ship will be a menace to anybody, Human or whatever, who gets at it. It's sort of our duty not to do a thing like that, you know? And I really don't want to go on as a zombie. And I see that beautiful yellow sun out there, the sun we saw all those days and nights down on the planet . . . like it's waiting for us . . . Syl?"

"Coati, I understand you."

"Of course, there're a lot of things I wanted to do; you d-did, too— maybe this is the b-big one—"

The recorder lapses to a fuzzy sound.

"Something has been erased," the deputy says.

It comes back in a minim or two with Coati's voice saying, "— didn't need to hear all that. The point is, we've decided. So—ow! Oh-h-h—*ow!* What?"

"Coati!" The small voice seems to be screaming. "Coati, I'm losing— I'm losing myself! Something wants to hurt you, to stop you—to make you go into cold-sleep—I'm fighting it— Oh, forgive me, forgive me—"

"OW! Hey, I forgive you, but— Oh, *ouch!* Wait, hold it, baby, I just have to set our course, and then I'll hop right into the chest. I *have* to set the computer; try to understand."

Undecipherable noise from the alien. Then, to everyone's surprise, the unmistakable sound of a young Human voice humming fills the room.

"I know that tune," the computer chief says suddenly. "It's old—wait— yes. It's 'Into the Heart of the Sun.' . . . She's trying to tell us what she's doing without alerting that maniacal parasite."

"We'd better listen closely," the deputy observes superfluously.

A moment later the humming gives place to a softly sung bar of words— yes, it's "Into the Heart of the Sun." It ends in a sharp yelp. "Hey, Syl, try not to, *please*—"

"I try! I try!"

"We get into cold-sleep just as soon as I possibly can. Don't hurt me, you doppelgänger, or I'll make a mistake and you'll end up as fried spores— Owwwww! For an amateur, you're a little d-devil, Syl." The voice seems to be trying to conceal the wail of real agony. Exec is reminded of the wounded patrolmen he tended as a young med-aid long ago during the Last War.

"I just have to regoogolate the fribilizer that keeps us from penetrating high g-fields," says Coati. "You wouldn't want *that* to happen, would you?"

Her own throat growls at her. "Hurry."

"That's an old nonsense phrase," Computers speaks up. " 'Googolating the fribilizer'—she's trying to tell us she's killing the automatic-drive override. Oh, good girl."

"And now I *must* send this message pipe off. It's in your interests, Syl; it shows you doing all those useful things. And I have to heat it first— Oh, ow—please let me, Syl, please try to let m-me—"

Sounds that might be a heat oven, roughly handled, punctuated by yelps from Coati. Her father is gripping his chair arms so hard they creak.

"Yes, I know that big yellow sun is getting pretty hot and bright. Don't let it worry you. If we go close by it, we'll save a whole leg of our trip. It's the only neat thing to do. Han Lu Han, anybody there? Here, I'll pull the bow blinds.

"And now the cassettes from Boney and Ko go in the pipe—*ow!*—and where's that little one from their bow camera? Syl, try to tell your primitive self you're just slowing me down with these jabs. Please, please— Ah, here it is. And out come the spores—I mean, the seeds that were in there. . . . That pipe is *hot*!

"And now it's time to say good-bye, put this in the pipe, and climb into the chest. I really hope the pipe's frequency can pull it through these g's. On second thought, maybe I'd like to see where we're going while it lasts. As long as I can stand the pain, I think I'll stay out and watch."

Loud sounds of the cassette being handled.

"Good-bye, all. To my folks, oh, I do love you, Dad and Mum. Maybe somebody at FedBase can explain—*OW*!! Oh . . . Oh . . . I can't . . . Hey, Syl, is there anybody you want to say good-bye to? Your mentor?"

A confused vocalization, then, faintly: "Yes. . . ."

"Remember Syl. She's the real stuff, she's doing this for Humans. For an alien race. She could have stopped me, believe it. . . . Bye, all."

A crash, and the recorder goes to silence.

"Han Lu Han," says the xenobiologist quietly into the silence. "He was that boy in the Lyrae mission. 'It's the only really neat thing to do.' He said that before he took the rescue run that killed him."

Exec clears his throat. "Myr Cass, we will send a reconnaissance mission to check the area. But I fear there is no reason to believe, or hope, that Myr Coati failed in her plan to eliminate the contagious menace of herself, her passenger, and the ship by flying into a sun. By the end of the message, she was close enough to feel its heat, and it was doubtless the effect of the gravity that delayed this message pipe so much longer than the preceding one, which was sent only a few days earlier. She had, moreover, carefully undone the precautions that prevent a ship on automatic drive from colliding with a star. Myr Cass, when confronted by a terrifying and painful dilemma capable of causing great harm to others, your daughter took the brave and honorable course, and we must be grateful to her."

Silence, as all contemplate the sudden ending of a bright young life. Two bright young lives.

"But you said she was alive and well when the message was sent." Coati's father makes a last, confused protest.

"Sir, I said she was compos mentis and probably in her ship," the deputy reminds him.

"Thank the gods her mother didn't come here. . . ."

"You can pinpoint the star she was headed for?" Exec asks Charts.

"Oh, yes. The B-K coordinates are good."

"Then, if nobody has a different idea, I suggest that it be appropriately named in the new ephemeris."

"Coati's Star," says Commo. People are rising to leave.

"And Syllobene," a quiet voice says. "Have we forgotten already?"

"Myr Cass, I think you may perhaps prefer to be alone for a moment," Exec tells him. "Anytime you wish to see me, I'll be at your service in my office."

"Thank you."

Exec leads his deputy out, and opts for a quiet lunch in their small private dining room. Added to the list of things that were on his mind before he entered the conference chamber to hear Coati's message are now the problem of when and how to contact the Eea; how to determine the degree of danger from their seeds or spores, in space near the promising GO suns; the Lost Colony question; whether to quarantine the area; and whether there is any chance of any seeds in FedBase itself from the earlier messages. Also, a sample of the chemical that Syllobene had immunized Coati with would seem to be a rather high priority.

But behind all these practical thoughts, an image floats in his mind's eye, accompanied by the sound of a light young voice humming. It's the image in silhouette of two children—one Human, the other not—advancing, hand in hand, toward an inferno of alien solar fire.

RACHEL IN LOVE

PAT MURPHY

P AT MURPHY was born in March 1955 in Spokane, Washington. She earned a B.A. in biology and general science from UC Santa Cruz in 1976; while there, she also participated in the science writing program. Her science articles have appeared in magazines and newspapers since 1976. From 1978 to 1982, she was a senior research writer in the educational graphics department at Sea World. Since 1982, she has worked in various writing/editorial capacities at the Exploratorium interactive science museum in San Francisco.

Her first published story was "Nightbird at the Window" in *Chrysalis 5* in 1979, and her first novel was *The Shadow Hunter.* Next came the fantasy *The Falling Woman,* which won the Nebula Award for best novel. It was a big year for Murphy, who also won the Nebula, Sturgeon Memorial, and Locus Awards for her novelette "Rachel in Love." Of her other novels, *The City, Not Long After* is science fiction; *Nadya* is dark fantasy; and related trio *There and Back Again, Wild Angel,* and *Adventures in Time and Space with Max Merriwell* are somewhere in between. Her collection *Points of Departure* won a Philip K. Dick Award, and her novelette "Bones" won the World Fantasy Award in 1991.

The story that follows is a powerful and uncomfortable look at gender, identity, and what it means to be human.

* * *

IT IS A SUNDAY MORNING in summer and a small brown chimpanzee named Rachel sits on the living room floor of a remote ranch house on the edge of the Painted Desert. She is watching a Tarzan movie on television. Her hairy arms are wrapped around her knees and she rocks back and forth with suppressed excitement. She knows that her father would say that she's too old for such childish amusements—but since Aaron is still sleeping, he can't chastise her.

On the television, Tarzan has been trapped in a bamboo cage by a band of wicked Pygmies. Rachel is afraid that he won't escape in time to save Jane from the ivory smugglers who hold her captive. The movie cuts to Jane, who is tied up in the back of a jeep, and Rachel whimpers softly to herself. She knows better than to howl: she peeked into her father's bedroom earlier, and he was still in bed. Aaron doesn't like her to howl when he is sleeping.

When the movie breaks for a commercial, Rachel goes to her father's room. She is ready for breakfast and she wants him to get up. She tiptoes to the bed to see if he is awake.

His eyes are open and he is staring at nothing. His face is pale and his lips are a purplish color. Dr. Aaron Jacobs, the man Rachel calls father, is not asleep. He is dead, having died in the night of a heart attack.

When Rachel shakes him, his head rocks back and forth in time with her shaking, but his eyes do not blink and he does not breathe. She places his hand on her head, nudging him so that he will waken and stroke her. He does not move. When she leans toward him, his hand falls limply to dangle over the edge of the bed.

In the breeze from the open bedroom window, the fine wisps of gray hair that he had carefully combed over his bald spot each morning shift and flutter, exposing the naked scalp. In the other room, elephants trumpet as they stampede across the jungle to rescue Tarzan. Rachel whimpers softly, but her father does not move.

Rachel backs away from her father's body. In the living room, Tarzan is swinging across the jungle on vines, going to save Jane. Rachel ignores the television. She prowls through the house as if searching for comfort—stepping into her own small bedroom, wandering through her father's laboratory. From the cages that line the walls, white rats stare at her with hot red eyes. A rabbit hops across its cage, making a series of slow dull thumps, like a feather pillow tumbling down a flight of stairs.

She thinks that perhaps she made a mistake. Perhaps her father is just sleeping. She returns to the bedroom, but nothing has changed. Her father lies open-eyed on the bed. For a long time, she huddles beside his body, clinging to his hand.

He is the only person she has ever known. He is her father, her teacher, her friend. She cannot leave him alone.

The afternoon sun blazes through the window, and still Aaron does not move. The room grows dark, but Rachel does not turn on the lights. She is waiting for Aaron to wake up. When the moon rises, its silver light shines through the window to cast a bright rectangle on the far wall.

Outside, somewhere in the barren rocky land surrounding the ranch house, a coyote lifts its head to the rising moon and wails, a thin sound that is as lonely as a train whistling through an abandoned station. Rachel joins in with a desolate howl of loneliness and grief. Aaron lies still and Rachel knows that he is dead.

WHEN RACHEL WAS YOUNGER, she had a favorite bedtime story. —Where did I come from? she would ask Aaron, using the abbreviated gestures of ASL, American Sign Language. —Tell me again.

"You're too old for bedtime stories," Aaron said.

—Please, she'd sign. —Tell me the story.

In the end, he always relented and told her. "Once upon a time, there was a little girl named Rachel," he said. "She was a pretty girl, with long golden hair like a princess in a fairy tale. She lived with her father and her mother and they were all very happy."

Rachel would snuggle contentedly beneath her blankets. The story, like any good fairy tale, had elements of tragedy. In the story, Rachel's father worked at a university, studying the workings of the brain and charting the electric fields that the nervous impulses of an active brain produced. But the other researchers at the university didn't understand Rachel's father; they distrusted his research and cut off his funding. (During this portion of the story, Aaron's voice took on a bitter edge.) So he left the university and took his wife and daughter to the desert, where he could work in peace.

He continued his research and determined that each individual brain produced its own unique pattern of fields, as characteristic as a fingerprint. (Rachel found this part of the story quite dull, but Aaron insisted on including it.) The shape of this "Electric Mind," as he called it, was determined by habitual patterns of thoughts and emotions. Record the Electric Mind, he postulated, and you could capture an individual's personality.

Then one sunny day, the doctor's wife and beautiful daughter went for a drive. A truck barreling down a winding cliffside road lost its brakes and met the car head-on, killing both the girl and her mother. (Rachel clung to Aaron's hand during this part of the story, frightened by the sudden evil twist of fortune.)

But though Rachel's body had died, all was not lost. In his desert lab, the doctor had recorded the electrical patterns produced by his daughter's brain. The doctor had been experimenting with the use of external magnetic fields to impose the patterns from one animal onto the brain of another. From an animal supply house, he obtained a young chimpanzee. He used a mixture of norepinephrin-based transmitter substances to boost the speed of neural processing in the chimp's brain, and then he imposed the pattern of his daughter's mind upon the brain of this young chimp, combining the two after his own fashion, saving his daughter in his own way. In the chimp's brain was all that remained of Rachel Jacobs.

The doctor named the chimp Rachel and raised her as his own daughter. Since the limitations of the chimpanzee larynx made speech very difficult, he instructed her in ASL. He taught her to read and to write. They were good friends, the best of companions.

By this point in the story, Rachel was usually asleep. But it didn't matter—she knew the ending. The doctor, whose name was Aaron Jacobs, and the chimp named Rachel lived happily ever after.

Rachel likes fairy tales and she likes happy endings. She has the mind of a teenage girl, but the innocent heart of a young chimp.

SOMETIMES, WHEN RACHEL looks at her gnarled brown fingers, they seem alien, wrong, out of place. She remembers having small, pale, delicate hands. Memories lie upon memories, layers upon layers, like the sedimentary rocks of the desert buttes.

Rachel remembers a blonde-haired fair-skinned woman who smelled sweetly of perfume. On a Halloween long ago, this woman (who was, in these memories, Rachel's mother) painted Rachel's fingernails bright red because Rachel was dressed as a gypsy and gypsies liked red. Rachel remembers the woman's hands: white hands with faintly blue veins hidden just beneath the skin, neatly clipped nails painted rose pink.

But Rachel also remembers another mother and another time. Her mother was dark and hairy and smelled sweetly of overripe fruit. She and Rachel lived in a wire cage in a room filled with chimps and she hugged Rachel to her hairy breast whenever any people came into the room. Rachel's mother groomed Rachel constantly, picking delicately through her fur in search of lice that she never found.

Memories upon memories: jumbled and confused, like random pictures clipped from magazines, a bright collage that makes no sense. Rachel remembers cages: cold wire mesh beneath her feet, the smell of fear around her. A man in a white lab coat took her from the arms of her hairy mother and pricked her with needles. She could hear her mother howling, but she could not escape from the man.

Rachel remembers a junior high school dance where she wore a new dress: she stood in a dark corner of the gym for hours, pretending to admire the crepe paper decorations because she felt too shy to search among the crowd for her friends.

She remembers when she was a young chimp: she huddled with five other adolescent chimps in the stuffy freight compartment of a train, frightened by the alien smells and sounds.

She remembers gym class: gray lockers and ugly gym suits that revealed her skinny legs. The teacher made everyone play softball, even Rachel who was unathletic and painfully shy. Rachel at bat, standing at the plate, was terrified to be the center of attention. "Easy out," said the catcher, a hard-edged girl who ran with the wrong crowd and always smelled of cigarette smoke. When Rachel swung at the ball and missed, the outfielders filled the air with malicious laughter.

Rachel's memories are as delicate and elusive as the dusty moths and butterflies that dance among the rabbit brush and sage. Memories of her girlhood never linger; they land for an instant, then take flight, leaving Rachel feeling abandoned and alone.

RACHEL LEAVES AARON'S body where it is, but closes his eyes and pulls the sheet up over his head. She does not know what else to do. Each day she waters the garden and picks some greens for the rabbits. Each day, she cares for the animals in the lab, bringing them food and refilling their water bottles. The weather is cool and Aaron's body does not smell too bad, though by the end of the week, a wide line of ants runs from the bed to the open window.

At the end of the first week, on a moonlit evening, Rachel decides to let the animals go free. She releases the rabbits one by one, climbing on a stepladder to reach down into the cage and lift each placid bunny out. She carries each one to the back door, holding it for a moment and stroking the soft warm fur. Then she sets the animal down and nudges it in the direction of the green grass that grows around the perimeter of the fenced garden.

The rats are more difficult to deal with. She manages to wrestle the large rat cage off the shelf, but it is heavier than she thought it would be. Though she slows its fall, it lands on the floor with a crash and the rats scurry to and fro within. She shoves the cage across the linoleum floor, sliding it down the hall, over the doorsill, and onto the back patio. When she opens the cage door, rats burst out like popcorn from a popper, white in the moonlight and dashing in all directions.

ONCE, WHILE AARON was taking a nap, Rachel walked along the dirt track that led to the main highway. She hadn't planned on going far. She just wanted to see what the highway looked like, maybe hide near the mailbox and watch a car drive past. She was curious about the outside world and her fleeting fragmentary memories did not satisfy that curiosity.

She was halfway to the mailbox when Aaron came roaring up in his old jeep. "Get in the car," he shouted at her. "Right now!" Rachel had never seen him so angry. She cowered in the jeep's passenger seat, covered with dust from the road, unhappy that Aaron was so upset. He didn't speak until they got back to the ranch house, and then he spoke in a low voice, filled with bitterness and suppressed rage.

"You don't want to go out there," he said. "You wouldn't like it out there. The world is filled with petty, narrow-minded, stupid people. They wouldn't understand you. And anyone they don't understand, they want to hurt. They hate anyone who's different. If they know that you're different, they punish you, hurt you. They'd lock you up and never let you go."

He looked straight ahead, staring through the dirty windshield. "It's not like the shows on TV, Rachel," he said in a softer tone. "It's not like the stories in books."

He looked at her then and she gestured frantically. —I'm sorry. I'm sorry.

"I can't protect you out there," he said. "I can't keep you safe."

Rachel took his hand in both of hers. He relented then, stroking her head. "Never do that again," he said. "Never."

Aaron's fear was contagious. Rachel never again walked along the dirt track and sometimes she had dreams about bad people who wanted to lock her in a cage.

. . .

TWO WEEKS AFTER Aaron's death, a black-and-white police car drives slowly up to the house. When the policemen knock on the door, Rachel hides behind the couch in the living room. They knock again, try the knob, then open the door, which she had left unlocked.

Suddenly frightened, Rachel bolts from behind the couch, bounding toward the back door. Behind her, she hears one man yell, "My God! It's a gorilla!"

By the time he pulls his gun, Rachel has run out the back door and away into the hills. From the hills she watches as an ambulance drives up and two men in white take Aaron's body away. Even after the ambulance and the police car drive away, Rachel is afraid to go back to the house. Only after sunset does she return.

Just before dawn the next morning, she wakens to the sound of a truck jouncing down the dirt road. She peers out the window to see a pale green pickup. Sloppily stenciled in white on the door are the words: PRIMATE RESEARCH CENTER. Rachel hesitates as the truck pulls up in front of the house. By the time she has decided to flee, two men are getting out of the truck. One of them carries a rifle.

She runs out the back door and heads for the hills, but she is only halfway to hiding when she hears a sound like a sharp intake of breath and feels a painful jolt in her shoulder. Suddenly, her legs give way and she is tumbling backward down the sandy slope, dust coating her red-brown fur, her howl becoming a whimper, then fading to nothing at all. She falls into the blackness of sleep.

THE SUN IS UP. Rachel lies in a cage in the back of the pickup truck. She is partially conscious and she feels a tingling in her hands and feet. Nausea grips her stomach and bowels. Her body aches.

Rachel can blink, but otherwise she can't move. From where she lies, she can see only the wire mesh of the cage and the side of the truck. When she tries to turn her head, the burning in her skin intensifies. She lies still, wanting to cry out, but unable to make a sound. She can only blink slowly, trying to close out the pain. But the burning and nausea stay.

The truck jounces down a dirt road, then stops. It rocks as the men get out. The doors slam. Rachel hears the tailgate open.

A woman's voice: "Is that the animal the County Sheriff wanted us to pick up?" A woman peers into the cage. She wears a white lab coat and her brown hair is tied back in a single braid. Around her eyes, Rachel can see small wrinkles, etched by years of living in the desert. The woman doesn't look evil. Rachel hopes that the woman will save her from the men in the truck.

"Yeah. It should be knocked out for at least another half hour. Where do you want it?"

"Bring it into the lab where we had the rhesus monkeys. I'll keep it there until I have an empty cage in the breeding area."

Rachel's cage scrapes across the bed of the pickup. She feels each bump and jar as a new pain. The man swings the cage onto a cart and the woman pushes the cart down a concrete corridor. Rachel watches the walls pass just a few inches from her nose.

The lab contains rows of cages in which small animals sleepily move. In the sudden stark light of the overhead fluorescent bulbs, the eyes of white rats gleam red.

With the help of one of the men from the truck, the woman manhandles Rachel onto a lab table. The metal surface is cold and hard, painful against Rachel's skin. Rachel's body is not under her control; her limbs will not respond. She is still frozen by the tranquilizer, able to watch, but that is all. She cannot protest or plead for mercy.

Rachel watches with growing terror as the woman pulls on rubber gloves and fills a hypodermic needle with a clear solution. "Mark down that I'm giving her the standard test for tuberculosis; this eyelid should be checked before she's moved in with the others. I'll add thiabendazole to her feed for the next few days to clean out any intestinal worms. And I suppose we might as well de-flea her as well," the woman says. The man grunts in response.

Expertly, the woman closes one of Rachel's eyes. With her open eye, Rachel watches the hypodermic needle approach. She feels a sharp pain in her eyelid. In her mind, she is howling, but the only sound she can manage is a breathy sigh.

The woman sets the hypodermic aside and begins methodically spraying Rachel's fur with a cold, foul-smelling liquid. A drop strikes Rachel's eye and burns. Rachel blinks, but she cannot lift a hand to rub her eye. The woman treats Rachel with casual indifference, chatting with the man as she spreads Rachel's legs and sprays her genitals. "Looks healthy enough. Good breeding stock."

Rachel moans, but neither person notices. At last, they finish their torture, put her in a cage, and leave the room. She closes her eyes, and the darkness returns.

. . .

RACHEL DREAMS. She is back at home in the ranch house. It is night and she is alone. Outside, coyotes yip and howl. The coyote is the voice of the desert, wailing as the wind wails when it stretches itself thin to squeeze through a crack between two boulders. The people native to this land tell tales of Coyote, a god who was a trickster, unreliable, changeable, mercurial.

Rachel is restless, anxious, unnerved by the howling of the coyotes. She is looking for Aaron. In the dream, she knows he is not dead, and she searches the house for him, wandering from his cluttered bedroom to her small room to the linoleum-tiled lab.

She is in the lab when she hears something tapping: a small dry scratching, like a wind-blown branch against the window, though no tree grows near the house and the night is still. Cautiously, she lifts the curtain to look out.

She looks into her own reflection: a pale oval face, long blonde hair. The hand that holds the curtain aside is smooth and white with carefully clipped fingernails. But something is wrong. Superimposed on the reflection is another face peering through the glass: a pair of dark brown eyes, a chimp face with red-brown hair and jug-handle ears. She sees her own reflection and she sees the outsider; the two images merge and blur. She is afraid, but she can't drop the curtain and shut the ape face out.

She is a chimp looking in through the cold, bright windowpane; she is a girl looking out; she is a girl looking in; she is an ape looking out. She is afraid and the coyotes are howling all around.

RACHEL OPENS HER EYES and blinks until the world comes into focus. The pain and tingling has retreated, but she still feels a little sick. Her left eye aches. When she rubs it, she feels a raised lump on the eyelid where the woman pricked her. She lies on the floor of a wire mesh cage. The room is hot and the air is thick with the smell of animals.

In the cage beside her is another chimp, an older animal with scruffy dark brown fur. He sits with his arms wrapped around his knees, rocking back and forth, back and forth. His head is down. As he rocks, he murmurs to himself, a meaningless cooing that goes on and on. On his scalp, Rachel can see a gleam of metal: a permanently implanted electrode protrudes from a shaven patch. Rachel makes a soft questioning sound, but the other chimp will not look up.

Rachel's own cage is just a few feet square. In one corner is a bowl of monkey pellets. A water bottle hangs on the side of the cage. Rachel ignores the food, but drinks thirstily.

Sunlight streams through the windows, sliced into small sections by the wire mesh that covers the glass. She tests her cage door, rattling it gently at first, then harder. It is securely latched. The gaps in the mesh are too small to admit her hand. She can't reach out to work the latch.

The other chimp continues to rock back and forth. When Rachel rattles the mesh of her cage and howls, he lifts his head wearily and looks at her. His red-rimmed eyes are unfocused; she can't be sure he sees her.

—Hello, she gestures tentatively. —What's wrong?

He blinks at her in the dim light. —Hurt, he signs in ASL. He reaches up to touch the electrode, fingering skin that is already raw from repeated rubbing.

—Who hurt you? she asks. He stares at her blankly and she repeats the question. —Who?

—Men, he signs.

As if on cue, there is the click of a latch and the door to the lab opens. A bearded man in a white coat steps in, followed by a clean-shaven man in a suit. The bearded man seems to be showing the other man around the lab. " . . . only preliminary testing, so far," the bearded man is saying. "We've been hampered by a shortage of chimps trained in ASL." The two men stop in front of the old chimp's cage. "This old fellow is from the Oregon center. Funding for the language program was cut back and some of the animals were dispersed to other programs." The old chimp huddles at the back of the cage, eyeing the bearded man with suspicion.

—Hungry? the bearded man signs to the old chimp. He holds up an orange where the old chimp can see it.

—Give orange, the old chimp gestures. He holds out his hand, but comes no nearer to the wire mesh than he must to reach the orange. With the fruit in hand, he retreats to the back of his cage.

The bearded man continues, "This project will provide us with the first solid data on neural activity during use of sign language. But we really need greater access to chimps with advanced language skills. People are so damn protective of their animals."

"Is this one of yours?" the clean-shaven man asks, pointing to Rachel. She cowers in the back of the cage, as far from the wire mesh as she can get.

"No, not mine. She was someone's household pet, apparently. The county sheriff had us pick her up." The bearded man peers into her cage.

Rachel does not move; she is terrified that he will somehow guess that she knows ASL. She stares at his hands and thinks about those hands putting an electrode through her skull. "I think she'll be put in breeding stock," the man says as he turns away.

Rachel watches them go, wondering at what terrible people these are. Aaron was right: they want to punish her, put an electrode in her head.

After the men are gone, she tries to draw the old chimp into conversation, but he will not reply. He ignores her as he eats his orange. Then he returns to his former posture, hiding his head and rocking himself back and forth.

Rachel, hungry despite herself, samples one of the food pellets. It has a strange medicinal taste, and she puts it back in the bowl. She needs to pee, but there is no toilet and she cannot escape the cage. At last, unable to hold it, she pees in one corner of the cage. The urine flows through the wire mesh to soak the litter below, and the smell of warm piss fills her cage. Humiliated, frightened, her head aching, her skin itchy from the flea spray, Rachel watches as the sunlight creeps across the room.

The day wears on. Rachel samples her food again, but rejects it, preferring hunger to the strange taste. A black man comes and cleans the cages of the rabbits and rats. Rachel cowers in her cage and watches him warily, afraid that he will hurt her, too.

When night comes, she is not tired. Outside, coyotes howl. Moonlight filters in through the high windows. She draws her legs up toward her body, then rests with her arms wrapped around her knees. Her father is dead, and she is a captive in a strange place. For a time, she whimpers softly, hoping to awaken from this nightmare and find herself at home in bed. When she hears the click of a key in the door to the room, she hugs herself more tightly.

A man in green coveralls pushes a cart filled with cleaning supplies into the room. He takes a broom from the cart, and begins sweeping the concrete floor. Over the rows of cages, she can see the top of his head bobbing in time with his sweeping. He works slowly and methodically, bending down to sweep carefully under each row of cages, making a neat pile of dust, dung, and food scraps in the center of the aisle.

THE JANITOR'S NAME is Jake. He is a middle-aged deaf man who has been employed by the Primate Research Center for the past seven years. He works night shift. The personnel director at the Primate Research Center likes Jake because he fills the federal quota for handicapped employees, and because he has not asked for a raise in five years. There have been some complaints about Jake—his work is often sloppy—but never enough to merit firing the man.

Jake is an unambitious, somewhat slow-witted man. He likes the Primate Research Center because he works alone, which allows him to drink on the job. He is an easy-going man, and he likes the animals. Sometimes, he brings treats for them. Once, a lab assistant caught him feeding an apple to a pregnant rhesus monkey. The monkey was part of an experiment on the effect of dietary restrictions on fetal brain development, and the lab assistant warned Jake that he would be fired if he was ever caught interfering with the animals again. Jake still feeds the animals, but he is more careful about when he does it, and he has never been caught again.

As Rachel watches, the old chimp gestures to Jake. —Give banana, the chimp signs. —Please banana. Jake stops sweeping for a minute and reaches down to the bottom shelf of his cleaning cart. He returns with a banana and offers it to the old chimp. The chimp accepts the banana and leans against the mesh while Jake scratches his fur.

When Jake turns back to his sweeping, he catches sight of Rachel and sees that she is watching him. Emboldened by his kindness to the old chimp, Rachel timidly gestures to him. —Help me.

Jake hesitates, then peers at her more closely. Both his eyes are shot with a fine lacework of red. His nose displays the broken blood vessels of someone who has been friends with the bottle for too many years. He needs a shave. But when he leans close, Rachel catches the scent of whiskey and tobacco. The smells remind her of Aaron and give her courage.

—Please help me, Rachel signs. —I don't belong here.

For the last hour, Jake has been drinking steadily. His view of the world is somewhat fuzzy. He stares at her blearily.

Rachel's fear that he will hurt her is replaced by the fear that he will leave her locked up and alone. Desperately she signs again. —Please please please. Help me. I don't belong here. Please help me go home.

He watches her, considering the situation. Rachel does not move. She is afraid that any movement will make him leave. With a majestic speed dictated by his inebriation, Jake leans his broom on the row of cages behind him and steps toward Rachel's cage again. —You talk? he signs. —I talk, she signs.

—Where did you come from?

—From my father's house, she signs. —Two men came and shot me and put me here. I don't know why. I don't know why they locked me in jail.

Jake looks around, willing to be sympathetic, but puzzled by her talk of jail. —This isn't jail, he signs. —This is a place where scientists raise monkeys.

Rachel is indignant. —I am not a monkey, she signs. —I am a girl.

Jake studies her hairy body and her jug-handle ears. —You look like a monkey.

Rachel shakes her head. —No. I am a girl.

Rachel runs her hands back over her head, a very human gesture of annoyance and unhappiness. She signs sadly, —I don't belong here. Please let me out.

Jake shifts his weight from foot to foot, wondering what to do. —I can't let you out. I'll get in big trouble.

—Just for a little while? Please?

Jake glances at his cart of supplies. He has to finish off this room and two corridors of offices before he can relax for the night.

—Don't go, Rachel signs, guessing his thoughts.

—I have work to do.

She looks at the cart, then suggests eagerly, —Let me out and I'll help you work.

Jake frowns. —If I let you out, you will run away.

—No, I won't run. I will help. Please let me out.

—You promise to go back?

Rachel nods.

Warily he unlatches the cage. Rachel bounds out, grabs a whisk broom from the cart, and begins industriously sweeping bits of food and droppings from beneath the row of cages. —Come on, she signs to Jake from the end of the aisle. —I will help.

When Jake pushes the cart from the room filled with cages, Rachel follows him closely. The rubber wheels of the cleaning cart rumble softly on the linoleum floor. They pass through a metal door into a corridor where the floor is carpeted and the air smells of chalk dust and paper.

Offices let off the corridor, each one a small room furnished with a desk, bookshelves, and a blackboard. Jake shows Rachel how to empty the wastebaskets into a garbage bag. While he cleans the blackboards, she wanders from office to office, trailing the trash-filled garbage bag.

At first, Jake keeps a close eye on Rachel. But after cleaning each blackboard, he pauses to sip whiskey from a paper cup. At the end of the corridor, he stops to refill the cup from the whiskey bottle that he keeps wedged between the Saniflush and the window cleaner. By the time he is halfway through the second cup, he is treating her like an old friend, telling her to hurry up so that they can eat dinner.

Rachel works quickly, but she stops sometimes to gaze out the office windows. Outside, moonlight shines on a sandy plain, dotted here and there with scrubby clumps of rabbit brush.

At the end of the corridor is a larger room in which there are several desks and typewriters. In one of the wastebaskets, buried beneath memos and candy-bar wrappers, she finds a magazine. The title is *Love Confessions* and the cover has a picture of a man and woman kissing. Rachel studies the cover, then takes the magazine, tucking it on the bottom shelf of the cart.

Jake pours himself another cup of whiskey and pushes the cart to another hallway. Jake is working slower now, and as he works he makes humming noises, tuneless sounds that he feels only as pleasant vibrations. The last few blackboards are sloppily done, and Rachel, finished with the wastebaskets, cleans the places that Jake missed.

They eat dinner in the janitor's storeroom, a stuffy windowless room furnished with an ancient grease-stained couch, a battered black-and-white television, and shelves of cleaning supplies. From a shelf, Jake takes the paper bag that holds his lunch: a baloney sandwich, a bag of barbecue potato chips, and a box of vanilla wafers. From behind the gallon jugs of liquid cleanser, he takes a magazine. He lights a cigarette, pours himself another cup of whiskey, and settles down on the couch. After a moment's hesitation, he offers Rachel a drink, pouring a shot of whiskey into a chipped ceramic cup.

Aaron never let Rachel drink whiskey, and she samples it carefully. At first the smell makes her sneeze, but she is fascinated by the way that the drink warms her throat, and she sips some more.

As they drink, Rachel tells Jake about the men who shot her and the woman who pricked her with a needle, and he nods. —The people here are crazy, he signs.

—I know, she says, thinking of the old chimp with the electrode in his head. —You won't tell them I can talk, will you?

Jake nods. —I won't tell them anything.

—They treat me like I'm not real, Rachel signs sadly. Then she hugs her knees, frightened at the thought of being held captive by crazy people. She considers planning her escape: she is out of the cage and she is sure she could outrun Jake. As she wonders about it, she finishes her cup of whiskey. The alcohol takes the edge off her fear. She sits close beside Jake on the couch, and the smell of his cigarette smoke reminds her of Aaron. For the first time since Aaron's death she feels warm and happy.

She shares Jake's cookies and potato chips and looks at the *Love Confessions* magazine that she took from the trash. The first story that she reads is about a woman named Alice. The headline reads: "I became a go-go dancer to pay off my husband's gambling debts, and now he wants me to sell my body."

Rachel sympathizes with Alice's loneliness and suffering. Alice, like Rachel, is alone and misunderstood. As Rachel slowly reads, she sips her second cup of whiskey. The story reminds her of a fairy tale: the nice man who rescues Alice from her terrible husband replaces the handsome prince who rescued the princess. Rachel glances at Jake and wonders if he will rescue her from the wicked people who locked her in the cage.

She has finished the second cup of whiskey and eaten half Jake's cookies when Jake says that she must go back to her cage. She goes reluctantly, taking the magazine with her. He promises that he will come for her again the next night, and with that she must be content. She puts the magazine in one corner of the cage and curls up to sleep.

SHE WAKES EARLY in the afternoon. A man in a white coat is wheeling a low cart into the lab.

Rachel's head aches with hangover and she feels sick. As she crouches in one corner of her cage, he stops the cart beside her cage and then locks the wheels. "Hold on there," he mutters to her, then slides her cage onto the cart.

The man wheels her through long corridors, where the walls are cement blocks, painted institutional green. Rachel huddles unhappily in the cage, wondering where she is going and whether Jake will ever be able to find her.

At the end of a long corridor, the man opens a thick metal door and a wave of warm air strikes Rachel. It stinks of chimpanzees, excrement, and rotting food. On either side of the corridor are metal bars and wire mesh. Behind the mesh, Rachel can see dark hairy shadows. In one cage, five adolescent chimps swing and play. In another, two females huddle together, grooming each other. The man slows as he passes a cage in which a big male is banging on the wire with his fist, making the mesh rattle and ring.

"Now, Johnson," says the man. "Cool it. Be nice. I'm bringing you a new little girlfriend."

With a series of hooks, the man links Rachel's cage with the cage next to

Johnson's and opens the doors. "Go on, girl," he says. "See the nice fruit." In the new cage is a bowl of sliced apples with an attendant swarm of fruit flies.

At first, Rachel will not move into the new cage. She crouches in the cage on the cart, hoping that the man will decide to take her back to the lab. She watches him get a hose and attach it to a water faucet. But she does not understand his intention until he turns the stream of water on her. A cold blast strikes her on the back and she howls, fleeing into the new cage to avoid the cold water. Then the man closes the doors, unhooks the cage, and hurries away.

The floor is bare cement. Her cage is at one end of the corridor and two walls are cement block. A door in one of the cement block walls leads to an outside run. The other two walls are wire mesh: one facing the corridor; the other, Johnson's cage.

Johnson, quiet now that the man has left, is sniffing around the door in the wire mesh wall that joins their cages. Rachel watches him anxiously. Her memories of other chimps are distant, softened by time. She remembers her mother; she vaguely remembers playing with other chimps her age. But she does not know how to react to Johnson when he stares at her with great intensity and makes a loud huffing sound. She gestures to him in ASL, but he only stares harder and huffs again. Beyond Johnson, she can see other cages and other chimps, so many that the wire mesh blurs her vision and she cannot see the other end of the corridor.

To escape Johnson's scrutiny, she ducks through the door into the outside run, a wire mesh cage on a white concrete foundation. Outside there is barren ground and rabbit brush. The afternoon sun is hot and all the other runs are deserted until Johnson appears in the run beside hers. His attention disturbs her and she goes back inside.

She retreats to the side of the cage farthest from Johnson. A crudely built wooden platform provides her with a place to sit. Wrapping her arms around her knees, she tries to relax and ignore Johnson. She dozes off for a while, but wakes to a commotion across the corridor.

In the cage across the way is a female chimp in heat. Rachel recognizes the smell from her own times in heat. Two keepers are opening the door that separates the female's cage from the adjoining cage, where a male stands, watching with great interest. Johnson is shaking the wire mesh and howling as he watches.

"Mike here is a virgin, but Susie knows what she's doing," one keeper was saying to the other. "So it should go smoothly. But keep the hose ready."

"Yeah?"

"Sometimes they fight. We only use the hose to break it up if it gets real bad. Generally, they do okay."

Mike stalks into Susie's cage. The keepers lower the cage door, trapping both chimps in the same cage. Susie seems unalarmed. She continues eating a slice of orange while Mike sniffs at her genitals with every indication of great interest. She bends over to let Mike finger her pink bottom, the sign of estrus.

Rachel finds herself standing at the wire mesh, making low moaning noises. She can see Mike's erection, hear his grunting cries. He squats on the floor of Susie's cage, gesturing to the female. Rachel's feelings are mixed: she is fascinated, fearful, confused. She keeps thinking of the description of sex in the *Love Confessions* story: When Alice feels Danny's lips on hers, she is swept away by the passion of the moment. He takes her in his arms and her skin tingles as if she were consumed by an inner fire.

Susie bends down and Mike penetrates her with a loud grunt, thrusting violently with his hips. Susie cries out shrilly and suddenly leaps up, knocking Mike away. Rachel watches, overcome with fascination. Mike, his penis now limp, follows Susie slowly to the corner of the cage, where he begins grooming her carefully. Rachel finds that the wire mesh has cut her hands where she gripped it too tightly.

IT IS NIGHT, and the door at the end of the corridor creaks open. Rachel is immediately alert, peering through the wire mesh and trying to see down to the end of the corridor. She bangs on the wire mesh. As Jake comes closer, she waves a greeting.

When Jake reaches for the lever that will raise the door to Rachel's cage, Johnson charges toward him, howling and waving his arms above his head. He hammers on the wire mesh with his fists, howling and grimacing at Jake. Rachel ignores Johnson and hurries after Jake.

Again Rachel helps Jake clean. In the laboratory, she greets the old chimp, but the animal is more interested in the banana that Jake has brought than in conversation. The chimp will not reply to her questions, and after several tries, she gives up.

While Jake vacuums the carpeted corridors, Rachel empties the trash, finding a magazine called *Modern Romance* in the same wastebasket that had provided *Love Confessions*.

Later, in the janitor's lounge, Jake smokes a cigarette, sips whiskey, and flips through one of his own magazines. Rachel reads love stories in *Modern Romance*.

Every once in a while, she looks over Jake's shoulder at grainy pictures of naked women with their legs spread wide apart. Jake looks for a long time at a picture of a blonde woman with big breasts, red fingernails, and purple-painted eyelids. The woman lies on her back and smiles as she strokes the pinkness between her legs. The picture on the next page shows her caressing her own breasts, pinching the dark nipples. The final picture shows her looking back over her shoulder. She is in the position that Susie took when she was ready to be mounted.

Rachel looks over Jake's shoulder at the magazine, but she does not ask questions. Jake's smell began to change as soon as he opened the magazine; the scent of nervous sweat mingles with the aromas of tobacco and whiskey. Rachel suspects that questions would not be welcome just now.

At Jake's insistence, she goes back to her cage before dawn.

OVER THE NEXT WEEK, she listens to the conversations of the men who come and go, bringing food and hosing out the cages. From the men's conversation, she learns that the Primate Research Center is primarily a breeding facility that supplies researchers with domestically bred apes and monkeys of several species. It also maintains its own research staff. In indifferent tones, the men talk of horrible things. The adolescent chimps at the end of the corridor are being fed a diet high in cholesterol to determine cholesterol's effects on the circulatory system. A group of pregnant females are being injected with male hormones to determine how that will affect the female offspring. A group of infants is being fed a low protein diet to determine adverse effects on their brain development.

The men look through her as if she were not real, as if she were a part of the wall, as if she were no one at all. She cannot speak to them; she cannot trust them.

Each night, Jake lets her out of her cage and she helps him clean. He brings treats: barbecue potato chips, fresh fruit, chocolate bars, and cookies. He treats her fondly, as one would treat a precocious child. And he talks to her.

At night, when she is with Jake, Rachel can almost forget the terror of the cage, the anxiety of watching Johnson pace to and fro, the sense of unreality that accompanies the simplest act. She would be content to stay with Jake forever, eating snack food and reading confessions magazines. He seems to like her company. But each morning, Jake insists that she must go back to the cage and the terror. By the end of the first week, she has begun plotting her escape.

Whenever Jake falls asleep over his whiskey, something that happens three nights out of five, Rachel prowls the center alone, surreptitiously gathering things that she will need to survive in the desert: a plastic jug filled with water, a plastic bag of food pellets, a large beach towel that will serve as a blanket on the cool desert nights, a discarded plastic shopping bag in which she can carry the other things. Her best find is a road map on which the Primate Center is marked in red. She knows the address of Aaron's ranch and finds it on the map. She studies the roads and plots a route home. Cross country, assuming that she does not get lost, she will have to travel about fifty miles to reach the ranch. She hides these things behind one of the shelves in the janitor's storeroom.

Her plans to run away and go home are disrupted by the idea that she is in love with Jake, a notion that comes to her slowly, fed by the stories in the confessions magazines. When Jake absent-mindedly strokes her, she is filled with a strange excitement. She longs for his company and misses him on the weekends when he is away. She is happy only when she is with him, following him through the halls of the center, sniffing the aroma of tobacco and whiskey that is his own perfume. She steals a cigarette from his pack and hides it in her cage, where she can savor the smell of it at her leisure.

She loves him, but she does not know how to make him love her back. Rachel knows little about love: she remembers a high school crush where she mooned after a boy with a locker near hers, but that came to nothing. She reads the confessions magazines and Ann Landers' column in the newspaper that Jake brings with him each night, and from these sources, she learns about romance. One night, after Jake falls asleep, she types a badly punctuated, ungrammatical letter to Ann. In the letter, she explains her situation and asks for advice on how to make Jake love her. She slips the letter into a sack labeled "Outgoing Mail," and for the next week she reads Ann's column with increased interest. But her letter never appears.

Rachel searches for answers in the magazine pictures that seem to fascinate Jake. She studies the naked women, especially the big-breasted woman with the purple smudges around her eyes.

One night, in a secretary's desk, she finds a plastic case of eyeshadow. She steals it and takes it back to her cage. The next evening, as soon as the Center is quiet, she upturns her metal food dish and regards her reflection in the shiny bottom. Squatting, she balances the eye shadow case on one knee and examines its contents: a tiny makeup brush and three shades of eye shadow—INDIAN BLUE, FOREST GREEN, and WILDLY VIOLET. Rachel chooses the shade labeled WILDLY VIOLET.

Using one finger to hold her right eye closed, she dabs her eyelid carefully with the makeup brush, leaving a gaudy orchid-colored smudge on her brown skin. She studies the smudge critically, then adds to it, smearing the color beyond the corner of her eyelid until it disappears in her brown fur. The color gives her eye a carnival brightness, a lunatic gaiety. Working with great care, she matches the effect on the other side, then smiles at herself in the glass, blinking coquettishly.

In the other cage, Johnson bares his teeth and shakes the mesh. She ignores him.

When Jake comes to let her out, he frowns at her eyes. —Did you hurt yourself? he asks.

—No, she says. Then, after a pause, —Don't you like it?

Jake squats beside her and stares at her eyes. Rachel puts a hand on his knee and her heart pounds at her own boldness. —You are a very strange monkey, he signs.

Rachel is afraid to move. Her hand on his knee closes into a fist; her face folds in on itself, puckering around the eyes.

Then, straightening up, he signs, —I liked your eyes better before.

He likes her eyes. She nods without taking her eyes from his face. Later, she washes her face in the women's restroom, leaving dark smudges the color of bruises on a series of paper towels.

RACHEL IS DREAMING. She is walking through the Painted Desert with her hairy brown mother, following a red rock canyon that Rachel somehow knows will lead her to the Primate Research center. Her mother is lagging behind: she does not want to go to the center; she is afraid. In the shadow of a rock outcropping, Rachel stops to explain to her mother that they must go to the center because Jake is at the center.

Rachel's mother does not understand sign language. She watches Rachel with mournful eyes, then scrambles up the canyon wall, leaving Rachel behind. Rachel climbs after her mother, pulling herself over the edge in time to see the other chimp loping away across the wind-blown red cinder-rock and sand.

Rachel bounds after her mother, and as she runs she howls like an abandoned infant chimp, wailing her distress. The figure of her mother wavers in the distance, shimmering in the heat that rises from the sand. The figure changes. Running away across the red sands is a pale blonde woman wearing a purple sweatsuit and jogging shoes, the sweet-smelling mother that Rachel remembers. The woman looks back and smiles at Rachel. "Don't howl like an ape, daughter," she calls. "Say Mama."

Rachel runs silently, dream running that takes her nowhere. The sand burns her feet and the sun beats down on her head. The blonde woman vanishes in the distance, and Rachel is alone. She collapses on the sand, whimpering because she is alone and afraid.

She feels the gentle touch of fingers grooming her fur, and for a moment, still half asleep, she believes that her hairy mother has returned to her. In the dream, she opens her eyes and looks into a pair of dark brown eyes, separated from her by wire mesh. Johnson. He has reached through a gap in the fence to groom her. As he sorts through her fur, he makes soft cooing sounds, gentle comforting noises.

Still half asleep, she gazes at him and wonders why she was so fearful. He does not seem so bad. He grooms her for a time, and then sits nearby, watching her through the mesh. She brings a slice of apple from her dish of food and offers it to him. With her free hand, she makes the sign for apple. When he takes it, she signs again: apple. He is not a particularly quick student, but she has time and many slices of apple.

ALL RACHEL'S PREPARATIONS are done, but she cannot bring herself to leave the center. Leaving the center means leaving Jake, leaving potato chips and whiskey, leaving security. To Rachel, the thought of love is always accompanied by the warm taste of whiskey and potato chips.

Some nights, after Jake is asleep, she goes to the big glass doors that lead to the outside. She opens the doors and stands on the steps, looking down into the desert. Sometimes a jackrabbit sits on its haunches in the rectangles of light that shine through the glass doors. Sometimes she sees kangaroo rats, hopping through the moonlight like rubber balls bouncing on hard pavement. Once, a coyote trots by, casting a contemptuous glance in her direction.

The desert is a lonely place. Empty. Cold. She thinks of Jake snoring softly in the janitor's lounge. And always she closes the door and returns to him.

Rachel leads a double life: janitor's assistant by night, prisoner and teacher by day. She spends her afternoons drowsing in the sun and teaching Johnson new signs.

On a warm afternoon, Rachel sits in the outside run, basking in the sunlight. Johnson is inside, and the other chimps are quiet. She can almost imagine she is back at her father's ranch, sitting in her own yard. She naps and dreams of Jake.

She dreams that she is sitting in his lap on the battered old couch. Her hand is on his chest: a smooth pale hand with red-painted fingernails. When she looks at the dark screen of the television set, she can see her reflection. She is a thin teenager with blonde hair and blue eyes. She is naked.

Jake is looking at her and smiling. He runs a hand down her back and she closes her eyes in ecstacy.

But something changes when she closes her eyes. Jake is grooming her as her mother used to groom her, sorting through her hair in search of fleas. She opens her eyes and sees Johnson, his diligent fingers searching through her fur, his intent brown eyes watching her. The reflection on the television screen shows two chimps, tangled in each other's arms.

Rachel wakes to find that she is in heat for the first time since she came to the center. The skin surrounding her genitals is swollen and pink.

For the rest of the day, she is restless, pacing to and fro in her cage. On his side of the wire mesh wall, Johnson is equally restless, following her when she goes outside, sniffing long and hard at the edge of the barrier that separates him from her.

That night, Rachel goes eagerly to help Jake clean. She follows him closely, never letting him get far from her. When he is sweeping, she trots after him with the dustpan and he almost trips over her twice. She keeps waiting for him to notice her condition, but he seems oblivious.

As she works, she sips from a cup of whiskey. Excited, she drinks more than usual, finishing two full cups. The liquor leaves her a little disoriented, and she sways as she follows Jake to the janitor's lounge. She curls up close beside him on the couch. He relaxes with his arms resting on the back of the couch, his legs stretching out before him. She moves so that she presses against him.

He stretches, yawns, and rubs the back of his neck as if trying to rub away stiffness. Rachel reaches around behind him and begins to gently rub his neck, reveling in the feel of his skin, his hair against the backs of her hands. The thoughts that hop and skip through her mind are confusing. Sometimes it seems that the hair that tickles her hands is Johnson's; sometimes, she knows it is Jake's. And sometimes it doesn't seem to matter. Are they really so different? They are not so different.

She rubs his neck, not knowing what to do next. In the confessions magazines, this is where the man crushes the woman in his arms. Rachel climbs into Jake's lap and hugs him, waiting for him to crush her in his arms. He blinks at her sleepily. Half asleep, he strokes her, and his moving hand brushes near her genitals. She presses herself against him, making a soft sound in her throat. She rubs her hip against his crotch, aware now of a slight change in his smell, in the tempo of his breathing. He blinks at her again, a little more awake now. She bares her teeth in a smile and tilts her head back to lick his neck. She can feel his hands on her shoulders, pushing her away, and she knows what he wants. She slides from his lap and turns, presenting him with her pink genitals, ready to be mounted, ready to have him penetrate her. She moans in anticipation, a low inviting sound.

He does not come to her. She looks over her shoulder and he is still sitting on the couch, watching her through half-closed eyes. He reaches over and picks up a magazine filled with pictures of naked women. His other hand drops to his crotch and he is lost in his own world.

Rachel howls like an infant who has lost its mother, but he does not look up. He is staring at the picture of the blonde woman.

Rachel runs down dark corridors to her cage, the only home she has. When she reaches her corridor, she is breathing hard and making small lonely whimpering noises. In the dimly lit corridor, she hesitates for a moment, staring into Johnson's cage. The male chimp is asleep. She remembers the touch of his hands when he groomed her.

From the corridor, she lifts the gate that leads into Johnson's cage and enters. He wakes at the sound of the door and sniffs the air. When he sees Rachel, he stalks toward her, sniffing eagerly. She lets him finger her genitals, sniff deeply of her scent. His penis is erect and he grunts in excitement. She turns and presents herself to him and he mounts her, thrusting deep inside. As he penetrates, she thinks, for a moment, of Jake and of the thin blonde teenage girl named Rachel, but then the moment passes. Almost against her will she cries out, a shrill exclamation of welcoming and loss.

After he withdraws his penis, Johnson grooms her gently, sniffing her genitals and softly stroking her fur. She is sleepy and content, but she knows that they cannot delay.

Johnson is reluctant to leave his cage, but Rachel takes him by the hand and leads him to the janitor's lounge. His presence gives her courage. She listens at the door and hears Jake's soft breathing. Leaving Johnson in the hall, she slips into the room. Jake is lying on the couch, the magazine draped over his legs. Rachel takes the equipment that she has gathered and stands for a moment, staring at the sleeping man. His baseball cap hangs on the arm of a broken chair, and she takes that to remember him by.

Rachel leads Johnson through the empty halls. A kangaroo rat, collecting seeds in the dried grass near the glass doors, looks up curiously as Rachel leads Johnson down the steps. Rachel carries the plastic shopping bag slung over her shoulder. Somewhere in the distance, a coyote howls, a long yapping wail. His cry is joined by others, a chorus in the moonlight.

Rachel takes Johnson by the hand and leads him into the desert.

A COCKTAIL WAITRESS, driving from her job in Flagstaff to her home in Winslow, sees two apes dart across the road, hurrying away from the bright beams of her headlights. After wrestling with her conscience (she does not want to be accused of drinking on the job), she notifies the county sheriff.

A local newspaper reporter, an eager young man fresh out of journalism school, picks up the story from the police report and interviews the waitress. Flattered by his enthusiasm for her story and delighted to find a receptive ear, she tells him details that she failed to mention to the police: one of the apes was wearing a baseball cap and carrying what looked like a shopping bag.

The reporter writes up a quick humorous story for the morning edition, and begins researching a feature article to be run later in the week. He knows that the newspaper, eager for news in a slow season, will play a human-interest story up big—kind of *Lassie, Come Home* with chimps.

JUST BEFORE DAWN, a light rain begins to fall, the first rain of spring. Rachel searches for shelter and finds a small cave formed by three tumbled boulders. It will keep off the rain and hide them from casual observers. She shares her food and water with Johnson. He has followed her closely all night, seemingly intimidated by the darkness and the howling of distant coyotes. She feels protective toward him. At the same time, having him with her gives her courage. He knows only a few gestures in ASL, but he does not need to speak. His presence is comfort enough.

Johnson curls up in the back of the cave and falls asleep quickly. Rachel sits in the opening and watches dawnlight wash the stars from the sky. The rain rattles against the sand, a comforting sound. She thinks about Jake. The baseball cap on her head still smells of his cigarettes, but she does not miss him. Not really. She fingers the cap and wonders why she thought she loved Jake.

The rain lets up. The clouds rise like fairy castles in the distance and the rising sun tints them pink and gold and gives them flaming red banners. Rachel remembers when she was younger and Aaron read her the story of Pinnochio, the little puppet who wanted to be a real boy. At the end of his adventures, Pinnochio, who has been brave and kind, gets his wish. He becomes a real boy.

Rachel had cried at the end of the story and when Aaron asked why, she had rubbed her eyes on the backs of her hairy hands. —I want to be a real girl, she signed to him. —A real girl.

"You are a real girl," Aaron had told her, but somehow she had never believed him.

The sun rises higher and illuminates the broken rock turrets of the desert. There is a magic in this barren land of unassuming grandeur. Some cultures send their young people to the desert to seek visions and guidance, searching for true thinking spawned by the openness of the place, the loneliness, the beauty of emptiness.

Rachel drowses in the warm sun and dreams a vision that has the clarity of truth. In the dream, her father comes to her. "Rachel," he says to her, "it doesn't matter what anyone thinks of you. You're my daughter."

—I want to be a real girl, she signs.

"You *are* real," her father says. "And you don't need some two-bit drunken janitor to prove it to you." She knows she is dreaming, but she also knows that her father speaks the truth. She is warm and happy and she doesn't need Jake at all. The sunlight warms her and a lizard watches her from a rock, scurrying for cover when she moves. She picks up a bit of loose rock that lies on the floor of the cave. Idly, she scratches on the dark red sandstone wall of the cave. A lopsided heart shape. Within it, awkwardly printed: Rachel and Johnson. Between them, a plus sign. She goes over the letters again and again, leaving scores of fine lines on the smooth rock surface. Then, late in the morning, soothed by the warmth of the day, she sleeps.

SHORTLY AFTER DARK, an elderly rancher in a pickup truck spots two apes in a remote corner of his ranch. They run away and lose him in the rocks, but not until he has a good look at them. He calls the police, the newspaper, and the Primate Center.

The reporter arrives first thing the next morning, interviews the rancher, and follows the men from the Primate Research Center as they search for evidence of the chimps. They find monkey shit near the cave, confirming that the runaways were indeed nearby. The news reporter, an eager and curious young man, squirms on his belly into the cave and finds the names scratched on the cave wall. He peers at it. He might have dismissed them as the idle scratchings of kids, except that the names match the names of the missing chimps. "Hey," he called to his photographer, "take a look at this."

The next morning's newspaper displays Rachel's crudely scratched letters. In a brief interview, the rancher mentioned that the chimps were carrying bags. "Looked like supplies," he said. "They looked like they were in for a long haul."

ON THE THIRD DAY, Rachel's water runs out. She heads toward a small town, marked on the map. They reach it in the early morning—thirst forces them to travel by day. Beside an isolated ranch house, she finds a faucet. She is filling her bottle when Johnson grunts in alarm.

A dark-haired woman watches from the porch of the house. She does not move toward the apes, and Rachel continues filling the bottle. "It's all right, Rachel," the woman, who has been following the story in the papers, calls out. "Drink all you want."

Startled, but still suspicious, Rachel caps the bottle and, keeping her eyes on the woman, drinks from the faucet. The woman steps back into the house. Rachel motions Johnson to do the same, signaling for him to hurry and drink. She turns off the faucet when he is done.

They are turning to go when the woman emerges from the house carrying a plate of tortillas and a bowl of apples. She sets them on the edge of the porch and says, "These are for you."

The woman watches through the window as Rachel packs the food into her bag. Rachel puts away the last apple and gestures her thanks to the woman. When the woman fails to respond to the sign language, Rachel picks up a stick and writes in the sand of the yard. "THANK YOU," Rachel scratches, then waves good-bye and sets out across the desert. She is puzzled, but happy.

THE NEXT MORNING'S NEWSPAPER includes an interview with the dark-haired woman. She describes how Rachel turned on the faucet and turned it off when she was through, how the chimp packed the apples neatly in her bag and wrote in the dirt with a stick.

The reporter also interviews the director of the Primate Research Center. "These are animals," the director explains angrily. "But people want to treat them like they're small hairy people." He describes the center as "primarily a breeding center with some facilities for medical research." The reporter asks some pointed questions about their acquisition of Rachel.

But the biggest story is an investigative piece. The reporter reveals that he has tracked down Aaron Jacobs' lawyer and learned that Jacobs left a will. In this will, he bequeathed all his possessions—including his house and surrounding land—to "Rachel, the chimp I acknowledge as my daughter."

THE REPORTER MAKES FRIENDS with one of the young women in the typing pool at the research center, and she tells him the office scuttlebutt: people suspect that the chimps may have been released by a deaf and drunken janitor, who was subsequently fired for negligence. The reporter, accompanied by a friend who can communicate in sign language, finds Jake in his apartment in downtown Flagstaff.

Jake, who has been drinking steadily since he was fired, feels betrayed by Rachel, by the Primate Center, by the world. He complains at length about Rachel: they had been friends, and then she took his baseball cap and ran away. He just didn't understand why she had run away like that.

"You mean she could talk?" the reporter asks through his interpreter.

—Of course she can talk, Jake signs impatiently. —She is a smart monkey.

The headlines read: "Intelligent chimp inherits fortune!" Of course, Aaron's bequest isn't really a fortune and she isn't just a chimp, but close enough. Animal rights activists rise up in Rachel's defense. The case is discussed on the national news. Ann Landers reports receiving a letter from a chimp named Rachel; she had thought it was a hoax perpetrated by the boys at Yale. The American Civil Liberties Union assigns a lawyer to the case.

BY DAY, RACHEL AND JOHNSON sleep in whatever hiding places they can find: a cave; a shelter built for range cattle; the shell of an abandoned car, rusted from long years in a desert gully. Sometimes Rachel dreams of jungle darkness, and the coyotes in the distance become a part of her dreams, their howling becomes the cries of fellow apes.

The desert and the journey have changed her. She is wiser, having passed through the white-hot love of adolescence and emerged on the other side. She dreams, one day, of the ranch house. In the dream, she has long blonde hair and pale white skin. Her eyes are red from crying and she wanders the house restlessly, searching for something that she has lost. When she hears coyotes howling, she looks through a window at the darkness outside. The face that looks in at her has jug-handle ears and shaggy hair. When she sees the face, she cries out in recognition and opens the window to let herself in.

By night, they travel. The rocks and sand are cool beneath Rachel's feet as she walks toward her ranch. On television, scientists and politicians discuss the ramifications of her case, describe the technology uncovered by investigation of Aaron Jacobs's files. Their debates do not affect her steady progress toward her ranch or the stars that sprinkle the sky above her.

It is night when Rachel and Johnson approach the ranch house. Rachel sniffs the wind and smells automobile exhaust and strange humans. From the hills, she can see a small camp beside a white van marked with the name of a local television station. She hesitates, considering returning to the safety of the desert. Then she takes Johnson by the hand and starts down the hill. Rachel is going home.

THE SCALEHUNTER'S BEAUTIFUL
DAUGHTER

LUCIUS SHEPARD

LUCIUS SHEPARD was born in Lynchburg, Virginia, in 1947 and published his first book, the poetry collection *Cantata of Death, Weakmind & Generation,* in 1967. However, it was only in 1983 that Shepard began to publish fiction of genre interest, with "The Taylorsville Reconstruction." The science fiction and fantasy field has a long tradition—exemplified perhaps by Robert Heinlein's stories of the late '30s and early '40s, Larry Niven's stories of the late '60s, John Varley's stories of the late '70s, and Greg Egan's stories of the '90s—of new writers producing impressive strings of short fiction. The work produced by Shepard between 1983 and 1993 is easily the equal of any of those, including as it does such major stories as "A Spanish Lesson," "R&R," "Salvador," and "The Jaguar Hunter." Shepard's short fiction from this period has been collected in two World Fantasy Award–winning volumes, *The Jaguar Hunter* and *The Ends of the Earth.* Shepard has also published SF/horror novel *Green Eyes,* SF novel *Life During Wartime,* novella *Kalimantan,* and horror novel *The Golden.*

In 1995 *The Encyclopedia of Science Fiction* said of Shepard's relationship to science fiction that "there is some sense that two ships may have passed in the night." Two years later Shepard returned from what he has since described as a career "pause," delivering a series of major short stories, starting with "Crocodile Rock" in 1999, followed by Hugo Award–winner

"Radiant Green Star" in 2000, and culminating in nearly 300,000 words of outstanding short fiction published in 2003. His latest books are the short novels *Colonel Rutherford's Colt* and *Floater,* and the mini-collection *Two Trains Running.* Forthcoming are the major new collection *Trujillo,* and the novels *A Handbook of American Prayer* and *Viator.*

One of Shepard's most impressive early achievements was the trio of fantasy stories "The Man Who Painted the Dragon Griaule," "The Scalehunter's Beautiful Daughter," and "The Father of Stones," which take the stuff of high fantasy and turns it completely on its head. Shepard once said in an interview that "I've always hated dragon stories, hated the entire elf-dragon-unicorn axis. The very notion of high fantasy causes my saliva to get thick and ropy. But as an exercise, I was attempting to create a dragon whom I could respect in the morning." The story that follows, which features the dragon Griaule who is "750 feet high at the midback, and from the tip of his tail to his nose he was six thousand feet long," is one of Shepard's finest. Shepard has recently completed a long, weird chronicle that features this and other tales of the great dragon.

* * *

I

NOT LONG AFTER THE CHRISTLIGHT of the world's first morning faded, when birds still flew to heaven and back, and even the wickedest things shone like saints, so pure was their portion of evil, there was a village by the name of Hangtown that clung to the back of the dragon Griaule, a vast mile-long beast who had been struck immobile yet not lifeless by a wizard's spell, and who ruled over the Carbonales Valley, controlling in every detail the lives of the inhabitants, making known his will by the ineffable radiations emanating from the cold tonnage of his brain. From shoulder to tail, the greater part of Griaule was covered with earth and trees and grass, from some perspectives appearing to be an element of the landscape, another hill among those that ringed the valley; except for sections cleared by the scalehunters, only a portion of his right side to the haunch, and his massive neck and head remained visible, and the head had sunk to the ground, its massive jaws halfway open, itself nearly as high as the crests of the surrounding hills. Situated almost eight hundred feet above the valley floor and directly behind the fronto-parietal plate, which overhung the place like a mossy cliff, the village consisted of several dozen shacks with shingled roofs and walls of weathered planking, and bordered a lake fed by a stream that ran down onto Griaule's back from an adjoining hill; it was hemmed in against the shore by thickets of chokecherry, stands of stunted oak and hawthornes, and but for the haunted feeling that pervaded the air, a vibrant stillness similar to the atmosphere of an old ruin, to someone standing beside the lake it would seem he was looking out upon an ordinary country settlement, one a touch less neatly ordered than most, littered as it was with the bones and entrails of skizzers and flakes and other parasites that infested the dragon, but nonetheless ordinary in the lassitude that governed it, and the shabby dress and hostile attitudes of its citizenry.

Many of the inhabitants of the village were scalehunters, men and women who scavenged under Griaule's earth-encrusted wings and elsewhere on his body, searching for scales that were cracked and broken, chipping off fragments and selling these in Port Chantay, where they were valued for their medicinal virtues. They were well paid for their efforts, but were treated as pariahs by the people of the valley, who rarely ventured onto the dragon, and their lives were short and fraught with unhappy incident, a circumstance they attributed to the effects of Griaule's displeasure at their presence. Indeed, his displeasure was a constant preoccupation, and they spent much of their earnings on charms that they believed would ward off its evil influence. Some wore bits of scale around their necks, hoping that this homage would communicate to Griaule the high regard in which they held him, and perhaps the most extreme incidence of this way of thinking was embodied by the nature given by the widower Riall to his daughter Catherine. On the day of her birth, also the day of his wife's death, he dug down beneath the floor of his shack until he reached Griaule's back, laying bare a patch of golden scale some six feet long and five feet wide, and from that day forth for the next eighteen years he forced her to sleep upon the scale, hoping that the dragon's essence would seep into her and so she would be protected against his wrath. Catherine complained at first about this isolation, but she came to enjoy the dreams that visited her, dreams of flying, of otherworldly climes (according to legend, dragons were native to another universe to which they traveled by flying into the sun); lying there sometimes, looking up through the plank-shored tunnel her father had dug, she would feel that she was not resting on a solid surface but was receding from the earth, falling into a golden distance.

Riall may or may not have achieved his desired end; but it was evident to the people of Hangtown that propinquity to the scale had left its mark on Catherine, for while Riall was short and swarthy (as his wife had also been), physically unprepossessing in every respect, his daughter had grown into a beautiful young woman, long-limbed and slim, with fine golden hair and lovely skin and a face of unsurpassed delicacy, seeming a lapidary creation with its voluptuous mouth and sharp cheekbones and large eloquent eyes, whose irises were so dark that they could be distinguished from the pupils only under the strongest of lights. Not alone in her beauty did she appear cut from different cloth from her parents; neither did she share their gloomy spirit and cautious approach to life. From earliest childhood she went without fear to every quarter of the dragon's surface, even into the darkness under the wing joints where few scalehunters dared go; she believed she had been immunized against ordinary dangers by her father's tactics, and she felt there was a bond between herself and the dragon, that her dreams and good looks were emblems of both a magical relationship and consequential destiny, and this feeling of invulnerability—along with the confidence instilled by her beauty—gave rise to a certain egocentricity and shallowness of character. She was often disdainful, careless in the handling of lovers' hearts, and though she did not stoop to duplicity—she had no need of that—she took pleasure in stealing the men whom other women loved. And yet she considered herself a good woman. Not a saint, mind you. But she honored her father and kept the house clean and did her share of work, and though she had her faults, she had taken steps—half-steps, rather—to correct them. Like most people, she had no clear moral determinant, depending upon taboos and specific circumstances to modify her behavior, and the "good," the principled, was to her a kind of intellectual afterlife to which she planned some day to aspire, but only after she had exhausted the potentials of pleasure and thus gained the experience necessary for the achievement of such an aspiration. She was prone to bouts of moodiness, as were all within the sphere of Griaule's influence, but generally displayed a sunny disposition and optimistic cast of thought. This is not to say, however, that she was a Pollyanna, an innocent. Through her life in Hangtown she was familiar with treachery, grief, and murder, and at eighteen she had already been with a wide variety of lovers. Her easy sexuality was typical of Hangtown's populace, yet because of her beauty and the jealousy it had engendered, she had acquired the reputation of being exceptionally wanton. She was amused, even somewhat pleased, by her reputation, but the rumors surrounding her grew more scurrilous, more deviant from the truth, and eventually there came a day when they were brought home to her with a savagery that she could never have presupposed.

Beyond Griaule's frontal spike, which rose from a point between his eyes, a great whorled horn curving back toward Hangtown, the slope of the skull flattened out into the top of his snout, and it was here that Catherine came one foggy morning, dressed in loose trousers and a tunic, equipped with scaling hooks and ropes and chisels, intending to chip off a sizeable piece of cracked scale she had noticed near the dragon's lip, a spot directly above one of the fangs. She worked at the piece for several hours, suspended by linkages of rope over Griaule's lower jaw. His half-open mouth was filled with a garden of evil-looking plants, the calloused surface of his forked tongue showing here and there between the leaves like nodes of red coral; his fangs were inscribed with intricate patterns of lichen, wreathed by streamers of fog and circled by raptors who now and then would plummet into the bushes to skewer some unfortunate lizard or vole. Epiphytes bloomed from splits in the ivory, depending long strings of interwoven red and purple blossoms. It was a compelling sight, and from time to time Catherine would stop working and lower herself in her harness until she was no more than fifty feet above the tops of the bushes and look off into the caliginous depths of Griaule's throat, wondering at the nature of the shadowy creatures that flitted there.

The sun burned off the fog, and Catherine, sweaty, weary of chipping, hauled herself up to the top of the snout and stretched out on the scales, resting on an elbow, nibbling at a honey pear and gazing out over the valley with its spiny green hills and hammocks of thistle palms and the faraway white buildings of Teocinte, where that very night she planned to dance and make love. The air became so warm that she stripped off her tunic and lay back, bare to the waist, eyes closed, daydreaming in the clean springtime heat. She had been drifting between sleep and waking for the better part of an hour, when a scraping noise brought her alert. She reached for her tunic and started to sit up; but before she could turn to see who or what had made the sound, something fell heavily across her ribs, taking her wind, leaving her gasping and disoriented. A hand groped her breast, and she smelled winey breath.

"Go easy, now," said a man's voice, thickened with urgency. "I don't want nothing half of Hangtown ain't had already."

Catherine twisted her head, and caught a glimpse of Key Willen's lean, sallow face looming above her, his sardonic mouth hitched at one corner in a half-smile.

"I told you we'd have our time," he said, fumbling with the tie of her trousers.

She began to fight desperately, clawing at his eyes, catching a handful of his long black hair and yanking. She threw herself onto her stomach, clutching at the edge of a scale, trying to worm out from beneath him; but he butted her in the temple, sending white lights shooting through her skull. Once her head had cleared, she found that he had flipped her onto her back, had pulled her trousers down past her hips and penetrated her with his fingers; he was working them in and out, his breath coming hoarse and rapid. She felt raw inside, and she let out a sharp, throat-tearing scream. She thrashed about, tearing at his shirt, his hair, screaming again and again, and when he clamped his free hand to her mouth, she bit it.

"You bitch! You . . . goddamn. . . ." He slammed the back of her head against the scale, climbed atop her, straddling her chest and pinning her shoulders with his knees. He slapped her, wrapped his hand in her hair, and leaned close, spittle flying to her face as he spoke. "You listen up, pig! I don't much care if you're awake . . . one way or the other, I'm gonna have my fun." He rammed her head into the scale again. "You hear me? Hear me?" He straightened, slapped her harder. "Hell, I'm having fun right now."

"Please!" she said, dazed.

"Please?" He laughed. "That mean you want some more?" Another slap. "You like it?"

Yet another slap.

"How 'bout that?"

Frantic, she wrenched an arm free, in reflex reaching up behind her head, searching for a weapon, anything, and as he prepared to slap her again, grinning, she caught hold of a stick—or so she thought—and swung it at him in a vicious arc. The point of the scaling hook, for such it was, sank into Key's flesh just back of his left eye, and as he fell, toppling sideways with only the briefest of outcries, the eye filled with blood, becoming a featureless crimson sphere like a rubber ball embedded in the socket. Catherine shrieked, pushed his legs off her waist and scrambled away, encumbered by her trousers, which had slipped down about her knees. Key's body convulsed, his heels drumming the scale. She sat staring at him for a long seamless time, unable to catch her breath, to think. But swarms of black flies, their translucent wings shattering the sunlight into prism, began landing on the puddle of blood that spread wide as a table from beneath Key's face, and she became queasy. She crawled to the edge of the snout and looked away across the checkerboard of fields below toward Port Chantay, toward an alp of bubbling cumulus building from the horizon. Her chest hollowed with cold, and she started to shake. The tremors passing through her echoed the tremor she had felt in Key's body when the hook had bit into his skull. All the sickness inside her, her shock and disgust at the violation, at confronting the substance of death, welled up in her throat and her stomach emptied. When she had finished she cinched her trousers tight, her fingers clumsy with the knot. She thought she should do something. Coil the ropes, maybe. Store the harness in her pack. But these actions, while easy to contemplate, seemed impossibly complex to carry out. She shivered and hugged herself, feeling the altitude, the distances. Her cheeks were feverish and puffy; flickers of sensation—she pictured them to be iridescent worms—tingled nerves in her chest and legs. She had the idea that everything was slowing, that time had flurried and was settling the way river mud settles after the passage of some turbulence. She stared off toward the dragon's horn. Someone was standing there. Coming toward her, now. At first she watched the figure approach with a defiant disinterest, wanting to guard her privacy, feeling that if she had to speak she would lose control of her emotions. But as the figure resolved into one of her neighbors back in Hangtown—Brianne, a tall young woman with brittle good looks, dark brown hair and an olive complexion—she relaxed from this attitude. She and Brianne were not friends; in fact, they had once been rivals for the same man. However, that had been a year and more in the past, and Catherine was relieved to see her. More than relieved. The presence of another woman allowed her to surrender to weakness, believing that in Brianne she would find a fund of natural sympathy because of their common sex.

"My God, what happened?" Brianne kneeled and brushed Catherine's hair back from her eyes. The tenderness of the gesture burst the dam of Catherine's emotions, and punctuating the story with sobs, she told of the rape.

"I didn't mean to kill him," she said. "I . . . I'd forgotten about the hook."

"Key was looking to get killed," Brianne said. "But it's a damn shame you had to be the one to help him along." She sighed, her forehead creased by a worry line. "I suppose I should fetch someone to take care of the body. I know that's not. . . ."

"No, I understand . . . it has to be done." Catherine felt stronger, more capable. She made as if to stand, but Brianne restrained her.

"Maybe you should wait here. You know how people will be. They'll see your face—" she touched Catherine's swollen cheeks "—and they'll be prying, whispering. It might be better to let the mayor come out and make his investigation. That way he can take the edge off the gossip before it gets started."

Catherine didn't want to be alone with the body any longer, but she saw the wisdom in waiting and agreed.

"Will you be all right?" Brianne asked.

"I'll be fine . . . but hurry."

"I will." Brianne stood; the wind feathered her hair, lifted it to veil the lower half of her face. "You're sure you'll be all right?" There was an odd undertone in her voice, as if it were really another question she was asking, or—and this, Catherine thought, was more likely—as if she were thinking ahead to dealing with the mayor.

Catherine nodded, then caught at Brianne as she started to walk away. "Don't tell my father. Let me tell him. If he hears it from you, he might go after the Willens."

"I won't say a thing, I promise."

With a smile, a sympathetic pat on the arm, Brianne headed back toward Hangtown, vanishing into the thickets that sprang up beyond the frontal spike. For a while after she had gone, Catherine felt wrapped in her consolation; but the seething of the wind, the chill that infused the air as clouds moved in to cover the sun, these things caused the solitude of the place and the grimness of the circumstance to close down around her, and she began to wish she had returned to Hangtown. She squeezed her eyes shut, trying to steady herself, but even then she kept seeing Key's face, his bloody eye, and remembering his hands on her. Finally, thinking that Brianne had had more than enough time to accomplish her task, she walked up past the frontal spike and stood looking out along the narrow trail that wound through the thickets on Griaule's back. Several minutes elapsed, and then she spotted three figures—two men and a woman—coming at a brisk pace. She shaded her eyes against a ray of sun that had broken through the overcast, and peered at them. Neither man had the gray hair and portly shape of Hangtown's mayor. They were lanky, pale, with black hair falling to their shoulders, and were carrying unsheathed knives. Catherine couldn't make out their faces, but she realized that Brianne must not have set aside their old rivalry, that in the spirit of vengeance she had informed Key's brothers of his death.

Fear cut through the fog of shock, and she tried to think what to do.

There was only one trail and no hope that she could hide in the thickets. She retreated toward the edge of the snout, stepping around the patch of drying blood. Her only chance for escape would be to lower herself on the ropes and take her refuge in Griaule's mouth; however, the thought of entering so ominous a place, a place shunned by all but the mad, gave her pause. She tried to think of alternatives, but there were none. Brianne would no doubt have lied to the Willens, cast her as the guilty party, and the brothers would never listen to her. She hurried to the edge, buckled on the harness and slipped over the side, working with frenzied speed, lowering in ten and fifteen foot drops. Her view of the mouth lurched and veered—a panorama of bristling leaves and head-high ferns, enormous fangs hooking up from the jaw and pitch-dark emptiness at the entrance to the throat. She was fifty feet from the surface when she felt the rope jerking, quivering; glancing up, she saw that one of the Willens was sawing at it with his knife. Her heart felt hot and throbbing in her chest, her palms were slick. She dropped half the distance to the jaw, stopping with a jolt that sent pain shooting through her spine and left her swinging back and forth, muddle-headed. She began another drop, a shorter one, but the rope parted high above and she fell the last twenty feet, landing with such stunning force that she lost consciousness.

She came to in a bed of ferns, staring up through the fronds at the dull brick-colored roof of Griaule's mouth, a surface festooned with spiky dark green epiphytes, like the vault of a cathedral that had been invaded by the jungle. She lay still for a moment, gathering herself, testing the aches that mapped her body to determine if anything was broken. A lump sprouted from the back of the head, but the brunt of the impact had been absorbed by her rear end, and though she felt pain there, she didn't think the damage was severe. Moving cautiously, wincing, she came to her knees and was about to stand when she heard shouts from above.

"See her?"

"Naw . . . you?"

"She musta gone deeper in!"

Catherine peeked between the fronds and saw two dark figures centering networks of ropes, suspended a hundred feet or so overhead like spiders with simple webs. They dropped lower, and panicked, she crawled on her belly away from the mouth, hauling herself along by gripping twists of dead vine that formed a matte underlying the foliage. After she had gone about fifty yards she looked back. The Willens were hanging barely a dozen feet above the tops of the bushes, and as she watched they lowered out of sight.

Her instincts told her to move deeper into the mouth, but the air was considerably darker where she now kneeled than where she had landed—a grayish green gloom—and the idea of penetrating the greater darkness of Griaule's throat stalled her heart. She listened for the Willens and heard slitherings, skitterings, and rustles. Eerie whistles that, although soft, were complex and articulated. She imagined that these were not the cries of tiny creatures but the gutterings of breath in a huge throat, and she had a terrifying sense of the size of the place, of her own relative insignificance. She couldn't bring herself to continue in deeper, and she made her way toward the side of the mouth, where thick growths of ferns flourished in the shadow. When she reached a spot at which the mouth sloped upward, she buried herself among the ferns and kept very still.

Next to her head was an irregular patch of pale red flesh, where a clump of soil had been pulled away by an uprooted plant. Curious, she extended a forefinger and found it cool and dry. It was like touching stone or wood, and that disappointed her; she had, she realized, been hoping the touch would affect her in some extreme way. She pressed her palm to the flesh, trying to detect the tic of a pulse, but the flesh was inert, and the rustlings and the occasional beating of wings overhead were the only signs of life. She began to grow drowsy, to nod, and she fought to keep awake. But after a few minutes she let herself relax. The more she examined the situation, the more convinced she became that the Willens would not track her this far; the extent of their nerve would be to wait at the verge of the mouth, to lay siege to her, knowing that eventually she would have to seek food and water. Thinking about water made her thirsty, but she denied the craving. She needed rest far more. And removing one of the scaling hooks from her belt, holding it in her right hand in case some animal less cautious than the Willens happened by, she pillowed her head against the pale red patch of Griaule's flesh and was soon fast asleep.

II

MANY OF CATHERINE'S dreams over the years had seemed sendings rather than distillations of experience, but never had she had one so clearly of that character as the dream she had that afternoon in Griaule's mouth. It was a simple dream, formless, merely a voice whose words less came to her ear than enveloped her, steeping her in their meanings, and of them she retained only a message of reassurance, of security, one so profound that it instilled in her a confidence that lasted even after she waked into a world gone black, the sole illumination being the gleams of reflected firelight that flowed along the curve of one of the fangs. It was an uncanny sight, that huge tooth glazed with fierce red shine, and under other circumstances she would have been frightened by it; but in this instance she did not react to the barbarity of the image and saw it instead as evidence that her suppositions concerning the Willens had been correct. They had built a fire near the lip and were watching for her, expecting her to bolt into their arms. But she had no intention of fulfilling their expectations. Although her confidence flickered on and off, although to go deeper into the dragon seemed irrational, she knew that any other course offered the certainty of a knife stroke across the neck. And, too, despite the apparent rationality of her decision, she had an unshakeable feeling that Griaule was watching over her, that his will was being effected. She had a flash vision of Key Willen's face, his gaping mouth and blood-red eye, and recalled her terror at his assault. However, these memories no longer harrowed her. They steadied her, resolving certain questions that—while she had never asked them—had always been there to ask. She hadn't been to blame in any way for the rape, she had not tempted Key. But she saw that she had left herself open to tragedy by her aimlessness, by her reliance on a vague sense of destiny to give life meaning. Now it appeared that her destiny was at hand, and she understood that its violent coloration might have been different had *she* been different, had she engaged the world with energy and not with a passive attitude. She hoped that knowing all this would prove important, but she doubted that it would, believing that she had gone too far on the wrong path for any degree of knowledge to matter.

It took all her self-control to begin her journey inward, feeling her way along the side of the throat, pushing through ferns and cobwebs, her hands encountering unfamiliar textures that made her skin crawl, alert to the burbling of insects and other night creatures. On one occasion she was close to turning back, but she heard shouts behind her, and fearful that the Willens were on her trail, she kept going. As she started down an incline, she saw a faint gleam riding the curve of the throat wall. The glow brightened, casting the foliage into silhouette, and eager to reach the source, she picked up her pace, tripping over roots, vines snagging her ankles. At length the incline flattened out, and she emerged into a large chamber, roughly circular in shape, its upper regions lost in darkness; upon the floor lay pools of black liquid; mist trailed across the surface of the pools, and whenever the mist lowered to touch the liquid, a fringe of yellowish red flame would flare up, cutting the shadows on the pebbled skin of the floor and bringing to light a number of warty knee-high protuberances that spouted among the pools— these were deep red in color, perforated around the sides, leaking pale threads of mist. At the rear of the chamber was an opening that Catherine assumed led farther into the dragon. The air was warm, dank, and a sweat broke out all over her body. She balked at entering the chamber; in spite of the illumination, it was less a human place than the mouth. But once again she forced herself onward, stepping carefully between the fires and, after discovering that the mist made her giddy, giving the protuberances a wide berth. Piercing whistles came from above. The notion that this might signal the presence of bats caused her to hurry, and she had covered half the distance across when a man's voice called to her, electrifying her with fear.

"Catherine!" he said. "Not so fast!"

She spun about, her scaling hook at the ready. Hobbling toward her was an elderly white-haired man dressed in the ruin of a silk frock coat embroidered with gold thread, a tattered ruffled shirt, and holed satin leggings. In his left hand he carried a gold-knobbed cane, and at least a dozen glittering rings encircled his bony fingers. He stopped an arms-length away, leaning on his cane, and although Catherine did not lower her hook, her fear diminished. Despite the eccentricity of his appearance, considering the wide spectrum of men and creatures who inhabited Griaule, he seemed comparatively ordinary, a reason for caution but no alarm.

"Ordinary?" The old man cackled. "Oh yes, indeed! Ordinary as angels, as unexceptional as the idea of God!" Before she had a chance to wonder at his knowledge of her thoughts, he let out another cackle. "How could I not know them? We are every one of us creatures of his thought, expressions of his whim. And here what is only marginally evident on the surface becomes vivid reality, inescapable truth. For here"—he poked the chamber floor with his cane—"here we live in the medium of his will." He hobbled a step closer, fixing her with a rheumy stare. "I have dreamed this moment a thousand times. I know what you will say, what you will think, what you will do. He has instructed me in all your particulars so that I may become your guide, your confidant."

"What are you talking about?" Catherine hefted her hook, her anxiety increasing.

"Not 'what,'" said the old man. "Who." A grin split the pale wrinkled leather of his face. "His Scaliness, of course."

"Griaule?"

"None other." The old man held out his hand. "Come along now, girl. They're waiting for us."

Catherine drew back.

The old man pursed his lips. "Well, I suppose you could return the way you came. The Willens will be happy to see you."

Flustered, Catherine said, "I don't understand. How can you know. . . ."

"Know your name, your peril? Weren't you listening? You are of Griaule, daughter. And more so than most, for you have slept at the center of his dreams. Your entire life has been prelude to this time, and your destiny will not be known until you come to the place from which his dreams arise . . . the dragon's heart." He took her hand. "My name is Amos Mauldry. Captain Amos Mauldry, at your service. I have waited years for you . . . years! I am to prepare you for the consummate moment of your life. I urge you to follow me, to join the company of the feelies and begin your preparation. But—" he shrugged "—the choice is yours. I will not coerce you more than I have done . . . except to say this. Go with me now, and when you return you will discover that you have nothing to fear of the Willen brothers."

He let loose of her hand and stood gazing at her with calm regard. She would have liked to disregard his words, but they were in such accord with all she had ever felt about her association with the dragon, she found that she could not. "Who," she asked, "are the feelies?"

He made a disparaging noise. "Harmless creatures. They pass their time in copulating and arguing among themselves over the most trivial of matters. Were they not of service to Griaule, keeping him free of certain pests, they would have no use whatsoever. Still, there are worse folk in the world, and they do have moments in which they shine." He shifted impatiently, tapped his cane on the chamber floor. "You'll meet them soon enough. Are you with me or not?"

Grudgingly, her hook at the ready, Catherine followed Mauldry toward the opening at the rear of the chamber and into a narrow, twisting channel illuminated by a pulsing golden light that issued from within Griaule's flesh. This radiance, Mauldry said, derived from the dragon's blood, which, while it did not flow, was subject to fluctuations in brilliance due to changes in its chemistry. Or so he believed. He had regained his lighthearted manner, and as they walked he told Catherine he had captained a cargo ship that plied between Port Chantay and the Pearl Islands.

"We carried livestock, breadfruit, whale oil," he said. "I can't think of much we didn't carry. It was a good life, but hard as hard gets, and after I re-tired . . . well, I'd never married, and with time on my hands, I figured I owed myself some high times. I decided I'd see the sights, and the sight I most wanted to see was Griaule. I'd heard he was the First Wonder of the World . . . and he was! I was amazed, flabbergasted. I couldn't get enough of seeing him. He was more than a wonder. A miracle, an absolute majesty of a creature. People warned me to keep clear of the mouth, and they were right. But I couldn't stay away. One evening—I was walking along the edge of the mouth—two scalehunters set upon me, beat and robbed me. Left me for dead. And I would have died if it hadn't been for the feelies." He clucked his tongue. "I suppose I might as well give you some of their background. It can't help but prepare you for them . . . and I admit they need preparing for. They're not in the least agreeable to the eye." He cocked an eye toward Catherine, and after a dozen steps more he said, "Aren't you going to ask me to proceed?"

"You didn't seem to need encouragement," she said.

He chuckled, nodding his approval. "Quite right, quite right." He walked on in silence, his shoulders hunched and head inclined, like an old turtle who'd learned to get about on two legs.

"Well?" said Catherine, growing annoyed.

"I knew you'd ask," he said, and winked at her. "I didn't know who they were myself at first. If I had known I'd have been terrified. There are about five or six hundred in the colony. Their numbers are kept down by child-birth mortality and various other forms of attrition. They're most of them the descendants of a retarded man named Feely who wandered into the mouth almost a thousand years ago. Apparently he was walking near the mouth when flights of birds and swarms of insects began issuing from it. Not just a few, mind you. Entire populations. Well sir, Feely was badly frightened. He was sure that some terrible beast had chased all these lesser creatures out, and he tried to hide from it. But he was so confused that instead of running away from the mouth, he ran into it and hid in the bushes. He waited for al-most a day . . . no beast. The only sign of danger was a muffled thud from deep within the dragon. Finally his curiosity overcame his fear, and he went into the throat." Mauldry hawked and spat. "He felt secure there. More se-cure than on the outside, at any rate. Doubtless Griaule's doing, that feeling. He needed the feelies to be happy so they'd settle down and be his extermi-nators. Anyway, the first thing Feely did was to bring in a madwoman he'd known in Teocinte, and over the years they recruited other madmen who happened along. I was the first sane person they'd brought into the fold. They're extremely chauvinistic regarding the sane. But of course they were directed by Griaule to take me in. He knew you'd need someone to talk to." He prodded the wall with his cane. "And now this is my home. More than a home. It's my truth, my love. To live here is to be transfigured."

"That's a bit hard to swallow," said Catherine.

"Is it, now? You of all those who dwell on the surface should understand the scope of Griaule's virtues. There's no greater security than that he offers, no greater comprehension than that he bestows."

"You make him sound like a god."

Mauldry stopped walking, looking at her askance. The golden light waxed bright, filling in his wrinkles with shadows, making him appear to be centuries old. "Well, what do you think he is?" he asked with an air of mild indignation. "What else could he be?"

Another ten minutes brought them to a chamber even more fabulous than the last. In shape it was oval, like an egg with a flattened bottom stood on end, an egg some one hundred and fifty feet high and a bit more than half that in diameter. It was lit by the same pulsing golden glow that had illuminated the channel, but here the fluctuations were more gradual and more extreme, ranging from a murky dimness to a glare approaching that of full daylight. The upper two thirds of the chamber wall was obscured by stacked ranks of small cubicles, leaning together at rickety angles, a geometry lacking the precision of the cells of a honeycomb, yet reminiscent of such, as if the bees that constructed it had been drunk. The entrances of the cubicles were draped with curtains, and lashed to their sides were ropes, rope ladders, and baskets that functioned as elevators, several of which were in use, lowering and lifting men and women dressed in a style similar to Mauldry: Catherine was reminded of a painting she had seen depicting the roof warrens of Port Chantay; but those habitations, while redolent of poverty and despair, had not as did these evoked an impression of squalid degeneracy, of order lapsed into the perverse. The lower portion of the chamber (and it was in this area that the channel emerged) was covered with a motley carpet composed of bolts of silk and satin and other rich fabrics, and seventy or eighty people were strolling and reclining on the gentle slopes. Only the center had been left clear, and there a gaping hole led away into yet another section of the dragon; a system of pipes ran into the hole, and Mauldry later explained that these carried the wastes of the colony into a pit of acids that had once fueled Griaule's fires. The dome of the chamber was choked with mist, the same pale stuff that had been vented from the protuberances in the previous chamber; birds with black wings and red markings on their heads made wheeling flights in and out of it, and frail scarves of mist drifted throughout. There was a sickly sweet odor to the place, and Catherine heard a murmurous rustling that issued from every quarter.

"Well," said Mauldry, making a sweeping gesture with his cane that included the entire chamber. "What do you think of our little colony?"

Some of the feelies had noticed them and were edging forward in small groups, stopping, whispering agitatedly among themselves, then edging forward again, all with the hesitant curiosity of savages; and although no signal had been given, the curtains over the cubicle entrances were being thrown back, heads were poking forth, and tiny figures were shinnying down the ropes, crowding into baskets, scuttling downward on the rope ladders, hundreds of people beginning to hurry toward her at a pace that brought to mind the panicked swarming of an anthill. And on first glance they seemed as alike as ants. Thin and pale and stooped, with sloping, nearly hairless skulls, and weepy eyes and thick-lipped slack mouths, like ugly children in their rotted silks and satins. Closer and closer they came, those in front pushed by the swelling ranks at their rear, and Catherine, unnerved by their stares, ignoring Mauldry's attempts to soothe her, retreated into the channel. Mauldry turned to the feelies, brandishing his cane as if it were a victor's sword, and cried, "She is here! He has brought her to us at last! She is here!"

His words caused several of those at the front of the press to throw back their heads and loose a whinnying laughter that went higher and higher in pitch as the golden light brightened. Others in the crowd lifted their hands, palms outward, holding them tight to their chests, and made little hops of excitement, and others yet twitched their heads from side to side, cutting their eyes this way and that, their expressions flowing between belligerence and confusion, apparently unsure of what was happening. This exhibition, clearly displaying the feelies' retardation, the tenuousness of their self-control, dismayed Catherine still more. But Mauldry seemed delighted and continued to exhort them, shouting, "She is here," over and over. His outcry came to rule the feelies, to orchestrate their movements. They began to sway, to repeat his words, slurring them so that their response was in effect a single word, "Shees'eer, Shees'eer," that reverberated through the chamber, acquiring a rolling echo, a hissing sonority, like the rapid breathing of a giant. The sound washed over Catherine, enfeebling her with its intensity, and she shrank back against the wall of the channel, expecting the feelies to break ranks and surround her; but they were so absorbed in their chanting, they appeared to have forgotten her. They milled about, bumping into one another, some striking out in anger at those who had impeded their way, others embracing and giggling, engaging in sexual play, but all of them keeping up the chorus of shouts.

Mauldry turned to her, his eyes giving back gleams of the golden light, his face looking in its vacuous glee akin to those of the feelies, and holding out his hands to her, his tone manifesting the bland sincerity of a priest, he said, "Welcome home."

III

CATHERINE WAS housed in two rooms halfway up the chamber wall, an apartment that adjoined Mauldry's quarters and was furnished with a rich carpeting of silks and furs and embroidered pillows; on the walls, also draped in these materials, hung a mirror with a gem-studded frame and two oil paintings—this bounty, said Mauldry, all part of Griaule's horde, the bulk of which lay in a cave west of the valley, its location known only to the feelies. One of the rooms contained a large basin for bathing, but since water was at a premium—being collected from points at which it seeped in through the scales—she was permitted one bath a week and no more. Still, the apartment and the general living conditions were on a par with those in Hangtown, and had it not been for the feelies, Catherine might have felt at home. But except in the case of the woman Leitha, who served her meals and cleaned, she could not overcome her revulsion at their inbred appearance and demented manner. They seemed to be responding to stimuli that she could not perceive, stopping now and then to cock an ear to an inaudible call or to stare at some invisible disturbance in the air. They scurried up and down the ropes to no apparent purpose, laughing and chattering, and they engaged in mass copulations at the bottom of the chamber. They spoke a mongrel dialect that she could barely understand, and they would hang on ropes outside her apartment, arguing, offering criticism of one another's dress and behavior, picking at the most insignificant of flaws and judging them according to an intricate code whose niceties Catherine was unable to master. They would follow her wherever she went, never sharing the same basket, but descending or ascending alongside her, staring, shrinking away if she turned her gaze upon them. With their foppish rags, their jewels, their childish pettiness and jealousies, they both irritated and frightened her; there was a tremendous tension in the way they looked at her, and she had the idea that at any moment they might lose their awe of her and attack.

She kept to her rooms those first weeks, brooding, trying to invent some means of escape, her solitude broken only by Leitha's ministrations and Mauldry's visits. He came twice daily and would sit among the pillows, declaiming upon Griaule's majesty, his truth. She did not enjoy the visits. The righteous quaver in his voice aroused her loathing, reminding her of the mendicant priests who passed now and then through Hangtown, leaving bastards and empty purses in their wake. She found his conversation for the most part boring, and when it did not bore, she found it disturbing in its constant references to her time of trial at the dragon's heart. She had no doubt that Griaule was at work in her life. The longer she remained in the colony, the more vivid her dreams became and the more certain she grew that his purpose was somehow aligned with her presence there. But the pathetic condition of the feelies shed a wan light on her old fantasies of a destiny entwined with the dragon's, and she began to see herself in that wan light, to experience a revulsion at her fecklessness equal to that she felt toward those around her.

"You are our salvation," Mauldry told her one day as she sat sewing herself a new pair of trousers—she refused to dress in the gilt and satin rags preferred by the feelies. "Only you can know the mystery of the dragon's heart, only you can inform us of his deepest wish for us. We've known this for years."

Seated amid the barbaric disorder of silks and furs, Catherine looked out through a gap in the curtains, watching the waning of the golden light. "You hold me prisoner," she said. "Why should I help you?"

"Would you leave us, then?" Mauldry asked. "What of the Willens?"

"I doubt they're still waiting for me. Even if they are, it's only a matter of which death I prefer, a lingering one here or a swift one at their hands."

Mauldry fingered the gold knob of his cane. "You're right," he said. "The Willens are no longer a menace."

She glanced up at him.

"They died the moment you went down out of Griaule's mouth," he said. "He sent his creatures to deal with them, knowing you were his at long last."

Catherine remembered the shouts she'd heard while walking down the incline of the throat. "What creatures?"

"That's of no importance," said Mauldry. "What is important is that you apprehend the subtlety of his power, his absolute mastery and control over your thoughts, your being."

"Why?'" she asked. "Why is that important?" He seemed to be struggling to explain himself, and she laughed. "Lost touch with your god, Mauldry? Won't he supply the appropriate cant?"

Mauldry composed himself. "It is for you, not I, to understand why you are here. You must explore Griaule, study the miraculous workings of his flesh, involve yourself in the intricate order of his being."

In frustration, Catherine punched at a pillow. "If you don't let me go, I'll die! This place will kill me. I won't be around long enough to do any exploring."

"Oh, but you will." Mauldry favored her with an unctuous smile. "That, too, is known to us."

Ropes creaked, and a moment later the curtains parted, and Leitha, a young woman in a gown of watered blue taffeta, whose bodice pushed up the pale nubs of her breasts, entered bearing Catherine's dinner tray. She set down the tray. "Be mo', ma'am?" she said. "Or mus' I later c'meah." She gazed fixedly at Catherine, her close-set brown eyes blinking, fingers plucking at the folds of her gown.

"Whatever you want," Catherine said.

Leitha continued to stare at her, and only when Mauldry spoke sharply to her did she turn and leave.

Catherine looked down disconsolately at the tray and noticed that in addition to the usual fare of greens and fruit (gathered from the dragon's mouth) there were several slices of underdone meat, whose reddish hue appeared identical to the color of Griaule's flesh. "What's this?" she asked, poking at one of the slices.

"The hunters were successful today," said Mauldry. "Every so often hunting parties are sent into the digestive tract. It's quite dangerous, but there are beasts there that can injure Griaule. It serves him that we hunt them, and their flesh nourishes us." He leaned forward, studying her face. "Another party is going out tomorrow. Perhaps you'd care to join them. I can arrange it if you wish. You'll be well protected."

Catherine's initial impulse was to reject the invitation, but then she thought that this might offer an opportunity for escape; in fact, she realized that to play upon Mauldry's tendencies, to evince interest in a study of the dragon, would be a wise move. The more she learned about Griaule's geography, the greater chance there would be that she would find a way out.

"You said it was dangerous. . . . How dangerous?"

"For you? Not in the least. Griaule would not harm you. But for the hunting party, well . . . lives will be lost."

"And they're going out tomorrow?"

"Perhaps the next day as well. We're not sure how extensive an infestation is involved."

"What kind of beast are you talking about?"

"Serpents of a sort."

Catherine's enthusiasm was dimmed, but she saw no other means of taking action. "Very well. I'll go with them tomorrow."

"Wonderful, wonderful!" It took Mauldry three tries to heave himself up from the cushion, and when at last he managed to stand, he leaned on his cane, breathing heavily. "I'll come for you early in the morning."

"You're going, too? You don't seem up to the exertion."

Mauldry chuckled. "It's true, I'm an old man. But where you're concerned, daughter, my energies are inexhaustible." He performed a gallant bow and hobbled from the room.

Not long after he had left, Leitha returned. She drew a second curtain across the entrance, cutting the light, even at its most brilliant, to a dim effusion. Then she stood by the entrance, eyes fixed on Catherine. "Wan' mo' fum Leitha?" she asked.

The question was not a formality. Leitha had made it plain by touches and other signs that Catherine had but to ask and she would come to her as a lover. Her deformities masked by the shadowy air, she had the look of a pretty young girl dressed for a dance, and for a moment, in the grip of loneliness and despair, watching Leitha alternately brightening and merging with gloom, listening to the unceasing murmur of the feelies from without, aware in full of the tribal strangeness of the colony and her utter lack of connection, Catherine felt a bizarre arousal.

But the moment passed, and she was disgusted with herself, with her weakness, and angry at Leitha and this degenerate place that was eroding her humanity. "Get out," she said coldly, and when Leitha hesitated, she shouted the command, sending the girl stumbling backward from the room. Then she turned onto her stomach, her face pressed into a pillow, expecting to cry, feeling the pressure of a sob building in her chest; but the sob never manifested, and she lay there, knowing her emptiness, feeling that she was no longer worthy of even her own tears.

BEHIND ONE OF the cubicles in the lower half of the chamber was hidden the entrance to a wide circular passage ringed by ribs of cartilage, and it was along this passage the next morning that Catherine and Mauldry, accompanied by thirty male feelies, set out upon the hunt. They were armed with swords and bore torches to light the way, for here Griaule's veins were too deeply embedded to provide illumination; they walked in a silence broken only by coughs and the soft scraping of their footsteps. The silence, such a contrast from the feelies' usual chatter, unsettled Catherine, and the flaring and guttering of the torches, the apparition of a backlit pale face turned toward her, the tingling acidic scent that grew stronger and stronger, all this assisted her impression that they were lost souls treading some byway in Hell.

Their angle of descent increased, and shortly thereafter they reached a spot from which Catherine had a view of a black distance shot through with intricate networks of fine golden skeins, like spiderwebs of gold in a night sky. Mauldry told her to wait, and the torches of the hunting party moved off, making it clear that they had come to a large chamber; but she did not understand just how large until a fire suddenly bloomed, bursting into towering flames: an enormous bonfire composed of sapling trunks and entire bushes. The size of the fire was impressive in itself, but the immense cavity of the stomach that it partially revealed was more impressive yet. It could not have been less than two hundred yards long, and was walled with folds of thin whitish skin figured by lacings and branchings of veins, attached to curving ribs covered with even thinner skin that showed their every articulation. A quarter of the way across the cavity, the floor declined into a sink brimming with a dark liquid, and it was along a section of the wall close to the sink that the bonfire had been lit, its smoke billowing up toward a bruised patch of skin some fifty feet in circumference with a tattered rip at the center. As Catherine watched the entire patch began to undulate. The hunting party gathered beneath it, ranged around the bonfire, their swords raised. Then, with ponderous slowness a length of thick white tubing was extruded from the rip, a gigantic worm that lifted its blind head above the hunting party, opened a mouth fringed with palps to expose a dark red maw and emitted a piercing squeal that touched off echoes and made Catherine put her hands to her ears. More and more of the worm's body emerged from the stomach wall, and she marveled at the courage of the hunting party, who maintained their ground. The worm's squealing became unbearably loud as smoke enveloped it; it lashed about, twisting and probing at the air with its head, and then, with an even louder cry, it fell across the bonfire, writhing, sending up showers of sparks. It rolled out of the fire, crushing several of the party; the others set to with their swords, hacking in a frenzy at the head, painting streaks of dark blood over the corpse-pale skin. Catherine realized that she had pressed her fists to her cheeks and was screaming, so involved was she in the battle. The worm's blood spattered the floor of the cavity, its skin was charred and blistered from the flames, and its head was horribly slashed, the flesh hanging in ragged strips. But it continued to squeal, humping up great sections of its body, forming an arch over groups of attackers and dropping down upon them. A third of the hunting party lay motionless, their limbs sprawled in graceless attitudes, the remnants of the bonfire—heaps of burning branches—scattered among them; the rest stabbed and sliced at the increasingly torpid worm, dancing away from its lunges. At last the worm lifted half its body off the floor, its head held high, silent for a moment, swaying with the languor of a mesmerized serpent. It let out a cry like the whistle of a monstrous tea kettle, a cry that seemed to fill the cavity with its fierce vibrations, and fell, twisting once and growing still, its maw half-open, palps twitching in the register of some final internal function.

The hunting party collapsed around it, winded, drained, some leaning on their swords. Shocked by the suddenness of the silence, Catherine went a few steps out into the cavity, Mauldry at her shoulder. She hesitated, then moved forward again, thinking that some of the party might need tending. But those who had fallen were dead, their limbs broken, blood showing on their mouths. She walked alongside the worm. The thickness of its body was three times her height, the skin glistening and warped by countless tiny puckers and tinged with a faint bluish cast that made it all the more ghastly.

"What are you thinking?" Mauldry asked.

Catherine shook her head. No thoughts would come to her. It was as if the process of thought itself had been canceled by the enormity of what she had witnessed. She had always supposed that she had a fair idea of Griaule's scope, his complexity, but now she understood that whatever she had once believed had been inadequate, and she struggled to acclimate to this new perspective. There was a commotion behind her. Members of the hunting party were hacking slabs of meat from the worm. Mauldry draped an arm about her, and by that contact she became aware that she was trembling.

"Come along," he said. "I'll take you home."

"To my room, you mean?" Her bitterness resurfaced, and she threw off his arm.

"Perhaps you'll never think of it as home," he said. "Yet nowhere is there a place more suited to you." He signaled to one of the hunting party, who came toward them, stopped to light a dead torch from a pile of burning branches.

With a dismal laugh, Catherine said, "I'm beginning to find it irksome how you claim to know so much about me."

"It's not you I claim to know," he said, "though it has been given me to understand something of your purpose. But—" he rapped the tip of his cane against the floor of the cavity "—he by whom you are most known, *him* I know well."

IV

CATHERINE MADE THREE escape attempts during the next two months, and thereafter gave up on the enterprise; with hundreds of eyes watching her, there was no point in wasting energy. For almost six months following the final attempt she became dispirited and refused to leave her rooms. Her health suffered, her thoughts paled, and she lay abed for hours, reliving her life in Hangtown, which she came to view as a model of joy and contentment. Her inactivity caused loneliness to bear in upon her. Mauldry tried his best to entertain her, but his mystical obsession with Griaule made him incapable of offering the consolation of a true friend. And so, without friends or lovers, without even an enemy, she sank into a welter of self-pity and began to toy with the idea of suicide. The prospect of never seeing the sun again, of attending no more carnivals at Teocinte . . . it seemed too much to endure. But either she was not brave enough or not sufficiently foolish to take her own life, and deciding that no matter how vile or delimiting the circumstance, it promised more than eternal darkness, she gave herself to the one occupation the feelies would permit her: the exploration and study of Griaule.

Like one of those enormous Tibetan sculptures of the Buddha constructed within a tower only a trifle larger than the sculpture itself, Griaule's unbeating heart was a dimpled golden shape as vast as a cathedral and was enclosed within a chamber whose walls left a gap six feet wide around the organ. The chamber could be reached by passing through a vein that had ruptured long ago and was now a wrinkled brown tube just big enough for Catherine to crawl along it; to make this transit and then emerge into that narrow space beside the heart was an intensely claustrophobic experience, and it took her a long, long while to get used to the process. Even after she had grown accustomed to this, it was still difficult for her to adjust to the peculiar climate at the heart. The air was thick with a heated stinging scent that reminded her of the brimstone stink left by a lightning stroke, and there was an atmosphere of imminence, a stillness and tension redolent of some chthonic disturbance that might strike at any moment. The blood at the heart did not merely fluctuate (and here the fluctuations were erratic, varying both in range of brilliance and rapidity of change); it circulated—the movement due to variations in heat and pressure through a series of convulsed inner chambers, and this eddying in conjunction with the flickering brilliance threw patterns of light and shadow on the heart wall, patterns as complex and fanciful as arabesques that drew her eye in. Staring at them, Catherine began to be able to predict what configurations would next appear and to apprehend a logic to their progression; it was nothing that she could put into words, but watching the play of light and shadow produced in her emotional responses that seemed keyed to the shifting patterns and allowed her to make crude guesses as to the heart's workings. She learned that if she stared too long at the patterns, dreams would take her, dreams notable for their vividness, and one particularly notable in that it recurred again and again.

The dream began with a sunrise, the solar disc edging up from the southern horizon, its rays spearing toward a coast strewn with great black rocks that protruded from the shallows, and perched upon them were sleeping dragons; as the sun warmed them, light flaring on their scales, they grumbled and lifted their heads and with the snapping sound of huge sails filling with wind, they unfolded their leathery wings and went soaring up into an indigo sky flecked with stars arranged into strange constellations, wheeling and roaring their exultation . . . all but one dragon, who flew only a brief arc before coming disjointed in midflight and dropping like a stone into the water, vanishing beneath the waves. It was an awesome thing to see, this tumbling flight, the wings billowing, tearing, the fanged mouth open, claws grasping for purchase in the air. But despite its beauty, the dream seemed to have little relevance to Griaule's situation. He was in no danger of falling, that much was certain. Nevertheless, the frequency of the dream's recurrence persuaded Catherine that something must be amiss, that perhaps Griaule feared an attack of the sort that had stricken the flying dragon. With this in mind she began to inspect the heart, using her hooks to clamber up the steep slopes of the chamber walls, sometimes hanging upside down like a blond spider above the glowing, flickering organ. But she could find nothing out of order, no imperfections—at least as far as she could determine—and the sole result of the inspection was that the dream stopped occurring and was replaced by a simpler dream in which she watched the chest of a sleeping dragon contract and expand. She could make no sense of it, and although the dream continued to recur, she paid less and less attention to it.

Mauldry, who had been expecting miraculous insights from her, was depressed when none were forthcoming. "Perhaps I've been wrong all these years," he said. "Or senile. Perhaps I'm growing senile."

A few months earlier, Catherine, locked into bitterness and resentment, might have seconded his opinion out of spite; but her studies at the heart had soothed her, infused her both with calm resignation and some compassion for her jailers—they could not, after all, be blamed for their pitiful condition—and she said to Mauldry, "I've only begun to learn. It's likely to take a long time before I understand what he wants. And that's in keeping with his nature, isn't it? That nothing happens quickly?"

"I suppose you're right," he said glumly.

"Of course I am," she said. "Sooner or later there'll be a revelation. But a creature like Griaule doesn't yield his secrets to a casual glance. Just give me time."

And oddly enough, though she had spoken these words to cheer Mauldry, they seemed to ring true.

She had started her explorations with minimal enthusiasm, but Griaule's scope was so extensive, his populations of parasites and symbiotes so exotic and intriguing, her passion for knowledge was fired and over the next six years she grew zealous in her studies, using them to compensate for the emptiness of her life. With Mauldry ever at her side, accompanied by small groups of the feelies, she mapped the interior of the dragon, stopping short of penetrating the skull, warned off from that region by a premonition of danger. She sent several of the more intelligent feelies into Teocinte, where they acquired beakers and flasks and books and writing materials that enabled her to build a primitive laboratory for chemical analysis. She discovered that the egg-shaped chamber occupied by the colony would—had the dragon been fully alive—be pumped full of acids and gasses by the contraction of the heart muscle, flooding the channel, mingling in the adjoining chamber with yet another liquid, forming a volatile mixture that Griaule's breath would—if he so desired—kindle into flame; if he did not so desire, the expansion of the heart would empty the chamber. She distilled from these liquids and from that she derived a potent narcotic that she named brianine after her nemesis, and from a lichen growing on the outer surface of the lungs, she derived a powerful stimulant. She catalogued the dragon's myriad flora and fauna, covering the walls of her rooms with lists and charts and notations on their behaviors. Many of the animals were either familiar to her or variants of familiar forms. Spiders, bats, swallows, and the like. But as was the case on the dragon's surface, a few of them testified to his other-worldly origins, and perhaps the most curious of them was Catherine's meta-hex (her designation for it), a creature with six identical bodies that thrived in the stomach acids. Each body was approximately the size and color of a worn penny, fractionally more dense than a jellyfish, ringed with cilia, and all were in a constant state of agitation. She had at first assumed the metahex to be six creatures, a species that traveled in sixes, but had begun to suspect otherwise when—upon killing one for the purposes of dissection—the other five bodies had also died. She had initiated a series of experiments that involved menacing and killing hundreds of the things, and had ascertained that the bodies were connected by some sort of field—one whose presence she deduced by process of observation—that permitted the essence of the creature to switch back and forth between the bodies, utilizing the ones it did not occupy as a unique form of camouflage. But even the metahex seemed ordinary when compared to the ghostvine, a plant that she discovered grew in one place alone, a small cavity near the base of the skull.

None of the colony would approach that region, warned away by the same sense of danger that had afflicted Catherine, and it was presumed that should one venture too close to the brain, Griaule would mobilize some of his more deadly inhabitants to deal with the interloper. But Catherine felt secure in approaching the cavity, and leaving Mauldry and her escort of feelies behind, she climbed the steep channel that led up to it, lighting her way with a torch, and entered through an aperture not much wider than her hips. Once inside, seeing that the place was lit by veins of golden blood that branched across the ceiling, flickering like the blown flame of a candle, she extinguished the torch; she noticed with surprise that except for the ceiling, the entire cavity—a boxy space some twenty feet long, about eight feet in height—was fettered with vines whose leaves were dark green, glossy, with complex veination and tips that ended in minuscule hollow tubes. She was winded from the climb, more winded—she thought—than she should have been, and she sat down against the wall to catch her breath; then, feeling drowsy, she closed her eyes for a moment's rest. She came alert to the sound of Mauldry's voice shouting her name. Still drowsy, annoyed by his impatience, she called out, "I just want to rest a few minutes!"

"A few minutes!" he cried. "You've been there three days! What's going on? Are you all right?"

"That's ridiculous!" She started to come to her feet, then sat back, stunned by the sight of a naked woman with long blond hair curled up in a corner not ten feet away, nestled so close to the cavity wall that the tips of leaves half-covered her body and obscured her face.

"Catherine!" Mauldry shouted. "Answer me!"

"I . . . I'm all right! Just a minute!"

The woman stirred and made a complaining noise.

"Catherine!"

"I said I'm all right!"

The woman stretched out her legs; on her right hip was a fine pink scar, hookshaped, identical to the scar on Catherine's hip, evidence of a childhood fall. And on the back of the right knee, a patch of raw, puckered skin, the product of an acid burn she'd suffered the year before. She was astonished by the sight of these markings, but when the woman sat up and Catherine understood that she was staring at her twin—identical not only in feature, but also in expression, wearing a resigned look that she had glimpsed many times in her mirror—her astonishment turned to fright. She could have sworn she felt the muscles of the woman's face shifting as the expression changed into one of pleased recognition, and in spite of her fear, she had a vague sense of the woman's emotions, of her burgeoning hope and elation.

"Sister," said the woman; she glanced down at her body, and Catherine had a momentary flash, of doubled vision, watching the woman's head decline and seeing as well naked breasts and belly from the perspective of the woman's eyes. Her vision returned to normal, and she looked at the woman's face . . . *her* face. Though she had studied herself in the mirror each morning for years, she had never had such a clear perception of the changes that life inside the dragon had wrought upon her. Fine lines bracketed her lips, and the beginnings of crows' feet radiated from the corners of her eyes. Her cheeks had hollowed, and this made her cheekbones appear sharper; the set of her mouth seemed harder, more determined. The high gloss and perfection of her youthful beauty had been marred far more than she had thought, and this dismayed her. However, the most remarkable change—the one that most struck her—was not embodied by any one detail but in the overall character of the face, in that it exhibited character, for—she realized—prior to entering the dragon it had displayed very little, and what little it had displayed had been evidence of indulgence. It troubled her to have this knowledge of the fool she had been thrust upon her with such poignancy.

As if the woman had been listening to her thoughts, she held out her hand and said, "Don't punish yourself, sister. We are all victims of our past."

"What are you?" Catherine asked, pulling back. She felt the woman was a danger to her, though she was not sure why.

"I am you." Again the woman reached out to touch her, and again Catherine shifted away. The woman's face was smiling, but Catherine felt the wash of her frustration and noticed that the woman had leaned forward only a few degrees, remaining in contact with the leaves of the vines as if there were some attachment between them that she could not break.

"I doubt that." Catherine was fascinated, but she was beginning to be swayed by the intuition that the woman's touch would harm her.

"But I am!" the woman insisted. "And something more, besides."

"What more?"

"The plant extracts essences," said the woman. "Infinitely small constructs of the flesh from which it creates a likeness free of the imperfections of your body. And since the seeds of your future are embodied by these essences, though they are unknown to you, I know them . . . for now."

"For now?"

The woman's tone had become desperate. "There's a connection between us . . . surely you feel it?"

"Yes."

"To live, to complete that connection, I must touch you. And once I do, this knowledge of the future will be lost to me. I will be as you . . . though separate. But don't worry. I won't interfere with you, I'll live my own life." She leaned forward again, and Catherine saw that some of the leaves were affixed to her back, the hollow tubes at their tips adhering to the skin. Once again she had an awareness of danger, a growing apprehension that the woman's touch would drain her of some vital substance.

"If you know my future," she said, "then tell me . . . will I ever escape Griaule."

Mauldry chose this moment to call out to her, and she soothed him by saying that she was taking some cuttings, that she would be down soon. She repeated her question, and the woman said, "Yes, yes, you will leave the dragon," and tried to grasp her hand. "Don't be afraid. I won't harm you."

The woman's flesh was sagging, and Catherine felt the eddying of her fear.

"Please!" she said, holding out both hands. "Only your touch will sustain me. Without it, I'll die!"

But Catherine refused to trust her.

"You must believe me!" cried the woman. "I am your sister! My blood is yours, my memories!" The flesh upon her arms had sagged into billows like the flesh of an old woman, and her face was becoming jowly, grossly distorted. "Oh, please! Remember the time with Stel below the wing . . . you were a maiden. The wind was blowing thistles down from Griaule's back like a rain of silver. And remember the gala in Teocinte? Your sixteenth birthday. You wore a mask of orange blossoms and gold wire, and three men asked for your hand. For God's sake, Catherine! Listen to me! The major . . . don't you remember him? The young major? You were in love with him, but you didn't follow your heart. You were afraid of love, you didn't trust what you felt because you never trusted yourself in those days."

The connection between them was fading, and Catherine steeled herself against the woman's entreaties, which had begun to move her more than a little bit. The woman slumped down, her features blurring, a horrid sight, like the melting of a wax figure, and then, an even more horrid sight, she smiled, her lips appearing to dissolve away from teeth that were themselves dissolving.

"I understand," said the woman in a frail voice, and gave a husky, glutinous laugh. "Now I see."

"What is it?" Catherine asked. But the woman collapsed, rolling onto her side, and the process of deterioration grew more rapid; within the span of a few minutes she had dissipated into a gelatinous grayish white puddle that retained the rough outline of her form. Catherine was both appalled and relieved; however, she couldn't help feeling some remorse, uncertain whether she had acted in self-defense or through cowardice had damned a creature who was by nature no more reprehensible than herself. While the woman had been alive—if that was the proper word—Catherine had been mostly afraid, but now she marveled at the apparition, at the complexity of a plant that could produce even the semblance of a human. And the woman had been, she thought, something more vital than mere likeness. How else could she have known her memories? Or could memory, she wondered, have a physiological basis? She forced herself to take samples of the woman's remains, of the vines, with an eye toward exploring the mystery. But she doubted that the heart of such an intricate mystery would be accessible to her primitive instruments. This was to prove a self-fulfilling prophecy, because she really did not want to know the secrets of the ghostvine, leery as to what might be brought to light concerning her own nature, and with the passage of time, although she thought of it often and sometimes discussed the phenomenon with Mauldry, she eventually let the matter drop.

V

THOUGH THE TEMPERATURE never changed, though neither rain nor snow fell, though the fluctuations of the golden light remained consistent in their rhythms, the seasons were registered inside the dragon by migrations of birds, the weaving of cocoons, the birth of millions of insects at once; and it was by these signs that Catherine—nine years after entering Griaule's mouth—knew it to be autumn when she fell in love. The three years prior to this had been characterized by a slackening of her zeal, a gradual wearing down of her enthusiasm for scientific knowledge, and this tendency became marked after the death of Captain Mauldry from natural causes; without him to serve as a buffer between her and the feelies, she was overwhelmed by their inanity, their woeful aspect. In truth, there was not much left to learn. Her maps were complete, her specimens and notes filled several rooms, and while she continued her visits to the dragon's heart, she no longer sought to interpret the dreams, using them instead to pass the boring hours. Again she grew restless and began to consider escape. Her life was being wasted, she believed, and she wanted to return to the world, to engage more vital opportunities than those available to her in Griaule's many-chambered prison. It was not that she was ungrateful for the experience. Had she managed to escape shortly after her arrival, she would have returned to a life of meaningless frivolity; but now, armed with knowledge, aware of her strengths and weaknesses, possessed of ambition and a heightened sense of morality, she thought she would be able to accomplish something of importance. But before she could determine whether or not escape was possible, there was a new arrival at the colony, a man whom a group of feelies—while gathering berries near the mouth—had found lying unconscious and had borne to safety. The man's name was John Colmacos, and he was in his early thirties, a botanist from the university at Port Chantay who had been abandoned by his guides when he insisted on entering the mouth and had subsequently been mauled by apes that had taken up residence in the mouth. He was lean, rawboned, with powerful, thick-fingered hands and fine brown hair that would never stay combed. His long jawed, horsey face struck a bargain between homely and distinctive, and was stamped with a perpetually inquiring expression, as if he were a bit perplexed by everything he saw. His blue eyes were large and intricate, the irises flecked with green and hazel, appearing surprisingly delicate in contrast to the rest of him.

Catherine, happy to have rational company, especially that of a professional in her vocation, took charge of nursing him back to health—he had suffered fractures of the arm and ankle, and was badly cut about the face; and in the course of this she began to have fantasies about him as a lover. She had never met a man with his gentleness of manner, his lack of pretense, and she found it most surprising that he wasn't concerned with trying to impress her. Her conception of men had been limited to the soldiers of Teocinte, the thugs of Hangtown, and everything about John fascinated her. For a while she tried to deny her feelings, telling herself that she would have fallen in love with almost anyone under the circumstances, afraid that by loving she would only increase her dissatisfaction with her prison; and, too, there was the realization that this was doubtless another of Griaule's manipulations, his attempt to make her content with her lot, to replace Mauldry with a lover. But she couldn't deny that under any circumstance she would have been attracted to John Colmacos for many reasons, not the least of which was his respect for her work with Griaule, for how she had handled adversity. Nor could she deny that the attraction was mutual. That was clear. Although there were awkward moments, there was no mooniness between them; they were both watching what was happening.

"This is amazing," he said one day while going through one of her notebooks, lying on a pile of furs in her apartment. "It's hard to believe you haven't had training."

A flush spread over her cheeks. "Anyone in my shoes, with all that time, nothing else to do, they would have done no less."

He set down the notebook and measured her with a stare that caused her to lower her eyes. "You're wrong," he said. "Most people would have fallen apart. I can't think of anybody else who could have managed all this. You're remarkable."

She felt oddly incompetent in the light of this judgment, as if she had accorded him ultimate authority and were receiving the sort of praise that a wise adult might bestow upon an inept child who had done well for once. She wanted to explain to him that everything she had done had been a kind of therapy, a hobby to stave off despair; but she didn't know how to put this into words without sounding awkward and falsely modest, and so she merely said, "Oh," and busied herself with preparing a dose of brianine to take away the pain in his ankle.

"You're embarrassed," he said. "I'm sorry . . . I didn't mean to make you uncomfortable."

"I'm not . . . I mean, I. . . ." She laughed. "I'm still not accustomed to talking."

He said nothing, smiling.

"What is it?" she said, defensive, feeling that he was making fun of her.

"What do you mean?"

"Why are you smiling?"

"I could frown," he said, "if that would make you comfortable."

Irritated, she bent to her task, mixing paste in a brass goblet studded with uncut emeralds, then molding it into a pellet.

"That was a joke," he said.

"I know."

"What's the matter?"

She shook her head. "Nothing."

"Look," he said. "I don't want to make you uncomfortable . . . I really don't. What am I doing wrong?"

She sighed, exasperated with herself. "It's not you," she said. "I just can't get used to you being here, that's all."

From without came the babble of some feelies lowering on ropes toward the chamber floor.

"I can understand that," he said. "I. . . ." He broke off, looked down and fingered the edge of the notebook.

"What were you going to say?"

He threw back his head, laughed. "Do you see how we're acting? Explaining ourselves constantly . . . as if we could hurt each other by saying the wrong word."

She glanced over at him, met his eyes, then looked away.

"What I meant was, we're not that fragile," he said, and then, as if by way of clarification, he hastened to add: "We're not that . . . vulnerable to one another."

He held her stare for a moment, and this time it was he who looked away and Catherine who smiled.

If she hadn't known she was in love, she would have suspected as much from the change in her attitude toward the dragon. She seemed to be seeing everything anew. Her wonder at Griaule's size and strangeness had been restored, and she delighted in displaying his marvelous features to John—the orioles and swallows that never once had flown under the sun, the glowing heart, the cavity where the ghostvine grew (though she would not linger there), and a tiny chamber close to the heart lit not by Griaule's blood but by thousands of luminous white spiders that shifted and crept across the blackness of the ceiling, like a night sky whose constellations had come to life. It was in this chamber that they engaged in their first intimacy, a kiss from which Catherine—after initially letting herself be swept away—pulled back, disoriented by the powerful sensations flooding her body, sensations both familiar and unnatural in that she hadn't experienced them for so long, and startled by the suddenness with which her fantasies had become real.

Flustered, she ran from the chamber, leaving John, who was still hobbled by his injuries, to limp back to the colony alone.

She hid from him most of that day sitting with her knees drawn up on a patch of peach-colored silk near the hole at the center of the colony's floor, immersed in the bustle and gabble of the feelies as they promenaded in their decaying finery. Though for the most part they were absorbed in their own pursuits, some sensed her mood and gathered around her, touching her, making the whimpering noises that among them passed for expressions of tenderness. Their pasty doglike faces ringed her, uniformly sad, and as if sadness were contagious, she started to cry. At first her tears seemed the product of her inability to cope with love, and then it seemed she was crying over the poor thing of her life, the haplessness of her days inside the body of the dragon; but she came to feel that her sadness was one with Griaule's, that this feeling of gloom and entrapment reflected his essential mood, and that thought stopped her tears. She'd never considered the dragon an object deserving of sympathy, and she did not now consider him such; but perceiving him imprisoned in a web of ancient magic, and the Chinese puzzle of lesser magics and imprisonments that derived from that original event, she felt foolish for having cried. Everything, she realized, even the happiest of occurrences, might be a cause for tears if you failed to see it in terms of the world that you inhabited; however, if you managed to achieve a balanced perspective, you saw that although sadness could result from every human action, you had to seize the opportunities for effective action which came your way and not question them, no matter how unrealistic or futile they might appear. Just as Griaule had done by finding a way to utilize his power while immobilized. She laughed to think of herself emulating Griaule even in this abstract fashion, and several of the feelies standing beside her echoed her laughter. One of the males, an old man with tufts of gray hair poking up from his pallid skull, shuffled near, picking at a loose button on his stiff, begrimed coat of silver-embroidered satin.

"Cat'rine mus' be easy sweetly, now?" he said. "No mo' bad t'ing?"

"No," she said. "No more bad thing."

On the other side of the hole a pile of naked feelies were writhing together in the clumsiness of foreplay, men trying to penetrate men, getting angry, slapping one another, then lapsing into giggles when they found a woman and figured out the proper procedure. Once this would have disgusted her, but no more. Judged by the attitudes of a place not their own, perhaps the feelies were disgusting; but this was their place, and Catherine's place as well, and accepting that at last, she stood and walked toward the nearest basket. The old man hustled after her, fingering his lapels in a parody of self-importance, and, as if he were the functionary of her mood, he announced to everyone they encountered, "No mo' bad t'ing, no mo' bad t'ing."

RIDING UP IN the basket was like passing in front of a hundred tiny stages upon which scenes from the same play were being performed—pale figures slumped on silks, playing with gold and bejeweled baubles—and gazing around her, ignoring the stink, the dilapidation, she felt she was looking out upon an exotic kingdom. Always before she had been impressed by its size and grotesqueness; but now she was struck by its richness, and she wondered whether the feelies' style of dress was inadvertent or if Griaule's subtlety extended to the point of clothing this human refuse in the rags of dead courtiers and kings. She felt exhilarated, joyful; but as the basket lurched near the level on which her rooms were located, she became nervous. It had been so long since she had been with a man, and she was worried that she might not be suited to him . . . then she recalled that she'd been prone to these worries even in the days when she had been with a new man every week.

She lashed the basket to a peg, stepped out onto the walkway outside her rooms, took a deep breath and pushed through the curtains, pulled them shut behind her. John was asleep, the furs pulled up to his chest. In the fading half-light, his face—dirtied by a few days' growth of beard—looked sweetly mysterious and rapt, like the face of a saint at meditation, and she thought it might be best to let him sleep; but that, she realized, was a signal of her nervousness, not of compassion. The only thing to do was to get it over with, to pass through nervousness as quickly as possible and learn what there was to learn. She stripped off her trousers, her shirt, and stood for a second above him, feeling giddy, frail, as if she'd stripped off much more than a few ounces of fabric. Then she eased in beneath the furs, pressing the length of her body to his. He stirred but didn't wake, and this delighted her;

she liked the idea of having him in her clutches, of coming to him in the middle of a dream, and she shivered with the apprehension of gleeful, childish power. He tossed, turned onto his side to face her, still asleep, and she pressed closer, marveling at how ready she was, how open to him. He muttered something, and as she nestled against him, he grew hard, his erection pinned between their bellies. Cautiously, she lifted her right knee atop his hip, guided him between her legs and moved her hips back and forth, rubbing against him, slowly, slowly, teasing herself with little bursts of pleasure. His eyelids twitched, blinked open, and he stared at her, his eyes looking black and wet, his skin stained a murky gold in the dimness. "Catherine," he said, and she gave a soft laugh, because her name seemed a power the way he had spoken it. His fingers hooked into the plump meat of her hips as he pushed and prodded at her, trying to find the right angle. Her head fell back, her eyes closed, concentrating on the feeling that centered her dizziness and heat, and then he was inside her, going deep with a single thrust, beginning to make love to her, and she said, "Wait, wait," holding him immobile, afraid for an instant, feeling too much, a black wave of sensation building, threatening to wash her away.

"What's wrong?" he whispered. "Do you want . . ."

"Just wait . . . just for a bit." She rested her forehead against his, trembling, amazed by the difference that he made in her body; one moment she felt buoyant, as if their connection had freed her from the restraints of gravity, and the next moment—whenever he shifted or eased fractionally deeper—she would feel as if all his weight were pouring inside her and she was sinking into the cool silks.

"Are you all right?"

"Mmm." She opened her eyes, saw his face inches away and was surprised that he didn't appear unfamiliar.

"What is it?" he asked.

"I was just thinking."

"About what?"

"I was wondering who you were, and when I looked at you, it was as if I already knew." She traced the line of his upper lip with her forefinger. "Who are you?"

"I thought you knew already."

"Maybe . . . but I don't know anything specific. Just that you were a professor."

"You want to know specifics?"

"Yes."

"I was an unruly child," he said. "I refused to eat onion soup, I never washed behind my ears."

His grasp tightened on her hips, and he thrust inside her, a few slow, delicious movements, kissing her mouth, her eyes.

"When I was a boy," he said, quickening his rhythm, breathing hard between the words, "I'd go swimming every morning. Off the rocks at Ayler's Point . . . it was beautiful. Cerulean water, palms. Chickens and pigs foraging. On the beach."

"Oh, God!" she said, locking her leg behind his thigh, her eyelids fluttering down.

"My first girlfriend was named Penny . . . she was twelve. Redheaded. I was a year younger. I loved her because she had freckles. I used to believe . . . freckles were . . . a sign of something. I wasn't sure what. But I love you more than her."

"I love you!" She found his rhythm, adapted to it, trying to take him all inside her. She wanted to see where they joined, and she imagined there was no longer any distinction between them, that their bodies had merged and were sealed together.

"I cheated in mathematics class, I could never do trigonometry. God . . . Catherine."

His voice receded, stopped, and the air seemed to grow solid around her, holding her in a rosy suspension. Light was gathering about them, frictive light from a strange heatless burning, and she heard herself crying out, calling his name, saying sweet things, childish things, telling him how wonderful he was, words like the words in a dream, important for their music, their sonority, rather than for any sense they made. She felt again the building of a dark wave in her belly. This time she flowed with it and let it carry her far.

VI

"LOVE'S STUPID," John said to her one day months later as they were sitting in the chamber of the heart, watching the complex eddying of golden light and whorls of shadow on the surface of the organ. "I feel like a damn sophomore. I keep finding myself thinking that I should do something noble. Feed the hungry, cure a disease." He made a noise of disgust. "It's as if I just woke up to the fact that the world has problems, and because I'm so happily in love, I want everyone else to be happy. But stuck. . . ."

"Sometimes I feel like that myself," she said, startled by this outburst. "Maybe it's stupid, but it's not wrong. And neither is being happy."

"Stuck in here," he went on, "there's no chance of doing anything for ourselves, let alone saving the world. As for being happy, that's not going to last . . . not in here, anyway."

"It's lasted six months," she said. "And if it won't last here, why should it last anywhere?"

He drew up his knees, rubbed the spot on his ankle where it had been fractured.

"What's the matter with you? When I got here, all you could talk about was how much you wanted to escape. You said you'd do anything to get out. It sounds now that you don't care one way or the other."

She watched him rubbing the ankle, knowing what was coming. "I'd like very much to escape. Now that you're here, it's more acceptable to me. I can't deny that. That doesn't mean I wouldn't leave if I had the chance. But at least I can think about staying here without despairing."

"Well, *I* can't! I. . . ." He lowered his head, suddenly drained of animation, still rubbing his ankle. "I'm sorry, Catherine. My leg's hurting again, and I'm in a foul mood." He cut his eyes toward her. "Have you got that stuff with you?"

"Yes." She made no move to get it for him.

"I realize I'm taking too much," he said. "It helps pass the time."

She bristled at that and wanted to ask if she was the reason for his boredom; but she repressed her anger, knowing that she was partly to blame for his dependency on the brianine, that during his convalescence she had responded to his demands for the drug as a lover and not as a nurse.

An impatient look crossed his face. "Can I have it?"

Reluctantly she opened her pack, removed a flask of water and some pellets of brianine wrapped in cloth, and handed them over. He fumbled at the cloth, hurrying to unscrew the cap of the flask, and then—as he was about to swallow two of the pellets—he noticed her watching him. His face tightened with anger, and he appeared ready to snap at her. But his expression softened, and he downed the pellets, held out two more. "Take some with me," he said. "I know I have to stop. And I will. But let's just relax today, let's pretend we don't have any troubles . . . all right?"

That was a ploy he had adopted recently, making her his accomplice in addiction and thus avoiding guilt; she knew she should refuse to join him, but at the moment she didn't have the strength for an argument. She took the pellets, washed them down with a swallow of water and lay back against the chamber wall. He settled beside her, leaning on one elbow, smiling, his eyes muddied-looking from the drug.

"You do have to stop, you know," she said.

His smile flickered, then steadied, as if his batteries were running low. "I suppose."

"If we're going to escape," she said, "you'll need a clear head."

He perked up at this. "That's a change."

"I haven't been thinking about escape for a long time. It didn't seem possible . . . it didn't even seem very important, anymore. I guess I'd given up on the idea. I mean just before you arrived, I'd been thinking about it again, but it wasn't serious . . . only frustration."

"And now?"

"It's become important again."

"Because of me, because I keep nagging about it?"

"Because of both of us. I'm not sure escape's possible, but I was wrong to stop trying."

He rolled onto his back, shielding his eyes with his forearm as if the heart's glow were too bright.

"John?" The name sounded thick and sluggish, and she could feel the drug taking her, making her drifty and slow.

"This place," he said. "This goddamn place."

"I thought"—she was beginning to have difficulty in ordering her words—"I thought you were excited by it. You used to talk. . . ."

"Oh, I am excited!" He laughed dully. "It's a storehouse of marvels. Fantastic! Overwhelming! It's too overwhelming. The feeling here. . . ." He turned to her. "Don't you feel it?"

"I'm not sure what you mean."

"How could you stand living here for all these years? Are you that much stronger than me, or are you just insensitive?"

"I'm . . ."

"God!" He turned away, stared at the heart wall, his face tattooed with a convoluted flow of light and shadow, then flaring gold. "You're so at ease here. Look at that." He pointed to the heart. "It's not a heart, it's a bloody act of magic. Every time I come here I get the feeling it's going to display a pattern that'll make me disappear. Or crush me. Or something. And you just sit there looking at it with a thoughtful expression as if you're planning to put in curtains or repaint the damn thing."

"We don't have to come here anymore."

"I can't stay away," he said, and held up a pellet of brianine. "It's like this stuff."

They didn't speak for several minutes . . . perhaps a bit less, perhaps a little more. Time had become meaningless, and Catherine felt that she was floating away, her flesh suffused with a rosy warmth like the warmth of lovemaking. Flashes of dream imagery passed through her mind: a clown's monstrous face; an unfamiliar room with tilted walls and three-legged blue chairs; a painting whose paint was melting, dripping. The flashes lapsed into thoughts of John. He was becoming weaker every day, she realized. Losing his resilience, growing nervous and moody. She had tried to convince herself that sooner or later he would become adjusted to life inside Griaule, but she was beginning to accept the fact that he was not going to be able to survive here. She didn't understand why, whether it was due—as he had said—to the dragon's oppressiveness or to some inherent weakness. Or a combination of both. But she could no longer deny it, and the only option left was for them to effect an escape. It was easy to consider escape with the drug in her veins, feeling aloof and calm, possessed of a dreamlike overview; but she knew that once it wore off she would be at a loss as to how to proceed.

To avoid thinking, she let the heart's patterns dominate her attention. They seemed abnormally complex, and as she watched she began to have the impression of something new at work, some interior mechanism that she had never noticed before, and to become aware that the sense of imminence that pervaded the chamber was stronger than ever before; but she was so muzzy-headed that she could not concentrate upon these things. Her eyelids drooped, and she fell into her recurring dream of the sleeping dragon, focusing on the smooth scaleless skin of its chest, a patch of whiteness that came to surround her, to draw her into a world of whiteness with the serene constancy of its rhythmic rise and fall, as unvarying and predictable as the ticking of a perfect clock.

OVER THE NEXT six months Catherine devised numerous plans for escape, but discarded them all as unworkable until at last she thought of one that—although far from foolproof—seemed in its simplicity to offer the least risk of failure. Though without brianine the plan would have failed, the process of settling upon this particular plan would have gone faster had drugs not been available; unable to resist the combined pull of the drug and John's need for companionship in his addiction, she herself had become an addict, and much of her time was spent lying at the heart with John, stupefied, too enervated even to make love. Her feelings toward John had changed; it could not have been otherwise, for he was not the man he had been. He had lost weight and muscle tone, grown vague and brooding, and she was concerned for the health of his body and soul. In some ways she felt closer than ever to him, her maternal instincts having been engaged by his dissolution; yet she couldn't help resenting the fact that he had failed her, that instead of offering relief, he had turned out to be a burden and a weakening influence; and as a result whenever some distance arose between them, she exerted herself to close it only if it was practical to do so. This was not often the case, because John had deteriorated to the point that closeness of any sort was a chore. However, Catherine clung to the hope that if they could escape, they would be able to make a new beginning.

The drug owned her. She carried a supply of pellets wherever she went, gradually increasing her dosages, and not only did it affect her health and her energy, it had a profound effect upon her mind. Her powers of concentration were diminished, her sleep became fitful, and she began to experience hallucinations. She heard voices, strange noises, and on one occasion she was certain that she had spotted old Amos Mauldry among a group of feelies milling about at the bottom of the colony chamber. Her mental erosion caused her to mistrust the information of her senses and to dismiss as delusion the intimations of some climactic event that came to her in dreams and from the patterns of light and shadow on the heart; and recognizing that certain of her symptoms—hearkening to inaudible signals and the like—were similar to the behavior of the feelies, she feared that she was becoming one of them. Yet this fear was not so pronounced as once it might have been. She sought now to be tolerant of them, to overlook their role in her imprisonment, perceiving them as unwitting agents of Griaule, and she could not be satisfied in hating either them or the dragon; Griaule and the subtle manifestations of his will were something too vast and incomprehensible to be a target for hatred, and she transferred all her wrath to Brianne, the woman who had betrayed her. The feelies seemed to notice this evolution in her attitude, and they became more familiar, attaching themselves to her wherever she went, asking questions, touching her, and while this made it difficult to achieve privacy, in the end it was their increased affection that inspired her plan.

One day, accompanied by a group of giggling, chattering feelies, she walked up toward the skull, to the channel that led to the cavity containing the ghostvine. She ducked into the channel, half-tempted to explore the cavity again; but she decided against this course and on crawling out of the channel, she discovered that the feelies had vanished. Suddenly weak, as if their presence had been an actual physical support, she sank to her knees and stared along the narrow passage of pale red flesh that wound away into a golden murk like a burrow leading to a shining treasure. She felt a welling up of petulant anger at the feelies for having deserted her. Of course she should have expected it. They shunned this area like. . . . She sat up, struck by a realization attendant to that thought. How far, she wondered, had the feelies retreated? Could they have gone beyond the side passage that opened into the throat? She came to her feet and crept along the passage until she reached the curve. She peeked around it, and seeing no one, continued on, holding her breath until her chest began to ache. She heard voices, peered around the next curve, and caught sight of eight feelies gathered by the entrance to the side passage, their silken rags agleam, their swords reflecting glints of the inconstant light. She went back around the curve, rested against the wall; she had trouble thinking, in shaping thought into a coherent stream, and out of reflex she fumbled in her pack for some brianine. Just touching one of the pellets acted to calm her, and once she had swallowed it she breathed easier. She fixed her eyes on the blurred shape of a vein buried beneath the glistening ceiling of the passage, letting the fluctuations of light mesmerize her. She felt she was blurring, becoming golden and liquid and slow, and in that feeling she found a core of confidence and hope.

There's a way, she told herself; *My God, maybe there really is a way.*

BY THE TIME she had fleshed out her plan three days later, her chief fear was that John wouldn't be able to function well enough to take part in it. He looked awful, his cheeks sunken, his color poor, and the first time she tried to tell him about the plan, he fell asleep. To counteract the brianine she began cutting his dosage, mixing it with the stimulant she had derived from the lichen growing on the dragon's lung, and after a few days, though his color and general appearance did not improve, he became more alert and energized. She knew the improvement was purely chemical, that the stimulant was a danger in his weakened state; but there was no alternative, and this at least offered him a chance at life. If he were to remain there, given the physical erosion caused by the drug, she did not believe he would last another six months.

It wasn't much of a plan, nothing subtle, nothing complex, and if she'd had her wits about her, she thought, she would have come up with it long before; but she doubted she would have had the courage to try it alone, and if there was trouble, then two people would stand a much better chance than one. John was elated by the prospect. After she had told him the particulars he paced up and down in their bedroom, his eyes bright, hectic spots of red dappling his cheeks, stopping now and again to question her or to make distracted comments.

"The feelies," he said. "We . . . uh . . . we won't hurt them?"

"I told you . . . not unless it's necessary."

"That's good, that's good." He crossed the room to the curtains drawn across the entrance. "Of course it's not my field, but . . ."

"John?"

He peered out at the colony through the gap in the curtains, the skin on his forehead washing from gold to dark. "Uh-huh."

"What's not your field?"

After a long pause he said, "It's not . . . nothing."

"You were talking about the feelies."

"They're very interesting," he said distractedly. He swayed, then moved sluggishly toward her, collapsed on the pile of furs where she was sitting. He turned his face to her, looked at her with a morose expression. "It'll be better," he said. "Once we're out of here, I'll . . . I know I haven't been . . . strong. I haven't been . . ."

"It's all right," she said, stroking his hair.

"No, it's not, it's not." Agitated, he struggled to sit up, but she restrained him, telling him not to be upset, and soon he lay still. "How can you love me?" he asked after a long silence.

"I don't have any choice in the matter." She bent to him, pushing back her hair so it wouldn't hang in his face, kissed his cheek, his eyes.

He started to say something, then laughed weakly, and she asked him what he found amusing.

"I was thinking about free will," he said. "How improbable a concept that's become. Here. Where it's so obviously not an option."

She settled down beside him, weary of trying to boost his spirits. She remembered how he'd been after his arrival: eager, alive, and full of curiosity despite his injuries. Now his moments of greatest vitality—like this one—were spent in sardonic rejection of happy possibility. She was tired of arguing with him, of making the point that everything in life could be reduced by negative logic to a sort of pitiful reflex if that was the way you wanted to see it. His voice grew stronger, this prompted—she knew—by a rush of the stimulant within his system.

"It's Griaule," he said. "Everything here belongs to him, even the most fleeting of hopes and wishes. What we feel, what we think. When I was a student and first heard about Griaule, about his method of dominion, the omnipotent functioning of his will, I thought it was foolishness pure and simple. But I was an optimist, then. And optimists are only fools without experience. Of course I didn't think of myself as an optimist. I saw myself as a realist. I had a romantic notion that I was alone, responsible for my actions, and I perceived that as being a noble beauty, a refinement of the tragic . . . that state of utter and forlorn independence. I thought how cozy and unrealistic it was for people to depend on gods and demons to define their roles in life. I didn't know how terrible it would be to realize that nothing you thought or did had any individual importance, that everything, love, hate, your petty likes and dislikes, was part of some unfathomable scheme. I couldn't comprehend how worthless that knowledge would make you feel."

He went on in this vein for some time, his words weighing on her, filling her with despair, pushing hope aside. Then, as if this monologue had aroused some bitter sexuality, he began to make love to her. She felt removed from the act, imprisoned within walls erected by his dour sentences; but she responded with desperate enthusiasm, her own arousal funded by a desolate prurience. She watched his spread-fingered hands knead and cup her breasts, actions that seemed to her as devoid of emotional value as those of a starfish gripping a rock; and yet because of this desolation, because she wanted to deny it and also because of the voyeuristic thrill she derived from watching herself being taken, used, her body reacted with unusual fervor. The sweaty film between them was like a silken cloth, and their movements seemed more accomplished and supple than ever before; each jolt of pleasure brought her to new and dizzying heights. But afterward she felt devastated and defeated, not loved, and lying there with him, listening to the muted gabble of the feelies from without, bathed in their rich stench, she knew she had come to the nadir of her life, that she had finally united with the feelies in their enactment of a perturbed and animalistic rhythm.

Over the next ten days she set the plan into motion. She took to dispensing little sweet cakes to the feelies who guarded her on her daily walks with John, ending up each time at the channel that led to the ghostvine. And she also began to spread the rumor that at long last her study of the dragon was about to yield its promised revelation. On the day of the escape, prior to going forth, she stood at the bottom of the chamber, surrounded by hundreds of feelies, more hanging on ropes just above her, and called out in ringing tones, "Today I will have word for you! Griaule's word! Bring together the hunters and those who gather food, and have them wait here for me! I will return soon, very soon, and speak to you of what is to come!"

The feelies jostled and pawed one another, chattering, tittering, hopping up and down, and some of those hanging from the ropes were so overcome with excitement that they lost their grip and fell, landing atop their fellows, creating squirming heaps of feelies who squalled and yelped and then started fumbling with the buttons of each other's clothing. Catherine waved at them, and with John at her side, set out toward the cavity, six feelies with swords at their rear.

John was terribly nervous and all during the walk he kept casting backward glances at the feelies, asking questions that only served to unnerve Catherine. "Are you sure they'll eat them?" he said. "Maybe they won't be hungry."

"They always eat them while we're in the channel," she said. "You know that."

"I know," he said. "But I'm just . . . I don't want anything to go wrong." He walked another half a dozen paces. "Are you sure you put enough in the cakes?"

"I'm sure." She watched him out of the corner of her eye. The muscles in his jaw bunched, nerves twitched in his cheek. A light sweat had broken on his forehead, and his pallor was extreme. She took his arm. "How do you feel?"

"Fine," he said. "I'm fine."

"It's going to work, so don't worry . . . please."

"I'm fine," he repeated, his voice dead, eyes fixed straight ahead.

The feelies came to a halt just around the curve from the channel, and Catherine, smiling at them, handed them each a cake; then she and John went forward and crawled into the channel. There they sat in the darkness without speaking, their hips touching. At last John whispered, "How much longer?"

"Let's give it a few more minutes . . . just to be safe."

He shuddered, and she asked again how he felt.

"A little shaky," he said. "But I'm all right."

She put her hand on his arm; his muscles jumped at the touch. "Calm down," she said, and he nodded. But there was no slackening of his tension.

The seconds passed with the slowness of sap welling from cut bark, and despite her certainty that all would go as planned, Catherine's anxiety increased. Little shiny squiggles, velvety darknesses blacker than the air, wormed in front of her eyes. She imagined that she heard whispers out in the passage. She tried to think of something else, but the concerns she erected to occupy her mind materialized and vanished with a superficial and formal precision that did nothing to ease her, seeming mere transparencies shunted across the vision of a fearful prospect ahead. Finally she gave John a nudge and they crept from the channel, made their way cautiously along the passage. When they reached the curve beyond which the feelies were waiting, she paused, listened. Not a sound. She looked out. Six bodies lay by the entrance to the side passage; even at that distance she could spot the half-eaten cakes that had fallen from their hands. Still wary, they approached the feelies, and as they came near, Catherine thought that there was something unnatural about their stillness. She knelt beside a young male, caught a whiff of loosened bowel, saw the rapt character of death stamped on his features and realized that in measuring out the dosages of brianine in each cake, she had not taken the feelies' slightness of build into account. She had killed them.

"Come on!" said John. He had picked up two swords; they were so short, they looked toylike in his hands. He handed over one of the swords and helped her to stand. "Let's go . . . there might be more of them!"

He wetted his lips, glanced from side to side. With his sunken cheeks and hollowed eyes, his face had the appearance of a skull, and for a moment, dumbstruck by the realization that she had killed, by the understanding that for all her disparagement of them, the feelies were human, Catherine failed to recognize him. She stared at them—like ugly dolls in the ruins of their gaud—and felt again that same chill emptiness that had possessed her when she had killed Key Willen. John caught her arm, pushed her toward the side passage; it was covered by a loose flap, and though she had become used to seeing the dragon's flesh everywhere, she now shrank from touching it. John pulled back the flap, urged her into the passage, and then they were crawling through a golden gloom, following a twisting downward course.

In places the passage was only a few inches wider than her hips, and they were forced to worm their way along. She imagined that she could feel the immense weight of the dragon pressing in upon her, pictured some muscle twitching in reflex, the passage constricting and crushing them. The closed space made her breathing sound loud, and for a while John's breathing sounded even louder, hoarse and labored. But then she could no longer hear it, and she discovered that he had fallen behind. She called out to him, and he said, "Keep going!"

She rolled onto her back in order to see him. He was gasping, his face twisted as if in pain. "What's wrong?" she cried, trying to turn completely, constrained from doing so by the narrowness of the passage.

He gave her a shove. "I'll be all right. Don't stop!"

"John!" She stretched out a hand to him, and he wedged his shoulder against her legs, pushing her along.

"Damn it . . . just keep going!" He continued to push and exhort her, and realizing that she could do nothing, she turned and crawled at an even faster pace, seeing his harrowed face in her mind's eye.

She couldn't tell how many minutes it took to reach the end of the passage; it was a timeless time, one long unfractionated moment of straining, squirming, pulling at the slick walls, her effort fueled by her concern; but when she scrambled out into the dragon's throat, her heart racing, for an instant she forgot about John, about everything except the sight before her. From where she stood the throat sloped upward and widened into the mouth, and through that great opening came a golden light, not the heavy mineral brilliance of Griaule's blood, but a fresh clear light, penetrating the tangled shapes of the thickets in beams made crystalline by dust and moisture—the light of day. She saw the tip of a huge fang hooking upward, stained gold with the morning sun, and the vault of the dragon's mouth above, with its vines and epiphytes. Stunned, gaping, she dropped her sword and went a couple of paces toward the light. It was so clean, so pure, its allure like a call. Remembering John, she turned back to the passage. He was pushing himself erect with his sword, his face flushed, panting.

"Look!" she said, hurrying to him, pointing at the light. "God, just look at that!" She steadied him, began steering him toward the mouth.

"We made it," he said. "I didn't believe we would."

His hand tightened on her arm in what she assumed was a sign of affection; but then his grip tightened cruelly, and he lurched backward.

"John!" She fought to hold on to him, saw that his eyes had rolled up into his head.

He sprawled onto his back, and she went down on her knees beside him, hands fluttering above his chest, saying, "John? John?" What felt like a shiver passed through his body, a faint guttering noise issued from his throat, and she knew, oh, she knew very well the meaning of that tremor, that signal passage of breath. She drew back, confused, staring at his face, certain that she had gotten things wrong, that in a second or two his eyelids would open. But they did not. "John?" she said, astonished by how calm she felt, by the measured tone of her voice, as if she were making a simple inquiry. She wanted to break through the shell of calmness, to let out what she was really feeling, but it was as if some strangely lucid twin had gained control over her muscles and will. Her face was cold, and she got to her feet, thinking that the coldness must be radiating from John's body and that distance would be a cure. The sight of him lying there frightened her, and she turned her back on him, folded her arms across her chest. She blinked against the daylight. It hurt her eyes, and the loops and interlacings of foliage standing out in silhouette also hurt her with their messy complexity, their disorder. She couldn't decide what to do. Get away, she told herself. Get out. She took a hesitant step toward the mouth, but that direction didn't make sense. No direction made sense, anymore.

Something moved in the bushes, but she paid it no mind. Her calm was beginning to crack, and a powerful gravity seemed to be pulling her back toward the body. She tried to resist. More movement. Leaves were rustling, branches being pushed aside. Lots of little movements. She wiped at her eyes. They were no tears in them, but something was hampering her vision, something opaque and thin, a tattered film. The shreds of her calm, she thought, and laughed . . . more a hiccup than a laugh. She managed to focus on the bushes and saw ten, twenty, no, more, maybe two or three dozen diminutive figures, pale mongrel children in glittering rags standing at the verge of the thicket. She hiccuped again, and this time it felt nothing like a laugh. A sob, or maybe nausea. The feelies shifted nearer, edging toward her. The bastards had been waiting for them. She and John had never had a chance of escaping.

Catherine retreated to the body, reached down, groping for John's sword. She picked it up, pointed it at them. "Stay away from me," she said. "Just stay away, and I won't hurt you."

They came closer, shuffling, their shoulders hunched, their attitudes fearful, but advancing steadily all the same.

"Stay away!" she shouted. "I swear I'll kill you!" She swung the sword, making a windy arc through the air. "I swear!"

The feelies gave no sign of having heard, continuing their advance, and Catherine, sobbing now, shrieked for them to keep back, swinging the sword again and again. They encircled her, standing just beyond range. "You don't believe me?" she said. "You don't believe I'll kill you? I don't have any reason not to." All her grief and fury broke through, and with a scream she lunged at the feelies, stabbing one in the stomach, slicing a line of blood across the satin and gilt chest of another. The two she had wounded fell, shrilling their agony, and the rest swarmed toward her. She split the skull of another, split it as easily as she might have a melon, saw gore and splintered bone fly from the terrible wound, the dead male's face nearly halved, more blood leaking from around his eyes as he toppled, and then the rest of them were on her, pulling her down, pummeling her, giving little fey cries. She had no chance against them, but she kept on fighting, knowing that when she stopped, when she surrendered, she would have to start feeling, and that she wanted badly to avoid. Their vapid faces hovered above her, seeming uniformly puzzled, as if unable to understand her behavior, and the mildness of their reactions infuriated her. Death should have frightened them, made them—like her—hot with rage. Screaming again, her thoughts reddening, pumped with adrenaline, she struggled to her knees, trying to shake off the feelies who clung to her arms. Snapping her teeth at fingers, faces, arms. Then something struck the back of her head, and she sagged, her vision whirling, darkness closing in until all she could see was a tunnel of shadow with someone's watery eyes at the far end. The eyes grew wider, merged into a single eye that became a shadow with leathery wings and a forked tongue and a belly full of fire that swooped down, open-mouthed, to swallow her up and fly her home.

VII

THE DRUG MODERATED Catherine's grief . . . or perhaps it was more than the drug. John's decline had begun so soon after they had met, it seemed she had become accustomed to sadness in relation to him, and thus his death had not overwhelmed her, but rather had manifested as an ache in her chest and a heaviness in her limbs, like small stones she was forced to carry about. To rid herself of that ache, that heaviness, she increased her use of the drug, eating the pellets as if they were candy, gradually withdrawing from life. She had no use for life any longer. She knew she was going to die within the dragon, knew it with the same clarity and certainty that accompanied all Griaule's sendings—death was to be her punishment for seeking to avoid his will, for denying his right to define and delimit her.

After the escape attempt, the feelies had treated her with suspicion and hostility; recently they had been absorbed by some internal matter, agitated in the extreme, and they had taken to ignoring her. Without their minimal companionship, without John, the patterns flowing across the surface of the heart were the only thing that took Catherine out of herself, and she spent hours at a time watching them, lying there half-conscious, registering their changes through slitted eyes. As her addiction worsened, as she lost weight and muscle tone, she became even more expert in interpreting the patterns, and staring up at the vast curve of the heart, like the curve of a golden bell, she came to realize that Mauldry had been right, that the dragon was a god, a universe unto itself with its own laws and physical constants. A god that she hated. She would try to beam her hatred at the heart, hoping to cause a rupture, a seizure of some sort; but she knew that Griaule was impervious to this, impervious to all human weapons, and that her hatred would have as little effect upon him as an arrow loosed into an empty sky.

One day almost a year after John's death she waked abruptly from a dreamless sleep beside the heart, sitting bolt upright, feeling that a cold spike had been driven down the hollow of her spine. She rubbed sleep from her eyes, trying to shake off the lethargy of the drug, sensing danger at hand. Then she glanced up at the heart and was struck motionless. The patterns of shadow and golden radiance were changing more rapidly than ever before, and their complexity, too, was far greater than she had ever seen; yet they were as clear to her as her own script: pulsings of darkness and golden eddies flowing, unscrolling across the dimpled surface of the organ. It was a simple message, and for a few seconds she refused to accept the knowledge it conveyed, not wanting to believe that this was the culmination of her destiny, that her youth had been wasted in so trivial a matter; but recalling all the clues, the dreams of the sleeping dragon, the repetitious vision of the rise and fall of its chest, Mauldry's story of the first feelie, the exodus of animals and insects and birds, the muffled thud from deep within the dragon after which everything had remained calm for a thousand years . . . she knew it must be true.

As it had done a thousand years before, and as it would do again a thousand years in the future, the heart was going to beat.

She was infuriated, and she wanted to reject the fact that all her trials and griefs had been sacrifices made for the sole purpose of saving the feelies. Her task, she realized, would be to clear them out of the chamber where they lived before it was flooded with the liquids that fueled the dragon's fires; and after the chamber had been emptied, she was to lead them back so they could go on with the work of keeping Griaule pest-free. The cause of their recent agitation, she thought, must have been due to their apprehension of the event, the result of one of Griaule's sendings; but because of their timid-

ity they would tend to dismiss his warning, being more frightened of the outside world than of any peril within the dragon. They would need guidance
to survive, and as once he had chosen Mauldry to assist her, now Griaule had
chosen her to guide the feelies.

She staggered up, as befuddled as a bird trapped between glass walls,
making little rushes this way and that; then anger overcame confusion, and
she beat with her fists on the heart wall, bawling her hatred of the dragon,
her anguish at the ruin he had made of her life. Finally, breathless, she collapsed, her own heart pounding erratically, trying to think what to do. She
wouldn't tell them, she decided; she would just let them die when the chamber flooded, and this way have her revenge. But an instant later she reversed
her decision, knowing that the feelies' deaths would merely be an inconvenience to Griaule, that he would simply gather a new group of idiots to serve
him. And besides, she thought, she had already killed too many feelies.
There was no choice, she realized; over the span of almost eleven years she
had been maneuvered by the dragon's will to this place and moment where,
by virtue of her shaped history and conscience, she had only one course of
action.

Full of muddle-headed good intentions, she made her way back to the
colony, her guards trailing behind, and when she had reached the chamber,
she stood with her back to the channel that led toward the throat, uncertain
of how to proceed. Several hundred feelies were milling about the bottom of
the chamber, and others were clinging to ropes, hanging together in front
of one or another of the cubicles, looking in that immense space like clusters of glittering, many-colored fruit; the constant motion and complexity
of the colony added to Catherine's hesitancy and bewilderment, and when
she tried to call out to the feelies, to gain their attention, she managed only
a feeble, scratchy noise. But she gathered her strength and called out again
and again, until at last they were all assembled before her, silent and staring,
hemming her in against the entrance to the channel, next to some chests that
contained the torches and swords and other items used by the hunters. The
feelies gawped at her, plucking at their gaudy rags; their silence seemed to
have a slow vibration. Catherine started to speak, but faltered; she took a
deep breath, let it out explosively and made a second try.

"We have to leave," she said, hearing the shakiness of her voice. "We
have to go outside. Not for long. Just for a little while . . . a few hours. The
chamber, it's going. . . ." She broke off, realizing that they weren't following
her. "The thing Griaule has meant me to learn," she went on in a louder

voice, "at last I know it. I know why I was brought to you. I know the purpose for which I have studied all these years. Griaule's heart is going to beat, and when it does the chamber will fill with liquid. If you remain here, you'll all drown."

The front ranks shifted, and some of the feelies exchanged glances, but otherwise they displayed no reaction.

Catherine shook her fists in frustration. "You'll die if you don't listen to me! You have to leave! When the heart contracts, the chamber will be flooded . . . don't you understand?" She pointed up to the mist-hung ceiling of the chamber. "Look! The birds . . . the birds have gone! They know what's coming! And so do you! Don't you feel the danger? I know you do!"

They edged back, some of them turning away, entering into whispered exchanges with their fellows.

Catherine grabbed the nearest of them, a young female dressed in ruby silks. "Listen to me!" she shouted.

"Liar, Cat'rine, liar," said one of the males, jerking the female away from her. "We not goin' be mo' fools."

"I'm not lying! I'm not!" She went from one to another, putting her hands on their shoulders, meeting their eyes in an attempt to impress them with her sincerity. "The heart is going to beat! Once . . . just once. You won't have to stay outside long. Not long at all."

They were all walking away, all beginning to involve themselves in their own affairs, and Catherine, desperate, hurried after them, pulling them back, saying, "Listen to me! Please!" Explaining what was to happen, and receiving cold stares in return. One of the males shoved her aside, baring his teeth in a hiss, his eyes blank and bright, and she retreated to the entrance of the channel, feeling rattled and disoriented, in need of another pellet. She couldn't collect her thoughts, and she looked around in every direction as if hoping to find some sight that would steady her; but nothing she saw was of any help. Then her gaze settled on the chests where the swords and torches were stored. She felt as if her head were being held in a vise and forced toward the chests, and the knowledge of what she must do was a coldness inside her head—the unmistakable touch of Griaule's thought. It was the only way. She saw that clearly. But the idea of doing something so extreme frightened her, and she hesitated, looking behind her to make sure that none of the feelies were keeping track of her movements. She inched toward the chests, keeping her eyes lowered, trying to make it appear that she was moving aimlessly. In one of the chests were a number of tinderboxes resting beside some torches; she stooped, grabbed a torch and one of the tinderboxes, and went walking briskly up the slope. She paused by the lowest rank of cubicles, noticed that some of the feelies had turned to watch her; when she lit the torch, alarm surfaced in their faces and they surged up the slope toward her. She held the torch up to the curtains that covered the entrance to the cubicle, and the feelies fell back, muttering, some letting out piercing wails.

"Please!" Catherine cried, her knees rubbery from the tension, a chill knot in her breast. "I don't want to do this! But you have to leave!"

A few of the feelies edged toward the channel, and encouraged by this, Catherine shouted, "Yes! That's it! If you'll just go outside, just for a little while, I won't have to do it!"

Several feelies entered the channel, and the crowd around Catherine began to erode, whimpering, breaking into tears, trickles of five and six at a time breaking away and moving out of sight within the channel, until there were no more than thirty of them left within the chamber, forming a ragged semi-circle around her. She would have liked to believe that they would do as she had suggested without further coercion on her part, but she knew that they were all packed into the channel or the chamber beyond, waiting for her to put down the torch. She gestured at the feelies surrounding her, and they, too, began easing toward the channel; when only a handful of them remained visible, she touched the torch to the curtains.

She was amazed by how quickly the fire spread, rushing like waves up the silk drapes, following the rickety outlines of the cubicles, appearing to dress them in a fancywork of reddish yellow flame, making crispy, chuckling noises. The fire seemed to have a will of its own, to be playfully seeking out all the intricate shapes of the colony and illuminating them, the separate flames chasing one another with merry abandon, sending little trains of fire along poles and stanchions, geysering up from corners, flinging out fiery fingers to touch tips across a gap.

She was so caught up in this display, her drugged mind finding in it an aesthetic, that she forgot all about the feelies, and when a cold sharp pain penetrated her left side, she associated this not with them but thought it a side-effect of the drug, a sudden attack brought on by her abuse of it. Then, horribly weak, sinking to her knees, she saw one of them standing next to her, a male with a pale thatch of thinning hair wisping across his scalp, holding a sword tipped with red, and she knew that he had stabbed her. She had the giddy urge to speak to him, not out of anger, just to ask a question that she wasn't able to speak, for instead of being afraid of the weakness invading her limbs, she had a terrific curiosity about what would happen next, and she had the irrational thought that her executioner might have the answer, that in his role as the instrument of Griaule's will he might have some knowledge of absolutes. He spat something at her, an accusation or an insult made inaudible by the crackling of the flames, and fled down the slope and out of the chamber, leaving her alone. She rolled onto her back, gazing at the fire, and the pain seemed to roll inside her as if it were a separate thing. Some of the cubicles were collapsing, spraying sparks, twists of black smoke boiling up, smoldering pieces of blackened wood tumbling down to the chamber floor, the entire structure appearing to ripple through the heat haze, looking unreal, an absurd construction of flaming skeletal framework and billowing, burning silks, and growing dizzy, feeling that she was falling upward into that huge fiery space, Catherine passed out.

She must have been unconscious for only a matter of seconds, because nothing had changed when she opened her eyes, except that a section of the fabric covering the chamber floor had caught fire. The flames were roaring, the snap and cracking of timbers as sharp as explosions, and her nostrils were choked with an acrid stink. With a tremendous effort that brought her once again to the edge of unconsciousness, she came to her feet, clutching the wound in her side, and stumbled toward the channel; at the entrance she fell and crawled into it, choking on the smoke that poured along the passageway. Her eyes teared from the smoke, and she wriggled on her stomach, pulling herself along with her hands. She nearly passed out half a dozen times before reaching the adjoining chamber, and then she staggered, crawled, stopping frequently to catch her breath, to let the pain of her wound subside, somehow negotiating a circuitous path among the pools of burning liquid and the pale red warty bumps that sprouted everywhere. Then into the throat. She wanted to surrender to the darkness there, to let go, but she kept going, not motivated by fear, but by some reflex of survival, simply obeying the impulse to continue for as long as it was possible. Her eyes blurred, and darkness frittered at the edges of her vision. But even so, she was able to make out the light of day, the menagerie of shapes erected by the interlocking branches of the thickets, and she thought that now she could stop, that this had been what she wanted—to see the light again, not to die bathed in the uncanny radiance of Griaule's blood.

She lay down, lowering herself cautiously among a bed of ferns, her back against the side of the throat, the same position—she remembered—in which she had fallen asleep that first night inside the dragon so many years before. She started to slip, to dwindle inside herself, but was alerted by a whispery rustling that grew louder and louder, and a moment later swarms of insects began to pour from the dragon's throat, passing overhead with a whirring rush and in such density that they cut off most of the light issuing from the mouth. Far above, like the shadows of spiders, apes were swinging on the vines that depended from the roof of the mouth, heading for the outer world, and Catherine could hear smaller animals scuttling through the brush. The sight of these flights made her feel accomplished, secure in what she had done, and she settled back, resting her head against Griaule's flesh, as peaceful as she could ever recall, almost eager to be done with life, with drugs and solitude and violence. She had a moment's worry about the feelies, wondering where they were; but then she realized that they would probably do no differently than had their remote ancestor, that they would hide in the thickets until all was calm.

She let her eyes close. The pain of the wound had diminished to a distant throb that scarcely troubled her, and the throbbing made a rhythm that seemed to be bearing her up. Somebody was talking to her, saying her name, and she resisted the urge to open her eyes, not wanting to be called back. She must be hearing things, she thought. But the voice persisted, and at last she did open her eyes. She gave a weak laugh on seeing Amos Mauldry kneeling before her, wavering and vague as a ghost, and realized that she was seeing things, too.

"Catherine," he said. "Can you hear me?"

"No," she said, and laughed again, a laugh that sent her into a bout of gasping; she felt her weakness in a new and poignant way, and it frightened her.

"Catherine?"

She blinked, trying to make him disappear; but he appeared to solidify as if she were becoming more part of his world than that of life. "What is it, Mauldry?" she said, and coughed. "Have you come to guide me to - heaven . . . is that it?"

His lips moved, and she had the idea that he was trying to reassure her of something; but she couldn't hear his words, no matter how hard she strained her ears. He was beginning to fade, becoming opaque, proving himself to be no more than a phantom; yet as she blacked out, experiencing a final moment of panic, Catherine could have sworn that she felt him take her hand.

SHE WALKED IN a golden glow that dimmed and brightened, and found herself staring into a face; after a moment, a long moment, because the face was much different than she had imagined it during these past few years, she recognized that it was hers. She lay still, trying to accommodate to this state of affairs, wondering why she wasn't dead, puzzling over the face and uncertain as to why she wasn't afraid; she felt strong and alert and at peace. She sat up and discovered that she was naked, that she was sitting in a small chamber lit by veins of golden blood branching across the ceiling, its walls obscured by vines with glossy dark green leaves. The body—her body—was lying on its back, and one side of the shirt it wore was soaked with blood. Folded beside the body was a fresh shirt, trousers, and resting atop these was a pair of sandals.

She checked her side—there was no sign of a wound. Her emotions were a mix of relief and self-loathing. She understood that somehow she had been conveyed to this cavity, to the ghostvine, and her essences had been transferred to a likeness, and yet she had trouble accepting the fact, because she felt no different than she had before . . . except for the feelings of peace and strength, and the fact that she had no craving for the drug. She tried to deny what had happened, to deny that she was now a thing, the bizarre contrivance of a plant, and it seemed that her thoughts, familiar in their ordinary process, were proofs that she must be wrong in her assumption. However, the body was an even more powerful evidence to the contrary. She would have liked to take refuge in panic, but her overall feeling of well-being prevented this. She began to grow cold, her skin pebbling, and reluctantly she dressed in the clothing folded beside the body. Something hard in the breast pocket of the shirt. She opened the pocket, took out a small leather sack; she loosed the tie of the sack and from it poured a fortune of cut gems into her hand: diamonds, emeralds, and sunstones. She put the sack back into the pocket, not knowing what to make of the stones, and sat looking at the body. It was much changed from its youth, leaner, less voluptuous, and in the repose of death, the face had lost its gloss and perfection, and was merely the face of an attractive woman . . . a disheartened woman. She thought she should feel something, that she should be oppressed by the sight, but she had no reaction to it; it might have been a skin she had shed, something of no more consequence than that.

She had no idea where to go, but realizing that she couldn't stay there forever, she stood and with a last glance at the body, she made her way down the narrow channel leading away from the cavity. When she emerged into the passage, she hesitated, unsure of which direction to choose, unsure, too, of which direction was open to her. At length, deciding not to tempt

Griaule's judgment, she headed back toward the colony, thinking that she would take part in helping them rebuild; but before she had gone ten feet she heard Mauldry's voice calling her name.

He was standing by the entrance to the cavity, dressed as he had been that first night—in a satin frock coat, carrying his gold-knobbed cane—and as she approached him, a smile broke across his wrinkled face, and he nodded as if in approval of her resurrection. "Surprised to see me?" he asked.

"I . . . I don't know," she said, a little afraid of him. "Was that you . . . in the mouth?"

He favored her with a polite bow. "None other. After things settled down, I had some of the feelies bear you to the cavity. Or rather I was the instrument that effected Griaule's will in the matter. Did you look in the pocket of your shirt?"

"Yes."

"Then you found the gems. Good, good."

She was at a loss for words at first. "I thought I saw you once before," she said finally. "A few years back."

"I'm sure you did. After my rebirth—" he gestured toward the cavity "—I was no longer of any use to you. You were forging your own path and my presence would have hampered your process. So I hid among the feelies, waiting for the time when you would need me." He squinted at her. "You look troubled."

"I don't understand any of this," she said. "How can I feel like my old self, when I'm obviously so different?"

"Are you?" he asked. "Isn't sameness or difference mostly a matter of feeling?" He took her arm, steered her along the passage away from the colony. "You'll adjust to it, Catherine. I have, and I had the same reaction as you when I first awoke." He spread his arms, inviting her to examine him. "Do I look different to you? Aren't I the same old fool as ever?"

"So it seems," she said drily. She walked a few paces in silence, then something occurred to her. "The feelies . . . do they. . . ."

"Rebirth is only for the chosen, the select. The feelies receive another sort of reward, one not given me to understand."

"You call this a reward? To be subject to more of Griaule's whims? And what's next for me? Am I to discover when his bowels are due to move?"

He stopped walking, frowning at her. "Next? Why, whatever pleases you, Catherine. I've been assuming that you'd want to leave, but you're free to do as you wish. Those gems I gave you will buy you any kind of life you desire."

"I can leave?"

"Most assuredly. You've accomplished your purpose here, and you're your own agent now. *Do* you want to leave?"

Catherine looked at him, unable to speak, and nodded.

"Well, then." He took her arm again. "Let's be off."

As they walked down to the chamber behind the throat and then into the throat itself, Catherine felt as one is supposed to feel at the moment of death, all the memories of her life within the dragon passing before her eyes with their attendant emotions—her flight, her labors and studies, John, the long hours spent beside the heart—and she thought that this was most appropriate, because she was not re-entering life but rather passing through into a kind of afterlife, a place beyond death that would be as unfamiliar and new a place as Griaule himself had once seemed. And she was astounded to realize that she was frightened of these new possibilities, that the thing she had wanted for so long could pose a menace and that it was the dragon who now offered the prospect of security. On several occasions she considered turning back, but each time she did, she rebuked herself for her timidity and continued on. However, on reaching the mouth and wending her way through the thickets, her fear grew more pronounced. The sunlight, that same light that not so many months before had been alluring, now hurt her eyes and made her want to draw back into the dim golden murk of Griaule's blood; and as they neared the lip, as she stepped into the shadow of a fang, she began to tremble with cold and stopped, hugging herself to keep warm.

Mauldry took up a position facing her, jogged her arm. "What is it?" he asked. "You seem frightened."

"I am," she said; she glanced up at him. "Maybe . . ."

"Don't be silly," he said. "You'll be fine once you're away from here. And"—he cocked his eye toward the declining sun—"you should be pushing along. You don't want to be hanging about the mouth when it's dark. I doubt anything would harm you, but since you're no longer part of Griaule's plan . . . well, better safe than sorry." He gave her a push. "Get along with you, now."

"You're not coming with me?"

"Me?" Mauldry chuckled. "What would I do out there? I'm an old man, set in my ways. No, I'm far better off staying with the feelies. I've become half a feely myself after all these years. But you're young, you've got a whole world of life ahead of you." He nudged her forward. "Do what I say, girl. There's no use in your hanging about any longer."

She went a couple of steps toward the lip, paused, feeling sentimental about leaving the old man; though they had never been close, he had been like a father to her . . . and thinking this, remembering her real father, whom she had scarcely thought of these last years, with whom she'd had the same lack of closeness, that made her aware of all the things she had to look forward to, all the lost things she might now regain. She moved into the thickets with a firmer step, and behind her, old Mauldry called to her for a last time.

"That's my girl!" he sang out. "You just keep going, and you'll start to feel at rights soon enough! There's nothing to be afraid of . . . nothing you can avoid, in any case! Goodbye, goodbye!"

She glanced back, waved, saw him shaking his cane in a gesture of farewell, and laughed at his eccentric appearance: a funny little man in satin rags hopping up and down in that great shadow between the fangs. Out from beneath that shadow herself, the rich light warmed her, seeming to penetrate and dissolve all the coldness that had been lodged in her bones and thoughts.

"Goodbye!" cried Mauldry. "Goodbye! Don't be sad! You're not leaving anything important behind, and you're taking the best parts with you. Just walk fast and think about what you're going to tell everyone. They'll be amazed by all you've done! Flabbergasted! Tell them about Griaule! Tell them what he's like, tell them all you've seen and all you've learned. Tell them what a grand adventure you've had!"

VIII

RETURNING TO HANGTOWN was in some ways a more unsettling experience than had been Catherine's flight into the dragon. She had expected the place to have changed, and while there *had* been minor changes, she had assumed that it would be as different from its old self as was she. But standing at the edge of the village, looking out at the gray weathered shacks ringing the fouled shallows of the lake, thin smoke issuing from tin chimneys, the cliff of the fronto-parietal plate casting its gloomy shadow, the chokecherry thickets, the hawthornes, the dark brown dirt of the streets, three elderly men sitting on cane chairs in front of one of the shacks, smoking their pipes and staring back at her with unabashed curiosity . . . superficially it was no different than it had been ten years before, and this seemed to imply that her years of imprisonment, her death and rebirth had been of small importance.

She did not demand that they be important to anyone else, yet it galled her that the world had passed through those years of ordeal without significant scars, and it also imbued her with the irrational fear that if she were to enter the village, she might suffer some magical slippage back through time and reinhabit her old life. At last, with a hesitant step, she walked over to the men and wished them a good morning.

"Mornin'," said a paunchy fellow with a mottled bald scalp and a fringe of gray beard, whom she recognized as Tim Weedlon. "What can I do for you, ma'am? Got some nice bits of scale inside."

"That place over there"—she pointed to an abandoned shack down the street, its roof holed and missing the door—"where can I find the owner?"

The other man, Mardo Koren, thin as a mantis, his face seamed and blotched, said, "Can't nobody say for sure. Ol' Riall died . . . must be goin' on nine, ten years back."

"He's dead?" She felt weak inside, dazed.

"Yep," said Tim Weedlon, studying her face, his brow furrowed, his expression bewildered. "His daughter run away, killed a village man name of Willen and vanished into nowhere . . . or so ever'body figured. Then when Willen's brothers turned up missin', people thought ol' Riall must done 'em. He didn't deny it. Acted like he didn't care whether he lived or died."

"What happened?"

"They had a trial, found Riall guilty." He leaned forward, squinting at her. "Catherine . . . is that you?"

She nodded, struggling for control. "What did they do with him?"

"How can it be you?" he said. "Where you been?"

"What happened to my father?"

"God, Catherine. You know what happens to them that's found guilty of murder. If it's any comfort, the truth come out finally."

"They took him in under the wing . . . they left him under the wing?" Her fists clenched, nails pricking hard into her palms. "Is that what they did?" He lowered his eyes, picked at a fray on his trouserleg.

Her eyes filled, and she turned away, facing the mossy overhang of the fronto-parietal plate. "You said the truth came out."

"That's right. A girl confessed to having seen the whole thing. Said the Willens chased you into Griaule's mouth. She woulda come forward sooner, but ol' man Willen had her feared for her life. Said he'd kill her if she told. You probably remember her. Friend of yours, if I recall. Brianne." She whirled around, repeated the name with venom.

"Wasn't she your friend?" Weedlon asked.

"What happened to her?"

"Why . . . nothing," said Weedlon. "She's married, got hitched to Zev Mallison. Got herself a batch of children. I 'spect she's home now if you wanna see her. You know the Mallison place, don'tcha?"

"Yes."

"You want to know more about it, you oughta drop by there and talk to Brianne."

"I guess . . . I will, I'll do that."

"Now tell us where you been, Catherine. Ten years! Musta been something important to keep you from home for so long."

Coldness was spreading through her, turning her to ice. "I was thinking, Tim . . . I was thinking I might like to do some scaling while I'm here. Just for old time's sake, you know." She could hear the shakiness in her voice and tried to smooth it out; she forced a smile. "I wonder if I could borrow some hooks."

"Hooks?" He scratched his head, still regarding her with confusion. "Sure, I suppose you can. But aren't you going to tell us where you've been? We thought you were dead."

"I will, I promise. Before I leave . . . I'll come back and tell you all about it. All right?"

"Well, all right." He heaved up from his chair. "But it's a cruel thing you're doing, Catherine."

"No crueler than what's been done to me," she said distractedly. "Not half so cruel."

"Pardon," said Tim. "How's that?"

"What?"

He gave her a searching look and said, "I was telling you it was a cruel thing, keeping an old man in suspense about where you've been. Why you're going to make the choicest bit of gossip we've had in years. And you came back with . . ."

"Oh! I'm sorry," she said. "I was thinking about something else."

THE MALLISON PLACE was among the larger shanties in Hangtown, half a dozen rooms, most of which had been added on over the years since Catherine had left; but its size was no evidence of wealth or status, only of a more expansive poverty. Next to the steps leading to a badly hung door was a litter of bones and mango skins and other garbage. Fruit flies hovered above a watermelon rind; a gray dog with its ribs showing slunk off around the corner, and there was a stink of fried onions and boiled greens. From inside came the squalling of a child. The shanty looked false to Catherine, an unassuming façade behind which lay a monstrous reality—the woman who had betrayed her, killed her father—and yet its drabness was sufficient to disarm her anger somewhat. But as she mounted the steps there was a thud as of something heavy falling, and a woman shouted. The voice was harsh, deeper than Catherine remembered, but she knew it must belong to Brianne, and that restored her vengeful mood. She knocked on the door with one of Tim Weedlon's scaling hooks, and a second later it was flung open and she was confronted by an olive-skinned woman in torn gray skirts—almost the same color as the weathered boards, as if she were the quintessential product of the environment—and gray streaks in her dark brown hair. She looked Catherine up and down, her face hard with displeasure, and said, "What do you want?"

It was Brianne, but Brianne warped, melted, disfigured as a waxwork might be disfigured by heat. Her waist gone, features thickened, cheeks sagging into jowls. Shock washed away Catherine's anger, and shock, too, materialized in Brianne's face. "No," she said, giving the word an abstracted value, as if denying an inconsequential accusation; then she shouted it: "No!" She slammed the door, and Catherine pounded on it, crying, "Damn you! Brianne!"

The child screamed, but Brianne made no reply.

Enraged, Catherine swung the hook at the door; the point sank deep into the wood, and when she tried to pull it out, one of the boards came partially loose; she pried at it, managed to rip it away, the nails coming free with a shriek of tortured metal. Through the gap she saw Brianne cowering against the rear wall of a dilapidated room, her arms around a little boy in shorts. Using the hook as a lever, she pulled loose another board, reached in and undid the latch. Brianne pushed the child behind her and grabbed a broom as Catherine stepped inside.

"Get out of here!" she said, holding the broom like a spear.

The gray poverty of the shanty made Catherine feel huge in her anger, too bright for the place, like a sun shining in a cave, and although her attention was fixed on Brianne, the peripheral details of the room imprinted themselves on her: the wood stove upon which a covered pot was steaming; an overturned wooden chair with a hole in the seat; cobwebs spanning the corners, rat turds along the wall; a rickety table set with cracked dishes and dust thick as fur beneath it. These things didn't arouse her pity or mute her anger; instead, they seemed extensions of Brianne, new targets for hatred. She moved closer, and Brianne jabbed the broom at her. "Go away," she said weakly. "Please . . . leave us alone!"

Catherine swung the hook, snagging the twine that bound the broom straws and knocking it from Brianne's hands. Brianne retreated to the corner where the wood stove stood, hauling the child along. She held up her hand to ward off another blow and said, "Don't hurt us."

"Why not? Because you've got children, because you've had an unhappy life?" Catherine spat at Brianne. "You killed my father!"

"I was afraid! Key's father . . ."

"I don't care," said Catherine coldly. "I don't care why you did it. I don't care how good your reasons were for betraying me in the first place."

"That's right! You never cared about anything!" Brianne clawed at her breast. "You killed my heart! You didn't care about Glynn, you just wanted him because he wasn't yours!"

It took Catherine a few seconds to dredge that name up from memory, to connect it with Brianne's old lover and recall that it was her callousness and self-absorption that had set the events of the past ten years in motion. But although this roused her guilt, it did not abolish her anger. She couldn't equate Brianne's crimes with her excesses. Still, she was confused about what to do, uncomfortable now with the very concept of justice, and she wondered if she should leave, just throw down the hook and leave vengeance to whatever ordering principle governed the fates in Hangtown. Then Brianne shifted her feet, made a noise in her throat and Catherine felt rage boiling up inside her.

"Don't throw that up to me," she said with flat menace. "Nothing I've done to you merited what you did to me. You don't even know what you did!" She raised the hook, and Brianne shrank back into the corner. The child twisted its head to look at Catherine, fixing her with brimming eyes, and she held back.

"Send the child away," she told Brianne.

Brianne leaned down to the child. "Go to your father," she said.

"No, wait," said Catherine, fearing that the child might bring Zev Mallison.

"Must you kill us both?" said Brianne, her voice hoarse with emotion. Hearing this, the child once more began to cry.

"Stop it," Catherine said to him, and when he continued to cry, she shouted it.

Brianne muffled the child's wails in her skirts. "Go ahead!" she said, her face twisted with fear. "Just do it!" She broke down into sobs, ducked her head and waited for the blow. Catherine stepped close to Brianne, yanked her head back by the hair, exposing her throat, and set the point of the hook against the big vein there. Brianne's eyes rolled down, trying to see the hook; her breath came in gaspy shrieks, and the child, caught between the two women, squirmed and wailed. Catherine's hand was trembling, and that slight motion pricked Brianne's skin, drawing a bead of blood. She stiffened, her eyelids fluttered down, her mouth fell open—an expression, at least so it seemed to Catherine, of ecstatic expectation. Catherine studied the face, feeling as if her emotions were being purified, drawn into a fine wire; she had an almost aesthetic appreciation of the stillness gathering around her, the hard poise of Brianne's musculature, the sensitive pulse in the throat that transmitted its frail rhythm along the hook, and she restrained herself from pressing the point deeper, wanting to prolong Brianne's suffering.

But then the hook grew heavy in Catherine's hands, and she understood that the moment had passed, that her need for vengeance had lost the immediacy and thrust of passion. She imagined herself skewering Brianne, and then imagined dragging her out to confront a village tribunal, forcing her to confess her lies, having her sentenced to be tied up and left for whatever creatures foraged beneath Griaule's wing. But while it provided her a measure of satisfaction to picture Brianne dead or dying, she saw now that anticipation was the peak of vengeance, that carrying out the necessary actions would only harm her. It frustrated her that all these years and the deaths would have no resolution, and she thought that she must have changed more than she had assumed to put aside vengeance so easily; this caused her to wonder again about the nature of the change, to question whether she was truly herself or merely an arcane likeness. But then she realized that the change had been her resolution, and that vengeance was an artifact of her old life, nothing more, and that her new life, whatever its secret character, must find other concerns to fuel it apart from old griefs and unworthy passions. This struck her with the force of a revelation, and she let out a long sighing breath that seemed to carry away with it all the sad vibrations of the past, all the residues of hates and loves, and she could finally believe that she was no longer the dragon's prisoner. She felt new in her whole being, subject to new compulsions, as alive as tears, as strong as wheat, far too strong and alive for this pallid environment, and she could hardly recall now why she had come.

She looked at Brianne and her son, feeling only the ghost of hatred, seeing them not as objects of pity or wrath, but as unfamiliar, irrelevant, lives trapped in the prison of their own self-regard, and without a word she turned and walked to the steps, slamming the hook deep into the boards of the wall, a gesture of fierce resignation, the closing of a door opening onto anger and the opening of one that led to uncharted climes, and went down out of the village, leaving old Tim Weedlon's thirst for gossip unquenched, passing along Griaule's back, pushing through thickets and fording streams, and not noticing for quite some time that she had crossed onto another hill and left the dragon far behind. Three weeks later she came to Cabrecavela, a small town at the opposite end of the Carbonales Valley, and there, using the gems provided her by Mauldry, she bought a house and settled in and began to write about Griaule, creating not a personal memoir but a reference work containing an afterword dealing with certain metaphysical speculations, for she did not wish her adventures published, considering them banal by comparison to her primary subjects, the dragon's physiology and ecology. After the publication of her book, which she entitled *The Heart's Millennium,* she experienced a brief celebrity; but she shunned most of the opportunities for travel and lecture and lionization that came her way, and satisfied her desire to impart the knowledge she had gained by teaching in the local school and speaking privately with those scientists from Port Chantay who came to interview her. Some of these visitors had been colleagues of John Colmacos, yet she never mentioned their relationship, believing that her memories of the man needed no modification; but perhaps this was less than an honest self-appraisal, perhaps she had not come to terms with that portion of her past, for in the spring five years after she had returned to the world she married one of these scientists, a man named Brian Ocoi, who in his calm demeanor and modest easiness of speech appeared cast from the same mold as Colmacos. From that point on little is known of her other than the fact that she bore two sons and confined her writing to a journal that has gone unpublished. However, it is said of her—as is said of all those who perform similar acts of faith in the shadows of other dragons yet unearthed from beneath their hills of ordinary-seeming earth and grass, believing that their bond serves through gentle constancy to enhance and not further delimit the boundaries of this prison world—from that day forward she lived happily ever after. Except for the dying at the end. And the heartbreak in-between.

The 1990s

TERRY BISSON

TERRY BISSON was born in February 1942, in Owensboro, Kentucky. After receiving a B.A. from the University of Louisville in 1964, he lived in New York scripting comics, editing the short-lived zine *Web of Horror,* and doing various hackwork for tabloids. He spent four years in the Red Rockers hippie commune in the Colorado mountains working as an auto mechanic, then returned to New York in 1976, serving as an editor and copywriter at Berkley and Avon until 1985. For the next five years, he ran "revolutionary mail order book service" Jacobin Books, and in the mid-'90s he was a consultant at HarperCollins. Bisson now lives in the San Francisco Bay Area.

Bisson's first novel was the fantasy *Wyrldmaker,* followed by novels where Americana blends with magical/SF themes, *Talking Man* and *Fire on the Mountain.* His short story "Bears Discover Fire" won the 1991 Hugo, Nebula, Locus, and Sturgeon Awards and is collected in *Bears Discover Fire and Other Stories.* His later novels combined serious SF with satire in *Voyage to the Red Planet, Pirates of the Universe,* and *The Pickup Artist.* Bisson was also chosen to complete Walter M. Miller Jr.'s novel *Saint Leibowitz and the Wild Horse Woman.* The short story "macs," which won the Hugo, Nebula, and Locus Awards, appears in the collection *In the Upper Room and Other Likely Stories* (2000). His most recent book is the novella "Dear Abbey."

Bisson has written often about America and Americana, seldom more famously than in this moving and often funny tale.

* * *

I WAS DRIVING WITH my brother, the preacher, and my nephew, the preacher's son, on I-65 just north of Bowling Green when we got a flat. It was Sunday night and we had been to visit Mother at the Home. We were in my car. The flat caused what you might call knowing groans since, as the old-fashioned one in my family (so they tell me), I fix my own tires, and my brother is always telling me to get radials and quit buying old tires.

But if you know how to mount and fix tires yourself, you can pick them up for almost nothing.

Since it was a left rear tire, I pulled over to the left, onto the median grass. The way my Caddy stumbled to a stop, I figured the tire was ruined. "I guess there's no need asking if you have any of that FlatFix in the trunk," said Wallace.

"Here, son, hold the light," I said to Wallace Jr. He's old enough to want to help and not old enough (yet) to think he knows it all. If I'd married and had kids, he's the kind I'd have wanted.

An old Caddy has a big trunk that tends to fill up like a shed. Mine's a '56. Wallace was wearing his Sunday shirt, so he didn't offer to help while I pulled magazines, fishing tackle, a wooden tool box, some old clothes, a comealong wrapped in a grass sack, and a tobacco sprayer out of the way, looking for my jack. The spare looked a little soft.

The light went out. "Shake it, son," I said.

It went back on. The bumper jack was long gone, but I carry a little quarter-ton hydraulic. I found it under Mother's old *Southern Livings,* 1978–1986. I had been meaning to drop them at the dump. If Wallace hadn't been along, I'd have let Wallace Jr. position the jack under the axle, but I got on my knees and did it myself. There's nothing wrong with a boy learning to change a tire. Even if you're not going to fix and mount them, you're still going to have to change a few in this life. The light went off again before I had the wheel off the ground. I was surprised at how dark the night was already. It was late October and beginning to get cool. "Shake it again, son," I said.

It went back on but it was weak. Flickery.

"With radials you just don't *have* flats," Wallace explained in that voice he uses when he's talking to a number of people at once; in this case, Wallace

Jr. and myself. "And even when you *do,* you just squirt them with this stuff called FlatFix and you just drive on. Three ninety-five the can."

"Uncle Bobby can fix a tire hisself," said Wallace Jr., out of loyalty I presume.

"*Him*self," I said from halfway under the car. If it was up to Wallace, the boy would talk like what Mother used to call "a helot from the gorges of the mountains." But drive on radials.

"Shake that light again," I said. It was about gone. I spun the lugs off into the hubcap and pulled the wheel. The tire had blown out along the sidewall. "Won't be fixing this one," I said. Not that I cared. I have a pile as tall as a man out by the barn.

The light went out again, then came back better than ever as I was fitting the spare over the lugs. "Much better," I said. There was a flood of dim orange flickery light. But when I turned to find the lug nuts, I was surprised to see that the flashlight the boy was holding was dead. The light was coming from two bears at the edge of the trees, holding torches. They were big, three-hundred pounders, standing about five feet tall. Wallace Jr. and his father had seen them and were standing perfectly still. It's best not to alarm bears.

I fished the lug nuts out of the hubcap and spun them on. I usually like to put a little oil on them, but this time I let it go. I reached under the car and let the jack down and pulled it out. I was relieved to see that the spare was high enough to drive on. I put the jack and the lug wrench and the flat into the trunk. Instead of replacing the hubcap, I put it in there too. All this time, the bears never made a move. They just held the torches up, whether out of curiosity or helpfulness, there was no way of knowing. It looked like there may have been more bears behind them, in the trees.

Opening three doors at once, we got into the car and drove off. Wallace was the first to speak. "Looks like bears have discovered fire," he said.

WHEN WE FIRST TOOK Mother to the Home, almost four years (forty-seven months) ago, she told Wallace and me she was ready to die. "Don't worry about me, boys," she whispered, pulling us both down so the nurse wouldn't hear. "I've drove a million miles and I'm ready to pass over to the other shore. I won't have long to linger here." She drove a consolidated school bus for thirty-nine years. Later, after Wallace left, she told me about her dream. A bunch of doctors were sitting around in a circle discussing her case. One said, "We've done all we can for her, boys, let's let her go." They all turned their hands up and smiled. When she didn't die that fall she seemed disappointed, though as spring came she forgot about it, as old people will.

In addition to taking Wallace and Wallace Jr. to see Mother on Sunday nights, I go myself on Tuesdays and Thursdays. I usually find her sitting in front of the TV, even though she doesn't watch it. The nurses keep it on all the time. They say the old folks like the flickering. It soothes them down.

"What's this I hear about bears discovering fire?" she said on Tuesday. "It's true," I told her as I combed her long white hair with the shell comb Wallace had brought her from Florida. Monday there had been a story in the Louisville *Courier-Journal,* and Tuesday one on NBC or *CBS Evening News*. People were seeing bears all over the state, and in Virginia as well. They had quit hibernating, and were apparently planning to spend the winter in the medians of the interstates. There have always been bears in the mountains of Virginia, but not here in western Kentucky, not for almost a hundred years. The last one was killed when Mother was a girl. The theory in the *Courier-Journal* was that they were following I-65 down from the forests of Michigan and Canada, but one old man from Allen County (interviewed on nationwide TV) said that there had always been a few bears left back in the hills, and they had come out to join the others now that they had discovered fire.

"They don't hibernate anymore," I said. "They make a fire and keep it going all winter."

"I declare," Mother said. "What'll they think of next!" The nurse came to take her tobacco away, which is the signal for bedtime.

EVERY OCTOBER, Wallace Jr. stays with me while his parents go to camp. I realize how backward that sounds, but there it is. My brother is a minister (House of the Righteous Way, Reformed), but he makes two thirds of his living in real estate. He and Elizabeth go to a Christian Success Retreat in South Carolina, where people from all over the country practice selling things to one another. I know what it's like not because they've ever bothered to tell me, but because I've seen the Revolving Equity Success Plan ads late at night on TV.

The schoolbus let Wallace Jr. off at my house on Wednesday, the day they left. The boy doesn't have to pack much of a bag when he stays with me. He has his own room here. As the eldest of our family, I hung on to the old home place near Smiths Grove. It's getting run down, but Wallace Jr. and I don't mind. He has his own room in Bowling Green, too, but since

Wallace and Elizabeth move to a different house every three months (part of the Plan), he keeps his .22 and his comics, the stuff that's important to a boy his age, in his room here at the home place. It's the room his dad and I used to share.

Wallace Jr. is twelve. I found him sitting on the back porch that overlooks the interstate when I got home from work. I sell crop insurance.

After I changed clothes, I showed him how to break the bead on a tire two ways, with a hammer and by backing a car over it. Like making sorghum, fixing tires by hand is a dying art. The boy caught on fast, though. "Tomorrow I'll show you how to mount your tire with the hammer and a tire iron," I said.

"What I wish is I could see the bears," he said. He was looking across the field to I-65, where the northbound lanes cut off the corner of our field. From the house at night, sometimes the traffic sounds like a waterfall.

"Can't see their fire in the daytime," I said. "But wait till tonight." That night CBS or NBC (I forget which is which) did a special on the bears, which were becoming a story of nationwide interest. They were seen in Kentucky, West Virginia, Missouri, Illinois (southern), and, of course, Virginia. There have always been bears in Virginia. Some characters there were even talking about hunting them. A scientist said they were heading into the states where there is some snow but not too much, and where there is enough timber in the medians for firewood. He had gone in with a video camera, but his shots were just blurry figures sitting around a fire. Another scientist said the bears were attracted by the berries on a new bush that grew only in the medians of the interstates. He claimed this berry was the first new species in recent history, brought about by the mixing of seeds along the highway. He ate one on TV, making a face, and called it a "new-berry." A climatic ecologist said that the warm winters (there was no snow last winter in Nashville, and only one flurry in Louisville) had changed the bears' hibernation cycle, and now they were able to remember things from year to year. "Bears may have discovered fire centuries ago," he said, "but forgot it." Another theory was that they had discovered (or remembered) fire when Yellowstone burned, several years ago.

The TV showed more guys talking about bears than it showed bears, and Wallace Jr. and I lost interest. After the supper dishes were done I took the boy out behind the house and down to our fence. Across the interstate and through the trees, we could see the light of the bears' fire. Wallace Jr. wanted to go back to the house and get his .22 and go shoot one, and I explained why that would be wrong. "Besides," I said, "a .22 wouldn't do much more to a bear than make it mad.

"Besides," I added, "it's illegal to hunt in the medians."

THE ONLY TRICK to mounting a tire by hand, once you have beaten or pried it onto the rim, is setting the bead. You do this by setting the tire upright, sitting on it, and bouncing it up and down between your legs while the air goes in. When the bead sets on the rim, it makes a satisfying "pop." On Thursday, I kept Wallace Jr. home from school and showed him how to do this until he got it right. Then we climbed our fence and crossed the field to get a look at the bears.

In northern Virginia, according to *Good Morning America,* the bears were keeping their fires going all day long. Here in western Kentucky, though, it was still warm for late October and they only stayed around the fires at night. Where they went and what they did in the daytime, I don't know. Maybe they were watching from the newberry bushes as Wallace Jr. and I climbed the government fence and crossed the northbound lanes. I carried an axe and Wallace Jr. brought his .22, not because he wanted to kill a bear but because a boy likes to carry some kind of a gun. The median was all tangled with brush and vines under the maple, oaks, and sycamores. Even though we were only a hundred yards from the house, I had never been there, and neither had anyone else that I knew of. It was like a created country. We found a path in the center and followed it down across a slow, short stream that flowed out of one grate and into another. The tracks in the gray mud were the first bear signs we saw. There was a musty but not really unpleasant smell. In a clearing under a big hollow beech, where the fire had been, we found nothing but ashes. Logs were drawn up in a rough circle and the smell was stronger. I stirred the ashes and found enough coals to start a new flame, so I banked them back the way they had been left.

I cut a little firewood and stacked it to one side, just to be neighborly.

Maybe the bears were watching us from the bushes even then. There's no way to know. I tasted one of the newberries and spit it out. It was so sweet it was sour, just the sort of thing you would imagine a bear would like.

THAT EVENING AFTER supper, I asked Wallace Jr. if he might want to go with me to visit Mother. I wasn't surprised when he said "yes." Kids have more consideration than folks give them credit for. We found her sitting on the concrete front porch of the Home, watching the cars go by on I-65. The nurse said she had been agitated all day. I wasn't surprised by that, either. Every fall as the leaves change, she gets restless, maybe the word is hopeful, again. I brought her into the dayroom and combed her long white hair. "Nothing but bears on TV anymore," the nurse complained, flipping the channels. Wallace Jr. picked up the remote after the nurse left, and we watched a CBS or NBC Special Report about some hunters in Virginia who had gotten their houses torched. The TV interviewed a hunter and his wife whose $117,500 Shenandoah Valley home had burned. She blamed the bears. He didn't blame the bears, but he was suing for compensation from the state since he had a valid hunting license. The state hunting commissioner came on and said that possession of a hunting license didn't prohibit (enjoin, I think, was the word he used) *the hunted* from striking back. I thought that was a pretty liberal view for a state commissioner. Of course, he had a vested interest in not paying off. I'm not a hunter myself.

"Don't bother coming on Sunday," Mother told Wallace Jr. with a wink. "I've drove a million miles and I've got one hand on the gate." I'm used to her saying stuff like that, especially in the fall, but I was afraid it would upset the boy. In fact, he looked worried after we left and I asked him what was wrong.

"How could she have drove a million miles?" he asked. She had told him 48 miles a day for 39 years, and he had worked it out on his calculator to be 336,960 miles.

"Have *driven*," I said. "And it's forty-eight in the morning and forty-eight in the afternoon. Plus there were the football trips. Plus, old folks exaggerate a little." Mother was the first woman school bus driver in the state. She did it every day and raised a family, too. Dad just farmed.

I USUALLY GET off the interstate at Smiths Grove, but that night I drove north all the way to Horse Cave and doubled back so Wallace Jr. and I could see the bears' fires. There were not as many as you would think from the TV—one every six or seven miles, hidden back in a clump of trees or under a rocky ledge. Probably they look for water as well as wood. Wallace Jr. wanted to stop, but it's against the law to stop on the interstate and I was afraid the state police would run us off.

There was a card from Wallace in the mailbox. He and Elizabeth were doing fine and having a wonderful time. Not a word about Wallace Jr., but the boy didn't seem to mind. Like most kids his age, he doesn't really enjoy going places with his parents.

. . .

ON SATURDAY AFTERNOON the Home called my office (Burley Belt Drought & Hail) and left word that Mother was gone. I was on the road. I work Saturdays. It's the only day a lot of part-time farmers are home. My heart literally skipped a beat when I called in and got the message, but only a beat. I had long been prepared. "It's a blessing," I said when I got the nurse on the phone.

"You don't understand," the nurse said. "Not *passed* away, gone. *Ran* away, gone. Your mother has escaped." Mother had gone through the door at the end of the corridor when no one was looking, wedging the door with her comb and taking a bedspread which belonged to the Home. What about her tobacco? I asked. It was gone. That was a sure sign she was planning to stay away. I was in Franklin, and it took me less than an hour to get to the Home on I-65. The nurse told me that Mother had been acting more and more confused lately. Of course they are going to say that. We looked around the grounds, which is only an acre with no trees between the interstate and a soybean field. Then they had me leave a message at the Sheriff's office. I would have to keep paying for her care until she was officially listed as Missing, which would be Monday.

It was dark by the time I got back to the house, and Wallace Jr. was fixing supper. This just involves opening a few cans, already selected and grouped together with a rubber band. I told him his grandmother had gone, and he nodded, saying, "She told us she would be." I called South Carolina and left a message. There was nothing more to be done. I sat down and tried to watch TV, but there was nothing on. Then, I looked out the back door, and saw the firelight twinkling through the trees across the northbound lane of I-65, and realized I just might know where to find her.

IT WAS DEFINITELY GETTING COLDER, so I got my jacket. I told the boy to wait by the phone in case the Sheriff called, but when I looked back, halfway across the field, there he was behind me. He didn't have a jacket. I let him catch up. He was carrying his .22, and I made him leave it leaning against our fence. It was harder climbing the government fence in the dark, at my age, than it had been in the daylight. I am sixty-one. The highway was busy with cars heading south and trucks heading north.

Crossing the shoulder, I got my pants cuffs wet on the long grass, already wet with dew. It is actually bluegrass.

The first few feet into the trees it was pitch black and the boy grabbed my hand. Then it got lighter. At first I thought it was the moon, but it was the high beams shining like moonlight into the treetops, allowing Wallace Jr. and me to pick our way through the brush. We soon found the path and its familiar bear smell.

I was wary of approaching the bears at night. If we stayed on the path we might run into one in the dark, but if we went through the bushes we might be seen as intruders. I wondered if maybe we shouldn't have brought the gun.

We stayed on the path. The light seemed to drip down from the canopy of the woods like rain. The going was easy, especially if we didn't try to look at the path but let our feet find their own way.

Then through the trees I saw their fire.

THE FIRE WAS mostly of sycamore and beech branches, the kind of fire that puts out very little heat or light and lots of smoke. The bears hadn't learned the ins and outs of wood yet. They did okay at tending it, though. A large cinnamon-brown northern-looking bear was poking the fire with a stick, adding a branch now and then from a pile at his side. The others sat around in a loose circle on the logs. Most were smaller black or honey bears; one was a mother with cubs. Some were eating berries from a hubcap. Not eating, but just watching the fire, my mother sat among them with the bedspread from the Home around her shoulders.

If the bears noticed us, they didn't let on. Mother patted a spot right next to her on the log and I sat down. A bear moved over to let Wallace Jr. sit on her other side.

The bear smell is rank but not unpleasant, once you get used to it. It's not like a barn smell, but wilder. I leaned over to whisper something to Mother and she shook her head. *It would be rude to whisper around these creatures that don't possess the power of speech,* she let me know without speaking. Wallace Jr. was silent, too. Mother shared the bedspread with us and we sat for what seemed hours, looking into the fire.

The big bear tended the fire, breaking up the dry branches by holding one end and stepping on them, like people do. He was good at keeping it going at the same level. Another bear poked the fire from time to time, but the others left it alone. It looked like only a few of the bears knew how to use fire, and were carrying the others along. But isn't that how it is with everything? Every once in a while, a smaller bear walked into the circle of firelight with an armload of wood and dropped it onto the pile. Median wood has a silvery cast, like driftwood.

Wallace Jr. isn't fidgety like a lot of kids. I found it pleasant to sit and stare into the fire. I took a little piece of Mother's Red Man, though I don't generally chew. It was no different from visiting her at the Home, only more interesting, because of the bears. There were about eight or ten of them. Inside the fire itself, things weren't so dull, either: little dramas were being played out as fiery chambers were created and then destroyed in a crashing of sparks. My imagination ran wild. I looked around the circle at the bears and wondered what *they* saw. Some had their eyes closed. Though they were gathered together, their spirits still seemed solitary, as if each bear was sitting alone in front of its own fire.

The hubcap came around and we all took some newberries. I don't know about Mother, but I just pretended to eat mine. Wallace Jr. made a face and spit his out. When he went to sleep, I wrapped the bedspread around all three of us. It was getting colder and we were not provided, like the bears, with fur. I was ready to go home, but not Mother. She pointed up toward the canopy of trees, where a light was spreading, and then pointed to herself. Did she think it was angels approaching from on high? It was only the high beams of some southbound truck, but she seemed mighty pleased. Holding her hand, I felt it grow colder and colder in mine.

WALLACE JR. WOKE ME UP by tapping on my knee. It was past dawn, and his grandmother had died sitting on the log between us. The fire was banked up and the bears were gone and someone was crashing straight through the woods, ignoring the path. It was Wallace. Two state troopers were right behind him. He was wearing a white shirt, and I realized it was Sunday morning. Underneath his sadness on learning of Mother's death, he looked peeved.

The troopers were sniffing the air and nodding. The bear smell was still strong. Wallace and I wrapped Mother in the bedspread and started with her body back out to the highway. The troopers stayed behind and scattered the bears' fire ashes and flung their firewood away into the bushes. It seemed a petty thing to do. They were like bears themselves, each one solitary in his own uniform.

There was Wallace's Olds 98 on the median, with its radial tires looking squashed on the grass. In front of it there was a police car with a trooper standing beside it, and behind it a funeral home hearse, also an Olds 98.

"First report we've had of them bothering old folks," the trooper said to Wallace. "That's not hardly what happened at all," I said, but nobody asked me to explain. They have their own procedures. Two men in suits got out of the hearse and opened the rear door. That to me was the point at which Mother departed this life. After we put her in, I put my arms around the boy. He was shivering even though it wasn't that cold. Sometimes death will do that, especially at dawn, with the police around and the grass wet, even when it comes as a friend.

We stood for a minute watching the cars and trucks pass. "It's a blessing," Wallace said. It's surprising how much traffic there is at 6:22 A.M.

THAT AFTERNOON, I went back to the median and cut a little firewood to replace what the troopers had flung away. I could see the fire through the trees that night.

I went back two nights later, after the funeral. The fire was going and it was the same bunch of bears, as far as I could tell. I sat around with them a while but it seemed to make them nervous, so I went home. I had taken a handful of newberries from the hubcap, and on Sunday I went with the boy and arranged them on Mother's grave. I tried again, but it's no use, you can't eat them.

Unless you're a bear.

JOHN KESSEL

J OHN KESSEL was born in Buffalo, New York, in 1950 and lives in
Raleigh, North Carolina, where he is a professor of American literature
at North Carolina State University. A writer of erudite short fiction
pieces that often make reference to, or are pastiches of popular culture,
Kessel made his first sale in 1975, and is best known for early stories
"Another Orphan" and "Buffalo." He has published a series of constantly
impressive short fiction, including several screwball comedies featuring series character Detlev Gruber (the most recent of which is "It's All True,"
and a series of science fiction stories set in the same world as recent
Sturgeon Award nominee "The Juniper Tree." Kessel's short fiction has
been collected in two volumes, *Meet Me in Infinity* and *The Pure Product,*
and he has published three novels: *Freedom Beach* (with James Patrick
Kelly), *Good News from Outer Space,* and *Corrupting Dr. Nice.*

Critic John Clute has said of Kessel's writing that he "seems to be one of
the writers capable of bending the tools of SF inward upon the human psyche"—something that happens in the possibly autobiographical tale that
follows.

* * *

IN APRIL OF 1934 H. G. Wells traveled to the United States, where he visited Washington, D.C., and met with President Franklin Delano Roosevelt. Wells, sixty-eight years old, hoped the New Deal might herald a revolutionary change in the U.S. economy, a step forward in an "Open Conspiracy" of rational thinkers that would culminate in a world socialist state. For forty years he'd subordinated every scrap of his artistic ambition to promoting this vision. But by 1934 Wells's optimism, along with his energy for saving the world, was waning.

While in Washington he asked to see something of the new social welfare agencies, and Harold Ickes, Roosevelt's Interior Secretary, arranged for Wells to visit a Civilian Conservation Corps camp at Fort Hunt, Virginia.

It happens that at that time my father was a CCC member at that camp. From his boyhood he had been a reader of adventure stories; he was a big fan of Edgar Rice Burroughs, and of H. G. Wells. This is the story of their encounter, which never took place.

IN BUFFALO IT'S COLD, but here the trees are in bloom, the mockingbirds sing in the mornings, and the sweat the men work up clearing brush, planting dogwoods and cutting roads is wafted away by warm breezes. Two hundred of them live in the Fort Hunt barracks high on the bluff above the Virginia side of the Potomac. They wear surplus army uniforms. In the morning, after a breakfast of grits, Sergeant Sauter musters them up in the parade yard, they climb onto trucks and are driven by forest service men out to wherever they're to work that day.

For several weeks Kessel's squad has been working along the river road, clearing rest stops and turnarounds. The tall pines have shallow root systems, and spring rain has softened the earth to the point where wind is forever knocking trees across the road. While most of the men work on the ground, a couple are sent up to cut off the tops of the pines adjoining the road, so if they do fall, they won't block it. Most of the men claim to be afraid of heights. Kessel isn't. A year or two ago back in Michigan he worked in a logging camp. It's hard work, but he is used to hard work. And at least he's out of Buffalo.

The truck rumbles and jounces out the river road, that's going to be the George Washington Memorial Parkway in our time, once the WPA project that will build it gets started. The humid air is cool now, but it will be hot again today, in the eighties. A couple of the guys get into a debate about whether the feds will ever catch Dillinger. Some others talk women. They're planning to go into Washington on the weekend and check out the dance halls. Kessel likes to dance; he's a good dancer. The fox trot, the lindy hop. When he gets drunk he likes to sing, and has a ready wit. He talks a lot more, kids the girls.

When they get to the site the foreman sets most of the men to work clearing the roadside for a scenic overlook. Kessel straps on a climbing belt, takes an ax and climbs his first tree. The first twenty feet are limbless, then climbing gets trickier. He looks down only enough to estimate when he's gotten high enough. He sets himself, cleats biting into the shoulder of a lower limb, and chops away at the road side of the trunk. There's a trick to cutting the top so that it falls the right way. When he's got it ready to go he calls down to warn the men below. Then a few quick bites of the axe on the opposite side of the cut, a shove, a crack and the top starts to go. He braces his legs, ducks his head and grips the trunk. The treetop skids off and the bole of the pine waves ponderously back and forth, with Kessel swinging at its end like an ant on a metronome. After the pine stops swinging he shinnies down and climbs the next tree.

He's good at this work, efficient, careful. He's not a particularly strong man—slender, not burly—but even in his youth he shows the attention to detail that, as a boy, I remember seeing when he built our house.

The squad works through the morning, then breaks for lunch from the mess truck. The men are always complaining about the food, and how there isn't enough of it, but until recently a lot of them were living in Hoovervilles—shack cities—and eating nothing at all. As they're eating a couple of the guys rag Kessel for working too fast. "What do you expect from a Yankee?" one of the southern boys says.

"He ain't a Yankee. He's a Polack."

Kessel tries to ignore them.

"Whyn't you lay off him, Turkel?" says Cole, one of Kessel's buddies.

Turkel is a big blond guy from Chicago. Some say he joined the CCCs to duck an armed robbery rap. "He works too hard," Turkel says. "He makes us look bad."

"Don't have to work much to make you look bad, Lou," Cole says. The others laugh, and Kessel appreciates it. "Give Jack some credit. At least he had enough sense to come down out of Buffalo." More laughter.

"There's nothing wrong with Buffalo," Kessel says.

"Except fifty thousand out-of-work Polacks," Turkel says.

"I guess you got no out-of-work people in Chicago," Kessel says. "You just joined for the exercise."

"Except he's not getting any exercise, if he can help it!" Cole says.

The foreman comes by and tells them to get back to work. Kessel climbs another tree, stung by Turkel's charge. What kind of man complains if someone else works hard? It only shows how even decent guys have to put up with assholes dragging them down. But it's nothing new. He's seen it before, back in Buffalo.

Buffalo, New York, is the symbolic home of this story. In the years preceding the First World War it grew into one of the great industrial metropolises of the United States. Located where Lake Erie flows into the Niagara River, strategically close to cheap electricity from Niagara Falls and cheap transportation by lakeboat from the Midwest, it was a center of steel, automobiles, chemicals, grain milling and brewing. Its major employers—Bethlehem Steel, Ford, Pierce Arrow, Gold Medal Flour, the National Biscuit Company, Ralston Purina, Quaker Oats, National Aniline—drew thousands of immigrants like Kessel's family. Along Delaware Avenue stood the imperious and stylized mansions of the city's old money, ersatz-Renaissance homes designed by Stanford White, huge Protestant churches, and a Byzantine synagogue. The city boasted the first modern skyscraper, designed by Louis Sullivan in the 1890s. From its productive factories to its polyglot work force to its class system and its boosterism, Buffalo was a monument to modern industrial capitalism. It is the place Kessel has come from—almost an expression of his personality itself—and the place he, at times, fears he can never escape. A cold, grimy city dominated by church and family, blinkered and cramped, forever playing second fiddle to Chicago, New York and Boston. It offers the immigrant the opportunity to find steady work in some factory or mill, but, though Kessel could not have put it into these words, it also puts a lid on his opportunities. It stands for all disappointed expectations, human limitations, tawdry compromises, for the inevitable choice of the expedient over the beautiful, for an American economic system that turns all things into commodities and measures men by their bank accounts. It is the home of the industrial proletariat.

It's not unique. It could be Youngstown, Akron, Detroit. It's the place my father, and I, grew up.

The afternoon turns hot and still; during a work break Kessel strips to the waist. About two o'clock a big black de Soto comes up the road and pulls off onto the shoulder. A couple of men in suits get out of the back, and one of them talks to the Forest Service foreman, who nods deferentially. The foreman calls over to the men.

"Boys, this here's Mr. Pike from the Interior Department. He's got a guest here to see how we work, a writer, Mr. H. G. Wells from England."

Most of the men couldn't care less, but the name strikes a spark in Kessel. He looks over at the little, pot-bellied man in the dark suit. The man is sweating; he brushes his mustache.

The foreman sends Kessel up to show them how they're topping the trees. He points out to the visitors where the others with rakes and shovels are leveling the ground for the overlook. Several other men are building a log rail fence from the treetops. From way above, Kessel can hear their voices between the thunks of his axe. H. G. Wells. He remembers reading "The War of the Worlds" in *Amazing Stories*. He's read *The Outline of History*, too. The stories, the history, are so large, it seems impossible that the man who wrote them could be standing not thirty feet below him. He tries to concentrate on the axe, the tree.

Time for this one to go. He calls down. The men below look up. Wells takes off his hat and shields his eyes with his hand. He's balding, and looks even smaller from up here. Strange that such big ideas could come from such a small man. It's kind of disappointing. Wells leans over to Pike and says something. The treetop falls away. The pine sways like a bucking bronco, and Kessel holds on for dear life.

He comes down with the intention of saying something to Wells, telling him how much he admires him, but when he gets down the sight of the two men in suits and his awareness of his own sweaty chest make him timid. He heads down to the next tree. After another ten minutes the men get back in the car, drive away. Kessel curses himself for the opportunity lost.

THAT EVENING AT the New Willard hotel, Wells dines with his old friends Clarence Darrow and Charles Russell. Darrow and Russell are in Washington to testify before a congressional committee on a report they have just submitted to the administration concerning the monopolistic effects of the National Recovery Act. The right wing is trying to eviscerate Roosevelt's program for large scale industrial management, and the Darrow Report is playing right into their hands. Wells tries, with little success, to convince Darrow of the short-sightedness of his position.

"Roosevelt is willing to sacrifice the small man to the huge corporations," Darrow insists, his eyes bright.

"The small man? Your small man is a romantic fantasy," Wells says. "It's not the New Deal that's doing him in—it's the process of industrial progress. It's the twentieth century. You can't legislate yourself back into 1870."

"What about the individual?" Russell asks.

Wells snorts. "Walk out into the street. The individual is out on the street corner selling apples. The only thing that's going to save him is some co-ordinated effort, by intelligent, selfless men. Not your free market."

Darrow puffs on his cigar, exhales, smiles. "Don't get exasperated, H.G. We're not working for Standard Oil. But if I have to choose between the bureaucrat and the man pumping gas at the filling station, I'll take the pump jockey."

Wells sees he's got no chance against the American mythology of the common man. "Your pump jockey works for Standard Oil. And the last I checked, the free market hasn't expended much energy looking out for his interests."

"Have some more wine," Russell says.

Russell refills their glasses with the excellent bordeaux. It's been a first rate meal. Wells finds the debate stimulating even when he can't prevail; at one time that would have been enough, but as the years go on the need to prevail grows stronger in him. The times are out of joint, and when he looks around he sees desperation growing. A new world order is necessary—it's so clear that even a fool ought to see it—but if he can't even convince radicals like Darrow, what hope is there of gaining the acquiescence of the shareholders in the utility trusts?

The answer is that the changes will have to be made over their objections. As Roosevelt seems prepared to do. Wells's dinner with the president has heartened him in a way that this debate cannot negate.

Wells brings up an item he read in the *Washington Post*. A lecturer for the communist party—a young Negro—was barred from speaking at the University of Virginia. Wells's question is, was the man barred because he was a communist or because he was Negro?

"Either condition," Darrow says sardonically, "is fatal in Virginia."

"But students point out the University has allowed communists to speak on campus before, and has allowed Negroes to perform music there."

"They can perform, but they can't speak," Russell says. "This isn't unusual. Go down to the Paradise Ballroom, not a mile from here. There's a Negro orchestra playing there, but no Negroes are allowed inside to listen."

"You should go to hear them anyway," Darrow says. "It's Duke Ellington. Have you heard of him?"

"I don't get on with the titled nobility," Wells quips.

"Oh, this Ellington's a noble fellow, all right, but I don't think you'll find him in the peerage," Russell says.

"He plays jazz, doesn't he?"

"Not like any jazz you've heard," Darrow says. "It's something totally new. You should find a place for it in one of your utopias."

All three of them are for helping the colored peoples. Darrow has defended Negroes accused of capital crimes. Wells, on his first visit to America almost thirty years ago, met with Booker T. Washington and came away impressed, although he still considers the peaceable co-existence of the white and colored races problematical.

"What are you working on now, Wells?" Russell asks. "What new improbability are you preparing to assault us with? Racial equality? Sexual liberation?"

"I'm writing a screen treatment based on *The Shape of Things to Come,*" Wells says.

He tells them about his screenplay, sketching out for them the future he has in his mind. An apocalyptic war, a war of unsurpassed brutality that will begin, in his film, in 1939. In this war, the creations of science will be put to the services of destruction in ways that will make the horrors of the Great War pale in comparison. Whole populations will be exterminated. But then, out of the ruins will arise the new world. The orgy of violence will purge the human race of the last vestiges of tribal thinking. Then will come the organization of the directionless and weak by the intelligent and purposeful. The new man. Cleaner, stronger, more rational. Wells can see it. He talks on, supplely, surely, late into the night. His mind is fertile with invention, still. He can see that Darrow and Russell, despite their Yankee individualism, are caught up by his vision. The future may be threatened, but it is not entirely closed.

FRIDAY NIGHT, back in the barracks at Fort Hunt, Kessel lies on his bunk reading a second-hand *Wonder Stories*. He's halfway through the tale of a scientist who invents an evolution chamber that progresses him through fifty thousand years of evolution in an hour, turning him into a big-brained telepathic monster. The evolved scientist is totally without emotions and wants to control the world. But his body's atrophied. Will the hero, a young engineer, be able to stop him?

At a plank table in the aisle a bunch of men are playing poker for cigarettes. They're talking about women and dogs. Cole throws in his hand and comes over to sit on the next bunk. "Still reading that stuff, Jack?"

"Don't knock it until you've tried it."

"Are you coming into D.C. with us tomorrow? Sergeant Sauter says we can catch a ride in on one of the trucks."

Kessel thinks about it. Cole probably wants to borrow some money. Two days after he gets his monthly pay he's broke. He's always looking for a good time. Kessel spends his leave more quietly; he usually walks into Alexandria—about six miles—and sees a movie or just walks around town. Still, he would like to see more of Washington. "Okay."

Cole looks at the sketchbook poking out from beneath Kessel's pillow. "Any more hot pictures?"

Immediately Kessel regrets trusting Cole. Yet there's not much he can say—the book is full of pictures of movie stars he's drawn. "I'm learning to draw. And at least I don't waste my time like the rest of you guys."

Cole looks serious. "You know, you're not any better than the rest of us," he says, not angrily. "You're just another Polack. Don't get so high-and-mighty."

"Just because I want to improve myself doesn't mean I'm high-and-mighty."

"Hey, Cole, are you in or out?" Turkel yells from the table.

"Dream on, Jack," Cole says, and returns to the game.

Kessel tries to go back to the story, but he isn't interested anymore. He can figure out that the hero is going to defeat the hyper-evolved scientist in the end. He folds his arms behind his head and stares at the knots in the rafters.

It's true, Kessel does spend a lot of time dreaming. But he has things he wants to do, and he's not going to waste his life drinking and whoring like the rest of them.

Kessel's always been different. Quieter, smarter. He was always going to do something better than the rest of them; he's well spoken, he likes to read. Even though he didn't finish high school he reads everything: *Amazing, Astounding, Wonder Stories.* He believes in the future. He doesn't want to end up trapped in some factory his whole life.

Kessel's parents immigrated from Poland in 1913. Their name was Kisiel, but his got Germanized in Catholic school. For ten years the family moved from one to another middle-sized industrial town, as Joe Kisiel bounced from job to job. Springfield. Utica. Syracuse. Rochester. Kessel remembers them loading up a wagon in the middle of the night with all their belongings in order to jump the rent on the run-down house in Syracuse. He remembers pulling a cart down to the Utica Club brewery, a nickel in his hand, to buy his father a keg of beer. He remembers them finally settling in the First Ward of Buffalo. The First Ward, at the foot of the Erie Canal, was an Irish neighborhood as far back as anybody could remember, and the Kisiels were the only Poles there. That's where he developed his chameleon ability to fit in, despite the fact he wanted nothing more than to get out. But he had to protect his mother, sister and little brothers from their father's drunken rages. When Joe Kisiel died in 1924 it was a relief, despite the fact that his son ended up supporting the family.

For ten years Kessel has strained against the tug of that responsibility. He's sought the free and easy feeling of the road, of places different from where he grew up, romantic places where the sun shines and he can make something entirely American of himself.

Despite his ambitions, he's never accomplished much. He's been essentially a drifter, moving from job to job. Starting as a pinsetter in a bowling alley, he moved on to a flour mill. He would have stayed in the mill only he developed an allergy to the flour dust, so he became an electrician. He would have stayed an electrician except he had a fight with a boss and got blacklisted. He left Buffalo because of his father; he kept coming back because of his mother. When the Depression hit he tried to get a job in Detroit at the auto factories, but that was plain stupid in the face of the universal collapse, and he ended up working up in the peninsula as a farm hand, then as a logger. It was seasonal work, and when the season was over he was out of a job. In the winter of 1933, rather than freeze his ass off in northern Michigan, he joined the CCC. Now he sends twenty-five of his thirty dollars a month back to his mother and sister in Buffalo. And imagines the future.

When he thinks about it, there are two futures. The first one is the one from the magazines and books. Bright, slick, easy. We, looking back on it, can see it to be the fifteen-cent utopianism of Hugo Gernsback's *Science and Invention* that flourished in the midst of the Depression. A degradation of the marvelous inventions that made Wells his early reputation, minus the social theorizing that drove Wells's technological speculations. The common man's boosterism. There's money to be made telling people like Jack Kessel about the wonderful world of the future.

The second future is Kessel's own. That one's a lot harder to see. It contains work. A good job, doing something he likes, using his skills. Not working for another man, but making something that would be useful for others. Building something for the future. And a woman, a gentle woman, for his wife. Not some cheap dancehall queen.

So when Kessel saw H. G. Wells in person, that meant something to him. He's had his doubts. He's twenty-nine years old, not a kid anymore. If he's ever going to get anywhere, it's going to have to start happening soon. He has the feeling that something significant is going to happen to him. Wells is a man who sees the future. He moves in that bright world where things make sense. He represents something that Kessel wants.

But the last thing Kessel wants is to end up back in Buffalo.

He pulls the sketchbook, the sketchbook he was to show me twenty years later, from under his pillow. He turns past drawings of movie stars: Jean Harlow, Mae West, Carole Lombard—the beautiful, unreachable faces of his longing—and of natural scenes: rivers, forests, birds—to a blank page. The page is as empty as the future, waiting for him to write upon it. He lets his imagination soar. He envisions an eagle, gliding high above the mountains of the West that he has never seen, but that he knows he will visit some day. The eagle is America; it is his own dreams. He begins to draw.

KESSEL DID NOT KNOW that Wells's life has not worked out as well as he planned. At that moment Wells is pining after the Russian émigré Moura Budberg, once Maxim Gorky's secretary, with whom Wells has been carrying on an off-and-on affair since 1920. His wife of thirty years, Amy Catherine "Jane" Wells, died in 1927. Since that time Wells has been adrift, alternating spells of furious pamphleteering with listless periods of suicidal depression. Meanwhile, all London is gossiping about the recent attack published in *Time and Tide* by his vengeful ex-lover Odette Keun. Have his mistakes followed him across the Atlantic to undermine his purpose? Does Darrow think him a jumped-up cockney? A moment of doubt overwhelms him. In the end, the future depends as much on the open-mindedness of men like Darrow as it does on a reorganization of society. What good is a guild of samurai if no one arises to take the job?

Wells doesn't like the trend of these thoughts. If human nature lets him down, then his whole life has been a waste.

But he's seen the president. He's seen those workers on the road. Those men climbing the trees risk their lives without complaining, for minimal pay. It's easy to think of them as stupid or desperate or simply young, but it's also possible to give them credit for dedication to their work. They don't seem to be ridden by the desire to grub and clutch that capitalism demands; if you look at it properly that may be the explanation for their ending up wards of the state. And is Wells any better? If he hadn't got an education he would have ended up a miserable draper's assistant.

Wells is due to leave for New York Sunday. Saturday night finds him sitting in his room, trying to write, after a solitary dinner in the New Willard. Another bottle of wine, or his age, has stirred something in Wells, and despite his rationalizations he finds himself near despair. Moura has rejected him. He needs the soft, supportive embrace of a lover, but instead he has this stuffy hotel room in a heat wave.

He remembers writing *The Time Machine,* he and Jane living in rented rooms in Sevenoaks with her ailing mother, worried about money, about whether the landlady would put them out. In the drawer of the dresser was a writ from the court that refused to grant him a divorce from his wife Isabel. He remembers a warm night, late in August—much like this one—sitting up late after Jane and her mother went to bed, writing at the round table before the open window, under the light of a paraffin lamp. One part of his mind was caught up in the rush of creation, burning, following the Time Traveller back to the sphinx, pursued by the Morlocks, only to discover that his machine is gone and he is trapped without escape from his desperate circumstance. At the same moment he could hear the landlady, out in the garden, fully aware that he could hear her, complaining to the neighbor about his and Jane's scandalous habits. On the one side, the petty conventions of a crabbed world; on the other, in his mind—the future, their peril and hope. Moths fluttering through the window beat themselves against the lampshade and fell onto the manuscript; he brushed them away unconsciously and continued, furiously, in a white heat. The time traveler, battered and hungry, returning from the future with a warning, and a flower.

He opens the hotel windows all the way but the curtains aren't stirred by a breath of air. Below, in the street, he hears the sound of traffic, and music. He decides to send a telegram to Moura, but after several false starts he finds he has nothing to say. Why has she refused to marry him? Maybe he is finally too old, and the magnetism of sex or power or intellect that has drawn women to him for forty years has finally all been squandered. The prospect of spending the last years remaining to him alone fills him with dread.

He turns on the radio, gets successive band shows: Morton Downey, Fats Waller. Jazz. Paging through the newspaper, he comes across an advertisement for the Ellington orchestra Darrow mentioned: it's at the ballroom just down the block. But the thought of a smoky room doesn't appeal to him. He considers the cinema. He has never been much for the "movies." Though he thinks them an unrivaled opportunity to educate, that promise has never been properly seized—something he hopes to do in *Things to Come*. The newspaper reveals an uninspiring selection: *20 Million Sweethearts,* a musical at the Earle, *The Black Cat,* with Boris Karloff and Bela Lugosi at the Rialto, and *Tarzan and His Mate* at the Palace. To these Americans he is the equivalent of this hack, Edgar Rice Burroughs. The books I read as a child, that fired my father's imagination and my own, Wells considers his frivolous apprentice work. His serious work is discounted. His ideas mean nothing.

Wells decides to try the Tarzan movie. He dresses for the sultry weather—Washington in spring is like high summer in London—and goes down to the lobby. He checks his street guide and takes the streetcar to the Palace Theater, where he buys an orchestra seat, for twenty-five cents, to see *Tarzan and His Mate.*

It is a perfectly wretched movie, comprised wholly of romantic fantasy, melodrama, and sexual innuendo. The dramatic leads perform with wooden idiocy surpassed only by the idiocy of the screenplay. Wells is attracted by the undeniable charms of the young heroine, Maureen O'Sullivan, but the film is devoid of intellectual content. Thinking of the audience at which such a farrago must be aimed depresses him. This is art as fodder. Yet the theater is filled, and the people are held in rapt attention. This only depresses Wells more. If these citizens are the future of America, then the future of America is dim. An hour into the film the antics of a comic chimpanzee, a scene of transcendent stupidity which nevertheless sends the audience into gales of laughter, drives Wells from the theater. It is still midevening. He wanders down the avenue of theaters, restaurants and clubs. On the sidewalk are beggars, ignored by the passersby. In an alley behind a hotel Wells spots a woman and child picking through the ashcans beside the restaurant kitchen.

Unexpectedly, he comes upon the marquee announcing DUKE ELLINGTON AND HIS ORCHESTRA. From within the open doors of the ballroom wafts the sound of jazz. Impulsively, Wells buys a ticket and goes in.

KESSEL AND HIS CRONIES have spent the day walking around the mall, which the WPA is re-landscaping. They've seen the Lincoln Memorial, the Capitol, the Washington Monument, the Smithsonian, the White House. Kessel has his picture taken in front of a statue of a soldier—a photo I have sitting on my desk. I've studied it many times. He looks forthrightly into the camera, faintly smiling. His face is confident, unlined.

When night comes they hit the bars. Prohibition was lifted only last year and the novelty has not yet worn off. The younger men get plastered, but Kessel finds himself uninterested in getting drunk. A couple of them set their minds on women and head for the Gayety Burlesque; Cole, Kessel and Turkel end up in the Paradise Ballroom listening to Duke Ellington.

They have a couple of drinks, ask some girls to dance. Kessel dances with a short girl with a southern accent who refuses to look him in the eyes. After thanking her he returns to the others at the bar. He sips his beer. "Not so lucky, Jack?" Cole says.

"She doesn't like a tall man," Turkel says.

Kessel wonders why Turkel came along. Turkel is always complaining about "niggers," and his only comment on the Ellington band so far has been to complain about how a bunch of jigs can make a living playing jungle music while white men sleep in barracks and eat grits three times a day. Kessel's got nothing against the colored, and he likes the music, though it's not exactly the kind of jazz he's used to. It doesn't sound much like Dixieland. It's darker, bigger, more dangerous. Ellington, resplendent in tie and tails, looks like he's enjoying himself up there at his piano, knocking out minimal solos while the orchestra plays cool and low.

Turning from them to look across the tables, Kessel sees a little man sitting alone beside the dance floor, watching the young couples sway in the music. To his astonishment he recognizes Wells. He's been given another chance. Hesitating only a moment, Kessel abandons his friends, goes over to the table and introduces himself.

"Excuse me, Mr. Wells. You might not remember me, but I was one of the men you saw yesterday in Virginia working along the road. The CCC?"

Wells looks up at a gangling young man wearing a khaki uniform, his olive tie neatly knotted and tucked between the second and third buttons of his shirt. His hair is slicked down, parted in the middle. Wells doesn't remember anything of him. "Yes?"

"I—I been reading your stories and books a lot of years. I admire your work."

Something in the man's earnestness affects Wells. "Please sit down," he says.

Kessel takes a seat. "Thank you." He pronounces "th" as "t" so that "thank" comes out "tank." He sits tentatively, as if the chair is mortgaged, and seems at a loss for words.

"What's your name?"

"John Kessel. My friends call me Jack."

The orchestra finishes a song and the dancers stop in their places, applauding. Up on the bandstand, Ellington leans into the microphone. "Mood Indigo," he says, and instantly they swing into it: the clarinet moans in low register, in unison with the muted trumpet and trombone, paced by the steady rhythm guitar, the brushed drums. The song's melancholy suits Wells's mood.

"Are you from Virginia?"

"My family lives in Buffalo. That's in New York."

"Ah—yes. Many years ago I visited Niagara Falls, and took the train through Buffalo." Wells remembers riding along a lakefront of factories spewing waste water into the lake, past heaps of coal, clouds of orange and black smoke from blast furnaces. In front of dingy rowhouses, ragged hedges struggled through the smoky air. The landscape of laissez faire. "I imagine the Depression has hit Buffalo severely."

"Yes sir."

"What work did you do there?"

Kessel feels nervous, but he opens up a little. "A lot of things. I used to be an electrician until I got blacklisted."

"Blacklisted?"

"I was working on this job where the super told me to set the wiring wrong. I argued with him but he just told me to do it his way. So I waited until he went away, then I sneaked into the construction shack and checked the blueprints. He didn't think I could read blueprints, but I could. I found out I was right and he was wrong. So I went back and did it right. The next day when he found out, he fired me. Then the so-and-so went and got me blacklisted."

Though he doesn't know how much credence to put in this story, Wells's sympathies are aroused. It's the kind of thing that must happen all the time. He recognizes in Kessel the immigrant stock that, when Wells visited the U.S. in 1906, made him skeptical about the future of America. He'd theorized that these Italians and Slavs, coming from lands with no democratic tradition, unable to speak English, would degrade the already corrupt political process. They could not be made into good citizens; they would not work well when they could work poorly, and given the way the economic deal was stacked against them would seldom rise high enough to do better.

But Kessel is clean, well-spoken despite his accent, and deferential. Wells realizes that this is one of the men who was topping trees along the river road.

Meanwhile, Kessel detects a sadness in Wells's manner. He had not imagined that Wells might be sad, and he feels sympathy for him. It occurs to him, to his own surprise, that he might be able to make *Wells* feel better. "So—what do you think of our country?" he asks.

"Good things seem to be happening here. I'm impressed with your President Roosevelt."

"Roosevelt's the best friend the working man ever had." Kessel pronounces the name "Roozvelt." "He's a man that—" he struggles for the words, "—that's not for the past. He's for the future."

It begins to dawn on Wells that Kessel is not an example of a class, or a sociological study, but a man like himself with an intellect, opinions, dreams. He thinks of his own youth, struggling to rise in a class-bound society. He leans forward across the table. "You believe in the future? You think things can be different?"

"I think they have to be, Mr. Wells."

Wells sits back. "Good. So do I."

Kessel is stunned by this intimacy. It is more than he had hoped for, yet it leaves him with little to say. He wants to tell Wells about his dreams, and at the same time ask him a thousand questions. He wants to tell Wells everything he has seen in the world, and to hear Wells tell him the same. He casts about for something to say.

"I always liked your writing. I like to read scientifiction."

"Scientifiction?"

Kessel shifts his long legs. "You know—stories about the future. Monsters from outer space. The Martians. The Time Machine. You're the best scientifiction writer I ever read, next to Edgar Rice Burroughs." Kessel pronounces "Edgar," "Eedgar."

"Edgar Rice Burroughs?"

"Yes."

"You *like* Burroughs?"

Kessel hears the disapproval in Wells's voice. "Well—maybe not as much as, as *The Time Machine*," he stutters. "Burroughs never wrote about monsters as good as your Morlocks."

Wells is nonplussed. "Monsters."

"Yes." Kessel feels something's going wrong, but he sees no way out. "But he does put more romance in his stories. That princess—Dejah Thoris?"

All Wells can think of is Tarzan in his loincloth on the movie screen, and the moronic audience. After a lifetime of struggling, a hundred books written to change the world, in the service of men like this, is this all his work has come to? To be compared to the writer of pulp trash? To "Edgar Rice Burroughs"? He laughs aloud.

At Wells's laugh, Kessel stops. He knows he's done something wrong, but he doesn't know what.

Wells's weariness has dropped down onto his shoulders again like an iron cloak. "Young man—go away," he says. "You don't know what you're saying. Go back to Buffalo."

Kessel's face burns. He stumbles from the table. The room is full of noise and laughter. He's run up against that wall again. He's just an ignorant Polack after all; it's his stupid accent, his clothes. He should have talked about something else—*The Outline of History,* politics. But what made him think he could talk like an equal with a man like Wells in the first place? Wells lives in a different world. The future is for men like him. Kessel feels himself the prey of fantasies. It's a bitter joke.

He clutches the bar, orders another beer. His reflection in the mirror behind the ranked bottles is small and ugly.

"Whatsa matter, Jack?" Turkel asks him. "Didn't he want to dance neither?"

AND THAT'S THE STORY, essentially, that never happened.

Not long after this, Kessel did go back to Buffalo. During the Second World War he worked as a crane operator in the 40-inch rolling mill of Bethlehem Steel. He met his wife, Angela Giorlandino, during the war, and they married in June 1945. After the war he quit the plant and became a carpenter. Their first child, a girl, died in infancy. Their second, a boy, was born in 1950. At that time Kessel began building the house that, like so many things in his life, he was never to entirely complete. He worked hard, had two more children. There were good years and bad ones. He held a lot of jobs. The recession of 1958 just about flattened him; our family had to go on welfare. Things got better, but they never got good. After the 1950s, the economy of Buffalo, like that of all U.S. industrial cities caught in the transition to a post-industrial age, declined steadily. Kessel never did work for himself, and as an old man was no more prosperous than he had been as a young one.

In the years preceding his death in 1946 Wells was to go on to further disillusionment. His efforts to create a sane world met with increasing frustration. He became bitter, enraged. Moura Budberg never agreed to marry him, and he lived alone. The war came, and it was, in some ways, even worse than he had predicted. He continued to propagandize for the socialist world state throughout, but with increasing irrelevance. The new leftists like Orwell considered him a dinosaur, fatally out of touch with the realities of world politics, a simpleminded technocrat with no understanding of the darkness of the human heart. Wells's last book, *Mind at the End of Its Tether,* proposed that the human race faced an evolutionary crisis that would lead to its extinction unless humanity leapt to a higher state of consciousness; a leap about which Wells speculated with little hope or conviction.

Sitting there in the Washington ballroom in 1934, Wells might well have understood that for all his thinking and preaching about the future, the future had irrevocably passed him by.

BUT THE STORY isn't quite over yet. Back in the Washington ballroom Wells sits humiliated, a little guilty for sending Kessel away so harshly. Kessel, his back to the dance floor, stares humiliated into his glass of beer. Gradually, both of them are pulled back from dark thoughts of their own inadequacies by the sound of Ellington's orchestra.

Ellington stands in front of the big grand piano, behind him the band: three saxes, clarinet, two trumpets, trombones, a drummer, guitarist, bass. "Creole Love Call," Ellington whispers into the microphone, then sits again at the piano. He waves his hand once, twice, and the clarinets slide into a low, wavering theme. The trumpet, muted, echoes it. The bass player and guitarist strum ahead at a deliberate pace, rhythmic, erotic, bluesy. Kessel and Wells, separate across the room, each unaware of the other, are alike drawn in. The trumpet growls a chorus of raucous solo. The clarinet follows, wailing. The music is full of pain and longing—but pain controlled, ordered, mastered. Longing unfulfilled, but not overpowering.

As I write this, it plays on my stereo. If anyone has a right to bitterness at thwarted dreams, a black man in 1934 had that right. That such men could, in such conditions, make this music opens a world of possibilities.

Through the music speaks a truth about art that Wells does not understand, but that I hope to: that art doesn't have to deliver a message in order to say something important. That art isn't always a means to an end but sometimes an end in itself. That art may not be able to change the world, but it can still change the moment.

Through the music speaks a truth about life that Kessel, sixteen years before my birth, doesn't understand, but that I hope to: that life constrained is not life wasted. That despite unfulfilled dreams, peace is possible.

Listening, Wells feels that peace steal over his soul. Kessel feels it too.

And so they wait, poised, calm, before they move on into their respective futures, into our own present. Into the world of limitation and loss. Into Buffalo.

EVEN THE QUEEN

CONNIE WILLIS

CONNIE WILLIS was born in 1945 and lives in Greeley, Colorado. Her first story, "The Secret of Santa Titicaca," was published in 1971, but she only began publishing regularly in the early '80s when she began to write full-time. Willis is best known for her short fiction, which has been gathered in three volumes, *Fire Watch, Impossible Things,* and *Miracle and Other Christmas Stories.* Her early stories include time travel story "Fire Watch," "All My Darling Daughters," "A Letter from the Clearys," "The Sidon in the Mirror," "Blued Moon," and "The Last of the Winnebagos."

Willis's first novel was the SF novel *Water Witch* (with Cynthia Felice)— one of several works that reflect the influence of Robert Heinlein on her work—and was followed by the substantial solo debut *Lincoln's Dreams* which won the John W. Campbell Memorial Award. Her second novel *Doomsday Book,* more typical of Willis's fiction and sharing the same mid-twenty-first century time-travel framing device as "Fire Watch," won the Hugo and Nebula Awards. It was followed by the short novels *Uncharted Territory, Remake,* and *Bellwether,* and major novel *Passage.* Willis has become one of the most celebrated writers in modern science fiction, and to date her fiction has won the Hugo Award eight times, the Nebula Award six times, the John W. Campbell Memorial Award, and the Locus Award nine times.

Feminism is not noted for its sense of humor, and attempting to bring a touch of comedy to "women's issues" is a hazardous path to take. And yet, that's just what Willis does in the very funny story that follows.

* * *

THE PHONE SANG as I was looking over the defense's motion to dismiss. "It's the universal ring," my law clerk Bysshe said, reaching for it. "It's probably the defendant. They don't let you use signatures from jail."

"No, it's not," I said. "It's my mother."

"Oh." Bysshe reached for the receiver. "Why isn't she using her signature?"

"Because she knows I don't want to talk to her. She must have found out what Perdita's done."

"Your daughter Perdita?" he asked, holding the receiver against his chest. "The one with the little girl?"

"No, that's Viola. Perdita's my younger daughter. The one with no sense."

"What's she done?"

"She's joined the Cyclists."

Bysshe looked enquiringly blank, but I was not in the mood to enlighten him. Or in the mood to talk to Mother. "I know exactly what Mother will say," I said. "She'll ask me why I didn't tell her, and then she'll demand to know what I'm going to do about it, and there is nothing I *can* do about it, or I obviously would have done it already."

Bysshe looked bewildered. "Do you want me to tell her you're in court?"

"No." I reached for the receiver. "I'll have to talk to her sooner or later." I took it from him. "Hello, Mother," I said.

"Traci," Mother said dramatically, "Perdita has become a Cyclist."

"I know."

"Why didn't you tell me?"

"I thought Perdita should tell you herself."

"Perdita!" She snorted. "She wouldn't tell me. She knows what I'd have to say about it. I suppose you told Karen."

"Karen's not here. She's in Iraq." The only good thing about this whole debacle was that thanks to Iraq's eagerness to show it was a responsible world community member and its previous penchant for self-destruction, my mother-in-law was in the one place on the planet where the phone service was bad enough that I could claim I'd tried to call her but couldn't get through, and she'd have to believe me.

The Liberation has freed us from all sorts of indignities and scourges, including Iraq's Saddams, but mothers-in-law aren't one of them, and I was almost happy with Perdita for her excellent timing. When I didn't want to kill her.

"What's Karen doing in Iraq?" Mother asked.

"Negotiating a Palestinian homeland."

"And meanwhile her granddaughter is ruining her life," she said irrelevantly. "Did you tell Viola?"

"I *told* you, Mother. I thought Perdita should tell all of you herself."

"Well, she didn't. And this morning one of my patients, Carol Chen, called me and demanded to know what I was keeping from her. I had no idea what she was talking about."

"How did Carol Chen find out?"

"From her daughter, who almost joined the Cyclists last year. *Her* family talked her out of it," she said accusingly. "Carol was convinced the medical community had discovered some terrible side-effect of ammenerol and were covering it up. I cannot believe you didn't tell me, Traci."

And I cannot believe I didn't have Bysshe tell her I was in court, I thought. "I told you, Mother. I thought it was Perdita's place to tell you. After all, it's her decision."

"Oh, Traci!" Mother said. "You cannot mean that!"

In the first fine flush of freedom after the Liberation, I had entertained hopes that it would change everything—that it would somehow do away with inequality and matriarchal dominance and those humorless women determined to eliminate the word "manhole" and third-person singular pronouns from the language.

Of course it didn't. Men still make more money, "herstory" is still a blight on the semantic landscape, and my mother can still say, "Oh, *Tra*ci!" in a tone that reduces me to pre-adolescence.

"Her decision!" Mother said. "Do you mean to tell me you plan to stand idly by and allow your daughter to make the mistake of her life?"

"What can I do? She's twenty-two years old and of sound mind."

"If she were of sound mind she wouldn't be doing this. Didn't you try to talk her out of it?"

"Of course I did, Mother."

"And?"

"And I didn't succeed. She's determined to become a Cyclist."

"Well, there must be something we can do. Get an injunction or hire a deprogrammer or sue the Cyclists for brainwashing. You're a judge, there must be some law you can invoke—"

"The law is called personal sovereignty, Mother, and since it was what made the Liberation possible in the first place, it can hardly be used against Perdita. Her decision meets all the criteria for a case of personal sovereignty: it's a personal decision, it was made by a sovereign adult, it affects no one else—"

"What about my practice? Carol Chen is convinced shunts cause cancer."

"Any effect on your practice is considered an indirect effect. Like secondary smoke. It doesn't apply. Mother, whether we like it or not, Perdita has a perfect right to do this, and we don't have any right to interfere. A free society has to be based on respecting others' opinions and leaving each other alone. We have to respect Perdita's right to make her own decisions."

All of which was true. It was too bad I hadn't said any of it to Perdita when she called. What I had said, in a tone that sounded exactly like my mother's, was "Oh, Per*di*ta!"

"This is all your fault, you know," Mother said. "I *told* you you shouldn't have let her get that tattoo over her shunt. And don't tell me it's a free society. What good is a free society when it allows my granddaughter to ruin her life?" She hung up.

I handed the receiver back to Bysshe.

"I really liked what you said about respecting your daughter's right to make her own decisions," he said. He held out my robe. "And about not interfering in her life."

"I want you to research the precedents on deprogramming for me," I said, sliding my arms into the sleeves. "And find out if the Cyclists have been charged with any free-choice violations—brainwashing, intimidation, coercion."

The phone rang, another universal. "Hello, who's calling?" Bysshe said cautiously. His voice became suddenly friendlier. "Just a minute." He put his hand over the receiver. "It's your daughter Viola."

I took the receiver. "Hello, Viola."

"I just talked to Grandma," she said. "You will not believe what Perdita's done now. She's joined the Cyclists."

"I know," I said.

"You *know*? And you didn't tell me? I can't believe this. You never tell me anything."

"I thought Perdita should tell you herself," I said tiredly.

"Are you kidding? She never tells me anything either. That time she had eyebrow implants she didn't tell me for three weeks, and when she got the laser tattoo she didn't tell me at all. *Twidge* told me. You should have called me. Did you tell Grandma Karen?"

"She's in Baghdad," I said.

"I know," Viola said. "I called her."

"Oh, Viola, you didn't!"

"Unlike you, Mom, I believe in telling members of our family about matters that concern them."

"What did she say?" I asked, a kind of numbness settling over me now that the shock had worn off.

"I couldn't get through to her. The phone service over there is terrible. I got somebody who didn't speak English, and then I got cut off, and when I tried again they said the whole city was down."

Thank you, I breathed silently. Thank you, thank you, thank you.

"Grandma Karen has a right to know, Mother. Think of the effect this could have on Twidge. She thinks Perdita's wonderful. When Perdita got the eyebrow implants, Twidge glued LED's to hers, and I almost never got them off. What if Twidge decides to join the Cyclists, too?"

"Twidge is only nine. By the time she's supposed to get her shunt, Perdita will have long since quit." I hope, I added silently. Perdita had had the tattoo for a year and a half now and showed no signs of tiring of it. "Besides, Twidge has more sense."

"It's true. Oh, Mother, how *could* Perdita do this? Didn't you tell her about how awful it was?"

"Yes," I said. "And inconvenient. And unpleasant and unbalancing and painful. None of it made the slightest impact on her. She told me she thought it would be fun."

Bysshe was pointing to his watch and mouthing, "Time for court."

"Fun!" Viola said. "When she saw what I went through that time? Honestly, Mother, sometimes I think she's completely brain-dead. Can't you have her declared incompetent and locked up or something?"

"No," I said, trying to zip up my robe with one hand. "Viola, I have to go. I'm late for court. I'm afraid there's nothing we can do to stop her. She's a rational adult."

"Rational!" Viola said. "Her eyebrows light up, Mother. She has Custer's Last Stand lased on her arm."

I handed the phone to Bysshe. "Tell Viola I'll talk to her tomorrow." I zipped up my robe. "And then call Baghdad and see how long they expect the phones to be out." I started into the courtroom. "And if there are any more universal calls, make sure they're local before you answer."

BYSSHE COULDN'T GET through to Baghdad, which I took as a good sign, and my mother-in-law didn't call. Mother did, in the afternoon, to ask if lobotomies were legal.

She called again the next day. I was in the middle of my Personal Sovereignty class, explaining the inherent right of citizens in a free society to make complete jackasses of themselves. They weren't buying it.

"I think it's your mother," Bysshe whispered to me as he handed me the phone. "She's still using the universal. But it's local. I checked."

"Hello, Mother," I said.

"It's all arranged," Mother said. "We're having lunch with Perdita at McGregor's. It's on the corner of Twelfth Street and Larimer."

"I'm in the middle of class," I said.

"I know. I won't keep you. I just wanted to tell you not to worry. I've taken care of everything."

I didn't like the sound of that. "What have you done?"

"Invited Perdita to lunch with us. I told you. At McGregor's."

"Who is 'us,' Mother?"

"Just the family," she said innocently. "You and Viola."

Well, at least she hadn't brought in the deprogrammer. Yet. "What are you up to, Mother?"

"Perdita said the same thing. Can't a grandmother ask her granddaughters to lunch? Be there at twelve-thirty."

"Bysshe and I have a court calendar meeting at three."

"Oh, we'll be done by then. And bring Bysshe with you. He can provide a man's point of view."

She hung up.

"You'll have to go to lunch with me, Bysshe," I said. "Sorry."

"Why? What's going to happen at lunch?"

"I have no idea."

ON THE WAY over to McGregor's, Bysshe told me what he'd found out about the Cyclists. "They're not a cult. There's no religious connection. They seem to have grown out of a pre-Liberation women's group," he said, looking at his notes, "although there are also links to the pro-choice movement, the University of Wisconsin, and the Museum of Modern Art."

"What?"

"They call their group leaders 'docents.' Their philosophy seems to be a mix of pre-Liberation radical feminism and the environmental primitivism of the eighties. They're floratarians and they don't wear shoes."

"Or shunts," I said. We pulled up in front of McGregor's and got out of the car. "Any mind control convictions?" I asked hopefully.

"No. A bunch of suits against individual members, all of which they won."

"On grounds of personal sovereignty."

"Yeah. And a criminal one by a member whose family tried to deprogram her. The deprogrammer was sentenced to twenty years, and the family got twelve."

"Be sure to tell Mother about that one," I said, and opened the door to McGregor's.

It was one of those restaurants with a morning glory vine twining around the *maître d*'s desk and garden plots between the tables.

"Perdita suggested it," Mother said, guiding Bysshe and me past the onions to our table. "She told me a lot of the Cyclists are floratarians."

"Is she here?" I asked, sidestepping a cucumber frame.

"Not yet." She pointed past a rose arbor. "There's our table."

Our table was a wicker affair under a mulberry tree. Viola and Twidge were seated on the far side next to a trellis of runner beans, looking at menus.

"What are you doing here, Twidge?" I asked. "Why aren't you in school?"

"I am," she said, holding up her LCD slate. "I'm remoting today."

"I thought she should be part of this discussion," Viola said. "After all, she'll be getting her shunt soon."

"My friend Kensy says she isn't going to get one, like Perdita," Twidge said.

"I'm sure Kensy will change her mind when the time comes," Mother said. "Perdita will change hers, too. Bysshe, why don't you sit next to Viola?"

Bysshe slid obediently past the trellis and sat down in the wicker chair at the far end of the table. Twidge reached across Viola and handed him a menu. "This is a great restaurant," she said. "You don't have to wear shoes." She held up a bare foot to illustrate. "And if you get hungry while you're waiting, you can just pick something." She twisted around in her chair, picked two of the green beans, gave one to Bysshe, and bit into the other one. "I bet she doesn't. Kensy says a shunt hurts worse than braces."

"It doesn't hurt as much as not having one," Viola said, shooting me a Now-Do-You-See-What-My-Sister's-Caused? look.

"Traci, why don't you sit across from Viola?" Mother said to me. "And we'll put Perdita next to you when she comes."

"If she comes," Viola said.

"I told her one o'clock," Mother said, sitting down at the near end. "So we'd have a chance to plan our strategy before she gets here. I talked to Carol Chen—"

"Her daughter nearly joined the Cyclists last year," I explained to Bysshe and Viola.

"*She* said they had a family gathering, like this, and simply talked to her daughter, and she decided she didn't want to be a Cyclist after all." She looked around the table. "So I thought we'd do the same thing with Perdita. I think we should start by explaining the significance of the Liberation and the days of dark oppression that preceded it—"

"*I* think," Viola interrupted, "we should try to talk her into just going off the ammenerol for a few months instead of having the shunt removed. If she comes. Which she won't."

"Why not?"

"Would you? I mean, it's like the Inquisition. Her sitting here while all of us 'explain' at her. Perdita may be crazy, but she's not stupid."

"It's hardly the Inquisition," Mother said. She looked anxiously past me toward the door. "I'm sure Perdita—" She stopped, stood up, and plunged off suddenly through the asparagus.

I turned around, half-expecting Perdita with light-up lips or a full-body tattoo, but I couldn't see through the leaves. I pushed at the branches.

"Is it Perdita?" Viola said, leaning forward.

I peered around the mulberry bush. "Oh, my God," I said.

It was my mother-in-law, wearing a black abayah and a silk yarmulke. She swept toward us through a pumpkin patch, robes billowing and eyes flashing. Mother hurried in her wake of trampled radishes, looking daggers at me.

I turned them on Viola. "It's your grandmother Karen," I said accusingly. "You told me you didn't get through to her."

"I didn't," she said. "Twidge, sit up straight. And put your slate down."

There was an ominous rustling in the rose arbor, as of leaves shrinking back in terror, and my mother-in-law arrived.

"Karen!" I said, trying to sound pleased. "What on earth are you doing here? I thought you were in Baghdad."

"I came back as soon as I got Viola's message," she said, glaring at everyone in turn. "Who's this?" she demanded, pointing at Bysshe. "Viola's new livein?"

"No!" Bysshe said, looking horrified.

"This is my law clerk, Mother," I said. "Bysshe Adams-Hardy."

"Twidge, why aren't you in school?"

"I *am,*" Twidge said. "I'm remoting." She held up her slate. "See? Math."

"I see," she said, turning to glower at me. "It's a serious enough matter to require my great-grandchild's being pulled out of school *and* the hiring of legal assistance, and yet you didn't deem it important enough to notify *me.* Of course, you *never* tell me anything, Traci."

She swirled herself into the end chair, sending leaves and sweet pea blossoms flying, and decapitating the broccoli centerpiece. "I didn't get Viola's cry for help until yesterday. Viola, you should never leave messages with Hassim. His English is virtually nonexistent. I had to get him to hum me your ring. I recognized your signature, but the phones were out, so I flew home. In the middle of negotiations, I might add."

"How *are* negotiations going, Grandma Karen?" Viola asked.

"They *were* going extremely well. The Israelis have given the Palestinians half of Jerusalem, and they've agreed to time-share the Golan Heights." She turned to glare momentarily at me. "*They* know the importance of communication." She turned back to Viola. "So why are they picking on you, Viola? Don't they like your new livein?"

"I am *not* her livein," Bysshe protested.

I have often wondered how on earth my mother-in-law became a mediator and what she does in all those negotiation sessions with Serbs and Catholics and North and South Koreans and Protestants and Croats. She takes sides, jumps to conclusions, misinterprets everything you say, refuses to listen. And yet she talked South Africa into a Mandelan government and would probably get the Palestinians to observe Yom Kippur. Maybe she just bullies everyone into submission. Or maybe they have to band together to protect themselves against her.

Bysshe was still protesting. "I never even met Viola till today. I've only talked to her on the phone a couple of times."

"You must have done something," Karen said to Viola. "They're obviously out for your blood."

"Not mine," Viola said. "Perdita's. She's joined the Cyclists."

"The Cyclists? I left the West Bank negotiations because you don't approve of Perdita joining a biking club? How am I supposed to explain this to the president of Iraq? She will *not* understand, and neither do I. A biking club!"

"The Cyclists do not ride bicycles," Mother said.

"They menstruate," Twidge said.

There was a dead silence of at least a minute, and I thought, it's finally happened. My mother-in-law and I are actually going to be on the same side of a family argument.

"All this fuss is over Perdita's having her shunt removed?" Karen said finally. "She's of age, isn't she? And this is obviously a case where personal sovereignty applies. You should know that, Traci. After all, you're a judge."

I should have known it was too good to be true.

"You mean you approve of her setting back the Liberation twenty years?" Mother said.

"I hardly think it's that serious," Karen said. "There are anti-shunt groups in the Middle East, too, you know, but no one takes them seriously. Not even the Iraqis, and they still wear the veil."

"Perdita is taking them seriously."

Karen dismissed Perdita with a wave of her black sleeve. "They're a trend, a fad. Like microskirts. Or those dreadful electronic eyebrows. A few women wear silly fashions like that for a little while, but you don't see women as a whole giving up pants or going back to wearing hats."

"But Perdita. . . ." Viola said.

"If Perdita wants to have her period, I say let her. Women functioned perfectly well without shunts for thousands of years."

Mother brought her fist down on the table. "Women also functioned *perfectly well* with concubinage, cholera, and corsets," she said, emphasizing each word with her fist. "But that is no reason to take them on voluntarily, and I have no intention of allowing Perdita—"

"Speaking of Perdita, where is the poor child?" Karen said.

"She'll be here any minute," Mother said. "I invited her to lunch so we could discuss this with her."

"Ha!" Karen said. "So you could browbeat her into changing her mind, you mean. Well, I have no intention of collaborating with you. *I* intend to listen to the poor thing's point of view with interest and an open mind. Respect, that's the key word, and one you all seem to have forgotten. Respect and common courtesy."

A barefoot young woman wearing a flowered smock and a red scarf tied around her left arm came up to the table with a sheaf of pink folders.

"It's about time," Karen said, snatching one of the folders away from her. "Your service here is dreadful. I've been sitting here ten minutes." She snapped the folder open. "I don't suppose you have Scotch."

"My name is Evangeline," the young woman said. "I'm Perdita's docent." She took the folder away from Karen. "She wasn't able to join you for lunch, but she asked me to come in her place and explain the Cyclist philosophy to you."

She sat down in the wicker chair next to me.

"The Cyclists are dedicated to freedom," she said. "Freedom from artificiality, freedom from body-controlling drugs and hormones, freedom from the male patriarchy that attempts to impose them on us. As you probably already know, we do not wear shunts."

She pointed to the red scarf around her arm. "Instead, we wear this as a badge of our freedom and our femaleness. I'm wearing it today to announce that my time of fertility has come."

"We had that, too," Mother said, "only we wore it on the back of our skirts."

I laughed.

The docent glared at me. "Male domination of women's bodies began long before the so-called 'Liberation,' with government regulation of abortion and fetal rights, scientific control of fertility, and finally the development of ammenerol, which eliminated the reproductive cycle altogether. This was all part of a carefully planned takeover of women's bodies, and by extension, their identities, by the male patriarchal regime."

"What an interesting point of view!" Karen said enthusiastically.

It certainly was. In point of fact, ammenerol hadn't been invented to eliminate menstruation at all. It had been developed for shrinking malignant tumors, and its uterine lining-absorbing properties had only been discovered by accident.

"Are you trying to tell us," Mother said, "that men *forced* shunts on women?! We had to *fight* everyone to get it approved by the FDA!"

It was true. What surrogate mothers and anti-abortionists and the fetal rights issue had failed to do in uniting women, the prospect of not having to menstruate did. Women had organized rallies, petitioned, elected senators, passed amendments, been excommunicated, and gone to jail, all in the name of Liberation.

"Men were *against* it," Mother said, getting rather red in the face. "And the religious right and the maxipad manufacturers, and the Catholic church—"

"They knew they'd have to allow women priests," Viola said.

"Which they did," I said.

"The Liberation hasn't freed you," the docent said loudly. "Except from the natural rhythms of your life, the very wellspring of your femaleness."

She leaned over and picked a daisy that was growing under the table. "We in the Cyclists celebrate the onset of our menses and rejoice in our bodies," she said, holding the daisy up. "Whenever a Cyclist comes into blossom, as we call it, she is honored with flowers and poems and songs. Then we join hands and tell what we like best about our menses."

"Water retention," I said.

"Or lying in bed with a heating pad for three days a month," Mother said.

"I think I like the anxiety attacks best," Viola said. "When I went off the ammenerol, so I could have Twidge, I'd have these days where I was convinced the space station was going to fall on me."

A middle-aged woman in overalls and a straw hat had come over while Viola was talking and was standing next to Mother's chair. "I had these mood swings," she said. "One minute I'd feel cheerful and the next like Lizzie Borden."

"Who's Lizzie Borden?" Twidge asked.

"She killed her parents," Bysshe said. "With an ax."

Karen and the docent glared at both of them. "Aren't you supposed to be working on your math, Twidge?" Karen said.

"I've always wondered if Lizzie Borden had PMS," Viola said, "and that was why—"

"No," Mother said. "It was having to live before tampons and ibuprofen. An obvious case of justifiable homicide."

"I hardly think this sort of levity is helpful," Karen said, glowering at everyone.

"Are you our waitress?" I asked the straw-hatted woman hastily.

"Yes," she said, producing a slate from her overalls pocket.

"Do you serve wine?" I asked.

"Yes. Dandelion, cowslip, and primrose."

"We'll take them all," I said.

"A bottle of each?"

"For now. Unless you have them in kegs."

"Our specials today are watermelon salad and *choufleur gratinée*," she said, smiling at everyone. Karen and the docent did not smile back. "You hand-pick your own cauliflower from the patch up front. The floratarian special is sautéed lily buds with marigold butter."

There was a temporary truce while everyone ordered. "I'll have the sweet peas," the docent said, "and a glass of rose water."

Bysshe leaned over to Viola. "I'm sorry I sounded so horrified when your grandmother asked if I was your livein," he said.

"That's okay," Viola said. "Grandma Karen can be pretty scary."

"I just didn't want you to think I didn't like you. I do. Like you, I mean."

"Don't they have soyburgers?" Twidge asked.

As soon as the waitress left, the docent began passing out the pink folders she'd brought with her. "These will explain the working philosophy of the Cyclists," she said, handing me one, "along with practical information on the menstrual cycle." She handed Twidge one.

"It looks just like those books we used to get in junior high," Mother said, looking at hers. " 'A Special Gift,' they were called, and they had all these pictures of girls with pink ribbons in their hair, playing tennis and smiling. Blatant misrepresentation."

She was right. There was even the same drawing of the fallopian tubes remembered from my middle school movie, a drawing that had always reminded me of *Alien* in the early stages.

"Oh, yuck," Twidge said. "This is disgusting."

"Do your math," Karen said.

Bysshe looked sick. "Did women really *do* this stuff?"

The wine arrived, and I poured everyone a large glass. The docent pursed her lips disapprovingly and shook her head. "The Cyclists do not use the artificial stimulants or hormones that the male patriarchy has forced on women to render them docile and subservient."

"How long do you menstruate?" Twidge asked.

"Forever," Mother said.

"Four to six days," the docent said. "It's there in the booklet."

"No, I mean, your whole life or what?"

"A woman has her menarche at twelve years old on the average and ceases menstruating at age fifty-five."

"I had my first period at eleven," the waitress said, setting a bouquet down in front of me. "At school."

"I had my last one on the day the FDA approved *ammenerol,*" Mother said.

"Three hundred and sixty-five divided by twenty-eight," Twidge said writing on her slate. "Times forty-three years." She looked up. "That's five hundred and fifty-nine periods."

"That can't be right," Mother said, taking the slate away from her. "It's at least five thousand."

"And they all start on the day you leave on a trip," Viola said.

"Or get married," the waitress said.

Mother began writing on the slate.

I took advantage of the ceasefire to pour everyone some more dandelion wine.

Mother looked up from the slate. "Do you realize with a period of five days, you'd be menstruating for nearly three thousand days? That's over eight solid years."

"And in between there's PMS," the waitress said, delivering flowers.

"What's PMS?" Twidge asked.

"Pre-menstrual syndrome was the name the male medical establishment fabricated for the natural variation in hormonal levels that signal the onset of menstruation," the docent said. "This mild and entirely normal fluctuation was exaggerated by men into a debility." She looked at Karen for confirmation.

"I used to cut my hair," Karen said.

The docent looked uneasy.

"Once I chopped off one whole side," Karen went on. "Bob had to hide the scissors every month. And the car keys. I'd start to cry every time I hit a red light."

"Did you swell up?" Mother asked, pouring Karen another glass of dandelion wine.

"I looked just like Orson Welles."

"Who's Orson Welles?" Twidge asked.

"Your comments reflect the self-loathing thrust on you by the patriarchy," the docent said. "Men have brainwashed women into thinking menstruation is evil and unclean. Women even called their menses 'the curse' because they accepted men's judgment."

"I called it the curse because I thought a witch must have laid a curse on me," Viola said. "Like in 'Sleeping Beauty.' "

Everyone looked at her.

"Well, I did," she said. "It was the only reason I could think of for such an awful thing happening to me." She handed the folder back to the docent. "It still is."

"I think you were awfully brave," Bysshe said to Viola, "going off the ammenerol to have Twidge."

"It was awful," Viola said. "You can't imagine."

Mother sighed. "When I got my period, I asked my mother if Annette had it, too."

"Who's Annette?" Twidge said.

"A Mouseketeer," Mother said and added, at Twidge's uncomprehending look, "on TV."

"High-rez," Viola said.

"The Mickey Mouse Club," Mother said.

"There was a high-rezzer called the Mickey Mouse Club?" Twidge said incredulously.

"They were days of dark oppression in many ways," I said.

Mother glared at me. "Annette was every young girl's ideal," she said to Twidge. "Her hair was curly, she had actual breasts, her pleated skirt was always pressed, and I could not imagine that she could have anything so *messy* and undignified. Mr. Disney would never have allowed it. And if Annette didn't have one, I wasn't going to have one either. So I asked my mother—"

"What did she say?" Twidge cut in.

"She said every woman had periods," Mother said. "So I asked her, 'Even the Queen of England?' and she said, 'Even the Queen.' "

"Really?" Twidge said. "But she's so *old*!"

"She isn't having it now," the docent said irritatedly. "I told you, menopause occurs at age fifty-five."

"And then you have hot flashes," Karen said, "and osteoporosis and so much hair on your upper lip you look like Mark Twain."

"Who's—" Twidge said.

"You are simply reiterating negative male propaganda," the docent interrupted, looking very red in the face.

"You know what I've always wondered?" Karen said, leaning conspiratorially close to Mother. "If Maggie Thatcher's menopause was responsible for the Falklands War."

"Who's Maggie Thatcher?" Twidge said.

The docent, who was now as red in the face as her scarf, stood up. "It is clear there is no point in trying to talk to you. You've all been completely brainwashed by the male patriarchy." She began grabbing up her folders. "You're blind, all of you! You don't even see that you're victims of a male conspiracy to deprive you of your biological identity, of your very womanhood. The Liberation wasn't a liberation at all. It was only another kind of slavery!"

"Even if that were true," I said, "even if it had been a conspiracy to bring us under male domination, it would have been worth it."

"She's right, you know," Karen said to Mother. "Traci's absolutely right. There are some things worth giving up anything for, even your freedom, and getting rid of your period is definitely one of them."

"Victims!" the docent shouted. "You've been stripped of your femininity, and you don't even care!" She stomped out, destroying several squash and a row of gladiolas in the process.

"You know what I hated most before the Liberation?" Karen said, pouring the last of the dandelion wine into her glass. "Sanitary belts."

"And those cardboard tampon applicators," Mother said.

"I'm never going to join the Cyclists," Twidge said.

"Good," I said.

"Can I have dessert?"

I called the waitress over, and Twidge ordered sugared violets. "Anyone else want dessert?" I asked. "Or more primrose wine?"

"I think it's wonderful the way you're trying to help your sister," Bysshe said, leaning close to Viola.

"And those Modess ads," Mother said. "You remember, with those glamorous women in satin brocade evening dresses and long white gloves, and below the picture was written, 'Modess, because. . . .' I thought Modess was a perfume."

Karen giggled. "I thought it was a brand of *champagne*!"

"I don't think we'd better have any more wine," I said.

THE PHONE STARTED singing the minute I got to my chambers the next morning, the universal ring.

"Karen went back to Iraq, didn't she?" I asked Bysshe.

"Yeah," he said. "Viola said there was some snag over whether to put Disneyland on the West Bank or not."

"When did Viola call?"

Bysshe looked sheepish. "I had breakfast with her and Twidge this morning."

"Oh." I picked up the phone. "It's probably Mother with a plan to kidnap Perdita. Hello?"

"This is Evangeline, Perdita's docent," the voice on the phone said. "I hope you're happy. You've bullied Perdita into surrendering to the enslaving male patriarchy."

"I have?" I said.

"You've obviously employed mind control, and I want you to know we intend to file charges." She hung up. The phone rang again immediately, another universal.

"What is the good of signatures when no one ever uses them?" I said and picked up the phone.

"Hi, Mom," Perdita said. "I thought you'd want to know I've changed my mind about joining the Cyclists."

"Really?" I said, trying not to sound jubilant.

"I found out they wear this red scarf thing on their arm. It covers up Sitting Bull's horse."

"That is a problem," I said.

"Well, that's not all. My docent told me about your lunch. Did Grandma Karen really tell you you were right?"

"Yes."

"Gosh! I didn't believe that part. Well, anyway, my docent said you wouldn't listen to her about how great menstruating is, that you all kept talking about the negative aspects of it, like bloating and cramps and crabbiness, and I said, 'What are cramps?' and she said, 'Menstrual bleeding frequently causes headaches and discomfort,' and I said, 'Bleeding?!? Nobody ever said anything about bleeding!' Why didn't you tell me there was blood involved, Mother?"

I had, but I felt it wiser to keep silent.

"And you didn't say a word about its being painful. And all the hormone fluctuations! Anybody'd have to be crazy to want to go through that when they didn't have to! How did you stand it before the Liberation?"

"They were days of dark oppression," I said.

"I *guess*! Well, anyway, I quit and now my docent is really mad. But I told her it was a case of personal sovereignty, and she has to respect my decision. I'm still going to become a floratarian, though, and I *don't* want you to try to talk me out of it."

I wouldn't dream of it," I said.

"You know, this whole thing is really your fault, Mom! If you'd told me about the pain part in the first place, none of this would have happened. Viola's right! You never tell us *anything*!"

GONE

JOHN CROWLEY

JOHN CROWLEY was born December 1942 in Presque Isle, Maine, and moved several times before settling in Indiana in 1953. Crowley attended Indiana University and earned a degree in English in 1964. He moved to New York and worked as a photographer's assistant, then tried to make a living as a freelance photographer and commercial artist. He became a freelance writer in 1966.

Crowley writes both science fiction and fantasy, often straddling both in the same book. His first three novels were mostly science fiction: *The Deep, Beasts,* and *Engine Summer* (collected as *Three Novels*). He moved into literary fantasy with the World Fantasy Award–winner *Little Big.* Mythology permeated his next book, *Aegypt,* the first volume of the Love and Sleep Quartet which to date also includes novels *Love and Sleep* and *Daemonomania.* The collection *Novelties* includes World Fantasy Award–winning novella "Great Work of Time." A second collection, *Antiquities: Seven Stories,* appeared in 1993. His short story "Gone," which follows, won the Locus Award in 1996. Crowley's most recent novel is *The Translator.* Upcoming is the retrospective story collection *Novelties and Antiquities: The Collected Stories of John Crowley.*

* * *

ELMERS AGAIN. You waited in a sort of exasperated amusement for yours, thinking that if you had been missed last time yours would likely be among the households selected this time, though how that process of selection went on no one knew, you only knew that a new capsule had been detected entering the atmosphere (caught by one of the thousand spy satellites and listening-and-peering devices that had been trained on the big Mother Ship in orbit around the moon for the past year) and though the capsule had apparently burned up in the atmosphere, that's just what had happened the time before, and then elmers everywhere. You could hope that you'd be skipped or passed over—there were people who had been skipped last time when all around them neighbors and friends had been visited or afflicted, and who would appear now and then and be interviewed on the news, though having nothing, after all, to say, it was the rest of us who had the stories—but in any case you started looking out the windows, down the drive, listening for the doorbell to ring in the middle of the day.

Pat Poynton didn't need to look out the window of the kids' bedroom where she was changing the beds, the only window from which the front door could be seen, when her doorbell rang in the middle of the day. She could almost hear, subliminally, every second doorbell on Ponader Drive, every second doorbell in South Bend go off just at that moment. She thought: Here's mine.

They had come to be called elmers (or Elmers) all over this country, at least, after David Brinkley had told a story on a talk show about how when they built the great World's Fair in New York in 1939, it was thought that people out in the country, people in places like Dubuque and Rapid City and South Bend, wouldn't think of making a trip East and paying five dollars to see all the wonders, that maybe the great show wasn't for the likes of them; and so the fair's promoters hired a bunch of people, ordinary-looking men with ordinary clothes wearing ordinary glasses and bow ties, to fan out to places like Vincennes and Austin and Brattleboro and just talk it up. Pretend to be ordinary folks who had been to the fair, and hadn't been high-hatted, no sirree, had a wonderful time, the wife too, and b'gosh had Seen the Future and could tell you the sight was worth the five dollars they were asking, which wasn't so much since it included tickets to all the shows and lunch. And all these men, whatever their real names were, were all called Elmer by the promoters who sent them out.

Pat wondered what would happen if she just didn't open the door. Would it eventually go away? It surely wouldn't push its way in, mild and blobby as it was (from the upstairs window she could see that it was the same as the last ones), and that made her wonder how after all they had all got inside—as far as she knew there weren't many who had failed to get at least a hearing. Some chemical hypnotic maybe that they projected, calming fear. What Pat felt standing at the top of the stair and listening to the doorbell pressed again (timidly, she thought, tentatively, hopefully) was amused exasperation, just like everyone else's: a sort of oh-Christ-no with a burble of wonderment just below it, and even expectation: for who wouldn't be at least intrigued by the prospect of his, or her, own lawn-mower, snow-shoveler, hewer of wood and drawer of water, for as long as it lasted?

"Mow your lawn?" it said when Pat opened the door. "Take out trash? Mrs. Poynton?"

Now actually in its presence, looking at it through the screen door, Pat felt most strongly a new part of the elmer feeling: a giddy revulsion she had not expected. It was so not human. It seemed to have been constructed to resemble a human being by other sorts of beings who were not human and did not understand very well what would count as human with other humans. When it spoke its mouth moved (*mouth-hole must move when speech is produced*) but the sound seemed to come from somewhere else, or from nowhere.

"Wash your dishes? Mrs. Poynton?"

"No," she said, as citizens had been instructed to say. "Please go away. Thank you very much."

Of course the elmer didn't go away, only stood bobbing slightly on the doorstep like a foolish child whose White Rose salve or Girl Scout cookies haven't been bought.

"Thank you very much," it said, in tones like her own. "Chop wood? Draw water?"

"Well gee," Pat said, and, helplessly, smiled.

What everyone knew, besides the right response to give to the elmer, which everyone gave and almost no one was able to stick to, was that these weren't the creatures or beings from the Mother Ship itself up above (so big you could see it, pinhead sized, crossing the face of the affronted moon) but some kind of creation of theirs, sent down in advance. An artifact, the official word was; some sort of protein, it was guessed; some sort of chemical process at the heart of it or head of it, maybe a DNA-based computer or something equally outlandish, but no one knew because of the way the first wave of them, flawed maybe, fell apart so quickly, sinking and melting like

the snowmen they sort of resembled after a week or two of mowing lawns
and washing dishes and pestering people with their Good Will Ticket, shriv-
eling into a sort of dry flocked matter and then into nearly nothing at all, like
cotton candy in the mouth.

"Good Will Ticket?" said the elmer at Pat Poynton's door, holding out to
her a tablet of something not paper, on which was written or printed or anyway somehow indited a little message. Pat didn't read it, didn't need to, you
had the message memorized by the time you opened your door to a second-
wave elmer like Pat's. Sometimes lying in bed in the morning in the bad hour
before the kids had to be got up for school Pat would repeat like a prayer
the little message that everybody in the world it seemed was going to be presented with sooner or later:

> Good Will
> You Mark Below
> All All Right With Love Afterwards
> Why Not Say Yes
> ☐ Yes

And no box for No, which meant—if it was a sort of vote, and experts
and officials (though how such a thing could have been determined Pat
didn't know) were guessing that's what it was, a vote to allow or to accept
the arrival or descent of the Mother Ship and its unimaginable occupants or
passengers—that you could only refuse to take it from the elmer: shaking
your head firmly and saying No clearly but politely, because even taking a
Good Will Ticket might be the equivalent of a Yes, and though what it
would be a Yes to exactly no one knew, there was at least a groundswell of
opinion in the think tanks that it meant acceding to or at least not resisting
World Domination.

You weren't, however, supposed to shoot your elmer. In places like
Idaho and Siberia that's what they were doing, you heard, though a bullet
or two didn't seem to make any difference to them, they went on pierced
with holes like characters in the Dick Tracy comics of long ago, smiling
shyly in at your windows, Rake your leaves? Yardwork? Pat Poynton was
sure that Lloyd would not hesitate to shoot, would be pretty glad that at last
something living or at least moving and a certified threat to freedom had at
last got before him to be aimed at. In the hall-table drawer Pat still had
Lloyd's 9mm Glock pistol, he had let her know he wanted to come get it but

he wasn't getting back into this house, she'd use it on him herself if he got close enough.

Not really, no, she wouldn't. And yet.

"Wash windows?" the elmer now said.

"Windows," Pat said, feeling a little of the foolish self-consciousness people feel who are inveigled by comedians or MCs into having conversations with puppets; wary in the same way too, the joke very likely being on her. "You do windows?"

It only bobbed before her like a big water toy.

"Okay," she said, and her heart filled. "Okay, come on in."

Amazing how graceful it really was; it seemed to navigate through the house and the furniture as though it were negatively charged to them, the way it drew close to the stove or the refrigerator and then was repelled gently away, avoiding collision. It seemed to be able to compact or compress itself, too, make itself smaller in small spaces, grow again to full size in larger spaces.

Pat sat down on the couch in the family room and watched. It just wasn't possible to do anything else but watch. Watch it take the handle of a bucket; watch it open the tops of bottles of cleansers and seem to inhale their odors to identify them; take up the squeegee and cloth she found for it. The world, the universe, Pat thought (it was the thought almost everyone thought who was just then taking a slow seat on his or her davenport in his or her family room or in his or her vegetable garden or junkyard or wherever and watching a second-wave elmer get its bearings and get down to work): how big the world, the universe is, how strange; how lucky I am to have learned it, to be here now seeing this.

So the world's work, its odd jobs anyway, were getting done as the humans who usually did them sat and watched, all sharing the same feelings of gratitude and glee, and not only because of the chores being done: it was that wonder, that awe, a universal neap tide of common feeling such as had never been experienced before, not by this species, not anyway since the days on the old old veldt when every member of it could share the same joke, the same dawn, the same amazement. Pat Poynton, watching hers, didn't hear the beebeep of the school-bus horn.

Most days she started watching the wall clock and her wristwatch alternately a good half hour before the bus's horn could be expected to be heard, like an anxious sleeper who continually awakes to check his alarm clock to see how close it has come to going off. Her arrangement with the driver was that he wouldn't let her kids off before tooting. He promised. She hadn't explained why.

But today the sounding of the horn had sunk away deeply into her back brain, maybe three minutes gone, where Pat at last reheard it or remembered having heard and not noticed it. She leapt to her feet, an awful certainty seizing her; she was out the door as fast as her heartbeat accelerated, and was coming down the front steps just in time to see down at the end of the block the kids disappearing into and slamming the door of Lloyd's classic Camaro (whose macho rumble Pat now realized she had also been hearing for some minutes). The cherry-red muscle car, Lloyd's other and more beloved wife, blew exhaust from double pipes that stirred the gutter's leaves, and leapt forward as though kicked.

She shrieked and spun around, seeking help; there was no one in the street. Two steps at a time, maddened and still crying out, she went up the steps and into the house, tore at the pretty little Hitchcock phone table, the phone spilling in parts, the table's legs leaving the floor, its jaw dropping and the Glock 9mm nearly falling out: Pat caught it and was out the door with it and down the street calling out her ex-husband's full name, coupled with imprecations and obscenities her neighbors had never heard her utter before, but the Camaro was of course out of hearing and sight by then.

Gone. Gone gone gone. The world darkened and the sidewalk tilted up toward her as though to smack her face. She was on her knees, not knowing how she had got to them, also not knowing whether she would faint or vomit.

She did neither, and after a time got to her feet. How had this gun, heavy as a hammer, got in her hand? She went back in the house and restored it to the raped little table, and bent to put the phone, which was whimpering urgently, back together.

She couldn't call the police; he'd said—in the low soft voice he used when he wanted to sound implacable and dangerous and just barely controlled, eyes rifling threat at her—that if she got the police involved in his family he'd kill all of them. She didn't entirely believe it, didn't entirely believe anything he said, but he had said it. She didn't believe the whole Christian survivalist thing he was supposedly into, thought he would not probably take them to a cabin in the mountains to live off elk as he had threatened or promised, would probably get no farther than his mother's house with them.

Please Lord let it be so.

The elmer hovered grinning in her peripheral vision like an accidental guest in a crisis as she banged from room to room getting her coat on and taking it off again, sitting to sob at the kitchen table, searching yelling for the cordless phone, where the hell had it been put this time. She called her mother, and wept. Then, heart thudding hard, she called his. One thing you didn't know about elmers (Pat thought this while she waited for her mother-in-law's long cheery phone-machine message to get over) was whether they were like cleaning ladies and handymen, and you were obliged not to show your feelings around them; or whether you were allowed to let go, as with a pet. Abstract question, since she had already.

The machine beeped and began recording her silence. She punched the phone off without speaking.

TOWARD EVENING SHE got the car out at last and drove across town to Mishiwaka. Her mother in law's house was unlit, and there was no car in the garage. She watched a long time, till it was near dark, and came back. There ought to have been elmers everywhere mowing lawns, taptapping with hammers, pulling wagonloads of kids. She saw none.

Her own was where she had left it. The windows gleamed as though coated with silver film.

"What?" she asked it. "You want something to do?" The elmer bounced a little in readiness and put out its chest—so, Pat thought, to speak—and went on smiling. "Bring back my kids," she said. "Go find them and bring them back."

It seemed to hesitate, bobbing between setting off on the job it had been given and turning back to refuse or maybe to await further explanation; it showed Pat its three-fingered cartoon hands, fat and formless. You knew, about elmers, that they would not take vengeance for you, or right wrongs. People had asked, of course they had. People wanted angels, avenging angels; believed they deserved them. Pat, too: she knew now that she wanted hers, wanted it right now.

She stared it down for a time, resentful; then she said forget it, sorry, just a joke, sort of; there's nothing really to do, just forget it, nothing more to do. She went past it, stepping first to one side as it did too and then to the other side; when she got by she went into the bathroom and turned on the water in the sink full force, and after a moment did finally throw up, a wrenching heave that produced nothing but pale sputum.

Toward midnight she took a couple of pills and turned on the TV.

What she saw immediately was two spread-eagled skydivers circling each other in the middle of the air, their orange suits rippling sharply in the wind of their descent. They drifted closer together, put gloved hands on each other's shoulders. Earth lay far below them, like a map. The announcer said it wasn't known just what happened, or what grievances they had, and at that moment one clouted the other in the face. Then he was grabbed by the other. Then the first grabbed the second. Then they flipped over in the air, each with an arm around the other's neck in love or rage, their other arms armwrestling in the air, or dancing, each keeping the other from releasing his chute. The announcer said thousands on the ground watched in horror, and indeed now Pat heard them, an awful moan or shriek from a thousand people, a noise that sounded just like awed satisfaction, as the two skydivers—locked, the announcer said, in deadly combat—shot toward the ground. The helicopter camera lost them and the ground camera picked them up, like one being, four legs thrashing; it followed them almost to the ground, when people rose up suddenly before the lens and cut off the view: but the crowd screamed, and someone right next to the camera said *What the hell.*

Pat Poynton had already seen these moments, seen them a couple of times. They had broken into the soaps with them. She pressed the remote. Demonic black men wearing outsize clothing and black glasses threatened her, moving to a driving beat and stabbing their forefingers at her. She pressed again. Police on a city street, her own city she learned, drew a blanket over someone shot. The dark stain on the littered street. Pat thought of Lloyd. She thought she glimpsed an elmer on an errand far off down the street, bobbing around a corner.

Press again.

That soothing channel where Pat often watched press conferences or speeches, awaking sometimes from half sleep to find the meeting over or a new one begun, the important people having left or not yet arrived, the backs of milling reporters and government people who talked together in low voices. Just now a senator with white hair and a face of exquisite sadness was speaking on the Senate floor. "I apologize to the gentleman," he said. "I wish to withdraw the word *snotty*. I should not have said it. What I meant by that word was: arrogant, unfeeling, self-regarding; supercilious; meanly relishing the discomfiture of your opponents and those hurt by your success. But I should not have said *snotty*. I withdraw *snotty*."

She pressed again, and the two skydivers again fell toward Earth.

What's wrong with us? Pat Poynton thought.

She stood, black instrument in her hand, a wave of nausea seizing her again. What's wrong with us? She felt as though she were drowning in a tide of cold mud, unstoppable; she wanted not to be here any longer, here amid this. She knew she did not, hadn't ever, truly belonged here at all. Her being here was some kind of dreadful sickening mistake.

"Good Will Ticket?"

She turned to face the great thing, gray now in the TV's light. It held out the little plate or tablet to her. All all right with love afterwards. There was no reason at all in the world not to.

"All right," she said. "All right."

It brought the ticket closer, held it up. It seemed to be not something it carried but a part of its flesh. She pressed her thumb against the square beside the YES. The little tablet yielded slightly to her pressure, like one of those nifty buttons on new appliances that feel, themselves, like flesh to press. Her vote registered, maybe.

The elmer didn't alter, or express satisfaction or gratitude, or express anything except the meaningless delight it had been expressing, if that's the word, from the start. Pat sat again on the couch and turned off the television. She pulled the afghan (his mother had made it) from the back of the couch and wrapped herself in it. She felt the calm euphoria of having done something irrevocable, though what exactly she had done she didn't know. She slept there awhile, the pills having grown importunate in her bloodstream at last; lay in the constant streetlight that tiger-striped the room, watched over by the unstilled elmer till gray dawn broke.

IN HER CHOICE, in the suddenness of it, what could almost be described as the insouciance of it if it had not been experienced as so urgent, Pat Poynton was not unique or even unusual; worldwide, polls showed, voting was running high against life on Earth as we know it and in favor of whatever it was that your YES was said to, about which opinions differed. The alecks of TV smart and otherwise detailed the rising numbers, and an agreement seemed to have been reached among them all, an agreement shared in by government officials and the writers of newspaper editorials, to describe this craven unwillingness to resist as a sign of decay, social sickness, repellently nonhuman behavior: the newspeople reported the trend toward mute surrender and knuckling under with the same faces they used for the relaying of stories about women who drowned their children or men who shot their wives to please their lovers, or of snipers in faraway places who brought down old women out gathering firewood; and yet what was actually funny to see (funny to Pat and those like her who had already felt the motion of the soul, the bone-weariness, too, that made the choice so obvious) was that in their smooth tanned faces was another look never before seen there, seen before only on the faces of the rest of us, in our own faces: a look for which Pat Poynton anyway had no name but knew very well, a kind of stricken longing: like, she thought, the bewildered look you see in kids' faces when they come to you for help.

It was true that a certain disruption of the world's work was becoming evident, a noticeable trend toward giving up, leaving the wheel, dropping the ball. People spent less time getting to the job, more time looking upward. But just as many now felt themselves more able to buckle down, by that principle according to which you get to work and clean your house before the cleaning lady comes. The elmers had been sent, surely, to demonstrate that peace and cooperation were better than fighting and selfishness and letting the chores pile up for others to do.

For soon they were gone again. Pat Poynton's began to grow a little listless almost as soon as she had signed or marked or accepted her Good Will Ticket, and by evening next day, though it had by then completed a list of jobs Pat had long since compiled but in her heart had never believed she would get around to, it had slowed distinctly. It went on smiling and nodding, like an old person in the grip of dementia, even as it began dropping tools and bumping into walls, and finally Pat, unwilling to witness its dissolution and not believing she was obliged to, explained (in the somewhat overdistinct way we speak to not real bright teenage baby-sitters or newly hired help who have just arrived from elsewhere and don't speak good English) that she had to go out and pick up a few things and would be back soon; and then she drove aimlessly out of town and up toward Michigan for a couple of hours.

Found herself standing at length on the dunes overlooking the lake, the dunes where she and Lloyd had first. He not the only one, though, only the last of a series that seemed for a moment both long and sad. Chumps. Herself, too, fooled bad, not once or twice, either.

Far off, where the shore of the silver water curved, she could see a band of dark firs, the northern mountains rising. Where he had gone or threatened to go. Lloyd had been part of a successful class-action suit against the company where he'd worked and where everybody had come down with Sick Building Syndrome, Lloyd being pissed off enough (though not ever really deeply affected as far as Pat could ever tell) to hold out with a rump group for a higher settlement, which they got, too, that was what got him the classic Camaro and the twenty acres of high woods. And lots of time to think.

Bring them back, you bastard, she thought; at the same time thinking that it was her, that she should not have done what she did, or should have done what she did not do; that she loved her kids too much, or not enough.

They would bring her kids back; she had become very sure of that, fighting down every rational impulse to question it. She had voted for an inconceivable future, but she had voted for it for only one reason: it would contain—had to contain—everything she had lost. Everything she wanted. That's what the elmers stood for.

She came back at nightfall and found the weird deflated spill of it strung out through the hallway and (why?) halfway down the stairs to the rec room, like the aftermath of a foam fire-extinguisher accident, smelling (Pat thought, others described it differently) like buttered toast; and she called the 800 number we all had memorized.

And then nothing. There were no more of them. If you had been missed you now waited in vain for the experience that had happened to nearly everyone else, uncertain why you had been excluded but able to claim that you, at least, would not have succumbed to their blandishments; and soon after it became apparent that there would be no more, no matter how well they would be received, because the Mother Ship or whatever exactly it was that was surely their origin also went away: not *away* in any trackable or pursuable direction, just away, becoming less distinct on the various tracking and spying devices, producing less data, fibrillating, becoming see-through finally and then unable to be seen. Gone. Gone gone gone.

And what then had we all acceded to, what had we betrayed ourselves and our leadership for, abandoning all our daily allegiances and our commitments so carelessly? Around the world we were asking questions like that, the kind that result in those forlorn religions of the abandoned and forgotten, the religions of those who have been expecting big divine things any moment and then find out they are going to get nothing but a long, maybe a more than lifelong, wait and a blank sky overhead. If their goal had been to make us just dissatisfied, restless, unable to do anything at all but wait to see what would now become of us, then perhaps they had succeeded; but Pat Poynton was certain they had made a promise and would keep it: the universe was not so strange, so unlikely, that such a visitation could occur and come to nothing. Like many others she lay awake looking up into the night sky (so to speak, up into the ceiling of her bedroom in her house on Ponader Drive, above or beyond which the night sky lay) and said over to herself the little text she had assented or agreed to: *Good will. You sign below. All all right with love afterwards. Why not say yes?*

At length she got up and belted her robe around her; she went down the stairs (the house so quiet, it had been quiet with the kids and Lloyd asleep in their beds when she had used to get up at five and make instant coffee and wash and dress to get to work but this was quieter) and put her parka on over her robe; she went out barefoot into the backyard.

Not night any longer but a clear October dawn, so clear the sky looked faintly green, and the air perfectly still: the leaves falling nonetheless around her, letting go one by one, two by two, after hanging on till now.

God, how beautiful, more beautiful somehow than it had been before she decided she didn't belong here; maybe she had been too busy trying to belong here to notice.

All all right with love afterwards. When though did afterwards start? When?

There came to her as she stood there a strange noise, far off and high up, a noise that she thought sounded like the barking of some dog pack, or maybe the crying of children let out from school, except that it wasn't either of those things; for a moment she let herself believe (this was the kind of mood a lot of people were understandably in) that this was it, the inrush or onrush of whatever it was that had been promised. Then out of the north a sort of smudge or spreading dark ripple came over the sky, and Pat saw that overhead a big flock of geese was passing, and the cries were theirs, though seeming too loud and coming from somewhere else or from everywhere.

Going south. A great ragged V spread out over half the sky.

"Long way," she said aloud, envying them their flight, their escape; and thinking then, No, they were not escaping, not from Earth, they were of Earth, born and raised, would die here, were just doing their duty, calling out maybe to keep their spirits up. Of Earth as she was.

She got it then, as they passed overhead, a gift somehow of their passage, though how she could never trace afterwards, only that whenever she thought of it she would think also of those geese, those cries, of encouragement or joy or whatever they were. She got it: in pressing her Good Will Ticket (she could see it in her mind, in the poor dead elmer's hand) she had not acceded or given in to something, not capitulated or surrendered, none of us had though we thought so and even hoped so: no she had made a promise.

"Well, yes," she said, a sort of plain light going on in her back brain, in many another, too, just then in many places, so many that it might have looked—to someone or something able to perceive it, someone looking down on us and our Earth from far above and yet able to perceive each of us one by one—like lights coming on across a darkened land, or like the bright pinpricks that mark the growing numbers of Our Outlets on a TV map, but that were actually our brains, Getting It one by one, brightening momentarily, as the edge of dawn swept westward.

They had not made a promise, she had: good will. She had said yes. And if she kept that promise it would all be all right, with love, afterwards: as right as it could be.

"Yes," she said again, and she raised her eyes to the sky, so vacant, more vacant now than before. Not a betrayal but a promise; not a letting go but a taking hold. Good only for as long as we, all alone here, kept it. All all right with love afterwards.

Why had they come, why had they gone to such effort, to tell us that, when we knew it all along? Who cared that much, to come to tell us? Would they come back, ever, to see how we'd done?

She went back inside, the dew icy on her feet. For a long time she stood in the kitchen (the door unshut behind her) and then went to the phone.

He answered on the second ring. He said hello. All the unshed tears of the last weeks, of her whole life probably, rose up in one awful bolus in her throat; she wouldn't weep though, no not yet.

"Lloyd," she said. "Lloyd, listen. We have to talk."

MANEKI NEKO

BRUCE STERLING

BRUCE STERLING was born April 1954 in Brownsville, Texas. He received a B.A. in journalism from the University of Texas in 1976. His first short story, "Man Made Self," appeared the same year. His first two novels, *Involution Ocean* and *The Artificial Kid,* were far-future adventures, the latter presaging the cyberpunk movement he is credited with creating. Sterling edited the cyberpunk anthology *Mirrorshades,* considered the definitive representation of the subgenre, and his near-future thriller *Islands in the Net* won the John W. Campbell Memorial Award. In 1990 he collaborated with William Gibson on the alternate history novel *The Difference Engine.* The future history novel *Schismatrix* introduced his Shaper-Mechanist universe, which pits bio-engineering against mathematics, also the setting of some of the stories in collection *Crystal Express* (*Schismatrix Plus* collected all the Shaper-Mechanist fiction in one volume).

After the nonfiction book *The Hacker Crackdown,* prompted by Sterling's concern for electronic civil liberties, he returned to fiction with near-future, high-tech scenarios in *Heavy Weather, Holy Fire,* and *Distraction,* which won the Arthur C. Clarke Award. He then backtracked to the recent past in the satirical fantasy *Zeitgeist,* which features Leggy Starlitz, protagonist of the novelettes "Hollywood," "Are You for '86?" and "The Littlest Jackal."

Sterling has produced a large and influential body of short fiction over his career, much of which has been collected in *Crystal Express, Globalhead,* and *A Good Old-Fashioned Future.* His novelette "Bicycle Repairman" won the Hugo Award and his novelette "Taklamakan" won the Hugo and the Locus Award. Sterling's nonfiction has appeared in the *New York Times, Wired, Nature, Newsday,* and *Time Digital.* His most recent book is *Tomorrow Now,* a nonfiction speculation on the future. Upcoming is the novel *The Zenith Angle.*

A "maneki neko" is a type of Japanese cat figurine that acts as a good luck charm for merchants and their businessmen. In the tale that follows Sterling uses the "maneki neko" as the starting point for a delightful look at the future of trust networks.

* * *

I CAN'T GO ON," his brother said.

Tsuyoshi Shimizu looked thoughtfully into the screen of his pasokon. His older brother's face was shiny with sweat from a late-night drinking bout. "It's only a career," said Tsuyoshi, sitting up on his futon and adjusting his pyjamas. "You worry too much."

"All that overtime!" his brother whined. He was making the call from a bar somewhere in Shibuya. In the background, a middle-aged office lady was singing karaoke, badly. "And the examination hells. The internal proficiency tests. The manager training programs. I never have time to live!"

Tsuyoshi grunted sympathetically. He didn't like these late-night videophone calls, but he felt obliged to listen. His big brother had always been a decent sort, before he had gone through the elite courses at Waseda University, joined a big corporation, and gotten professionally ambitious.

"My back hurts," his brother groused. "I have an ulcer. My hair is going gray. And I know they'll fire me. No matter how loyal you are to the big companies, they have no loyalty to their employees any more. It's no wonder that I drink."

"You should get married," Tsuyoshi offered.

"I can't find the right girl. Women never understand me." He shuddered. "Tsuyoshi, I'm truly desperate. The market pressures and the competition are crushing me. I can't breathe. My life has got to change. I'm thinking of taking the vows. I'm serious! I want to renounce this whole modern world."

Tsuyoshi was alarmed. "You're very drunk, right?"

His brother leaned closer to the screen. "Life in a monastery sounds truly good to me. It's so quiet there. You recite the sutras. You consider your existence. There are rules to follow, and rewards that make sense. It's just the way that Japanese business used to be, back in the good old days."

Tsuyoshi grunted skeptically.

"Last week I went out to a special place in the mountains . . . a monastery on Mount Aso," his brother confided. "The monks there, they know about people in trouble, people who are burned out by modern life. The monks protect you from the world. No computers, no phones, no faxes, no e-mail, no overtime, no commuting, nothing at all. It's beautiful, and it's peaceful, and nothing ever happens there. Really, it's like paradise."

"Listen, older brother," Tsuyoshi said, "you're not a religious man by nature. You're a section chief for a big import-export company."

"Well . . . maybe religion won't work for me. I did think of running away to America. Nothing much ever happens there, either."

Tsuyoshi smiled. "That sounds much better! America is a good vacation spot. A long vacation is just what you need! Besides, the Americans are real friendly since they gave up their handguns."

"But I can't go through with it," his brother wailed. "I just don't dare. I can't just wander away from everything that I know and trust to the kindness of strangers."

"That always works for me," Tsuyoshi said. "Maybe you should try it." Tsuyoshi's wife stirred uneasily on the futon. Tsuyoshi lowered his voice. "Sorry, but I have to hang up now. Call me before you do anything rash."

"Don't tell Dad," Tsuyoshi's brother said. "He worries so."

"I won't tell Dad." Tsuyoshi cut the connection and the screen went dark.

Tsuyoshi's wife rolled over, heavily. She was seven months pregnant. She stared at the ceiling, puffing for breath. "Was that another call from your brother?" she said.

"Yeah. The company just gave him another promotion. More responsibilities. He's celebrating."

"That sounds nice," his wife said tactfully.

NEXT MORNING, Tsuyoshi slept late. He was self-employed, so he kept his own hours. Tsuyoshi was a video format upgrader by trade. He transferred old videos from obsolete formats into the new high-grade storage media. Doing this properly took a craftsman's eye. Word of Tsuyoshi's skills had gotten out on the network, so he had as much work as he could handle. At ten A.M., the mailman arrived. Tsuyoshi abandoned his breakfast of raw egg and miso soup, and signed for a shipment of flaking, twentieth-century analog television tapes. The mail also brought a fresh overnight shipment of strawberries, and a jar of homemade pickles.

"Pickles!" his wife enthused. "People are so nice to you when you're pregnant."

"Any idea who sent us that?"

"Just someone on the network."

"Great."

Tsuyoshi booted his mediator, cleaned his superconducting heads and examined the old tapes. Home videos from the 1980s. Someone's grandmother as a child, presumably. There had been a lot of flaking and loss of polarity in the old recording medium.

Tsuyoshi got to work with his desktop fractal detail generator, the image stabilizer and the interlace algorithms. When he was done, Tsuyoshi's new digital copies would look much sharper, cleaner, and better composed than the original primitive videotape.

Tsuyoshi enjoyed his work. Quite often he came across bits and pieces of videotape that were of archival interest. He would pass the images on to the net. The really big network databases, with their armies of search engines, indexers, and catalogs, had some very arcane interests. The net machines would never pay for data, because the global information networks were noncommercial. But the net machines were very polite and had excellent net etiquette. They returned a favor for a favor, and since they were machines with excellent, enormous memories, they never forgot a good deed.

Tsuyoshi and his wife had a lunch of ramen with naruto, and she left to go shopping. A shipment arrived by overseas package service. Cute baby clothes from Darwin, Australia. They were in his wife's favorite color, sunshine yellow.

Tsuyoshi finished transferring the first tape to a new crystal disk. Time for a break. He left his apartment, took the elevator and went out to the corner coffeeshop. He ordered a double iced mocha cappuccino and paid with a chargecard.

His pokkecon rang. Tsuyoshi took it from his belt and answered it. "Get one to go," the machine told him.

"Okay," said Tsuyoshi, and hung up. He bought a second coffee, put a lid on it and left the shop.

A man in a business suit was sitting on a park bench near the entrance of Tsuyoshi's building. The man's suit was good, but it looked as if he'd slept in it. He was holding his head in his hands and rocking gently back and forth. He was unshaven and his eyes were red-rimmed.

The pokkecon rang again. "The coffee's for him?" Tsuyoshi said.

"Yes," said the pokkecon. "He needs it."

Tsuyoshi walked up to the lost businessman. The man looked up, flinching warily, as if he were about to be kicked. "What is it?" he said.

"Here," Tsuyoshi said, handing him the cup. "Double iced mocha cappuccino."

The man opened the cup, and smelled it. He looked up in disbelief. "This is my favorite kind of coffee. . . . Who are you?"

Tsuyoshi lifted his arm and offered a hand signal, his fingers clenched like a cat's paw. The man showed no recognition of the gesture. Tsuyoshi shrugged, and smiled. "It doesn't matter. Sometimes a man really needs a coffee. Now you have a coffee. That's all."

"Well. . . ." The man cautiously sipped his cup, and suddenly smiled. "It's really great. Thanks!"

"You're welcome." Tsuyoshi went home.

His wife arrived from shopping. She had bought new shoes. The pregnancy was making her feet swell. She sat carefully on the couch and sighed.

"Orthopedic shoes are expensive," she said, looking at the yellow pumps. "I hope you don't think they look ugly."

"On you, they look really cute," Tsuyoshi said wisely. He had first met his wife at a video store. She had just used her credit card to buy a disk of primitive black-and-white American anime of the 1950s. The pokkecon had urged him to go up and speak to her on the subject of Felix the Cat. Felix was an early television cartoon star and one of Tsuyoshi's personal favorites.

Tsuyoshi would have been too shy to approach an attractive woman on his own, but no one was a stranger to the net. This fact gave him the confidence to speak to her. Tsuyoshi had soon discovered that the girl was delighted to discuss her deep fondness for cute, antique, animated cats. They had lunch together. They'd had a date the next week. They'd had spent Christmas Eve together in a love hotel. They had a lot in common.

She had come into his life through a little act of grace, a little gift from Felix the Cat's magic bag of tricks. Tsuyoshi had never gotten over feeling grateful for this. Now that he was married and becoming a father, Tsuyoshi Shimizu could feel himself becoming solidly fixed in life. He had a man's role to play now. He knew who he was, and he knew where he stood. Life was good to him.

"You need a haircut, dear," his wife told him.

"Sure."

His wife pulled a gift box out of her shopping bag. "Can you go to the Hotel Daruma, and get your hair cut, and deliver this box for me?"

"What is it?" Tsuyoshi said.

Tsuyoshi's wife opened the little wooden gift box. A maneki neko was nestled inside white foam padding. The smiling ceramic cat held one paw upraised, beckoning for good fortune.

"Don't you have enough of those yet?" he said. "You even have maneki neko underwear."

"It's not for my collection. It's a gift for someone at the Hotel Daruma."

"Oh."

"Some foreign woman gave me this box at the shoestore. She looked American. She couldn't speak Japanese. She had really nice shoes, though. . . ."

"If the network gave you that little cat, then you're the one who should take care of that obligation, dear."

"But dear"—she sighed—"my feet hurt so much, and you could do with a haircut anyway, and I have to cook supper, and besides, it's not really a nice maneki neko, it's just cheap tourist souvenir junk. Can't you do it?"

"Oh, all right," Tsuyoshi told her. "Just forward your pokkecon prompts onto my machine, and I'll see what I can do for us."

She smiled. "I knew you would do it. You're really so good to me."

Tsuyoshi left with the little box. He wasn't unhappy to do the errand, as it wasn't always easy to manage his pregnant wife's volatile moods in their small six-tatami apartment. The local neighborhood was good, but he was hoping to find bigger accommodations before the child was born. Maybe a place with a little studio, where he could expand the scope of his work. It was very hard to find decent housing in Tokyo, but word was out on the net. Friends he didn't even know were working every day to help him. If he kept up with the net's obligations, he had every confidence that some day something nice would turn up.

Tsuyoshi went into the local pachinko parlor, where he won half a liter of beer and a train charge-card. He drank the beer, took the new train card and wedged himself into the train. He got out at the Ebisu station, and turned on his pokkecon Tokyo street map to guide his steps. He walked past places called Chocolate Soup, and Freshness Physique, and The Aladdin Mai-Tai Panico Trattoria.

He entered the Hotel Daruma and went to the hotel barber shop, which was called the Daruma Planet Look. "May I help you?" said the receptionist.

"I'm thinking, a shave and a trim," Tsuyoshi said.

"Do you have an appointment with us?"

"Sorry, no." Tsuyoshi offered a hand gesture.

The woman gestured back, a jerky series of cryptic finger movements.

Tsuyoshi didn't recognize any of the gestures. She wasn't from his part of the network.

"Oh well, never mind," the receptionist said kindly. "I'll get Nahoko to look after you."

Nahoko was carefully shaving the fine hair from Tsuyoshi's forehead when the pokkecon rang. Tsuyoshi answered it.

"Go to the ladies' room on the fourth floor," the pokkecon told him.

"Sorry, I can't do that. This is Tsuyoshi Shimizu, not Ai Shimizu. Besides, I'm having my hair cut right now."

"Oh, I see," said the machine. "Recalibrating." It hung up.

Nahoko finished his hair. She had done a good job. He looked much better. A man who worked at home had to take special trouble to keep up appearances. The pokkecon rang again.

"Yes?" said Tsuyoshi.

"Buy bay rum aftershave. Take it outside."

"Right." He hung up. "Nahoko, do you have bay rum?"

"Odd you should ask that," said Nahoko. "Hardly anyone asks for bay rum any more, but our shop happens to keep it in stock."

Tsuyoshi bought the aftershave, then stepped outside the barbershop. Nothing happened, so he bought a manga comic and waited. Finally a hairy, blond stranger in shorts, a tropical shirt, and sandals approached him. The foreigner was carrying a camera bag and an old-fashioned pokkecon. He looked about sixty years old, and he was very tall.

The man spoke to his pokkecon in English. "Excuse me," said the pokkecon, translating the man's speech into Japanese. "Do you have a bottle of bay rum aftershave?"

"Yes I do." Tsuyoshi handed the bottle over. "Here."

"Thank goodness!" said the man, his words relayed through his machine. "I've asked everyone else in the lobby. Sorry I was late."

"No problem," said Tsuyoshi. "That's a nice pokkecon you have there."

"Well," the man said, "I know it's old and out of style. But I plan to buy a new pokkecon here in Tokyo. I'm told that they sell pokkecons by the basketfull in Akihabara electronics market."

"That's right. What kind of translator program are you running? Your translator talks like someone from Osaka."

"Does it sound funny?" the tourist asked anxiously.

"Well, I don't want to complain, but. . . ." Tsuyoshi smiled. "Here, let's trade meishi. I can give you a copy of a brand-new freeware translator."

"That would be wonderful." They pressed buttons and squirted copies of their business cards across the network link.

Tsuyoshi examined his copy of the man's electronic card and saw that his name was Zimmerman. Mr. Zimmerman was from New Zealand. Tsuyoshi activated a transfer program. His modern pokkecon began transferring a new translator onto Zimmerman's machine.

A large American man in a padded suit entered the lobby of the Daruma. The man wore sunglasses, and was sweating visibly in the summer heat. The American looked huge, as if he lifted a lot of weights. Then a Japanese woman followed him. The woman was sharply dressed, with a dark blue dress suit, hat, sunglasses, and an attache case. She had a haunted look.

Her escort turned and carefully watched the bellhops, who were bringing in a series of bags. The woman walked crisply to the reception desk and began making anxious demands of the clerk.

"I'm a great believer in machine translation," Tsuyoshi said to the tall man from New Zealand. "I really believe that computers help human beings to relate in a much more human way."

"I couldn't agree with you more," said Mr. Zimmerman, through his machine. "I can remember the first time I came to your country, many years ago. I had no portable translator. In fact, I had nothing but a printed phrasebook. I happened to go into a bar, and . . . "

Zimmerman stopped and gazed alertly at his pokkecon. "Oh dear, I'm getting a screen prompt. I have to go up to my room right away."

"Then I'll come along with you till this software transfer is done," Tsuyoshi said.

"That's very kind of you." They got into the elevator together. Zimmerman punched for the fourth floor. "Anyway, as I was saying, I went into this bar in Roppongi late at night, because I was jetlagged and hoping for something to eat . . ."

"Yes?"

"And this woman . . . well, let's just say this woman was hanging out in a foreigner's bar in Roppongi late at night, and she wasn't wearing a whole lot of clothes, and she didn't look like she was any better than she ought to be. . . ."

"Yes, I think I understand you."

"Anyway, this menu they gave me was full of kanji, or katakana, or romanji, or whatever they call those, so I had my phrasebook out, and I was trying very hard to puzzle out these pesky ideograms . . ." The elevator opened and they stepped into the carpeted hall of the hotel's fourth floor.

"So I opened the menu and I pointed to an entree, and I told this girl. . . ." Zimmerman stopped suddenly, and stared at his screen. "Oh dear, something's happening. Just a moment."

Zimmerman carefully studied the instructions on his pokkecon. Then he pulled the bottle of bay rum from the baggy pocket of his shorts, and unscrewed the cap. He stood on tiptoe, stretching to his full height, and carefully poured the contents of the bottle through the iron louvers of a ventilation grate, set high in the top of the wall.

ZIMMERMAN SCREWED the cap back on neatly, and slipped the empty bottle back in his pocket. Then he examined his pokkecon again. He frowned, and shook it. The screen had frozen. Apparently Tsuyoshi's new translation program had overloaded Zimmerman's old-fashioned operating system. His pokkecon had crashed.

Zimmerman spoke a few defeated sentences in English. Then he smiled, and spread his hands apologetically. He bowed, and went into his room, and shut the door.

The Japanese woman and her burly American escort entered the hall. The man gave Tsuyoshi a hard stare. The woman opened the door with a passcard. Her hands were shaking.

Tsuyoshi's pokkecon rang. "Leave the hall," it told him. "Go downstairs. Get into the elevator with the bellboy."

Tsuyoshi followed instructions.

The bellboy was just entering the elevator with a cart full of the woman's baggage. Tsuyoshi got into the elevator, stepping carefully behind the wheeled metal cart. "What floor, sir?" said the bellboy.

"Eight," Tsuyoshi said, ad-libbing. The bellboy turned and pushed the buttons. He faced forward attentively, his gloved hands folded.

The pokkecon flashed a silent line of text to the screen. "Put the gift box inside her flight bag," it read.

Tsuyoshi located the zippered blue bag at the back of the cart. It was a matter of instants to zip it open, put in the box with the maneki neko, and zip the bag shut again. The bellboy noticed nothing. He left, tugging his cart.

Tsuyoshi got out on the eighth floor, feeling slightly foolish. He wandered down the hall, found a quiet nook by an ice machine and called his wife. "What's going on?" he said.

"Oh, nothing." She smiled. "Your haircut looks nice! Show me the back of your head."

Tsuyoshi held the pokkecon screen behind the nape of his neck.

"They do good work," his wife said with satisfaction. "I hope it didn't cost too much. Are you coming home now?"

"Things are getting a little odd here at the hotel," Tsuyoshi told her. "I may be some time."

His wife frowned. "Well, don't miss supper. We're having bonito."

Tsuyoshi took the elevator back down. It stopped at the fourth floor. The woman's American companion stepped onto the elevator. His nose was running and his eyes were streaming with tears.

"Are you all right?" Tsuyoshi said.

"I don't understand Japanese," the man growled. The elevator doors shut.

The man's cellular phone crackled into life. It emitted a scream of anguish and a burst of agitated female English. The man swore and slammed his hairy fist against the elevator's emergency button. The elevator stopped with a lurch. An alarm bell began ringing.

The man pried the doors open with his large hairy fingers and clambered out into the fourth floor. He then ran headlong down the hall.

The elevator began buzzing in protest, its doors shuddering as if broken. Tsuyoshi climbed hastily from the damaged elevator, and stood there in the hallway. He hesitated a moment. Then he produced his pokkecon and loaded his Japanese-to-English translator. He walked cautiously after the American man.

THE DOOR TO their suite was open. Tsuyoshi spoke aloud into his pokkecon. "Hello?" he said experimentally. "May I be of help?"

The woman was sitting on the bed. She had just discovered the maneki neko box in her flight bag. She was staring at the little cat in horror.

"Who are you?" she said, in bad Japanese.

Tsuyoshi realized suddenly that she was a Japanese American. Tsuyoshi had met a few Japanese Americans before. They always troubled him. They looked fairly normal from the outside, but their behavior was always bizarre. "I'm just a passing friend," he said. "Something I can do?"

"Grab him, Mitch!" said the woman in English. The American man rushed into the hall and grabbed Tsuyoshi by the arm. His hands were like steel bands.

Tsuyoshi pressed the distress button on his pokkecon.

"Take that computer away from him," the woman ordered in English. Mitch quickly took Tsuyoshi's pokkecon away, and threw it on the bed. He deftly patted Tsuyoshi's clothing, searching for weapons. Then he shoved Tsuyoshi into a chair.

The woman switched back to Japanese. "Sit right there, you. Don't you dare move." She began examining the contents of Tsuyoshi's wallet.

"I beg your pardon?" Tsuyoshi said. His pokkecon was lying on the bed. Lines of red text scrolled up its little screen as it silently issued a series of emergency net alerts.

The woman spoke to her companion in English. Tsuyoshi's pokkecon was still translating faithfully. "Mitch, go call the local police."

Mitch sneezed uncontrollably. Tsuyoshi noticed that the room smelled strongly of bay rum. "I can't talk to the local cops. I can't speak Japanese." Mitch sneezed again.

"Okay, then I'll call the cops. You handcuff this guy. Then go down to the infirmary and get yourself some antihistamines, for Christ's sake."

Mitch pulled a length of plastic whipcord cuff from his coat pocket and attached Tsuyoshi's right wrist to the head of the bed. He mopped his streaming eyes with a tissue. "I'd better stay with you. If there's a cat in your luggage, then the criminal network already knows we're in Japan. You're in danger."

"Mitch, you may be my bodyguard, but you're breaking out in hives."

"This just isn't supposed to happen," Mitch complained, scratching his neck. "My allergies never interfered with my job before."

"Just leave me here and lock the door," the woman told him. "I'll put a chair against the knob. I'll be all right. You need to look after yourself."

Mitch left the room.

The woman barricaded the door with a chair. Then she called the front desk on the hotel's bedside pasocon. "This is Louise Hashimoto in room 434. I have a gangster in my room. He's an information criminal. Would you call the Tokyo police, please? Tell them to send the organized crime unit. Yes, that's right. Do it. And you should put your hotel security people on full alert. There may be big trouble here. You'd better hurry." She hung up.

Tsuyoshi stared at her in astonishment. "Why are you doing this? What's all this about?"

"So you call yourself Tsuyoshi Shimizu," said the woman, examining his credit cards. She sat on the foot of the bed and stared at him. "You're yakuza of some kind, right?"

"I think you've made a big mistake," Tsuyoshi said.

Louise scowled. "Look, Mr. Shimizu, you're not dealing with some Yankee tourist here. My name is Louise Hashimoto and I'm an assistant federal prosecutor from Providence, Rhode Island, USA." She showed him a magnetic ID card with a gold official seal.

"It's nice to meet someone from the American government," said Tsuyoshi, bowing a bit in his chair. "I'd shake your hand, but it's tied to the bed."

"You can stop with the innocent act right now. I spotted you out in the hall earlier, and in the lobby, too, casing the hotel. How did you know my body-guard is violently allergic to bay rum? You must have read his medical records."

"Who, me? Never!"

"Ever since I discovered you network people, it's been one big pattern," said Louise. "It's the biggest criminal conspiracy I ever saw. I busted this software pirate in Providence. He had a massive network server and a whole bunch of AI freeware search engines. We took him in custody, we bagged all his search engines, and catalogs, and indexers. . . . Later that very same day, these *cats* start showing up."

"Cats?"

Louise lifted the maneki neko, handling it as if it were a live eel. "These little Japanese voodoo cats. Maneki neko, right? They started showing up everywhere I went. There's a china cat in my handbag. There's three china cats at the office. Suddenly they're on display in the windows of every antique store in Providence. My car radio starts making meowing noises at me."

"You *broke* part of the network?" Tsuyoshi said, scandalized. "You took someone's machines away? That's terrible! How could you do such an inhuman thing?"

"You've got a real nerve complaining about that. What about *my* machinery?" Louise held up her fat, eerie-looking American pokkecon. "As soon as I stepped off the airplane at Narita, my PDA was attacked. Thousands and thousands of email messages. All of them pictures of cats. A denial-of-service attack! I can't even communicate with the home office! My PDA's useless!"

"What's a PDA?"

"It's a PDA, my Personal Digital Assistant! Manufactured in Silicon Valley!"

"Well, with a goofy name like that, no wonder our pokkecons won't talk to it."

Louise frowned grimly. "That's right, wise guy. Make jokes about it. You're involved in a malicious software attack on a legal officer of the United States Government. You'll see." She paused, looking him over. "You know, Shimizu, you don't look much like the Italian mafia gangsters I have to deal with, back in Providence."

"I'm not a gangster at all. I never do anyone any harm."

"Oh no?" Louise glowered at him. "Listen pal, I know a lot more about your setup, and your kind of people, than you think I do. I've been studying your outfit for a long time now. We computer cops have names for your kind of people. Digital panarchies. Segmented, polycephalous, integrated influence networks. What about all these *free goods and services* you're getting all this time?"

She pointed a finger at him. "Ha! Do you ever pay *taxes* on those? Do you ever *declare* that income and those benefits? All the free shipments from other countries! The little homemade cookies, and the free pens and pencils and bumper stickers, and the used bicycles, and the helpful news about fire sales. . . . You're a tax evader! You're living through kickbacks! And bribes! And influence peddling! And all kinds of corrupt off-the-books transactions!"

Tsuyoshi blinked. "Look, I don't know anything about all that. I'm just living my life."

"Well, your network gift economy is undermining the lawful, government approved, regulated economy!"

"Well," Tsuyoshi said gently, "maybe my economy is *better* than your economy."

"Says who?" she scoffed. "Why would anyone think that?"

"It's better because we're *happier* than you are. What's wrong with acts of kindness? Everyone likes gifts. Midsummer gifts. New Year's Day gifts. Year-end presents. Wedding presents. Everybody likes those."

"Not the way you Japanese like them. You're totally crazy for gifts."

"What kind of society has no gifts? It's barbaric to have no regard for common human feelings."

Louise bristled. "You're saying I'm barbaric?"

"I don't mean to complain," Tsuyoshi said politely, "but you do have me tied up to your bed."

Louise crossed her arms. "You might as well stop complaining. You'll be in much worse trouble when the local police arrive."

"Then we'll probably be waiting here for quite a while," Tsuyoshi said. "The police move rather slowly, here in Japan. I'm sorry, but we don't have as much crime as you Americans, so our police are not very alert."

The pasocon rang at the side of the bed. Louise answered it. It was Tsuyoshi's wife.

"Could I speak to Tsuyoshi Shimizu please?"

"I'm over here, dear," Tsuyoshi called quickly. "She's kidnapped me! She tied me to the bed!"

"Tied to her *bed*?" His wife's eyes grew wide. "That does it! I'm calling the police!"

Louise quickly hung up the pasocon. "I haven't kidnapped you! I'm only detaining you here until the local authorities can come and arrest you."

"Arrest me for what, exactly?"

Louise thought quickly. "Well, for poisoning my bodyguard by pouring bay rum into the ventilator."

"But I never did that. Anyway, that's not illegal, is it?"

The pasocon rang again. A shining white cat appeared on the screen. It had large, staring, unearthly eyes.

"Let him go," the cat commanded in English.

Louise shrieked and yanked the pasocon's plug from the wall.

Suddenly the lights went out. "Infrastructure attack!" Louise squealed. She rolled quickly under the bed.

The room went gloomy and quiet. The air conditioner had shut off. "I think you can come out," Tsuyoshi said at last, his voice loud in the still room. "It's just a power failure."

"No it isn't," Louise said. She crawled slowly from beneath the bed, and sat on the mattress. Somehow, the darkness had made them more intimate. "I know very well what this is. I'm under attack. I haven't had a moment's peace since I broke that network. Stuff just happens to me now. Bad stuff. Swarms of it. It's never anything you can touch, though. Nothing you can prove in a court of law."

She sighed. "I sit in chairs, and somebody's left a piece of gum there. I get free pizzas, but they're not the kind of pizzas I like. Little kids spit on my sidewalk. Old women in walkers get in front of me whenever I need to hurry."

The shower came on, all by itself. Louise shuddered, but said nothing. Slowly, the darkened, stuffy room began to fill with hot steam.

"My toilets don't flush," Louise said. "My letters get lost in the mail. When I walk by cars, their theft alarms go off. And strangers stare at me. It's always little things. Lots of little tiny things, but they never, ever stop. I'm up against something that is very very big, and very very patient. And it knows all about me. And it's got a million arms and legs. And all those arms and legs are all people."

There was the noise of scuffling in the hall. Distant voices, confused shouting.

Suddenly the chair broke under the doorknob. The door burst open violently. Mitch tumbled through, the sunglasses flying from his head. Two hotel security guards were trying to grab him. Shouting incoherently in English, Mitch fell headlong to the floor, kicking and thrashing. The guards lost their hats in the struggle. One tackled Mitch's legs with both his arms, and the other whacked and jabbed him with a baton.

Puffing and grunting with effort, they hauled Mitch out of the room. The darkened room was so full of steam that the harried guards hadn't even noticed Tsuyoshi and Louise.

Louise stared at the broken door. "Why did they do that to him?"

Tsuyoshi scratched his head in embarrassment. "Probably a failure of communication."

"Poor Mitch! They took his gun away at the airport. He had all kinds of technical problems with his passport. . . . Poor guy, he's never had any luck since he met me."

There was a loud tapping at the window. Louise shrank back in fear. Finally she gathered her courage, and opened the curtains. Daylight flooded the room.

A window-washing rig had been lowered from the roof of the hotel, on cables and pulleys. There were two window-washers in crisp gray uniforms. They waved cheerfully, making little catpaw gestures.

There was a third man with them. It was Tsuyoshi's brother.

One of the washers opened the window with a utility key. Tsuyoshi's brother squirmed into the room. He stood up and carefully adjusted his coat and tie.

"This is my brother," Tsuyoshi explained.

"What are you doing here?" Louise said.

"They always bring in the relatives when there's a hostage situation," Tsuyoshi's brother said. "The police just flew me in by helicopter and landed me on the roof." He looked Louise up and down. "Miss Hashimoto, you just have time to escape."

"What?" she said.

"Look down at the streets," he told her. "See that? You hear them? Crowds are pouring in from all over the city. All kinds of people, everyone with wheels. Street noodle salesmen. Bicycle messengers. Skateboard kids. Takeout delivery guys."

Louise gazed out the window into the streets, and shrieked aloud. "Oh no! A giant swarming mob! They're surrounding me! I'm doomed!"

"You are not doomed," Tsuyoshi's brother told her intently. "Come out the window. Get onto the platform with us. You've got one chance, Louise. It's a place I know, a sacred place in the mountains. No computers there, no phones, nothing." He paused. "It's a sanctuary for people like us. And I know the way."

She gripped his suited arm. "Can I trust you?"

"Look in my eyes," he told her. "Don't you see? Yes, you can trust me. We have everything in common."

Louise stepped out the window. She clutched his arm, the wind whipping at her hair. The platform creaked rapidly up and out of sight.

Tsuyoshi stood up from the chair. When he stretched out, tugging at his handcuffed wrist, he was just able to reach his pokkecon with his fingertips. He drew it in, and clutched it to his chest. Then he sat down again, and waited patiently for someone to come and give him freedom.

The 2000s

BORDER GUARDS

GREG EGAN

GREG EGAN was born in Perth, Western Australia, in 1961 and earned a Bachelor of Science in mathematics from the University of Western Australia before attending the National Film and Television School. He gave up a career in filmmaking—which inspired the early surreal novel *An Unusual Angle*—for science fiction, and has supported himself as a computer programmer when not writing full-time.

Egan began publishing short fiction in the '80s, but his most impressive work is the extensive body of short fiction published during the '90s, which includes "Reasons to Be Cheerful," "Learning to Be Me," "Cocoon," "Luminous," the Hugo Award–winning "The Planck Dive," and the Hugo and Locus Award–winning story "Oceanic." His unique view of cutting-edge science has established him as one of the world's most important writers of science fiction. He has been represented in every volume of the U.S.-based *Year's Best Science Fiction* since 1991. Egan's short fiction has been collected in *Axiomatic* and *Luminous*.

Egan's first major novel—the first of his Nature of Consciousness books—was *Quarantine*; it was followed by the John W. Campbell Memorial Award–winner *Permutation City, Distress, Diaspora, Teranesia,* and radical space opera *Schild's Ladder.*

* * *

IN THE EARLY AFTERNOON of his fourth day out of sadness, Jamil was wandering home from the gardens at the centre of Noether when he heard shouts from the playing field behind the library. On the spur of the moment, without even asking the city what game was in progress, he decided to join in.

As he rounded the corner and the field came into view, it was clear from the movements of the players that they were in the middle of a quantum soccer match. At Jamil's request, the city painted the wave function of the hypothetical ball across his vision, and tweaked him to recognise the players as the members of two teams without changing their appearance at all. Maria had once told him that she always chose a literal perception of colour-coded clothing instead; she had no desire to use pathways that had evolved for the sake of sorting people into those you defended and those you slaughtered. But almost everything that had been bequeathed to them was stained with blood, and to Jamil it seemed a far sweeter victory to adapt the worst relics to his own ends than to discard them as irretrievably tainted.

The wave function appeared as a vivid auroral light, a quicksilver plasma bright enough to be distinct in the afternoon sunlight, yet unable to dazzle the eye or conceal the players running through it. Bands of colour representing the complex phase of the wave swept across the field, parting to wash over separate rising lobes of probability before hitting the boundary and bouncing back again, inverted. The match was being played by the oldest, simplest rules: semi-classical, non-relativistic. The ball was confined to the field by an infinitely high barrier, so there was no question of it tunnelling out, leaking away as the match progressed. The players were treated classically: their movements pumped energy into the wave, enabling transitions from the game's opening state—with the ball spread thinly across the entire field—into the range of higher-energy modes needed to localise it. But localisation was fleeting; there was no point forming a nice sharp wave packet in the middle of the field in the hope of kicking it around like a classical object. You had to shape the wave in such a way that all of its modes—cycling at different frequencies, travelling with different velocities—would come into phase with each other, for a fraction of a second, within the goal itself. Achieving that was a matter of energy levels, and timing.

Jamil had noticed that one team was under-strength. The umpire would be skewing the field's potential to keep the match fair, but a new participant would be especially welcome for the sake of restoring symmetry. He watched the faces of the players, most of them old friends. They were frowning with concentration, but breaking now and then into smiles of delight at their small successes, or their opponents' ingenuity.

He was badly out of practice, but if he turned out to be dead weight he could always withdraw. And if he misjudged his skills, and lost the match with his incompetence? No one would care. The score was nil all; he could wait for a goal, but that might be an hour or more in coming. Jamil communed with the umpire, and discovered that the players had decided in advance to allow new entries at any time.

Before he could change his mind, he announced himself. The wave froze, and he ran on to the field. People nodded greetings, mostly making no fuss, though Ezequiel shouted, "Welcome back!" Jamil suddenly felt fragile again; though he'd ended his long seclusion four days before, it was well within his power, still, to be dismayed by everything the game would involve. His recovery felt like a finely balanced optical illusion, a figure and ground that could change roles in an instant, a solid cube that could evert into a hollow.

The umpire guided him to his allotted starting position, opposite a woman he hadn't seen before. He offered her a formal bow, and she returned the gesture. This was no time for introductions, but he asked the city if she'd published a name. She had: Margit.

The umpire counted down in their heads. Jamil tensed, regretting his impulsiveness. For seven years he'd been dead to the world. After four days back, what was he good for? His muscles were incapable of atrophy, his reflexes could never be dulled, but he'd chosen to live with an unconstrained will, and at any moment his wavering resolve could desert him.

The umpire said, "Play." The frozen light around Jamil came to life, and he sprang into motion.

Each player was responsible for a set of modes, particular harmonics of the wave that were theirs to fill, guard, or deplete as necessary. Jamil's twelve modes cycled at between 1,000 and 1,250 milliHertz. The rules of the game endowed his body with a small, fixed potential energy, which repelled the ball slightly and allowed different modes to push and pull on each other through him, but if he stayed in one spot as the modes cycled, every influence he exerted would eventually be replaced by its opposite, and the effect would simply cancel itself out.

To drive the wave from one mode to another, you needed to move, and to drive it efficiently you needed to exploit the way the modes fell in and out of phase with each other: to take from a 1,000 milliHertz mode and give to a 1,250, you had to act in synch with the quarter-Hertz beat between them. It was like pushing a child's swing at its natural frequency, but rather than setting a single child in motion, you were standing between two swings and acting more as an intermediary: trying to time your interventions in such a way as to speed up one child at the other's expense. The way you pushed on the wave at a given time and place was out of your hands completely, but by changing location in just the right way you could gain control over the interaction. Every pair of modes had a spatial beat between them—like the moiré pattern formed by two sheets of woven fabric held up to the light together, shifting from transparent to opaque as the gaps between the threads fell in and out of alignment. Slicing through this cyclic landscape offered the perfect means to match the accompanying chronological beat.

Jamil sprinted across the field at a speed and angle calculated to drive two favourable transitions at once. He'd gauged the current spectrum of the wave instinctively, watching from the sidelines, and he knew which of the modes in his charge would contribute to a goal and which would detract from the probability. As he cut through the shimmering bands of colour, the umpire gave him tactile feedback to supplement his visual estimates and calculations, allowing him to sense the difference between a cyclic tug, a to and fro that came to nothing, and the gentle but persistent force that meant he was successfully riding the beat.

Chusok called out to him urgently, "Take, take! Two-ten!" Everyone's spectral territory overlapped with someone else's, and you needed to pass amplitude from player to player as well as trying to manage it within your own range. *Two-ten*—a harmonic with two peaks across the width of the field and ten along its length, cycling at 1,160 milliHertz—was filling up as Chusok drove unwanted amplitude from various lower-energy modes into it. It was Jamil's role to empty it, putting the amplitude somewhere useful. Any mode with an even number of peaks across the field was unfavourable for scoring, because it had a node—a zero point between the peaks—smack in the middle of both goals.

Jamil acknowledged the request with a hand signal and shifted his trajectory. It was almost a decade since he'd last played the game, but he still knew the intricate web of possibilities by heart: he could drain the two-ten harmonic into the three-ten, five-two and five-six modes—all with "good parity," peaks along the centre-line—in a single action.

As he pounded across the grass, carefully judging the correct angle by sight, increasing his speed until he felt the destructive beats give way to a steady force like a constant breeze, he suddenly recalled a time—centuries before, in another city when he'd played with one team, week after week, for forty years. Faces and voices swam in his head. Hashim, Jamil's ninety-eighth child, and Hashim's granddaughter Laila had played beside him. But he'd burnt his house and moved on, and when that era touched him at all now it was like an unexpected gift. The scent of the grass, the shouts of the players, the soles of his feet striking the ground, resonated with every other moment he'd spent the same way, bridging the centuries, binding his life together. He never truly felt the scale of it when he sought it out deliberately; it was always small things, tightly focused moments like this, that burst the horizon of his everyday concerns and confronted him with the astonishing vista.

The two-ten mode was draining faster than he'd expected; the see-sawing centre-line dip in the wave was vanishing before his eyes. He looked around, and saw Margit performing an elaborate Lissajous manoeuvre, smoothly orchestrating a dozen transitions at once. Jamil froze and watched her, admiring her virtuosity while he tried to decide what to do next; there was no point competing with her when she was doing such a good job of completing the task Chusok had set him.

Margit was his opponent, but they were both aiming for exactly the same kind of spectrum. The symmetry of the field meant that any scoring wave would work equally well for either side—but only one team could be the first to reap the benefit, the first to have more than half the wave's probability packed into their goal. So the two teams were obliged to cooperate at first, and it was only as the wave took shape from their combined efforts that it gradually became apparent which side would gain by sculpting it to perfection as rapidly as possible, and which would gain by spoiling it for the first chance, then honing it for the rebound.

Penina chided him over her shoulder as she jogged past, "You want to leave her to clean up four-six, as well?" She was smiling, but Jamil was stung; he'd been motionless for ten or fifteen seconds. It was not forbidden to drag your feet and rely on your opponents to do all the work, but it was regarded as a shamefully impoverished strategy. It was also very risky, handing them the opportunity to set up a wave that was almost impossible to exploit yourself.

He reassessed the spectrum, and quickly sorted through the alternatives.

Whatever he did would have unwanted side effects; there was no magic way to avoid influencing modes in other players' territory, and any action that would drive the transitions he needed would also trigger a multitude of others, up and down the spectrum. Finally, he made a choice that would weaken the offending mode while causing as little disruption as possible.

Jamil immersed himself in the game, planning each transition two steps in advance, switching strategy half-way through a run if he had to, but staying in motion until the sweat dripped from his body, until his calves burned, until his blood sang. He wasn't blinded to the raw pleasures of the moment, or to memories of games past, but he let them wash over him, like the breeze that rose up and cooled his skin with no need for acknowledgement. Familiar voices shouted terse commands at him; as the wave came closer to a scoring spectrum every trace of superfluous conversation vanished, every idle glance gave way to frantic, purposeful gestures. To a bystander, this might have seemed like the height of dehumanisation: twenty-two people reduced to grunting cogs in a pointless machine. Jamil smiled at the thought but refused to be distracted into a complicated imaginary rebuttal. Every step he took was the answer to that, every hoarse plea to Yann or Joracy, Chusok or Maria, Eudore or Halide. These were his friends, and he was back among them. Back in the world.

The first chance of a goal was thirty seconds away, and the opportunity would fall to Jamil's team; a few tiny shifts in amplitude would clinch it. Margit kept her distance, but Jamil could sense her eyes on him constantly—and literally feel her at work through his skin as she slackened his contact with the wave. In theory, by mirroring your opponent's movements at the correct position on the field you could undermine everything they did, though in practice not even the most skilful team could keep the spectrum completely frozen. Going further and spoiling was a tug of war you didn't want to win too well: if you degraded the wave too much, your opponent's task—spoiling your own subsequent chance at a goal—became far easier.

Jamil still had two bad-parity modes that he was hoping to weaken, but every time he changed velocity to try a new transition, Margit responded in an instant, blocking him. He gestured to Chusok for help; Chusok had his own problems with Ezequiel, but he could still make trouble for Margit by choosing where he placed unwanted amplitude. Jamil shook sweat out of his eyes; he could see the characteristic "stepping stone" pattern of lobes forming, a sign that the wave would soon converge on the goal, but from the middle of the field it was impossible to judge their shape accurately enough to know what, if anything, remained to be done.

Suddenly, Jamil felt the wave push against him. He didn't waste time looking around for Margit; Chusok must have succeeded in distracting her. He was almost at the boundary line, but he managed to reverse smoothly, continuing to drive both the transitions he'd been aiming for.

Two long lobes of probability, each modulated by a series of oscillating mounds, raced along the sides of the field. A third, shorter lobe running along the centre-line melted away, reappeared, then merged with the others as they touched the end of the field, forming an almost rectangular plateau encompassing the goal.

The plateau became a pillar of light, growing narrower and higher as dozens of modes, all finally in phase, crashed together against the impenetrable barrier of the field's boundary. A shallow residue was still spread across the entire field, and a diminishing sequence of elliptical lobes trailed away from the goal like a staircase, but most of the wave that had started out lapping around their waists was now concentrated in a single peak that towered above their heads, nine or ten metres tall.

For an instant, it was motionless.

Then it began to fall.

The umpire said, "Forty-nine point eight."

The wave packet had not been tight enough.

Jamil struggled to shrug off his disappointment and throw his instincts into reverse. The other team had fifty seconds, now, to fine-tune the spectrum and ensure that the reflected packet was just a fraction narrower when it reformed, at the opposite end of the field.

As the pillar collapsed, replaying its synthesis in reverse, Jamil caught sight of Margit. She smiled at him calmly, and it suddenly struck him: *She'd known they couldn't make the goal. That was why she'd stopped opposing him.* She'd let him work towards sharpening the wave for a few seconds, knowing that it was already too late for him, knowing that her own team would gain from the slight improvement.

Jamil was impressed; it took an extraordinary level of skill and confidence to do what she'd just done. For all the time he'd spent away, he knew exactly what to expect from the rest of the players, and in Margit's absence he would probably have been wishing out loud for a talented newcomer to make the game interesting again. Still, it was hard not to feel a slight sting of resentment. Someone should have warned him just how good she was.

With the modes slipping out of phase, the wave undulated all over the field again, but its reconvergence was inevitable: unlike a wave of water or sound, it possessed no hidden degrees of freedom to grind its precision into entropy. Jamil decided to ignore Margit; there were cruder strategies than mirror-blocking that worked almost as well. Chusok was filling the two-ten mode now; Jamil chose the four-six as his spoiler. All they had to do was keep the wave from growing much sharper, and it didn't matter whether they achieved this by preserving the status quo, or by nudging it from one kind of bluntness to another.

The steady resistance he felt as he ran told Jamil that he was driving the transition, unblocked, but he searched in vain for some visible sign of success. When he reached a vantage point where he could take in enough of the field in one glance to judge the spectrum properly, he noticed a rapidly vibrating shimmer across the width of the wave. He counted nine peaks: good parity. Margit had pulled most of the amplitude straight out of his spoiler mode and fed it into *this*. It was a mad waste of energy to aim for such an elevated harmonic, but no one had been looking there, no one had stopped her.

The scoring pattern was forming again, he only had nine or ten seconds left to make up for all the time he'd wasted. Jamil chose the strongest good-parity mode in his territory, and the emptiest bad one, computed the velocity that would link them, and ran.

He didn't dare turn to watch the opposition goal; he didn't want to break his concentration. The wave retreated around his feet, less like an Earthly ebb tide than an ocean drawn into the sky by a passing black hole. The city diligently portrayed the shadow that his body would have cast, shrinking in front of him as the tower of light rose.

The verdict was announced. "Fifty point one."

The air was filled with shouts of triumph—Ezequiel's the loudest, as always. Jamil sagged to his knees, laughing. It was a curious feeling, familiar as it was: he cared, and he didn't. If he'd been wholly indifferent to the outcome of the game there would have been no pleasure in it, but obsessing over every defeat—or every victory—could ruin it just as thoroughly. He could almost see himself walking the line, orchestrating his response as carefully as any action in the game itself.

He lay down on the grass to catch his breath before play resumed. The outer face of the microsun that orbited Laplace was shielded with rock, but light reflected skywards from the land beneath it crossed the 100,000 kilometre width of the 3-toroidal universe to give a faint glow to the planet's nightside. Though only a sliver was lit directly, Jamil could discern the full disk of the opposite hemisphere in the primary image at the zenith: continents and oceans that lay, by a shorter route, 12,000 or so kilometres beneath him. Other views in the lattice of images spread across the sky were from different angles, and showed substantial crescents of the dayside itself. The one thing you couldn't find in any of these images, even with a telescope, was your own city. The topology of this universe let you see the back of your head, but never your reflection.

JAMIL'S TEAM LOST, three nil. He staggered over to the fountains at the edge of the field and slaked his thirst, shocked by the pleasure of the simple act. Just to be alive was glorious now, but once he felt this way, anything seemed possible. He was back in synch, back in phase, and he was going to make the most of it, for however long it lasted.

He caught up with the others, who'd headed down towards the river. Ezequiel hooked an arm around his neck, laughing. "Bad luck, Sleeping Beauty! You picked the wrong time to wake. With Margit, we're invincible."

Jamil ducked free of him. "I won't argue with that." He looked around. "Speaking of whom—"

Penina said, "Gone home. She plays, that's all. No frivolous socialising after the match."

Chusok added, "Or any other time." Penina shot Jamil a glance that meant: not for want of trying on Chusok's part.

Jamil pondered this, wondering why it annoyed him so much. On the field, she hadn't come across as aloof and superior. Just unashamedly good.

He queried the city, but she'd published nothing besides her name. Nobody expected—or wished—to hear more than the tiniest fraction of another person's history, but it was rare for anyone to start a new life without carrying through something from the old as a kind of calling card, some incident or achievement from which your new neighbours could form an impression of you.

They'd reached the riverbank. Jamil pulled his shirt over his head. "So what's her story? She must have told you something."

Ezequiel said, "Only that she learnt to play a long time ago; she won't say where or when. She arrived in Noether at the end of last year, and grew a house on the southern outskirts. No one sees her around much. No one even knows what she studies."

Jamil shrugged, and waded in. "Ah well. It's a challenge to rise to." Penina laughed and splashed him teasingly. He protested, "I *meant* beating her at the game."

Chusok said wryly, "When you turned up, I thought you'd be our secret weapon. The one player she didn't know inside out already."

"I'm glad you didn't tell me that. I would have turned around and fled straight back into hibernation."

"I know. That's why we all kept quiet." Chusok smiled. "Welcome back."

Penina said, "Yeah, welcome back, Jamil."

Sunlight shone on the surface of the river. Jamil ached all over, but the cool water was the perfect place to be. If he wished, he could build a partition in his mind at the point where he stood right now, and never fall beneath it. Other people lived that way, and it seemed to cost them nothing. Contrast was overrated; no sane person spent half their time driving spikes into their flesh for the sake of feeling better when they stopped. Ezequiel lived every day with the happy boisterousness of a five-year-old; Jamil sometimes found this annoying, but then any kind of disposition would irritate someone. His own stretches of meaningless sombreness weren't exactly a boon to his friends.

Chusok said, "I've invited everyone to a meal at my house tonight. Will you come?"

Jamil thought it over, then shook his head. He still wasn't ready. He couldn't force-feed himself with normality; it didn't speed his recovery, it just drove him backwards.

Chusok looked disappointed, but there was nothing to be done about that. Jamil promised him, "Next time. OK?"

Ezequiel sighed. "What are we going to do with you? You're worse than Margit!" Jamil started backing away, but it was too late. Ezequiel reached him in two casual strides, bent down and grabbed him around the waist, hoisted him effortlessly onto one shoulder, then flung him through the air into the depths of the river.

JAMIL WAS WOKEN by the scent of wood smoke. His room was still filled with the night's grey shadows, but when he propped himself up on one elbow and the window obliged him with transparency, the city was etched clearly in the predawn light.

He dressed and left the house, surprised at the coolness of the dew on his feet. No one else in his street seemed to be up; had they failed to notice the smell, or did they already know to expect it? He turned a corner and saw the rising column of soot, faintly lit with red from below. The flames and the ruins were still hidden from him, but he knew whose house it was.

When he reached the dying blaze, he crouched in the heat-withered garden, cursing himself. Chusok had offered him the chance to join him for his last meal in Noether. Whatever hints you dropped, it was customary to tell no one that you were moving on. If you still had a lover, if you still had young children, you never deserted them. But friends, you warned in subtle ways. Before vanishing.

Jamil covered his head with his arms. He'd lived through this countless times before, but it never became easier. If anything it grew worse, as every departure was weighted with the memories of others. His brothers and sisters had scattered across the branches of the New Territories. He'd walked away from his father and mother when he was too young and confident to realise how much it would hurt him, decades later. His own children had all abandoned him eventually, far more often than he'd left them. It was easier to leave an ex-lover than a grown child: something burned itself out in a couple, almost naturally, as if ancestral biology had prepared them for at least that one rift.

Jamil stopped fighting the tears. But as he brushed them away, he caught sight of someone standing beside him. He looked up. It was Margit.

He felt a need to explain. He rose to his feet and addressed her. "This was Chusok's house. We were good friends. I'd known him for ninety-six years."

Margit gazed back at him neutrally. "Boo hoo. Poor baby. You'll never see your friend again."

Jamil almost laughed, her rudeness was so surreal. He pushed on, as if the only conceivable, polite response was to pretend that he hadn't heard her. "No one is the kindest, the most generous, the most loyal. It doesn't matter. That's not the point. Everyone's unique. Chusok was Chusok." He banged a fist against his chest, utterly heedless now of her contemptuous words. "There's a hole in me, and it will never be filled." That was the truth, even though he'd grow around it. *He should have gone to the meal, it would have cost him nothing.*

"You must be a real emotional Swiss cheese," observed Margit tartly.

Jamil came to his senses. "Why don't you fuck off to some other universe? No one wants you in Noether."

Margit was amused. "You *are* a bad loser."

Jamil gazed at her, honestly confused for a moment; the game had slipped his mind completely. He gestured at the embers. "What are you doing here? Why did you follow the smoke, if it wasn't regret at not saying goodbye to him when you had the chance?" He wasn't sure how seriously to take Penina's light-hearted insinuation, but if Chusok had fallen for Margit, and it had not been reciprocated, that might even have been the reason he'd left.

She shook her head calmly. "He was nothing to me. I barely spoke to him."

"Well, that's your loss."

"From the look of things, I'd say the loss was all yours."

He had no reply. Margit turned and walked away.

Jamil crouched on the ground again, rocking back and forth, waiting for the pain to subside.

JAMIL SPENT THE NEXT week preparing to resume his studies. The library had near-instantaneous contact with every artificial universe in the New Territories, and the additional lightspeed lag between Earth and the point in space from which the whole tree-structure blossomed was only a few hours. Jamil had been to Earth, but only as a tourist; land was scarce, they accepted no migrants. There were remote planets you could live on, in the home universe, but you had to be a certain kind of masochistic purist to want that. The precise reasons why his ancestors had entered the New Territories had been forgotten generations before—and it would have been presumptuous to track them down and ask them in person—but given a choice between the then even-more-crowded Earth, the horrifying reality of interstellar distances, and an endlessly extensible branching chain of worlds which could be traversed within a matter of weeks, the decision wasn't exactly baffling.

Jamil had devoted most of his time in Noether to studying the category of representations of Lie groups on complex vector spaces—a fitting choice, since Emmy Noether had been a pioneer of group theory, and if she'd lived to see this field blossom she would probably have been in the thick of it herself. Representations of Lie groups lay behind most of physics: each kind of subatomic particle was really nothing but a particular way of representing the universal symmetry group as a set of rotations of complex vectors. Organising this kind of structure with category theory was ancient knowledge, but Jamil didn't care; he'd long ago reconciled himself to being a student, not a discoverer. The greatest gift of consciousness was the ability to take the patterns of the world inside you, and for all that he would have relished the thrill of being the first at anything, with ten-to-the-sixteenth people alive that was a futile ambition for most.

In the library, he spoke with fellow students of his chosen field on other worlds, or read their latest works. Though they were not researchers, they could still put a new pedagogical spin on old material, enriching the connections with other fields, finding ways to make the complex, subtle truth easier to assimilate without sacrificing the depth and detail that made it worth knowing in the first place. They would not advance the frontiers of knowledge. They would not discover new principles of nature, or invent new technologies. But to Jamil, understanding was an end in itself.

He rarely thought about the prospect of playing another match, and when he did the idea was not appealing. With Chusok gone, the same group could play ten-to-a-side without Jamil to skew the numbers. Margit might even choose to swap teams, if only for the sake of proving that her current team's monotonous string of victories really had been entirely down to her.

When the day arrived, though, he found himself unable to stay away. He turned up intending to remain a spectator, but Ryuichi had deserted Ezequiel's team, and everyone begged Jamil to join in.

As he took his place opposite Margit, there was nothing in her demeanour to acknowledge their previous encounter: no lingering contempt, but no hint of shame either. Jamil resolved to put it out of his mind; he owed it to his fellow players to concentrate on the game.

They lost, five nil.

Jamil forced himself to follow everyone to Eudore's house, to celebrate, commiserate, or as it turned out, to forget the whole thing. After they'd eaten, Jamil wandered from room to room, enjoying Eudore's choice of music but unable to settle into any conversation. No one mentioned Chusok in his hearing.

He left just after midnight. Laplace's near-full primary image and its eight brightest gibbous companions lit the streets so well that there was no need for anything more. Jamil thought: Chusok might have merely travelled to another city, one beneath his gaze right now. And wherever he'd gone, he might yet choose to stay in touch with his friends from Noether.

And his friends from the next town, and the next?

Century after century?

Margit was sitting on Jamil's doorstep, holding a bunch of white flowers in one hand.

Jamil was irritated. "What are you doing here?"

"I came to apologise."

He shrugged. "There's no need. We feel differently about certain things. That's fine. I can still face you on the playing field."

"I'm not apologising for a difference of opinion. I wasn't honest with you. I was cruel." She shaded her eyes against the glare of the planet and looked up at him. "You were right: it was my loss. I wish I'd known your friend."

He laughed curtly. "Well, it's too late for that."

She said simply, "I know."

Jamil relented. "Do you want to come in?" Margit nodded, and he instructed the door to open for her. As he followed her inside, he said, "How long have you been here? Have you eaten?"

"No."

"I'll cook something for you."

"You don't have to do that."

He called out to her from the kitchen, "Think of it as a peace offering. I don't have any flowers."

Margit replied, "They're not for you. They're for Chusok's house."

Jamil stopped rummaging through his vegetable bins, and walked back into the living room. "People don't usually do that in Noether."

Margit was sitting on the couch, staring at the floor. She said, "I'm so lonely here. I can't bear it any more."

He sat beside her. "Then why did you rebuff him? You could at least have been friends."

She shook her head. "Don't ask me to explain."

Jamil took her hand. She turned and embraced him, trembling miserably. He stroked her hair. "Sssh."

She said, "Just sex. I don't want anything more."

He groaned softly. "There's no such thing as that."

"I just need someone to touch me again."

"I understand." He confessed, "So do I. But that won't be all. So don't ask me to promise there'll be nothing more."

Margit took his face in her hands and kissed him. Her mouth tasted of wood smoke.

Jamil said, "I don't even know you."

"No one knows anyone, any more."

"That's not true."

"No, it's not," she conceded gloomily. She ran a hand lightly along his arm. Jamil wanted badly to see her smile, so he made each dark hair thicken and blossom into a violet flower as it passed beneath her fingers.

She did smile, but she said, "I've seen that trick before."

Jamil was annoyed. "I'm sure to be a disappointment all round, then. I expect you'd be happier with some kind of novelty. A unicorn, or an amoeba."

She laughed. "I don't think so." She took his hand and placed it against her breast. "Do you ever get tired of sex?"

"Do you ever get tired of breathing?"

"I can go for a long time without thinking about it."

He nodded. "But then one day you stop and fill your lungs with air, and it's still as sweet as ever."

Jamil didn't know what he was feeling any more. Lust. Compassion. Spite. She'd come to him hurting, and he wanted to help her, but he wasn't sure that either of them really believed this would work.

Margit inhaled the scent of the flowers on his arm. "Are they the same colour? Everywhere else?"

He said, "There's only one way to find out."

JAMIL WOKE IN THE EARLY HOURS of the morning, alone. He'd half expected Margit to flee like this, but she could have waited till dawn. He would have obligingly feigned sleep while she dressed and tip-toed out.

Then he heard her. It was not a sound he would normally have associated with a human being, but it could not have been anything else.

He found her in the kitchen, curled around a table leg, wailing rhythmically. He stood back and watched her, afraid that anything he did would only make things worse. She met his gaze in the half light, but kept up the mechanical whimper. Her eyes weren't blank; she was not delirious, or hallucinating. She knew exactly who, and where, she was.

Finally, Jamil knelt in the doorway. He said, "Whatever it is, you can tell me. And we'll fix it. We'll find a way."

She bared her teeth. "You can't *fix it,* you stupid child." She resumed the awful noise.

"Then just tell me. Please?" He stretched out a hand towards her. He hadn't felt quite so helpless since his very first daughter, Aminata, had come to him as an inconsolable six-year-old, rejected by the boy to whom she'd declared her undying love. He'd been twenty-four years old; a child himself. More than a thousand years ago. *Where are you now, Nata?*

Margit said, "I promised. I'd never tell."

"Promised who?"

"Myself."

"Good. They're the easiest kind to break."

She started weeping. It was a more ordinary sound, but it was even more chilling. She was not a wounded animal now, an alien being suffering some incomprehensible pain. Jamil approached her cautiously; she let him wrap his arms around her shoulders.

He whispered, "Come to bed. The warmth will help. Just being held will help."

She spat at him derisively, "It won't bring her back."

"Who?"

Margit stared at him in silence, as if he'd said something shocking.

Jamil insisted gently, "Who won't it bring back?" She'd lost a friend, badly, the way he'd lost Chusok. That was why she'd sought him out. He could help her through it. They could help each other through it.

She said, "It won't bring back the dead."

MARGIT WAS seven thousand five hundred and ninety-four years old. Jamil persuaded her to sit at the kitchen table. He wrapped her in blankets, then fed her tomatoes and rice, as she told him how she'd witnessed the birth of his world.

The promise had shimmered just beyond reach for decades. Almost none of her contemporaries had believed it would happen, though the truth should have been plain for centuries: *the human body was a material thing*. In time, with enough knowledge and effort, it would become possible to safeguard it from any kind of deterioration, any kind of harm. Stellar evolution and cosmic entropy might or might not prove insurmountable, but there'd be aeons to confront those challenges. In the middle of the twenty-first century, the hurdles were aging, disease, violence, and an overcrowded planet.

"Grace was my best friend. We were students." Margit smiled. "Before everyone was a student. We'd talk about it, but we didn't believe we'd see it happen. It would come in another century. It would come for our great-great-grandchildren. We'd hold infants on our knees in our twilight years and tell ourselves: *this one will never die*.

"When we were both twenty-two, something happened. To both of us." She lowered her eyes. "We were kidnapped. We were raped. We were tortured."

Jamil didn't know how to respond. These were just words to him: he knew their meaning, he knew these acts would have hurt her, but she might as well have been describing a mathematical theorem. He stretched a hand across the table, but Margit ignored it. He said awkwardly, "This was . . . the Holocaust?"

She looked up at him, shaking her head, almost laughing at his naivete. "Not even one of them. Not a war, not a pogrom. Just one psychopathic man. He locked us in his basement, for six months. He'd killed seven women." Tears began spilling down her cheeks. "He showed us the bodies. They were buried right where we slept. He showed us how we'd end up, when he was through with us."

Jamil was numb. He'd known all his adult life what had once been possible—what had once happened, to real people—but it had all been consigned to history long before his birth. In retrospect it seemed almost inconceivably stupid, but he'd always imagined that the changes had come in such a way that no one still living had experienced these horrors. There'd been no escaping the bare minimum, the logical necessity: his oldest living ancestors must have watched their parents fall peacefully into eternal sleep. But not this. Not a flesh-and-blood woman, sitting in front of him, who'd been forced to sleep in a killer's graveyard.

He put his hand over hers, and choked out the words. "This man . . . *killed* Grace? He killed your friend?"

Margit began sobbing, but she shook her head. "No, no. We got out!" She twisted her mouth into a smile. "Someone stabbed the stupid fucker in a bar-room brawl. We dug our way out while he was in hospital." She put her face down on the table and wept, but she held Jamil's hand against her cheek. He couldn't understand what she'd lived through, but that didn't mean he couldn't console her. Hadn't he touched his mother's face the same way, when she was sad beyond his childish comprehension?

She composed herself, and continued. "We made a resolution, while we were in there. If we survived, there'd be no more empty promises. No more day dreams. What he'd done to those seven women—and what he'd done to us—would become impossible."

And it had. Whatever harm befell your body, you had the power to shut off your senses and decline to experience it. If the flesh was damaged, it could always be repaired or replaced. In the unlikely event that your jewel itself was destroyed, everyone had backups, scattered across universes. No human being could inflict physical pain on another. In theory, you could still be killed, but it would take the same kind of resources as destroying a galaxy. The only people who seriously contemplated either were the villains in very bad operas.

Jamil's eyes narrowed in wonder. She'd spoken those last words with such fierce pride that there was no question of her having failed.

"*You* are Ndoli? You invented the jewel?" As a child, he'd been told that the machine in his skull had been designed by a man who'd died long ago.

Margit stroked his hand, amused. "In those days, very few Hungarian women could be mistaken for Nigerian men. I've never changed my body that much, Jamil. I've always looked much as you see me."

Jamil was relieved; if she'd been Ndoli himself, he might have succumbed to sheer awe and started babbling idolatrous nonsense. "But you worked with Ndoli? You and Grace?"

She shook her head. "We made the resolution, and then we floundered. We were mathematicians, not neurologists. There were a thousand things going on at once: tissue engineering, brain imaging, molecular computers. We had no real idea where to put our efforts, which problems we should bring our strengths to bear upon. Ndoli's work didn't come out of the blue for us, but we played no part in it.

"For a while, almost everyone was nervous about switching from the brain to the jewel. In the early days, the jewel was a separate device that learned its task by mimicking the brain, and it had to be handed control of the body at one chosen moment. It took another fifty years before it could be engineered to replace the brain incrementally, neuron by neuron, in a seamless transition throughout adolescence."

So Grace had lived to see the jewel invented, but held back, and died before she could use it? Jamil kept himself from blurting out this conclusion; all his guesses had proved wrong so far.

Margit continued. "Some people weren't just nervous, though. You'd be amazed how vehemently Ndoli was denounced in certain quarters. And I don't just mean the fanatics who churned out paranoid tracts about 'the machines' taking over, with their evil inhuman agendas. Some people's antagonism had nothing to do with the specifics of the technology. They were opposed to immortality, in principle."

Jamil laughed. "*Why?*"

"Ten thousand years' worth of sophistry doesn't vanish overnight," Margit observed dryly. "Every human culture had expended vast amounts of intellectual effort on the problem of coming to terms with death. Most religions had constructed elaborate lies about it, making it out to be something other than it was—though a few were dishonest about life, instead. But even most secular philosophies were warped by the need to pretend that *death was for the best*.

"It was the naturalistic fallacy at its most extreme—and its most transparent, but that didn't stop anyone. Since any child could tell you that death was meaningless, contingent, unjust, and abhorrent beyond words, it was a hallmark of sophistication to believe otherwise. Writers had consoled themselves for centuries with smug puritanical fables about immortals who'd long for death—who'd *beg* for death. It would have been too much to expect all those who were suddenly faced with the reality of its banishment to confess that they'd been whistling in the dark. And would-be moral philosophers—mostly those who'd experienced no greater inconvenience in their lives than a late train or a surly waiter—began wailing about the destruction of the human spirit by this hideous blight. We needed death and suffering, to put steel into our souls! Not horrible, horrible *freedom and safety*!"

Jamil smiled. "So there were buffoons. But in the end, surely they swallowed their pride? If we're walking in a desert and I tell you that the lake you see ahead is a mirage, I might cling stubbornly to my own belief, to save myself from disappointment. But when we arrive, and I'm proven wrong, I *will* drink from the lake."

Margit nodded. "Most of the loudest of these people went quiet in the end. But there were subtler arguments, too. Like it or not, all our biology and all of our culture *had* evolved in the presence of death. And almost every righteous struggle in history, every worthwhile sacrifice, had been against suffering, against violence, against death. Now, that struggle would become impossible."

"Yes." Jamil was mystified. "But only because it had triumphed."

Margit said gently, "I know. There was no sense to it. And it was always my belief that anything worth fighting for—over centuries, over millennia—was worth attaining. It *can't* be noble to toil for a cause, and even to die for it, unless it's also noble to succeed. To claim otherwise isn't sophistication, it's just a kind of hypocrisy. If it's better to travel than arrive, you shouldn't start the voyage in the first place.

"I told Grace as much, and she agreed. We laughed together at what we called the *tragedians:* the people who denounced the coming age as the age without martyrs, the age without saints, the age without revolutionaries. There would never be another Gandhi, another Mandela, another Aung San Suu Kyi—and yes, that *was* a kind of loss, but would any great leader have sentenced humanity to eternal misery, for the sake of providing a suitable backdrop for eternal heroism? Well, some of them would have. But the down-trodden themselves had better things to do."

Margit fell silent. Jamil cleared her plate away, then sat opposite her again. It was almost dawn.

"Of course, the jewel was not enough," Margit continued. "With care, Earth could support forty billion people, but where would the rest go? The jewel made virtual reality the easiest escape route: for a fraction of the space, a fraction of the energy, it could survive without a body attached. Grace and I weren't horrified by that prospect, the way some people were. But it was not the best outcome, it was not what most people wanted, the way they wanted freedom from death.

"So we studied gravity, we studied the vacuum."

Jamil feared making a fool of himself again, but from the expression on her face he knew he wasn't wrong this time. *M. Osvát and G. Füst*. Co-authors of the seminal paper, but no more was known about them than those abbreviated names. "You gave us the New Territories?"

Margit nodded slightly. "Grace and I."

Jamil was overwhelmed with love for her. He went to her and knelt down to put his arms around her waist. Margit touched his shoulder. "Come on, get up. Don't treat me like a god, it just makes me feel old."

He stood, smiling abashedly. Anyone in pain deserved his help—but if he was not in her debt, the word had no meaning.

"And Grace?" he asked.

Margit looked away. "Grace completed her work, and then decided that she was a tragedian, after all. Rape was impossible. Torture was impossible. Poverty was vanishing. Death was receding into cosmology, into metaphysics. It was everything she'd hoped would come to pass. And for her, suddenly faced with that fulfilment, everything that remained seemed trivial.

"One night, she climbed into the furnace in the basement of her building. Her jewel survived the flames, but she'd erased it from within."

IT WAS MORNING NOW. Jamil was beginning to feel disoriented; Margit should have vanished in daylight, an apparition unable to persist in the mundane world.

"I'd lost other people who were close to me," she said. "My parents. My brother. Friends. And so had everyone around me, then. I wasn't special: grief was still commonplace. But decade by decade, century by century, we shrank into insignificance, those of us who knew what it meant to lose someone for ever. We're less than one in a million, now.

"For a long time, I clung to my own generation. There were enclaves, there were ghettos, where everyone understood the old days. I spent two hundred years married to a man who wrote a play called *We Who Have Known the Dead*—which was every bit as pretentious and self-pitying as you'd guess from the title." She smiled at the memory. "It was a horrible, self-devouring world. If I'd stayed in it much longer, I would have followed Grace. I would have begged for death."

She looked up at Jamil. "It's people like you I want to be with: *people who don't understand*. Your lives aren't trivial, any more than the best parts of our own were: all the tranquillity, all the beauty, all the happiness that made the sacrifices and the life-and-death struggles worthwhile.

"The tragedians were wrong. They had everything upside-down. Death never gave meaning to life: it was always the other way round. All of its gravitas, all of its significance, was stolen from the things it ended. But the value of life always lay entirely in itself—not in its loss, not in its fragility.

"Grace should have lived to see that. She should have lived long enough to understand that the world hadn't turned to ash."

Jamil sat in silence, turning the whole confession over in his mind, trying to absorb it well enough not to add to her distress with a misjudged question. Finally, he ventured, "Why do you hold back from friendship with us, though? Because we're just children to you? Children who can't understand what you've lost?"

Margit shook her head vehemently. "I don't *want you* to understand! People like me are the only blight on this world, the only poison." She smiled at Jamil's expression of anguish, and rushed to silence him before he could swear that she was nothing of the kind. "Not in everything we do and say, or everyone we touch: I'm not claiming that we're tainted, in some fatuous mythological sense. But when I left the ghettos, I promised myself that I wouldn't bring the past with me. Sometimes that's an easy vow to keep. Sometimes it's not."

"You've broken it tonight," Jamil said plainly. "And neither of us have been struck down by lightning."

"I know." She took his hand. "But I was wrong to tell you what I have, and I'll fight to regain the strength to stay silent. I stand at the border between two worlds, Jamil. I remember death, and I always will. But my job now is to guard that border. To keep that knowledge from invading your world."

"We're not as fragile as you think," he protested. "We all know something about loss."

Margit nodded soberly. "Your friend Chusok has vanished into the crowd. That's how things work now: how you keep yourselves from suffocating in a jungle of endlessly growing connections, or fragmenting into isolated troupes of repertory players, endlessly churning out the same lines.

"You have your little deaths—and I don't call them that to deride you. But I've seen both. And I promise you, they're not the same."

IN THE WEEKS that followed, Jamil resumed in full the life he'd made for himself in Noether. Five days in seven were for the difficult beauty of mathematics. The rest were for his friends.

He kept playing matches, and Margit's team kept winning. In the sixth game, though, Jamil's team finally scored against her. Their defeat was only three to one.

Each night, Jamil struggled with the question. What exactly did he owe her? Eternal loyalty, eternal silence, eternal obedience? She hadn't sworn him to secrecy; she'd extracted no promises at all. But he knew she was trusting him to comply with her wishes, so what right did he have to do otherwise?

Eight weeks after the night he'd spent with Margit, Jamil found himself alone with Penina in a room in Joracy's house. They'd been talking about the old days. Talking about Chusok.

Jamil said, "Margit lost someone, very close to her."

Penina nodded matter-of-factly, but curled into a comfortable position on the couch and prepared to take in every word.

"Not in the way we've lost Chusok. Not in the way you think at all."

Jamil approached the others, one by one. His confidence ebbed and flowed. He'd glimpsed the old world, but he couldn't pretend to have fathomed its inhabitants. What if Margit saw this as worse than betrayal—as a further torture, a further rape?

But he couldn't stand by and leave her to the torture she'd inflicted on herself.

Ezequiel was the hardest to face. Jamil spent a sick and sleepless night beforehand, wondering if this would make him a monster, a corrupter of children, the epitome of everything Margit believed she was fighting.

Ezequiel wept freely, but he was not a child. He was older than Jamil, and he had more steel in his soul than any of them.

He said, "I guessed it might be that. I guessed she might have seen the bad times. But I never found a way to ask her."

THE THREE LOBES OF PROBABILITY converged, melted into a plateau, rose into a pillar of light.

The umpire said, "Fifty-five point nine." It was Margit's most impressive goal yet.

Ezequiel whooped joyfully and ran towards her. When he scooped her up in his arms and threw her across his shoulders, she laughed and indulged him. When Jamil stood beside him and they made a joint throne for her with their arms, she frowned down at him and said, "You shouldn't be doing this. You're on the losing side."

The rest of the players converged on them, cheering, and they started down towards the river. Margit looked around nervously. "What is this? We haven't finished playing."

Penina said, "The game's over early, just this once. Think of this as an invitation. We want you to swim with us. We want you to talk to us. We want to hear everything about your life."

Margit's composure began to crack. She squeezed Jamil's shoulder. He whispered, "Say the word, and we'll put you down."

Margit didn't whisper back; she shouted miserably, "What do you want from me, you parasites? I've won your fucking game for you! What more do you want?"

Jamil was mortified. He stopped and prepared to lower her, prepared to retreat, but Ezequiel caught his arm.

Ezequiel said, "We want to be your border guards. We want to stand beside you."

Christa added, "We can't face what you've faced, but we want to understand. As much as we can."

Joracy spoke, then Yann, Narcyza, Maria, Halide. Margit looked down on them, weeping, confused.

Jamil burnt with shame. He'd hijacked her, humiliated her. He'd made everything worse. She'd flee Noether, flee into a new exile, more alone than ever.

When everyone had spoken, silence descended. Margit trembled on her throne.

Jamil faced the ground. He couldn't undo what he'd done. He said quietly, "Now you know our wishes. Will you tell us yours?"

"Put me down."

Jamil and Ezequiel complied.

Margit looked around at her teammates and opponents, her children, her creation, her would-be friends.

She said, "I want to go to the river with you. I'm seven thousand years old, and I want to learn to swim."

HELL IS THE ABSENCE OF GOD

TED CHIANG

TED CHIANG was born in Port Jefferson, New York, and graduated from Brown University in Providence, Rhode Island, with a degree in computer science. He attended Clarion the same year and took a job in Seattle as a technical writer in the computer industry. Although he's published just eight stories in twelve years, Chiang has won an impressive number of honors: the John W. Campbell New Writer Award in 1992, a Nebula Award for "Tower of Babylon" (1990), another Nebula and the Theodore Sturgeon Memorial Award for "Story of Your Life" (1998), a Sidewise Award for "Seventy-Two Letters" (2000), and the Locus and Hugo Awards for "Hell Is the Absence of God" (2001). His entire body of short fiction has been collected in the Locus Award–winning collection *Stories of Your Life and Others*. He lives in Bellevue, Washington.

* * *

THIS IS THE STORY of a man named Neil Fisk, and how he came to love God. The pivotal event in Neil's life was an occurrence both terrible and ordinary: the death of his wife Sarah. Neil was consumed with grief after she died, a grief that was excruciating not only because of its intrinsic magnitude, but because it also renewed and emphasized the previous pains of his life. Her death forced him to reexamine his relationship with God, and in doing so he began a journey that would change him forever.

Neil was born with a congenital abnormality that caused his left thigh to be externally rotated and several inches shorter than his right; the medical term for it was proximal femoral focus deficiency. Most people he met assumed God was responsible for this, but Neil's mother hadn't witnessed any visitations while carrying him; his condition was the result of improper limb development during the sixth week of gestation, nothing more. In fact, as far as Neil's mother was concerned, blame rested with his absent father, whose income might have made corrective surgery a possibility, although she never expressed this sentiment aloud.

As a child Neil had occasionally wondered if he was being punished by God, but most of the time he blamed his classmates in school for his unhappiness. Their nonchalant cruelty, their instinctive ability to locate the weaknesses in a victim's emotional armor, the way their own friendships were reinforced by their sadism: he recognized these as examples of human behavior, not divine. And although his classmates often used God's name in their taunts, Neil knew better than to blame Him for their actions.

But while Neil avoided the pitfall of blaming God, he never made the jump to loving Him; nothing in his upbringing or his personality led him to pray to God for strength or for relief. The assorted trials he faced growing up were accidental or human in origin, and he relied on strictly human resources to counter them. He became an adult who—like so many others—viewed God's actions in the abstract until they impinged upon his own life. Angelic visitations were events that befell other people, reaching him only via reports on the nightly news. His own life was entirely mundane; he worked as a superintendent for an upscale apartment building, collecting rent and performing repairs, and as far as he was concerned, circumstances were fully capable of unfolding, happily or not, without intervention from above.

This remained his experience until the death of his wife.

It was an unexceptional visitation, smaller in magnitude than most but no different in kind, bringing blessings to some and disaster to others. In this instance the angel was Nathanael, making an appearance in a downtown shopping district. Four miracle cures were effected: the elimination of carcinomas in two individuals, the regeneration of the spinal cord in a paraplegic, and the restoration of sight to a recently blinded person. There were also two miracles that were not cures: a delivery van, whose driver had fainted at the sight of the angel, was halted before it could overrun a busy sidewalk; another man was caught in a shaft of Heaven's light when the angel departed, erasing his eyes but ensuring his devotion.

Neil's wife Sarah Fisk had been one of the eight casualties. She was hit by flying glass when the angel's billowing curtain of flame shattered the storefront window of the café in which she was eating. She bled to death within minutes, and the other customers in the café—none of whom suffered even superficial injuries—could do nothing but listen to her cries of pain and fear, and eventually witness her soul's ascension toward Heaven.

Nathanael hadn't delivered any specific message; the angel's parting words, which had boomed out across the entire visitation site, were the typical *Behold the power of the Lord.* Of the eight casualties that day, three souls were accepted into Heaven and five were not, a closer ratio than the average for deaths by all causes. Sixty-two people received medical treatment for injuries ranging from slight concussions to ruptured eardrums to burns requiring skin grafts. Total property damage was estimated at $8.1 million, all of it excluded by private insurance companies due to the cause. Scores of people became devout worshipers in the wake of the visitation, either out of gratitude or terror.

Alas, Neil Fisk was not one of them.

AFTER A VISITATION, it's common for all the witnesses to meet as a group and discuss how their common experience has affected their lives. The witnesses of Nathanael's latest visitation arranged such group meetings, and family members of those who had died were welcome, so Neil began attending. The meetings were held once a month in a basement room of a large church downtown; there were metal folding chairs arranged in rows, and in the back of the room was a table holding coffee and doughnuts. Everyone wore adhesive name tags made out in felt-tip pen.

While waiting for the meetings to start, people would stand around, drinking coffee, talking casually. Most people Neil spoke to assumed his leg was a result of the visitation, and he had to explain that he wasn't a witness, but rather the husband of one of the casualties. This didn't bother him particularly; he was used to explaining about his leg. What did bother him was the tone of the meetings themselves, when participants spoke about their reaction to the visitation: most of them talked about their newfound devotion to God, and they tried to persuade the bereaved that they should feel the same.

Neil's reaction to such attempts at persuasion depended on who was making it. When it was an ordinary witness, he found it merely irritating. When someone who'd received a miracle cure told him to love God, he had to restrain an impulse to strangle the person. But what he found most disquieting of all was hearing the same suggestion from a man named Tony Crane; Tony's wife had died in the visitation too, and he now projected an air of groveling with his every movement. In hushed, tearful tones he explained how he had accepted his role as one of God's subjects, and he advised Neil to do likewise.

Neil didn't stop attending the meetings—he felt that he somehow owed it to Sarah to stick with them—but he found another group to go to as well, one more compatible with his own feelings: a support group devoted to those who'd lost a loved one during a visitation, and were angry at God because of it. They met every other week in a room at the local community center, and talked about the grief and rage that boiled inside of them.

All the attendees were generally sympathetic to one another, despite differences in their various attitudes toward God. Of those who'd been devout before their loss, some struggled with the task of remaining so, while others gave up their devotion without a second glance. Of those who'd never been devout, some felt their position had been validated, while others were faced with the near impossible task of becoming devout now. Neil found himself, to his consternation, in this last category.

Like every other nondevout person, Neil had never expended much energy on where his soul would end up; he'd always assumed his destination was Hell, and he accepted that. That was the way of things, and Hell, after all, was not physically worse than the mortal plane.

It meant permanent exile from God, no more and no less; the truth of this was plain for anyone to see on those occasions when Hell manifested itself. These happened on a regular basis; the ground seemed to become transparent, and you could see Hell as if you were looking through a hole in the floor. The lost souls looked no different than the living, their eternal bodies resembling mortal ones. You couldn't communicate with them—their exile from God meant that they couldn't apprehend the mortal plane where His actions were still felt—but as long as the manifestation lasted you could hear them talk, laugh, or cry, just as they had when they were alive.

People varied widely in their reactions to these manifestations. Most devout people were galvanized, not by the sight of anything frightening, but at being reminded that eternity outside paradise was a possibility. Neil, by contrast, was one of those who were unmoved; as far as he could tell, the lost souls as a group were no unhappier than he was, their existence no worse than his in the mortal plane, and in some ways better: his eternal body would be unhampered by congenital abnormalities.

Of course, everyone knew that Heaven was incomparably superior, but to Neil it had always seemed too remote to consider, like wealth or fame or glamour. For people like him, Hell was where you went when you died, and he saw no point in restructuring his life in hopes of avoiding that. And since God hadn't previously played a role in Neil's life, he wasn't afraid of being exiled from God. The prospect of living without interference, living in a world where windfalls and misfortunes were never by design, held no terror for him.

Now that Sarah was in Heaven, his situation had changed. Neil wanted more than anything to be reunited with her, and the only way to get to Heaven was to love God with all his heart.

THIS IS NEIL'S STORY, but telling it properly requires telling the stories of two other individuals whose paths became entwined with his. The first of these is Janice Reilly.

What people assumed about Neil had in fact happened to Janice. When Janice's mother was eight months pregnant with her, she lost control of the car she was driving and collided with a telephone pole during a sudden hailstorm, fists of ice dropping out of a clear blue sky and littering the road like a spill of giant ball bearings. She was sitting in her car, shaken but unhurt, when she saw a knot of silver flames—later identified as the angel Bardiel—float across the sky. The sight petrified her, but not so much that she didn't notice the peculiar settling sensation in her womb. A subsequent ultrasound revealed that the unborn Janice Reilly no longer had legs; flipperlike feet grew directly from her hip sockets.

Janice's life might have gone the way of Neil's, if not for what happened two days after the ultrasound. Janice's parents were sitting at their kitchen table, crying and asking what they had done to deserve this, when they received a vision: the saved souls of four deceased relatives appeared before them, suffusing the kitchen with a golden glow. The saved never spoke, but their beatific smiles induced a feeling of serenity in whoever saw them. From that moment on, the Reillys were certain that their daughter's condition was not a punishment.

As a result, Janice grew up thinking of her legless condition as a gift; her parents explained that God had given her a special assignment because He considered her equal to the task, and she vowed that she would not let Him down. Without pride or defiance, she saw it as her responsibility to show others that her condition did not indicate weakness, but rather strength.

As a child, she was fully accepted by her schoolmates; when you're as pretty, confident, and charismatic as she was, children don't even notice that you're in a wheelchair. It was when she was a teenager that she realized that the able-bodied people in her school were not the ones who most needed convincing. It was more important for her to set an example for other handicapped individuals, whether they had been touched by God or not, no matter where they lived. Janice began speaking before audiences, telling those with disabilities that they had the strength God required of them.

Over time she developed a reputation, and a following. She made a living writing and speaking, and established a nonprofit organization dedicated to promoting her message. People sent her letters thanking her for changing their lives, and receiving those gave her a sense of fulfillment of a sort that Neil had never experienced.

This was Janice's life up until she herself witnessed a visitation by the angel Rashiel. She was letting herself into her house when the tremors began; at first she thought they were of natural origin, although she didn't live in a geologically active area, and waited in the doorway for them to subside. Several seconds later she caught a glimpse of silver in the sky and realized it was an angel, just before she lost consciousness.

Janice awoke to the biggest surprise of her life: the sight of her two new legs, long, muscular, and fully functional.

She was startled the first time she stood up: she was taller than she expected. Balancing at such a height without the use of her arms was unnerving, and simultaneously feeling the texture of the ground through the soles of her feet made it positively bizarre. Rescue workers, finding her wandering down the street dazedly, thought she was in shock until she—marveling at her ability to face them at eye level—explained to them what had happened.

When statistics were gathered for the visitation, the restoration of Janice's legs was recorded as a blessing, and she was humbly grateful for her good fortune. It was at the first of the support group meetings that a feeling of guilt began to creep in. There Janice met two individuals with cancer who'd witnessed Rashiel's visitation, thought their cure was at hand, and been bitterly disappointed when they realized they'd been passed over. Janice found herself wondering, why had she received a blessing when they had not?

Janice's family and friends considered the restoration of her legs a reward for excelling at the task God had set for her, but for Janice, this interpretation raised another question. Did He intend for her to stop? Surely not; evangelism provided the central direction of her life, and there was no limit to the number of people who needed to hear her message. Her continuing to preach was the best action she could take, both for herself and for others.

Her reservations grew during her first speaking engagement after the visitation, before an audience of people recently paralyzed and now wheelchairbound. Janice delivered her usual words of inspiration, assuring them that they had the strength needed for the challenges ahead; it was during the Q&A that she was asked if the restoration of her legs meant she had passed her test. Janice didn't know what to say; she could hardly promise them that one day their marks would be erased. In fact, she realized, any implication that she'd been rewarded could be interpreted as criticism of others who remained afflicted, and she didn't want that. All she could tell them was that she didn't know why she'd been cured, but it was obvious they found that an unsatisfying answer.

Janice returned home disquieted. She still believed in her message, but as far as her audiences were concerned, she'd lost her greatest source of credibility. How could she inspire others who were touched by God to see their condition as a badge of strength, when she no longer shared their condition?

She considered whether this might be a challenge, a test of her ability to spread His word. Clearly God had made her task more difficult than it was before; perhaps the restoration of her legs was an obstacle for her to overcome, just as their earlier removal had been.

This interpretation failed her at her next scheduled engagement. The audience was a group of witnesses to a visitation by Nathanael; she was often invited to speak to such groups in the hopes that those who suffered might draw encouragement from her. Rather than sidestep the issue, she began with an account of the visitation she herself had recently experienced. She explained that while it might appear she was a beneficiary, she was in fact facing her own challenge: like them, she was being forced to draw on resources previously untapped.

She realized, too late, that she had said the wrong thing. A man in the audience with a misshapen leg stood up and challenged her: was she seriously suggesting that the restoration of her legs was comparable to the loss of his wife? Could she really be equating her trials with his own?

Janice immediately assured him that she wasn't, and that she couldn't imagine the pain he was experiencing. But, she said, it wasn't God's intention that everyone be subjected to the same kind of trial, but only that each person face his or her own trial, whatever it might be. The difficulty of any trial was subjective, and there was no way to compare two individuals' experiences. And just as those whose suffering seemed greater than his should have compassion for him, so should he have compassion for those whose suffering seemed less.

The man was having none of it. She had received what anyone else would have considered a fantastic blessing, and she was complaining about it. He stormed out of the meeting while Janice was still trying to explain.

That man, of course, was Neil Fisk. Neil had had Janice Reilly's name mentioned to him for much of his life, most often by people who were convinced his misshapen leg was a sign from God. These people cited her as an example he should follow, telling him that her attitude was the proper response to a physical handicap. Neil couldn't deny that her leglessness was a far worse condition than his distorted femur. Unfortunately, he found her attitude so foreign that, even in the best of times, he'd never been able to learn anything from her. Now, in the depths of his grief and mystified as to why she had received a gift she didn't need, Neil found her words offensive.

In the days that followed, Janice found herself more and more plagued by doubts, unable to decide what the restoration of her legs meant. Was she being ungrateful for a gift she'd received? Was it both a blessing and a test? Perhaps it was a punishment, an indication that she had not performed her duty well enough. There were many possibilities, and she didn't know which one to believe.

THERE IS ONE OTHER PERSON who played an important role in Neil's story, even though he and Neil did not meet until Neil's journey was nearly over. That person's name is Ethan Mead.

Ethan had been raised in a family that was devout, but not profoundly so. His parents credited God with their above-average health and their comfortable economic status, although they hadn't witnessed any visitations or received any visions; they simply trusted that God was, directly or indirectly, responsible for their good fortune. Their devotion had never been put to any serious test, and might not have withstood one; their love for God was based in their satisfaction with the status quo.

Ethan was not like his parents, though. Ever since childhood he'd felt certain that God had a special role for him to play, and he waited for a sign telling him what that role was. He'd have liked to have become a preacher, but felt he hadn't any compelling testimony to offer; his vague feelings of expectation weren't enough. He longed for an encounter with the divine to provide him with direction.

He could have gone to one of the holy sites, those places where—for reasons unknown—angelic visitations occurred on a regular basis, but he felt that such an action would be presumptuous of him. The holy sites were usually the last resort of the desperate, those people seeking either a miracle cure to repair their bodies or a glimpse of Heaven's light to repair their souls, and Ethan was not desperate. He decided that he'd been set along his own course, and in time the reason for it would become clear. While waiting for that day, he lived his life as best he could: he worked as a librarian, married a woman named Claire, raised two children. All the while, he remained watchful for signs of a greater destiny.

Ethan was certain his time had come when he became witness to a visitation by Rashiel, the same visitation that—miles away—restored Janice Reilly's legs. Ethan was by himself when it happened; he was walking toward his car in the center of a parking lot, when the ground began to shudder. Instinctively he knew it was a visitation, and he assumed a kneeling position, feeling no fear, only exhilaration and awe at the prospect of learning his calling.

The ground became still after a minute, and Ethan looked around, but didn't otherwise move. Only after waiting for several more minutes did he rise to his feet. There was a large crack in the asphalt, beginning directly in front of him and following a meandering path down the street. The crack seemed to be pointing him in a specific direction, so he ran alongside it for several blocks until he encountered other survivors, a man and a woman climbing out of a modest fissure that had opened up directly beneath them. He waited with the two of them until rescuers arrived and brought them to a shelter.

Ethan attended the support group meetings that followed and met the other witnesses to Rashiel's visitation. Over the course of a few meetings, he became aware of certain patterns among the witnesses. Of course there were those who'd been injured and those who'd received miracle cures. But there were also those whose lives were changed in other ways: the man and woman he'd first met fell in love and were soon engaged; a woman who'd been pinned beneath a collapsed wall was inspired to become an EMT after being rescued. One business owner formed an alliance that averted her impending bankruptcy, while another whose business was destroyed saw it as a message that he change his ways. It seemed that everyone except Ethan had found a way to understand what had happened to them.

He hadn't been cursed or blessed in any obvious way, and he didn't know what message he was intended to receive. His wife Claire suggested that he consider the visitation a reminder that he appreciate what he had, but Ethan found that unsatisfying, reasoning that *every* visitation—no matter where it occurred—served that function, and the fact that he'd witnessed a visitation firsthand had to have greater significance. His mind was preyed upon by the idea that he'd missed an opportunity, that there was a fellow witness whom he was intended to meet but hadn't. This visitation had to be the sign he'd been waiting for; he couldn't just disregard it. But that didn't tell him what he was supposed to do.

Ethan eventually resorted to the process of elimination: he got hold of a list of all the witnesses, and crossed off those who had a clear interpretation of their experience, reasoning that one of those remaining must be the person whose fate was somehow intertwined with his. Among those who were confused or uncertain about the visitation's meaning would be the one he was intended to meet.

When he had finished crossing names off his list, there was only one left: JANICE REILLY.

IN PUBLIC NEIL WAS ABLE to mask his grief as adults are expected to, but in the privacy of his apartment, the floodgates of emotion burst open. The awareness of Sarah's absence would overwhelm him, and then he'd collapse on the floor and weep. He'd curl up into a ball, his body racked by hiccuping sobs, tears and mucus streaming down his face, the anguish coming in ever-increasing waves until it was more than he could bear, more intense than he'd have believed possible. Minutes or hours later it would leave, and he would fall asleep, exhausted. And the next morning he would wake up and face the prospect of another day without Sarah.

An elderly woman in Neil's apartment building tried to comfort him by telling him that the pain would lessen in time, and while he would never forget his wife, he would at least be able to move on. Then he would meet someone else one day and find happiness with her, and he would learn to love God and thus ascend to Heaven when his time came.

This woman's intentions were good, but Neil was in no position to find any comfort in her words. Sarah's absence felt like an open wound, and the prospect that someday he would no longer feel pain at her loss seemed not just remote, but a physical impossibility. If suicide would have ended his pain, he'd have done it without hesitation, but that would only ensure that his separation from Sarah was permanent.

The topic of suicide regularly came up at the support group meetings, and inevitably led to someone mentioning Robin Pearson, a woman who used to come to the meetings several months before Neil began attending. Robin's husband had been afflicted with stomach cancer during a visitation by the angel Makatiel. She stayed in his hospital room for days at a stretch, only for him to die unexpectedly when she was home doing laundry. A nurse who'd been present told Robin that his soul had ascended, and so Robin had begun attending the support group meetings.

Many months later, Robin came to the meeting shaking with rage. There'd been a manifestation of Hell near her house, and she'd seen her husband among the lost souls. She'd confronted the nurse, who admitted to lying in the hopes that Robin would learn to love God, so that at least she would be saved even if her husband hadn't been. Robin wasn't at the next meeting, and at the meeting after that the group learned she had committed suicide to rejoin her husband.

None of them knew the status of Robin's and her husband's relationship in the afterlife, but successes were known to happen; some couples had indeed been happily reunited through suicide. The support group had attendees whose spouses had descended to Hell, and they talked about being torn between wanting to remain alive and wanting to rejoin their spouses. Neil wasn't in their situation, but his first response when listening to them had been envy: if Sarah had gone to Hell, suicide would be the solution to all his problems.

This led to a shameful self-knowledge for Neil. He realized that if he had to choose between going to Hell while Sarah went to Heaven, or having both of them go to Hell together, he would choose the latter: he would rather she be exiled from God than separated from him. He knew it was selfish, but he couldn't change how he felt: he believed Sarah could be happy in either place, but he could only be happy with her.

Neil's previous experiences with women had never been good. All too often he'd begin flirting with a woman while sitting at a bar, only to have her remember an appointment elsewhere the moment he stood up and his shortened leg came into view. Once, a woman he'd been dating for several weeks broke off their relationship, explaining that while she herself didn't consider his leg a defect, whenever they were seen in public together other people assumed there must be something wrong with her for being with him, and surely he could understand how unfair that was to her?

Sarah had been the first woman Neil met whose demeanor hadn't changed one bit, whose expression hadn't flickered toward pity or horror or even surprise when she first saw his leg. For that reason alone it was predictable that Neil would become infatuated with her; by the time he saw all the sides of her personality, he'd completely fallen in love with her. And because his best qualities came out when he was with her, she fell in love with him too.

Neil had been surprised when Sarah told him she was devout. There weren't many signs of her devotion—she didn't go to church, sharing Neil's dislike for the attitudes of most people who attended—but in her own, quiet way she was grateful to God for her life. She never tried to convert Neil, saying that devotion would come from within or not at all. They rarely had any cause to mention God, and most of the time it would've been easy for Neil to imagine that Sarah's views on God matched his own.

This is not to say that Sarah's devotion had no effect on Neil. On the contrary, Sarah was far and away the best argument for loving God that he had ever encountered. If love of God had contributed to making her the person she was, then perhaps it did make sense. During the years that the two of them were married, his outlook on life improved, and it probably would have reached the point where he was thankful to God, if he and Sarah had grown old together.

Sarah's death removed that particular possibility, but it needn't have closed the door on Neil's loving God. Neil could have taken it as a reminder that no one can count on having decades left. He could have been moved by the realization that, had he died with her, his soul would've been lost and the two of them separated for eternity. He could have seen Sarah's death as a wake-up call, telling him to love God while he still had the chance.

Instead Neil became actively resentful of God. Sarah had been the greatest blessing of his life, and God had taken her away. Now he was expected to love Him for it? For Neil, it was like having a kidnapper demand love as ransom for his wife's return. Obedience he might have managed, but sincere, heartfelt love? That was a ransom he couldn't pay.

This paradox confronted several people in the support group. One of the attendees, a man named Phil Soames, correctly pointed out that thinking of it as a condition to be met would guarantee failure. You couldn't love God as a means to an end, you had to love Him for Himself. If your ultimate goal in loving God was a reunion with your spouse, you weren't demonstrating true devotion at all.

A woman in the support group named Valerie Tommasino said they shouldn't even try. She'd been reading a book published by the humanist movement; its members considered it wrong to love a God who inflicted such pain, and advocated that people act according to their own moral sense instead of being guided by the carrot and the stick. These were people who, when they died, descended to Hell in proud defiance of God.

Neil himself had read a pamphlet of the humanist movement; what he most remembered was that it had quoted the fallen angels. Visitations of fallen angels were infrequent, and caused neither good fortune nor bad; they weren't acting under God's direction, but just passing through the mortal plane as they went about their unimaginable business. On the occasions they appeared, people would ask them questions: Did they know God's intentions? Why had they rebelled? The fallen angels' reply was always the same: *Decide for yourselves. That is what we did. We advise you to do the same.*

Those in the humanist movement had decided, and if it weren't for Sarah, Neil would've made the identical choice. But he wanted her back, and the only way was to find a reason to love God.

Looking for any footing on which to build their devotion, some attendees of the support group took comfort in the fact that their loved ones hadn't suffered when God took them, but instead died instantly. Neil didn't even have that; Sarah had received horrific lacerations when the glass hit her. Of course, it could have been worse. One couple's teenage son had been trapped in a fire ignited by an angel's visitation, and received full-thickness burns over eighty percent of his body before rescue workers could free him; his eventual death was a mercy. Sarah had been fortunate by comparison, but not enough to make Neil love God.

Neil could think of only one thing that would make him give thanks to God, and that was if He allowed Sarah to appear before him. It would give him immeasurable comfort just to see her smile again; he'd never been visited by a saved soul before, and a vision now would have meant more to him than at any other point in his life.

But visions don't appear just because a person needs one, and none ever came to Neil. He had to find his own way toward God.

The next time he attended the support group meeting for witnesses of Nathanael's visitation, Neil sought out Benny Vasquez, the man whose eyes had been erased by Heaven's light. Benny didn't always attend because he was now being invited to speak at other meetings; few visitations resulted in an eyeless person, since Heaven's light entered the mortal plane only in the brief moments that an angel emerged from or reentered Heaven, so the eyeless were minor celebrities, and in demand as speakers to church groups.

Benny was now as sightless as any burrowing worm: not only were his eyes and sockets missing, his skull lacked even the space for such features, the cheekbones now abutting the forehead. The light that had brought his soul as close to perfection as was possible in the mortal plane had also deformed his body; it was commonly held that this illustrated the superfluity of physical bodies in Heaven. With the limited expressive capacity his face retained, Benny always wore a blissful, rapturous smile.

Neil hoped Benny could say something to help him love God. Benny described Heaven's light as infinitely beautiful, a sight of such compelling majesty that it vanquished all doubts. It constituted incontrovertible proof that God should be loved, an explanation that made it as obvious as $1+1=2$. Unfortunately, while Benny could offer many analogies for the effect of Heaven's light, he couldn't duplicate that effect with his own words. Those who were already devout found Benny's descriptions thrilling, but to Neil, they seemed frustratingly vague. So he looked elsewhere for counsel.

Accept the mystery, said the minister of the local church. If you can love God even though your questions go unanswered, you'll be the better for it.

Admit that you need Him, said the popular book of spiritual advice he bought. When you realize that self-sufficiency is an illusion, you'll be ready.

Submit yourself completely and utterly, said the preacher on the television. Receiving torment is how you prove your love. Acceptance may not bring you relief in this life, but resistance will only worsen your punishment.

All of these strategies have proven successful for different individuals; any one of them, once internalized, can bring a person to devotion. But these are not always easy to adopt, and Neil was one who found them impossible.

Neil finally tried talking to Sarah's parents, which was an indication of how desperate he was: his relationship with them had always been tense. While they loved Sarah, they often chided her for not being demonstrative enough in her devotion, and they'd been shocked when she married a man who wasn't devout at all. For her part, Sarah had always considered her parents too judgmental, and their disapproval of Neil only reinforced her opinion. But now Neil felt he had something in common with them—after all, they were all mourning Sarah's loss—and so he visited them in their suburban colonial, hoping they could help him in his grief.

How wrong he was. Instead of sympathy, what Neil got from Sarah's parents was blame for her death. They'd come to this conclusion in the weeks after Sarah's funeral; they reasoned that she'd been taken to send him a message, and that they were forced to endure her loss solely because he hadn't been devout. They were now convinced that, his previous explanations notwithstanding, Neil's deformed leg was in fact God's doing, and if only he'd been properly chastened by it, Sarah might still be alive.

Their reaction shouldn't have come as a surprise: throughout Neil's life, people had attributed moral significance to his leg even though God wasn't responsible for it. Now that he'd suffered a misfortune for which God was unambiguously responsible, it was inevitable that someone would assume he deserved it. It was purely by chance that Neil heard this sentiment when he was at his most vulnerable, and it could have the greatest impact on him.

Neil didn't think his in-laws were right, but he began to wonder if he might not be better off if he did. Perhaps, he thought, it'd be better to live in a story where the righteous were rewarded and the sinners were punished, even if the criteria for righteousness and sinfulness eluded him, than to live in a reality where there was no justice at all. It would mean casting himself in the role of sinner, so it was hardly a comforting lie, but it offered one reward that his own ethics couldn't: believing it would reunite him with Sarah.

Sometimes even bad advice can point a man in the right direction. It was in this manner that his in-laws' accusations ultimately pushed Neil closer to God.

MORE THAN ONCE when she was evangelizing, Janice had been asked if she ever wished she had legs, and she had always answered—honestly—no, she didn't. She was content as she was. Sometimes her questioner would point out that she couldn't miss what she'd never known, and she might feel differently if she'd been born with legs and lost them later on. Janice never denied that. But she could truthfully say that she felt no sense of being incomplete, no envy for people with legs; being legless was part of her identity. She'd never bothered with prosthetics, and had a surgical procedure been available to provide her with legs, she'd have turned it down. She had never considered the possibility that God might restore her legs.

One of the unexpected side effects of having legs was the increased attention she received from men. In the past she'd mostly attracted men with amputee fetishes or sainthood complexes; now all sorts of men seemed drawn to her. So when she first noticed Ethan Mead's interest in her, she thought it was romantic in nature; this possibility was particularly distressing since he was obviously married.

Ethan had begun talking to Janice at the support group meetings, and then began attending her public speaking engagements. It was when he suggested they have lunch together that Janice asked him about his intentions, and he explained his theory. He didn't know *how* his fate was intertwined with hers; he knew only that it was. She was skeptical, but she didn't reject his theory outright. Ethan admitted that he didn't have answers for her own questions, but he was eager to do anything he could to help her find them. Janice cautiously agreed to help him in his search for meaning, and Ethan promised that he wouldn't be a burden. They met on a regular basis and talked about the significance of visitations.

Meanwhile Ethan's wife Claire grew worried. Ethan assured her that he had no romantic feelings toward Janice, but that didn't alleviate her concerns. She knew that extreme circumstances could create a bond between individuals, and she feared that Ethan's relationship with Janice—romantic or not—would threaten their marriage.

Ethan suggested to Janice that he, as a librarian, could help her do some research. Neither of them had ever heard of a previous instance where God had left His mark on a person in one visitation and removed it in another. Ethan looked for previous examples in hopes that they might shed some light on Janice's situation. There were a few instances of individuals receiving multiple miracle cures over their lifetimes, but their illnesses or disabilities had always been of natural origin, not given to them in a visitation. There was one anecdotal report of a man being struck blind for his sins, changing his ways, and later having his sight restored, but it was classified as an urban legend.

Even if that account had a basis in truth, it didn't provide a useful precedent for Janice's situation: her legs had been removed before her birth, and so couldn't have been a punishment for anything she'd done. Was it possible that Janice's condition had been a punishment for something her mother or father had done? Could her restoration mean they had finally earned her cure? She couldn't believe that.

If her deceased relatives were to appear in a vision, Janice would've been reassured about the restoration of her legs. The fact that they didn't made her suspect something was amiss, but she didn't believe that it was a punishment. Perhaps it had been a mistake, and she'd received a miracle meant for someone else; perhaps it was a test, to see how she would respond to being given too much. In either case, there seemed only one course of action: she would, with utmost gratitude and humility, offer to return her gift. To do so, she would go on a pilgrimage.

Pilgrims traveled great distances to visit the holy sites and wait for a visitation, hoping for a miracle cure. Whereas in most of the world one could wait an entire lifetime and never experience a visitation, at a holy site one might only wait months, sometimes weeks. Pilgrims knew that the odds of being cured were still poor; of those who stayed long enough to witness a visitation, the majority did not receive a cure. But they were often happy just to have seen an angel, and they returned home better able to face what awaited them, whether it be imminent death or life with a crippling disability. And of course, just living through a visitation made many people appreciate their situations; invariably, a small number of pilgrims were killed during each visitation.

Janice was willing to accept the outcome whatever it was. If God saw fit to take her, she was ready. If God removed her legs again, she would resume the work she'd always done. If God let her legs remain, she hoped she would receive the epiphany she needed to speak with conviction about her gift.

She hoped, however, that her miracle would be taken back and given to someone who truly needed it. She didn't suggest to anyone that they accompany her in hopes of receiving the miracle she was returning, feeling that that would've been presumptuous, but she privately considered her pilgrimage a request on behalf of those who were in need.

Her friends and family were confused at Janice's decision, seeing it as questioning God. As word spread, she received many letters from followers, variously expressing dismay, bafflement, and admiration for her willingness to make such a sacrifice.

As for Ethan, he was completely supportive of Janice's decision, and excited for himself. He now understood the significance of Rashiel's visitation for him: it indicated that the time had come for him to act. His wife Claire strenuously opposed his leaving, pointing out that he had no idea how long he might be away, and that she and their children needed him too. It grieved him to go without her support, but he had no choice. Ethan would go on a pilgrimage, and at the next visitation, he would learn what God intended for him.

NEIL'S VISIT TO SARAH'S parents caused him to give further thought to his conversation with Benny Vasquez. While he hadn't gotten a lot out of

Benny's words, he'd been impressed by the absoluteness of Benny's devotion. No matter what misfortune befell him in the future, Benny's love of God would never waver, and he would ascend to Heaven when he died. That fact offered Neil a very slim opportunity, one that had seemed so unattractive he hadn't considered it before; but now, as he was growing more desperate, it was beginning to look expedient.

Every holy site had its pilgrims who, rather than looking for a miracle cure, deliberately sought out Heaven's light. Those who saw it were always accepted into Heaven when they died, no matter how selfish their motives had been; there were some who wished to have their ambivalence removed so they could be reunited with their loved ones, and others who'd always lived a sinful life and wanted to escape the consequences.

In the past there'd been some doubt as to whether Heaven's light could indeed overcome *all* the spiritual obstacles to becoming saved. The debate ended after the case of Barry Larsen, a serial rapist and murderer who, while disposing of the body of his latest victim, witnessed an angel's visitation and saw Heaven's light. At Larsen's execution, his soul was seen ascending to Heaven, much to the outrage of his victims' families. Priests tried to console them, assuring them—on the basis of no evidence whatsoever—that Heaven's light must have subjected Larsen to many lifetimes' worth of penance in a moment, but their words provided little comfort.

For Neil this offered a loophole, an answer to Phil Soames's objection; it was the one way that he could love Sarah more than he loved God, and still be reunited with her. It was how he could be selfish and still get into Heaven. Others had done it; perhaps he could too. It might not be just, but at least it was predictable.

At an instinctual level, Neil was averse to the idea: it sounded like undergoing brainwashing as a cure for depression. He couldn't help but think that it would change his personality so drastically that he'd cease to be himself. Then he remembered that everyone in Heaven had undergone a similar transformation; the saved were just like the eyeless except that they no longer had bodies. This gave Neil a clearer image of what he was working toward: no matter whether he became devout by seeing Heaven's light or by a lifetime of effort, any ultimate reunion with Sarah couldn't re-create what they'd shared in the mortal plane. In Heaven, they would both be different, and their love for each other would be mixed with the love that all the saved felt for everything.

This realization didn't diminish Neil's longing for a reunion with Sarah.

In fact it sharpened his desire, because it meant that the reward would be the same no matter what means he used to achieve it; the shortcut led to precisely the same destination as the conventional path.

On the other hand, seeking Heaven's light was far more difficult than an ordinary pilgrimage, and far more dangerous. Heaven's light leaked through only when an angel entered or left the mortal plane, and since there was no way to predict where an angel would first appear, light-seekers had to converge on the angel after its arrival and follow it until its departure. To maximize their chances of being in the narrow shaft of Heaven's light, they followed the angel as closely as possible during its visitation; depending on the angel involved, this might mean staying alongside the funnel of a tornado, the wavefront of a flash flood, or the expanding tip of a chasm as it split apart the landscape. Far more light-seekers died in the attempt than succeeded.

Statistics about the souls of failed light-seekers were difficult to compile, since there were few witnesses to such expeditions, but the numbers so far were not encouraging. In sharp contrast to ordinary pilgrims who died without receiving their sought-after cure, of which roughly half were admitted into Heaven, every single failed light-seeker had descended to Hell. Perhaps only people who were already lost ever considered seeking Heaven's light, or perhaps death in such circumstances was considered suicide. In any case, it was clear to Neil that he needed to be ready to accept the consequences of embarking on such an attempt.

The entire idea had an all-or-nothing quality to it that Neil found both frightening and attractive. He found the prospect of going on with his life, trying to love God, increasingly maddening. He might try for decades and not succeed. He might not even have that long; as he'd been reminded so often lately, visitations served as a warning to prepare one's soul, because death might come at any time. He could die tomorrow, and there was no chance of his becoming devout in the near future by conventional means.

It's perhaps ironic that, given his history of not following Janice Reilly's example, Neil took notice when she reversed her position. He was eating breakfast when he happened to see an item in the newspaper about her plans for a pilgrimage, and his immediate reaction was anger: how many blessings would it take to satisfy that woman? After considering it more, he decided that if she, having received a blessing, deemed it appropriate to seek God's assistance in coming to terms with it, then there was no reason he, having received such terrible misfortune, shouldn't do the same. And that was enough to tip him over the edge.

. . .

HOLY SITES WERE INVARIABLY in inhospitable places: one was an atoll in the middle of the ocean, while another was in the mountains at an elevation of 20,000 feet. The one that Neil traveled to was in a desert, an expanse of cracked mud reaching miles in every direction; it was desolate, but it was relatively accessible and thus popular among pilgrims. The appearance of the holy site was an object lesson in what happened when the celestial and terrestrial realms touched: the landscape was variously scarred by lava flows, gaping fissures, and impact craters. Vegetation was scarce and ephemeral, restricted to growing in the interval after soil was deposited by floodwaters or whirlwinds and before it was scoured away again.

Pilgrims took up residence all over the site, forming temporary villages with their tents and camper vans; they all made guesses as to what location would maximize their chances of seeing the angel while minimizing the risk of injury or death. Some protection was offered by curved banks of sandbags, left over from years past and rebuilt as needed. A site-specific paramedic and fire department ensured that paths were kept clear so rescue vehicles could go where they were needed. Pilgrims either brought their own food and water or purchased them from vendors charging exorbitant prices; everyone paid a fee to cover the cost of waste removal.

Light-seekers always had off-road vehicles to better cross rough terrain when it came time to follow the angel. Those who could afford it drove alone; those who couldn't formed groups of two or three or four. Neil didn't want to be a passenger reliant on another person, nor did he want the responsibility of driving anyone else. This might be his final act on Earth, and he felt he should do it alone. The cost of Sarah's funeral had depleted their savings, so Neil sold all his possessions in order to purchase a suitable vehicle: a pickup truck equipped with aggressively knurled tires and heavy-duty shock absorbers.

As soon as he arrived, Neil started doing what all the other light-seekers did: crisscrossing the site in his vehicle, trying to familiarize himself with its topography. It was on one of his drives around the site's perimeter that he met Ethan; Ethan flagged him down after his own car had stalled on his return from the nearest grocery story, eighty miles away. Neil helped him get his car started again, and then, at Ethan's insistence, followed him back to his campsite for dinner. Janice wasn't there when they arrived, having gone to visit some pilgrims several tents over; Neil listened politely while Ethan—

heating prepackaged meals over a bottle of propane—began describing the events that had brought him to the holy site.

When Ethan mentioned Janice Reilly's name, Neil couldn't mask his surprise. He had no desire to speak with her again, and immediately excused himself to leave. He was explaining to a puzzled Ethan that he'd forgotten a previous engagement when Janice arrived.

She was startled to see Neil there, but asked him to stay. Ethan explained why he'd invited Neil to dinner, and Janice told him where she and Neil had met. Then she asked Neil what had brought him to the holy site. When he told them he was a light-seeker, Ethan and Janice immediately tried to persuade him to reconsider his plans. He might be committing suicide, said Ethan, and there were always better alternatives than suicide. Seeing Heaven's light was not the answer, said Janice; that wasn't what God wanted. Neil stiffly thanked them for their concern, and left.

During the weeks of waiting, Neil spent every day driving around the site; maps were available, and were updated after each visitation, but they were no substitute for driving the terrain yourself. On occasion he would see a light-seeker who was obviously experienced in off-road driving, and ask him—the vast majority of the light-seekers were men—for tips on negotiating a specific type of terrain. Some had been at the site for several visitations, having neither succeeded nor failed at their previous attempts. They were glad to share tips on how best to pursue an angel, but never offered any personal information about themselves. Neil found the tone of their conversation peculiar, simultaneously hopeful and hopeless, and wondered if he sounded the same.

Ethan and Janice passed the time by getting to know some of the other pilgrims. Their reactions to Janice's situation were mixed: some thought her ungrateful, while others thought her generous. Most found Ethan's story interesting, since he was one of the very few pilgrims seeking something other than a miracle cure. For the most part, there was a feeling of camaraderie that sustained them during the long wait.

Neil was driving around in his truck when dark clouds began coalescing in the southeast, and the word came over the CB radio that a visitation had begun. He stopped the vehicle to insert earplugs into his ears and don his helmet; by the time he was finished, flashes of lightning were visible, and a light-seeker near the angel reported that it was Barakiel, and it appeared to be moving due north. Neil turned his truck east in anticipation and began driving at full speed.

There was no rain or wind, only dark clouds from which lightning emerged. Over the radio other light-seekers relayed estimates of the angel's direction and speed, and Neil headed northeast to get in front of it. At first he could gauge his distance from the storm by counting how long it took for the thunder to arrive, but soon the lightning bolts were striking so frequently that he couldn't match up the sounds with the individual strikes.

He saw the vehicles of two other light-seekers converging. They began driving in parallel, heading north, over a heavily cratered section of ground, bouncing over small ones and swerving to avoid the larger ones. Bolts of lightning were striking the ground everywhere, but they appeared to be radiating from a point south of Neil's position; the angel was directly behind him, and closing.

Even through his earplugs, the roar was deafening. Neil could feel his hair rising from his skin as the electric charge built up around him. He kept glancing in his rearview mirror, trying to ascertain where the angel was while wondering how close he ought to get.

His vision grew so crowded with afterimages that it became difficult to distinguish actual bolts of lightning among them. Squinting at the dazzle in his mirror, he realized he was looking at a continuous bolt of lightning, undulating but uninterrupted. He tilted the driver's-side mirror upward to get a better look, and saw the source of the lightning bolt, a seething, writhing mass of flames, silver against the dusky clouds: the angel Barakiel.

It was then, while Neil was transfixed and paralyzed by what he saw, that his pickup truck crested a sharp outcropping of rock and became airborne. The truck smashed into a boulder, the entire force of the impact concentrated on the vehicle's left front end, crumpling it like foil. The intrusion into the driver's compartment fractured both of Neil's legs and nicked his left femoral artery. Neil began, slowly but surely, bleeding to death.

He didn't try to move; he wasn't in physical pain at the moment, but he somehow knew that the slightest movement would be excruciating. It was obvious that he was pinned in the truck, and there was no way he could pursue Barakiel even if he weren't. Helplessly, he watched the lightning storm move further and further away.

As he watched it, Neil began crying. He was filled with a mixture of regret and self-contempt, cursing himself for ever thinking that such a scheme could succeed. He would have begged for the opportunity to do it over again, promised to spend the rest of his days learning to love God, if only he could live, but he knew that no bargaining was possible and he had only himself to blame. He apologized to Sarah for losing his chance at being re-united with her, for throwing his life away on a gamble instead of playing it safe. He prayed that she understood that he'd been motivated by his love for her, and that she would forgive him.

Through his tears he saw a woman running toward him, and recognized her as Janice Reilly. He realized his truck had crashed no more than a hundred yards from her and Ethan's campsite. There was nothing she could do, though; he could feel the blood draining out of him, and knew that he wouldn't live long enough for a rescue vehicle to arrive. He thought Janice was calling to him, but his ears were ringing too badly for him to hear anything. He could see Ethan Mead behind her, also starting to run toward him.

Then there was a flash of light and Janice was knocked off her feet as if she'd been struck by a sledgehammer. At first he thought she'd been hit by lightning, but then he realized that the lightning had already ceased. It was when she stood up again that he saw her face, steam rising from newly featureless skin, and he realized that Janice had been struck by Heaven's light.

Neil looked up, but all he saw were clouds; the shaft of light was gone. It seemed as if God were taunting him, not only by showing him the prize he'd lost his life trying to acquire while still holding it out of reach, but also by giving it to someone who didn't need it or even want it. God had already wasted a miracle on Janice, and now He was doing it again.

It was at that moment that another beam of Heaven's light penetrated the cloud cover and struck Neil, trapped in his vehicle.

Like a thousand hypodermic needles the light punctured his flesh and scraped across his bones. The light unmade his eyes, turning him into not a formerly sighted being, but a being never intended to possess vision. And in doing so the light revealed to Neil all the reasons he should love God.

He loved Him with an utterness beyond what humans can experience for one another. To say it was unconditional was inadequate, because even the word "unconditional" required the concept of a condition and such an idea was no longer comprehensible to him: every phenomenon in the universe was nothing less than an explicit reason to love Him. No circumstance could be an obstacle or even an irrelevancy, but only another reason to be grateful, a further inducement to love. Neil thought of the grief that had driven him to suicidal recklessness, and the pain and terror that Sarah had experienced before she died, and still he loved God, not in spite of their suffering, but because of it.

He renounced all his previous anger and ambivalence and desire for answers. He was grateful for all the pain he'd endured, contrite for not previ-

ously recognizing it as the gift it was, euphoric that he was now being granted this insight into his true purpose. He understood how life was an unde-
served bounty, how even the most virtuous were not worthy of the glories of
the mortal plane.

For him the mystery was solved, because he understood that everything
in life is love, even pain, especially pain.

So minutes later, when Neil finally bled to death, he was truly worthy of
salvation.

And God sent him to Hell anyway.

ETHAN SAW ALL OF THIS. He saw Neil and Janice remade by Heaven's
light, and he saw the pious love on their eyeless faces. He saw the skies become clear and the sunlight return. He was holding Neil's hand, waiting for
the paramedics, when Neil died, and he saw Neil's soul leave his body and
rise toward Heaven, only to descend into Hell.

Janice didn't see it, for by then her eyes were already gone. Ethan was the
sole witness, and he realized that this was God's purpose for him: to follow
Janice Reilly to this point and to see what she could not.

When statistics were compiled for Barakiel's visitation, it turned out that
there had been a total of ten casualties, six among light-seekers and four
among ordinary pilgrims. Nine pilgrims received miracle cures; the only individuals to see Heaven's light were Janice and Neil. There were no statistics
regarding how many pilgrims had felt their lives changed by the visitation,
but Ethan counted himself among them.

Upon returning home, Janice resumed her evangelism, but the topic of
her speeches has changed. She no longer speaks about how the physically
handicapped have the resources to overcome their limitations; instead she,
like the other eyeless, speaks about the unbearable beauty of God's creation.
Many who used to draw inspiration from her are disappointed, feeling
they've lost a spiritual leader. When Janice had spoken of the strength she
had as an afflicted person, her message was rare, but now that she's eyeless,
her message is commonplace. She doesn't worry about the reduction in her
audience, though, because she has complete conviction in what she evangel-
izes.

Ethan quit his job and became a preacher so that he too could speak
about his experiences. His wife Claire couldn't accept his new mission and
ultimately left him, taking their children with her, but Ethan was willing to
continue alone. He's developed a substantial following by telling people

what happened to Neil Fisk. He tells people that they can no more expect justice in the afterlife than in the mortal plane, but he doesn't do this to dissuade them from worshiping God; on the contrary, he encourages them to do so. What he insists on is that they not love God under a misapprehension, that if they wish to love God, they be prepared to do so no matter what His intentions. God is not just, God is not kind, God is not merciful, and understanding that is essential to true devotion.

As for Neil, although he is unaware of any of Ethan's sermons, he would understand their message perfectly. His lost soul is the embodiment of Ethan's teachings.

For most of its inhabitants, Hell is not that different from Earth; its principal punishment is the regret of not having loved God enough when alive, and for many that's easily endured. For Neil, however, Hell bears no resemblance whatsoever to the mortal plane. His eternal body has well-formed legs, but he's scarcely aware of them; his eyes have been restored, but he can't bear to open them. Just as seeing Heaven's light gave him an awareness of God's presence in all things in the mortal plane, so it has made him aware of God's absence in all things in Hell. Everything Neil sees, hears, or touches causes him distress, and unlike in the mortal plane this pain is not a form of God's love, but a consequence of His absence. Neil is experiencing more anguish than was possible when he was alive, but his only response is to love God.

Neil still loves Sarah, and misses her as much as he ever did, and the knowledge that he came so close to rejoining her only makes it worse. He knows his being sent to Hell was not a result of anything he did; he knows there was no reason for it, no higher purpose being served. None of this diminishes his love for God. If there were a possibility that he could be admitted to Heaven and his suffering would end, he would not hope for it; such desires no longer occur to him.

Neil even knows that by being beyond God's awareness, he is not loved by God in return. This doesn't affect his feelings either, because unconditional love asks nothing, not even that it be returned.

And though it's been many years that he has been in Hell, beyond the awareness of God, he loves Him still. That is the nature of true devotion.

OCTOBER IN THE CHAIR

NEIL GAIMAN

NEIL GAIMAN was born in England in 1960, and worked as a free-lance journalist before co-editing *Ghastly Beyond Belief* (with Kim Newman) and writing *Don't Panic: The Official Hitchhiker's Guide to the Galaxy Companion.* He started writing graphic novels and comics with *Violent Cases* in 1987, and with the seventy-five installments of the award-winning series *The Sandman* established himself as one of the leading comics writers of his generation. His first novel, *Good Omens* (with Terry Pratchett), appeared in 1991, and was followed by *Neverwhere, Stardust,* and the Locus Award–winners *American Gods* and *Coraline.* His most recent books are *The Sandman: Endless Nights* and picture book *The Wolves in the Walls* (with long time collaborator Dave McKean). Gaiman's work has won the Hugo, World Fantasy, Bram Stoker, Locus, Geffen, International Horror Guild, Mythopoeic, and Will Eisner Comic Industry Awards. Upcoming among many other projects, is the novel *The Anansi Boys.* Gaiman moved to the United States in 1992 with his wife and three children, and currently lives near Minneapolis.

Gaiman moves with admirable ease from one form to another, and has published everything from poetry and song lyrics to picture books and full-length novels for adults. It's something that underscores that he is, first and foremost, a storyteller. In the tale that follows, he deftly enters the autumnal territory of Ray Bradbury. . . .

* * *

—*FOR RAY BRADBURY*

OCTOBER WAS IN THE CHAIR, so it was chilly that evening, and the leaves were red and orange and tumbled from the trees that circled the grove. The twelve of them sat around a campfire roasting huge sausages on sticks, which spat and crackled as the fat dripped onto the burning applewood, and drinking fresh apple cider, tangy and tart in their mouths.

April took a dainty bite from her sausage, which burst open as she bit into it, spilling hot juice down her chin. "Beshrew and suck-ordure on it," she said.

Squat March, sitting next to her, laughed, low and dirty, and then pulled out a huge, filthy handkerchief. "Here you go," he said.

April wiped her chin. "Thanks," she said. "The cursed bag-of-innards burned me. I'll have a blister there tomorrow."

September yawned. "You are *such* a hypochondriac," he said, across the fire. "And such *lan*guage." He had a pencil-thin mustache, and was balding in the front, which made his forehead seem high, and wise.

"Lay off her," said May. Her dark hair was cropped short against her skull, and she wore sensible boots. She smoked a small, brown cigarillo which smelled heavily of cloves. "She's sensitive."

"Oh puhlease," said September. "Spare me."

October, conscious of his position in the chair, sipped his apple cider, cleared his throat, and said, "Okay. Who wants to begin?" The chair he sat in was carved from one large block of oak wood, inlaid with ash, with cedar, and with cherrywood. The other eleven sat on tree stumps equally spaced about the small bonfire. The tree stumps had been worn smooth and comfortable by years of use.

"What about the minutes?" asked January. "We always do minutes when I'm in the chair."

"But you aren't in the chair now, are you, dear?" said September, an elegant creature of mock solicitude.

"What about the minutes?" repeated January. "You can't ignore them."

"Let the little buggers take care of themselves," said April, one hand running through her long blond hair. "And I think September should go first."

September preened and nodded. "Delighted," he said.

"Hey," said February. "Hey-hey-hey-hey-hey-hey-hey. I didn't hear the chairman ratify that. Nobody starts till October says who starts, and then nobody else talks. Can we have maybe the tiniest semblance of order here?" He peered at them, small, pale, dressed entirely in blues and grays.

"It's fine," said October. His beard was all colors, a grove of trees in autumn, deep brown and fire orange and wine red, an untrimmed tangle across the lower half of his face. His cheeks were apple red. He looked like a friend, like someone you had known all your life. "September can go first. Let's just get it rolling."

September placed the end of his sausage into his mouth, chewed daintily, and drained his cider mug. Then he stood up and bowed to the company and began to speak.

"Laurent DeLisle was the finest chef in all of Seattle; at least, Laurent DeLisle thought so, and the Michelin stars on his door confirmed him in his opinion. He was a remarkable chef, it is true—his minced lamb brioche had won several awards, his smoked quail and white truffle ravioli had been described in the *Gastronome* as 'the tenth wonder of the world.' But it was his wine cellar . . . ah, his wine cellar . . . that was his source of pride and his passion.

"I understand that. The last of the white grapes are harvested in me, and the bulk of the reds: I appreciate fine wines, the aroma, the taste, the aftertaste as well.

"Laurent DeLisle bought his wines at auctions, from private wine lovers, from reputable dealers: he would insist on a pedigree for each wine, for wine frauds are, alas, too common, when the bottle is selling for perhaps five, ten, a hundred thousand dollars, or pounds, or euros.

"The treasure—the jewel—the rarest of the rare and the *ne plus ultra* of his temperature-controlled wine cellar was a bottle of 1902 Château Lafitte. It was on the wine list at $120,000, although it was, in true terms, priceless, for it was the last bottle of its kind."

"Excuse me," said August politely. He was the fattest of them all, his thin hair combed in golden wisps across his pink pate.

September glared down at his neighbor. "Yes?"

"Is this the one where some rich dude buys the wine to go with the dinner, and the chef decides that the dinner the rich dude ordered isn't good enough for the wine, so he sends out a different dinner, and the guy takes one mouthful, and he's got, like, some rare allergy and he just dies like that, and the wine never gets drunk after all?"

September said nothing. He looked a great deal.

"Because if it is, you told it before. Years ago. Dumb story then. Dumb story now." August smiled. His pink cheeks shone in the firelight.

September said, "Obviously pathos and culture are not to everyone's taste. Some people prefer their barbecues and beer, and some of us like—"

February said, "Well, I hate to say this, but he kind of does have a point. It has to be a new story."

September raised an eyebrow and pursed his lips. "I'm done," he said abruptly. He sat down on his stump.

They looked at each other across the fire, the months of the year.

JUNE, HESITANT AND CLEAN, raised her hand and said, "I have one about a guard on the X-ray machines at LaGuardia Airport, who could read all about people from the outlines of their luggage on the screen, and one day she saw a luggage X ray so beautiful that she fell in love with the person, and she had to figure out which person in the line it was, and she couldn't, and she pined for months and months. And when the person came through again she knew it this time, and it was the man, and he was a wizened old Indian man and she was pretty and black and, like twenty-five, and she knew it would never work out and she let him go, because she could also see from the shapes of his bags on the screen that he was going to die soon."

October said, "Fair enough, young June. Tell that one."

JUNE STARED AT HIM, like a spooked animal. "I just did," she said.

October nodded. "So you did," he said, before any of the others could say anything. And then he said, "Shall we proceed to my story, then?"

February sniffed. "Out of order there, big fella. The man in the chair only tells his story when the rest of us are through. Can't go straight to the main event."

May was placing a dozen chestnuts on the grate above the fire, deploying them into patterns with her tongs. "Let him tell his story if he wants to," she said. "God knows it can't be worse than the one about the wine. And I have things to be getting back to. Flowers don't bloom by themselves. All in favor?"

"You're taking this to a formal vote?" February said. "I cannot believe this. I cannot believe this is happening." He mopped his brow with a hand-ful of tissues, which he pulled from his sleeve.

Seven hands were raised. Four people kept their hands down—February, September, January, and July. ("I don't have anything personal on this," said July apologetically. "It's purely procedural. We shouldn't be set-ting precedents.")

"It's settled then," said October. "Is there anything anyone would like to say before I begin?"

"Um. Yes. Sometimes," said June, "sometimes I think somebody's watch-ing us from the woods and then I look and there isn't anybody there. But I still think it."

April said, "That's because you're crazy."

"Mm," said September, to everybody. "She's sensitive but she's still the cruelest."

"Enough," said October. He stretched in his chair. He cracked a cobnut with his teeth, pulled out the kernel, and threw the fragments of shell into the fire, where they hissed and spat and popped, and he began.

THERE WAS A BOY, *October said,* who was miserable at home, although they did not beat him. He did not fit well, not his family, not his town, nor even his life. He had two older brothers, who were twins, older than he was, and who hurt him or ignored him, and were popular. They played football: some games one twin would score more and be the hero, and some games the other would. Their little brother did not play football. They had a name for their brother. They called him the Runt.

They had called him the Runt since he was a baby, and at first their mother and father had chided them for it.

The twins said, "But he *is* the runt of the litter. Look at *him.* Look at *us.*" The boys were six when they said this. Their parents thought it was cute. A name like "the Runt" can be infectious, so pretty soon the only person who called him Donald was his grandmother, when she telephoned him on his birthday, and people who did not know him.

Now, perhaps because names have power, he was a runt: skinny and small and nervous. He had been born with a runny nose, and it had not stopped running in a decade. At mealtimes, if the twins liked the food they would steal his; if they did not, they would contrive to place their food on his plate and he would find himself in trouble for leaving good food uneaten.

Their father never missed a football game, and would buy an ice cream afterward for the twin who had scored the most, and a consolation ice cream for the other twin, who hadn't. Their mother described herself as a newspaperwoman, although she mostly sold advertising space and subscriptions: she had gone back to work full-time once the twins were capable of taking care of themselves.

The other kids in the boy's class admired the twins. They had called him Donald for several weeks in first grade, until the word trickled down that his brothers called him the Runt. His teachers rarely called him anything at all, although among themselves they could sometimes be heard to say that it was a pity that the youngest Covay boy didn't have the pluck or the imagination or the life of his brothers.

The Runt could not have told you when he first decided to run away, nor when his daydreams crossed the border and became plans. By the time he admitted to himself that he was leaving he had a large Tupperware container hidden beneath a plastic sheet behind the garage containing three Mars bars, two Milky Ways, a bag of nuts, a small bag of licorice, a flashlight, several comics, an unopened packet of beef jerky, and thirty-seven dollars, most of it in quarters. He did not like the taste of beef jerky, but he had read that explorers had survived for weeks on nothing else, and it was when he put the packet of beef jerky into the Tupperware box and pressed the lid down with a pop that he knew he was going to have to run away.

He had read books, newspapers, and magazines. He knew that if you ran away you sometimes met bad people who did bad things to you; but he had also read fairy tales, so he knew that there were kind people out there, side by side with the monsters.

The Runt was a thin ten-year-old, with a runny nose, and a blank expression. If you were to try to pick him out of a group of boys, you'd be wrong. He'd be the other one. Over at the side. The one your eye slipped over.

All through September he put off leaving. It took a really bad Friday, during the course of which both of his brothers sat on him (and the one who sat on his face broke wind, and laughed uproariously) to decide that whatever monsters were waiting out in the world would be bearable, perhaps even preferable.

Saturday, his brothers were meant to be looking after him, but soon they went into town to see a girl they liked. The Runt went around the back of the garage and took the Tupperware container out from beneath the plastic sheeting. He took it up to his bedroom. He emptied his schoolbag onto his bed, filled it with his candies and comics and quarters and the beef jerky. He filled an empty soda bottle with water.

The Runt walked into the town and got on the bus. He rode west, ten-dollars-in-quarters' worth of west, to a place he didn't know, which he thought was a good start, then he got off the bus and walked. There was no sidewalk now, so when cars came past he would edge over into the ditch, to safety.

The sun was high. He was hungry, so he rummaged in his bag and pulled out a Mars bar. After he ate it he found he was thirsty, and he drank almost half of the water from his soda bottle before he realized he was going to have to ration it. He had thought that once he got out of the town he would see springs of fresh water everywhere, but there were none to be found. There was a river, though, that ran beneath a wide bridge.

The Runt stopped halfway across the bridge to stare down at the brown water. He remembered something he had been told in school: that, in the end, all rivers flowed into the sea. He had never been to the seashore. He clambered down the bank and followed the river. There was a muddy path along the side of the riverbank, and an occasional beer can or plastic snack packet to show that people had been that way before, but he saw no one as he walked.

He finished his water.

He wondered if they were looking for him yet. He imagined police cars and helicopters and dogs, all trying to find him. He would evade them. He would make it to the sea.

The river ran over some rocks, and it splashed. He saw a blue heron, its wings wide, glide past him, and he saw solitary end-of-season dragonflies, and sometimes small clusters of midges, enjoying the Indian summer. The blue sky became dusk gray, and a bat swung down to snatch insects from the air. The Runt wondered where he would sleep that night.

Soon the path divided, and he took the branch that led away from the river, hoping it would lead to a house, or to a farm with an empty barn. He walked for some time, as the dusk deepened, until, at the end of the path, he found a farmhouse, half tumbled down and unpleasant-looking. The Runt walked around it, becoming increasingly certain as he walked that nothing could make him go inside, and then he climbed over a broken fence to an abandoned pasture, and settled down to sleep in the long grass with his schoolbag for his pillow.

He lay on his back, fully dressed, staring up at the sky. He was not in the slightest bit sleepy.

"They'll be missing me by now," he told himself. "They'll be worried."

He imagined himself coming home in a few years' time. The delight on his family's faces as he walked up the path to home. Their welcome. Their love. . . .

He woke some hours later, with the bright moonlight in his face. He could see the whole world—as bright as day, like in the nursery rhyme, but pale and without colors. Above him, the moon was full, or almost, and he imagined a face looking down at him, not unkindly, in the shadows and shapes of the moon's surface.

A voice said, "Where do you come from?"

He sat up, not scared, not yet, and looked around him. Trees. Long grass. "Where are you? I don't see you?"

Something he had taken for a shadow moved, beside a tree on the edge of the pasture, and he saw a boy of his own age.

"I'm running away from home," said the Runt.

"Whoa," said the boy. "That must have taken a whole lot of guts."

THE RUNT GRINNED with pride. He didn't know what to say.

"You want to walk a bit?" said the boy.

"Sure," said the Runt. He moved his schoolbag, so it was next to the fence post, so he could always find it again.

They walked down the slope, giving a wide berth to the old farmhouse.

"Does anyone live there?" asked the Runt.

"Not really," said the other boy. He had fair, fine hair that was almost white in the moonlight. "Some people tried a long time back, but they didn't like it, and they left. Then other folk moved in. But nobody lives there now. What's your name?"

"Donald," said the Runt. And then, "But they call me the Runt. What do they call you?"

The boy hesitated. "Dearly," he said.

"That's a cool name."

Dearly said, "I used to have another name, but I can't read it anymore."

They squeezed through a huge iron gateway, rusted part open, part closed into position, and they were in the little meadow at the bottom of the slope.

"This place is cool," said the Runt.

There were dozens of stones of all sizes in the small meadow. Tall stones, bigger than either of the boys, and small ones, just the right size for sitting on. There were some broken stones. The Runt knew what sort of a place this was, but it did not scare him. It was a loved place.

"Who's buried here?" he asked.

"Mostly okay people," said Dearly. "There used to be a town over there. Past those trees. Then the railroad came and they built a stop in the next town over, and our town sort of dried up and fell in and blew away. There's bushes and trees now, where the town was. You can hide in the trees and go into the old houses and jump out."

The Runt said, "Are they like that farmhouse up there? The houses?" He didn't want to go in them, if they were.

"No," said Dearly. "Nobody goes in them, except for me. And some animals, sometimes. I'm the only kid around here."

"I figured," said the Runt.

"Maybe we can go down and play in them," said Dearly.

"That would be pretty cool," said the Runt.

It was a perfect early October night: almost as warm as summer, and the harvest moon dominated the sky. You could see everything.

"Which one of these is yours?" asked the Runt.

Dearly straightened up proudly, and took the Runt by the hand. He pulled him over to an overgrown corner of the field. The two boys pushed aside the long grass. The stone was set flat into the ground, and it had dates carved into it from a hundred years before. Much of it was worn away, but beneath the dates it was possible to make out the words DEARLY DE-PARTED WILL NEVER BE FORG.

"Forgotten, I'd wager," said Dearly.

"Yeah, that's what I'd say too," said the Runt.

They went out of the gate, down a gully, and into what remained of the old town. Trees grew through houses, and buildings had fallen in on themselves, but it wasn't scary. They played hide-and-seek. They explored. Dearly showed the Runt some pretty cool places, including a one-room cottage that he said was the oldest building in that whole part of the country. It was in pretty good shape, too, considering how old it was.

"I can see pretty good by moonlight," said the Runt. "Even inside. I didn't know that it was so easy."

"Yeah," said Dearly. "And after a while you get good at seeing even when there ain't any moonlight."

The Runt was envious.

"I got to go to the bathroom," said the Runt. "Is there somewhere around here?"

Dearly thought for a moment. "I don't know," he admitted. "I don't do that stuff anymore. There are a few outhouses still standing, but they may not be safe. Best just to do it in the woods."

"Like a bear," said the Runt.

He went out the back, into the woods which pushed up against the wall of the cottage, and went behind a tree. He'd never done that before, in the open air. He felt like a wild animal. When he was done he wiped himself with fallen leaves. Then he went back out the front. Dearly was sitting in a pool of moonlight, waiting for him.

"How did you die?" asked the Runt.

"I got sick," said Dearly. "My maw cried and carried on something fierce. Then I died."

"If I stayed here with you," said the Runt, "would I have to be dead too?"

"Maybe," said Dearly. "Well, yeah. I guess."

"What's it like? Being dead?"

"I don't mind it," admitted Dearly. "Worst thing is not having anyone to play with."

"But there must be lots of people up in that meadow," said the Runt. "Don't they ever play with you?"

"Nope," said Dearly. "Mostly, they sleep. And even when they walk, they can't be bothered to just go and see stuff and do things. They can't be bothered with me. You see that tree?"

It was a beech tree, its smooth gray bark cracked with age. It sat in what must once have been the town square, ninety years before.

"Yeah," said the Runt.

"You want to climb it?"

"It looks kind of high."

"It is. Real high. But it's easy to climb. I'll show you."

It was easy to climb. There were handholds in the bark, and the boys went up the big beech tree like a couple of monkeys, like pirates, like warriors. From the top of the tree one could see the whole world. The sky was starting to lighten, just a hair, in the east.

Everything waited. The night was ending. The world was holding its breath, preparing to begin again.

"This was the best day I ever had," said the Runt.

"Me too," said Dearly. "What are you going to do now?"

"I don't know," said the Runt.

He imagined himself going on, walking across the world, all the way to the sea. He imagined himself growing up and growing older, bringing himself up by his bootstraps. Somewhere in there he would become fabulously wealthy. And then he would go back to the house with the twins in it, and he would drive up to their door in his wonderful car, or perhaps he would turn up at a football game (in his imagination the twins had neither aged nor grown) and look down at them, in a kindly way. He would buy them all—the twins, his parents—a meal at the finest restaurant in the city, and they would tell him how badly they had misunderstood him and mistreated him. They would apologize and weep, and through it all he would say nothing. He would let their apologies wash over him. And then he would give each of them a gift, and afterward he would leave their lives once more, this time for good.

It was a fine dream.

In reality, he knew, he would keep walking, and be found tomorrow, or the day after that, and go home and be yelled at and everything would be the same as it ever was, and day after day, hour after hour until the end of time he'd still be the Runt, only they'd be mad at him for leaving.

"I have to go to bed soon," said Dearly. He started to climb down the big beech tree.

Climbing down the tree was harder, the Runt found. You couldn't see where you were putting your feet, and had to feel around for somewhere to put them. Several times he slipped and slid, but Dearly went down ahead of him, and would say things like "Just a little to the right now," and they both made it down just fine.

The sky continued to lighten, and the moon was fading, and it was harder to see. They clambered back through the gully. Sometimes the Runt wasn't sure that Dearly was there at all, but when he got to the top, he saw the boy waiting for him.

They didn't say much as they walked up to the meadow filled with stones. The Runt put his arm over Dearly's shoulder, and they walked in step up the hill.

"Well," said Dearly. "Thanks for stopping by."

"I had a good time," said the Runt.

"Yeah," said Dearly. "Me too."

Down in the woods somewhere a bird began to sing.

"If I wanted to stay—?" said the Runt, all in a burst. Then he stopped. *I might never get another chance to change it,* thought the Runt. He'd never get to the sea. They'd never let him.

Dearly didn't say anything, not for a long time. The world was gray. More birds joined the first.

"I can't do it," said Dearly eventually. "But *they* might."

"Who?"

"The ones in there." The fair boy pointed up the slope to the tumble-down farmhouse with the jagged broken windows, silhouetted against the dawn. The gray light had not changed it.

The Runt shivered. "There's people in there?" he said. "I thought you said it was empty."

"It ain't empty," said Dearly. "I said nobody lives there. Different things." He looked up at the sky. "I got to go now," he added. He squeezed the Runt's hand. And then he just wasn't there any longer.

The Runt stood in the little graveyard all on his own, listening to the bird-song on the morning air. Then he made his way up the hill. It was harder by himself.

He picked up his schoolbag from the place he had left it. He ate his last Milky Way and stared at the tumbledown building. The empty windows of the farmhouse were like eyes, watching him.

It was darker inside there. Darker than anything.

He pushed his way through the weed-choked yard. The door to the farmhouse was mostly crumbled away. He stopped at the doorway, hesitat-ing, wondering if this was wise. He could smell damp, and rot, and some-thing else underneath. He thought he heard something move, deep in the house, in the cellar, maybe, or the attic. A shuffle, maybe. Or a hop. It was hard to tell.

Eventually, he went inside.

NOBODY SAID ANYTHING. October filled his wooden mug with apple cider when he was done, and drained it, and filled it again.

"It was a story," said December. "I'll say that for it." He rubbed his pale blue eyes with a fist. The fire was almost out.

"What happened next?" asked June nervously. "After he went into the house?"

May, sitting next to her, put her hand on June's arm. "Better not to think about it," she said.

"Anyone else want a turn?" asked August. There was no reply. "Then I think we're done."

"That needs to be an official motion," pointed out February.

"All in favor?" said October. There was a chorus of "Ayes." "All against?" Silence. "Then I declare this meeting adjourned."

They got up from the fireside, stretching and yawning, and walked away into the wood, in ones and twos and threes, until only October and his neighbor remained.

"Your turn in the chair next time," said October.

"I know," said November. He was pale, and thin lipped. He helped October out of the wooden chair. "I like your stories. Mine are always too dark."

"I don't think so," said October. "It's just that your nights are longer. And you aren't as warm."

"Put it like that," said November, "and I feel better. I suppose we can't help who we are."

"That's the spirit," said his brother. And they touched hands as they walked away from the fire's orange embers, taking their stories with them back into the dark.

NOVEL/SF NOVEL

2003	*The Years of Rice and Salt,* Kim Stanley Robinson
2002	*Passage,* Connie Willis
2001	*The Telling,* Ursula K. Le Guin
2000	*Cryptonomicon,* Neal Stephenson
1999	*To Say Nothing of the Dog,* Connie Willis
1998	*The Rise of Endymion,* Dan Simmons
1997	*Blue Mars,* Kim Stanley Robinson
1996	*The Diamond Age,* Neal Stephenson
1995	*Mirror Dance,* Lois McMaster Bujold
1994	*Green Mars,* Kim Stanley Robinson
1993	*Doomsday Book,* Connie Willis
1992	*Barrayar,* Lois McMaster Bujold
1991	*The Fall of Hyperion,* Dan Simmons
1990	*Hyperion,* Dan Simmons
1989	*Cyteen,* C.J. Cherryh
1988	*The Uplift War,* David Brin
1987	*Speaker for the Dead,* Orson Scott Card
1986	*The Postman,* David Brin
1985	*The Integral Trees,* Larry Niven
1984	*Startide Rising,* David Brin
1983	*Foundation's Edge,* Isaac Asimov
1982	*The Many-Colored Land,* Julian May

1981   *The Snow Queen,* Joan D. Vinge
1980   *Titan,* John Varley
1979   *Dreamsnake,* Vonda N. McIntyre
1978   *Gateway,* Frederik Pohl
1977   *Where Late the Sweet Birds Sang,* Kate Wilhelm
1976   *The Forever War,* Joe Haldeman
1975   *The Dispossessed,* Ursula K. Le Guin
1974   *Rendezvous with Rama,* Arthur C. Clarke
1973   *The Gods Themselves,* Isaac Asimov
1972   *The Lathe of Heaven,* Ursula K. Le Guin
1971   *Ringworld,* Larry Niven

FANTASY NOVEL

2003   *The Scar,* China Miéville
2002   *American Gods,* Neil Gaiman
2001   *A Storm of Swords,* George R.R. Martin
2000   *Harry Potter and the Prisoner of Azkaban,* J.K. Rowling
1999   *A Clash of Kings,* George R.R. Martin
1998   *Earthquake Weather,* Tim Powers
1997   *A Game of Thrones,* George R.R. Martin
1996   *Alvin Journeyman,* Orson Scott Card
1995   *Brittle Innings,* Michael Bishop
1994   *The Innkeeper's Song,* Peter S. Beagle
1993   *Last Call,* Tim Powers
1992   *Beauty,* Sheri S. Tepper
1991   *Tehanu: The Last Book of Earthsea,* Ursula K. Le Guin
1990   *Prentice Alvin,* Orson Scott Card
1989   *Red Prophet,* Orson Scott Card
1988   *Seventh Son,* Orson Scott Card
1987   *Soldier of the Mist,* Gene Wolfe
1986   *Trumps of Doom,* Roger Zelazny
1985   *Job: A Comedy of Justice,* Robert A. Heinlein
1984   *The Mists of Avalon,* Marion Zimmer Bradley
1983   *The Sword of the Lictor,* Gene Wolfe
1982   *The Claw of the Conciliator,* Gene Wolfe
1981   *Lord Valentine's Castle,* Robert Silverberg
1980   *Harpist in the Wind,* Patricia A. McKillip
1978   *The Silmarillion,* J.R.R. Tolkien

HORROR/DARK FANTASY NOVEL

1999   *Bag of Bones,* Stephen King
1997   *Desperation,* Stephen King
1996   *Expiration Date,* Tim Powers

1995   *Fires of Eden,* Dan Simmons
1994   *The Golden,* Lucius Shepard
1993   *Children of the Night,* Dan Simmons
1992   *Summer of Night,* Dan Simmons
1991   *The Witching Hour,* Anne Rice
1990   *Carrion Comfort,* Dan Simmons
1989   *Those Who Hunt the Night* (aka *Immortal Blood),* Barbara Hambly

FIRST NOVEL

2003   *A Scattering of Jades,* Alexander C. Irvine
2002   *Kushiel's Dart,* Jacqueline Carey
2001   *Mars Crossing,* Geoffrey A. Landis
2000   *The Silk Code,* Paul Levinson
1999   *Brown Girl in the Ring,* Nalo Hopkinson
1998   *The Great Wheel,* Ian R. MacLeod
1997   *Whiteout,* Sage Walker
(tie)   *Reclamation,* Sarah Zettel
1996   *The Bohr Maker,* Linda Nagata
1995   *Gun, with Occasional Music,* Jonathan Lethem
1994   *Cold Allies,* Patricia Anthony
1993   *China Mountain Zhang,* Maureen F. McHugh
1992   *The Cipher,* Kathe Koja
1991   *In the Country of the Blind,* Michael F. Flynn
1990   *Orbital Decay,* Allen Steele
1989   *Desolation Road,* Ian McDonald
1988   *War for the Oaks,* Emma Bull
1987   *The Hercules Text,* Jack McDevitt
1986   *Contact,* Carl Sagan
1985   *The Wild Shore,* Kim Stanley Robinson
1984   *Tea with the Black Dragon,* R.A. MacAvoy
1983   *Courtship Rite,* Donald Kingsbury
1982   *Starship & Haiku,* Somtow Sucharitkul
1981   *Dragon's Egg,* Robert L. Forward

YOUNG ADULT NOVEL

2003   *Coraline,* Neil Gaiman

NOVELLA

2003   "The Tain," China Miéville
2002   "The Finder," Ursula K. Le Guin
2001   "Radiant Green Star," Lucius Shepard
2000   "Orphans of the Helix," Dan Simmons
1999   "Oceanic," Greg Egan

1998 ". . . Where Angels Fear to Tread," Allen Steele
1997 "Bellwether," Connie Willis
1996 "Remake," Connie Willis
1995 "Forgiveness Day," Ursula K. Le Guin
1994 "Mefisto in Onyx," Harlan Ellison
1993 "Barnacle Bill the Spacer," Lucius Shepard
1992 "The Gallery of His Dreams," Kristine Kathryn Rusch
1991 "A Short, Sharp Shock," Kim Stanley Robinson
1990 "The Father of Stones," Lucius Shepard
1989 "The Scalehunter's Beautiful Daughter," Lucius Shepard
1988 "The Secret Sharer," Robert Silverberg
1987 "R&R," Lucius Shepard
1986 "The Only Neat Thing to Do," James Tiptree Jr.
1985 "PRESS ENTER [#]," John Varley
1984 "Her Habiline Husband," Michael Bishop
1983 "Souls," Joanna Russ
1982 "Blue Champagne," John Varley
1981 "Nightflyers," George R.R. Martin
1980 "Enemy Mine," Barry B. Longyear
1979 "The Persistence of Vision," John Varley
1978 "Stardance," Spider & Jeanne Robinson
1977 "The Samurai and the Willows," Michael Bishop
1976 "The Storms of Windhaven," Lisa Tuttle & George R.R. Martin
1975 "Born with the Dead," Robert Silverberg
1974 "The Death of Doctor Island," Gene Wolfe
1973 "The Gold at the Starbow's End," Frederik Pohl

NOVELETTE

2003 "The Wild Girls," Ursula K. Le Guin
2002 "Hell Is the Absence of God," Ted Chiang
2001 "The Birthday of the World," Ursula K. Le Guin
2000 "Huddle," Stephen Baxter
(tie) "Border Guards," Greg Egan
1999 "The Planck Dive," Greg Egan
(tie) "Taklamakan," Bruce Sterling
1998 "Newsletter," Connie Willis
1997 "Mountain Ways," Ursula K. Le Guin
1996 "When the Old Gods Die," Mike Resnick
1995 "The Martian Child," David Gerrold
1994 "Death in Bangkok," Dan Simmons
1993 "Danny Goes to Mars," Pamela Sargent
1992 "All Dracula's Children," Dan Simmons
1991 "Entropy's Bed at Midnight," Dan Simmons

1990   "Dogwalker," Orson Scott Card
1989   "The Function of Dream Sleep," Harlan Ellison
1988   "Rachel in Love," Pat Murphy
1987   "Thor Meets Captain America," David Brin
1986   "Paladin of the Lost Hour," Harlan Ellison
1985   "Bloodchild," Octavia E. Butler
1984   "The Monkey Treatment," George R.R. Martin
1983   "Djinn, No Chaser," Harlan Ellison
1982   "Guardians," George R.R. Martin
1981   "The Brave Little Toaster," Thomas M. Disch
1980   "Sandkings," George R.R. Martin
1979   "The Barbie Murders," John Varley
1977   "The Bicentennial Man," Isaac Asimov
1976   "The New Atlantis," Ursula K. Le Guin
1975   "Adrift Just Off the Islets of Langerhans: Latitude 38° 54' N, Longitude 77° 00'
       13" W," Harlan Ellison

SHORT STORY/SHORT FICTION

2003   "October in the Chair," Neil Gaiman
2002   "The Bones of the Earth," Ursula K. Le Guin
2001   "The Missing Mass," Larry Niven
2000   "macs," Terry Bisson
1999   "Maneki Neko," Bruce Sterling
1998   "Itsy Bitsy Spider," James Patrick Kelly
1997   "Gone," John Crowley
1996   "The Lincoln Train," Maureen F. McHugh
1995   "None So Blind," Joe Haldeman
1994   "Close Encounter," Connie Willis
1993   "Even the Queen," Connie Willis
1992   "Buffalo," John Kessel
1991   "Bears Discover Fire," Terry Bisson
1990   "Lost Boys," Orson Scott Card
1989   "Eidolons," Harlan Ellison
1988   "Angel," Pat Cadigan
1987   "Robot Dreams," Isaac Asimov
1986   "With Virgil Oddum at the East Pole," Harlan Ellison
1985   "Salvador," Lucius Shepard
1984   "Beyond the Dead Reef," James Tiptree Jr.
1983   "Sur," Ursula K. Le Guin
1982   "The Pusher," John Varley
1981   "Grotto of the Dancing Deer," Clifford D. Simak
1980   "The Way of Cross and Dragon," George R.R. Martin
1979   "Count the Clock That Tells the Time," Harlan Ellison

1978   "Jeffty Is Five," Harlan Ellison
1977   "Tricentennial," Joe Haldeman
1976   "Croatoan," Harlan Ellison
1975   "The Day Before the Revolution," Ursula K. Le Guin
1974   "The Deathbird," Harlan Ellison
1973   "Basilisk," Harlan Ellison
1972   "The Queen of Air and Darkness," Poul Anderson
1971   "The Region Between," Harlan Ellison

COLLECTION

2003   *Stories of Your Life and Others,* Ted Chiang
2002   *Tales from Earthsea,* Ursula K. Le Guin
2001   *Tales of Old Earth,* Michael Swanwick
2000   *The Martians,* Kim Stanley Robinson
1999   *The Avram Davidson Treasury,* Avram Davidson, edited by Robert Silverberg &
       Grania Davis
1998   *Slippage,* Harlan Ellison
1997   *None So Blind,* Joe Haldeman
1996   *Four Ways to Forgiveness,* Ursula K. Le Guin
1995   *Otherness,* David Brin
1994   *Impossible Things,* Connie Willis
1993   *The Collected Stories of Robert Silverberg Volume 1: Secret Sharers,* Robert
       Silverberg
1992   *Night of the Cooters: More Neat Stories,* Howard Waldrop
1991   *Maps in a Mirror: The Short Fiction of Orson Scott Card,* Orson Scott Card
1990   *Patterns,* Pat Cadigan
1989   *Angry Candy,* Harlan Ellison
1988   *The Jaguar Hunter,* Lucius Shepard
1987   *Blue Champagne,* John Varley
1986   *Skeleton Crew,* Stephen King
1985   *The Ghost Light,* Fritz Leiber
1984   *Unicorn Variations,* Roger Zelazny
1983   *The Compass Rose,* Ursula K. Le Guin
1982   *Sandkings,* George R.R. Martin
1981   *The Barbie Murders,* John Varley
1980   *Convergent Series,* Larry Niven
1979   *The Persistence of Vision,* John Varley
1977   *A Song for Lya,* George R.R. Martin
1976   *The Wind's Twelve Quarters,* Ursula K. Le Guin
1975   *The Best of Fritz Leiber,* Fritz Leiber

ANTHOLOGY

2003 *The Year's Best Science Fiction: Nineteenth Annual Collection,* Gardner Dozois, ed. (St. Martin's)

2002 *The Year's Best Science Fiction: Eighteenth Annual Collection,* Gardner Dozois, ed.

2001 *The Year's Best Science Fiction: Seventeenth Annual Collection,* Gardner Dozois, ed.

2000 *Far Horizons,* Robert Silverberg, ed.

1999 *Legends,* Robert Silverberg, ed.

1998 *The Year's Best Science Fiction: Fourteenth Annual Collection,* Gardner Dozois, ed.

1997 *The Year's Best Science Fiction: Thirteenth Annual Collection,* Gardner Dozois, ed.

1996 *The Year's Best Science Fiction: Twelfth Annual Collection,* Gardner Dozois, ed.

1995 *The Year's Best Science Fiction: Eleventh Annual Collection,* Gardner Dozois, ed.

1994 *The Year's Best Science Fiction: Tenth Annual Collection,* Gardner Dozois, ed.

1993 *The Year's Best Science Fiction: Ninth Annual Collection,* Gardner Dozois, ed.

1992 *Full Spectrum 3,* Lou Aronica, Amy Stout & Betsy Mitchell, eds.

1991 *The Year's Best Science Fiction: Seventh Annual Collection,* Gardner Dozois, ed.

1990 *The Year's Best Science Fiction: Sixth Annual Collection,* Gardner Dozois, ed.

1989 *Full Spectrum,* Lou Aronica & Shawna McCarthy, eds.

1988 *The Year's Best Science Fiction: Fourth Annual Collection,* Gardner Dozois, ed.

1987 *The Year's Best Science Fiction: Third Annual Collection,* Gardner Dozois, ed.

1986 *Medea: Harlan's World,* Harlan Ellison, ed.

1985 *Light Years and Dark,* Michael Bishop, ed.

1984 *The Best Science Fiction of the Year #12,* Terry Carr, ed.

1983 *The Best Science Fiction of the Year #11,* Terry Carr, ed.

1982 *Shadows of Sanctuary,* Robert Lynn Asprin, ed.

1981 *The Magazine of Fantasy & Science Fiction: A 30 Year Retrospective,* Edward L. Ferman, ed.

1980 *Universe 9,* Terry Carr, ed.

1979 *The Best Science Fiction of the Year #7,* Terry Carr, ed.

1977 *The Best Science Fiction of the Year #5,* Terry Carr, ed.

1976 *Epoch,* Roger Elwood & Robert Silverberg, eds.

1971 *The Science Fiction Hall of Fame,* Robert Silverberg, ed.

NONFICTION/RELATED/REFERENCE BOOK

2003 *Tomorrow Now: Envisioning the Next Fifty Years,* Bruce Sterling

2002 *Being Gardner Dozois,* Michael Swanwick

2001 *On Writing,* Stephen King

2000 *Sixty Years of Arkham House,* S.T. Joshi

1999 *The Dreams Our Stuff Is Made Of: How Science Fiction Conquered the World,* Thomas M. Disch

1998 *The Encyclopedia of Fantasy,* John Clute & John Grant, eds.

1997 *Look at the Evidence,* John Clute

1996 *Science Fiction: The Illustrated Encyclopedia,* John Clute

1995 *I,. Asimov: A Memoir,* Isaac Asimov

1994   *The Encyclopedia of Science Fiction,* John Clute & Peter Nicholls, eds.

1993   *Dinotopia,* James Gurney

1992   *Science-Fiction: The Early Years,* Everett F. Bleiler

1991   *Science Fiction Writers of America Handbook,* Kristine Kathryn Rusch & Dean Wesley Smith, eds.

1990   *Grumbles from the Grave,* Robert A. Heinlein

1989   *First Maitz,* Don Maitz

1988   *Watchmen,* Alan Moore & Dave Gibbons

1987   *Trillion Year Spree,* Brian W. Aldiss (with David Wingrove)

1986   *Benchmarks: Galaxy Bookshelf,* Algis Budrys

1985   *Sleepless Nights in the Procrustean Bed,* Harlan Ellison

1984   *Dream Makers, Volume II,* Charles Platt

1983   *The Engines of the Night,* Barry N. Malzberg

1982   *Danse Macabre,* Stephen King

1981   *In Joy Still Felt: The Autobiography of Isaac Asimov, 1954–1978,* Isaac Asimov

1980   *The Science Fiction Encyclopedia,* Peter Nicholls, ed.

1979   *The Way the Future Was,* Frederik Pohl

1976   *Alternate Worlds, the Illustrated History of Science Fiction,* James Gunn

ART BOOK

2003   *Spectrum 9: The Best in Contemporary Fantastic Art,* Cathy Fenner & Arnie Fenner, eds.

2002   *Spectrum 8: The Best in Contemporary Fantastic Art,* Cathy Fenner & Arnie Fenner, eds.

2001   *Spectrum 7: The Best in Contemporary Fantastic Art,* Cathy Fenner & Arnie Fenner, eds.

2000   *Science Fiction of the 20th Century,* Frank M. Robinson

1999   *Spectrum 5: The Best in Contemporary Fantastic Art,* Cathy Fenner & Arnie Fenner, eds.

1998   *Infinite Worlds: The Fantastic Visions of Science Fiction Art,* Vincent Di Fate

1997   *Spectrum 3: The Best in Contemporary Fantastic Art,* Cathy Burnett & Arnie Fenner eds., with Jim Loehr

1996   *Spectrum 2: The Best in Contemporary Fantastic Art,* Cathy Burnett & Arnie Fenner, eds.

1995   *Spectrum: The Best in Contemporary Fantastic Art,* Cathy Burnett & Arnie Fenner, eds.

1994   *The Art of Michael Whelan: Scenes/Visions,* Michael Whelan

1980   *Barlowe's Guide to Extraterrestrials,* Wayne Douglas Barlowe & Ian Summers

1979   *Tomorrow and Beyond,* Ian Summers, ed.

EDITOR

1989–2993   Gardner Dozois

BOOK PUBLISHER

1988–2003   Tor
1984–1987   Ballantine/Del Rey
1983   Pocket/Timescape
1982   Pocket/Timescape
1981   Ballantine/Del Rey
1980   Ballantine/Del Rey
1978   Ballantine/Del Rey
1977   Ballantine
1972–1974   Ballantine

ARTIST (PROFESSIONAL)

2003   Bob Eggleton
2002   Michael Whelan
2001   Bob Eggleton
1980–2000   Michael Whelan
1979   Boris Vallejo
1976/77   Rick Sternbach
1974/75   Frank Kelly Freas

ORIGINAL ANTHOLOGY

1975   *Universe 4,* Terry Carr, ed.
1974   *Astounding,* Harry Harrison, ed.
1973   *Again, Dangerous Visions,* Harlan Ellison, ed.
1972   *Universe 1,* Terry Carr, ed.

REPRINT ANTHOLOGY/COLLECTION

1975   *Before the Golden Age,* Isaac Asimov, ed.
1974   *The Best Science Fiction of the Year #2,* Terry Carr, ed.
1973   *The Best Science Fiction of the Year,* Terry Carr, ed.
1972   *World's Best Science Fiction: 1971,* Donald A. Wollheim & Terry Carr, eds.

FANZINE

1977   *Locus*
1976   *Locus*
1975   *Outworlds*
1971–1974   *Locus*

SINGLE FANZINE ISSUE

1971   *Locus*

CRITIC

1977   Spider Robinson

1976   Richard Geis
1975   P. Schuyler Miller
1974   Richard E. Geis

FAN WRITER
1973   Terry Carr
1972   Charlie Brown
1971   Harry Warner Jr.

FAN CRITIC
1971   Ted Pauls

PUBLISHER - HARDCOVER
1976   Science Fiction Book Club
1975   Science Fiction Book Club

PUBLISHER - PAPERBACK
1976   Ballantine
1975   Ballantine

PAPERBACK COVER ARTIST
1973   Frank Kelly Freas
1972   Gene Szafran
1971   Leo & Diane Dillon

MAGAZINE ARTIST
1973   Frank Kelly Freas
1972   Frank Kelly Freas

FAN ARTIST
1975   Tim Kirk
1974   Tim Kirk
1973   Bill Rotsler
1972   Bill Rotsler
1971   Alicia Austin

FAN CARTOONIST
1971   Bill Rotsler

CONVENTION
1972   Noreascon

The founder and publisher of *Locus* magazine, CHARLES N. BROWN has been involved in science fiction and fantasy for more than sixty years. The editor of *Locus* for more than thirty years, Charles has won more Hugo Awards (twenty-three) than anyone else and is one of the most respected names in the genre. He lives in Oakland, California.

JONATHAN STRAHAN cofounded *Eidolon: The Journal of Australian Science Fiction and Fantasy,* and is currently the reviews editor of *Locus.* He lives in Perth, western Australia, with his wife, former *Locus* managing editor Marianne Jablon, and their two daughters.

www.locusmag.org

Locus, The Magazine of the Science Fiction and Fantasy Field, is available from: Locus Publications, P.O. Box 13305, Oakland, CA 94661, USA. For credit-card orders, call 510-339-9198, fax 510-339-8144, use our website www.locusmag.com, or e-mail locus@locusmag.com. All subscriptions are payable in U.S. funds. Canadians, please use bank or postal money orders, not personal checks. Subscription rates: *USA* $30.00 for 6 issues (periodical); $52.00 for 12 issues (periodical). *CANADA and MEXICO* $32.00 for 6 issues (periodical); $55.00 for 12 issues (periodical). E-mail for international rates.

COPYRIGHT NOTICES